'This is an author that does not pull his punches . . . A gripping, and at times genuinely shocking, read' *SFX Magazine*

Alarums

and

Blood Games

headline

ALARUMS first published in Great Britain in 1993
by HEADLINE PUBLISHING GROUP

BLOOD GAMES first published in Great Britain in 1992
by HEADLINE PUBLISHING GROUP

First published in this omnibus edition in 2006
by HEADLINE PUBLISHING GROUP

A HEADLINE paperback

1

0 7553 3175 3 (ISBN-10)
978 0 7553 3175 8 (ISBN-13)

Typeset in Janson by Avon DataSet Ltd, Bidford on Avon, Warwickshire

Printed and bound in Great Britain by
Mackays of Chatham plc, Chatham, Kent

Headline's policy is to use papers that are natural, renewable and recyclable
products and made from wood grown in sustainable forests. The logging and
manufacturing processes are expected to conform to the environmental
regulations of the country of origin.

HEADLINE PUBLISHING GROUP
A division of Hodder Headline
338 Euston Road
London NW1 3BH

www.headline.co.uk
www.hodderheadline.com

Alarums

TO KATHLEEN AND KELLY LAYMON,
MY MOM AND DAD,
WHO BROUGHT ME INTO THE WORLD
AND RAISED ME WITH LOVE
AND HAVE ALWAYS STOOD BESIDE ME
– FROM ME WITH LOVE –

E'en the Daws and Jackals trembled with Afright
As strange Alarums, crying Chaos, bruited through the Night.

'The Portent'
Henry Loveworth

Chapter One

Bodie fidgeted, trying to find a comfortable way to sit on the straight-backed chair. It was impossible. The chair had been designed by a sadist.

The music, too.

He could be at a movie right now. Or back at his apartment, sprawled in his lounge chair, reading a book. Instead, here he was in Wesley Hall on a chair grinding his butt bones to powder, listening to a string quartet.

The music fairly lilted.

Boring as hell. Doug Kershaw or Charlie Daniels, now those are a couple of guys who know how to treat a violin.

Melanie, of course, wouldn't be caught dead stomping her foot and sawing out a lively number.

She sat there as stately as a mortician, stiff-backed and prim, playing what sounded like the background score of 'Four Wimps at Tea-Time'.

Melancholy Melanie.

She looked like a poet contemplating suicide. Thin, almost cadaverous. Glossy black hair hanging to her shoulders. Big, gloomy eyes set in a face so white it seemed nearly translucent. A very long, pale, vulnerable neck. And the choker, of course – one of those velvet bands around her neck.

Bodie found her chokers very erotic. Especially when that was all she had on.

'If I unfasten that,' he had once asked, 'will your head fall off?'

'Perhaps.'

Straddling Melanie, he'd reached behind her neck to remove the narrow ribbon.

She'd whispered, 'Not yet,' held onto her ears, then said, 'Now.'

Sensitive and haunted, but not without a sense of humor.

Bodie shifted his position on the chair. Crossing his legs helped a little. He'd been smart enough, this time, to take a front row seat. At the last concert, he'd been so boxed in that even the small relief of crossing his legs had been impossible. He checked his wristwatch. Ten till nine. Fifty minutes down, seventy to go. He wondered if he could survive that long.

A number ended to quiet applause, and Bodie clapped harder than anyone.

They'll think I'm truly appreciative, he thought. They'll be right. I appreciate the fact that it's over.

Melanie looked at him. Her expression didn't change. Distant, solemn and rather haughty, befitting the occasion. Bodie winked.

Melanie quickly turned her eyes away, but blushed. The color suffused her creamy neck and face. She squirmed just a bit, then stiffened her back even more than before, tucked down her chin firmly against the violin and waited, rigid, for the music to resume.

The new tune sounded much like the last one.

Here we go again.

Bodie glanced at his wristwatch again. Only two minutes had passed.

Don't worry, he told himself. This *will* end. Eventually. Then freedom. Stretch. Get the kinks out. A nice long walk to Sparkey's. A salami pizza, a pitcher of beer. Relief.

All you've got to do is hold on until ten o'clock.

Does anyone really *enjoy* this music? he wondered. The hall was pretty crowded. Everyone here couldn't possibly be the lover, relative, or friend of a performer. Well, plenty of them were students and teachers from the music department. They probably eat it up, the same way Melanie . . .

She jerked as if she'd been kicked in the back, but nobody was behind her. She flung her arms across her face. The violin fell to her lap. The cello player to her left dodged the tip of her flying bow. She made strangled, gasping sounds. The violin dropped to the floor as tremors jolted her body.

Bodie leaped up and ran to her.

A seizure?

Heart attack? Epileptic fit?

He lurched to a stop in front of Melanie, careful not to step on the violin, and grabbed her wrists. Her rigid arms jumped and twitched in his grip as if an electric current were sizzling through them.

'Melanie!' His voice had no effect.

He forced her arms down and pinned them to the sides of her thrashing body. Her face was inches from his – twisted and gray, eyes rolled back so that only the whites showed. Her tongue lolled out. Spittle dribbled down her chin. Her wheezing breath was hot on Bodie's face.

Somebody bumped into him. He realized they were surrounded by a crowd. People murmured to each other, some asked questions, some called out advice.

'Get back!' he snapped.

He was scared. He'd never been so scared. Melanie looked as if she were being killed – ripped apart inside or electrocuted.

'Paramedics,' said a voice behind him. 'I'll call the paramedics.'

'Yeah, quick!' Bodie yelled.

3

Melanie's chair suddenly tipped back as she rammed her feet against the floor. Bodie tugged her arms. The chair thumped down and she lurched against him. Bodie, off balance, staggered backward. Someone tried to catch him, but failed. He tumbled to the floor, Melanie on top. Her forehead smashed his nose.

Suddenly, the quaking stopped and the stiffness went out of her. She lay motionless. Bodie tasted blood, felt it trickling down his throat and dribbling along his upper lip and cheeks. 'Are you okay?' he asked.

Melanie shook her head. 'I have to go home,' she muttered. She looked up at the crowd clustered around them. 'I'm sorry,' she said, and burst into tears.

They assured everyone that they were both all right. The paramedics hadn't been called yet. Bodie turned down an offered ride to the hospital. Handkerchief pressed to his nose, he explained that he would take Melanie to the hospital himself, for a checkup. She nodded in agreement, red-eyed but no longer crying. 'We'll be fine,' she said. 'Thank you. Thank you all for your concern.'

A member of the quartet brought Melanie's instrument case to her. 'Everything's in there,' the girl told her. 'Your violin's fine.'

Some of the group stayed with them as they left the auditorium – offering sympathy or encouragement, asking questions, ready to help in case of a relapse. Professor Trueblood, head of the music department, preceded them and opened doors. 'My car's just around in back,' he said. 'I'll drive you to the emergency room, I insist.'

'Really, I'm fine,' Melanie told him. 'Thank you, anyway. I'm fine.'

'I'll take care of her,' Bodie said through his sodden handkerchief.

'You're in some need of attention yourself, young man.'

'I'll be all right.'

Professor Trueblood watched from the door of Wesley Hall as they hurried down the concrete stairs. Once away from him, they walked slowly side by side.

They walked through the warm night in silence. Then Melanie asked, 'How's your nose?'

'It'll live.' He sniffed. 'I think the bleeding's stopped.'

'I'm sorry I hurt you.'

'It's nothing.' He looked at her. 'Are you going to tell me what happened?'

'Oh, Bodie,' she whispered. Her arm slipped around his back, her small hand warm on his hip. 'It's something terrible.'

'I know. I saw.'

'Not that. I mean . . . *what I saw.*'

'What you saw?'

'My dad. It must've been Dad. Or my sister.' Her hand tightened on Bodie's hip. 'God. He . . . he must be dead. One of them, anyway. I . . . damn it.' She sobbed. 'I don't know which one. But Dad, I think. When it happened last time, it was Mom.'

Bodie stopped. He turned and stared down into her glistening eyes. Her sorrow made a thickness in his throat and a tight hurt in his chest. But her words . . . What was she saying?

He tucked the handkerchief into his pocket and gently took hold of her shoulders. Too late, he realized he had blood on his fingers. 'I want to understand,' he said.

Melanie stiffened. She lowered her head and wiped her nose with a cuff. 'There was something coming at me,' she said in a shaky voice. 'Only not at *me*. It was dark and noisy and running at me and I knew I had to get out of the way or it would kill me, but I didn't have time, it was too fast and it got me. It got me.'

Bodie pulled her gently against him. She lowered her face against the side of his neck. He felt its wetness, the tickle of her eyelashes. 'That's what happened in your mind?' he whispered. 'While you were . . . shaking and stuff?'

He felt her nod. 'Jesus,' he muttered.

'When it happened before, I was eleven and at summer camp. It was Mom that time.'

She had told Bodie about the loss of her mother, the woman slipping in the bathtub, smashing her head and drowning. 'You had a vision or whatever then – like tonight?' he asked.

'Not exactly like tonight. But yes. That's why I know Dad's dead.'

'You don't *know* it,' Bodie said. 'Not for sure.'

She didn't answer.

'Come on. Let's get back to the apartment. You can call home. Maybe everything's fine.'

In their apartment two blocks from campus, Bodie stood in silence behind Melanie while she dialed. Her head was down. On the shoulders of her white blouse were the rust-colored marks left by his fingers.

She listened to the phone for a long time, then hung up and turned to him. 'Nobody answered.'

Bodie looked at his wristwatch. Nine-thirty. It would be eight-thirty, Pacific time. 'Maybe they went out for dinner or something. Why don't you try again in an hour or so?'

'It won't do any good.'

'You can't be sure,' he said. 'How many times have you had these . . . visions?'

'Only once like this. Strong like this. When Mom was killed.'

'How come you never told me about it?'

She was silent for a moment. Her arms tightened around him. 'I didn't want you thinking I'm a weirdo.'

'Hell, I already knew that.'

'I love you, Bodie.'

'See? That proves you're a weirdo.'

'Yeah.'

'Look, what do you want to do?'

'Go home.'

'Right now?'

'Yeah. I've got to. I can't stand it.'

'Do you want me to go with you?'

'Do you mind?'

'No, of course not.'

'You can drive back in time for your Monday classes, and I can just stay there until . . .' She shrugged.

'Maybe we'll find out everything's all right.'

She didn't answer.

As they held each other, Bodie thought about the trip. Her father's home in Brentwood, California, was probably more than eight hours from Phoenix. If they got away by ten, they would reach the house around six in the morning, five o'clock Pacific time.

A long drive, especially going without sleep. But Bodie felt a stir of excitement about making the trip – a journey through the desert night, Melanie at his side, maybe stopping along the way at a diner for coffee. It would be like a little adventure, even though the occasion for it was anything but joyful.

'Let's pack up,' he said, 'and get going.'

Chapter Two

'He set fire to house. He think, "Ha ha, I burn up body, no body." He think, "Me clever fella." Not so clever. Take more than house on fire to dispose of corpse. All he do, he cook it like side of beef.'

The Los Angeles County Medical Examiner grinned and nodded sagely as his remark brought a few chuckles and moans from his audience. Pen looked around. The dapper little oriental, a cross between Quincy and Charlie Chan, had his listeners spellbound. They were eating it up.

She was glad she'd finally worked up the courage to come to one of these meetings. Even though she had sold only one story so far, she felt special to be sitting among so many mystery writers.

Gary Beatty leaned sideways on his seat, shoulder brushing against her. He took a thin cigar from his mouth. 'The man's got good patter,' he said, twitching his lip like Sam Spade. 'Too bad he don't talk English.'

Gary was the first person she'd met here tonight. She had arrived early, found a parking place on a sidestreet beside the Greater Los Angeles Press Club, rushed with her umbrella through the rain, and barely gotten seated at the Press Club bar before he climbed onto the stool beside her.

'Heyyy, Allen,' he greeted the bartender.

'Gary, how are you?' Allen, an oriental, spoke with a voice like Paul McCartney. 'What can I get you, eh? Coors or Bud?'

'Make it a Coors.'

Allen finished preparing Pen's vodka-tonic and set it in front of her. Pen unsnapped her handbag. Gary shook his head. 'It's on me,' he said.

'No, really . . .'

'Never look a gift-drink in the mouth.'

'Well . . .'

'Don't make me twist your arm, babe. We both might enjoy it too much.'

She'd stayed with Gary, talking and drinking, for twenty minutes. Then he'd led her up to the meeting room.

'This'll separate the men from the sissies,' Gary said as the overhead lights went out.

'Do you think he'll show bodies?' Pen asked.

Gary tipped back his head and blew out a smoke ring. 'I wouldn't be at all surprised.'

The first slides showed the Los Angeles Medical Examiner's headquarters building and fleet of golden vans. As they appeared on the screen, the coroner gave statistics about the size of his department, its annual budget, the number of bodies handled during the previous year, the previous month. Gary, Pen noticed, was taking notes. 'We do booming business,' the coroner said. Rather gleefully.

Then it started getting bad.

A slide of the autopsy room. Stainless steel operating tables. Trays of surgical instruments. Scales for weighing excised organs. Slanted tables with drains at their lower ends to catch the run-off.

Pen realized she was holding her breath. She let it out, inhaled deeply, and took a drink of the vodka-tonic she'd brought up with her from the bar.

The next slide showed a sunlit field. One of the golden

vans was near a couple of police cars. Several men stood in knee-high weeds near the top of the picture. 'Nice spot for picnic, but we have customer.' The projector clicked and hummed. The customer appeared.

A woman. She was sprawled face-down. Her skin looked bluish-gray and puffy. The bottoms of her feet were dirty. Surrounding her were the shoes and ankles of men from the previous shot. 'She not be here long. Overnight, maybe.'

A close-up of her buttocks. What had looked in the longer view like a dark smudge was now obviously the contusion surrounding a bite. 'Our killer make big mistake. Love bites. Teeth marks not fingerprints, but almost. Good for us, bad for him. Maybe we get saliva sample. If he secreter, we get blood type from saliva. Pin him down good.'

The picture changed.

A different naked woman. Heavier than the other one. She was face-down on a table in the autopsy room. The little man stepped close to the screen and pointed a finger at her rump. Both buttocks were a deep, grayish purple. 'Post-mortem lividity. When heart stop pumping, gravity act on blood. Blood sink.' He pointed out other blotches on her shoulder-blades and the backs of her legs. 'Look like world's worst hickey. But we know she supine after death. Can't fool Mother Nature.'

Gary groaned. 'What a wit,' he muttered.

Pen took a deep, shaky breath. She felt light-headed and a little weak. Something's wrong, she thought. Too much vodka? She wanted to take another sip, but she didn't dare.

The next slide showed a man.

He was stretched out on a table. A blue cloth covered his face. He was naked. His skin was red. 'This not post-mortem lividity, this not sunburn, this cyanosis.' He went on. Pen kept glancing at the corpse's limp penis, and forcing her eyes away from it, and looking again.

She shut her eyes. Her face felt cold and numb. She rubbed it with her hand. It was wet.

This, she thought, is what they call a cold sweat.

Christ.

What am I doing here?

Then came a close-up of a gaunt, dead face. A man with whiskers. And a white speck of something in the hair of his left nostril. 'Nature always at work,' said the chipper coroner.

Pen's ears were ringing.

He pointed at the speck. 'Fly eggs. Fly eggs like little clocks, very handy. We know they left after death, so . . .'

Pen set her drink on the floor and picked up her umbrella and handbag. She rose on wobbly legs, side-stepped past Gary's knees, and made her way along the side of the room until she reached the head of the stairs. The narrow staircase looked steep. She paused, wondering if she dare try to descend. Damn well better, she thought. Gotta get out of here before I toss my cookies.

Hooking the umbrella handle over her left wrist, she clutched the wooden hand-rail and started down.

Her mouth kept filling with saliva. The staircase looked darker than it should. When she blinked, it had an electric blue aura. She clung to the railing, sliding her hand down it, prepared to grip it firmly if her legs should give out.

You're gonna faint or barf, she thought. One or the other.

God, what a disaster.

Fly eggs.

She gagged, her throat straining and tears coming to her eyes.

Then she was at the bottom of the staircase, breathing

deeply of the fresh, cool breeze. It helped. The rain sounded pleasant spattering the courtyard in front of her. It seemed to be coming down harder than before.

She still felt shaky, but her vision was better and the cold tightness in her stomach seemed to be easing. She pursed her lips and stretched her mouth wide. The numbness had left her cheeks.

Opening her umbrella, she wondered what to do. One thing was certain, she couldn't go back upstairs. That left two alternatives: either cross the courtyard to the Press Club bar and wait there for the meeting to end, or go home.

Gary might stop by the bar after the meeting ended. But there was no guarantee of that. And if he should show up, it might lead to trouble.

Probably end up trying to fend him off.

Better just leave.

She stepped out of the entryway. The rain drummed on her umbrella as she hurried through the courtyard and down the concrete steps to the parking lot.

Twenty minutes later, she closed the apartment door behind her and hooked the dripping umbrella over its knob. Rump against the door to steady herself, she pulled off her boots. She carried them into the bedroom, turning on lights as she went.

It felt good to get out of her clothes. She hung up the damp skirt in the closet, slipped her feet into an old pair of moccasins, and put on her robe. The robe was soft against her skin.

In the bathroom, she switched on the heat light. Then she went to the kitchen and removed a bottle of Burgundy from the refrigerator.

A glass of wine, a good book, a long hot bath – the life of luxury. Worth coming home for.

The cork came out with a low, ringing pop.

She carried the bottle into the dining area and took a crystal glass from the cabinet. Back in the bathroom, she filled the glass. She took a drink, the wine cool and tart in her mouth, warm after she swallowed. Its heat flowed downward, spreading.

Nice, she thought.

This will be very nice, far superior to sitting in the Press Club bar.

Something might have developed with Gary.

Forget it.

He just would've tried to pull something. They all do. If you don't come across, they try to force you. The hell with them.

She set down the glass and bottle beside the tub – near the far end so they would be easy to reach once she was in. Kneeling, she stoppered the drain and turned the water on. She got the temperature right, almost too hot to bear, then dried her hands and went to get a book.

Her loosely belted robe hung open. She left it that way, feeling too lazy and comfortable to bother closing it.

She switched on the light in the spare bedroom, her office. Resting on the corner of her desk was the new Dean R. Koontz book. It was getting good, but it was a hardbound. No risking a hardbound in the bath.

She started toward her bookshelves and yelped in pain as a corner of the desk gouged her thigh. Clutching herself, she whirled around and dropped onto the chair.

'Je*sus*,' she hissed.

When the pain subsided, she lifted her hand. No blood on

her leg, but a layer of skin was peeled back, ruffled and white, leaving a patch of shiny pink flesh.

She let out a trembling breath.

Damn it, why didn't I look where I was going? It'll feel great when the hot water hits it.

From where she sat, she could hear the bath water.

She started to stand up.

And noticed the telephone answering machine beside her typewriter. Its red light was on. She looked more closely.

Four calls while she was gone? A busy night.

She rewound the tape, pressed the playback button, then turned away and headed for the bookshelves.

'Hello, honey.' Pen didn't recognize the man's voice. 'Sorry you're away. I wanted to talk to you about my big hard cock and your hot juicy cunt.'

The words pounded her breath away. She spun around, stared at the brown plastic recorder.

'How'd you like me to fuck your brains out, huh? Yeah, I'll stick it right up . . .'

She lunged at the desk, arm out, stiff finger set to jab the voice to silence. The machine beat her to it, a quiet beep signaling the end of the message.

Pen's legs felt weak. She braced herself over the desk, elbows locked, hands flat on the cool wood.

Second message.

Same voice.

'How'd you like it if I stuck my tongue up . . .'

She stabbed the stop button.

Shut her eyes. Lowered her head. Took deep breaths as her heart slammed.

Goddamn demented sicko. Good thing I wasn't home. Better fly eggs than . . .

14

Pen opened her eyes. Glimpsed the blond tuft between her legs. Jerked the robe shut and pulled its belt tight. Looked at the machine.

Maybe the bastard quit after two calls.

She pressed the fast forward button, watching the counter turn. Okay, third message. '. . . come in your mouth. I want to shoot my load down . . .'

She shoved the eject control. The cassette flipped up. She tore it from the machine and threw it.

Chapter Three

They were heading west on Highway 10, an hour out of Phoenix, the headbeams of the VW van pushing ahead of them through the darkness and lighting more than Bodie cared to see beyond the breakdown lane.

The fencing over there had snagged a lot of tumbleweed. That seemed to be its sole purpose.

Beyond the fence was nothing.

Nada.

Hell, there's plenty out there, he thought. Plenty of rocks and sand and cacti and tarantulas and scorpions. And tumbleweed.

He remembered an old episode of *Thriller* or *Outer Limits* (hard to keep the two shows straight) where a couple got stuck in an area very much like this and the goddamn tumbleweeds got them. Surrounded them, closed in, and . . .

A pale shape the size of a trashcan scooted into the path of his headlights. Bodie's foot jumped to the brake pedal. Before he could ram it down, the thing had already blown past his lane.

A tumbleweed, must've hopped the fence.

It looked like a giant hairball of dead sticks.

Skeletal.

The back of his neck tingled.

'It's coming for us,' he said – quoting his favorite line from *The Night of the Living Dead*. He tried to smile.

Melanie turned toward him. Her face was a pale oval with dark smudges for eyes and lips. 'Just a joke,' he said. She didn't answer. 'Remember that old *Thriller*? Maybe it was *The Outer Limits*. This couple was . . . Hey, would you say something?'

'I was so awful to him. I never stopped blaming him for . . . what happened to Mom. I know it wasn't his fault, but he was right there in the house. If he'd only heard her fall . . . If *I'd* been there, instead of away at camp.'

'Who sent you to the camp?' Bodie asked.

'They did. Mom and Dad. I didn't even want to go, but they said it would be a growth experience. They felt I was too dependent and introverted, that camp would help "bring me out". I didn't have any choice about going. I know I shouldn't hold myself responsible for Mom's accident. Dad either. It wasn't his fault any more than mine. But what you know and what you feel don't always match up. So things were never right between Dad and me after that. I tried . . . I just couldn't forgive him, or myself. Then he went and remarried.'

'Right away?'

'No. I was a sophomore in high school. That really broke it. I mean, here he was pushing sixty and Joyce was like twenty-six. It was disgusting. I couldn't handle it. I moved in with my sister and lived with her till I finished high school. I just couldn't . . .' Her voice trembled. 'Now he's dead, and I'll never . . .' She began to weep.

'You don't know for sure he's dead,' Bodie told her.

'I know. I know.'

'We'll find a gas station. There's got to be one around here someplace. I want you to call again.'

'It won't do any good.'

'You've sure got a lot of faith in that vision of yours. You might just have it all wrong.'

She sniffed and didn't answer.

'You admitted, yourself, that you weren't sure who the victim was. You thought it might be your father *or* your sister.'

'It was Dad.'

'*Now* you're sure?'

'Yes.'

'You know, maybe this is one of those things where a person sees into the future. Precognition? If it is, then maybe going there might be part of some design to prevent it from happening. Possible?'

'I don't know,' Melanie muttered.

Not a flat-out denial. Bodie felt that he had made a breakthrough . . . at least opened a crack in her certainty. 'When you had the vision about your mother, was it before or after her accident?'

'Right at the same time. I had it while she was drowning.'

'Okay, that's your one major experience with this kind of thing. This time could be entirely different. In fact, when you start thinking about it, the second time with anything is almost never the same as the first. Think about it. Your first drink, your first date with a guy. Look at the first time you had sex. I know for a fact it was different the second time around – a whole new ball game, so to speak.'

17

'I'm glad you find this amusing.'

'I'm just trying to help, Mel. You're all upset about this thing, but it's possible that your vision wasn't what you think. I'm just saying that maybe your father – or whoever – is still okay. Maybe this was a warning, and you're meant to get there in time to prevent whatever you saw.'

'I guess it's possible,' she admitted. But there was no conviction in her voice.

It *is* possible, he told himself.

Hell, it's possible that the whole damned episode was a figment of her imagination. All that guilt revolving around her father, probably a subconscious wish for him to croak, God only knows what other hang-ups are ticking away in her head. An emotional time-bomb that finally blew.

He decided to keep that theory to himself.

The last thing she needed right now was Bodie suggesting she'd flipped her gourd.

We'll find out soon enough, he thought. If it turns out that her father got his ticket canceled tonight . . .

Bodie saw an oasis ahead. Lights, buildings, a Shell sign high atop a pole. Coming up fast.

He eased his van onto the exit ramp, a single lane curving away toward the Shell station, a second station across from it with a lighted wooden sign announcing 'Bargain Gas', a Denny's restaurant, and a squat adobe building decorated with blinking blue neon that read, 'Bingo's Bar and Grill'.

Melanie leaned across the seat for a look at the gas gauge. 'You've got half a tank,' she said.

'Better safe than sorry.'

'I guess I might as well call while we're stopped,' she said. She didn't sound eager.

Bodie stopped beside the self-service pumps at the

Shell station. Straight ahead, at the edge of the lot, stood a pair of public telephones. 'Do you want to call while I fill her up?'

'I have to use the john.'

They both climbed out of the van. Bodie stepped to the pump, unhooked the nozzle and shoved down the start lever. He watched Melanie. She was walking with her head down, looking depressed and vulnerable. Not much different from the way she usually looked, a way that made Bodie want to hold and comfort her. He found his eyes lingering on the seat of her corduroys, loose-fitting pants that almost but not quite hid the moving curves of her buttocks. He imagined slipping his hands down the waistband. The cool smoothness. He wondered if she was wearing panties.

She's probably wearing them tonight, he thought. Sex would've been the furthest thing from her mind when she'd changed clothes for the trip.

She vanished around a corner of the building. Bodie took off the gas cap and thrust the spout into the neck of his tank.

It's these balmy Arizona nights, he thought. A guy can't help getting a little horny.

If she phones and everyone is fine, maybe he would pull off the highway . . .

Cut it out.

It's always terrific in the back of the van. A certain risk of exposure that adds to the whole . . .

The nozzle shut off. He hooked it back onto the pump, capped his tank, and headed for the office. He was nearly there when Melanie appeared, striding past the corner of the building, rubbing her hands on her cords.

'No towels?' he asked.

'One of those stupid blower machines.'

19

'I'll move the van over by the phones.'

She nodded, and kept on walking. Bodie continued to the office. He paid for the gas, and came out.

Melanie was standing at one of the phones, searching inside her purse.

The filling station was deserted except for Bodie's van. He decided not to move it, after all, and headed for Melanie. She looked up at him. 'Problem?' he called.

'I've only got a quarter.'

He took out his wallet. 'Make it a card call,' he told her. 'Mine's here somewhere.' By the time he reached her, he had found his calling card.

'Thanks,' she said.

He explained how to use it.

Melanie turned away and dropped her quarter into the slot. As she dialed, Bodie stepped close against her back. He held her shoulders gently. 'It'll be all right,' he said. She nodded, her hair caressing his chin and mouth.

She read off the card numbers to the operator.

He felt her body tighten.

'It's ringing,' she said.

He rubbed her shoulders, felt the bra straps under the crisp fabric of her blouse.

'Nobody's answering,' she said.

'Give it some time.' Bodie pressed his lips to the back of her head. Her hair had a faint, pleasant aroma of lemons.

'It's no use. Nobody's home.'

She hung up. A quarter clanked and skidded into the coin return. She fingered it out, turned around, and looked up at Bodie with her wide, hurt eyes.

'I wish I could make everything all right,' he said.

'I know.'

'Look, maybe there's someone else you could call. A neighbor?'

She bit down on her lower lip, frowned.

And suddenly started digging in her purse. Her hand came out with a small, red booklet.

Pen's eyes moved across the page, following the lines of words. She thought she was reading the paperback novel. Her eyes traced over its sentences, and she wasn't aware that none of their meaning reached her mind.

Sorry you're away, I wanted to talk to you.

What if he calls again?

My big hard cock . . . your hot juicy cunt.

He's out there somewhere, a sicko, and he's thinking about *me.*

Maybe right now reaching for his phone.

Pen turned a page of the book. Her eyes followed the words and she listened, expecting to hear the distant jangle of her telephone. All she heard was a slow drip of water near her feet.

He might never call again.

Oh, he will. He will.

Four calls already tonight.

Probably four, though she'd only listened to three of them.

He likes the sound of my voice.

Four times, she had talked to him. *Hello. I'm sorry, but I'm unable to answer your call at this time. If you'd like to leave me your name and . . .*' Four times, her voice had traveled the wires and come out close to his ear like an intimate whisper. She saw him alone in a room with her voice. The lights were off so he could pretend that more than her voice was there – that his hand was Pen's hand stroking him in the darkness, or Pen's mouth sucking him, or . . .

21

That's it for the answering machine.

He won't get another chance to use my voice.

Give it away. Give it to Dad. 'I don't want the damn thing,' he would say. 'Do the world a favor and deep-six it.' Good joke, though. Gift-wrap it and watch his face when he tears open the package. Pen smiled as she imagined his reaction.

Hey, she thought. Congratulations, you're thinking about Dad, not that . . .

How'd you like it if I stuck my tongue up . . .

Damn it.

Her thighs jumped shut, sweeping up a wave of hot water that lapped the undersides of her breasts. She turned a page and continued reading. 'Penny squirmed under the bed . . .' Hey, this gal has my name! She turned back a few pages. The name Penny popped out at her from almost every paragraph. Who's Penny? What's going on? Scanning what she had read so far, she realized that none of it had registered.

With a sigh, she sat up, reached over the side of the tub, and set the book on the floor beside the wine bottle. Her glass, resting on the edge of the tub, was empty. She picked it up, brought the bottle in with her, and filled the glass.

Ought to get myself smashed real good, she thought.

She drank half the wine in the glass, then poured to the top and set the bottle down carefully on the rim of the tub.

Get good and polluted, maybe you'll crack your head getting out, and . . . like mother like daughter. No more worries about your friendly neighborhood pervert.

Being careful not to spill, she eased down again into the liquid heat. Lower this time. Her head sank against the air-filled backrest. She held the glass close to her face and stared through the clear purple Burgundy.

The color of post-mortem lividity.

Mom . . .

Christ, don't start thinking about her.

This has certainly turned into a banner night.

Some creep I don't even know . . .

How do I know I don't know him?

The voice.

He could've changed his voice, disguised it.

These kinds of guys, though, don't they usually call strangers? Open the phone book, pick a name, any name, as long as it isn't a man's. Not much to be said for the old ploy of using your initial. He sees P. Conway, he knows it's not a Peter.

'No Peter here,' she mumbled. 'No, indeed.'

She tried for a drink.

Too late, she realized she should have sat up for it.

The rim was almost to her lips before the base of the glass met her chest. A quick tip. Wine sloshed into her mouth, spilled down her chin. Choking, she lurched up. She tried to hold her mouthful of wine, realized it would spurt out her nose if she didn't get rid of it, and coughed it out. The wine turned the water pink between her legs.

She coughed, sniffed, took a deep breath that made her lungs ache.

Neat play.

She blinked tears out of her eyes.

Go Mom one better, drown on a mouthful of Charles Krug.

Death, where is thy sting?

The pink cloud spread out and vanished, but the sweet aroma of the wine filled Pen's nostrils.

She drank what was left in her glass, then set the glass aside.

Sliding her feet up the bottom of the tub, she raised her knees out of the water. Leaned foward. Sniffed them. A pleasant odor, but if she did nothing about it she might be sorry. It would stick with her like spilled perfume, cloying after a while, even nauseating.

A banner night. Star-spangled.

She spread her knees wide, leaned between them, and tugged the chain of the drain stopper. The rubber disk came up with a belch. A small whirlpool appeared on the water's surface, and the level began to drop.

A quick shower.

She hated showers.

You can't hear a damn thing.

The Manson family could break down your door, Norman Bates could waltz in singing 'Mammy', the telephone . . .

You could fall down and split your skull.

Especially after you've had a few snorts.

She hated showers.

What're you gonna do, you smell like a guided tour of wine country?

She turned her head. The empty glass and the half-empty bottle of wine stood on the tub's rim. She would have to move them out of the way. The book on the floor, too. Showers could be very messy.

She reached for the bottle.

The telephone rang.

Her whole body lurched. Her hand struck the bottle's neck. With a quick grab, she caught the teetering bottle and held it steady.

The phone rang again.

YOU BASTARD, YOU HAVE NO RIGHT!

Each jangle was a blow smashing against Pen's heart, pounding her breath away.

She saw herself climb from the tub and rush, streaming water, into her office. Snatching up the phone. *You rotten degenerate shit, if you ever call me again . . .*

No, that's what he wants. My voice, my fear.

Give him a blast with your whistle.

The police whistle was on her key ring. The key ring was in her purse. In the living room. On the coffee table.

Grab it and blast his ear off.

That'll wilt your big, hard cock you goddamn . . .

The ringing finally stopped.

She let go of the wine bottle.

She listened. She heard her thumping heart, her quick shaky breaths, the water gurgling down the drain, silence beyond the locked bathroom door.

He knows I'm home, now. The tape didn't talk to him, he knows I'm home.

The tub emptied. The drain went quiet.

Pen sat there. Wet. The wet turned cold. She was shivering.

She sat there, hunched over, knees up, breasts against her legs, arms hugging her shins. Teeth clamped shut to keep them from clicking.

Droplets of water squirmed down her skin.

The thing to do now is . . . is what?

Make it so he can't call back.

She squeezed her legs harder.

Right now.

Pen let go, unhuddled, lost the comfort of warm firm legs tight together and tight to her breasts.

She felt very naked, very vulnerable as she stood up and lifted a leg over the side of the tub.

It rings now, she thought, I fall, crack my head open.

She swung her other leg over.

Both feet on the bathmat.

Your timing's off, you creep.

She felt as if she had tricked him, won a small victory.

Then there was the soft dry warmth of her towel. It rubbed the wetness away. It eased the chill. It calmed the shivers. Her teeth unclenched, and she noticed the ache in her jaw muscles.

When she finished, the towel smelled of Burgundy.

She wrapped it snugly around her breasts and tucked in a corner to hold it in place.

At the door, she gripped the knob and hesitated.

Don't clutch up again, she told herself. He's not out there. It's perfectly safe.

She turned the knob. The lock button popped with a loud, springy ping. She pulled the door open and stared through a gap the width of her head. Lights from the living room, her office, and her bedroom glowed through the hallway. Nothing looked wrong. But it all looked wrong, strangely mutated and alien.

A voice on a tape, and the world shifts.

She listened.

There was the faint hum of her refrigerator, nothing else.

A drop of water trickled off her rump and skidded down the back of her leg. Reaching a hand around, she smeared it away.

Wait a while longer, why don't you? Stand here till he calls again.

She stepped into the hallway. Glanced into her bedroom as she passed its door.

Nobody jumped out at her.

Of course not. I've got a bad case of the willies, that's all.

She stopped at her office door. Saw the cassette on the carpet, the answering machine beside the typewriter.

First things first.

At the end of the hallway, she made a quick scan of the living room. Her eyes swept to the door. The guard chain hung in place.

Satisfied?

Pen wasn't satisfied, but she felt her shoulders ease down a bit.

She stepped into the kitchen. From the hallway came enough light for her purposes, but she flicked the kitchen switch anyway to kill the shadows.

Just above the switch panel, her telephone was fixed to the wall. She wrapped a hand around it and pulled. The metal plate stayed on the wall, its jack hole empty. She placed the disconnected phone on top of her refrigerator.

One down, one to go.

With swift long strides, she returned to her office. She carefully avoided the desk corner that had earlier gouged her leg.

The answering machine. The phone. Their cords dropped off the edge of the desk, hung nearly straight down the gap between the side of the desk and the bookshelves, then curved upward and vanished behind the books.

Pen sidestepped. She dropped to a squat, held herself steady with one hand on the desk corner, and reached into the gap with her left hand. Her fingertips found the cords. She followed them, twisting sideways, slipping her hand over the book tops. Her towel fell. The phone blared, jolting her heart and ripping her breath away. With a cry of fright and rage, she hurled herself forward. Her right shoulder rammed the desk, shoving it, turning it. Another blast from the phone.

Her knees hit the carpet. She squirmed, wedging herself into the gap, shelves digging into her hip and ribs, the desk edge scraping across her right breast. The phone shrieked in her ear. She writhed, teeth bared, whimpering, and her fingers found the phone jack. She yanked it from the wall.

Silence.

She eased herself free.

Her trembling fingers grasped the towel. She dragged it with her as she moved backward on her knees.

Eyes fixed on the phone.

The next best thing to being there.

Chapter Four

'This *is* Friday night,' Bodie said. 'People go out.'

'I know,' Melanie muttered. She was slumped in the passenger seat, knees up, feet against the dash. She had been like that since they left the service station. Staring straight ahead, but too low to see out the windshield. 'Maybe it was Pen it happened to,' she said.

Maybe it's no one, Bodie thought. 'Worrying about it won't do any good. Why don't you go in back and try to get some sleep?'

She didn't answer. She didn't move. She stayed curled up, head pushed forward by the seat back. Bodie wondered how she could breathe in that position.

'Doesn't your sister go out on dates?' he asked.

'No.'

'No?'

'Well, sometimes, I suppose. Hardly ever.'

'What is she, fat and ugly?'

Melanie turned her head. In the dim light, her face was a blur. Bodie couldn't read her expression, but he guessed that she wasn't amused.

'Just trying to cheer you up,' he explained.

'She's beautiful,' Melanie said.

'As beautiful as you?'

'Yeah, I'm a regular Bo Derek.'

'You look great to me.'

'You haven't seen Pen.' There was no admiration in Melanie's voice. Her monotone sounded just slightly resentful.

'She sure has a terrible name,' Bodie said.

'Who notices?'

'Me.'

'You haven't seen her yet.'

'What does she look like?'

'The Playmate of the Year.'

'Which year?'

'Any year.'

'I can't wait to meet her.'

'I'll bet.'

Bodie reached over. He patted the back of Melanie's upraised leg. When she didn't protest, he slid his hand down the soft corduroy and caressed her rump. 'I'm not big on Playmates,' he said.

'You . . .'

'I know, I haven't seen Pen yet. Her favorite books must be *The Prophet* and *Jonathan Livingston Seagull*.'

Melanie humphed.

'So why doesn't she go out with guys?'

'She's got a problem with them.'

'Ah.'

'Not "ah". It's not like that. It's just that they're always hitting on her. They've been hitting on her since she was – God only knows – twelve or thirteen. She got tired of it, that's all.'

'That's some problem.'

'It can be. I suppose. I wouldn't know.'

Bodie leaned closer to Melanie. His fingertips found the center seam of her corduroys. He stroked along it, feeling her heat through the fabric. He pressed harder, rubbed. Melanie caught her breath.

'Not now,' she said.

He took his hand away.

Melanie lowered her feet to the floor and sat up straight. 'I'm sorry,' she muttered.

'No, I understand.'

'It's my *family*. Dad or Pen . . .'

'I know. I'd be upset, too. But it is Friday night. Just because nobody answered their phones, you shouldn't jump to conclusions. All you've really got to go on is that vision or whatever it was.'

'You think it was just my imagination.'

'I didn't say that.'

'It's what you're thinking.'

'No, but I do think that's possible. You're carrying around all this resentment and guilt about your father – about your sister, too, apparently. I'm no shrink, but –'

'That's right, you're not.'

'I'm just trying to help.'

'I'm not a mental case.'

'Melanie . . .'

'If you didn't believe me, you should've said so in the first place. I could've come by myself.' Her voice climbed higher, trembling. 'I don't need this. It's hard enough . . .' She inhaled with a sob. 'Forget it.'

'Hey, come on,' Bodie said softly.

She got up, squeezed between the two seats, and disappeared into the rear of the van.

Good work, Bodie thought. He sighed.

Christ, you can't win.

You'd think she would jump at the possibility that her vision was a false alarm. Does she *want* it to be true?

We're talking about her father or sister biting it, for Christsake.

Yeah, maybe she does want it true. In the back of her mind. Wishful thinking. All right for *you*, Dad. You had it coming – let Mom drown, then married a tramp young enough to be your daughter. Take *that*, Pen. That'll teach you – think you can get away with looking like a goddamn Playmate of the Year?

I've gotta see this Pen.

I'll bet you do, Melanie said, her voice bitter in his mind.

She wants them to pay.

Vengeance is sweet, and a whole lot sweeter if you're there to see it happen, arrange for a little telepathic connection so you can feel their agony as their bodies get smashed.

Bodies smashed. Now that's convenient, isn't it? What did she say? It was noisy and running at her, and too fast for her to get out of the way. Like a car or a train. Some kind of vehicle.

That'll smash you up pretty good. Disfigurement. The gorgeous sister who always got the guys – maybe some guys

31

you wanted for yourself – gets nailed by a car. The Playmate of the Year body turned to a broken pile of gore. Take *that*, you bitch. *Now* who's the pretty one?

Bodie didn't like the way his thoughts were going. He turned the radio on. Dolly Parton, 'Singles Bars and Single Women'. He left the volume low to keep the sound from disturbing Melanie.

Maybe she'll fall asleep back there. Sleep, that knits the raveled sleeve of care. She could use it. A couple of hours of forgetting about her damned vision.

Maybe we shouldn't have called.

Especially her sister.

That made it a whole lot worse, finding out that Pen wasn't home, either.

Where was she? Maybe out at a movie or something. But maybe Pen had been notified of her father's accident and she'd left her place to be with him. At the hospital. At the morgue.

Or the reverse: Pen the victim, her father the one called away from home.

One way or the other. That's why nobody answered.

I'm as bad as she is, Bodie thought. Face it, I'm half expecting the vision to turn out real.

If it wasn't telepathy or something, it was a mental blowout and Melanie's running on a flat.

For her sake, it better be real.

You don't want that, either.

What you've got here, old pal, is one of your basic no-win situations.

Heads you've lost your dad or sister, tails you've lost your mind.

Not me, Melanie. I'm just along for the ride.

Don't you wish.

She's part of me, like it or not. Her problems are my problems. It got that way, somehow.

When he first saw Melanie, she was walking toward him with her books clutched to her chest, her head down, a frown on her face. It was a sunny Friday, late enough in the afternoon so that most classes were over and everyone around the campus seemed cheerful and relaxed. Everyone except this girl mourning over the cracks in the walkway.

Bodie felt sorry for her. He also felt intrigued. She looked lovely, fragile – ethereal – and quite obviously down in the dumps.

Badly in need of rescue.

She was still several yards ahead of him, still gazing at the walk, and he knew she would pass him without looking up.

So he fished a quarter out of his pocket. He gave it an underhand toss. It clinked on the concrete, bounced, landed on its edge and rolled in a crazy zig-zag toward the girl. Bodie knew, from the slight side-to-side motions of her head, that she was watching the quarter's approach. As it took a swerve to the right, she lengthened her stride. Her sandal slapped it flat. Her frown was gone when she raised her face and met Bodie's eyes. She looked rather satisfied with herself – pleased that she had succeeded in halting the runaway coin.

'Thanks,' he said. 'It got away from me.'

She didn't say a word. She was now looking edgy. Maybe feeling intimidated because she was a freshman – so obviously a freshman – and he was old enough to be a grad student or even an instructor. She took one step backward.

Bodie crouched to pick up the quarter.

She wore a knee-length skirt. She had slim, pale legs. They

had no tan at all. Their whiteness made them seem blatantly naked.

Bodie had a difficult time forcing his gaze away from them.

He peeled the quarter off the sidewalk, and stood.

The girl's face was red. One of her fine, black eyebrows was curled upward in a pretty good imitation of a question mark. Bodie guessed that she had noticed the inspection of her legs.

I'm done for, he thought.

The girl sidestepped, ready to be on her way.

Bodie sidestepped, too.

'Excuse me,' she said. Her voice trembled. 'Please, I'm in a hurry.' She stepped the other way. Again, Bodie blocked her.

She gave up trying to dodge past him. Standing still, she looked into his eyes and caught her lower lip between her teeth.

'I'm sorry if I upset you,' he said.

'I'm not upset.'

'And I was *not* staring at your legs,' he added.

'There's nothing *wrong* with my legs,' she said.

'Really?' He didn't know why he said that. He could think of nothing else to say.

'My legs are fine,' she insisted.

'And dandy,' Bodie said. 'They're a couple of the dandiest legs I've seen in a long time.'

'Yeah, I'll bet.' She watched him with narrowed eyes.

Either she has a leg problem that I didn't notice, Bodie thought, or her self-image needs an overhaul.

'In fact,' he said, 'I couldn't help wondering what the rest of them looked like.'

'I've only got the two.'

'That isn't what I . . .' He realized she had made a joke.

Taken totally by surprise, he burst out laughing. The girl didn't laugh, but a corner of her mouth turned up in a rather wry half-smile.

'I've got this-here quarter,' Bodie said. He flipped it in the air and caught it. 'What-say we mosey over to the student union and I'll buy you a Dr Pepper?'

She accepted the offer.

It started that way: a tossed coin, a look at her legs, a misunderstanding, and a joke that made things right.

Melanie seemed perplexed that he found her attractive. She made nervous jokes about being skinny and plain.

The next night at the drive-in, when he fumbled under the back of her blouse to unhook her bra, she said, 'You'll be sorry.' He said, 'Don't be ridiculous.' He got it open and reached around to the front and she grabbed his wrist. 'Don't,' she said. She was weeping, her tears making silver slicks down her face in the light from the movie screen. 'It's padded,' she sobbed. 'So?' She let go of his hand. He moved it to her breast. 'See?' she asked. And Bodie said, 'That's not so bad, Herman.' She laughed through her sobs, and elbowed him. The breast was warm and smooth. It wasn't large, but it filled his hand. The nipple felt very big. The other breast was the same. His hand wandered from one to the other. He wanted them in his mouth, but when he tried to unbutton her blouse, Melanie stopped him. 'Not here,' she gasped. They left the drive-in and Bodie drove to his apartment.

When he opened the door, she stood rigid and gazed into the dark room with wide, frightened eyes. Bodie took her hand. It felt like ice. It trembled. 'Nothing to worry about,' he said, and led her inside. He turned on the lights.

'I don't know about this,' she said. Her voice sounded high and tight.

'Neither do I,' Bodie said to calm her down. 'Let's just watch some TV.'

A quick, jerking nod.

'We don't have to do anything,' he told her.

'Okay.'

He turned on the television. Leaving Melanie on the sofa, he went into the kitchen and poured wine. Then he sat down beside her. She used both hands on her glass, trying to hold it steady. As she took a sip, she watched Bodie raise his glass. They both saw the surface of his wine shimmer. He was shaking a little, himself.

'What are *you* so nervous about?' Melanie asked.

'Who, me?'

'Yeah, you.'

They stared into each other's eyes. For a long time.

'We *don't* have to do anything,' she told him. Smiling, she set her glass on the table.

Bodie put down his glass.

They kissed. They held each other. She was trembling, but she was the one who eased *him* down onto the sofa. They lay on their sides, their bodies together. She still trembled, but she untucked his shirt and unbuttoned it and spread it open and caressed his chest. Bodie followed her lead. Soon, they were both bare to the waist. Bodie kissed her mouth, her eyes, her long neck with its black velvet choker. He stroked and held and squeezed her breasts while her hands roamed his back.

Her hands didn't venture below Bodie's belt. He abided by the unspoken rule, and kept his own hands from straying lower on Melanie.

He realized, soon, that this was as far as Melanie was willing to take it. The lower half was out of bounds. Squirm and rub, but hands off and clothes on.

He realized something else.

Melanie was a virgin.

She had to be.

The lower half wasn't just out of bounds, it was not even on the map.

Bodie would be her first.

If he could just get her pants off . . . That might not be easy, though.

Better not try it.

Maybe tomorrow night, or . . .

Melanie's hand pushed under his belt. Her cool fingers curled around his penis.

My God, he thought.

As her fingers slid, he opened the waist of her corduroys.

The corduroys ended up beneath her. Bodie didn't know it. He didn't know much of anything. He was dazed above her, inside her at last but only partway, holding back, aching with the feel of her slick tightness hugging him, needing in all the way but holding back, not wanting to hurt her though her fingers dug into his buttocks, urging him deeper and she panted, 'Harder . . . In . . . Push!' And, at last, he pushed. Flinching rigid, Melanie gasped, 'Oh!' in a high hurt voice and thrust up against him. He went deep. All the way. All of him inside and it was past bearing and he erupted, throbbing and pumping.

She held him. She stroked his hair. She wouldn't let him up. He mumbled lazily about not wanting to crush her, but she told him not to worry about it.

Bodie fell asleep. When he woke up, he was still on top of Melanie. He was still inside her. He felt *glued* to her. 'I think we're stuck,' he said.

'Good.' She smiled and kissed the tip of his nose.

'I think we really *are* stuck.'

'Something must've dried.'

He pulled free as gently as he could, but it hurt her. Her lips peeled back with pain.

Bodie looked down. 'Not a pretty sight.'

Melanie sat up. She looked. 'Yuck.'

'I guess we'd better take a shower.'

They took a shower. Bodie, Melanie, and Melanie's corduroy pants. When they were finished, only the cords were still bloodstained. 'They'll never be the same,' Bodie said.

Melanie smiled. 'Neither will I.'

She's part of me, like it or not. Her problems are my problems. It got that way very fast and maybe not on purpose, but that's how it is and that's why I'm driving through the desert night with a psychic or a nut case in the back of the van.

'I'm sorry,' she said near his ear.

He felt a rush of affection.

'Forgive me?' she asked.

'You had every right to be upset.'

She eased forward between the seats and rested a hand on Bodie's thigh. He looked at her. The bare arm led to a bare shoulder. Below the shoulder was the mound of a breast. A small breast, its nipple large and dark. 'Why don't you find a place to pull off the freeway?' she suggested.

'Are you sure?'

The answer was Melanie's hand sliding to his groin.

Bodie started looking for an off-ramp.

Chapter Five

After a quick shower to get rid of the wine smell, Pen dried herself with a fresh towel. She put a bandage on her scraped thigh, slipped into her moccasins, and put her robe on. Then she picked up the empty glass and the wine bottle.

Polish it off, she thought, and maybe you'll be able to sleep.

You'll sleep, all right. You'll be dead to the world, and maybe that's not such a grand plan.

You might even have a visitor.

Don't even *think* about that.

I'd damn well better think about that. He has my phone number, so he must have my address. It's right there in the directory for him. The answering machine is off, so he knows I'm here. What if he decides to come over?

They don't do that, she told herself, and opened the bathroom door. She walked quickly to the kitchen and put the wine bottle into the refrigerator. Then she rinsed out her glass at the sink.

Crank callers don't pay visits.

Who says so?

Fictional cops. In books, on TV, in the movies. *He's just a crank caller, ma'am. No reason to be alarmed. These guys who get their jollies phoning up women, they're timid mice afraid of their own shadows. That's how come they use the phone, 'cause it's anonymous and safe. You've got nothing to worry about.*

That's what they say, those fictional cops. And the next thing you know, the caller who's a timid mouse is sneaking through the gal's house with a butcher knife, intent upon carving her up.

Pen turned off the faucet. She set the glass in the sink. As she dried her hands, she looked across the kitchen. In the dining area stood her table surrounded by four sturdy, straight-backed chairs.

She carried one of them into the living room, moved her umbrella aside, and tilted the chair backward, wedging its top rail under the doorknob.

'That'll slow him down,' she muttered.

She didn't need to check the windows; they'd been closed and latched since last weekend. With dowel rods in the runners to keep the windows from being slid open, they were secure.

Real secure, she thought. Glass.

If he wants in badly enough . . .

He would have to be crazy. There are fifteen other apartments in this complex, all with windows facing the courtyard and pool. If he smashes a window – if I scream – someone will hear.

Would anyone come to help?

Probably. Manny Hammond, for instance. There's a guy would jump at the chance to rush to my rescue. Wouldn't that be wonderful. Better him than nobody, I suppose. By a small margin.

Pen returned to the kitchen. The butcher block on her counter held eight knives. She took the two largest knives into her bedroom. She placed one on the nightstand. Crouching, she set the other on the carpet just beneath the edge of her bed.

In case we end up on the floor . . .

Are you serious? she wondered.

Must be, I'm doing it.

She realized that she didn't want to leave the nightstand knife in plain sight. She took a copy of *Publishers Weekly* from her magazine stand and spread it open on top of the weapon.

Okay, you're in good shape now.

You're in good shape, all right, if paranoia's good shape. You're acting totally bonkers.

Yeah? Better safe than – her mind flashed a picture of the coroner's slide, the naked woman face-down on the autopsy table, buttocks purple. *World's worst hickey*.

One more knife, she decided, and returned to the kitchen for it. She placed this knife on the floor beneath the other side of the bed.

Back in the living room, she unplugged her stereo and removed its extension cord. Kneeling in her bedroom entryway, she ran an end of the cord through the gap between the door and the frame, over the top of the lower hinge. She brought the plug back through under the hinge, made a knot, and yanked. The cord held firm. She drew it across the doorway and tied its other end around the rear leg of her dresser.

Standing, she admired her work.

'Have a nice trip,' she said.

What else might she . . . ?

Isn't this *enough*? I'm certifiable.

This is enough, she decided.

She turned off the bedroom lights.

Other lights in her apartment were still on. She had intended to leave them on. But the dark line of her trip cord was plainly visible across the bottom of the doorway.

It won't do much good if he can see it.

Pen stepped over the cord and made her way through the apartment.

She wished she could leave all the rooms bright. But darkness would work against him in more ways than just hiding the cord.

41

You really are expecting him to show up?

No, not really. All right, yes. Yes, I think he'll show up. Maybe.

She'd been raped once. She didn't intend to let it ever happen again.

Maybe I should get the hell out of here.

She stepped over the cord. She sat on the edge of her bed.

I could drive over to Dad's house and spend the night there. Or go over to a friend's. Abby or Jane or Loretta – any one of them would be glad to let me stay. I can't just barge in, though. I'd have to call first. Plug in a phone, call, get dressed, go out in the rain.

What'll that solve? she asked herself.

It'll get me through the night.

But what about tomorrow night and the night after that?

'Fuck it,' she muttered.

If he's going to come, let him come.

She got up and turned off the lights. She took off her robe, draped it over a chair, slipped out of her moccasins, and climbed into bed. The cool, smooth sheets felt wonderful. The heat of her body warmed them. Snuggling, she buried her face in her pillow.

You're *really* planning to sleep in the raw?

I always do.

This isn't always. You want to be starkers when he jumps you?

If. *If.*

Pen felt cozy. She didn't want to leave the comfort of the bed. But she forced herself to sit up, turn on the bedside lamp, and swing her feet to the floor.

There was a naked woman in the mirror, walking toward Pen. Her face made a mocking snarl, a lip curling up, baring teeth.

'Yeah, I know, it's all your fault.'

The rotten bastard doesn't even know what I look like, she thought. He probably picked my name at random. I could be a refugee from the ugly farm, he'd still be giving me grief.

I'm a woman, that's all he cares about.

A pair of breasts and a vagina.

I want to talk to you . . .

A chill squirmed up her body.

She bent and tugged open a drawer. She pulled out a pair of powder blue silk pajamas. She put them on, the cool fabric sliding over her skin like oil. Clinging, revealing.

Better than her nightgowns, though.

A lot better than nothing at all.

She rubbed her arms, feeling the goosebumps through the slick fabric.

The woman in the mirror sneered at her, obviously disgusted with the whole situation.

Pen took off the pajamas and put them back into the drawer. She opened the top drawer, saw that she was down to her last four pairs of good panties, and searched near the back of the drawer until she found some old ones. They were ragged and the elastic was limp. Perfect.

She found an old, frayed bra and put it on. Then a pair of jeans. Calvins. The tightest jeans she owned.

So tight they peeled the bandage off her thigh.

She fastened them.

The woman in the mirror rolled her eyes upward. *You're a clown*.

Okay, I'm a clown.

She put on a baggy blue sweatshirt.

Her tightly encased legs made it hard to bend over, but she managed, and put on socks. Then she crossed to her closet and took out a pair of cowboy boots. She put them on. They had pointed toes. Great for kicking.

Looking down at herself, she shook her head.

Thank God I'm alone. Bad enough that *I* know I've flipped out.

Dressed like this, she wasn't about to get inside her sheets. She remade her bed, leaving the pillow out, then turned off the lights and lay down. On her back.

Great. Like taking a nap on the couch.

Bonkers.

So what's the alternative? Pretend nothing's wrong? *Don't* brace the front door, *don't* booby-trap the bedroom entrance, *don't* arm myself? Curl up naked and cozy under the sheets as if there isn't a guy out there who maybe wants to rape me?

She closed her eyes. Her lids felt spring-loaded. Keeping them shut took an effort. She pulled the pillow over her face. Folded her hands on her belly.

I'll never fall asleep this way, she thought.

Maybe that's best.

I can catch up on my sleep tomorrow after sunrise. I'll be safe once it's daylight. Just lie here and relax. Try to think pleasant thoughts, fat chance.

Instead of pleasant thoughts, Pen found herself wondering whether there were any other precautions she might take. Call the police? They'd probably tell her to get an unlisted number. But that wouldn't stop the creep from dropping by when he got the urge.

If I just had a gun.

Well, you don't.

Maybe pick one up tomorrow.

There's a waiting period for handguns, she knew from story research. About two weeks.

But I could walk out of a store tomorrow with a shotgun. I think. Yeah, the waiting period only applies to pistols, doesn't it?

So buy a shotgun.

Then what? Sleep with it?

Yeah . . .

Pen opened her eyes. She was curled on her side, legs spread out as if she were running. The leg on the bottom was numb. The tight jeans had cut off its circulation.

She didn't remember turning onto her side. Had she fallen asleep? Opening her eyes, she squinted at the lighted face of the alarm clock. Three-thirty.

Asleep, all right, but not for long enough.

Her leg tingled painfully as she rolled onto her back.

She shut her eyes again.

And heard a footstep. Her heart slammed her breath away. She lay rigid, listening. She heard only the thud of her heart. Then another quiet, scraping step. Not inside the apartment, but on the concrete walkway just outside her window.

The window was above her face.

She rolled, dropped her knees to the floor, and slid the knife out from under the magazine. Still on her knees, she crept away from the bed. She rose to her feet and leaned against the wall at the far end of the window.

With one finger, she eased out the edge of the curtain a fraction of an inch. No face. She widened the gap enough to see out with both eyes.

Someone was there, all right.

She took a breath so deep that her chest strained against her bra and she heard a quiet ripping sound from somewhere along the back of the garment. She let the air out slowly. Very tired all of a sudden, she leaned her shoulder against the wall. She continued to peer out the window.

So much for your lurking degenerate, she thought.

At the door of the corner apartment, only a couple of yards beyond the end of Pen's long window, Alicia Bonner was wrapped around her boyfriend. The eighteen-year-old girl, who apparently took her fashion cues from the *Mad Max* movies, wore boots that made quiet, shuffling sounds on the walkway as she adjusted her stance against the apartment door.

The overhang of the roof sheltered Alicia and her friend from the rain.

One of Alicia's hands shoved under the belt at the rear of the guy's jeans. She squirmed, her thighs hugging his upthrust leg.

My big hard cock and your hot juicy cunt . . .

There should be a way to erase your mind, Pen thought. Rewind, press a button, and erase the voice as easily as you might remove it from magnetic tape.

Patent it, you'd make a bundle.

She heard whispers through her window.

How long are they going to be at it?

As long as it takes. Right.

Pen put the knife on the table, lay down on her bed, drew the pillow down over her face, and sighed.

As long as they stay out there, she realized, I don't need to worry about my friend.

Friend?

Go to sleep.

In spite of the pillow over her head, she could hear the rain, sometimes a shuffling boot, sometimes a whisper.

Thanks for the sentry duty, kids.

She found herself relaxing, easing toward sleep.

Gotta pee.

Not too badly yet. But better get it over with.

Moaning, she forced herself to climb out of bed. She unbuttoned her jeans as she crossed the dark room, and was pulling the zipper down when her boot stopped in mid-stride.

Oh, yeah.

The trip cord.

Oh, shit.

Her other foot flew forward to catch her, but the cord hooked it back.

Both feet snagged, she yelped and threw out her arms as she dived through the doorway. The far wall of the corridor pounded a forearm aside and smashed the top of her head.

Stars. A galaxy. Whirling bright.

Ringing. Pen heard ringing.

I'd better get the phone.

But somebody was digging a fork into her brain through a neat round hole in her skull. Prodding around, prying out bite-size chunks of gray matter.

I'd better get the phone while I still have enough brains left to . . .

Wait. I killed the phones.

Him.

How does he make the phones ring when they're not plugged in?

It's not the phones, it's the doorbell.

Her stomach clenched. Her heart hammered, shooting bolts of pain through her head.

Groaning, she clutched the top of her head.

No hole there. A tender lump the size of a split golf ball.

The ringing stopped.

Pen opened her eyes. The hallway was dim with the vague blue-gray gloom of early morning.

She was sprawled belly-down on the floor, her cheek itchy against the carpet. She pushed herself up to her hands and knees, squeezing her eyes tight as pain surged through her head.

You're lucky you didn't kill yourself, the way . . .

Sounds from the front door. Someone trying the knob? A scrape and click of metal against metal.

Pen unhooked her feet from the trip cord and thrust herself up. She leaped it, rushed across her room and snatched the knife off the nightstand. Her head pounded. The back of her neck had burning steel rods that rammed into the base of her brain with each step as she ran, jumped the cord, and sprinted down the corridor to the living room.

The front door was open!

Only a few inches, but enough to admit the hand.

The hand was clutching the back of the chair, shaking it, trying to work it out from under the knob.

Chapter Six

'Hurry!'

'I'm trying.'

'Let me try.'

'I'm getting it.'

'Come *on*.'

With his left hand on the outside knob, Bodie pulled the door tight against his right arm. The chair inside slipped down a bit. He tugged at it. He was pretty sure he could get it out of the way, but he wondered what Melanie would ask him to do about the security chain. Kick the door open and rip its mounting from the wall?

Then came a thud of footfalls. Someone charging toward the other side of the door.

'You bastard!'

He lurched back against Melanie, jerked his arm from the gap. A long blade jabbed out. He stumbled backward as fast as the blade approached him. Almost. Its point nicked his side.

His feet tangled with Melanie's. He fell against her. The bars of the balcony's guard rail rang as Melanie hit them.

An arm in the blue sleeve of a sweatshirt waved the knife, blindly slicing the air.

'Pen!' Melanie blurted.

The arm stopped. The blade tilted upward. The arm withdrew from the opening. A moment later, half a face appeared in the gap, a single eye staring out through strands of blond hair. And lower, one breast in the same blue sweatshirt worn by the knife-wielding arm.

'Melanie?'

The half-face and breast went away. The door shut. Bodie heard the chair bump the door, heard the security chain rattle. Then the door swung open wide.

This is the Playmate of the Year? Bodie thought. This is the Weird Sister. Double, double toil and trouble . . .

At least she had put down the knife. Trembling fingers parted the hair away from her face. She muttered, 'My God, I could've killed you.'

'Just a flesh wound, ma'am,' he drawled. Holding his side, he got to his feet.

Pen bent forward and looked around as if to see whether anyone had witnessed the assault. 'Come in,' she whispered.

Bodie held back and let Melanie enter first. Pen shut the door behind him. She leaned against it. She looked haggard, distracted. 'I don't . . . I'm so sorry. I don't know what to say.'

'What's going on?' Melanie asked.

She shrugged. Her jeans were open, smooth skin showing above a triangle of white panties. She seemed to realize this at the same moment as Bodie. She raised the zipper and buttoned the waist. 'I had some trouble,' she murmured. She rubbed the back of her neck. 'Come on, we'd better get a bandage.'

They followed her into a short corridor. Passing a bedroom, Bodie saw an electrical cord stretched across the bottom of the doorway.

What the hell is going on? he thought.

In the bathroom, she asked him to sit down and take off his shirt. He lowered the toilet cover and sat on it. As he removed his shirt, Pen took disinfectant and a tin of Band-aids out of the medicine cabinet. She moistened a washcloth at the sink.

'I'll do that,' Melanie said.

Crouching beside him, she cleaned away the blood and pressed the balled cloth to his cut. With his arm raised, Bodie watched. She took the cloth away. There was a quarter-inch gash below his last rib. Blood welled out. Melanie covered it again.

Pen unwrapped a Band-aid. 'I don't understand,' she said in a haggard voice. 'What are you doing here?'

'I had a vision,' Melanie explained.

Pen frowned. 'Of me?'

'I'm not sure.' She lifted the washcloth and squirted disinfectant onto the wound. The cool spray made Bodie flinch. As blood began to trickle out again, she took the bandage from her sister and pressed it firmly in place. 'There,' she said.

'Thanks.'

'You came all the way from Phoenix . . . because of a *vision*?'

'That's right.' Melanie stood up. 'This is Bodie, by the way.'

'I'm sorry I hurt you, Bodie,' she said, looking so sorry that he feared she might begin to cry.

'No sweat.'

'I thought you were . . . someone else.'

'Who?' Melanie asked.

'I don't know. I got these calls last night. Obscene calls.' She turned away. She reached into the medicine cabinet, took down a bottle of prescription pills, apparently realized her mistake, put that bottle back and slipped her fingers around the plastic bottle beside it. Aspirin. After filling a cup with water, she swallowed four of the tablets. 'I'm such a wreck,' she muttered. 'I smashed my head up.'

Melanie met Bodie's eyes. 'See? Didn't I tell you?' She turned to Pen. 'I knew you were in some kind of terrible trouble. My vision – it was like the one I had when Mom drowned.'

'Well, I'm not dead, anyway. Though that might be preferable, the way I feel right now.' She made a smile that was very much like a grimace. Rubbing her face, she said, 'Have you two eaten?'

'We drove straight through,' Bodie said. Except for an hour parked on a desolate road – a stop, he suspected, that had to do with Melanie wanting him properly satisfied before his encounter with the gorgeous sister.

'Why don't I get us some breakfast?'

As they headed for the kitchen, Melanie noticed the cord across the bedroom entrance. 'What's that?' she asked.

'A precaution. I was . . . I managed to convince myself he'd break in. Last night.'

'The caller?'

'Yeah.'

'Was it someone you know?'

'I don't think so.'

They entered the kitchen.

'Just an anonymous obscene phone caller?'

'*Just*?'

'They're usually harmless,' Melanie pointed out.

'So I've heard.'

'How did you get hurt?' Bodie asked.

'I tripped on the wire. Hoist on my own petard,' she added, a wry smile lifting a corner of her mouth. 'Bacon and eggs?'

'Great. I'm starving.'

Melanie nodded, crouched, and took a pan out of the cupboard.

Pen took out a coffee filter.

'I can make the coffee,' Bodie told her. 'Why don't you sit down and relax?'

'Sitting down won't help, I'm afraid. What I need is about twelve hours of sleep.' Her trembling hand spilled some coffee grounds onto the counter as she dumped scoopsful into the filter. 'I'm so wasted.' She frowned. '*You* two must be exhausted. You drove all night, and . . .' Her voice just stopped as if the rest of her sentence wasn't worth the effort.

'Let's get some food in us first,' Melanie said. She started peeling off strips of bacon and arranging them in the skillet. 'Why don't you tell us what happened?'

Pen emptied a container of water into the top of her coffee machine. Then she leaned against the counter. She rubbed the back of her neck again. 'Like I said, I got these obscene phone calls.'

'What did the guy say?' Melanie asked.

Pen glanced at Bodie, and lowered her eyes. 'Never mind what he said. It was pretty bad.'

'What did *you* say?'

'Nothing. He was on my answering machine.'

Melanie lit up. 'You've got him on tape?'

'Yeah.'

'Fabulous. Let's hear what he had to say.'

Pen shook her head.

Bodie frowned. '*We* called you last night. Mel did.' He looked at Melanie. 'You didn't get the answering machine, did you?'

'No.'

'What time was that?' Pen asked.

'Around ten, your time.'

'Ten?' She moaned. 'That was you? I'd turned off the answering machine by then. I was taking a bath. I thought you were *him*. So I got out and disconnected the . . .' She frowned. 'Did you call twice?'

'Just once,' Melanie said.

Pen's lip curled up.

Melanie turned on the burner under the skillet. 'So what happened after you disconnected the phones?'

'That's when I got to thinking he might come over.'

'What made you think that?'

'Why *shouldn't* I think that? He made it pretty plain that he wanted to . . . mess with me.'

'But that kind of guy almost never . . .'

53

'*Almost*. I know. But maybe this guy is the exception. I mean, he had my phone number so he obviously had my address. Anyway, I decided to be ready for him. That's why I blocked the door and strung that damn cord. Just to be ready, you know? Just in case. That's why I had the knife. So in the middle of the night I forgot about the cord and took a header into the wall.'

She looked sideways at the coffee machine. The glass pot was full. She took mugs down from a cupboard. Her hand trembled badly as she filled them. She gave a mug to Bodie.

'Do you still think the guy might come over?' he asked.

She shrugged. 'What's to stop him?'

'We're here now. I guess Mel's vision paid off.'

'Yeah,' Pen said. 'It was right on target this time.'

'We'll keep watch for you,' Melanie said. 'You can sleep all day if you want.'

'I may have to.'

When breakfast was done, Melanie and her friend both insisted that she get some sleep. She went into the bathroom and drank a glassful of Alka-Seltzer. When she came out, Bodie was kneeling in her bedroom doorway, removing the cord.

'Don't worry about anything,' he told her.

She thanked him. Then she turned to Melanie and hugged her tightly. 'It's great to see you again, kiddo.' She ruffled Melanie's hair.

Alone in her room with the door shut, she turned back the covers of her bed. The sheets looked wonderful. There was no need any more for the confining, protective clothes. She took them off. Because of Bodie being in the apartment, however, she put on pajamas before crawling into bed.

She eased the pillow over her eyes to block out the morning

light. Her neck felt stiff, but her head no longer ached badly. The food and aspirin had helped. She took a deep breath. She felt pretty good, considering.

Her ordeal was over, at least for now. Maybe it was over for good.

She had over-reacted, that's for sure.

Damn near cracked her skull. Damn near broke her neck. Damn near stabbed Bodie.

I *did* stab him.

He was very nice about it.

Nice guy.

Lucky Mel.

Lucky me, having them both here.

But how long would they stay? She hadn't asked. They'd have to go back to school soon, maybe even tomorrow.

Don't worry about that now.

Nothing to worry about now.

She rolled over, the pajamas sliding against her skin, the covers up around her neck, and fell asleep.

'Do you think we can both fit on the couch?' Bodie asked.

'Who can sleep?'

'Me,' he said. 'I'm beat. *I* didn't sack out in the van for the last half of the trip, remember?'

'I don't know about you, but I want to hear the tape.'

'I don't think Pen would want us to.'

'She doesn't have to find out.'

Bodie sat on the couch. He patted the cushion beside him. 'I'll talk dirty to you.'

'Not funny. Whatever the guy said, it scared the hell out of her. I've never seen her like this.'

'I thought maybe she was *always* maniacal.'

'Come on.'

Bodie stood up. His heart pounded fast and he stood motionless, waiting for a light-headed feeling to pass.

'You okay?'

'My body's telling me to sack out.'

'So sack out,' Melanie told him, sounding a trifle annoyed. 'I'll listen to the tape alone.'

'That's all right. I'm up.'

He followed her. She wandered around the apartment, searching for the machine. Apparently, Pen hadn't owned it when Melanie was living with her. Finally, she led the way into an office next to Pen's bedroom. The answering machine was on the desk. Empty.

Melanie scowled at it. 'The cassette's gotta be around here someplace,' she whispered.

She searched the waste basket.

Bodie found the cassette on the carpet at the far end of the room. He turned it in his hand. It didn't look damaged.

'Close the door,' Melanie whispered.

He quietly shut the door and returned to the desk. Melanie slipped the cassette into the up-tilted holder and snapped it into place. She rewound the tape. And played it.

'Hello, honey. Sorry you're away . . .'

Melanie turned the volume lower.

The voice sounded nasty. It would've sounded nasty reading a McDonald's menu, Bodie thought. But the things it said . . . He pictured Pen listening, imagined how she must have felt. Alone in the apartment. Exposed to the sick mind of a stranger, violated and scared.

The tape only permitted a brief message. But the bastard had time to tell her what he wanted to do before a beep cut him off mid-sentence.

'I don't see what she was so upset about,' Melanie muttered. 'Just your standard obscene . . .'

'How'd you like it if I stuck my . . .'

'This is really sick,' Bodie whispered over the continuing voice.

'It's not *that* bad,' Melanie said. 'Pen's gotta be nuts to let this stuff upset her so much. I've had some bad calls. They never freaked *me* out like that.'

The guy's time ran out, but he called again. 'Suck me, honey. Open up wide. Suck me off. I want to come in your mouth. I want to shoot my load down your throat. Come on, open up. Open wide, you whore. Yes, yes. Take me in, swallow my cock and – *beeeeep.*'

Three down, one to go.

Bodie took a deep breath.

The fourth message started.

'Pen, it's Joyce. Your father's been in a terrible accident. I'm at the emergency room of the Beverlywood Medical Center on Pico. You'd better get here as soon as you can.'

Chapter Seven

Pen struggled awake. Someone was knocking on her door. Why was her door shut, and who . . . ? She remembered. Melanie's here. And her boyfriend, Bodie. The guy I stabbed.

What if I'd killed him?

She seemed to shrink inside.

The door opened and Melanie's face appeared in the gap. She looked hurt and confused. 'You'd better get dressed.'

'What's wrong?'

'We listened to the tape.'

Pen's throat went tight. 'Well, damn it, thanks a bunch. You and Bodie both?'

'Joyce was on it.'

'Huh?'

'On your tape. Dad's been hurt. They took him to an emergency room. Joyce didn't say how he was, just that he'd been in a terrible accident.'

'God. Oh, no.'

'We'd better get over there.'

'Yeah. Yeah. I'll just be a minute.'

The door shut.

Pen sprang from the bed. She flung her pajamas off.

An accident. Dad.

In a daze, she took panties from her drawer and stepped into them. She was still pulling them up as she rushed to her closet. She tugged a pair of white slacks off a hanger, put them on, and grabbed the nearest blouse. It was burgundy, silken, too dressy for the slacks. She didn't care. She put it on and pushed her feet into sandals while she fastened the buttons. She let the blouse hang out. She zipped her pants on the way to the door.

'. . . call her,' Bodie was saying as she entered the living room. 'She could tell you how he's doing.'

'I guess.'

'Call Joyce?' Pen asked. 'Yeah.' She turned back and went into the kitchen. Her disconnected telephone was still on top of the refrigerator. She pulled it down and plugged it into the wall. With a shaky hand, she dialed. Melanie appeared beside her.

A busy signal.

She hung up. 'It's busy.'

Melanie, closing her eyes, let out a long breath as if having the news postponed was a blessing.

Pen drew the girl gently against her. Melanie's arms went around her and she rested her forehead against the side of Pen's neck. Her breath felt hot through the blouse. 'Don't worry, okay?'

'I'm scared.'

'So am I.'

'What if he's dead?'

'He's not. Joyce would've said so.' But my phones were unplugged, Pen thought. Joyce might've tried to call back. 'Come on, Mel. Let's go.' She eased the girl away. 'Do you know where they took him?'

'The Beverlywood Medical Center.'

'Okay. It's not far.'

They hurried down to the front of the apartment building. Bodie offered to drive. His blue van was parked at the curb. Pen rode in the passenger seat and gave directions, while Melanie crouched behind the gap and hung onto the seat backs.

The numbness in Pen wouldn't pass. None of this seemed real.

'Make a right on Pico,' she said.

When Pen finally saw the hospital at the end of the next block, she felt as if she were in an elevator and its floor had dropped out from under her feet.

'That's it,' she gasped.

Bodie swung his van to the curb. 'Is this close enough?'

'Fine,' Melanie said.

It's as close as I ever want to get, Pen thought.

They climbed out. Bodie fed the meter. Melanie took his hand, and Pen led the way.

The morning sky was deep blue. The mild breeze, smelling fresh after last night's rain, drifted Pen's blouse against her skin. She noticed that it felt good, and she wondered how anything could feel good at this moment with her stomach clenched and her shaking legs barely able to hold her up – with her father in the building up ahead . . .

He has to be alive. He has to be. Please.

A woman approaching, pushing a baby stroller.

He always wanted a grandchild.

Only a week ago, he'd said, 'I'm not getting any younger, you know. Why don't you go out like a good daughter and get yourself knocked up?'

Pen's throat tightened. Her eyes started to burn.

Christ now, don't cry.

He's all right, damn it.

Don't fall apart in front of Melanie. Hold it together.

She glanced back. Melanie was holding Bodie's hand and gazing at the sidewalk. Bodie met her eyes. She wondered how he must feel, finding himself in the middle of a family tragedy. Probably wishing he'd never left Phoenix. First he gets stabbed, now this.

At the corner, Pen turned toward the crosswalk. She pushed a button on the light post to activate the WALK sign, and waited. Across Pico Boulevard was a driveway marked 'Ambulance Entrance'. A police car was parked at the curb.

The WALK sign went green. She stepped off the curb and a hand clamped her shoulder from behind. It jerked her to a halt. A red blur steaked by, roaring, hitting her with its slipstream. As she staggered backwards a step, she saw the low rear-end of a speeding Porsche.

'Asshole ran the red light,' Bodie muttered.

Pen turned to him. He took his hand off her shoulder. 'Thanks. Guess I'd better watch where I'm going.'

Melanie had a hand pressed to her heart. She looked wide-eyed and breathless as if someone had just jumped at her in the dark.

'You okay?' Pen asked her.

She nodded.

The DON'T WALK sign was already flashing, so they waited through another cycle of the traffic lights. When the WALK sign returned, Pen checked the intersection before leaving the curb.

On the other side, she headed for the ambulance driveway, realized she shouldn't try entering there, and turned around in confusion. She shrugged, stepped past Bodie and Melanie, and spotted a doorway facing Beverly Drive.

Her numbness seemed to spread and deepen as the glass doors parted.

She stepped into a reception room. A young woman gnawing her lower lip glanced nervously at her and looked away. She was on a bench, holding the hand of a tow-head no older than five who was bent forward to peer at a black woman with a bloody rag wrapped around her arm. The black woman, on a chair along the far wall, held her arm and rocked herself back and forth, humming softly. She had a blank look in her eyes. The child stopped staring at her long enough to eye the three new arrivals, apparently checking them for injuries.

Pen turned to the office enclosure on her left. Through the glass partition, she saw two women in white uniforms. One was seated at a desk. The other, heavy and wearing her brown hair in a Prince Valiant cut, looked up from her paperwork, smiled at Pen, and approached the window.

Pen froze.

She was here – a few steps, a few words, a few moments away from learning the truth – and the weight of it paralyzed her. She couldn't move. Her legs shook. She stared at the woman and gasped for breath.

Bodie stepped around her. He leaned close to the window. 'We got word that a Whit Conway was brought here yesterday after an accident. These are his daughters. They're awfully anxious to find out how he is.'

The woman looked down at something out of sight below the counter front. 'That's Whitman Conway?'

'Yes.'

'He was admitted via ambulance last night, accompanied by his spouse.' She stopped talking, but continued to read whatever gave the information.

Pen's stomach gave a little flip.

Melanie took hold of her hand.

'His admitting diagnosis was fracture of the patellae bilaterally . . .'

'What does that mean?' Bodie asked.

'Both kneecaps were broken. His right upper arm was also fractured,' she added, bypassing the medical jargon. She rubbed her mouth. 'He also had a severe head injury. He was unconscious when they brought him in.'

Melanie's hand flinched in Pen's grip.

'He was admitted to the hospital for surgery. I only have the ER records here, so you'll need to check the main hospital for his current condition.'

She gave directions to Bodie. He nodded, then asked, 'Does it say how he got hurt?'

'He was struck by an automobile while crossing a street in Beverly Hills. A hit and run.'

Bodie thanked her. He led the way to a door at the rear of the room. Pen and Melanie followed him into a corridor.

Hit by a car. Pen thought of her own close call on the boulevard outside, but in her mind Bodie didn't stop her and the car broke her knees back. She flew headfirst at the windshield.

Dad.

A severe head injury.

Surgery.

At least he's not dead, she told herself. At least he wasn't dead when he left the emergency room.

The woman would've known, wouldn't she, if he'd died later on? Maybe not. Or maybe she knew, but preferred to let someone else break the news.

They came out of the corridor into a lobby. Double glass doors faced Pico. A woman was seated behind an information desk.

'I'll try to find out what's going on,' Bodie said. 'Why don't you two have a seat?'

Pen nodded. She guided Melanie to a sofa near the wall, and they sat down.

Bodie spoke to the woman at the desk. She made a telephone call, said something to Bodie. He came back and sat beside Melanie. 'A doctor's going to come out and talk to us.'

They waited.

Pen rubbed her sweaty hands on her pants.

I'm sorry, we did everything humanly possible.

A man came through a doorway at the far side of the lobby. He walked straight toward them. He was not the old, weary physician Pen had expected. He looked young, not much over thirty, handsome and energetic. He belonged in tennis whites, but he wore gray slacks and an open white jacket, a

63

shirt of Stuart plaid and a solid green tie, loosely knotted. He carried a clipboard.

Pen tried to read his expression. It was business-like. It gave nothing away.

Bodie was already standing.

Pen forced herself up. Melanie hesitated, then stood.

'I'm Dr Gray,' he said, and shook hands with Bodie. 'I'm the neurosurgeon who operated on Mr Conway.' He had a pleasant voice, a pleasant smile.

'How is he?' Melanie asked, her voice a choked whisper.

'Your father's in a stable condition.'

His words tore the fog from Pen's mind.

Dad's all right.

The tears came and she thought, it's okay, oh my God, he's not dead, he's okay. 'Can we see him?' she asked. Blubbering. I'm blubbering. I don't care.

'Certainly. But we need to talk first. Will you step this way?'

Talk.

It's not okay.

Dr Gray led them into an office. They sat on soft chairs and he sat on the edge of his desk, facing them.

'Your father sustained what we call a subdural hematoma. The impact from the accident caused blood vessels inside his skull to rupture. We operated on him immediately after he was admitted last night to open the skull, relieve the pressure of the blood build-up inside, and stop the bleeding. The surgery went well. However, your father did sustain a certain amount of brain damage, which is almost inevitable considering the trauma he experienced.' Frowning, Dr Gray rubbed his cheek as if checking for whiskers. 'I've seen patients in worse condition than your father make full and complete recoveries. I've seen others who weren't so fortunate. But your father is in excellent physical shape for a man his age, so we can be somewhat optimistic about the outcome. At present, however, he's comatose.'

'He's in a *coma*?' Bodie asked.

'He hasn't regained consciousness since the time of the accident. He is in no immediate danger, however. We have him on life support systems, and his condition is being constantly monitored. His vital signs are good.'

'You think he'll come out of it, though?' Bodie asked.

'There's just no way of knowing. He might pull out of it today or next week . . .'

'Or never,' Melanie said.

'That's also a possibility. But we're doing everything we can for him.'

Chapter Eight

Bodie stood at the foot of the bed. Melanie, beside him, stared at her father while Pen went to the man's side and took hold of his hand.

A sheet covered him to the chest. Tubes ran into his nostrils and arms. The top of his head was wrapped in bandages.

The cardiac monitor had a jagged green line and beeped regularly just as such machines did on television – which was the extent of Bodie's exposure to such things until now. The respirator made a chirping sound as it pumped air into the man's lungs. Somewhere, Bodie had heard the term 'bird respirator'. He supposed they were called that because of the noise.

All very interesting.

He wanted the hell out of there.

The doctor had made it sound pretty good, almost as if the coma was just a minor setback. But the old guy, bandaged and hooked up from every direction, looked like a Victor Frankenstein experiment on a bad day.

'Dad, it's Penny. The doctor says you're going to be fine. Melanie's here, too.'

'Hi, Dad,' Melanie said.

'You're going to be fine,' Pen repeated.

His chest rose and fell, but he didn't twitch an eyelid. The cardiac monitor beeped at the same rate as before.

Good thing this isn't a television show, Bodie thought, or the line on the screen of the heart machine would go flat about now and you'd get that long whining noise.

So far, so good.

He didn't want to be around, though, when it happened.

A long time seemed to pass before Dr Gray suggested they leave. 'You could come back this evening at eight and see him for a few minutes. Maybe his condition will have improved by then.'

Pen squeezed her father's hand. 'We'll see you tonight, Dad.' She let go and backed away.

Melanie said nothing – as if she knew there wasn't any point.

They left the room. Dr Gray led them to the elevator and tried once again to reassure them before he departed.

As the elevator doors began to close, a voice called, 'Could you hold that?' Bodie pushed the 'Doors Open' button. An orderly swung a gurney around and rolled it inside. On the gurney was a wasted, sallow-faced old woman with greasy hair. Bodie, wishing he could go back in time and let the doors shut her out, tried to hold his breath as the elevator descended.

Hospitals. Charming places.

The old crone had a bad case of impending demise, and he hoped it wasn't catching.

Finally, the doors glided open and he hurried out. The orderly and his ghastly patient stayed. They were going down. What was down in the basement? Isn't that where hospitals took their dead? She wasn't quite ready for that yet.

Dropping back, Bodie walked alongside Melanie to the lobby doors. And then he was in the sunlight, in the fresh untainted air. Well, there was a slight odor of exhaust fumes from the cars rushing by on Pico, but that was far better than the hospital air with its smells of floor wax and disinfectant and, far worse, its secret under-smell of decay and death.

'It's nice to be out of there,' Pen said.

They waited at the corner. The WALK sign came on. An RTD bus went ahead through the intersection as if traffic signals were meant only for cars. Bodie thought of the Porsche that almost nailed Pen.

A dangerous city.

If things had turned out a little differently, Dr Gray might've spent the morning inside *her* head.

I need sleep, Bodie thought as he crossed the road. 'Maybe we should check into a motel,' he said.

'Why don't you two stay at my place?' Pen suggested. Her voice was a weary monotone. 'You can use my bed. I'll use the couch.'

Bodie felt a little flip of excitement. 'Fine with me.'

'I don't know,' Melanie said. She, too, sounded tired. 'Maybe a motel.'

'There's no hurry,' Pen told her. 'You can decide later. Right now, I think we should go over and see Joyce.'

'What for?'

'She's Dad's wife.'

'Some wife. She wasn't even there. How come she wasn't there? Isn't a wife supposed to stay with her husband when he's half dead in the hospital?'

'He's not half dead.'

'Really? Three-quarters? Seven-eighths?'

'Cut it out, Mel.'

'*Mom* would've stayed with him.'

'They only let *us* stay for about five minutes.'

'There's a waiting room.'

'Look, for all we know Joyce could've spent the whole night there.'

'I'll just bet she did.'

'Maybe you'd better *not* see her, if you're going to act this way.'

'I've got a great idea. Why don't you go and see her without us. Give her my regards.'

'Okay.'

They reached Bodie's van and climbed in. He started the engine. 'Where to?' he asked.

'My apartment, I guess,' Pen said. 'I'll take my car over to Dad's place, and you guys can catch up on your sleep.'

'Never mind,' Melanie said from behind them. 'I want to see her, after all.'

'Are you sure?'

'Yeah, I'm sure. I've got a few questions I'd like to ask.'

Pen turned in her seat to look at her. The movement

twisted her blouse slightly, opening a gap between two of its buttons. Bodie saw smooth, shadowed skin on the side of her breast. 'Such as?' Pen asked.

'Such as where was she when Dad got hit.'

'She was with him,' Bodie said. 'She was there when he was brought into the emergency room.'

'How come *she* wasn't hurt?'

'We'll find out,' Pen said. Her blouse was drawn tight against her breast. The glossy fabric was molded to it, filled, rounded, puckered just a bit in the shape of a disk at the very front. Bodie looked again at the skin inside the small opening. Then he put on his safety harness. 'But let's not make it an inquisition,' Pen added. 'Joyce is Dad's wife, regardless of what you might think of her. Dad loves her, so we have to treat her with respect. Okay?'

'I guess so.'

Pen turned to the front.

'Which way do I go?' Bodie asked, looking at her face and being careful not to lower his eyes. Her face wasn't bad to look at, either.

'Make a left at the light.'

He nodded, checked the side mirror for traffic, and pulled out.

He realized that he was now feeling pretty good – a vast change from a few minutes ago.

Looking at Pen hadn't hurt any.

If we stay with her, I'll get plenty of opportunities.

He wished he hadn't mentioned a motel. It was pretty clear that Melanie would rather stay at a motel than at Pen's apartment.

It'll work out, he thought.

I'll plead penury.

* * *

Except for Pen giving occasional instructions on where to turn, the sisters were silent during the drive. Bodie imagined they must both be dwelling on the situation, wondering how their father got hit and whether he would recover. Maybe remembering times they'd spent with him.

Melanie had more than the tragedy to cope with. She also had her burden of guilt.

She'd been holding a lot of grudges, blaming him for the death of her mother, apparently dumping on him with a vengeance when he married Joyce.

She was probably wishing she'd been nicer to him.

'You'd better get to the right,' Pen said.

He eased over. They were on San Vicente, and the air streaming in through the open window was cooler than it had been a few minutes ago. Bodie suspected they were approaching the ocean, though there was no sign of it ahead.

The road had a wide, grassy center strip that appeared to be a haven for joggers.

Must be great for the lungs, Bodie thought, running your little heart out down the middle of a busy street.

'You'd better slow down,' Pen said. 'It's coming up, and you really can't see the road until you're almost on top of it.'

Bodie checked the mirror, then took his foot off the gas pedal. The area over there was heavily wooded. He couldn't see the road yet.

He flicked the arm of his turn signal, eased down on the brake, spotted the side road concealed among bushes and trees, and turned onto it. He drove slowly along the single lane. Though he could see no houses, he found evidence of their presence: patches of fence visible behind shrubbery and vines, mail boxes on weathered posts, now and then a garage, an occasional driveway entrance with a gate, a few cars parked half on the road so that he had to steer carefully around them.

The cars were not slouches: a Jaguar, a Porsche, a Ferrari, a Mercedes that looked incredibly huge and alien among the sleek sports cars.

'You can pull over behind the Mercedes,' Pen told him.

Speaking of alien – his VW van in with these ritzy vehicles. Folks would figure it must belong to the help. Caterers, perhaps. A party at the Conway residence.

A wake.

He maneuvered his van over to the right as far as possible. Bushes scraped its side. It was still jutting an uncomfortable distance into the road, but no more so than the Mercedes.

He hopped down. Instead of trying to squeeze through the passenger door, Pen swung her legs onto the driver's seat and scooted across. She gripped the steering wheel to pull herself along. Bodie tried not to look at her blouse.

He held out his hand. Pen took it, and he helped her out. 'Thank you.'

He let go of her hand, perhaps a bit too quickly. Melanie had pushed the seatback forward. He moved in, gently gripped her upper arm, and steadied her as she stepped down.

They walked past the gray Mercedes. Melanie frowned at it.

Near the front of the car stood a mailbox like the others along the road. This one bore the name CONWAY in black metal letters.

A gap in the bushes revealed a wooden gate. Farther up the road, a break in the foliage made way for a garage. The closed garage door was only a yard off the road. Must be dicey backing out, Bodie thought.

Pen, leading the way, unlatched the front gate and swung it

open. She stepped through, followed by Melanie. Bodie went next and closed the gate.

The lawn was a trim carpet of grass. Most of it was shaded by trees, which blocked Bodie's view of the house's upper story. The walkway led past a small, concrete fountain. In the center of the fountain stood a pudgy cherub wearing a mischievous leer and nothing else. Water spurted from his brass penis, splashing into the pool.

Bodie wondered if Whit was responsible for that. It was the mark, he thought, of either upper class sophistication at its worst, or a nice bit of nasty wit. The latter, he hoped. He could like a guy who got a kick out of pissing statues.

The white stucco house had the look of a hacienda. An open porch ran the length of it, shadowed by a red tile roof. A dozen flower pots were suspended by rope from the porch ceiling. Beyond them were some white, wrought-iron chairs and a love seat which couldn't be very comfortable but looked cheery. There were big windows on each side of the front door.

Pen stepped onto the porch and rang the doorbell.

Bodie heard chimes inside.

The door was opened by a young woman with a grief-twisted face who gasped, 'Oh, honey,' and threw her arms around Pen. After a quick hug and a kiss on the cheek, she seemed to notice the other sister. 'Melanie?'

Melanie received a hug and kiss while she stood motionless with her arms hanging. She didn't resist, just took it like a kid being greeted by a distant, annoying relation.

Done with the hugging, Joyce shook her head. 'It's so awful. I'm so glad you're both here.'

'Melanie drove in last night,' Pen said. She looked around. 'This is her friend, Bodie.'

Bodie said, 'Nice to meet you,' and stepped forward to shake the offered hand.

Step-mom looked about the right age to be an older sister, and had the sleek features of a fashion model. Right now, she was showing a white jumpsuit belted in at her waist. It had zippered pockets at the breasts and thighs, and one long zipper down the front. Each zipper had a big, dangling golden tab for easy opening.

She wore a thin gold chain around her neck.

She had a soft tan, curving cheeks, coral eyes, and thin eyebrows that were a shade darker than her blond hair. The hair was cut in a boyish, pixie style as if meant to show off her ears. She wore big, hoop earrings.

Whit, quite obviously, had been a very lucky man before last night.

'Please,' she said. 'Come in.'

She led them across a red tile foyer. In spite of the jumpsuit's loose fit, her walking drew it taut against her buttocks.

The living room had a plush carpet of the same burgundy shade as Pen's blouse. It also had a man on the sofa, who got to his feet as they entered.

Melanie stopped short.

'Harrison,' Pen said in a low voice.

'He's been such a sweetheart through all this,' Joyce said.

'Pen,' he said. He looked and sounded somber. He took her hand and patted it. 'I'm so sorry.'

She pulled her hand from his grip.

Harrison turned to Melanie, shaking his head. He picked up her dangling hand and squeezed it. 'A terrible thing,' he said. 'Terrible.'

Joyce said, 'This is Melanie's friend, Dobie.'

'Bodie,' he corrected, and shook hands with Harrison.

The man had a firm grip. He was somewhat taller than Bodie, maybe six-two. He was slim, but he had muscles inside his polo shirt. Bodie squeezed the guy's hand a little harder than necessary. 'Harrison Donner. I'm Whit's law partner and an old friend of the family.'

The old friend of the family must've been pushing thirty.

'Nice to meet you,' Bodie said, giving his voice some extra force.

The man had a calm, self-assured quality that wasn't arrogance, but almost.

I'm sure he's a great guy, Bodie thought. A real sport.

He no doubt belonged to the Mercedes outside, though a Porsche seemed more in character.

'Why doesn't everyone sit down and make themselves comfortable?' Joyce suggested. 'I'll get us some coffee.' She went out.

Harrison returned to his place on the sofa. Pen looked around the room until he was seated, then went to the far end of the sofa. Bodie sidestepped to a stuffed chair and sat down. Melanie sat on the carpet at his feet. She rested an arm on his knee. He stroked her arm.

'Have you been to the hospital?' Harrison asked.

'We were just there,' Pen said.

'Joyce and I were there through the operation. I think she's holding up quite well under the circumstances.'

Melanie's other hand covered Bodie's hand, pressed it gently, and stayed there.

'Were you at the accident?' Pen asked.

He shook his head. 'Joyce phoned me from the emergency room. She'd called you first, but you apparently weren't home and she got your answering machine. She needed someone to be with her.'

'So naturally she called you,' Melanie said.

'*You* weren't exactly available, young lady. Joyce did, in fact, put a call through to your number in Phoenix to no avail.'

'We were probably already on our way,' Bodie said.

Harrison looked puzzled.

Joyce came in carrying a silver tray. She set it on the table in front of Harrison and began to pour coffee into china cups. When they were full, she inquired about cream and sugar. No takers. She passed out the cups. She was shaking enough to make them clitter against their saucers.

Taking one for herself, she sat in a chair near Pen's end of the sofa – about as far from Harrison as the furniture would allow.

To Bodie, her choice of seats had a guilty look.

She obviously knew how it must appear to the sisters, finding her here with Harrison.

Bodie felt a little sorry for her.

Harrison resumed his puzzled expression. He directed it at Pen. 'Let me see whether I understand the sequence of events, here. Melanie and her friend were already en route to L.A. at the time Joyce attempted to call her. Therefore, you telephoned her with the news of the accident last night. So tell me, where have you been since then? You didn't phone? You didn't visit the hospital until this morning? Weren't you at all concerned about your father's condition?'

'Harrison, stop it,' Joyce said.

Pen looked grateful for the support. 'The thing is,' she said, 'I didn't get your message until this morning.' She frowned at Harrison. 'I don't even know why we're discussing this. All that really counts is Dad. I mean, Mel and I don't even know how he got hit.' To Joyce, she said, 'Were you with him?'

The woman nodded.

'We'll get to that in good time,' Harrison went on. 'I'd like to find out how Melanie learned about the accident if you didn't tell her last night.'

'Why are you so concerned about it?' Melanie asked.

'Let's just say that inconsistencies trouble me. I'm an attorney, after all. A good portion of my time is devoted to hunting them out. It's how one goes about discovering the truth.'

'You want the truth?'

Harrison nodded.

'I saw it happen.'

'Oh?'

'In a vision.'

'Let me get this straight. Are we talking ESP, telepathy, that sort of thing?'

'That's right,' Melanie said.

'And this vision of yours prompted you to make the trip?'

'She called here first,' Bodie pointed out. 'Nobody was home.'

Harrison leaned forward, planting his elbows on his knees and gazing at her. 'This is amazing,' he said. 'What time did you experience this vision?'

Melanie shrugged.

'About five till nine,' Bodie answered. 'That would be five till eight, Pacific time.'

Harrison arched an eyebrow and looked at Joyce.

'That's just when it happened,' Joyce confirmed. She was looking a trifle spooked.

'What, exactly, did you see?'

'I saw Dad get run down by a car.'

'Can you describe the car?'

'I don't think so.'

'The driver?'

She shook her head.

'It's too bad your vision couldn't have been a little more detailed. Information of that kind wouldn't be admissible, of course, but if it led to establishing the identity of the driver, we might find enough evidence to pin him down. I hate the thought of someone getting away with this.'

Pen turned to Joyce. 'You were there. Didn't you see what happened?'

'Not very well. It was dark and raining. All I know for sure is that it was a sports car. I can't even be sure of the color.'

'You didn't catch the license plate?'

'It all happened so fast.'

'How *did* it happen?' Melanie asked.

'We went out to dinner at Gerards.'

'That's in Beverly Hills,' Harrison explained. 'On Cañon.'

Pen nodded. 'I've been there. It's Dad's favorite restaurant.'

'We went there for your birthday this year,' Joyce said. 'Do you remember his parking spot?'

'The bank lot across the street.'

'That's where he parked last night. It's where he always parks when we go to Gerards.' She looked at Harrison. 'Whit would walk blocks to avoid leaving his car in the hands of a parking attendant.'

'Don't I know,' he said.

'Destruction Derby rejects,' Pen added, apparently quoting her father.

'Anyway, since it was raining, he let me out in front of the restaurant. I told him he should just have the boy take his car. I mean, it was pouring, he was going to get soaked. But he said, "Rain'll dry. I'm not turning this buggy over to that toenail." He called the car-hop a toenail. Not to his face, but . . . Anyway, I got out and stood under the canopy to wait for him. He drove across the street and parked behind the bank. It's right on the corner, you know. The bank, not the lot. The lot's in the rear, and I guess he didn't want to go to the corner and use the crosswalk because it was out of the way. So he just cut right across the street. The light at the corner was red and there weren't any cars coming. Not from the other way, either. Then suddenly this car was hitting him.' She pressed her lips together in a tight line and stared down at the coffee cup on her lap. When she spoke again, her voice was pitched higher than before, and trembling. 'I didn't even see it till it hit him. I guess I was looking at something else. I saw him step off the curb, and there wasn't any traffic, and then I heard this awful sound and looked and he was like rolling over the top of this sports car. It never even slowed down or anything after it hit him. Whit . . . he was lying in the road and the light had turned green and all these *other* cars were starting to come at him. I ran out and . . . none of them hit him. I, you know, waved them off.'

'God Almighty,' Pen muttered.

'Did anyone in those other cars see him get hit?' Bodie asked.

'I don't know. The first cars, they just slowed down and went around me and kept going. Three or four did that. Then someone stopped, but he hadn't seen anything.'

'What about the restaurant's car-hop or doorman?' Pen asked.

'They didn't see it. The doorman was showing a party inside, and the parking guys were off parking cars. Anyway, someone called the police, I guess. They showed up and then an ambulance.' She sighed deeply. She was silent for a few moments. Staring down into her coffee cup, she said, 'It's so hard to believe something like that could happen.'

'How *could* it happen?' Melanie asked. 'That car coming out of nowhere like that.'

'It undoubtedly made a right turn onto Cañon,' Harrison said, 'and the driver didn't see him until it was too late.'

Melanie whispered, 'The bastard. He's not going to get away with it.'

Chapter Nine

'He . . . or she,' Harrison said, 'may lose some sleep over it, if he wasn't too drunk to know it even happened, but unless someone comes up with the license number of his car, he will get away with it. I've had any number of cases involving phantom cars. Without the license number, you're dead in the water.'

'I don't even care who did it,' Joyce confessed. 'I mean, I *care*, but . . .'

'And well you should,' Harrison told her. 'Retribution – and getting him off the streets – aside, we're talking here about a personal injury suit of rather staggering proportions. Assuming the driver was insured . . .'

'How can you even *think* about a lawsuit right now? Whit's lying in a hospital room, half . . .' She cut herself off.

Half-dead, Bodie finished for her. Or three-quarters? Seven-eighths? The phrase seemed to be making its rounds.

'I'm sorry,' Harrison told her. 'I shouldn't have brought it up. It's a moot point, anyway. We'll probably never know who the driver was.'

Joyce lifted her cup and took a sip. Apparently, whatever remained of her coffee had grown cold. She made a face, then got up from her chair and set the cup and saucer onto the table. Returning to her seat, she managed a smile and said to Melanie, 'I hope you won't be rushing back to school.'

'Not right away,' Melanie told her. 'I want to stay around until . . .' She shrugged. 'We haven't really discussed it, but I can't go back while Dad's the way he is. Bodie may have to go back, though. He's got a teaching assistantship.'

'I can make arrangements for someone else to cover my classes,' he said. 'For a few days, at least.'

'There's plenty of room for both of you here,' Joyce said.

Bodie thought about Pen's offer. He would rather stay at her place – no question. 'I don't know,' he said.

'It wouldn't be any trouble. You can't just go off to some motel. I'm sure Whit wouldn't allow it, if he were here. So as long as you're in town, this is home. All right?'

'All right,' Melanie said. 'Thank you.'

Pen lowered her eyes. She looked as if the rejection had hurt her, but she didn't speak up.

Neat play, Mel.

'Have you eaten yet?' Joyce asked.

'Pen gave us breakfast,' Bodie said.

'Well, you two must be exhausted. Maybe you'd like to freshen up.'

'I could sure use some sleep,' Melanie told her.

'Fine. Why don't you go ahead and get some rest? Do you have your things?'

'Out in the van.'

'Fine. Harrison, why don't you give them a hand with their luggage? I'll get out some clean sheets and towels.'

'Pen, are you staying?' Bodie asked.

'Well . . .'

'There's no need to rush off,' Joyce said. 'Besides, I'm sure you have a lot of catching up to do with your sister.'

Pen hesitated.

'You don't want to be alone,' Bodie told her.

'No, I suppose not.' She nodded to Joyce. 'If you don't mind, I could use a little rack time myself. Rough night.'

'It's all settled, then.' She bobbed her head briskly.

'I'll give you that hand with the bags,' Harrison said.

'No need,' Bodie told him. 'We haven't got much.'

'I guess I'll be on my way, then.'

Bodie expected Joyce to protest. She'd been eager enough to keep everyone else at the house. But she stood up as Harrison rose from the sofa, and said, 'Thanks so much for everything. I don't know what I would've done.'

'Just give me a call if you need me.'

'I will. Thanks again.'

'You'll be going over to see Whit tonight?' he asked.

Joyce nodded.

'Keep me posted.'

'Certainly.'

'I'm sure it'll all turn out fine. Whit's a tough old bird. He won't let a little thing like this keep him down.'

They all said goodbye, and Harrison turned away. Joyce didn't see him to the door.

Joyce poked her head through the bedroom doorway. 'I put some fresh washcloths and towels in the bathroom. If you need anything you can't find, just give a yell.'

'Thank you,' Bodie said.

She left. Bodie continued helping Melanie put clean sheets on the bed. 'Did this used to be your room?' he asked.

'It was. All new furniture, though.'

'Good thing. I bet you didn't have a bed like this.' It was a strange bed, unlike any that Bodie had seen before, a single with a space beneath it for a second bed. They had rolled out the bottom section, Joyce showing them how to raise it level with the other mattress. 'Nice that she didn't give us any grief about sleeping together.'

'She knows I live with you.'

'Still, some people . . .'

'She isn't my mother.'

'She seems nice.'

Melanie raised an eyebrow. Removing a leather toilet kit from her suitcase, she said, 'Back in a minute.'

Bodie sat on the bed. He rubbed his face. He felt vague and a little nauseous. Sleep would take care of that. And sleep would be a welcome release from having to face all this. A lot was going on. More than he wanted to think about.

Melanie came back.

'Do you have to use the john?' she asked.

'Yeah.'

'It's at the end of the hall.'

He got up slowly and crouched over his suitcase to take out his toothbrush and paste.

'When you go by,' Melanie told him, 'take a peek into the master bedroom.'

He did as she asked. In the bathroom, he brushed the fuzz off his teeth, washed his face and used the toilet. Then he returned.

Melanie shut the door. 'Did you see the bed?'

'Yeah. Something special about it?'

'It wasn't made.'

'No.' The covers and top sheet had been left in a messy heap near the foot of the bed. 'So?'

'So who used it? More to the point, when?'

'I don't know.'

'Guess.'

Bodie sat down and pulled his shoes off. Getting out of his shoes felt wonderful. He hadn't been aware of how hot and cramped his feet had been. 'It doesn't have to be that. Joyce and your father might've been using it before they took off for the restaurant.'

'I doubt it.'

He peeled off his damp socks, and sighed. 'Or maybe Joyce took a nap after she got home from the hospital.'

'She came back with Harrison. They used that bed last night. Joyce and Harrison. Dad's bed.'

Wearily, Bodie shook his head. 'And she just left the bed messed up for all to see?'

'She didn't know we'd show up.'

'She wouldn't have left it like that. Not if she'd been screwing around with Harrison. Even if she didn't make the bed right away, she would've found some excuse to get up here and fix it after we arrived. Or at least close the door.'

'Not necessarily.'

Bodie shrugged. 'If you say so,' he said, taking off his shirt. 'But I think she would've made some effort to cover up, don't you?'

'You'd think so.'

He unfastened his pants, stood and pulled them down along with his shorts. He stepped out of them and climbed between the smooth, cool sheets.

Hell, he thought, they probably did. A rotten damn thing to do, but they probably did. Maybe they'd been at each other behind Whit's back for a long time. Or Joyce just needed comfort, last night, and Harrison had obliged.

Melanie took off her blouse. She left her bra on. Her small breasts, the dark flesh of her nipples, showed through the transparent fabric.

And Bodie remembered Pen in the van, the gap between her buttonholes, the shadowy glimpse of her breast.

He felt a warm stir. The sheet began to rise between his legs, so he rolled onto his side.

Melanie unfastened her pants.

'You know,' Bodie said, 'Pen invited us to stay with *her*.'

'She doesn't have room.'

'She has a good-sized bed. She offered to use the couch.'

'Pen wouldn't be very comfortable on a couch.' Melanie draped her blouse and pants over the back of a chair. She faced Bodie. 'I suppose you wanted us to stay with her.'

'She's your sister. And I'm a little surprised you'd want to be under the same roof with Joyce, the way you feel about her.'

'Maybe I want to keep an eye on her.'

'I doubt if she'll be boffing Harrison with us in the house.'

'The bitch.' Melanie removed her bra and panties. Wearing only her velvet choker, she stepped to the foot of the bed. Bodie watched her crawl over the mattress, pull back the blanket and sheet, and cover herself. She lay on her back, staring at the ceiling.

'I think Pen really wants us to stay with her,' he said.

'Then she should've spoken up.'

'She'd already made the offer.'

'We would've been tripping over each other.'

'Haven't you forgotten something?'

'More than likely.'

'The telephone calls.'

'Big deal. A few dirty calls.'

'They were a big deal to your sister. I think she's frightened, and I don't blame her. *I'd* be nervous about staying there alone, if I were her.'

Melanie's head turned. She stared at him across the joining beds. 'You just want to see her in a nightie.'

'There's that, too,' he said, and smiled.

Melanie didn't smile.

Bodie scooted across the bed and kissed her. He whispered, 'Sleep tight,' then rolled over and shut his eyes.

Waking up, Pen lifted her face off the warm pocket of the pillow. She felt wonderful. Then she saw where she was and remembered her father. A dark heaviness spread through her.

He'll be all right, she told herself.

We'll see him tonight.

And Melanie's here. Thank God Melanie's here. Going through this alone would've been so much worse.

Maybe Dad'll be better when we see him.

She pushed herself up and sat on the edge of the bed. She had slept in her clothes. Her slick, burgundy blouse was twisted around her torso. The weight of her body had pressed wrinkles into it. She straightened it, but the wrinkles remained.

Maybe Bodie would drive her to her apartment so she could change before going to the hospital.

The apartment. The phone calls.

Fear began to knot her. She tried to push it aside.

That business doesn't count, she told herself. Not with Dad in the hospital.

But the fear grew.

Pen quickly stood up. In front of the bureau mirror, she brushed her hair. Then she left the room and hurried downstairs. The living room was empty, but voices came from the den. As she approached, she heard Bodie speaking over the quiet dialogue from the television.

'. . . a PhD in English literature. Which is probably a totally useless thing to have, but I fancy myself as a slightly eccentric professor in a patched jacket . . .' He smiled at Pen as she entered. He was slumped in an armchair, feet crossed at the ankles, one hand holding a Corona beer against his belt buckle.

Joyce, on the couch, was sipping a glass of white wine.

'Don't stop,' Pen said to Bodie.

'All through,' he told her.

'You plan to be an English professor?'

'Since I don't have any useful talents.'

Smiling, Pen sat on the couch.

'Let me get you something to drink,' Joyce offered.

'Wine would be great.'

Leaving the room, Joyce said over her shoulder, 'Pen's a writer.'

'I write mysteries,' she said. 'But I've only sold one so far. It was just a short story.'

'That's terrific. As I understand it, the world's full of would-be writers who've never had *any*thing published.'

'Do you have any ambitions along those lines?'

'Nope. I'd rather spend my time reading good stuff than writing lousy stuff. Do you have a normal job?'

'I don't know how normal it is, but I'm a certified shorthand reporter. I spend most of my time trotting around to law offices to take down depositions.'

'It must be a good source for story ideas.'

She nodded. 'I've met some very strange people. The main thing, though, is that I can pick and choose assignments. I only work when I want to – which is most of the time because I *do* like to eat, pay my rent, little things like that.'

'No desire to be an attorney?'

'That'd be a full-time career. I don't have room for it.'

'Wouldn't leave you time for your writing?'

'Not enough. And I'd rather write.'

'I'd like to read your stuff.'

'It ain't Updike.'

'Ah, but is it Hammett?'

'No. It's pretty good Pen Conway, though.'

A grin spread over Bodie's face.

Joyce came in carrying a bottle of white wine and a glass. She filled the glass for Pen, gave herself a refill, and sat down. 'I guess I should start thinking about supper.'

'Don't,' Bodie said. 'I'll save you the trouble, if everyone likes pizza. I know Melanie does.'

'Where *is* Melanie?' Pen asked.

'Still asleep. I was in L.A. a couple of years ago and had this great pizza at some place not far from here.'

'That must have been La Barbera's,' Pen said.

'Right, that's the place. Is it still around?'

'Sure.'

'Why don't I drive over and pick one up?'

'Oh,' Joyce said, 'that's a lot of trouble.'

'No more trouble than you making something for all of us. Besides, I've really got a craving for that stuff. It's the best pizza I've ever tasted.'

'If you feel that strongly about it,' Joyce said. 'The least I can do is call in the order. What kind should we get?'

'Melanie doesn't like mushrooms.'

'How about salami?' Pen suggested. 'Mushrooms on half.'

'Sounds good to me.'

Joyce took a sip of wine, then left to make the call.

'Maybe you could give me directions,' Bodie said.

'I can do better than that,' Pen told him. 'I'll go with you and act as navigator.'

'I'd be glad to have you along. Maybe you'd better stay here, though. Melanie might come down while we're gone, and I don't think she'd like the idea that both of us went off without her. Besides, you might be needed as a referee.'

Pen frowned.

Bodie glanced over his shoulder as if to make sure that Joyce wasn't returning. 'Melanie wasn't too happy about finding that Harrison fellow here. She thinks there was maybe some hanky-panky going on.'

'It crossed my mind, too,' Pen admitted.

'Anyway, I don't know whether she'd say anything, but it might help the situation if you're around.'

'I suppose you're right.'

Bodie sat up straight and drank the last of his beer. 'So. How do I get to La Barbera's from here?'

'Easy.'

While she was explaining the directions, Joyce returned, opening her purse. 'They said it should be ready in half an hour.'

'This is my treat,' Bodie told her.

'No, really, I insist.' She took out a twenty-dollar bill.

Bodie waved it off. 'No way,' he said, and Joyce didn't argue.

When Bodie was gone, Joyce said, 'He seems like a very nice young man.'

'Yeah. I'd say Melanie lucked out. She's been involved with some awful twerps.'

'I wouldn't know about that.' Joyce sat down and took a sip of wine. She turned sideways, sliding a knee onto the couch and resting an arm on the back. 'I'm glad she's staying. It's awful that it took something like this to get her here, but maybe we'll finally have a chance to . . . mend fences. It would be nice if she could like me.' Joyce smiled a little sadly. 'Why couldn't she be more like you?'

'Melanie sees things differently.'

'Don't I know it? I'm young enough to be Whit's daughter, a cold-hearted gold digger and a slut.'

'That about sums it up.'

'I *love* Whit.'

'You'd have a hard time convincing Melanie of that.'

'I shouldn't have to,' Joyce said. 'But it would be such a relief if she could learn to accept me. We don't have to be buddies. Just . . . I can *feel* the chill. Even when she's trying to act pleasant, there's always this chill.'

'I know.'

'Like I'm a spider, or something, and she'd like to step on me.'

Chapter Ten

Pen climbed the stairs and went down the corridor to Melanie's room. She knocked lightly on the door.

'Who is it?'

'Me.' She entered and shut the door.

Melanie, on the bed, was covered to the chest. Her shoulders were bare.

'I wanted to make sure you were awake. Bodie went to get pizza. He should've been back by now, but . . .'

'Where'd he go?'

'La Barbera's. He's been gone over an hour. Hope he didn't get lost.'

'Did he go alone?'

Pen nodded. 'I offered to show him the way, but he thought I should stay here with you and Joyce.'

'Joyce,' she muttered.

'Try and be nice to her, okay?'

'Nice. Sure. What do you think Harrison was doing here?'

'I don't think you should jump to conclusions.'

'Did you happen to notice the master bedroom?'

'No.'

'Well, I did. The bed's been used.'

'That doesn't prove much. If she had anything to hide, don't you think she would've tidied up after herself?'

'That's what Bodie said.' Tossing the covers aside, Melanie crawled off the bed. She walked casually toward the corner of the room where her suitcase lay open on the floor. There were no tan lines on her skin. Apparently, she still believed in avoiding the sun. Areas of her back, buttocks and calves had a red hue from lying in bed.

They forced Pen to remember the coroner's slides.

Post-mortem lividity.

Dad. What if he . . .

The hospital would have called.

'You always *were* pals with that bitch,' Melanie said, squatting beside the suitcase.

'She's all right.'

Melanie found panties. She stood up, stepped into them, and turned to face Pen. She looked like a bizarre stranger: her sunless skin, her black hair, her black choker, her black lace panties. 'Harrison does get around,' she said.

'Cut it out.'

'I guess you and Joyce have quite a lot in common.'

'For God's sake, Mel.'

Melanie laughed softly. Shaking her head, she turned away and crouched over her suitcase.

The redness behind her shoulders had faded a little.

'I guess I should wear something decent for the hospital,' she said.

'Unless we make a stop by my apartment on the way over, I'm stuck with what I've got on.'

'Bodie thinks we should be staying with you.'

'The offer's still open,' Pen said.

'Do you *want* us to?' Melanie took a frilly white blouse from her suitcase and put it on.

'You'd probably be more comfortable here,' Pen admitted. 'Besides, you already told Joyce you'd stay.'

'That can be changed.'

'No. It wouldn't be nice.'

'Bodie thinks you're afraid to stay there alone.'

'How flattering.'

'Are you?'

She shrugged, but Melanie's back was to her. 'A little bit, maybe. Nothing I can't handle.'

Melanie lifted out a black skirt.

'We're not going to a funeral tonight,' Pen said.

'Not tonight.'

'You're really going to wear that?'

'Bodie likes me in black.'

91

'Oh. That's different.'

'You approve, then?'

'I approve.'

Bodie shook his head, rolled his eyes upward. 'What happened? Disaster. God save me from the streets of Los Angeles. It all started when I couldn't get over into the right-hand turn lane from San Vicente onto Wilshire. That resulted in quite a detour. When I finally did get to the restaurant, they didn't have our pizza. Apparently, something got screwed up with the phone order – they lost it or something. So I had to reorder and wait around while they made it.' He blew out a long breath. 'At any rate, here I am. An older man but wiser.'

As they ate the pizza, they agreed that it was well worth his trouble.

By six o'clock, they were done eating.

That left an hour and a half before time to set out for the hospital.

Joyce went upstairs to bathe and change her clothes.

In the living room, Pen sat in an armchair. Melanie and Bodie took the couch, sitting close together, Melanie's hand on his leg. They talked. But there was no talk of Joyce or Harrison or Dad, as if the subjects were taboo.

Pen's uneasiness grew as the time passed. She had difficulty sitting still, and her chest had a tightness that made breathing a struggle. Finally, she got off her chair. She lay on the floor, knees upraised. That seemed to help.

'Are you all right?' Bodie asked.

'Just nerves,' she said.

'Maybe you need a Valium or something,' Melanie said.

'Don't think so.' She rubbed her face. 'I could use a good snootful, though.'

92

'You've *had* a pretty good snootful.'

'Hardly. A few glasses of wine do not a snootful make.'

'Pen thinks that she can't be a writer without being a drunk.'

'I'm not a drunk. Tonight, however, I might prefer it.'

'What's stopping you?'

'I don't want to make an ass out of myself staggering into the hospital.'

Joyce entered the room. She wore a white pullover that looked like cashmere, a gray jacket and matching pleated skirt, hose and high heels.

Joyce and Melanie, both in skirts. Me in my white jeans. Great, Pen thought.

She should've asked Bodie to run her over to her apartment after dinner so she could put on a dress.

So who cares? she asked herself. Who am I out to impress, the nurses? Dad isn't likely to notice. And if he does . . .

She pictured him awake, sitting up in bed, breathing for himself, the tubes and wires disconnected.

Don't get your hopes up.

They would've called.

'Are you feeling all right?' Joyce asked, staring down at her.

'I'm fine.'

'Too much wine,' Melanie said.

'Not enough.' Pen sat up. 'Is it about time to go?'

'Pretty soon,' Joyce said. 'I'd be glad to do the driving,' she told Bodie.

'Fine.'

Joyce slipped the Lincoln Continental into an open space of curb on Pico Boulevard, and they climbed out.

Pen, realizing they wouldn't have to walk across the road, thought about the car that had come so close to running her down that morning. A Porsche. A sports car.

A sports car had hit Dad.

The same one that almost got me?

That's crazy, she told herself. *Just a coincidence. Don't try to make something out of it.*

The night air chilled the material of her blouse. Shivering, she folded her arms across her chest and clamped her teeth together.

Melanie, ahead of her, walked stiffly with her shoulders hunched, but she was pressed against Bodie's side and his arm was around her back. That had to help.

The warmth of the hospital lobby felt good.

They entered an elevator. Bodie pushed the button for Dad's floor. The piped-in music was an orchestral version of 'Bridge Over Troubled Water'. Pen wondered if the tune had been selected for purposes of irony.

When they left the elevator, Joyce led the way to the nurses' station. A nurse guided them down the corridor and opened the door to Dad's room.

He wasn't awake, sitting up, breathing for himself.

He looked the same.

He looked dead.

Pen's eyes darted to the cardiac monitor. The line on the screen jigged with each heartbeat. Every jump of the line was accompanied by a beep.

Joyce went to the bedside and squeezed his hand.

The rhythm of his heart didn't change.

He has no idea we're even here, Pen thought.

'It's Joyce. Can you hear me? Can you understand me?' Joyce waited as if for a reply. 'Your daughters are here.

Melanie came all the way from Phoenix to be with you. We're all pulling for you, Whit. You're going to be all right. You'll be just fine.' She was silent for a little while. Then she looked around at the others. 'Could I be alone with him for a few minutes?'

They went out to the hallway. Pen closed the door.

'Why doesn't she want us in there?' Melanie whispered.

'She's his wife,' Pen said. 'She wants a little privacy with him.'

'He's in a *coma*.'

'A little privacy with a gal like Joyce might pull him out of it,' Bodie suggested.

Melanie glared at him.

'Sorry,' he muttered. 'My big mouth.'

'Don't worry about it,' Pen said, more to her sister than to Bodie.

'I wonder what she is doing in there.'

'Talking to him, I should imagine,' Pen said. 'About things that don't concern you and me.'

'Maybe she's telling him to go ahead and die.'

Melanie, so prim and Victorian in her choker and frilly white blouse and black skirt, had spoken the unthinkable and was staring at Pen as if she thought Pen was dimwitted for not realizing the obvious.

'My God, Mel,' she muttered.

'If Dad dies, she gets Harrison, the insurance, the inheritance . . .'

'Have you lost your mind?'

'She might even pull the plug on him.'

'Alarms would go off,' Bodie whispered. He was frowning, shaking his head. 'I think . . . the machines are tied in to the nurses' station. If anything like that happened . . .'

'She wouldn't *do* that,' Pen said.

'Oh, no?'

'Melanie, Jesus.'

Melanie swung open the door.

Gazing past her shoulder, Pen saw Joyce turn her head in surprise. She was bent over the bed, straightening a blanket at Dad's shoulders. She pressed a hand to her chest and smiled nervously. 'You startled me.'

'Sorry,' Pen said. 'Is everything all right?'

'Fine. I was about to ask you back in.'

They entered the room.

'Did he . . . make any kind of response?'

'I'm afraid not.'

Pen followed Melanie closer to the bed and bumped her when she jerked to a rigid stop.

Melanie began to groan.

Joyce looked puzzled, then alarmed.

Melanie's back arched and she suddenly quaked. She pressed her fists to the sides of her head.

'What's she doing?' Joyce blurted. 'My God!'

Pen's mind seemed to freeze as she stood at the back of her twitching, moaning sister.

'Don't worry,' Bodie said. *He* sounded worried. 'It's like last . . .'

Melanie lurched against Pen. Bodie stopped her from falling. With Bodie at her back, Pen braced herself up and wrapped her arms around Melanie's chest. The girl's whole body jumped with spastic shudders. Pen kept her face turned away to avoid the thrashing head.

'You got her?' Bodie gasped.

'Yeah.'

'You got her? Don't let her fall.'

'Should I get help?' Joyce asked.

'No. It'll be okay.'

'What's *wrong* with her?'

Melanie's head snapped back, striking Pen's jaw just below the ear. The pain was a hot jolt. She squeezed her eyes shut, but didn't let go of Melanie.

'You okay?' Bodie asked.

Pen heard him through a ringing in her ear.

'Ease her down. Try to ease her down.'

She felt Bodie's hands on her sides, pushing at her ribcage to steady her as she sank to a crouch. The strain lessened when Melanie's rump met the floor.

Abruptly, her body went limp. Her head sagged forward. She took deep breaths.

'Are you okay?' Pen asked.

The head bobbed slightly.

Bodie's hands went away from Pen. He stepped to the front and knelt beside Melanie. 'How you doing?' he asked in a gentle voice.

'Okay, I guess.'

'Another vision?'

'I . . . I think so.'

He helped her up. Pen, rising to her feet, rubbed her sore jaw. She stretched her mouth open wide. It made her ear hurt.

'What was it?' Bodie asked.

'I don't know.'

He stroked Melanie's cheeks.

'I can't remember. Just that it was awful. But I lost it. Like sometimes when you wake up from a nightmare and it's gone.'

'Is she all right now?' Joyce asked.

It struck Pen as interesting that the question wasn't directed to Melanie – as if a more reliable opinion were required.

Nodding, Bodie put his arms around her. She clung to him, face pressed to the side of his neck. One of Bodie's hands was motionless at the center of her back. The other patted her gently.

Pen watched.

She worked her jaw from side to side.

Then she saw her father on the bed, oblivious to it all. She went to him.

'I'm sorry I made such a scene,' Melanie said when they were back in the car.

'Are you certain you're all right?' Joyce asked.

'Yeah.'

'Do those things happen often?'

'No. Hardly ever.'

'It sure scared the hell out of me.'

'I'm sorry.'

'As long as you're all right.' Joyce pulled away from the curb. She glanced toward Pen. 'Where to? Would you like to come back with us, or . . . ?'

'We're not far from my apartment.'

'You're welcome to spend the night at the house.'

'Why don't you?' Bodie suggested from the back seat.

'Pen got a couple of obscene phone calls last night,' Melanie explained. 'She's pretty frightened.'

'I'm not frightened,' Pen insisted, wishing Melanie had kept quiet about the situation. It was personal. Joyce didn't need to know about it. 'They made me a little nervous,' she said, 'but I'm okay now.'

Am I? she wondered.

She didn't look forward to being alone in the apartment.

On the other hand, getting away by herself might be a relief.

A long, hot bath. Sleep in her own bed.

How'd you like me to fuck your brains out?

She felt a hot rush of dread.

It won't get any better, she told herself, by staying somewhere else. It might even get worse.

'Why don't you go ahead and take me to my apartment?' she said.

'Are you sure?'

'It was just a voice on a phone. I can't let a little thing like that get to me.'

'Obscene phone calls,' Melanie said. 'Everybody gets them. I've had a few.'

'Me, too,' Joyce said.

'What did you do?' Melanie asked her.

'I just hung up, but I'll admit I was pretty edgy for a while.'

'They never do anything but call,' Melanie went on. 'I think they have to get their jollies over the phone because they're afraid of women. The phone is safe and anonymous. They never actually pay a visit.'

'I wouldn't say never,' Bodie told them. 'There was a story in the news a couple of months ago about a woman who was getting calls like that. The day after she got an unlisted number, she was raped and murdered. Apparently, changing number made the guy feel rejected.'

'Oh, thank you very much, Bodie,' Pen said. 'That's just what I wanted to hear.'

'I think you have a right to be worried, that's all. I didn't like the sound of that guy.'

'They all sound like that,' Melanie said.

'The calls were recorded on my answering machine,' Pen explained to Joyce.

'Whit won't let me get one of those things.'

'I've heard him on the subject,' Pen said. 'Dad likes answering machines about as much as he likes car-hops.'

Joyce turned off Pico and headed up the sidestreet toward Pen's apartment. 'You're sure you wouldn't rather stay with us?' She sounded as if she really wanted Pen to join them for the night – maybe to keep an eye on Melanie in case of another 'vision'.

'No,' she said. 'I'll be okay. Maybe I'll come by in the morning, though.'

'Do,' Joyce urged her. 'Come early, and we'll all have a nice breakfast together.'

'You've got a deal.'

Joyce eased the Lincoln to a stop across from Pen's apartment building. Pen swung her door open. For a moment, she was ready to back down.

'See you in the morning,' Melanie said.

'Right. See you then.' She started to step out.

'I'll go up with you,' Bodie said, 'and check the place out.'

She felt a surge of relief. 'Thank you. I'd like that.'

'I'll go, too,' Melanie said.

Outside the car, she put herself between Pen and Bodie, and latched onto his hand.

They walked to the iron gate, and Bodie swung it open. Pen went through first. She heard their footsteps close behind her as she cut across the courtyard toward the stairway. Party sounds of music, loud voices and laughter came from one of the apartments on the second floor. Though the pool lights were off, she spotted a couple in the whirlpool at the far end. She couldn't see who they were. She probably, in fact, wouldn't have recognized them even in light. Most of the other tenants were strangers to her. She preferred it that way.

Melanie and Bodie followed her up the stairs and along the balcony to her door. While she hunted for her keys, they caught up.

'A lot of activity around here,' Melanie said.

'Saturday night.'

'Does that guy, Manny, still live here?' Melanie asked.

'Oh yes.'

She pushed her key into the lock, twisted it, and opened the door. Reaching inside, she flicked a light switch.

The lamp by the couch came on.

On the carpet at her feet lay a square, white envelope – the kind that birthday cards came in. She crouched over it. There was no stamp, no address. P. CONWAY was written in large, crooked letters.

Picking up the envelope, she could feel that it was empty.

'Someone must've slipped it under my door,' she muttered.

'I don't like this,' Bodie said.

She turned the envelope over, and felt her legs go weak as she read its scribbled message:

I CAME AND YOU WEREN'T HOME. TOO BAD. NEXT TIME I'LL COME WHEN YOU ARE. SEE YOU SOON.

Chapter Eleven

'Let me see.'

Pen handed the envelope to Bodie. He held it out to the side so that Melanie could read it, too.

'I guess you'd better come back with us,' Melanie said.

'Yeah,' Pen muttered. 'Let me get a few things.'

They waited in the living room.

'This is starting to look serious,' Melanie said. 'I mean, I never thought he might come after her.'

'It doesn't surprise me much,' Bodie said. 'The way that guy sounded on the phone . . . he sounded like he meant it.'

'Maybe she'd better go to the police.'

'Yeah.'

Melanie took the envelope from him and studied both sides. She pursed it open to make sure it was empty. Turning around, she stared at the place on the carpet where Pen had found it. Her shoulders rose as she took a deep breath. She sighed the breath out. Her head lowered, and she shook it slowly from side to side. 'The guy was actually here,' she said in a weary voice.

'Lucky thing Pen wasn't.'

'I feel like such a jerk.'

Bodie put a hand low on her back. Her skin was warm through the blouse. 'Don't worry about it,' he said.

'I feel like I'm in the goddamn *Twilight Zone*. Dad. This.'

'Pen almost getting hit this morning,' Bodie added.

'I'd forgotten about that.'

'I hadn't. And if you want to talk *Twilight Zone*, there're your visions. It's too bad you can't remember the one at the hospital.'

'I remember it,' she said. She turned and looked into Bodie's eyes. 'I remembered it *then*. I just didn't want to talk about it in front of the others.'

'What was it?'

'Later. I'll tell you when we're alone.'

'We're alone now.'

'Pen.'

Bodie could hear her in another room. Footsteps. Drawers opening.

'She'll be done in a minute,' Melanie said.

'Why don't you want her to know about it? Does it involve her?'

'In a way.'

'Come on, what is it?'

'No. I said later. It's just between you and me.'

'Okay,' he muttered. 'Later.'

'Don't be mad at me.'

'I'm not mad.'

'Yes you are,' she sulked.

' "True!" ' he blurted. ' "Nervous – very, very dreadfully nervous I had been and am; but why *will* you say that I am mad?" '

' "The disease had sharpened my senses," ' came Pen's voice from the other side of the room, ' "not destroyed, not dulled them." '

Bodie grinned at her.

Melanie, looking perplexed, switched her gaze from Bodie to Pen.

'*The Tell-Tale Heart*,' Pen explained.

'We oughtta take our show on the road,' Bodie said. The hurt glance from Melanie made him regret the suggestion. 'Ready to go?'

'All set.' Pen had a small suitcase at her side, a purse hanging from her shoulder. She wore the same white jeans as before, but her burgundy blouse had been replaced by a plaid flannel shirt that was neatly tucked in. She wore a suede jacket over the shirt, its front open, the dangling ends of its belt swaying as she walked.

Bodie watched her take a few steps. There was just enough difference in the look and motion of her shirt to indicate, in Bodie's judgement, that she had taken the opportunity to put on a bra.

'I'll carry that,' he said, reaching for the suitcase.

'Thank you.'

As she passed it to him, the telephone clamored. Her hand jerked and the suitcase slipped from Bodie's fingers, thumped the floor. Pen stood rigid. She flinched as the phone rang again.

'Want me to get it?' Bodie asked.

She didn't look capable of answering.

'*I* will.' Melanie rushed past him.

He hurried behind her to the kitchen and watched her snatch up the receiver. 'Hello?' Pause. 'No, this isn't Pen. May I tell her who is calling?' She listened, then covered the mouthpiece and called, 'It's some guy named Gary.'

'Okay,' Pen said. She came up beside Melanie and took the phone. 'Hello? . . . Right, this is *the* Pen Conway . . . Of course I remember you. "Never look a gift drink in the mouth." '

Bodie felt like a snoop, listening, but Melanie hadn't left so he stayed, too. Besides, he told himself, the guy didn't know if Pen would remember him, so they couldn't be on intimate terms.

'I guess it was the slides,' she said. 'I thought I was going to barf . . . Right, I just drove home . . . I was tempted, but I didn't know for sure whether you'd come down afterwards . . . Oh, really?' Pen fooled with the top button of her shirt. She frowned slightly. 'Tonight? I really can't . . . No, it's a family situation. I really couldn't. Look, why don't you give me your number? When this situation is settled, I'll call you.' She nodded, but didn't write down his number. 'Got it . . . I will. Thanks for calling, Gary . . . Goodnight.' She hung up. 'A guy I met last night at the mystery writers meeting.' She unplugged the phone and set it on top of the refrigerator. 'We'd better go. Joyce'll think we've abandoned her.'

In the living room, Pen stopped and looked down at the envelope on the coffee table where Melanie had left it.

'Should we take it with us?' Melanie asked.

Pen picked it up and crumpled it into a ball.

'Hey, don't ruin it! That's evidence.'

'Evidence of what?' Pen asked her sister. Without waiting for a reply, she headed again for the kitchen.

'Maybe you should show it to the police,' Melanie called.

Pen didn't answer. She came back without the envelope.

'You threw it away?'

'Do you think I want it looking at me when I come back?'

'Bodie and I were talking. We think you should go to the police.'

Pen left the lamp on. They stepped outside. She pulled the door shut and rattled the knob. Walking along the balcony toward the stairs, she looked back at them. 'I'm not going to the police. First off, they've got bigger problems to worry about. Second, there's certainly not sufficient evidence to identify the creep even if they did care.' With a hand on the metal railing, she started down. 'They'd just advise me to get an unlisted number or move out. Besides, they'd want to hear the tape.'

And that, Bodie guessed, might be the real reason she didn't want the police involved. He couldn't blame her. They would insist on listening to the tape. Pen would be there with them as it played, as that piece of scum talked about fucking her, sticking his tongue in her, coming in her mouth. Hearing it again, herself, would be awful enough. But to have a couple of strangers listening, maybe wondering just how it would be to do those things to Pen . . . and they *would* wonder exactly that, Bodie thought. A man couldn't help it.

'What are you going to do?' Melanie asked.

'I don't know yet. Move out, maybe. Or buy a gun.'

'I guess I'll turn in,' Joyce said shortly after they returned to her house. 'It's early, though. Feel free to stay up as long as you want. Watch some TV, have a snack, a drink, whatever.' To Pen, she added, 'You know where everything is.'

'Would it be all right to use the jacuzzi?' Pen asked.

'Sure. That'd be nice on a night like this. I'd join you but . . . I'm the one who didn't get a nap this afternoon.'

They told her goodnight, and she went upstairs.

'You two interested?' Pen asked, looking at Melanie.

'I don't think so. But you go ahead.'

'Are you sure?'

Bodie wanted to go in the jacuzzi. Badly. He said nothing.

'We didn't bring our suits,' Melanie said.

One of Pen's shoulders rose and fell just slightly. 'Dad has some spare trunks he keeps around for guests. One of those should be fine for Bodie. You could wear your underthings or whatever,' she told Melanie.

'Or nothing,' Bodie suggested.

'Hardy har,' Melanie said.

'I'll go turn the heat on.'

Melanie dropped onto the sofa, slouched back, and folded her hands behind her head. She watched Pen walk away, then turned her eyes to Bodie.

He shrugged. With a smile to hide his disappointment, he sat beside Melanie. He put a hand on her thigh. 'I think the jacuzzi would be neat.'

'We'd freeze getting out.'

'I don't mind.'

'I'll bet.'

'What's that supposed to mean?'

'You just want to see Pen with her clothes off.'

He laughed softly, then moved his hand higher. He slid her skirt against the warm smoothness of her skin. 'I'm not interested in Pen.'

'I've seen you looking at her.'

'Of course I look at her. I do that. When people are in my presence, I look at them. It's a defense against collisions.'

'Yeah, makes jokes.'

'Should I turn my head away when she's in the room?'

'It's not funny,' Melanie said.

'I know it's not,' he told her. 'I'm sorry. I suppose I have been looking at her. She is attractive.'

'Tell me about it.'

'But she's not you, Melanie. You're the one I love.'

He got his hand out from between her legs as she suddenly twisted around. She threw her arms around him and hugged him hard. Her face pressed the side of his neck. He lightly stroked her back.

'In spite of your weirdness,' he kidded.

'I'm so messed up.'

'You're fine.'

'No, I'm not.'

Bodie noticed a figure enter his peripheral vision. Turning his head just a bit, he saw Pen at the corner of the room. She halted, then backstepped quietly past the banister's newel post and crept up the stairs.

When she's ready to go in, Bodie thought, she'll have to come down those stairs and I'll be right here.

He felt eager, guilty.

'Have I been rotten to her?' Melanie asked.

'To Pen? I wouldn't say rotten, exactly. I know you have this rivalry or inferiority complex or something about her, but I think she could use a little more understanding from you. It isn't just *your* father who's in the hospital. He's Pen's father, too.'

'I know,' she said in a voice full of pain.

'And she also has this business of the obscene caller to deal with. Either one of those situations is pretty damned traumatic, and she's had both of them dumped on her at the same time. I'm sure she'd appreciate a little support.'

Nodding, Melanie eased out of his arms. Her eyes were red and wet. She rubbed them dry with her sleeve.

Bodie stroked the back of her head. 'Are you all right?'

She sniffed. 'I don't know why you put up with me.'

'Neither do I, but what the hell.'

With a hint of a smile, she dropped back against the cushion. She let out a long sigh. Bodie leaned back, shoulder touching hers, and took hold of her hand.

'I'll try not to be such a pain in the ass,' she said.

'Me, too.' He squeezed her hand. She returned the squeeze. Later, he said, 'I would like to go in the jacuzzi.'

'Oh yeah?'

'Why don't we wait till Pen's finished? It'll be just you and me and the hot, bubbling water.'

'We'd still freeze getting out.'

'Who cares?'

Pen started down the stairway.

Bodie covered his eyes.

Melanie elbowed him.

He lowered his hands and watched Pen come down the stairs. She wore a royal blue robe that reached to mid-thigh, and had a folded towel under one arm.

'You do have a bathing suit on under that?' Melanie asked.

'Sure. I packed one tonight. I had this in mind.'

'We'll meet you in there,' Melanie said, and stood up.

'Great.'

Fabulous, Bodie thought.

At the bottom of the stairs, Pen said, 'Dad keeps those spare trunks in the linen closet by the bathroom. No rush, though. The water won't be good and hot for a while yet.'

Bodie, still amazed by Melanie's decision, followed her upstairs. She led him to the linen closet and pulled out two swimsuits. One was striped and baggy, so he chose the other – bikini trunks of thin, stretch nylon.

'You'll look sweet in those,' Melanie said.

'Better sweet than nerdy.'

She found two large towels, led Bodie to the bedroom.

When the trunks were on, he lifted his shirttail for Melanie's inspection.

'Cute. Real cute.'

The clinging fabric not only bulged at his crotch, but showed his penis in some detail. He let the shirttail fall. 'What the hell, it'll be dark out there.'

Melanie raised an eyebrow, but didn't protest.

'I'll keep my back to your sister,' he said.

'You'd *better*.' Melanie went to the door.

'Aren't you going to change?'

'Into what?'

He shrugged. This is getting better and better, he thought. He followed her downstairs and out the back door. Shivering, he took one of the towels and wrapped it around his waist.

The patio was bright beneath a floodlight. Looking around, Bodie spotted a Weber grill, an umbrella table with chairs, and a couple of loungers. No sign of Pen or the hot spa.

But he heard a hum of machinery off in the distance. It made a steady, high noise like a window air-conditioning unit.

'This way,' Melanie said.

He followed her off the lighted patio, into the darkness beyond. They walked on flagstones set in the grass. There were a lot of trees back here. Looking all around, Bodie could see no sign of neighboring houses.

He ducked beneath the low branches of lemon trees that hung over the walkway.

Then he spotted a gazebo with trellis walls on three sides and no top. The front side was open. Within was the elevated tub, Pen's head and shoulders visible in the moonlight.

'Welcome,' Pen said as they approached. 'I brought us some refreshments.' On the edge beside her stood a wine bottle and glass, and two bottles of beer. She had a wine glass in her hand.

Bodie dipped his fingers into the water. It felt like a hot bath.

Pen, stretching an arm out behind her, flicked a switch. A red light came on at the bottom. She wore a bikini that was probably white but looked pink in the swirling red-hued water. Bodie quickly turned to Melanie. 'Ladies first,' he said.

Melanie, standing sideways, put a hand on the wooden platform surrounding the pool and stepped out of her shoes.

She took off her blouse, folded it carefully, and placed it on the platform beside the towels. She was naked from the waist up. Her skin shimmered with a rosy glow. Her nipples were stiff and jutting. Bodie, watching, felt his penis push at his flimsy, yielding swimsuit. Melanie's small breasts lifted and flattened slightly as she raised her arms to unfasten her choker. Her eyes were on him. She removed her skirt, folded it, and put it on top of the blouse. She wore brief panties of black lace. Leaving them on, she climbed the wooden stairs and stepped down into the pool. 'Oh, that feels good,' she said, and crouched until the water frothed around her shoulders. Wisps of steam circled her face.

Bodie unbuttoned his shirt. 'Can you see the house from here?' he asked, and turned his back to the women. No, he couldn't see the house through the bushes and trees. More important, the girls couldn't see his front. As he took off his shirt, he glanced down. His suit was sticking out badly.

He wished he'd picked the other trunks.

He turned around, holding the shirt low, and casually started to fold it as he climbed the stairs. He kept folding it as he looked into the water and spotted the three submerged steps. Fortunately, Pen turned away to reach for the wine bottle. He tossed the shirt onto Melanie's pile of clothes, and hurried down. The hot water covered him to the belly.

He squatted. Moving backward, he found the tile bench with his rump. He reclined and stretched out his legs in Melanie's direction. His feet touched hers. She was sitting off to his right. Pen was straight across from him.

'How do you like it?' Melanie asked.

'Fantastic.'

Pen handed a glass of wine to Melanie, then lifted a beer bottle off the ledge and leaned toward Bodie. Her bikini was the kind that tied behind the neck. Its cords looked pale against the wet glossy skin of her chest. Her breasts were below the surface, blurred by the bubbling water. Bodie took the beer bottle and thanked her.

Easing back against the wall, he took a sip. The beer was cold and good. The hot water caressed him. His suit was so skimpy and thin that he felt naked.

'The beer's great,' he said.

Pen nodded. Her blond hair was damp and straggly from the steam, and Bodie liked the way a few tendrils curled over her forehead and in front of her ears. She took a sip of wine. She was sitting up fairly straight to drink it. Her wet arm looked sleek. The tops of her breasts were just above the surface, now, lapped by moving water. Through the swirl, Bodie could see the rest of her bikini top, her tawny skin below it, the patch of pink-tinted fabric between her legs with cords stretched to her hips, the length of her legs. But the bubbling water distorted all he saw to vague, shifting blurs.

'Dad wanted to put in a swimming pool,' Melanie said. 'There wasn't room with all the trees. He didn't want any of them taken out, so he settled for this.'

'This is nice,' Bodie said.

'Especially when the weather's a little chilly,' Pen added. 'And it almost always is, at night.'

'We're only a couple of miles from the ocean,' Melanie said. She lifted her wine glass to her lips and sat up a bit more. Her breasts came out of the water. They shimmered wet in the red glow and their dark nipples stood erect.

If she's trying to steal my attention from Pen, Bodie thought, she's succeeding.

He scooted across the slick tile bench until he was directly across from her.

'Maybe you should take Bodie to the beach tomorrow,' Pen suggested. 'Over by Venice, it's a real carnival on the weekends. On Ocean Front Walk? Have you ever been there?' she asked Bodie.

'A couple of years ago. I wouldn't mind seeing it again.'

'It's a thought,' Melanie said. She looked at Pen. 'Would you like to come along if we go?'

'I think I'll start looking for a new apartment.'

'You're really going to move?'

'Probably.' Pen turned to give herself a refill.

Melanie shook her head. 'That's pretty drastic.' She lowered her wine glass. The edge of its base bent her right nipple downward. The glass eased lower. Her nipple, released, sprang up straight.

Bodie squirmed and took a drink of beer.

'I'm not sure I can stay at that place of mine any more.' Pen took a drink. Then she tilted back her head and stared at the sky. 'Would anyone mind if I turn off the lights?'

'Fine,' Melanie said.

There goes my view, Bodie thought. 'All right.'

Pen reached over the edge of the platform, and the red glow died.

The half moon was almost straight overhead. An airliner passed near it. Bodie could only see a few stars.

He looked down. The women were indistinct, pale shapes of faces and shoulders, invisible below the water's surface.

'It's peaceful this way,' Pen said.

'Dark, too,' said Bodie.

Melanie put down her glass and slipped forward. She came over to Bodie's side of the pool and eased onto the bench. Her arm slid against his. She was covered to the shoulders. The pale mounds of her breasts were barely visible through the water, and Bodie couldn't see anything below them. He put a hand on her leg.

'I'm glad we decided to come out with you,' she told Pen. 'I'd forgotten how glorious this feels.'

Bodie felt his hand being lifted off her thigh. Something was pushed against his palm. He closed his fingers around it. A small cloth of some . . . Melanie's panties.

She took them away from him and guided his hand up her leg.

'Do you still stay away from the jacuzzi at your apartment?' Melanie asked in a calm voice.

'Still do,' Pen said.

'When I was staying with her, she never went in the pool or sunbathed or anything.'

'I didn't like the idea of strangers looking at me.'

Bodie nodded. He didn't trust his voice. His hand was taken to its destination and released. His fingers slid against Melanie. His heart raced. He tried to breathe normally. He felt as if his erection might split the front of his swimsuit.

Melanie squirmed slightly against his fingers.

And suddenly it was all wrong.

What the hell was he doing?

He moved his hand to Melanie's leg. She gripped his wrist and gently urged it back, but he pulled his hand free and stood up. 'I think I'll go back in, now,' he said, trying to keep his voice steady. 'I'm starting to feel a little sick. It's probably the heat and the beer, I don't know. I'll see you two later.'

He climbed out, wrapped the towel around his shoulders, picked up his shirt, and hurried down to the concrete slab.

'So long,' Pen said. Her voice sounded strange.

'See you later,' Melanie said.

Bodie shivered all the way back to the house – but it was Melanie that made him grit his teeth.

What in God's name went on in that mind of hers!

Be fair, he told himself. Maybe she just got horny and lost control. That'd be perfectly understandable. Hell, yes.

But he *knew* that wasn't it.

Handing her panties to him. Like a dog dropping a ball at his feet. Come on, play with me.

Play with me in front of my sister.

It'll be our little secret.

Unless, of course, she happens to notice. And that would be even better, wouldn't it?

Bodie stopped at the door, quickly wiped his legs to make sure he wouldn't drip on the floor, then entered the house.

Chapter Twelve

Groggy and hot after the wine and the long time in the spa, Pen stepped into the shower. The cool water pelted her, slid down her body. She wore her bikini to rinse the chlorine from it. Then she took it off, wrung it out and draped it over the shower door.

She wondered at Melanie. The girl had actually gone into the spa topless.

No big deal, Pen thought. I would've been naked in there, myself, except for them.

Well, that's the point, isn't it? If Melanie had gone in just with Bodie, or just with me . . . but we were both in there. That's what makes it so strange.

Like she was trying to prove something. To Bodie or to me? Maybe to herself.

Pen wondered if Bodie's abrupt departure had anything to do with Melanie's behavior. She'd been sitting right next to him. Maybe put a hand inside his trunks?

Thinking about it, Pen felt a warm, trembling stir. She stopped sliding the soap over her body, set it in the dish, and turned to face the spray.

Give the girl a break, she told herself. Melanie's only trying to protect her interests – keep Bodie for herself. It's probably worse because of Dad. Something like that throws your emotions out of whack, distorts your perspective.

I should let her know I don't have designs on Bodie.

Sure. She wouldn't believe it, though.

Pen shampooed her hair. When she was done in the shower, she stepped out and dried herself. She brushed her teeth. She used the toilet.

The cool shower hadn't been enough to take away the heat from the spa and wine, and a light film of moisture made her robe cling to her skin when she put it on.

In the hallway, she turned off the overhead lights and stepped quickly past the closed door of Joyce's room. Melanie's door was also shut. A strip of light showed through the space beneath it. Passing the door, Pen heard a radio. And Melanie.

Breathless, quick moans from Melanie not quite hidden by the smooth voice of Kenny Rogers.

Pen rushed into her room and shut the door. Wiped her sweaty face with a sleeve of her robe. The sound of music came faintly through the wall. She stood motionless, listening, but didn't hear Melanie.

Tossing her robe onto the bed, she stepped to the window and opened it. The night breeze came in, chilling her damp body.

The radio voice now sounded like Waylon Jennings and she heard a muffled outcry that gave her stomach a flip.

She hurried to her suitcase, took out her hair drier, sat at the dressing table, and turned it on. The noise of the blower obliterated the sounds of the music and Melanie.

She entered the hospital room, and the bed was empty. 'Where's Dad?' she asked. 'Did he go home?'

'Wouldn't you like to know?' the doctor said, grinning. He was short and skinny, with black hair.

'Where's Dad?' she asked.

'First show me your tits.'

'Go to hell.'

'Don't be a tease. I know you want me.' He tugged her bikini top.

I knew I should've dressed up before coming here.

The bikini tore away. She crossed her arms over her breasts.

'It's all right, I'm a doctor.' He twirled his stethoscope. 'Let me just see about your ticker.'

Pen wasn't at all sure about this. Probably a trick of some kind. But he could tell her where Dad was. She lowered her arms.

The doctor bent over and pressed the metal disk to her nipple. 'Cough,' he said.

He's no doctor. My heart isn't there. A real doctor would know that.

'I don't hear it. You'd better lie down.'

'What for?'

'So I can fuck your brains out.'

117

'You're *him*!'

She rammed a knife into his belly so hard it doubled him over and lifted him off his feet. He hit the floor with his hands and knees. 'Where's Dad?'

'You didn't have to kill me.'

'You're not dead, you're talking.'

'I'm gonna *get* you!'

She ran from the room and looked back when she heard rushing footsteps behind her. The man was chasing her, pulling the knife from his belly as he ran. Blood flew from his wound, spraying out, painting the floor and wall in front of him.

Pen jabbed the elevator button.

He ran closer and closer, waving the knife overhead.

Come on, elevator!

Oh shit oh shit!

Pen hopped from foot to foot. She pounded on the elevator door.

The man wore a wild grin. He started to laugh, blood exploding from his mouth and nostrils.

The elevator doors slid open. Pen jumped inside. He lunged for her, but the doors shut in time, trapping his arm at the elbow.

The elevator started down. His arm glided up to the ceiling, broke off and dropped to the floor. He kept his grip on the knife. His arm rolled. The blade lifted, pointed at Pen, made little circles. Pen backed away from it. The elevator gained speed. Plummeted.

Where is it going?

Why doesn't it slow down?

It'll stop suddenly and I'm supposed to fall on the knife, but I won't.

She sat on the elevator floor.

Outfoxed you, you bastard.

The elevator stopped smoothly without the expected jolt. The doors parted.

Beyond them was darkness.

The lighted indicator above the elevator door read 'B'.

This is the basement. Somebody turned off the lights, that's all.

Oddly, the severed arm on the floor with the knife twirling in its hand didn't worry Pen half so much as the darkness outside the elevator.

The basement. That's where the corpses are kept. The patients who didn't make it. Stored in drawers.

She sidestepped around the arm and stopped at the edge of the elevator floor. She peered into the pitch black.

She didn't want to go out there.

Her heart pounded with terror, and she struggled for breath.

'Hello?' she called. 'Anyone there?'

No answer came.

Of course not. The dead don't talk.

She called out again. 'Hello?'

'Help me,' came the distant, muffled voice of her father.

'I'll be right there!'

If she could just find a light switch. She reached outside the elevator, felt along the wall, and a cold hand grabbed her wrist.

'Yyeee-ahh!!!'

Pen lurched awake and heard the last of her outcry in the dark room. She sat up, panting.

'God almighty,' she muttered.

She drew a sleeve across her face to wipe the sweat away. Her pajamas felt glued to her skin.

One hell of a nightmare. She tried to remember it; and

recalled searching for a light switch, someone clutching her hand. There must've been more to the dream, but the rest was gone.

Somewhere, she'd heard that you need to stay awake for three or four minutes – if you fall asleep any sooner, you might find yourself back in the same nightmare.

No thank you.

Besides, her mouth was dry, she had a slight headache, and she needed to urinate.

She got up, plucked the pajamas away from her back and buttocks, and opened her door. The hallway was dark. One of its light switches was on the wall just outside her door. She almost reached for it, but thoughts of the nightmare sent a chill crawling up her skin. She felt the tingle of gooseflesh on her thighs and forearms, the nape of her neck, her forehead. The skin of her nipples grew tight and stiff.

It was just a goddamn nightmare, she told herself.

Still, she couldn't reach for the switch.

She turned on her bedroom lamp instead. It cast a pool of light into the hallway. No one was there, waiting to grab her. Of course not.

Feeling more at ease, she walked silently to the bathroom. She used the toilet. She found Tylenol in the medicine cabinet and washed down two pills. On the way back to her room, she paused in front of Melanie's door. The strip of light at its bottom was gone. No sound came from inside. She continued to her own room, stepped through the doorway, and stopped fast.

Bodie, in a rumpled bathrobe, stood facing her window. 'Are you decent?' he asked quietly without looking around.

Pen eased the door shut. She took a shaky breath. 'I'm decent,' she said. 'What are you doing here?'

He turned around. His hands were clasped at his waist. His eyes looked nervous. He made a feeble smile that quickly died. 'I just need to talk to you for a couple of minutes. I'm sorry for barging in.'

'It's all right,' she said. Her voice sounded strangely muted and husky.

Good Christ, she thought. He came to my room. What *is* this?

She sat on the edge of her bed. Folded her trembling hands. Took a deep breath. Looked down at herself, found her top button open, fastened it, and refolded her hands.

Bodie came around to a straight-backed chair beside her dresser. His sandy brown hair was mussed. His robe was tightly shut, tied at the waist with its cloth belt. He held it together over his thighs as he sat down.

'You yelled or something,' he said.

'Yeah. A nightmare. A real winner.'

'Are you okay?'

She nodded.

'I wasn't going to come over, but I heard that, and then you walked past our door. I figured this might be the time. I was lying awake, thinking about . . .' He hesitated.

'About what?'

'Telling you.'

Telling me what? she wondered. Her heart hammered.

'Bodie,' she whispered, 'you shouldn't have come here.'

'I know, I know. Melanie'd kill me . . .'

'Could you blame her?'

'I can't keep this thing to myself.'

'You hardly know me.'

'I know I can trust you. I think we've got some real trouble about to go down.'

Pen frowned, relieved, a little disappointed, confused.

'What are you talking about?'

'Remember in the hospital room? How Melanie wigged out?'

'Remember? Are you kidding?'

'She said she didn't know what her vision was about, but that wasn't true. She remembered the whole thing. And she told me about it in the room tonight.'

Before or after you screwed her? Pen wondered, and immediately felt angry at herself for thinking it. 'What did she say?'

'It was the accident again. She saw the car speeding toward her, like before, only this time she saw the driver. She said the driver was Harrison Donner.'

'Oh, man,' Pen muttered. 'Is she sure?'

'She seemed very sure.'

'Harrison hit Dad?'

'Melanie thinks it was a conspiracy, that Harrison and Joyce planned it together.'

'Was that in her vision, too?'

'It's a theory she came up with. The way she explained it, Joyce knew in advance about their plan to eat at Gerard's – probably even called in the reservation herself. She also knew that your father always left his car in that bank parking lot, so he'd have to cross Cañon to get to the restaurant. She filled in Harrison, and he was waiting – maybe parked at the curb. When your father started across . . .' Bodie's hands lifted off his knees, hovered a moment, and dropped down again.

'What you're saying . . . Melanie thinks they conspired to murder Dad?'

'That's about it. I'm not convinced she's right, but it *could've* been set up that way. I don't see any holes in it, do you?'

'Harrison couldn't count on there not being any witnesses.'

'If the situation didn't look favorable, he had the option of aborting. For all we know, they used a similar set-up half a dozen times before last night, and called it off each time for one reason or another – witnesses, too much traffic, whatever.'

'You've given it a lot of thought,' Pen said.

'Two hours' worth, between the time she told me and the time I came over here.'

Pen realized she was shivering. It may have been Bodie's story. It may have been the breeze from the window chilling the nightmare sweat on her pajamas.

Bodie sat stiff in the chair, legs pressed together, hands gripping his knees.

'Are you cold?' she asked.

'A little,' he admitted.

It crossed her mind to invite him onto the bed. They could cover up.

I don't believe so, she told herself.

'I'll shut the window,' she said.

'I'll do it.'

As he went to the window, Pen dropped onto her side, reached to the foot of her bed, and sat up, dragging the knitted comforter. She held it out to Bodie when he returned.

He thanked her, wrapped it around his body, and sat on the chair. 'That's a lot better,' he said.

Pen scooted back on the mattress. She crossed her legs. She drew a blanket up behind her and draped it over her shoulders. 'So,' she said. 'What's the motive?'

'Joyce and Harrison are lovers.'

'Do you think they really are?'

Bodie shrugged. 'I don't know. It's possible. It's likely, I guess.'

'Okay. Suppose they are. That's hardly a motive for murder. Getting a divorce is a cinch in this state, and she'd come out of it with a pretty good settlement.'

'Half?'

Pen shook her head. 'They've been married almost three years. She'd probably get half of what Dad earned after the date of their marriage, plus maybe a couple of years of alimony.'

'But if she . . .' Bodie hesitated.

'Kills him.'

'Yeah. She gets it all. Plus his life insurance.'

'That'd depend on his will and on who's named as beneficiaries in the insurance policies. I imagine Melanie and I would get some of it.' Pen frowned. 'Melanie talked about all that at the hospital. Remember? She blurted out something about Joyce getting Harrison and the insurance and inheritance if Dad would die. Then she burst into the room to "save" him.'

'Thought Joyce was planning to pull the plug.'

'And that's when she had her vision,' Pen said. 'She'd barely gotten through the door when it started.'

Bodie pulled the comforter more tightly around himself. 'Are you thinking that she faked it?'

Pen considered the possibility, remembered Melanie thrashing in her arms, moaning. 'I don't think she faked the attack. But I wonder if her suspicions couldn't have triggered it somehow. She already suspected Joyce and Harrison were lovers and she thought that Joyce might want Dad to die, so it's just one more small step to the idea that Joyce and Harrison conspired to run him down. Her subconscious, maybe, took that step for her.'

'And gave her the attack,' Bodie said. 'I don't know. I had

pretty much that same idea about the episode she had at the concert last night. She didn't know whether it was you or her father who got creamed, but she was carrying a real load of anger and guilt about both of you, so I got the feeling that her vision might be some kind of perverse wish-fulfillment.'

Pen gazed at him.

'I don't mean she *wanted* you dead. Just that she couldn't handle her feelings about either one of you. And her mind shorted out. Gave her the vision. But what she saw in that trance turned out to be right. Maybe this one is, too.'

'They aren't always,' Pen said, and felt a small tremor in her stomach.

'She was right about her mother, wasn't she?'

'But there were other times. Like the night of Dad and Joyce's wedding. They were flying to Hawaii for their honeymoon. Melanie and I were here at the house and she threw a pretty good fit. When she came out of it, she said the airliner had blown up in mid-air.'

Bodie pursed his lips as if to whistle, but no sound came out.

'Obviously,' Pen said, 'she was wrong on that one. No airliner at all went down that night, much less the one carrying Dad and Joyce.'

'She wasn't happy about the marriage, I know that.'

'She was outraged by it. She felt that Dad was betraying the memory of our mother, and that Joyce was a whore after Dad for his money. That's why she moved in with me before they got back from their honeymoon. She couldn't stand either of them.

'Then there was her vision about me,' Pen said. Her stomach fluttered again and she suddenly felt uncomfortably warm. She shrugged the blanket off her shoulders. She took a deep breath. Talking about this, she realized, would be difficult. But Bodie needed to know.

'It was the summer before my senior year at college. I always came home for the summers. Melanie was fifteen. She'd started going with this guy, Steve Wells, who'd just graduated high school. He was seventeen or eighteen, I guess.'

'She likes older men,' Bodie said.

It forced a smile from Pen. 'Yeah, apparently so. Anyway, he spent quite a lot of time here.' She hesitated.

'And he fell for you,' Bodie said.

Pen nodded. 'Did Melanie tell you about this?'

'She didn't have to. The way she is about you, it's obvious something of that kind must've happened along the way.'

'God, it's not like I did anything to encourage him. I mean, I was nice to him. I didn't ignore him. But I never . . . flirted with him or anything like that.'

Bodie's face grew slightly red.

Pen didn't want to think about what his blush might mean. She fingered the cuff of her pajama leg. 'So he was here for dinner one night. Dad barbequed out back. After we ate, Dad had to leave. There was a meeting or something, I forget.'

'Let me guess,' Bodie said. 'The three of you went in the jacuzzi.'

Pen met his eyes.

'We didn't have the jacuzzi then.'

'Oh.'

'Melanie fell asleep on the couch. We'd had margaritas with supper, and she was pretty much looped. I went into the kitchen to make coffee, and Steve followed me. It was awful. He blurted out about how he'd lost interest in Melanie the minute he laid eyes on me, and the only reason he kept going with her was so he could come to the house and see me. I told him to forget it, I wouldn't have anything to do with him and if he'd lost interest in Melanie he should get the hell out of her life. It took him a while to get the message. But when he did, he left.

'Melanie didn't wake up for a couple more hours. In the meantime, I'd taken a bath and put on a nightgown. I was reading in bed when Melanie came into my room. She asked where Steve was, and I said he'd gone home. I didn't tell her what had gone on. I figured it was his responsibility, you know?'

'Yeah,' Bodie said. 'Why should you get stuck with breaking the news?'

'Anyway, all of a sudden Melanie threw a fit. Her eyes rolled up and she started shaking. She fell on the floor. I was scared. I didn't know what was going on. But then she came out of it and looked at me as if I were some kind of monster. She went nuts. She called me . . . some pretty awful names. She said Steve and I had made it together while she was zonked out on the couch. I told her that we hadn't done anything, but she wouldn't believe me. That's because she'd *seen* it. She'd seen it all, in glorious detail, while she was rolling around drooling on my bedroom carpet.'

Pen was shaking by the time she finished. She let out a long breath, then waited, staring at the edge of her mattress until she felt reasonably calm again. 'I denied it, and Steve denied it when she phoned him. But to this day she's convinced we both lied, that we actually . . . screwed . . . while she was sleeping off her margaritas. She has total faith in those visions of hers.'

Bodie was frowning. The frown had started early in Pen's story, and stayed. 'It has to be terrible, getting blamed like that for something you didn't do.'

'Yeah. It almost makes you wish you'd done something to deserve it.'

A corner of Bodie's mouth curled up. 'Should've slept with the guy.'

'He wasn't my type.' Pen felt a smile come to her own face. 'At any rate, that was probably more than you wanted to hear, but . . .'

'Not at all. It tells me a lot about you and Melanie – this thing she has about you. It's been putting a certain strain on *me*, you know.'

'I can imagine. I'm sure she thinks we just can't wait to jump in the sack together.' Immediately, Pen wished she hadn't said that. She felt a heat wash over her face. 'Let's get back to her visions,' she said.

'Right. Her visions.'

'She's had at least two that were totally off: Steve and I, and the airliner that didn't blow up.'

'She doesn't believe she was wrong about you and Steve,' Bodie said, 'but you'd think the business about the airliner explosion would've shaken her faith a bit.'

'You'd think so.'

'Well, this thing tonight has her absolutely convinced that Harrison's the one who ran down your father. She's also sure that Joyce helped set it up. And she plans to do something about it.'

'Like what?' Pen asked.

'She said, "They're gonna pay." '

'She's thinking about revenge?'

'It looks that way.'

'Oh, Jesus.'

'That's why I had to talk to you. I think we need to do something.'

'Maybe you'd better take her back to Phoenix.'

'I don't think she'd go along with that.'

'What's your idea, then?' Pen asked.

'The main thing is, we need to keep an eye on her.'

'She's never been violent. That I know about.'

'Nobody ever tried to kill her father before.'

'We don't know that they . . .'

'*She* knows. She's absolutely certain. And I think there's a possibility that she's right. Those visions of hers have been on the mark more often than not.'

'I'd say they're about fifty-fifty.'

'I think she's right about those two being lovers. What do you think?'

'I'm not convinced,' Pen said, 'but I have my suspicions.'

'If they *are*, it's conceivable that they did decide to eliminate your father.'

'That's pretty hard to buy.'

'People commit murder every day.'

'I know that.'

'And the people they kill, more often than not, are friends or members of the family.'

Pen nodded. 'I've done some research on the subject.'

Bodie shrugged the comforter off his shoulders and leaned forward, elbows on knees. 'I'm not saying they're guilty. The thing is, Melanie thinks they are. She might or might not be right, but there's a strong chance she'll do something about it. I say we not only keep an eye on her, we help her.'

'Help her do what?'

'Nail them,' Bodie said.

'*What?*'

'Only we control Melanie, we channel her. First, we convince her that the vision isn't enough. Then we offer to help investigate. I think she'll go along with that.'

'And *do* we investigate?'

'Just some minor-league snooping. Who knows? We might actually turn up some evidence.'

'Fat chance.'

'If we do, we take it to the police. If we turn up zilch, at least we've kept Melanie out of trouble for a while, and maybe she'll even end up convinced they had nothing to do with it.'

'One problem. I'm not supposed to know about this vision she had, and I don't imagine she'd be overjoyed to find out you snuck into my bedroom to fill me in.'

'Tell her that you're suspicious. Right now, she thinks you'd take Joyce's side.'

'Did she say that?'

Bodie nodded.

'I guess I can't blame her.'

'But if you let her know that you have doubts of your own about Joyce, I think she'll see you as an ally and confide in you.'

'It's like conspiring against her.'

'Joyce?'

'Melanie.' She sighed. 'I don't know. If we start looking for clues or whatever, we might just end up feeding her delusion.'

'If it *is* a delusion.'

'Yeah, if. And if she's right, I'd be as anxious as anyone to see those two get what's coming to them.'

'Tell Melanie that.'

'Maybe I'd better.'

'I think she'll be glad to know you're with her.'

'Maybe.'

Bodie stood up. 'I'd better get out of here.' He lifted the comforter and carried it to the foot of Pen's bed. 'Talk about feeding delusions . . . if she woke up and found out I was over here . . .' He put the comforter on the bed. 'She'd never, no way, believe it was innocent.'

'I don't know how innocent it was.'

Bodie's eyes widened.

'I didn't mean *that*.' Again, she felt herself blush. 'I meant the way we're plotting against her.'

Bodie nodded and went to the door. He paused with a hand on the knob, and looked back at Pen. 'The times are out of joint,' he said.

'I think that should be Melanie's line.'

He smiled. 'Goodnight, Pen.'

'Goodnight.'

Chapter Thirteen

Melanie was not in the room.

Bodie snuggled down and shut his eyes again. The bed felt too warm and cozy to leave. Briefly, he wondered where Melanie had gone.

Then he pictured Pen in her room last night sitting cross-legged on her bed: her mussed golden hair, her blue eyes, the light sprinkle of freckles across her nose. He saw the shiny blue pajama shirt open at her throat, the way it lay smooth over the mounds of her breasts and how it draped her lap. The pants legs were stretched taut to her knees. Her ankles were slim and bare.

Bodie ached as he lingered on the image of her. If only . . . If only what?

Maybe if she had started to cry. She hadn't been close to it, though. But if she *had* cried, he could've comforted her – moved to the bed and put an arm around her, and she would've turned to him. He could've held her gently as she wept. Kissed her.

God, to kiss her. Just to hold and kiss her.

Thinking about it made a hollow ache in his chest.

Don't worry, Melanie, he thought, it'll never happen.

If Whit dies . . .

Nice thought. Damn.

But to hold her, to kiss her.

He remembered his shock of alarm when Pen had asked, last night, if he was cold. For just an instant he'd feared – and hoped – that she would ask him to come to the bed. No funny stuff, she would've said. Promise? Oh, yes.

It didn't happen.

Nothing happened.

Not quite nothing. She hadn't told him to go away. They'd sat for a long time, alone in her room, she in her pajamas and he in his robe, and they'd talked. She'd told him things, shared secrets. There had been an intimacy to it all.

Thank God for Melanie's vision. Without that for an excuse . . . It was not an excuse, he told himself. It was his *reason* for going to her room.

His intentions had been entirely honorable.

But God, what if something *had* happened!

It didn't. It won't. Don't even think about it.

Suppose she'd said, 'Bodie, I've been lying awake thinking about you, wishing you were here with me. I love you. I can't help myself.'

With a moan, he tossed his covers aside and got out of bed. When he was dressed, he stepped into the hallway. The bathroom door was shut. He heard water running – someone

132

about to take a bath? So he combed his hair in the bedroom, then went downstairs.

From the silence, he guessed that nobody else was around. Someone had been in the kitchen, though. He poured himself a mug of hot coffee.

On the center of the kitchen table was a note folded in half to make it stand like a tent. Bodie picked it up.

Hi!
I've gone to Mass and I have some errands to run. Expect me when you see me. Make yourselfs at home. Their's bacon and eggs in the fridge as well as coffee cake in the freezer. So help yourselfs.

Love,
Joyce

Good speller, Bodie thought, and put the note down.

Gone to mass? That would mean she's Catholic. Will you be confessing today, Joyce? And what sort of sins will you be whispering in the Father's ear? Adultery? Attempted murder?

Beyond the glass door, the patio was bright with sunlight. Bodie stepped to the door. He gripped its handle. He saw Pen off to the left, reclined on a lounger and reading a paperback. She wore a blue and yellow plaid blouse and white shorts. Her legs were stretched out, long and slender, her bare feet crossed at the ankles. She had a coffee mug in one hand.

Bodie wanted to go out there and pull up a chair beside her.

What could it hurt?

He didn't know what it could hurt, but maybe she wanted time to herself and maybe Melanie would put in an appearance

133

full of suspicion and maybe he had just damn well not find himself alone with Pen first thing in the morning.

So he backed away from the door.

He carried his coffee mug into the living room. The Sunday *Los Angeles Times* was on a lamp table. He searched through it until he found the book section, then sat on the couch to read it while he drank his coffee and waited.

When his mug was empty, he returned to the kitchen. He filled it. He stepped to the door and looked out again. Pen was still on the lounger. Her knees were drawn up, and she held the book open against her thighs. Her hair glinted in the sunlight.

With a sigh, he turned away. He took his coffee back to the living room and sat down. This is crazy, he thought, and I'm a rat. She's Melanie's sister, for Godsake.

I haven't done anything.

And I'd better not.

It would probably blow up in my face, anyway. Even if Pen were interested in me (a damn big if), she's loyal to Melanie. Look what happened when that Steve character put moves on her.

Bodie found the newspaper's 'Calendar' section and began to look at the movie ads.

Then Melanie came down the stairs. She wore her tan corduroys and a gray sleeveless sweatshirt with the neck stretched out so it hung below one shoulder. Her choker was black.

'Where is everyone?' she asked as she approached him.

Bodie stood up. 'I don't know where your sister is. Joyce went to mass.'

'Mass?' She smirked.

'All squeaky clean?' he asked, and stroked the back of her head. Her thick black hair felt damp. She moved against him, and they kissed. Her hands slipped into the rear pockets of his pants. As they rubbed him, Bodie eased his own hands under her sweatshirt. Her skin felt smooth. There were no straps. He ran his hands up and down her back. Velvety. Warm. Bare. She felt wonderful and she was his and he was nuts to want Pen when he already had Melanie. He pushed a hand beneath the waistband of her cords.

'Aren't you ever *not* horny?' she whispered against his lips.

'Not when you're around.'

She smiled slightly. She kissed him again, then eased away. 'I wonder if the bitch left us something to eat.'

'Bacon and eggs in the fridge, coffee cake in the freezer.'

They headed for the kitchen.

'She sure got out of here early,' Melanie said.

'Think she's avoiding us?'

'I'd avoid us, if I were her.' Melanie lifted the note off the kitchen table. 'Mass. That's rich. Wants us to think she went off to pray for Dad?'

'Maybe she did.'

'Yeah, to pray he dies.'

Bodie stepped over to the door. 'Oh, there's Pen. I wonder if she's eaten yet.'

'Ask her.'

He slid open the door. The sound made her look around. 'Good morning,' he said.

'Hi, Bodie.'

His heart beat a little faster. 'Are you hungry?'

Nodding, she swung her legs off the lounger and stood up. Bodie caught himself staring at her legs as she walked toward him. He turned away.

'It's wonderful out there,' she said and entered the kitchen. 'I never sit out at my place.'

'Maybe you can find a new apartment with a private patio,' Melanie said.

'I should try. Sleep well?' she asked.

'Fine,' Melanie answered.

'Me, too,' said Bodie. 'Zonked right out.'

'The jacuzzi will do that to you. That and the booze.' She met Bodie's gaze and looked away. 'I was out like a light.'

'Did you see Joyce's note?' Bodie asked.

'Guess she's making herself scarce. Who could blame her?'

'What do you mean?' Bodie asked.

'Just that she can't be very comfortable around Dad's family. She's obviously sleeping with Harrison, after all.'

'I thought you didn't believe that,' Melanie said. 'What changed your mind?'

'Being around her, I guess. I can't even put my finger on it, but there's something about her. Maybe the way she's been acting – I don't know – ingratiating. It's as if she has a guilty conscience so she's bending over backwards to be sweet. You add that to the fact that Harrison was here yesterday morning . . . and what you told me about the bed.' Pen frowned at her sister. 'It makes me think that maybe you've been right about her all along. She wouldn't be sleeping with Harrison if she loved Dad.'

'She never loved Dad,' Melanie said. 'She just wanted his money.'

'But that doesn't mean she tried to kill him,' Bodie pointed out.

Melanie stabbed him with her eyes.

He grimaced. 'Woops.'

'What are you talking about?' Pen asked. 'Tried to kill *Dad*?'

Bodie tried to look sorry for his slip of the tongue. With a shrug, he said, 'Maybe you'd better tell her, Melanie.'

'*Neat* play.'

'It just came out.'

'I wish somebody would tell me what the hell's going on,' Pen demanded. 'My God, I think I have a right to know. He's my father, too.'

Leaning back against the refrigerator door, Melanie folded her arms across her chest. She sighed, gave Bodie another fierce glance, then met Pen's eyes. 'Joyce and Harrison fixed it up so Dad would get hit by the car.'

Pen's eyes went wide. Her mouth dropped open. She shook her head. 'That's insane,' she muttered.

'I *told* you she wouldn't listen.'

'Go on,' Bodie urged. 'Tell her the rest.'

'What's the point?'

Bodie looked at Pen. 'Harrison was driving the car that ran your father down. Melanie saw him. It was that vision she had last night in the hospital room.'

'I saw him behind the windshield,' Melanie said. 'It was as if I were looking with Dad's eyes.'

'You can't make an accusation like that based on nothing more than . . . your imagination.'

'It wasn't my imagination.'

'Maybe it was telepathy,' Bodie suggested. 'Maybe your father communicated it to her.'

'Don't tell me *you* believe it, too?'

'I don't know. I guess maybe I do.'

'You're both bananas.'

Bodie wondered if, perhaps, Pen was playing it a bit *too* skeptical.

'Joyce made the dinner reservations,' Melanie said, a certain eagerness sneaking into her voice. 'She knew Dad always parked behind the bank, knew he'd have to cross the street. Harrison parked and waited till Dad started across.'

'It could've happened that way,' Bodie said.

'It *did*.'

'You'd need proof,' Pen told her. 'You can't base this whole thing on some kind of psychic experience.'

'Let's *get* proof,' Bodie suggested.

'I already know,' Melanie said.

'Your visions aren't always right,' Pen pointed out. 'Remember Dad's honeymoon?'

'That was a fluke.'

'Maybe this is a fluke.'

'It's not.'

'Then let's get some proof we can take to the police,' Bodie said.

Melanie sighed.

'We'd need to take a look at Harrison's car,' Pen said. 'If he hit Dad, the car might've sustained some damage. And there'd be . . . traces. Even if he tried to wash it off . . .'

'Joyce claimed it was a sports car,' Bodie said. 'Harrison drives a Mercedes.'

'Joyce could've lied,' Melanie said.

'Harrison owns a Porsche,' said Pen. 'He has a Mercedes and a Porsche.'

'You *would* know that.' Melanie smirked at Bodie. 'They were lovers, you know.'

'We were *not* lovers.'

'Uh-huh, sure.'

'We went out a few times, that's all.'

'Do you know where he lives?' Bodie asked.

'Of course she does.'

Bodie wished he hadn't found out about Pen and Harrison.

Thoughts of them together . . . 'Let's drive out to his place,' he said quickly, 'and see if we can get a look at his Porsche.'

Melanie shrugged. 'I guess it can't hurt.'

'Why don't we have breakfast first?' Bodie suggested. 'I'm starving.'

'You and your stomach.'

'Harrison's house is only a few miles from here,' Pen said. 'Why don't we eat afterwards?'

'Two against one,' he said. 'It ain't fair.'

Bodie drove west on San Vicente. Melanie sat in the van's passenger seat. Pen, crouched behind them, held onto the seatbacks, her left hand inches from Bodie's shoulder. Her face was in the gap, and he saw it each time he looked to the right. Her shampoo, or perfume, had a fresh clean scent.

Bodie's stomach didn't feel right – maybe simple hunger, maybe being so close to Pen, or maybe a reaction to finding out about her and Harrison. Lovers? She'd denied it. But she had admitted going with him. Bodie didn't like that. The guy was movie-star handsome, cool and smooth.

Drives a fucking Porsche.

An asshole.

Even if they hadn't been lovers, Pen must've liked him. They must've kissed. He must've had his hands on her.

Such thoughts didn't improve the condition of Bodie's stomach.

Whatever went on between them, he told himself, it's over now. Pen doesn't seem to like him. Maybe he dumped her. I hope she's the one who did the dumping.

'Make a left at the light,' she said.

Bodie steered into the turn pocket and waited for the green arrow.

'You know,' Melanie said, 'he probably didn't use his own car.'

'He's arrogant enough,' said Pen. 'Maybe he did.'

'Arrogant doesn't mean stupid.'

'It's still worth checking,' Bodie told them, and made the turn.

'You'll want to hang a right on the third street down.'

He nodded.

'Either rented a car or stole one.'

'Not necessarily,' Pen said. 'Renting would leave a trail.'

'He could've paid cash.'

'You have to show ID. Maybe he's got a fake ID, but that's tricky to pull off. The driver's license has your photo.'

'It's not *that* tricky,' Melanie argued.

'Besides, the rental person could identify him.'

'Not if he wore a disguise.'

'I don't think he'd do anything that elaborate – and risky. As you said, he's not stupid. He would know that the simpler he made it, the less chance of tripping up.'

Bodie turned right. The residential street was shaded by trees. The houses, mostly two stories, looked old but well kept. A peaceful neighborhood, its occupants probably well-off if not filthy rich.

'Two blocks,' Pen told him. 'Then make a left.'

'He must've stolen it, then,' Melanie said.

'That's not so simple, either. It's not as easy as they make it look on TV. Especially if we're talking about a sports car. You can't just jump in and hotwire the thing in five seconds and take off. You've got to bypass the steering wheel lock – and most of these newer cars have alarm systems.'

'Sports cars get stolen all the time,' Melanie told her.

'Mostly by pros, guys with the equipment to pull the ignition . . .'

'You sound like a pro yourself,' Bodie said.

'I've written about this kind of stuff. I had to do some research.'

'I just can't believe he would use his own car,' Melanie said.

'There must be a thousand Porsches in L.A. At least. He slaps some stolen plates on his Porsche before he goes after Dad, and he's home free as long as he doesn't take it in for repairs. He's got the Mercedes. He can leave the Porsche in his garage for a few weeks, then maybe get it repaired out of state. Turn here, Bodie, then take the first left.'

He slowed, steered around the corner, saw the intersection a short distance ahead, and flicked the arm of his turn signal.

'It'll be the third house on the right,' Pen said.

'What'll we do,' Bodie asked, 'drop in and ask to see his Porsche?'

'Just go by, for starters. Don't even slow down.'

Even as he made the turn, he spotted Harrison's gray Mercedes parked in the driveway of the third house.

'Damn it,' Melanie muttered.

'Too bad he's not at mass with Joyce,' Bodie said.

Harrison's home, unlike those of his neighbors, was a single-story ranch house. It looked more modern than the others. Red brick, a red tile roof, white trim. In front of the Mercedes stood a wrought-iron gate.

Pen's head blocked Bodie's view as she strained forward between the seats to look out Melanie's window. When she settled back, they were beyond the house.

'The Porsche must be in his garage,' she said.

'So what'll we do?' Bodie asked.

'We can't do anything while he's there.'

'Why don't we get some breakfast?'

'All right.'

He stopped at the corner, waited for a Mustang to go by, then drove through the intersection and saw, parked at the curb, a black Lincoln Continental. His heart gave a kick.

'My God,' Melanie gasped.

Bodie hit the brakes.

Pen leaned forward again. 'It's Dad's, all right.'

'Are you sure?'

'That pipe holder on the dash? I gave it to him for Christmas a few years ago.'

Bodie shook his head. 'Guess who's not at mass.'

'That miserable bitch,' Pen muttered. 'She really *is* making it with . . . oh, man. Oh, that dirty . . .'

'*I* knew it all along.' Melanie sounded proud of herself.

'God, if Dad ever found out he'd die. How could she *do* something like this!' Pen dropped backward out of sight. 'I want to go home,' she said in a small voice.

Bodie started his van moving again.

'*Not* to her home.' She sniffed. 'I never want to see her again.'

Melanie grinned.

'Your apartment?' Bodie asked.

'Please.'

'What about the caller?'

'Who cares?'

Chapter Fourteen

Bodie insisted on escorting Pen up to her apartment. Melanie stayed with them. This time, no note had been left under the door.

'Are you sure you'll be all right here?' Bodie asked.

'I just need to be alone.'

'I don't know why you're so upset all of a sudden,' Melanie said. 'I thought you already believed they were screwing around. All that happened is that we confirmed it.'

'Yeah, we confirmed it. I'll see you guys later, okay? Could you do me a real favor and bring my stuff over sometime? I really don't want to go back there unless I have to.'

'Sure, we'll do that,' Bodie said. 'Maybe you should reconnect one of your phones in case we need to get in touch about something.'

She nodded.

Then they were gone.

Pen sat on her sofa, propped her elbows on her knees, and rested her chin on her hands. She stared at the wall.

Hell no, she hadn't believed that Joyce was making it with Harrison. She'd suspected it, of course, but she hadn't *believed*. It was too damned outrageous.

Probably in Harrison's bed right now, this instant, fucking. And Dad in the hospital, barely alive.

And yeah they did it yesterday, too. Right from the hospital to Dad's home and fucked in Dad's bed.

What kind of scum is she?

The kind of scum, maybe, who *would* try to kill Dad. Why not? A piece of shit like that doesn't have any conscience.

143

How about Harrison?

Yeah, how about him.

Dad trusted him, treated him like a son, thought I'd lost my mind when I refused to see the guy any more, probably had our wedding all planned in his head and was looking forward to the grandchildren. I damn near wept at the pitiful look on his face. 'You two are so perfect for each other.' Right, Dad, but he's a shallow egocentric sadistic sleaze. Only I couldn't hurt you by telling on him. Big mistake.

Hey, Dad, this apple of your eye Harrison raped me. What do you think about that? He wasn't any too gentle about it, either. Want to see the bruises, the teethmarks?

Trembling, Pen leaned back against the cushions of the sofa. She hugged a corduroy-covered pillow to her chest.

She'd been a fool to let him take her to his home that night.

But they'd had dinner at Scandia where he'd been charming and amusing and they had shared two bottles of cabernet sauvignon after the margaritas. She was feeling no pain by the time they left.

'What're we doing here?' she asked when she found his car stopped in the driveway of his house.

'*The Maltese Falcon.* Starts in five minutes. You want to watch it, don't you?'

'We're gonna watch TV?'

'Have some coffee, sober up, drive you home after.'

Her mind whispered a warning, but she ignored it. They went inside. She sat on the couch. Harrison took off his jacket and necktie, and turned on the television. He went into the kitchen to make coffee. When he returned, he sat beside her. He held her hand, but that was all right.

He went away during the first commercial and came back with mugs of coffee.

'I bet you didn't know I was a private eye. A regular Sam Spade.'

'*You* were a private eye?'

'Bet you didn't know that.'

'Bet I don't believe it.'

He went away. Pen drank some coffee. He came back with a shoe box and sat beside her, the box on his lap. He lifted out a holstered revolver. 'My snub-nose .38,' he said.

Here we are, drunk, and he's got a gun in his hand. 'Let's see,' she said. He handed it to her. She removed it from the holster and turned the barrel toward her face.

'Hey, watch out.'

The bullet heads were visible inside the cylinder holes. 'Christ, it's loaded.'

'Of course.'

She put it on the coffee table at their knees. 'Ever shoot someone?'

'No, but I had to draw it a couple times. The firm I worked for did some security work.'

'Must've been exciting.'

'At first. It got boring fast. What *was* exciting was the repos.'

He took a leather wallet from the box and handed it to her. She opened it. Inside was a silver badge engraved, 'Special Agent'. The card holder showed his ID indicating that he was an agent of Robert Abrams Private Investigations, Inc. 'Amazing,' Pen said. 'You really were a private eye.'

'For two years while I was in law school. I needed the money and I figured it'd be good experience. Get a load of these babies.' He lifted a pair of handcuffs out of the box.

'Ever use these?'

'Sure. I made a couple of arrests. Show you how it's done?'

'I don't know.'

'Hey, you wanta be a writer, don't you? You gotta know this stuff. Here, stand up.'

'What are you gonna do?'

'You're a suspect. I just got the drop on you.' He stood, aiming his index finger at her, stuffing the cuffs into his pocket. 'On your feet.'

Laughing, Pen stood.

'Over to the wall.'

She bumped the lamp table, grabbed the base of the shaking lamp until it stopped wobbling, then stepped to the wall. 'This is just an excuse to frisk me,' she said.

'Hands against the wall.'

She raised them overhead, pressed them to the paneling.

Harrison poked her side. 'Don't try any funny stuff.'

'That what you said really?'

'I think I said, "Move and yer dead meat." '

'That's even worse.'

One of his feet hooked around Pen's right ankle and jerked her foot backward. He did the same to her other foot. Without the wall's support, she would've fallen on her face.

'Now I've got you immobilized,' Harrison said. 'You need both hands to hold you up.'

'True.'

He stuck his finger against her back and began to pat her down using his left hand.

Here it comes, she thought. 'Don't get carried away, huh?'

'Gotta make sure you ain't packin'.'

He ran his hand down her sides and her legs. He stayed away from her breasts and groin and rump. Pen was

146

impressed. Maybe I've got him wrong, she thought. Maybe he's okay, after all.

'Okay, you're clean,' he said. He snapped a cuff around her right wrist and pulled her arm down behind her back. He brought her left arm down, pulling her away from the wall, and snapped the other cuff around her wrist. 'Any questions?'

'Got a key for these?' Pen asked and turned around.

And saw the look on his face.

'Now the prisoner is in my control.'

'Harrison.'

'You're under arrest.'

'Let me go.'

'Uh-uh.'

She backed against the wall. 'Don't.'

He reached behind her neck to untie the cords of her gown.

'I'll scream.'

'Then I'll stuff something in your mouth, and that'll make it a little tough for you to breathe. Just relax.' The cords loosened. He drew them down, uncovering her breasts. His eyes were glassy, his face deep red. He pulled at the gown until it slipped to Pen's feet. He licked his lips. He squeezed her breasts.

'I'll have you arrested,' she said, her voice shaking. 'You'll get disbarred.'

'Bullshit. It's common knowledge you've been going with me. You came over here after an expensive dinner. Who's gonna believe you were forced into anything?' His hands slid down her body. He pushed his fingers under the elastic of her pantyhose.

'Bastard!' She kneed him, but missed the target, caught him instead in the thigh.

He cried out, staggered backward, then lunged at her, a shoulder driving her hard against the wall. A fist smashed her belly. Breath blasting out, she sagged.

Then she was on the floor, dazed and fighting for air as he yanked the pantyhose down her legs. 'It's time, baby,' he muttered. 'It's time.' He pulled her panties off. 'Time to pay the piper, babe. Can't string a guy along forever.' He tugged his belt open. 'A guy can just take so much. What does it take, huh? I'm not good enough for you? Maybe you're a dyke, huh? Is that it?' He flung his slacks aside.

'Bastard,' she gasped.

'That's me, that's me.' He tugged down his underpants and stepped out of them. 'And what are you? Fuckin' iceberg. What's it take to get in your pants, huh? Act of fuckin' Congress?' He made a sharp laugh. 'Handcuffs, that's what it takes.' He kicked her legs apart, dropped to his knees between them and tore off his shirt.

'Don't.'

'Time to pay the piper, babe. I'm gonna fuck your brains out. And know what? You're gonna like it. Yeah. When's the last time you got your brains fucked out?'

'No!'

What did he say?

Fuck your brains out.

Did he really say that? That's what the guy on the phone said.

Pen felt tears trickling from the corners of her eyes.

She was slumped backward on the sofa, teeth clenched, pillow squeezed to her chest, legs pressed together so tightly that they ached. She sat up. She wiped her tears on the shoulder of her blouse. Her right ear felt wet inside. It had caught a tear. She wrapped a fingertip with her shirttail and swabbed out the ear.

Christ, the rape.

Harrison had been very apologetic about it. Later that night. The next morning on the telephone. He'd even sent a dozen long-stemmed red roses. Pen knew he wasn't remorseful, just afraid she might tell on him.

I was drunk, I didn't know what I was doing.

You knew, all right.

I'm gonna fuck your brains out.

Could Harrison be the one who phoned Friday night? The voice hadn't sounded like his. Maybe he disguised it.

But why would he call me? He and Joyce . . .

It wasn't him, Pen told herself.

Are you sure?

She went into the bathroom. She blew her nose. In the mirror, her eyes were red, the lids pink and swollen. They narrowed suddenly.

She hurried into her office. The tape cassette was still in the answering machine where Melanie and Bodie had left it. She rewound and played it.

Listening to the voice, she saw Harrison kneeling over her, naked. Her stomach clenched. Her heart pounded. Her legs felt weak. She was on the floor, Harrison thrusting into her, biting her, her arms cuffed behind her back fiery with pain, the foul words filling her head.

Then came Joyce's voice. She switched off the answering machine and sank onto the desk chair.

The voice hadn't sounded at all like Harrison.

The man who'd made those filthy calls, who'd left the note under her door, wasn't Harrison.

But he had Harrison's soul.

'Fuck you, buddy,' she muttered, 'and the horse you rode in on.'

Bodie finished reading the Traffic Collision Report and passed it to Melanie. The detective on the other side of the desk was busy at his computer terminal. He was a touch typist, and fast. Hardly fits the stereotype of the two-fingered cop, Bodie thought. But then, this is Beverly Hills. He supposed that Beverly Hills cops weren't quite typical.

When Melanie finished reading, she set the report on the detective's desk. He swiveled his chair and faced them. 'Did you find what you were looking for?' he asked in a pleasant voice.

He looked younger than Bodie.

'There was only the one witness?' Bodie asked.

'The spouse? She's the only one we know about at this time.'

'What happens now?' Bodie asked.

'We've put out a notice to all the auto body shops in L.A. and Orange Counties. They're instructed to let us know if a sports car is brought in with front end damage. Also, we're checking auto theft reports. If a driver gets involved in a hit-and-run, usually the first thing he'll do is report his vehicle stolen.'

'That makes sense,' Bodie said.

'We've had better than two dozen reports of stolen autos since the time of the accident, and we're looking into them. I think there's a good chance that one of them will turn out to be the vehicle that struck Mr Conway.'

'I hope so,' Bodie told him. He looked at Melanie.

'I guess that's all,' Melanie said, and stood up. 'Thank you for helping us.'

'That's what I'm here for. If I can be of any further assistance, don't hesitate to call or come by.' He handed his business card to Melanie. She looked at it and nodded.

'Why didn't you tell him?' Bodie asked as they crossed the parking lot.

'I never intended to.'

'They might have focused their investigation on Harrison.'

'What would I say, that I know the bastard did it because I'm psychic?'

'At least you could've told about him and Joyce having an affair.'

'So could you.'

'I didn't think it was my place to bring up something like that. I mean, it's your family. If you wanted it out, you had the opportunity.' He opened the van door for Melanie, went around to the driver's side, and climbed in.

'Let's go back to Harrison's place,' she said. 'Maybe they're gone by now.'

Pen hesitated at the door and wiped her sweaty hands on her shorts. Calm down, she told herself. There's no reason to be nervous. You're not going in for a physical or to have a cavity filled. Nothing bad will happen. What do you think, they're going to grill you?

She opened the door and stepped inside.

There were several other customers, but she felt conspicuous, an alien who had no right to be here. A trickle of sweat dribbled down her side. She pressed her arm against it, blotting it with her blouse.

Some of her tension eased when she spotted a book rack over near the counter. Books. Familiar territory. She stepped to the rack and saw *The Shooter's Bible*. Her copy at home was probably five years old, its information outdated. She lifted one of the heavy volumes off the rack, flipped through its pages, then tucked it under her arm to buy.

I'm not so out of place, after all, she thought. I probably know more about firearms than a lot of the people who come in here.

I know that revolvers don't have safety switches. A silencer is fine on an automatic, but stupid on a revolver because noise escapes around the cylinder. You don't get shot by a shell – that's the part of the cartridge that stays in the chamber. And it doesn't get ejected if you're talking revolvers. An automatic, all you've got to do is hold the trigger down but with a semi-auto you've got to pull the trigger for each shot. A .357 magnum will take .38 caliber ammo.

Hell, I'm not totally ignorant.

Feeling more confident, she turned away from the book rack and walked up an aisle. She could see rifles and shotguns standing upright in wall racks behind the counter at the far end of the store.

She stopped in front of the glass display case. The clerk at the far end was ringing up boxes of ammunition for a man in a safari jacket.

Inside the case were handguns, telescopic rifle sights, handcuffs, knives . . .

Handcuffs.

She stared.

They had cut off her circulation so her hands went numb. Their edges had left deep grooves in her wrists and red marks that turned to bruises just above her buttocks. She had felt them under her, digging in as Harrison rammed.

'Could I show you a pair of those bracelets?'

Pen looked up, surprised to find the clerk in front of her.

'Uh, no. No thank you.' She lifted *The Shooter's Bible* onto the counter. 'I'd like to get this. A gun, too.'

He nodded. His head, on top of a long neck, looked too small for his body. His tightly curled blond hair was cut short and his mustache was nearly invisible. He blinked at her through wire-rimmed glasses. 'Would this be for personal defense, or perhaps . . . ?'

'Personal defense,' Pen said.

His small head bobbed some more. 'That narrows it down. You'll want something lightweight but with some stopping power.' His head tipped down and swiveled as he searched the case. 'We have a mean little Walther PPK, a seven-shot semi-auto. You'd probably want either the .32 or the .380.' Crouching, he reached down to slide open the back of the case.

'No,' Pen said. 'Actually, I was thinking in terms of a shotgun.'

His pale eyebrows lifted.

'A 12-gauge shotgun.'

He stood up straight. There seemed to be admiration in his eyes. 'You *do* want stopping power.'

'That's what it's all about.'

He turned away. He lifted a shotgun down from the wall rack. 'This is your Marlin 12-gauge pump-action, walnut stock and fore-end, all steel action and parts. A five-shot magazine with your standard shells, or four if you use the magnum shells.'

'Magnum?'

'They're three inches long, not two and three-quarters like your standard shells. High velocity buckshot loads.'

'I see.'

'Here, try this on for size.' He passed the shotgun to Pen.

It was heavy. It felt dangerous. She liked it. But she didn't know what to do now that she was holding it. After peering down its sight ramp, she handed it back to the man.

'The perfect weapon for home defense,' he told her. Then, speaking softly as if sharing a secret, he said, 'You're in your home at night, somebody breaks in – nobody in the world is going to mess with you, you've got one of these babies. Not even a guy with a handgun. He just has to know you've got it and he's gone. I mean *gone*.' A grin spread over the young man's face. 'Odds are, you won't even have to fire a shot. You shut your bedroom door. You hear him coming. You wait till he's just outside the door, then you . . .' His arm jerked, snapping the pump-action back and forth with a snick and clatter of steel. 'He hears that and he knows what you've got. He's out of there. Best deterrent in the world – just the *sound* of it cocking.'

'Sounds good to me,' Pen said. 'How much is it?'

'Two-twenty-five, and I'll throw in a box of those magnums.'

'I'll take it.'

'Great.'

'How many shells to a box?'

'Five.'

'Give me an extra four boxes, then.'

'You'll want a cleaning kit.'

She nodded.

Driving home, Pen felt pleased with herself. She had really done it – really bought herself a shotgun.

She wished she'd had it Friday night. Things would've been different. No cord stretched across her doorway, for starters. No header into the wall, damn near splitting open her skull.

Wouldn't have panicked.

Wouldn't have stabbed Bodie.

It had cost a bundle, but it was worth every dime.

Besides, she told herself, just moving to a new apartment would've cost more than the shotgun.

And it would've been running away.

You don't run, now. You don't run ever.

You've got a 12-gauge pumpgun with magnum high-velocity buckshot loads.

You hold your ground.

Chapter Fifteen

They drove past Harrison's house. His Mercedes was still parked in the driveway. Joyce's Lincoln Continental was still at the curb on the next block.

'Why don't we go on back to your Dad's place?' Bodie suggested. 'We can pick up Pen's things and take them over to her.'

'Okay,' Melanie said.

Bodie didn't like it that Pen would be staying at her apartment. He would miss her. No more chances to be in the spa with her. No more sneaking into her room after Melanie was asleep.

Maybe they could talk her into returning.

Maybe *I* could. No help could be expected from Melanie on that. Remind Pen about the caller, the note left under her door, frighten her into coming back. If I push too hard, though, Melanie won't like it – might suspect I have something more on my mind than Pen's safety.

At least I'll have a chance to see her again when we take the suitcase over.

Maybe she's already changed her mind. She's had some time to cool off. With a little luck, maybe the caller struck again.

Bodie turned onto San Vicente and thought about calling her, himself. Use Joyce's phone. He'd have to get away from Melanie long enough . . .

What if Pen recognized his voice?

I want to come in your mouth.

I want to spread your legs and stick my cock up your . . .

I can't talk to her that way. Not a chance.

I could just call her up and say nothing. That'd spook her.

A rotten trick, but it might really be dangerous for her to stay alone in that apartment. The guy just might pay a visit.

Bodie wondered if she had reconnected her phones.

'Have you decided what to do about school?' Melanie asked.

He shook his head.

'You don't have to stay here, you know. All this . . . it's not your problem.'

'Trying to get rid of me?' he asked, and grinned at her.

'I just don't want you to feel that you *have* to stick around. You've got those classes to teach, and . . . There's no telling how long Dad might last.'

'He might surprise you and recover.'

'Yeah, sure,' she muttered.

'I'll stay a few days. Besides, I want to help you get to the bottom of this business with Joyce and Harrison.'

'That won't take long,' Melanie said.

'You've got a plan in mind?'

She shrugged.

'We could always beat Joyce with a rubber hose until she spills the beans,' he suggested.

'Good idea.'

He turned and drove slowly up the narrow lane to the house.

Inside, he said, 'Do you think we could eat before I keel over?'

'Sure.'

Melanie found hot dogs in the refrigerator, buns in the freezer. She put them in the microwave. While they heated, she filled two glasses with Pepsi and found an open bag of potato chips. Bodie ate some chips while he waited. They were a little stale, chewy and with a strange under-taste that reminded him of drinking water from a garden hose.

Melanie put the steaming buns and hot dogs on plates. Bodie lathered his buns with mustard. They sat at the kitchen table to eat.

'I guess you should pack up Pen's things when we're done.'

Melanie chewed.

'Want me to help?'

'You'd like that,' she said.

Indeed I would, he thought. 'I can wait down here.'

And call Pen?

And breathe.

It'd be for her own good.

But when they finished eating, it was Melanie who went to the telephone. She dialed 411.

'Who are you calling?'

'Directory assistance.'

'I *know* that.'

'Santa Monica,' she said into the receiver. 'Harrison Donner. On Twenty-first Street.'

Bodie's back stiffened.

Melanie pressed down on the cut-off button, let it up, and began to dial.

'What the hell are you doing?'

'You'll see.'

'That's what I'm afraid of.'

'Hello. Harrison? This is Melanie Conway . . . Just fine. Dad's come out of it . . . Yeah. I'm calling from the hospital. He's just come out of his coma . . . Yeah, isn't it great? Anyway, the thing is, he says he has to talk to you . . . No, I don't know what it's about but I guess it's pretty important. Could you come right over? . . . Great. See you in a few minutes.' She hung up.

Bodie stared at her.

'Let's get going,' she said.

'What . . . ?'

'We're gonna take a look at his Porsche,' she said.

'Good Christ, Mel.'

Pen sat on the sofa with the shotgun box heavy across her lap. She opened it and lifted out the weapon. The wood and steel were glossy in the light from the window at her back. There was a faint, pleasant odor of oil.

Though she'd never fired a shotgun, a boyfriend had taken her out to the hills near Valencia one Saturday and they'd had a fine time plinking cans with revolvers and his rifle. The rifle was a .30 caliber lever-action. She remembered the way it crashed her shoulder when she fired it. And the godawful noise.

The shotgun would probably be similar.

She raised it, pressed it firmly to her shoulder, and sighted along the narrow strip of steel that ran the length of the barrel to a bead on its muzzle.

Paul's rifle had had a telescopic sight. With that, she'd hit the cans more often than not.

With this – if she ever actually needed to use it – her target wouldn't be more than twenty feet away. She couldn't possibly miss.

She worked the pump. It made a sliding snick-clack. Her finger curled around the trigger, but she didn't squeeze it.

The thing's not loaded, she told herself. It shouldn't be. But if it is, you'll blast your wall open.

She set the shotgun across her knees and spent the next few minutes studying its instruction booklet. Then she checked the chamber. Empty. She pulled the trigger. Click. Then she opened a box of cartridges and fed four of them into the magazine.

Leaving the weapon uncocked, she pressed a switch to activate the safety. She worked the switch back and forth a few times until she felt familiar with it.

All set, she thought.

She had already decided on the best place to keep it. She carried the shotgun into her bedroom, knelt beside her bed, and pushed it beneath the draping side of her coverlet.

Then she lay down on the bed.

Someone's here!

She threw herself off the mattress, snatched out the shotgun, swept its barrel high to clear the bed, and swung it toward the door.

'Pow,' she whispered.

She shook her head. She felt a little silly, like a kid playing soldier, but she returned the shotgun to its place. This time, she took off her shoes and got beneath the covers. She tried the maneuver again. The covers slowed her down, but not by much.

She practiced three more times, then stripped off the sheets and pillow cases and piled them on the floor.

Sunday. Laundry day.

You're home now, you're not running away, you might as well do your regular chores as if nothing has changed.

Bodie drove past Harrison's house. The Mercedes was no longer in the driveway.

'It worked,' Melanie said.

'Sure it worked. But what's he going to think when he gets to the hospital and finds out you lied?'

'It'll sure make him wonder, won't it?' Melanie didn't sound bothered.

'He'll wonder, all right.'

On the next block, Bodie found an empty stretch of curb where the Continental had been. He pulled over and parked.

'What time is it now?' Melanie asked as they met on the sidewalk.

Bodie checked his wristwatch. 'Twelve-forty.'

'Good.'

'It's kind of tight, if you ask me.' He hurried to stay with her.

'No problem. I phoned at twelve-thirty. Say it took five minutes for them to clear out. Should take them fifteen minutes to reach the hospital, at least five to find out they were tricked, and fifteen to get back here. And that's assuming they're real fast about it. So we should be all right till ten after one.'

'Right. So we check his garage and get away clean as a

whistle. Only what the hell are you going to say when Harrison wants to know about your call?'

'That'll depend on what his Porsche looks like, won't it?'

'It damn well better be smashed up.'

The driveway gates beneath the porte cochere were seven feet high and locked. Bodie looked at the gate's mechanism. 'It opens by remote,' he said.

Melanie didn't hesitate. She hurried onto the porch, walked across it and boosted herself onto its low brick wall. Then she swung her legs over and dropped onto the driveway behind the gate.

With a groan of despair, Bodie did the same. He followed Melanie toward the garage.

This really bites, he thought. It's crazy.

The driveway was bordered by a high fence, but the neighbor's house was two stories. He could see its upstairs windows.

If someone happened to be looking down . . .

He imagined a police car swinging into the driveway.

Oh man, oh man.

Behind Harrison's house, the narrow driveway flared out in front of the two-car garage.

Melanie tugged at the handle, trying to lift the garage door.

'That'll be on remote, too,' Bodie told her.

'You try.'

It's no use, he thought. But he pulled hard on the handle. The door didn't budge.

The door had no windows.

A walkway led around the corner of the garage. It led to a side door with glass panels.

Melanie cupped her hands against one of the windows and peered inside. 'There it is,' she said.

'How does it look?'

'Dark.' She tried the knob, shook her head, then turned toward Bodie.

'Let's give it up,' he said.

'Do you want to kick the door open?'

'Are you kidding? Christ, we're already trespassing. Do you want to end up in *jail*?'

She glanced sideways. Then her arm shot back. Bodie flinched, stunned and disbelieving, as her elbow rammed one of the lower windows. The glass blasted inward, shards clinking and shattering as they hit the garage floor.

'Mel!'

'I'm not giving up,' she said. Reaching through the broken window, she opened the door. 'You can wait here if you're scared.'

'Let's make it quick and get out of here.'

Inside, the garage was cool and dark. Bodie quickly shut the door.

Melanie flipped a switch. An overhead bulb came on. The Porsche, on the far side of the garage, gleamed fire-engine red.

Bodie glanced around as they walked toward it. Along the near wall were wash basins, a clothes washer and drier, shelves stacked with cardboard boxes. Closer to the garage door were rakes, a power lawn mower, shovels, bags of fertilizer. The stale, dank odor of the garage was mixed with the smells of fertilizer and gasoline.

Bodie shivered. It was the cool, closed-in air. It was *being* here.

God, this is insane.

Melanie stopped in front of the Porsche. Her eyes roamed its windshield and hood.

They looked fine to Bodie. He moved to her side as she crouched to inspect the headlights, grill and bumper.

'Not a scratch,' Bodie said.

'It just means he probably didn't use this car. He still could've stolen or rented one.'

'That'll be pretty tricky to prove.'

'God *damn* it!'

'Come on, let's get out of here.'

She followed Bodie to the door. After opening it, he twisted his hand on the inside knob to smear the fingerprints. Then he pulled it shut and did the same to the outside knob.

Melanie, well ahead of him, walked quickly to the back door of the house. She opened it and stood peering inside as Bodie ran to her.

'No!' he snapped. He grabbed her shoulder.

'What time is it?'

'Mel, no. We can't.'

'Come on, what time is it?'

He checked. 'Ten till one.'

'We've got at least fifteen minutes.'

'What do you want to do in there?' he asked. His voice was shaky, his heart thumping wildly.

'Just take a quick look around.'

'God, Mel.'

'There might be evidence. *I'm* going in.'

'No!'

'Let go of me.'

He dropped his hand from her shoulder.

He entered the kitchen behind Melanie. He felt sick. Breaking into the garage was bad enough. *This* was utter madness.

He realized he wanted badly to urinate.

If we're caught in here . . .

Why the hell didn't Harrison lock his back door?

Maybe someone's here!

Don't even think that.

The house was silent.

What if he's got a silent alarm?

'What if he's got a silent alarm?' Bodie whispered. 'It might be tied in directly to the police or a security patrol.'

Melanie ignored him.

'Two minutes,' he said. 'You've got two minutes, then we're out of here even if I have to drag you.'

They passed a bathroom. He could sure use it. He didn't dare.

He followed Melanie into a bedroom.

The covers and top sheet hung off the foot of the king-size bed. The pillows were mashed. Near the center of the blue satin bottom sheet was a wet place.

Melanie, leaning over, swiped at it with her forefinger. She rubbed her fingertip with the ball of her thumb, then sniffed it.

Bodie struggled not to gag.

She turned to him. A corner of her mouth twitched. 'Guess we know what *they've* been doing.'

Bodie grabbed her wrist. 'We're getting out of here *now*.'

'Okay, okay, don't pull.'

Letting go, he rushed ahead of her – out the bedroom, down a corridor to the living room, across the living room to the foyer. He opened the front door. Melanie stepped out. He twisted his hand on the knob, remembered that Melanie had left prints on the back door, and wondered if he should race through the house to wipe them off.

A patrol car might be racing toward the house right now.

He stepped outside and pulled the door shut by its edge.

They walked slowly over the flagstones to the sidewalk.

When they reached the end of the block, Bodie realized they were safe. He filled his lungs. His heart was still hammering. He still had to urinate, but the need wasn't as strong as before.

They climbed into the van. He pulled away. 'Thank God that's over,' he said.

'We didn't accomplish much.'

'We found out Harrison's car isn't smashed up. And I presume your sniff-test eliminated the possibility that their relationship was purely Platonic.'

'I wish I could be there when they get back from the hospital.'

'They'd no doubt have some very interesting comments about you.'

'That's right.'

'You should've thought about that before you made the call.'

'I did. My message wasn't just to get rid of them. It was to worry them, stir things up.'

'I'm sure you succeeded. And when Harrison finds the busted garage window, he'll really get stirred up. He'll know exactly who did it. And why.'

'That's right,' she said calmly.

'Maybe we'd better move in with Pen.'

'Oh, you'd like that.'

'What I *wouldn't* like is facing Harrison after what we did. He'll know what we were up to.'

'I don't care what he thinks.'

'Do you care what he might do?'

'He won't bring in the cops, if that's what you're afraid of.'

'If he's innocent . . .'

'He isn't innocent.'

'If he's *not* innocent, that's even worse.'

When they entered the house, Bodie hurried ahead of Melanie. 'My teeth are floating,' he said.

'Hey, I left my purse in the van.'

He tossed the keys to her and rushed into the bathroom. He swung the door shut, unzipped, aimed at the toilet and released the tight hold he'd been keeping for so long. He sighed. He counted the seconds until he was done. Sixty-three. No record. His record was ninety-eight seconds one night last year after walking back to his apartment from a beer drinking session at Sparkey's.

He zipped up, flushed the toilet, and washed his hands.

Melanie should wash *her* hands, he thought. She actually touched that stuff. And sniffed it.

The girl is definitely mad.

He dried his hands and left the bathroom.

Melanie didn't seem to be back yet. He went to the kitchen. The thoughts of Sparkey's had whetted his thirst. He found several bottles of Corona beer in the refrigerator. Taking one out, he felt a small tug of guilt.

It's not as if I'm stealing the thing, he told himself. Joyce said we should make ourselves at home.

He searched a drawer, found a bottle opener, and pried off the cap.

She might not be quite so generous, however, if she knew what we've been doing.

Hell, it isn't her beer, anyway. It's Whit's. He's the bread-winner around here, the beer-winner. He certainly wouldn't begrudge me a brew. Look what I've gone through on his behalf.

Bodie took a drink. It was cold and very good. He sat at the table and drank some more.

Poor sod, he thought. They certainly screwed you over, Whit. Your law partner and your dear wife. You'll have some nasty surprises if you ever come to.

But did they run you down? Ah, there's the question.

Nice to make them pay, if they did.

And how do we go about that? Harrison, the slime, was smart enough not to use his own car. So where do we go from here?

I guess we don't *have* to go anywhere from here. Melanie has already hurled the crapola into the fan. We only have to sit back and watch where it flies.

Perchance to duck.

Taking her one long time to fetch her purse.

Bodie suddenly knew why.

He set down his beer bottle and sighed.

'Melanie,' he muttered. 'Oh, for Christsake.'

He walked out to the street. His van was gone, all right.

Chapter Sixteen

Pen carried her laundry basket down the stairs and past the pool in the courtyard. The apartment building was silent and she saw no one. A typical Sunday afternoon. The tenants were either gone, or hidden away in their rooms.

She entered the short passageway between the courtyard

and alley. The utility room's door stood ajar. It was supposed to be kept locked to prevent vandalism and unauthorized use of the machines. Alicia, from the corner apartment, had told her once about walking in on a shopping cart lady doing her wash – a filthy woman who screeched and jibbered like a lunatic when Alicia confronted her.

Pen set down her basket and swung the door wide. She peered into the gloom. Seeing no one, she reached around the corner and turned on the overhead light. The room looked deserted. The two washers and two driers were silent. She picked up her basket and entered.

The washing machines were top loaders. She opened each and looked inside. They were empty.

My lucky day, she thought.

She had separated her laundry before coming down. Bending over her basket, she lifted out a bundle of white fabrics. A sock fell to the floor on its way to the machine. She squatted to pick it up.

'Beautiful ass.'

She flinched. Her head snapped around so fast she hurt her neck.

In the doorway stood Manny Hammond from 202. He'd played football at USC and usually wore a jersey to remind everyone of his glory days. This afternoon, he wasn't wearing the jersey – just a pair of faded red gym shorts and thongs. The shorts were extremely tight.

'You startled me,' Pen said. She picked up the sock and dropped it into the machine.

'You gotta loosen up.'

'I'll keep that in mind.'

Damn it, where'd he come from?

'Aren't you missing a game on TV?' she asked.

'Why would I watch a game when I can watch you?' He leaned against the doorframe, crossed his ankles, and folded his arms across his massive chest.

With a sigh, Pen crouched to pick up her bleach and detergent. She could feel his gaze. She straightened up. Her hand trembled as she filled the measuring cup.

'Gotcha rattled, huh?'

'You didn't have to sneak up on me like that,' she said, keeping her eyes away from him as she dumped the detergent, then the bleach, into the washer. She closed the lid. She turned on the machine and heard water rush in.

'Why don't you toss in the rest?' he suggested, grinning. 'That stuff you got on looks like it could use a good wash.'

'Some other time.'

'No time like the present. Come on, honey, it's laundry day. Get *everything* good and clean.'

She glared at him, heat spreading over her face. 'Why don't you take a hike, Manny?'

He grinned. 'Bet you say that to all the guys.'

'Just the jerks.' Embarrassed and angry, she picked up her basket and tumbled its contents into the other washer.

'You aren't a dyke, are you?'

'Shut the hell up.'

'I mean, 'cause it'd be a shame, a piece like you. A real loss to mankind.'

She didn't bother with the measuring cup. She shook the detergent into the machine and set the basket aside.

'Yeah, I guess you are a dyke.'

She slammed the lid down and whirled around. 'I'm not a lesbian and you're a piece of shit.'

He looked amused. 'That's no way to talk. Glad to hear you're not a dyke, though. So what is it, you just frigid?'

Seething, Pen turned away. She started the washer and picked up her empty basket. With a shaking hand, she set the detergent and bleach inside it. She held the basket with its edge against her belly and faced Manny.

'Not leaving already, are you?' He stepped into the middle of the doorway.

'Please move,' she said.

'When was the last time you had a good fucking?'

'Get out of my way.'

'That's gotta be your problem, you know. And I'm just the guy to help you with that.' He lowered a hand and patted the front of his shorts. It was obvious from the bulge that he had an erection. 'I'm well equipped to handle that problem for you, honey. Wanta see?' Grinning, he drew the shorts down a fraction.

'Stop it.'

'Tell you what. Why don't you toss these in with your stuff? *All* your stuff. Know what I mean? And I'll show you what it's like to . . .'

'Move,' Pen said and walked toward him, the basket braced in front of her.

'Hey, now. This is your big chance.'

'Move!' she yelled in his face.

He flinched and stepped aside.

Pen walked past him, half expecting to be grabbed.

He muttered, 'Cunt.' But he kept his hands to himself.

She hurried through the doorway, out of the shadowed area and into the sunlight. She was trembling and she had a hard time catching her breath. At the foot of the stairs, she looked back.

Manny, standing near the corner of the pool, raised his middle finger and rotated it.

Pen hurried up the stairs, along the balcony to her apartment, and unlocked the door. Inside, she leaned against the door. Her chest hurt. She panted for air.

The filthy bastard.

When was the last time you had a good fucking?

I wanted to talk to you about my big hard cock and your hot juicy cunt.

Her legs folded. She slid down the door and stared over the tops of her upraised knees.

Manny?

The voice wasn't quite the same, but he could've disguised it when he made the calls.

Manny.

Over in 202. With a clear view of her front door and windows. Knowing who she saw and when. Knowing when she was here and when she was gone and when she went to bed.

Knowing when she was alone.

Manny.

Melanie must have made it.

She would've been back around one-twenty, no later than one-thirty, if she'd reached Harrison's house, found his Mercedes in the driveway, and given up.

So she must've beaten him back to the house, snuck in the back door, and hidden herself. In the closet, or maybe under the bed.

Bodie looked at his wristwatch. Two minutes had passed since the last time. It was now five till two.

If Melanie had turned back, she would've been here half an hour ago.

He stared at the empty beer bottle as he turned it slowly in his fingers.

And what, perchance, do *I* do about this curious turn of events?

For starters, have another beer.

Bodie got up and took another Corona from the refrigerator. He opened it. This one, he took outside. He stretched out on the lounger. The mild breeze kept the sun from feeling too hot. Closing his eyes, he pictured the way Pen had looked this morning when she was on the same lounger.

He took a drink.

What was she doing right now? Had she gone out to find a new apartment? Was she wondering why they hadn't shown up yet with her things?

Hey, I'm stranded here. I'd bring the stuff to you if I could. I'd rather, by far, be there than here.

As soon as Melanie gets back.

That could be a while.

She's stuck there until she has a chance to sneak out.

They might, of course, catch her.

I could walk over there. Wouldn't take more than half an hour.

Or phone Pen. She has a car. We drive over to Harrison's and then what? Knock on the door and ask for Melanie? Real cute.

But the thought of phoning Pen made his heart quicken. He could tell her about Melanie. They could discuss the situation. Maybe she would even come over. They'd be alone in the house. Oh, come off it, he told himself.

I'd better call her.

He set his beer bottle on the table and went into the house. He dialed Directory Assistance, gave Pen's city and name to the live operator and heard a computer voice give the number. He wrote it on a wall pad, and dialed.

He let the phone ring ten times, then hung up.

He went outside again and sat in the sun. He drank some beer and put the bottle down. He shut his eyes.

So much for having a visitor.

He could call a cab and go over to Pen's place. There's a thought.

Hi. Just dropped by to see how you're doing. Where's Melanie? Oh, she's hiding in Harrison's house, gathering clues.

Pen, finding herself incapable of reading after her return from the laundry room, had turned on the television and sat gazing at its screen, her mind preoccupied with swirling, disjointed thoughts about her encounter with Manny, the calls, her father, the shotgun, whether she should move to a new apartment after all, Joyce and Harrison betraying her father and possibly trying to murder him, Melanie's 'vision', Bodie in her bedroom last night, Melanie's jealousy.

Then had come the blare of her timer's alarm, and the need to go down again to the laundry room.

The shotgun was out of the question, so she'd taken a steak knife along, wrapped in a towel beneath her arm.

Transferring her damp laundry from the washing machines to a drier, she had expected Manny to sneak in, maybe even assault her this time, but he never showed up.

Now she was waiting again. In a few minutes, the drying cycle would finish and she would have to return once more. The towel with the knife inside lay on the table in front of her. She wouldn't go down there without it.

Maybe Manny was all talk. He hadn't *tried* anything.

Maybe I should forget the knife.

That was a hard-on in his shorts, and he wanted to stick it

in me. He made that pretty damn obvious. If I'd shown the slightest interest, he would've had me on the floor and . . .

Manny isn't the caller.

Manny didn't slip the note under the door.

Manny confronts you in the laundry room, half naked, and tries to bully you into putting out. He's not the type to make anonymous telephone calls.

Pen slumped back on the sofa, frowning at the television screen.

There had been, she realized, a certain comfort in believing it was Manny. He was real and known, an enemy to protect herself against. Not a faceless presence, not a stranger out there somewhere, wanting her. Better Manny with his smirk and his pecs and his bulging gym shorts than . . .

She jerked rigid at the sudden jangle of a bell.

I want to come . . .

Not the phone, the timer.

She stood up, patted the pocket of her shorts to make sure she had her keys, then picked up the towel with the knife inside. She clamped the towel under her arm, lifted the laundry basket, and left her apartment.

Manny's curtains were open. She didn't see him at any of the windows, but that proved nothing; he could be standing back a few feet, concealed in the dimness of a room, watching her undetected.

She hurried along the balcony and down the stairs. Walking past the pool, she heard faint music from one of the apartments. A sign of life. She found that reassuring.

She had left the laundry room locked, and it was locked when she reached it.

Manny, of course, would have a key of his own.

Setting the basket down, Pen dug into her pocket and took

out the keys. She unlocked the door, swung it open, and peered inside.

Nobody there.

She flicked the light on. Then she toed her basket through the doorway and shut herself inside.

The drier still rumbled.

She had set it for an hour.

It should've stopped five minutes ago.

Picking up her basket, she stepped over to the machine. The timer dial showed that it still had three or four minutes to run.

I must've set my kitchen timer wrong, Pen told herself.

Either that, or someone had been in here and fooled with the dial on the drier.

I am so damn paranoid. I've gotta cut it out.

Bending over, she curled her fingers around the handle of the drier's door. Suddenly, she was afraid to open it.

Anything might be inside.

How about a dead, mangled cat? A note tied to its tail: 'How about a little pussy?'

You're losing your grip, Pen old pal.

She forced herself to open the door. The machine went silent and her breath snagged as the corner of a sheet flopped out.

Crouching, she looked into the dark drum. Nothing seemed to be in there except her laundry.

She reached inside and clutched warm fabric with both hands.

Tiny, needle-sharp teeth didn't nip her fingers.

Of course not.

There's nothing wrong except in my mind.

She lifted out a bundle of laundry and dropped it into the basket.

Shit, she thought as she reached in again. Plenty is wrong. The whole damn world is caving in.

But nobody left me a gift.

You hope.

Quickly, she finished unloading the machine.

She pressed the towel-wrapped knife into the soft pile of her laundry, lifted her basket, and hurried from the room.

Half the pool was in shadow, but she walked in sunlight and shook her head.

A dead cat in the drier.

Hungry rats?

God Almighty, things are bad enough without me *inventing* nasty little surprises.

She reached the bottom of the stairs.

Almost safe.

Climbing them, she imagined Manny staring out his window at her.

He's the least of my worries, she told herself. He's a creep, but he isn't the caller. I can handle him.

She was tempted to look around as she walked along the balcony, but if he was watching she really didn't want to know. She unlocked her door, entered, and nudged it shut with her rump.

Safe.

The door was locked behind her. The phones were disconnected. The shotgun was under the bed.

No one can touch me now.

Pen took a few long, slow breaths, trying to calm herself, then carried the basket into her bedroom and upended it on the mattress.

She began to sort her laundry: sheets and pillow cases in one pile, another pile for clothes that would need to be ironed,

176

a third for undergarments. When the sorting was done, she carried her brassieres two at a time to her dresser and stacked them neatly in a drawer. Then she folded her panties. Except for the tattered white pair she'd worn to bed Friday night, the panties were new and skimpy and brightly colored – red, blue, pink, lavender.

Her black panties weren't there.

She knew she had worn them.

So where are they?

She searched the two remaining piles, thinking the black panties may have been caught in a blouse or sheet. They weren't there. She checked the basket, the floor beside the bed. Then she looked once more through the laundry, more carefully this time, lifting each article and shaking it, expecting the panties to flutter out.

They didn't.

'Goddamn it,' she whispered.

Her chest felt tight.

She must have left the panties inside the washer or drier. They were small and dark, easily missed when removing the rest of her clothes from the machines. Normally, she ran her hands around the metal to make certain nothing was left behind. But she hadn't done that today. Too preoccupied. Too careless. Too eager to get back to the safety of her room.

Good move.

She didn't want to go back down. She wanted to stay right here, locked in with the phones unplugged, maybe have a glass of wine and take a long, hot bath.

Better get the panties before someone else does.

She hurried out and was halfway down the stairs when she realized she had forgotten her knife.

She quickly patted the pocket of her shorts and didn't feel the bulge of her keys. Her heart galloped. She slapped her other front pocket. She *never* kept them in that pocket, but that's exactly where they were.

Thank God.

Really great if you'd locked yourself out.

Striding alongside the pool, she pulled the key case from her pocket and had the proper key out, ready in her hand, by the time she reached the laundry room.

Inside, she bent over the washing machine to peer inside, felt between the wings of its agitator and ran her fingers under the top in case the panties were clinging there. She crouched in front of the drier and swept a hand around the inside drum. She even checked the washing machine she had used for her white laundry. Then she searched the floor.

The panties were definitely gone.

Someone had come in and taken them.

Manny? What if it *wasn't* Manny?

Tight and cold inside, Pen hurried back to her apartment. She leaned against the door, shaking.

Calm down.

Calm down, *hell*. Someone took my panties – wanted them and stole them and *has* them.

Watched me come and go from the laundry room.

I've got to get out of here.

Chapter Seventeen

After waking up, Bodie wandered over to the gazebo. He slipped his fingers through the cool water of the spa, and remembered last night in the swirling heat, Pen so beautiful, Melanie topless and flirting and later bottomless as well, so urgently striving to keep Bodie's attention from her sister.

Where is she now? Crouched in Harrison's closet? Hiding beneath his bed? Maybe caught.

He supposed he should do something about it, but what?

Stepping around the wooden platform, he found the controls. Turn a knob, flick a switch, he could probably get the water hot.

Go ahead.

He did.

The machinery hummed and the clear surface stirred a bit. Lowering an arm into the water, he felt along the side until a warm current pushed at his wrist.

He returned to the house. Upstairs, he found the bikini trunks he'd worn last night and put them on. With a towel draping his bare shoulders, he went down to the kitchen. He took a beer from the refrigerator, opened it, and walked out to the spa. He climbed in.

The water made him shiver, but he sat in front of the lead-in pipe. The water from there blew warm against his back.

He was sitting where Pen had sat last night.

Closing his eyes, he pictured the way she had looked – her face shimmering in the red glow, her blond hair the color of a harvest moon, a few damp locks clinging to her forehead, the shiny satin of her wet shoulders, the way the water rippled over the tops of her breasts.

The water felt warmer, now.

'Hi.'

Bodie's eyes flew open. For a moment, he couldn't believe that Pen was standing there. But she was, oh yes. 'Hello,' he said.

'I didn't think anyone was here.'

'Just me.'

'Where's everyone else?'

'Joyce is still . . . out.'

Pen nodded, an angry look flaring for a moment in her eyes. 'Melanie's sort of abandoned me here.'

She climbed up, left her sandals on the platform, and sat on the edge with her legs hanging in the water. 'It could be hotter.'

He shrugged. His heart was thudding.

'I freaked out a little bit, staying over there alone.'

'I called you earlier.'

Her eyebrows lifted.

'I guess you weren't home.'

'I haven't plugged in my phones. Not yet. Who knows, maybe never.'

'That bad, huh?'

'I know it's silly.'

'I don't think so.'

'Thanks. What did you call about?'

'Why don't you put on your suit and come in?'

'Is that why you called?'

'I called about Melanie.'

Pen nodded for him to go on.

'We went back to Harrison's. First, we went to the police station, but we didn't find out much. Then we went to

Harrison's. He and Joyce were still there so we came back to the house and Melanie phoned him – said your father had come out of his coma and wanted to see him.'

'Are you serious?'

'It worked. We sped back there and he was gone, so we broke into his garage for a peek at the Porsche.'

'What do you mean, you broke in?'

'Melanie smashed a window.'

'Jesus H. Christ, and you *let* her do all this stuff?' Pen didn't sound angry at him, just perplexed.

'Well, not exactly. I didn't know what she was up to. When she phoned Harrison with that wild story, I had no idea what she was going to say till it was out of her mouth. Even then, I couldn't believe my ears. The same with breaking the garage window – she just *did* it. I was ready to call it quits, and the next thing I know she's driving her elbow through the glass.'

'You were supposed to stop her from doing crazy stuff. That was the whole idea behind investigating Harrison.'

'Well, part of the idea was to look for evidence.'

'Did you find any?'

'The Porsche looked fine. If he's the one who hit your father, he must've used a different car.'

She nodded. 'It figures. He's too smart to use his own car for something like that.' Leaning back, she braced herself up with stiff arms. She rolled her head around as if trying to work kinks out of her neck muscles. Her untucked plaid blouse had slipped upward, showing a triangle of skin between the last button and the waist of her shorts. At the top of the opening was her navel. A little more belly was exposed as she raised one hand to rub the back of her neck.

'Headache?' Bodie asked.

'Not yet. Just a stiff neck. I've been a little tense.'

'The hot water would do it good.'

'You're determined to get me in there.' She smiled slightly as she said it.

Bodie smiled back. 'Nah.'

'All we'd need is for Melanie to come back and find me in there with you.'

'Not much worse than if she'd found me in your bedroom last night.'

'True. But I don't think we should press our luck. Where *is* she, anyway?'

'I'm not exactly sure.'

'Where do you *think* she is?'

'In Harrison's house, spying on the suspects.'

'*What?*'

'I don't know for sure.'

Pen sat up straight. Frowning, she leaned forward a bit as if to hear him better. Her hands settled on her thighs. 'She's *in* his house?'

'That's my guess. When we were there before, the back door was unlocked.'

'So she went in, of course.'

'We both did.'

'Good God.'

Bodie shrugged. 'I figured, what the hell, we'd already broken into the guy's garage.'

'So did you find anything in the house?'

He ran a few euphemisms through his mind. Semen by any other name . . . 'There was some indication that they had, indeed, been making the beast with two backs.'

Pen blushed. She said, 'You're so literary.'

'A regular Robert B. Parker.'

'Nothing . . . more incriminating?'

'We didn't linger. I dragged Melanie out of there as fast as I could.'

'But you think she's there now?'

'She wasn't exactly eager to leave. We no sooner got back here than she took off in my van. That was around one o'clock. She's been gone ever since.'

'That was almost *three* hours ago!'

'I know, I know. And I'm just sitting here.' Reaching back, he picked up his bottle of beer and took a drink. 'Want some?'

'Bodie!'

'Have *you* got any ideas?'

She reached out a hand. Bodie stood. She glanced down his body and quickly away as he waded forward a step and gave her the bottle. She drank from it, head tilted back and eyes sliding shut for a moment. She handed the bottle back to him. 'Thanks.' She rubbed her hand on her bare thigh. It left a moist smear.

Bodie sat down, the hot water climbing to his shoulders. He raised the bottle to his mouth, felt it against his lips. Seconds ago, Pen's lips had been here.

'That stupid damn idiot,' she muttered. She shook her head. 'Sorry. I shouldn't be ... What were you planning to do, just wait around and hope she comes back?'

'Something like that. If she is in Harrison's house, she's hiding somewhere. So she might not be able to just take off when she wants to. Basically, she's stuck there until she can find a chance to sneak out. Even when the chance *comes*, she might not take it. I mean, the girl has to be pretty desperate or she wouldn't have gone in there in the first place. She probably figures this is her last, best chance to get the goods on those two.'

Pen was nodding. She understood and agreed. 'On the other hand, maybe she's been caught.'

'I know.'

'What if they *are* the ones who . . . did this to Dad?'

'Then Melanie's in plenty of trouble.'

'Or worse.'

'But if they haven't caught her and we go charging to the rescue . . .'

'We can't just *wait*.'

'We don't want to blow it for Melanie, though. She'll never forgive us if we rush in and pull her out before she's had a chance to hear something really incriminating.'

'I can live without her forgiveness. I've been getting along without it this long.' Pen's eyes took on a frantic look. 'He's got a *gun*, Bodie. Harrison has a gun.'

'All the more reason not to charge in on him.'

'I bought a shotgun today.'

'Oh, great. We can have a shoot-out.'

'He might *kill* her. I know him. He's capable of . . . almost anything.'

'Okay. We'll do something. I don't know what, but . . .'

'We have to.'

Bodie took a drink of beer and stood up. Pen continued to sit on the edge, right beside the steps. Turning around, he reached over the side and turned off the heat.

'Maybe we can come up with a plan,' she said, still sitting there.

Bodie waded toward the steps.

'I don't know what,' she said.

'We'll think of something.' His throat felt tight. He stared straight ahead so he wouldn't have to see where she was looking as he climbed the first step and felt the water level slide down to his thighs. The bikini trunks hugged him.

Pen stood up. Bodie, pulling the towel off his shoulders,

offered it to her. 'Want to dry your legs?' he asked.

'Thanks.' She took it and bent over, her hair swaying at the sides of her face as she ran the towel down her legs. She gave it back to him. She stepped into her sandals.

'Would you hold this for me?' he asked.

She took the beer bottle. As he dried himself, she moved past him and stepped down from the platform.

Looking up at him, she said, 'We need a way to trick them out of the house.'

'Like phoning to say your father wants to see them?'

'Oh, sure. Right.' Her glance flicked downward and quickly aside. She squinted as if peering at something in the bushes. 'I don't know,' she said, and took a sip of beer.

Bodie, done with drying, wrapped the towel around his waist and climbed down the stairs.

Pen stepped backward. She followed him toward the house. 'You know,' she said, 'Melanie might not even *be* at Harrison's house. She could've gone anywhere. I mean, she didn't come out and tell you where she was going?'

'No, she didn't.'

'Before we do anything else, we should drive by and see if your van's in the neighborhood.'

'I'd like to take a quick shower first.'

'Go on ahead.'

He pulled open the sliding glass door, stepped aside to let Pen pass, and entered the kitchen behind her. The seat of her white shorts was soiled a little. He let his gaze glide down the backs of her legs. 'I'll hurry,' he said.

Pen stayed in the kitchen and Bodie went upstairs. He tried not to think about the fact that he was alone in the house with her, but he could think of little else. His insides felt quivery.

Nothing's going to happen, he told himself. Don't get excited. You wouldn't dare, and she wouldn't go for it. Neither of you wants to stab Melanie in the back.

But he left the bathroom door unlocked. He peeled the swimsuit down his legs and wrung it out over the sink.

Pen's white bikini was hanging over the top runner of the shower door. It would get wet if he left it there. He pulled it down. Saw her wearing it in the hot spa. Saw her taking it off here in the bathroom. Tempted to caress the garment, he quickly draped it over a towel rod.

He showered. He imagined Pen sneaking in and sliding back the frosted door. She was naked. *Mind if I join you?*

Don't torment yourself, he thought. She won't.

She didn't.

When he was done, he walked down the hallway to the bedroom with a towel wrapped around his waist. Quickly, he dressed and went downstairs. He found Pen on the living room sofa, leaning back with her legs stretched out. Her purse was beside her, its strap over her shoulder. 'Ready to go?' she asked.

'I guess so.'

They went out to her car. Bodie, in the passenger seat, watched her climb in and start the engine. She turned the car around. On San Vicente, she lowered the visor to shield her eyes from the late afternoon sun. Below the visor's shadow, soft down on her cheek and over her lip shone golden in the sunlight.

She looked at him.

'Just thinking,' he said.

'Oh?'

He hadn't been thinking about anything, just admiring Pen's face. 'What if Melanie's not there?' he asked.

'I guess that would be quite a relief.'

'If she's not there, where is she?'

Pen shook her head slightly. 'More to the point, what'll we do if she *is* there?'

'Who knows?'

'I wish she'd just stayed in Phoenix.'

The words hurt Bodie.

'I don't mean you,' Pen said as if she knew.

'I brought her out.'

'You were just being gallant. I bet you're sorry now, though, aren't you? Got yourself right in the middle of a real mess.'

'It has its compensations.'

Pen kept her eyes on the road.

I shouldn't have said that, Bodie thought. Lord!

'Yeah,' Pen said. 'I heard Melanie compensating you last night. Thin walls.'

For a moment, Bodie didn't understand. Then he realized she had heard them in bed.

That wasn't what I meant by compensation, Bodie thought.

It's what she *thinks* I meant.

Good thing.

My God, she heard us screwing.

'I guess we should've turned the radio higher,' he said.

'She probably wanted me to hear,' Pen said. 'The way she was acting last night, it wouldn't surprise me.'

'Wanted you to hear?'

'So I'd know she had something I didn't.'

Me?

She's talking about me, here.

'Trying to make you jealous?' he heard himself ask. His voice sounded distant.

'It wouldn't surprise me,' she said.

'*Were* you?' He couldn't believe he had asked that.

'Jealous?' She glanced at him. 'What do you think?'

He swallowed. 'I wouldn't . . . hazard a guess.'

'And I won't hazard an answer. If I say yes I was jealous, I'm as much as asking you to put moves on me, and I couldn't do that to Melanie. If I say no, you're insulted.'

'Good point.'

'Let's just stay friends.'

'Good idea.'

'Better keep an eye out for your van.'

He realized that she had just turned onto Harrison's street. The Mercedes was parked in his driveway. Joyce's Continental was at the curb in front of his house.

'Interesting,' Pen said. 'She didn't bother parking up the road this time.'

'Their secret love's no big secret any more.'

'Mel's call saw to that.' Pen turned the corner. 'I wonder what they had to say about *that*.'

'Whatever it was, Melanie probably heard some of it.'

'If she's there.'

They found Bodie's van parked on the opposite side of the block.

Pen pulled in behind it. Bodie got out. He peered through its windows and returned to the car. 'She's not inside.'

'She really is in Harrison's place.'

'Looks that way.'

'Any bright ideas?' Pen asked.

'Leave her there.'

'Brilliant.'

'I'm serious. She got herself in there, and I suspect she's perfectly capable of extricating herself when the time is right.'

'What if she's not? What if they already have her? What if

they came back from the hospital and *said* things, talked about running down Dad, and then caught Melanie?'

'Then the situation takes a quantum leap into Shitsville. But I'd prefer to believe that hasn't happened. For all we know right now, those two had nothing to do with the hit-and-run. They aren't going to . . . get violent with Melanie . . . just because she knows they're having an affair.'

Pen looked at him. Her eyes were somber. 'We can't just leave her there,' she said in a whisper.

'I know.'

'But you said . . .'

'Just trying to talk us out of doing something stupid.'

'Like what?'

'I'll go in and get her. Alone. You stay in the car and get the cops if we don't come out in five minutes.'

'That's your plan?' Pen asked.

'Great, huh? Simple and direct.'

'He's got a gun.'

'He won't shoot anyone. Not with you waiting.'

'I don't like it.'

'What's your plan?'

'Why don't *I* go in and you wait in the car?'

'I can think of one excellent reason.'

'What?'

'Because I won't let you.'

Chapter Eighteen

Pen steered her car into the driveway and parked behind Harrison's Mercedes. She kept the engine running.

Bodie took off his wristwatch. Handing it to Pen, he said, 'Five minutes.'

'I'm frightened.'

'Not me.'

'Yeah, I can tell.'

'It's been nice knowing you.'

'Very funny.'

Bodie climbed from the car. He felt as if his breath had been knocked out. His legs seemed ready to collapse, but he forced them to move, one after the other, until he reached the front door.

He pressed the doorbell. Chimes rang inside the house.

He struggled to breathe.

He wondered whether Pen had started the five-minute countdown when he left the car, or planned to wait until he was inside.

He reached up to ring the bell again, and the door opened.

Harrison arched a single eyebrow. He wore a blue warm-up suit with white stripes down the sleeves and legs, and he didn't hold a gun. 'What have we here?' he asked.

'Sorry to bother you,' Bodie said, trying without success to keep his voice from shaking.

Harrison leaned sideways and looked past him. 'One accounted for. Where's the other sister, trapped in a telephone booth?'

'Could I come in and talk to you?'

He stepped back to let Bodie enter. 'I take it you've been selected to represent the grievance committee.'

'Something like that.'

He shut the door behind Bodie. 'What's on your mind, punching me out?'

'No, thanks.'

'Then what?'

'We know about you and Joyce.'

Harrison smirked. 'That's rather obvious at this point. You're way off base, however, if you think I had anything to do with running down Whit.'

Bodie's stomach dropped. 'I don't know what you're . . .'

'Oh, you weren't in on the cute little telephone call or breaking into my garage?'

Bodie's eyes caught movement off to the side. Turning his head, he saw Joyce lean against the entryway from the hall. She wore a bathrobe that was too large for her. The sleeves were rolled above her wrists. 'When I get back to my house tonight,' she said, 'I want all three of you gone. I never want to see any of you again.'

'Fine,' Bodie said.

'Who's going to pay for the garage window?' Harrison asked.

'Melanie,' Bodie said, and wondered if his voice was loud enough to carry to her hiding place.

'I knew it,' Joyce said.

'That crazy little bitch.'

'Listen, mister . . .'

'No, you listen. We don't appreciate being the targets of this lunatic vendetta, and the courts have remedies . . .'

'MELANIE!'

'What the fuck are . . . ?'

'MELANIE, GET OUT HERE!!!'

Joyce clenched her robe tight and stood there rigid, a look of alarm on her face.

'Is she *here*?' Harrison raged. 'Goddamn it, if that little bitch is in my house . . . !'

Bodie stepped past him.

Harrison clamped his shoulder. Whirling, Bodie knocked the hand away. 'We'll be out of here in a . . .'

Joyce shrieked. Harrison's glower changed to shock. Bodie spun around in time to see Joyce slam against the floor with Melanie on her back. Straddling her rump, Melanie tore at her hair, jerked her head up and smacked a fist into her cheek.

Bodie, rammed aside by Harrison, fell against a chair. He shoved himself up. As he raced across the room, he saw Harrison grab Melanie by the neck of her sweatshirt and try to hoist her off Joyce. The loose, sleeveless sweatshirt flew up her body, covered her face, caught her arms for an instant, then released her. Harrison staggered off balance, waving the empty shirt at the ceiling. He landed on his rump.

Melanie, naked to the waist, punched the back of Joyce's neck.

Harrison was getting up.

Bodie, ignoring him, grabbed Melanie's arm and dragged her off Joyce.

'Leave go!' Melanie yelled.

'Come on!'

She stumbled along on her knees, pulled by Bodie.

'Everybody calm down!' he shouted. 'We're getting out of here. We're going.'

'Crazy bitch!' Joyce shrieked.

Harrison moved in.

'Leave her *alone*!' Bodie warned.

Harrison kicked. The toe of his running shoe smashed Melanie in the ribs just below her armpit. Her hand jerked from Bodie's grip. She tumbled, her face striking the edge of a table. Bodie snatched her sweatshirt. Harrison, hanging onto it, lunged against him. Hooking an arm around Harrison's head, he twisted and flung the man over his hip. As Harrison hit the floor, Bodie dropped and drove a knee into his belly. Harrison's breath blasted out. 'I told you to *leave her alone!*' He tore the sweatshirt from Harrison's grip.

Melanie was on her knees, hanging onto the table with one hand while she pressed the other hand to her cheek. Blood spilled out between her fingers. Her side had a red scuff from the kick.

Crouching, Bodie gave her the sweatshirt. He glimpsed a small gash over her cheekbone before she pressed the sweatshirt against it. 'Come on,' he said gently. 'Let's get going.' Hands beneath her armpits, he lifted her. She was very heavy for a moment. Then her legs were supporting her weight. He steered her toward the door.

'I'm gonna . . . get the cops on you!' Harrison yelled.

Bodie looked around. The man was curled on his side, hugging his stomach. 'Go ahead, asshole. But you'd better have a good alibi for Friday night.'

'Fuckin' lunatics! Both of you!'

Joyce, on her knees, clutched her robe shut with both hands and stared through strings of hanging hair. She said nothing.

Melanie got the door open.

Bodie, with an arm around her back, helped her down the porch stairs. It was still daylight and the sweatshirt was pressed to her face, but her breasts were hidden beneath her arms.

Pen, looking stunned, rushed around her car and opened the rear door. 'My God, what happened?'

'Let's get out of here.'

Melanie ducked into the back seat. Bodie followed her. Pen ran to the other side and flung herself behind the steering wheel. She shot her car out of the driveway and sped forward. 'Where to?'

'My van.'

'Should we take her to emergency? What happened to her?'

'A small cut below the eye. She fell against a table.'

'I'm okay,' Melanie muttered.

'We'd better take her to emergency,' Pen said.

'*I'm all right.*'

'I have a first aid kit in my van.' Bodie pulled her down so that her head rested on his lap. 'Let me take a look.' He lifted the sweatshirt away from her cheek. The cut was half an inch below her left eye. Blood filled the wound and began leaking out. He dabbed it away.

'What went on in there?' Pen asked. 'Was there a fight?'

'A wee scuffle.'

'You sure nailed Harrison,' Melanie said, smiling up at him.

'Why don't you put this on?'

Sitting up, she slipped her arms through the sleeve holes. She drew the sweatshirt down over her head, then lifted the bottom of it and held the cloth against her wound. Her left breast stuck out like someone peering from under a stage curtain. It had a smear of blood beside the nipple.

'Did you find out anything?' Pen asked.

'They know we suspect them,' Bodie said.

'What about you, Mel? Where were you all afternoon?'

'In the bedroom. Under the bed.'

'What did you hear?'

194

'They did it, all right.'

'Hit Dad?'

'Yeah.'

'What did they say?'

'Not now. I don't . . . feel too good.'

'She caught a kick in the ribs, too.'

Pen stopped behind the van. Melanie gave the keys to Bodie, and he opened the rear doors. He was glad to see that she had lowered her sweatshirt before leaving the car.

All three climbed into the van. As Bodie shut the doors, Melanie lay down on the sleeping bag. She raised the blood-spotted sweatshirt to her cheek.

Bodie took out his first aid kit. He spread disinfectant cream on her cut, then applied a bandage.

Pen, crouching at his side, asked, 'Now what should we do? Go to the police?'

'I don't think so,' Bodie said. 'Melanie was in the house illegally. And she's the one who started the fight. I imagine we could both wind up charged with all kinds of shit.'

'Great,' Pen muttered.

'As it is, Harrison threatened to call the cops on us. I'm not sure he has the guts to go through with it, though.'

She looked down at Melanie. 'Did you actually hear him admit to hitting Dad with the car?'

'Yes.'

'What about Joyce?'

'She was in on it. They did it together, just like I thought.'

Chapter Nineteen

Pen finished packing and waited in the living room. Bodie came down a few minutes later, carrying luggage. Melanie was behind him. She had washed the blood from her face and changed into a clean white blouse.

'Can we stay with you?' Melanie asked.

'Of course,' Pen said. She looked at Bodie. 'Are you sure you shouldn't drive back tonight?'

'Well . . .'

'I'm not eager to get rid of you, but if Harrison presses charges you'd be better off out of state.'

'He won't press charges,' Melanie said. 'He knows we'd tell everything.'

'It probably would be better,' Bodie admitted, 'to get a good night's sleep before starting out. We'll leave first thing in the morning.'

'Fine.'

Not fine, Pen thought. She didn't want them to leave at all. But she'd known they couldn't stay long. Starting tomorrow, they would both be missing school and Bodie had classes to teach. Also, it was best that they go back as soon as possible before Melanie got a chance to make more trouble.

She was surprised, however, by Melanie's apparent willingness to return in the morning.

We'd better watch her, she thought.

'I'll stop by a fast-food place,' Bodie said, 'and get us all some supper.'

'There's a Jack-in-the-Box . . .'

He nodded. 'I saw it. What would you like?'

'Tacos would be fine. They've got great tacos.'

Outside, Pen hesitated in front of the door. 'I wonder if we should leave the house keys.'

'Screw that,' Melanie said. 'It's still Dad's house. Joyce doesn't have any right to be kicking us out.'

'I suppose not.'

Melanie went with Bodie to his van. Pen climbed into her car and followed them out to San Vicente.

Driving back to her apartment, she wondered if Melanie would change her mind about leaving in the morning. It hardly seemed possible that she would abandon her hopes of nailing Joyce and Harrison, especially now that she'd apparently heard them admit their guilt.

She must have a plan. Maybe she intends to sneak out, tonight. And do what? God only knows. She'd been crazy enough to hide in Harrison's house – and attack Joyce.

We'd just better make damn sure she doesn't get away from us. Even if it means staying awake all night.

When Pen parked in front of her apartment building, she considered waiting in her car for them to show up. The stop for food should only take them five minutes.

Don't be a chicken, she told herself. If you're not going to move out – and that was the whole point of buying the shotgun – you'd better get used to the place again.

He took my panties. He was here this afternoon. Maybe he's a tenant like Manny.

But not Manny. Someone else.

I can't go on living here, she realized.

Nor could she move out of her car seat.

It'll be all right with Bodie here.

Tomorrow, I'll find a new place. I'll stay in a motel for as long as . . .

Tomorrow, Bodie will be gone.

He has to go. He has to get Melanie away from all this.

I wouldn't mind getting away from all this, myself.

I can't go anywhere, though. Not while Dad's the way he is.

Should call the hospital. Maybe go over there tonight.

What if Joyce is there?

We have to do something about those two. They can't get away with it.

I could go to the police tomorrow and tell them everything. If they focus their investigation on Harrison, they might turn something up. I'll do that. Unless they show up here, first, to arrest Melanie and Bodie.

At least we got her out of Harrison's house in one piece.

Bodie was right, we should've left her there. She probably would've managed to sneak out on her own with nobody the wiser.

Or maybe not.

They might've caught her. God only knows what Harrison would've done.

It was the right move.

What's *their* next move? They know the three of us are onto them. What'll they do about it? Maybe nothing. Harrison's an attorney, he knows we haven't got any evidence.

Maybe it's too much that we suspect them.

So what's he going to do, kill the three of us?

That would bring down an awful lot of heat. He wouldn't risk it unless he was feeling mighty desperate.

Melanie and Bodie will be gone tomorrow. Once he finds that out, it'll relieve the pressure. And once I've gone to the cops, I'll have done my share of the damage. He won't have any motive, then, to shut me up.

We just need to get through the night.

In her mind, Pen saw Harrison kick open the apartment door and rush in, his .38 blasting. A slug smashed Melanie in the chest, slamming her down. She and Bodie ran, but a bullet caught him in the back. She made it to her bedroom, whipped the shotgun around and cut Harrison in half when he lunged through the doorway. She hurried into the living room. Melanie was dead, but Bodie still breathed. You'll be all right, she told him. You'll be fine.

Real nice, she thought. I kill off my sister and let Bodie survive.

Pen knew *she* wasn't psychic. That was Melanie's department. But she recognized the value of daydreams. What she had imagined was a possible scenario. Unlikely, but possible.

Just in case, she would brace the door with a chair and keep her shotgun within reach.

Harrison, she told herself, would have to be insane to barge in shooting.

But he does have the gun.

And those handcuffs.

A former private eye. How come he didn't have to give back the badge and ID when he stopped working for that agency? Maybe he claimed he lost them. A couple of items like that could be very useful, especially if a guy is into rape.

Not as useful as the handcuffs.

Don't start thinking about that, she warned herself. Get off it quick.

But something he'd said that night . . . something about the job. What was it? Ever shoot someone? No, but he'd drawn his gun a couple of times. Said it was a boring job.

Except for the repos.

Holy shit!

She flinched as someone rapped on her window. Melanie looked in at her. Pen climbed out of the car.

'Been here long?' Bodie asked. He had sacks of food in his hands.

Pen shook her head. 'Just a few minutes.' Should she tell them about Harrison, that he'd had experience stealing cars and might even own the tools for it?

Might just set off Melanie.

A midnight search for the tools?

Let's not rock the boat. Save it for the police.

She took out her suitcase and led the way through the front gate. Heading for the stairs, she swept her eyes across all the apartments surrounding the pool. Did *he* live in one of them? Pen knew only a few of the tenants. He might be one she didn't know.

But he knows me.

He has my panties.

He'd like to fuck my brains out and . . .

Stop it!

She hurried up the stairs, telling herself to stay calm. The creep wouldn't try anything tonight, not with Bodie here.

And this is my last night here, you filthy scum. Tough luck.

She opened her apartment door and looked down at the carpet. No message had been slipped under the door during her absence.

While she and Melanie set the kitchen table, Bodie went down to get the rest of the luggage.

'Are you really going to leave tomorrow?' Pen asked.

'I guess so. I'll come back if Dad . . . changes.'

'Do you want to go over to the hospital tonight?'

'What's the point? He's just . . . it's like he's dead. I can't stand to see him that way.' Melanie sank into a chair and held her head. 'I just want to forget everything. I want to sleep.'

'How do you feel?'

'I've got an awful headache.'

'I'll get you some aspirin.' Pen went into the bathroom and opened the medicine cabinet. As she reached for the Excedrin, she saw a bottle of sleeping pills. They were Quaaludes, 150 mg, a drug she had been prescribed by her doctor when she complained of insomnia during a bad period following the rape. The expiration date had passed. But the pills shouldn't cause any harm. Even if they weren't quite as strong as they had once been, a couple of them should certainly knock out Melanie for the night. And put a stop to any plan she might have for sneaking out, later on.

Pen's hands trembled as she shook two of the tablets onto her palm.

It's a dirty trick, she thought.

They'll wipe her out. Bodie and I won't have to spend the night standing guard over her.

She put away the bottle. With the two pills in her hand, she left the bathroom.

Bodie was sitting down at the table when she entered the kitchen. She took a tumbler from the cupboard and filled it with water. 'I got Mel some aspirin,' she said.

Bodie nodded.

She set the glass in front of Melanie and dropped the pills into her palm. 'It's a new brand,' she said. 'They're extra-strength. They may make you a little drowsy, but . . .'

'Fine,' Melanie said. She cupped them to her mouth and drank half the water.

'You don't have blurred vision or nausea, do you?' Bodie asked her.

201

'No. Just a headache.'

'Better lie down after you eat,' Bodie said.

'Yeah.'

Pen got a bottle of beer for Bodie and poured wine for herself and Melanie to drink with the meal. Sitting down, she took her tacos from their paper envelopes and put them on her plate. Bodie and Melanie unwrapped their bacon cheeseburgers. Bodie had bought an order of nachos for each of them – tortilla chips smothered with melted cheese and green chilis.

'All we're missing is a mariachi band,' Bodie said.

'I should've whipped up some margaritas,' said Pen. It was just as well that she hadn't, she realized; she wouldn't have dared give Melanie the sleeping pills. Some wine on top of the pills might not cause a problem. Tequilla and triple sec, though . . .

'Why don't you tell Pen what happened this afternoon?' Bodie suggested.

Melanie raised a shoulder. 'Not much to tell,' she said, and took a bite of her burger.

'Apparently,' Bodie said, 'they had quite a lot to say about the three of us. None of it very flattering.'

'Harrison *really* tore into you,' Melanie said, looking rather gleefully at Pen. 'He used names on you that'd make that caller of yours blush.'

'Sweet of him,' Pen muttered, and bit into a taco.

'Yeah. He thinks you were the brains behind my phone call and breaking into his garage. Said you're out to get him.'

'Did he happen to say why?'

'Told Joyce it was because he dumped you.'

'Is that so.'

'Said he'd fix your wagon.'

202

'My wagon isn't broken.'

'Said he'd like to ream your ass,' Melanie added.

Bodie set down his beer. 'I should've laid waste to that prick when I had the chance.'

'What did he say about the accident?' Pen asked.

'They know we know. First thing Harrison did when they got back was check the garage. He had it figured out even before he found the broken window that the call was a trick to get rid of him so we could check out his car. When he came back in, he said to Joyce, "I knew it. Those fucks are onto us." Then he told her not to worry, we'd never be able to prove anything.'

'He was probably right about that,' Bodie said.

'Joyce is afraid Dad saw Harrison driving. She thought maybe they should inject air into his veins.'

Pen stiffened. 'At the hospital?'

'Yeah. But Harrison told her they'd be idiots to do anything that risky since Dad probably wouldn't ever come to, anyway. He said they should wait and see. Even if Dad *does* revive, there's only a slight chance he'll have any memory of the accident.'

Bodie nodded. 'It's very unlikely that he would remember. I fell off a roof when I was a kid, and I *still* can't remember falling.'

'What were you doing on a roof?' Pen asked.

'I don't know. I ate lunch about an hour before it happened, but the rest of it's a blank until I woke up in an ambulance.'

'That's how Peter Hurkos became psychic,' Melanie said. 'Fell off a ladder or a roof or something.'

'Well, it didn't make me psychic. Thank God. One around here is . . .'

'One too many?' Melanie supplied, and raised an eyebrow.

Bodie looked annoyed for a moment, then just somber. 'I was going to say, "One is enough." '

'I bet.'

'Cut it out,' Pen told her.

Melanie fixed Pen with a knowing gaze. 'I'm sure *you* can't wait to get rid of me.'

'Hey, look, we're on your side.'

'Then how come you're both so eager to get me back to Phoenix?'

'It's for your own good,' Bodie told her.

'Oh, sure.'

'Look what you did today,' Pen said, trying to keep her voice calm. 'You broke God knows how many laws . . .'

'Lot of good *the law* is.'

'Christ, you went ape, you actually assaulted Joyce.'

'She tried to kill our father!'

'Maybe so.'

'No maybes.'

'On top of that, you put yourself in real danger. Bodie, too. You both could've ended up killed because of that dumb stunt you pulled.'

'And you were safe in the car.'

'Hey,' Bodie said, 'somebody had to stay out to get help in case the shit hit the fan. Pen wanted to go in instead of me.'

'Sure, stick up for her.'

'*Damn it!*' Bodie slammed his bottle down on the table. Pen flinched. Melanie jumped, then burst into tears and rushed from the kitchen.

Bodie watched her go. He looked at Pen, shook his head, and muttered, 'Sorry.'

'She was asking for it.'

'I know, but . . .' With a sigh, he pushed back his chair and stood up. 'I'd better apologize to her, or something.'

* * *

Bodie found her in Pen's room, lying on the bed with a pillow hugged over her eyes. He sat beside her.

'Leave me alone,' she mumbled.

'Hey, I'm sorry I lost my temper. Why don't you come on back and finish eating?'

'I'm not hungry.'

'Don't you want to grow up to be big and strong?'

'Ha ha ha.'

'Come on, Mel.'

'I just want to sleep. I'm tired and I've got a headache.'

'You'll feel better if you come out and finish your hamburger.'

'No, I won't.'

Bodie put his hand on her belly. Her skin was warm through the blouse. 'I don't like seeing you upset.'

She sniffed. 'You're both against me.'

'No we're not. Maybe we were a little quick to snap at you, but it's been pretty tense. We didn't know what was happening to you while you were in that house.'

'I was fine.'

'We didn't know that. We were really worried, and the only reason we worried is because we love you. Nobody's *against* you. Well, maybe Joyce and Harrison.'

Her mouth trembled into a smile. She pushed the pillow away from her face and drew it down beneath her head. With fingertips, she brushed the tears from her face. She took a deep breath and let it out slowly. 'I didn't mean to cause you so much trouble.'

'It's all right. Hey, it was kind of exciting.'

'Did Pen really want to go in and get me herself?'

'Yeah. I had to threaten her bodily harm to keep her in the car.'

'I shouldn't have talked to her like that.'

'I'm sure she understands. The past couple of days have been tough on all of us.'

'Would you close the curtains for me?'

Bodie got up. He found the draw cord and pulled, shutting out the late afternoon light.

'I'll come out as soon as I feel better.'

'I'll stay.'

'No, go ahead and finish eating.'

'Are you sure?'

'Yeah. Just don't eat up the rest of my burger. I'll be out a little later.'

Bodie bent over the bed. He kissed her gently on the lips. 'Sleep tight,' he whispered.

Leaving the room, he started to pull the door shut. Then he realized that Melanie might get the wrong idea, so he left it wide open.

He returned to the kitchen. Pen, still at the table, looked over her shoulder as he approached. 'How is she?'

'Fine. She wants to take a nap.'

'That's probably a good idea.'

'She warned me not to polish off her dinner.'

'I guess she is feeling better.'

Bodie sat down across the table from Pen. He felt relieved to have Melanie out of the way, and guilty about the feeling. His bacon cheeseburger was no longer warm. It still tasted good. He washed down a mouthful with beer.

'She doesn't seem very happy about going back tomorrow,' Pen said.

'I'm not overjoyed by the prospect, myself.'

'I'd think you might be glad to get out of this.'

'I don't like the idea of leaving you holding the bag.

Melanie made a real mess of things, and you'll be left with the consequences.'

'I'll be okay. I wasn't involved in the hairy stuff. With you and Melanie gone, Harrison might figure he's won. He'll probably pretend the whole thing never happened. He's good at that.'

'What do you mean?'

Pen shook her head. 'He won't try anything with me.'

'I hope you're right. But Melanie said he thinks you were behind all this today.'

'Let him think what he wants.' Pen lifted a chip to her mouth. Some cheese clung to her upper lip. She chewed, then licked it off. 'Maybe you shouldn't tell Melanie – at least not before you're gone – but I plan to visit the police tomorrow and tell them everything.'

Bodie frowned. 'Do you think that's a good idea?'

'It's self-preservation, for one thing. Once I've talked to the police and accused those two, I don't think they'd dare to come after me. It wouldn't look good if anything happened to me after that. Besides, I plan to make believers out of the cops. Maybe they'll turn up some evidence.'

'Better them than us.'

'That's for sure,' Pen agreed.

'I don't know where we'd go from here, anyway.'

'Melanie might have a few ideas about that.' She glanced around as if to make sure that her sister wasn't sneaking through the kitchen, then said, 'I suspect she might have one last move up her sleeve. It's a long time from now till morning.'

'Yeah,' Bodie said. 'Yeah, I see what you mean. She takes a nap now, and sneaks out tonight after you and I are asleep. I wouldn't put it past her. We'll have to make sure she doesn't get the chance.'

Chapter Twenty

When they finished eating, Pen and Bodie cleaned off the table. Pen wrapped the remains of Melanie's burger and put it in the refrigerator. She took out a can of coffee and began to prepare a pot.

'Good idea,' Bodie said. 'It's going to be a long night.'

'We could sleep in shifts,' Pen said.

'I didn't bring one.'

She laughed. 'You can borrow one of mine.'

'A tempting offer,' Bodie said. He excused himself and headed for the hallway.

While he was gone, apparently to use the toilet, Pen finished making the coffee. Then she carried a kitchen chair to the front door and tipped it backward, bracing its back under the knob. Just like Friday night, she thought, and remembered her terror the next morning when she saw an arm reaching in, trying to dislodge the chair. It had been Bodie, though, and she'd stabbed him.

'I don't think that will keep Mel in,' Bodie said as he entered the living room.

She smiled at him. 'Oh, darn.'

'What's it for?'

'Just in case.'

'You afraid Harrison might try something?'

'I doubt it. But you never know.'

'You're about the most cautious person I've ever met.'

'A streak of paranoia,' she said. 'I think it runs in the family.'

Bodie sat near an end of the sofa. 'A broken clock has the right time twice a day, and even paranoids have enemies.'

'Sometimes imaginary enemies. Look how I stabbed you yesterday.'

'A mere nick.'

'Fortunately. But it shows what can happen if you lose control.'

'Hell, I was trying to force my way in. You didn't know who I was. I'd say the attack was justified.'

'Justified, maybe, but a mistake. The coffee's probably ready.'

She went into the kitchen, filled two mugs, and brought them out. She gave one to Bodie. 'Did you look in on Melanie?'

'She's zonked out.'

'Good. I need to get something.' Pen set her mug on the table and went to her bedroom. The closed curtains kept out the dim evening light. Melanie was a vague shape on the bed. Pen crept close to her. She heard the girl's long, slow breaths.

Zonked, all right.

With those Quaaludes in her, she wouldn't be waking up for a very, very long time.

Pen thought of her father in a coma.

I did this to Melanie.

She'll come out of it, Dad won't.

Yes, he will. He has to.

Crouching, Pen slipped the shotgun out from under the bed. She carried it back into the living room. Bodie's eyes widened. 'What, me worry?' Pen asked.

'Lordy lordy, I'd sure hate to get on your bad side.'

'Damn right. I'm one bad dude.'

'Can I see it?'

'Sure. It's loaded, by the way.'

'Wouldn't do much good otherwise.'

She handed it to him, then picked up her coffee mug and sat at the other end of the sofa. She turned sideways to face him, bringing her knees up against the back cushion.

'A beaut,' Bodie said. He shouldered the weapon, aimed it across the room, lowered it onto his lap and stroked its walnut stock. 'Real nice.'

'I just bought it this morning.'

'Twelve-gauge?'

Pen nodded. 'With special magnum cartridges.'

'Wicked. I guess Harrison better not mess with *you*.'

'I didn't have him in mind,' she said, and took a drink of coffee as Bodie turned to look at her.

'The caller?'

'Yeah.'

'I'd almost forgotten about him. All this other stuff going on.'

'I wish I could forget about him,' she said, and drank more coffee. 'I'd better put that shotgun someplace.' She set her mug on the table.

Bodie leaned sideways and passed the weapon to her.

She stood up. 'I want to keep it handy in case.'

'You don't want Melanie to spot it,' Bodie advised.

'You must be a mind reader.' She propped the shotgun against the wall between the front door and the end of the sofa, hidden behind the curtains. Then she pulled the draw cord. The curtains skidded shut. 'A symptom of paranoia,' she said. 'You don't want people looking in.'

'An uncle of mine was killed that way,' Bodie told her. 'He was in his living room one night with the lights on and the drapes open. Someone out on the street plinked him.'

'My God, really?'

'It was just one of those random things. I guess he made an irresistible target.'

Pen shook her head. 'The things that happen in this world.'

'Can't be too careful.'

'My motto.' She turned on a lamp. 'More coffee?'

'Sure.'

She took the mugs into the kitchen, filled them and returned. She gave a mug to Bodie, then sat at her end of the sofa. 'It's all a little frightening,' she said.

' "We are here as on a darkling plain swept with confused alarms of struggle and flight . . ." '

' "Where ignorant armies clash by night," ' Pen said. Bodie grinned. 'Hey, how about letting me read one of your stories?'

Pen's stomach did a little flip. 'Okay,' she said. 'If you're sure . . .'

'Sure.'

Nervously, she took another drink of coffee. Then she got up and went to the bookcase. She pulled down a copy of *Ellery Queen's Mystery Magazine* and handed it to Bodie. 'Remember, William Faulkner I ain't.'

'They paid you for this, right?'

'Yep.'

'Then, Faulkner or not, it's quite an accomplishment.'

'Thanks,' she muttered. 'Page 93.'

He opened the magazine and began to read.

My story, Pen thought. She was pleased, but embarrassed. She didn't know what to do with herself while he read it, so she crouched over her suitcase and took out the paperback she had started reading Friday night in the tub.

She sat on the sofa and opened it.

Bodie turned a page.

She wondered if he liked the story so far.

It was pretty shallow, really.

She tried to read the paperback, but her gaze kept straying

211

from the page to Bodie at the other end of the sofa. His face looked solemn. He brushed a hank of light brown hair off his forehead, but it flopped down again.

Pen forgot about the book on her lap and forgot to worry about Bodie's reaction to her short story. She stared at him – his hair glossy in the lamplight, his shirt rumpled in front from the way he was slouched, one foot propped on the other knee, the old running shoe half off and dangling from his toes, a disk of pink skin showing through a hole in the heel of his sock.

She wanted to scoot over the sofa to his side.

Ah, but you won't, she told herself.

Melanie's out for the count.

Don't even consider it.

Bodie, eyes still on the story, shook his head and muttered, 'Oh, my God.' He closed the magazine. He looked at Pen and shook his head some more. He grinned. 'Man, I was worried sick about her and all the time *she's* the one hunting *them*.'

'Does that mean you liked it?'

'You reversed everything. The final line of the story, you turned it all upside-down. Yeah, I think it's terrific. Nice writing, too. I felt as if I were inside her, feeling everything she felt, going through it all. Really nice. If you turned this in to me as a student, I'd give it an A minus.'

Pen, delighted, forced herself to scowl. 'Why the minus?'

'To keep you from getting cocky.'

She laughed. 'Thanks, anyway.'

'Do you have some more I could read?'

'That's the only published one.'

'I don't care.'

'Let's quit while I'm ahead.'

'Come on,' he said. 'We've got all night.'

And only tonight, Pen thought. I don't want to spend it all watching him read my stories. 'Well, maybe one more.'

She drank the rest of her coffee, then went into her office and turned on the light. She felt shaky and excited.

She needed badly to use the bathroom – all that coffee. But she sat at her desk and slid open the deep bottom drawer. Each of the manila folders was labeled with a story title. She flipped through them with trembling fingers.

Better pick one fast, she thought, before I burst.

She pulled out the folder for 'The McDougal Stone' and opened it on her lap. On top of the paper-clipped manuscript were three rejection slips.

Maybe he can tell me what's wrong with it.

Hell, I thought it was good.

She took out the manuscript and put the folder away.

As she stood up, her eyes met the answering machine. The voice filled her head, tearing apart her good feelings, turning her insides cold and tight. She looked quickly at the window. Its curtains were shut.

He can't see me.

Maybe he saw the light come on. If he lives in the building . . .

But he can't call and he knows I'm not alone. Nothing to worry about. Not tonight.

He has my panties.

She rushed out of the office and some of her fear eased when she entered the living room and saw Bodie in the lamplight, looking so calm and comfortable – and happy.

'This one's been rejected a few times,' she said, handing the story to him.

'Must really stink.'

She laughed. 'Back in a minute,' she said, and hurried to the bathroom. Bodie had left the toilet seat down. Very considerate. She quickly opened her white shorts and pulled them down her legs. She hooked her thumbs under the sides of her panties, tugged them down, and sat.

And stared at the skimpy lace panties drawn taut between her ankles.

Bodie heard the toilet flush. Expecting Pen to return in a few seconds, he watched the dark entrance to the hallway. And waited.

Apparently, she wasn't coming back right away.

He read more of the story, and almost finished it before he heard a door open. Pen's footsteps were slow and quiet in the hallway. Then she stepped into the living room.

She raised a hand in a hesitant greeting. A smile faltered on her face. Her nose was a little red and her eyes were red and puffy. 'More coffee?' she asked in a chipper voice.

'No thanks. Are you all right?'

Nodding, she sat at her end of the sofa. 'Finished the story yet?'

'No. What's wrong? You've been crying.'

'It's ridiculous.'

'It can't be ridiculous if it upset you that much.' Leaning forward, he dropped the manuscript onto the coffee table. He turned toward Pen. She was bent forward, elbows on knees, her head drooping. Bodie, frowning, scooted closer and put his hand on her back. She didn't flinch or tell him to stop. He rubbed her gently between the shoulder blades, aware of her warm smoothness through the blouse.

'Ever get the feeling that you've lost your grip?'

'Slipped a few cogs?'

She nodded. The hair hanging over her face shimmered in the lamplight.

'Yeah,' Bodie said. 'Sometimes. What happened?'

'It's that guy who called Friday night. Even with everything else, I haven't been able to get him off my mind.'

'That's understandable.'

'My God, he had me so rattled that I stabbed you. I mean, I blew everything out of proportion. I put that stupid trip-cord across my doorway and damn near cracked my head open, then I stabbed you, for Christsake.'

'I'm not complaining.'

'I was so messed up, I actually believed he would come here and try to rape me. I was certain of it.'

'There was a real danger that he might,' Bodie said. 'I was worried, too.'

'Then he left that message under my door. I was petrified. But I thought, I'm not going to let him run my life. I won't let him scare me away. So I went out this morning and bought the shotgun. I'll fix him, right? Just let him come. The shotgun's a magic wand – wave it and I'm safe. Only the thing is, I got back here and I was alone and I was *still* scared, damn it. But I wasn't going to let him get to me, right? So I go down to the laundry room and some creep puts moves on me and I'm so messed up I think *he's* the caller. I actually take a knife with me when I go back down. I probably would've stabbed *him* if he'd shown up again. That would've been real cute. Stab two innocent guys in two days. Maybe I could go down in the *Guinness Book of World Records*.'

'You shouldn't be so hard on yourself,' Bodie whispered.

'Oh, you haven't heard the good one yet. Talk about paranoia. When I went to put away my laundry, something wasn't there. A pair of underpants. Neat, huh? My obscene caller snuck into the laundry room and stole my panties. That really freaked me out. He not only knows where I live, but he is *here* and spying on me, maybe even a tenant in the building, and he's got my goddamn panties. Only here's the thing.' Pen's voice quavered. She turned her head toward Bodie. Strands of hair hung across her face and her eyes were shiny. 'Here's the real corker.' Her chin trembled. 'I was wearing them the whole time. I had 'em *on*. Nobody stole them. I've been wearing them all day. I've got them on right now.' She made a choking sound that may have been an attempted laugh but came out as a sob. 'How's that for nuts, huh?'

'Oh, Pen,' he whispered. He stroked her hair.

Then she was turning, putting her arms around him, weeping with her face against his chest.

'It's all right,' he said. 'It's all right.' He sank against the cushion, holding her gently. He stroked her hair, her back. She felt big in his arms, broader across the back than Melanie. A breast was pressing against him. He told himself to ignore it. Just holding her gave him a good, warm, comfortable feeling and he didn't want the extra guilt of growing aroused but he couldn't help it.

'I have to tell you something,' he said, and eased her away.

She nodded and sniffed, her face close to his, her hands on his sides.

'This is all my fault,' Bodie said.

Pen shook as she took a deep breath.

'Partly my fault, anyway.'

She had a confused look in her eyes.

'That caller of yours . . . he never came here. He made the telephone calls, but he didn't come here. Remember how it took me so long to pick up the pizza last night? I didn't get lost. I stopped by a drugstore and bought a birthday card. I used its envelope. I'm the one who left that message under your door.'

'No, you didn't. You're just trying to make me feel better.'

'I'm sorry. It was a dumb trick.'

'No, you . . .'

'I really did it.'

'*Why?*'

'So you wouldn't stay here last night. I heard that guy's voice on the tape. I was afraid . . . afraid he *might* come over. I didn't want you to be here alone. And I knew you were frightened about staying and it was just Melanie forcing you into it.'

Pen stared into his eyes.

'A dumb trick,' he said again. 'I should have known it would make things worse for you. Hell, I *did* know. I just didn't care. I wanted you over at the house no matter what.'

'Because you were worried about me?'

'Yeah.'

Leave it at that, he warned himself.

I've gone this far. I have to finish.

'And also . . . because it wasn't fair. You'd asked us to stay with you and I knew we should – it was the right thing to do because you asked first and you really needed us here and I thought we should stay with you but Melanie went and told Joyce we'd stay at her house. She only did it to spite you.'

'She did it to keep you away from me,' Pen said.

'I know. I didn't *want* me away from you.'

'Oh, Bodie.'

'Well . . .'

'I guess it's not much of a surprise,' Pen said.

'Happens all the time,' he said. 'Melanie shows up with a boyfriend and he falls all over you. I know I'm a jerk. We'll be gone in the morning, and that'll be the end of it.'

She curled a warm hand behind his neck. 'The end of it,' she whispered. 'I know. Tonight's our . . . Those tablets I gave Melanie before we ate? They weren't aspirin. They were sleeping pills. Strong ones. She won't be getting up tonight.'

'My God.'

'I was afraid she might try to sneak out later,' Pen said. 'That's why I did it. Not for this. Not so we could be alone.'

Bodie shook his head.

'It's no worse than you writing that note, is it?'

'Better,' he heard himself say. 'A lot better. We're quite a tricky pair, you and me.'

'I'm not proud of drugging her, but . . . I'm going to miss you so much, Bodie.' She lifted her face to him and they kissed.

We shouldn't, he thought.

Pen's mouth was warm and moist.

He felt giddy. He felt like a high school kid somehow miraculously being kissed by the one girl he'd been longing for, the girl admired only from a distance and daydreamed about. It seemed unreal.

He put his arms around her. She sank against him, pressing him into the cushion.

Oh, this is real.

Her weight on him was real. Her breasts pushing against his chest were real. And her mouth, open against his, and her tongue, and her breath going into him.

Pen's mouth eased away. His lips were wet. She stared at him, her eyes moving a fraction from side to side. He felt as if he could see into them, but not deeply enough. He wanted to look into her mind, to be inside with her thoughts and feelings.

'What are we gonna do?' she whispered.

'About what?'

'Us.' Her eyes, so close to his, kept moving just a bit, looking from his left eye to his right and back again.

'What do you want to do?' he asked.

'It's not that simple.'

'Why not?'

'I can't hurt her, Bodie. I won't.'

'She's asleep. You said . . .'

'What about after tonight?'

Bodie's heart sped up.

'We'll work something out,' he said. His voice sounded as desperate as he felt.

'How?'

'I don't know.'

'Neither do I,' Pen said. She leaned forward against him, her forehead resting in the curve of his neck. He stroked her back.

'I can't lose you. All my life I've been hoping that some-day . . .'

'Pen and Bodie sitting in a tree, k-i-s-s-i-n-g.'

Pen lurched in his arms.

Beyond the doorway, barely visible in the darkness of the hall, stood Melanie.

Chapter Twenty-one

Melanie dug a hand into a pocket of her corduroy pants. The hand came out with two pills in its palm. 'I knew they weren't aspirin,' she said, her voice flat. She stared at Pen with blank eyes. 'You gave me sleeping pills. So you could have the night with Bodie. So you could seduce him.'

'Oh, man,' Bodie muttered.

'That's not the reason,' Pen said. 'I was afraid you'd sneak out and go after Harrison.'

'Slut,' Melanie said calmly.

'Mel!' Bodie snapped.

Her head turned slowly toward him. 'What?' she asked.

'Don't talk that way. She's on your side. We both are.'

'You want me out of the way.'

'Don't be crazy.'

A placid, humorless smile curled Melanie's lips.

My God, Pen thought, what have we done to her?

Bodie turned to Pen. 'We'd better leave,' he said. 'I don't think we should wait for morning. I'll take her back now.'

'Yeah.'

'We can't leave,' Melanie said. 'You haven't fucked her yet. You have to fuck her. Everyone has to fuck her.' The mild way she said it, smiling, made goosebumps crawl up Pen's back.

Bodie stood up. He stepped around the coffee table, passed in front of Melanie, and picked up the two suitcases he had left near the wall after bringing them up from the van. Melanie, standing motionless, followed him with an empty gaze.

Pen got to her feet. She removed the chair from under the knob and opened the door.

Bodie looked at her with such agony that she wanted to throw her arms around him. 'It'll be all right,' he said.

'I don't think so.'

'She'll get over this once we're away.'

Will she? Pen thought. I won't, and neither will you.

'Come on, Melanie,' he said gently.

She walked toward him, her dead eyes staying on Pen. 'First came love,' she chanted in a low voice, 'then came marriage, then came Penny with a baby carriage.'

'Bye,' Bodie said.

She nodded.

Then they were out the door. Stepping onto the balcony, Pen watched her sister follow Bodie to the stairs and down. When they were out of sight, she heard the courtyard gate squeak open and shut. She folded her arms over her breasts for warmth against the night chill. She pressed her bare legs together. She clamped her teeth shut so they wouldn't click.

Then came the faint sound of Bodie's van starting up.

That's it, she thought. They're going.

'Hey babe, I'll warm you up,' Manny called out his door.

She didn't feel annoyed or threatened. She felt nothing about him. He didn't matter.

Stepping inside her apartment, she closed the door. She slipped the guard chain into place and looked at the chair she had used earlier to brace the door shut.

Why bother?

She wasn't afraid. She thought vaguely that she should be pleased she was no longer afraid, but she just didn't care.

She plugged her kitchen telephone back into the wall.

Let the bastard call, she thought. He can't hurt me. Sticks and stones can break my bones, but words . . .

Pen and Bodie sitting in a tree, k-i-s-s-i-n-g.

Words can never hurt me.

How could everything have gone so wrong?

They're gone. I'll never see Bodie again.. Melanie hates my guts. She thinks I . . . she's right.

Bodie. Oh, God, Bodie.

She wandered into her bedroom and turned on the light. She wanted to lie down, to sleep, to forget.

Not even nine o'clock.

Nine. They'd missed visiting hours at the hospital.

She had hardly even given her father a thought, today.

I'll go see him tomorrow, she promised herself.

In the bathroom, she brushed her teeth and washed her face. She returned to her bedroom. She took off her clothes, her panties last.

Sitting on the edge of the bed, she held the panties in her hands.

Nobody took them. All in my head.

We have nothing to fear but ourselves.

She dropped them to the floor, turned off the lamp, and crawled between the sheets of her bed. The sheets were cool at first on her naked body, then warm.

She thought about Bodie driving through the night, Melanie silent in the passenger seat. Was he trying to apologize? Would Melanie listen? Or was she too far gone, lost in a private world of pain?

Don't feel too sorry for her, Pen thought. Bodie and I, we've got our own world of pain, and all because we didn't want to hurt her.

But we did.

We hurt her good. Ourselves, too.

Goddamn it.

Why didn't she take the pills!

Maybe it's best this way. If she'd stayed asleep, Bodie and I . . . we would've ended up making love.

Probably.

No probably.

Don't think about it. Just don't think.

She drew the extra pillow down and hugged it tightly to her breasts.

She remembered the feel of kissing him.

The needle on Bodie's gas gauge showed that he was down to a quarter of a tank. He was driving south on Robertson Boulevard. If he remembered correctly, he was only a couple of miles from the on-ramp to the Santa Monica Freeway. Once on the freeway, stopping for gas would be a lot of trouble.

As he waited at a traffic light, he saw a self-service station on the other side of the intersection.

The light turned green. He rolled through the intersection and swung into the station. He stopped beside the pumps. He took his key from the ignition. Twisting around, he peered into the dark rear of the van and said, 'I'll be back in a minute.'

Melanie didn't answer.

What if she's not back there?

She has to be. Bodie knew he would've heard the rear doors open if she had tried to sneak out.

But he wondered.

Turning on the light, he saw Melanie stretched out flat on the sleeping bag, her hands folded on her belly. 'Are you all right?' he asked.

She said nothing. She didn't move.

'Don't worry about it,' he said. 'Okay? Nothing happened between me and Pen. There's no point brooding over it.'

She didn't respond.

Bodie climbed from the van. He put the keys in his pants pocket and took out his wallet as he walked toward the office cubicle. Along the way, he glanced back a few times.

He didn't really expect Melanie to bolt, but she'd been full of surprises lately.

He slipped his credit card into the trough beneath the glass partition. The swarthy, grinning man on the other side picked it up. Bodie told him the number of the pump he planned to use, then headed for the van.

Even though he'd tried to keep an eye on it, he cautioned himself to make sure, before driving off, that Melanie was still inside.

She's not going anywhere, he thought. She's in shock or something.

He pushed the pump nozzle into his tank and held the lever down.

She'll probably be fine tomorrow. Just pissed as hell and full of accusations. She'll probably dump *me*, and save me the trouble.

When the flow clicked off, Bodie shoved the nozzle into place on the side of the pump. He screwed his gas cap on tightly and started for the office.

It's less than a month till the end of the semester. One way or another, we'll be finished by then and I'll come back to Pen.

Bodie scooped up his credit card and signed the slip. He tore off the customer receipt and dropped the rest into the trough. The man thanked him.

He headed back for the van.

He climbed in, turned on the light and checked the rear. Melanie was still lying there. She looked as if she hadn't moved a muscle the whole time he was filling the tank.

He turned off the overhead lights, dug out his keys, and started the engine.

Maybe I'll luck out, he thought, and she'll stay this way the whole trip.

He drove onto a sidestreet, stopped at the corner, then made a right onto Robertson. On the track again, he wondered whether to make a right or a left when he reached the freeway.

Just wait for the signs.

Whichever way goes east – you know you don't want to end up at the ocean.

Maybe by summer there will be a vacancy in Pen's apartment building.

He stopped for a traffic light.

The real question is, can I wait for the semester to end? I have to. Gotta finish the MA.

He heard a quiet sound of movement behind him.

At least Melanie's not paralyzed.

I could always drive over on weekends. Once I've settled the situation with Melan . . .

Pain blasted through Bodie's head.

Pen jerked awake, gasping and shaking, her heart thundering.

A bell was ringing.

Someone at the door!

It blared again.

The telephone?

She hurled herself off the bed and rushed across her room,

afraid the caller might hang up before she could reach the phone – afraid he might not.

Who?

She hoped it was Bodie. It could be anyone.

The obscene caller. Harrison or Joyce. The hospital.

My God, don't let it be bad news!

Maybe a wrong number, a salesman.

The phone rang again.

The hallway was faintly lighted from the living room lamp she hadn't bothered to turn off.

She slapped a hand against the kitchen doorframe to stop herself, reached around the corner and snatched up the phone. 'Hello?'

'This is *you*, isn't it?'

She knew the voice. Her skin seemed to shrink. She felt it tighten and prickle.

'Not a recording, this time?'

'No.'

'Do you know who I am?'

'What do you want?' she asked, her voice trembling.

'I want to talk. I've missed you. Have you been away?'

Hang up, she thought. Sure. If I do, he'll just call again.

Or come over. He knows I'm here.

Pen remembered the shotgun. She'd left it in the living room, propped against the wall near the door, hidden behind the curtains.

Let him come over. Give him a big surprise.

'Or were you just afraid to pick up the phone? You're not scared of me, honey, are you?'

'Why should I be scared?' she asked, trying to steady her voice.

He laughed. It was a quiet, dry laugh that made a cold place in her stomach.

'I've been hoping you'd call again,' she told him.

'Really?'

'Those things you said . . . I've listened to the tape so many times. I love it.'

'Makes you hot?'

'It sure does. I'm getting hot right now.'

'What are you wearing?' he asked.

Not a stitch. Pen wished she'd grabbed her robe on the way to the phone.

He can't see me.

'Jeans. And a sweater.'

'A brassiere?' he hissed.

She almost said yes. She wanted to be wearing one. She wanted to be dressed in tight, heavy clothes. She had never felt so exposed and vulnerable.

Don't back out now, she told herself.

Shivering, she said, 'No.'

'Ah, fabulous. A sweater and no brassiere. I can see it. Yes. Oh, my cock is getting big and hot. Do you know what I'd like to do? I'd like to lift your sweater and suck your tits.'

'Would you like me to take it off?' she asked.

'Oh, yes.'

What the hell am I doing? she wondered. Am I mad? 'There,' she said, 'it's off.'

He sighed. 'Are your nipples hard?'

She looked down. They were hard. But not because of desire. 'They sure are,' she said.

'I'd like to rub my cock on them. Would you like that?'

'I sure would.'

'Oh, I know it, I know it. Wouldn't you like to take off your pants?'

'Sure. Just a second.'

'And your underpants, too. I want you naked.'

She heard his raspy breathing. As she listened, she leaned against the doorframe. She rubbed her cold legs together. Looking down, she saw that her thighs were spickled with goosebumps.

'Okay,' she said. 'I'm naked. Are you?'

'Of course. And oh, my cock is *huge*. He wants you.'

'He?'

'Spike.'

Almost funny, she thought. The creep's got a name for his penis. A dog's name, Spike. But also a term for a very large nail.

'I bet Spike's big and powerful,' she said. 'I wish I could feel him.' She heard the words. This isn't me. This is a character in one of my stories, talking to a madman.

'What would you do with him?'

'I'd pet him. He likes to be petted, I bet.'

'Oh, yes.'

'Then I'd suck on him.'

'Oh, honey!'

'I'd suck on Spike till he throbbed in my mouth and I'd swallow every delicious drop and then I'd lick him clean.'

I'm as mad as he is.

Method in my madness, tra-la, tra-la.

'Would you like that?' she asked in a husky voice.

'Oh, yes, yes. Then what?'

'Wouldn't *you* like to know?'

'Tell me.'

'Why don't you come over and find out?'

'Tell me first.'

'I'd rub you all over with honey. And then you'd rub me all over with more, so we're all slick and sticky. Then we'd lick it off each other and when it's all gone, I'd spread my legs and . . .'

'Yes yes!'

'Oh God I'm hot! Let's not talk about it.'

'Please.'

'I want you to fuck me. I want Spike in my cunt. You want that, don't you?'

'YES!'

'Come over.'

'What?'

'Now.'

There was silence except for his harsh breathing.

'Or are you just one of those guys who likes to talk about it? All words and no action?'

He laughed, that same dry chuckle like rustling paper. 'You'll find out. I'll *ream* you, honey. I'll fuck your brains out!'

'So get over here and do it. No more talk.'

More breathing.

God, am I really going to blow his head off?

You damn betcha.

Magnum loads.

I can't do it.

Oh, no? Oh, no?

'Come on, lover,' she whispered. 'I'm *hot*! I want you! I've gotta have you! Get over here!'

'Yeah. Yeah. Okay. Just tell me where you live.'

What?

'You *know* where I live.'

'I will once you tell me.'

'My address is right in the phone book.'

'So what's your name, you sweet stuff?'

'You don't know my *name*?'

'Fuck, no. I just dialed some numbers. Wrote 'em down so I could call you back, but . . .'

Pen slammed down the phone. With a tug at its plastic base, she removed it from the wall jack.

For a long time, she stood leaning against the doorframe, gasping, arms folded across her breasts, legs tight together. She trembled badly. She knew that she should be feeling relief, even triumph.

Instead, she felt sick.

Knowing such a man was out there, even though she would get her number changed and he would be out of her life forever.

Knowing what she had said to him.

The foulness.

And knowing, worst of all, that she had actually tried to lure him to her.

To kill him with the shotgun.

She felt soiled.

Pushing herself away from the wall, she walked on shaky legs down the hallway toward the bathroom.

Bodie woke up and groaned at the pain in his head. He felt as if his lids were all that held his eyes inside his sockets, that if he opened them, his eyes might burst out from the pressure behind them.

He also felt ready to throw up.

Must've really tied one on last night. He couldn't remember getting smashed, but . . .

What the hell was he lying on? Not a bed.

He rubbed the surface.

Grass. Dewy grass.

He opened his eyes. The pain and nausea swelled. He thrust himself to his hands and knees and vomited. The spasms wracked him, driving white-hot nails into the base of his skull. When he had finished, he knelt above the mess and clutched his head. The hand above his right ear pressed against an enormous lump.

Not a hangover. I've been . . .

He'd been driving, taking Melanie back to Phoenix.

A crash? He must've crashed and been thrown clear of the van. Melanie!

He turned his head, groaning at the new surge of pain. The van was nowhere in sight. Neither was a road. Bodie was on his knees behind a hedge. To his right was a field with playground equipment near the far corner. Turning some more, he saw a building – a school?

Where the hell am I? What am I doing here?

Bodie pushed himself carefully to his feet and stood motionless, waiting for a wave of dizziness to pass. He dragged a handkerchief from his pocket, blew his nose, and dropped the handkerchief to the grass. Then he walked slowly through an opening in the bushes.

He found himself on a sidewalk. In front of him was a narrow street, homes on the other side. Cars were parked along the street, but not his van. To his left, about a block away, was a busy road with cars passing through its intersection. He walked toward it and tried to remember.

I was at Pen's apartment. With her on the sofa. We kissed. Oh, we did kiss. It had been so . . . and then Melanie came in. She was supposed to be asleep but she hadn't taken the pills.

Should've taken the damn pills. Acting very weird. Time to get her out of there, take her back to Phoenix. She was in the back of the van, wouldn't talk. I stopped for gas. Then what?

He could remember signing his credit card slip, but nothing after that.

But we didn't crash. If we crashed, where's the van?

He gingerly fingered the bump on the side of his head.

Melanie . . . could she have hit me with something? Must've. Knocked me out. While I was *driving*? Maybe I was stopped at a light. She could've knocked me out, shoved me over to the passenger seat and got behind the wheel.

Wasn't ready to go back to Phoenix.

Found the school yard, unloaded me, and dragged me behind the bushes.

Strong enough to do that?

They say crazy people . . .

Crazy.

She's gone after someone.

Unfinished business.

Pen?

Bodie's head throbbed.

She's gone after Pen.

No, maybe not, maybe it's Harrison and Joyce. That's okay. Who gives a shit?

But what if it's Pen? What'll Melanie do to her?

Bodie stopped at the corner of the busy street. It was Robertson Boulevard, just as he'd suspected, and he could see the freeway overpass in the distance.

He had to warn Pen.

He raised his left hand to check his wristwatch.

The watch was gone.

No way to know how long he'd been unconscious in the field.

232

If it was only a few minutes, he might still have time to warn her.

He spotted pay phones across the road.

He slapped the rear pocket of his pants. His wallet was gone. He shoved a hand into his front pocket. No change.

No way to phone Pen. No way to warn her.

He started to run.

Bolts of pain shot through his head but he didn't slow down.

I won't make it in time, he thought. It might already be too late.

What'll Melanie do to her?

All my fault.

Oh shit oh shit oh shit!

The pain!

I've got to save her!

Ahead of Bodie, a man came out of a burger joint with a bag of food, crossed the sidewalk, and stepped in front of a parked Cadillac.

'Hey,' Bodie called, rushing toward him. 'Mister! Can you give me a ride? Please? It's really urgent.'

'Are you nuts?'

'Somebody's gonna get killed. All I need is a ride. It won't take long. Please!'

The man chuckled, shook his head, and reached into his pocket for the keys. 'Does this look like a taxi, pal?'

'I'm not kidding, mister. It's an *emergency*!'

'Fuck off.' He turned toward the door of his car.

Bodie grabbed his jacket, spun him around, and smashed a fist into his belly. He was fat and soft. His breath whooshed out. He doubled over and Bodie chopped the back of his neck. The man's knees hit the pavement. Bodie yanked him forward by the back of his jacket, and he flopped.

'I'm sorry, mister. I'll make sure you get it back.'

He tore the keys from the man's limp fingers, unlocked the driver's door, and jumped in. As he started the car, the man's face appeared in front of the bumper.

Bodie shot the car backwards. The man crawled toward it, yelling.

The road was clear.

Bodie whipped the car around in a U-turn and floored the gas pedal.

God Almighty, he thought, what have I done?

Assault and battery, grand theft. *Jesus!*

Just don't let the cops stop me.

Though he ached to keep the accelerator floored, he lowered his speed to forty-five.

He checked the rearview mirror.

No cars on his tail.

No one had seen him rip off the guy's Caddy and come after him. Lucky lucky.

A red traffic light.

Damn!

He didn't dare run it.

He pounded his fist on the steering wheel while he waited for the green.

'Come on, come on!'

It changed. He rammed the car forward.

I stole this thing.

I beat that guy up and took his car.

Oh, we got us a crime wave, folks.

Top o' the world, Ma!

God Almighty.

Yesterday a mild-mannered student, today a felon.

He felt a tickle in his throat. A giggle? It might come out a scream.

Almost there.

Let her be all right. Please, God, let her be all right.

Bodie swung onto Pen's street.

Almost there. Let her be all right.

Dead on the floor, her body torn by knife wounds, blank eyes staring at the ceiling . . .

No, no, no!

He was on her block, darting his eyes from side to side, looking for his van. He jerked the car to a stop in front of her building. Still no sign of the van, but Melanie might've parked it around a corner.

He leaped from the car, dashed across the street, threw open the iron gate and ran to the stairs. He charged up the stairs three at a time and raced along the balcony to her door. Light shone through the curtains of the picture window. He pounded on the door. 'Pen!' he called. 'Pen, it's Bodie!'

Seconds passed.

He pounded again.

The door was opened.

By Pen, wearing a blue velour bathrobe.

She looked all right. She looked wonderful. She had a worried look in her eyes.

'Is Melanie here?' Bodie asked.

Pen shook her head.

Bodie stepped inside. He swung the door shut, put his arms around Pen, and hugged her hard.

Chapter Twenty-two

It felt so good to see him, to have him back, to hold him. She squeezed him tightly. She didn't want to know why he was here, what had gone wrong. She wanted only to go on holding him.

He was panting for air, and she could feel the beat of his heart against her chest.

'Are you okay?' she whispered after a while.

'I am now. Except for a splitting headache.'

'I'll get you some aspirin.'

'I'll go with you.'

He followed her. 'What happened?' she asked.

'I don't know for sure. I guess Melanie brained me.'

Pen looked back at him, frowning. 'She *hit* you?'

'I woke up in a school playground over near the freeway. The van was gone. I was afraid she'd come here.'

'I haven't seen her.'

In the bathroom, Pen opened the medicine cabinet. She took out the bottle of aspirin and swung the mirrored door shut.

Bodie, behind her, slipped his arms around her waist. Pen watched him in the mirror. His face, above her right shoulder, looked pale and hurt.

'I was so afraid she might have done something to you,' he said.

'Oh, Bodie.'

One of his hands slipped inside her robe. The hand was cool against her skin. It moved slowly upward and held her breast. Sighing, she leaned back against him. She hooked a thumb under the cloth belt of her robe and pulled. The belt fell open. Bodie parted the front of her robe. She saw him gazing at her in the mirror. His face, still pale, no longer looked tight with pain. His hands drifted lightly over her breasts, palms brushing her rigid nipples. He held her breasts. He squeezed them and Pen squirmed, moaning. As his hands curled beneath them, the sides of his thumbs rubbed across her nipples, making her breath catch.

His hands roamed downward, caressing her belly, sliding over her hips and down her thighs. Then they began moving gently upward. Pen closed her eyes. The hands slipped away, returning to her hips.

The aspirin bottle fell from Pen's fingers. She took Bodie's right hand and guided it between her legs. He moaned when he touched her there. Pen's legs went weak. His hand pressed her, and she writhed against it.

I'm sorry, Melanie, she thought. I'm sorry, I don't care, we tried.

She eased Bodie's hand away and turned around. The robe fell from her shoulders. Bodie's hands moved down her back, cupped her buttocks.

With trembling fingers, she began to unbutton his shirt.

'What about Melanie?' he whispered.

'I don't care any more. She hurt you. She doesn't deserve you.'

'She must've gone over to Harrison's.'

'No.' Pen didn't want to think about Melanie.

'I don't like the idea of chasing after her, but I can't just let her . . .'

'Let her what?'

'I don't know. I have to go after her, though.'

Pen leaned against Bodie's chest. He held her gently. 'I'll go with you,' she said.

His hands slid up her back as she crouched to pick up her robe. They caressed her shoulders. She stood, turned away, and lifted the plastic aspirin bottle out of the sink where it had fallen. 'You'd better take some,' she said. She gave him the bottle, then waited at his side while he cupped water from the faucet and swallowed four of the tablets.

She walked ahead of him to the bedroom. He stood in the doorway, watching as she hung her robe on the closet door.

'Were you asleep?' he asked.

'Earlier I was. Then I got a call. From *him*.'

'Oh, no.'

She opened a dresser drawer and lifted out a pair of blue panties. 'We talked,' she said, stepping into them. Balancing on one foot, then the other, she pulled on a pair of white socks. She looked at Bodie. He was gazing at her, his mouth open a little. 'It turns out the guy won't be coming over. He doesn't know where I live, or even who I am. I'll get a new phone number and that'll be the end of him.'

'How'd he get your number?'

'Just dialed it at random.'

'My God.'

'All that worry for nothing. There was never any way he could've . . . paid me a visit.'

'That's great.'

'Yeah,' Pen muttered. She squatted and opened the bottom drawer. She took out a pair of faded blue sweatpants and put them on. She tossed the matching sweatshirt onto her bed. Still naked from the waist up and feeling Bodie's gaze, she went to the closet. She took out her running shoes and carried them to the bed. There, she sat down. She put them on and tied the laces. Picking up her sweatshirt, she walked toward him.

'Trying to rub it in?' he asked.

'It's *your* idea to go after her. See what you're missing?'

He smiled slightly, staring into Pen's eyes as he touched her breasts. 'Things have a funny way of working out.'

'Real funny,' Pen said, arching her back as he caressed her. 'If she hadn't whacked me, we'd be on our way to Phoenix.'

'She's be safe.'

'I wouldn't . . . be here with you.'

Her breath went ragged as he pressed her nipples. 'Oh God, Bodie.'

'Worth a bump on the head.'

'We'd . . . better go.'

His hands lowered and held her sides. She pulled the sweatshirt down over her head.

'I wish we *could* just forget about her,' he said.

'We can't.'

'I know.'

'Do you really think she went to Harrison's?'

Bodie nodded.

'What'll we do, go over there again?'

'I guess so.'

They walked down the hallway to the living room. Pen picked up her purse and slung its strap over her shoulder. At the end of the sofa, she swept the curtain aside and lifted her shotgun.

'Are you kidding?'

'Just in case.'

'If we need that, we're really in deep shit.'

'I know he's got a .38.'

'Here, let me take it.'

'I can handle it.'

'If it comes to shooting, I'd better do it.'

239

'What are you, some kind of a sexist?'

'Right on, babe.' He held out his hands for the shotgun.

Pen shook her head. 'We can't just walk around with this.' She slipped the barrel inside her baggy sweatpants. It was cold against the side of her leg. She raised her sweatshirt and pulled it down over the stock.

'Can you walk with it there?'

'I can try.' Holding it against her side, she stepped onto the balcony. Bodie shut the door. He went ahead of her, glancing back occasionally as she limped to the stairs and made her way slowly down them. She kept her right leg stiff.

At the bottom, he took hold of her left arm.

He opened the gate for her.

She hobbled along beside him.

When they reached her car, she eased the shotgun down her leg until its muzzle rested on the pavement. Clamping her arm to the stock, she took her keys out of her purse and opened the door. She looked around. Saw no one. Lifted her sweatshirt over the stock. Pulled the shotgun out of her pants and quickly swung it into the car.

'I'll be in the Cadillac,' Bodie said, and nodded toward the street.

Pen saw the big car parked on the other side. 'Where'd you get . . . ?'

'Tell you later. Follow me. Just a couple of blocks, then I'll ditch it and we'll be on our way.'

Pen climbed into her car. When the headlights of the Cadillac came on, she backed onto the road. She followed the Caddy down the block, away from Pico.

Where on earth did he get that thing? she wondered. He must have stolen it. No other possibility. He'd been stranded . . . worried about me. Actually stole a car in order to get to me.

He could wind up in prison.

Though frightened for him, Pen felt grateful. He'd put himself on the line for her, risked his freedom, his future.

'Get out of there,' she whispered.

He kept driving.

'Come on, come on.' She checked her rearview, half expecting to see a police cruiser, but the street behind her was clear. 'Damn it, Bodie! Come on!'

He turned right.

Pen followed. And let out a long breath when he pulled over to a curb. But he didn't get out.

'What're you *doing*?' she blurted. Driving slowly past the car, she glanced inside and saw him leaning across the seats. A light shone from the open glove compartment.

Just beyond the Cadillac, she stopped. She killed her headlights to darken her license plates – in case someone should notice Bodie abandoning the stolen car and getting into hers.

'Hurry, would you?' she muttered.

Finally, he climbed out. Pen leaned across the passenger seat, shouldering over the shotgun, and unlatched the door. She grabbed the barrel in time to keep the gun from falling out as he opened the door. Straightening up, she pulled it with her. The interior light was on, but just for a moment. Then the door bumped shut and darkness came back.

Pen drove away with her headlights off. 'I thought you were going to stay in there all night,' she said.

'I had to find the registration. I'll try to call the owner when I get the chance, tell him where to find his car.' Then he told Pen how he had stolen it.

Pen listened, stunned.

'I didn't even think about it,' he said. 'All of a sudden, I was just doing it. The funny thing is, I don't even feel very guilty. I'm just glad I wasn't caught.'

Pen turned the corner and put on her headlights. 'Me, too.'

'I've never done anything like that before.' He sounded apologetic.

Pen reached over and squeezed his hand. 'If you think I'm going to hold it against you . . . I feel badly that you hurt the man, but . . . hey, the gallant knight can't come to the rescue if he ain't got a charger.'

'Only thing is,' he muttered, 'the damsel wasn't in distress.'

'You didn't know that.'

'It's the thought that counts, right?'

She glanced at him. Her throat felt tight. 'The thought counts plenty. You better believe it.'

Bodie's fingers tightened around her hand.

Pen stopped for a traffic light at Pico. 'I guess I'll go surface streets,' she said. 'Either way, it'll take a while to reach Harrison's.'

'Take the slowest route.'

'You don't mean that.'

'I know.'

The light changed. Driving through the intersection, she looked up the road and saw the hospital in the distance. She thought of her father lying in bed, kept alive by tubes. 'I didn't even go and see him today,' she said.

'We'll go tomorrow.'

We. The word made her feel good. 'You're not going back to Phoenix tonight?'

'It's a little late for that. Besides, things have changed. Things *have* changed, haven't they?'

'A lot,' Pen assured him.

'You're not going to let Melanie . . . ?'

'She smashed you on the head. She might've killed you, doing a thing like that. She lost whatever claim she had.'

'I don't think she'll see it that way.'

'Tough.' Pen made a left onto Olympic, and picked up speed.

'What's the hurry?' Bodie asked.

'You got me,' Pen said, but she didn't slow down. 'Melanie's had about an hour to do whatever she wanted to do.'

'What do you think she *is* doing?'

'Who knows? I was absolutely certain she planned to murder you. I was wrong about that, thank God. Who knows? I just hope it's all over before we get there.'

'I don't want anything to happen to her.'

'I don't either, but . . .'

'It'll be our fault. We pushed her over the edge, Bodie. Whatever happens, we're responsible. You and me.'

'Don't forget she spent the afternoon under Harrison's bed. That was before she caught us together.'

'Did you see the look on her face when she found us on the sofa?'

'I'm not saying she wasn't upset. But the fact that she didn't take the pills *proves* she planned to sneak out.'

'She thought I wanted to put her out so you and I could be alone.' Pen sped up to make it through a yellow light. 'Maybe she was right. I didn't consciously do it for that reason, but . . . maybe it was in the back of my mind.'

'Whatever our guilt may be,' Bodie said, 'we're doing our penance now. We could be back in your apartment. Instead, we're racing to the rescue.'

'Or to pick up the pieces.'

* * *

Harrison's Mercedes stood in the driveway of his house. Joyce's Continental was no longer parked in front.

'Playing it smart,' Pen said as she drove slowly past the front of the house. 'For all they know, we've been to the police. Wouldn't look too good if Joyce spent the night with him.'

'So she went home,' Bodie said.

'And where's Melanie?'

Bodie shrugged. He had been checking both sides of the street for his van, but so far hadn't spotted it. 'Keep going,' he said. 'Maybe she left it in back.'

Pen turned, then turned again. She drove past Harrison's block, then made another right, returned to his street and stopped at the corner. 'What do you think?'

'Don't ask me,' Bodie said. 'I've been wrong twice already.'

'She must've gone to Dad's.'

'The house? That'd be my guess, too. This is looking better and better. I figured we'd have a run-in with Harrison. Of course, he might've gone there with Joyce. In her car.'

'I doubt it,' Pen said. 'They probably split up.'

'Should we check his place?'

Shaking her head, Pen made a left turn on Harrison's street, heading away. 'We're looking for Melanie,' she said.

She waited for a break in the traffic on 26th Street, then turned left.

'I just hope . . .'

'What?' she asked.

'Melanie might've already been to Harrison's. They might've . . . gotten her. That could be why the van wasn't there. Maybe Harrison drove her away in it. Joyce would've followed in her car to pick him up after they . . . disposed of her.'

Pen glanced at him. In the dim gray light from the street-lamps, her eyes were wide, her lips twisted.

'It's just a possibility,' he said, wishing he'd kept the theory to himself.

'If he's hurt Melanie . . .'

'We'll probably find her at your dad's house.'

Pen stopped for a red light at San Vicente. Leaning forward, she pressed her forehead against the top of the steering wheel.

Bodie reached over. He rubbed her back through the soft sweatshirt. 'It'll be all right,' he said.

'Will it? Dad's in a coma. Melanie . . . God knows.' She turned her head. Her face was a mask of agony. 'It's all my fault.'

'It's Harrison's,' Bodie said.

A car horn beeped behind them.

The light had gone green, and the car ahead of them was moving into the intersection. Pen turned right onto San Vicente.

'I could have stopped it all,' she said. 'If I hadn't kept my mouth shut. I didn't want to hurt Dad. It would've been such a blow to him. He thought Harrison was such a terrific guy. But if I'd told . . . maybe the bastard would be in prison right now, though I doubt it. Would've been tough convincing a jury I wasn't asking for it. But it might've changed everything. I should've told, damn it.'

Bodie, breathless, stared at her. He felt as if he'd been kicked in the stomach. 'Asking for it?'

'Harrison raped me.'

'No.'

'I should've told.'

'Were you . . . hurt?'

She faced Bodie. She nodded. Tears were glistening in her

eyes. They looked silver in the streetlights. 'I was battered up some,' she murmured.

'Did you fight him?'

'As much as I could,' she said, her voice shaking. 'He had me handcuffed.'

Bodie groaned.

'He worked on me . . . for a long time.' With the back of her wrist, she wiped tears off her cheek. 'I haven't been with a man since then.' Sniffing, she looked at Bodie. 'You'll be the first – if you still want me, now that you know . . .'

'Oh, Pen.' He put a hand on her thigh and squeezed it gently through her sweatpants. Heat seemed to flow up his arm. 'I've never wanted anyone the way I want you.'

'It doesn't bother you that . . . ?'

'I'd like to kill the bastard,' Bodie muttered.

'I never told anyone,' she said. 'I just pretended it never happened, and Harrison acted as if it really *hadn't* happened, and after a while it was almost as if . . .'

'A way to live with it,' Bodie said.

'I should've told. Maybe none of this would've happened.' She rubbed a sleeve across her face.

Bodie stroked her leg as she slowed the car and turned left onto the narrow road leading to her father's house. He wished he could pull her into his arms and hold her tight and make all the pain go away – her pain and his own.

Harrison had raped her. Handcuffed her, beaten her up, fucked her.

The scum.

The piece of shit.

'Bodie, you're hurting me.'

'I'm sorry.' He unclamped his fingers from Pen's thigh and wrapped them around the steel of the shotgun's barrel.

Then he looked along the roadside for his van. They drove slowly past a Ferrari, a Porsche, a Jaguar.

Pen stopped her car in front of the garage. 'She's not here. It must be like you said and they took her away in the van.'

'Drive on a little further.'

Pen steered around a bend in the road and there was Bodie's van, snug against a leafy hedge. Bodie felt his bowels tighten.

Pen shifted to reverse, twisted herself sideways, hooked an arm over the seatback, and looked out the rear window. She backed up slowly.

Bodie gazed at her.

It seemed important, somehow, to see what she looked like right now and to keep it for a memory and never lose it.

The dim silhouette of her face. The pale white of her eye and the silver trail of a tear leading down from its corner. The flow of soft hair. The way her lower lip was caught between her teeth. The curve of her jawline. The hollow of her throat. The way her breasts pushed out her sweatshirt, forming soft mounds, the right higher than the left because her right arm was raised onto the seatback.

His gaze followed Pen's left arm to the steering wheel. The sleeve was drawn up above her slim wrist. Her hand, moving the wheel slightly from side to side, seemed small and fragile. He looked at the way her sweatpants were gathered over her lap, and how they draped her thighs. Then he looked again at her face.

So beautiful. All of her. And she's mine now.

I'll never let anything bad happen to her again, he thought, and felt a terrible hollow ache of loss because he knew it was an empty promise. The future would hurt them both, kill them both sooner or later no matter what.

Pen stopped the car broadside in front of the garage door.

She set the brake, shut off the headlights, and turned to Bodie.

He lifted the shotgun out of the way. He put his arms around her and drew her gently against him. They kissed. He slipped his hands beneath the sweatshirt, moved them up the velvety skin of her back.

'I wish we didn't have to go in there,' she whispered.

'We don't have to.'

Pen kissed him lightly, then eased herself away. She took the key from the ignition. She opened her door.

Bodie climbed out, taking the shotgun with him.

Chapter Twenty-three

Pen stopped at the front door and searched through her keys with trembling fingers. 'I wish we knew whether Joyce is here,' she said.

'The garage have any windows?'

'No.'

She found the house key and opened the door. She started to enter, but Bodie put a hand on her shoulder. He stepped inside. Pen followed.

And heard Melanie's voice.

'. . . here alone, or I'll kill her . . . I don't think you want to do that. I've got a paper here that the cops would find very interesting.'

Pen silently shut the door and followed Bodie across the foyer.

'You'll see when you get here. You'd better make it quick. I'll kill her if you're not here in ten minutes.'

She hung up as they stepped into the den.

'Melanie?'

She turned around. 'The lovebirds,' she said, staring at them through strands of black hair. She stroked the hair away from her face, her fingertips drawing stripes of blood across her forehead. Her white blouse was untucked, its front smeared with blood as if she had used it repeatedly to wipe her hands.

'Oh, Mel,' Pen muttered, 'what have you done?'

With a smirk, she raised a sheet of paper.

Bodie took it from her and studied it.

'You guys would've let them get away with killing Dad.'

'They didn't kill him,' Pen said.

Melanie's lips quivered. 'You just wanted to take Bodie away from me. That was all you cared about. You didn't care what they did to Dad.'

'Of course I care,' Pen said, realizing that Melanie now seemed more coherent than she'd been when Bodie took her away from the apartment. More coherent, but no less crazy.

The girl's lips peeled up, a dog snarl that changed into a sick grin. 'You cared about spreading your legs.'

Bodie handed the paper to Pen. Its edges had bloody fingerprints. She read the shaky handwriting:

This is my confession. I, Joyce Conway, conspired with Harrison Donner to murder my husband, Whit Conway. We were lovers behind his back. We wanted him dead so as to get his insurance and inheratence.

'That was Harrison you told to come over?' Bodie asked.

'Who else.'

'He'll probably show up with a goddamn SWAT team.'
'I don't think so.'

I let Harrison in on where and when we planned to have dinner and he waited in his car. When Whit started to cross the street, he hit him with the car. It was a stolen car, as he didn't want to use his own.

Joyce's signature was scribbled at the bottom in the same handwriting as the confession.

'Where is she?' Bodie asked.

'Want to see her?' Melanie looked at her wristwatch. It was Bodie's. 'I guess we have a few minutes.' She took the paper from Pen and stepped past them. As they followed her to the stairway, she glanced back. 'We'll have to hide before Harrison shows up. The element of surprise, you know.'

At the bottom of the stairs, Bodie looked at Pen. His face was gray. He took her hand. His fingers felt like ice.

They rushed up the stairs behind Melanie. She led the way along the corridor.

Pen knew they would find carnage. She felt light-headed and numb. The lights seemed too dim. When she blinked, an electric-blue aura surrounded Melanie. Pen was nauseous. Just like Friday night, she thought, the mystery writers' meeting, the coroner's shock-show.

Post-mortem lividity, bite marks on the corpse's buttock, the gray penis of the dead man, fly eggs in the nostril.

I've gotta get out of here.

Fresh air.

Bodie stopped her at the door of the master bedroom. 'Wait here,' he said.

Pen leaned against the doorframe, her back to the room.

Bodie let go of her hand. He stepped past her. Sliding down, Pen hung her head and stared between her knees at the carpet.

I shouldn't, she thought. Shouldn't let him face it alone. It'll help him if I'm there.

She forced herself to stand.

She heard nothing from inside the room.

Turning to the doorway, she saw Bodie and Melanie standing side by side. Their backs were toward her. Their bodies blocked her view of whatever they were looking at. Whatever? Joyce.

Pen walked slowly closer.

She smelled blood, and gagged. Quickly, she lifted the front of her sweatshirt. She pressed the soft fabric to her nose and mouth. It had a fresh scent that masked the coppery odor of the blood. She stopped gagging. She blinked the tears from her eyes and stepped to Bodie's side.

Joyce, on a straight-backed chair, gazed at her from a crimson face. She blinked away the blood that dribbled into her eyes from her cut forehead. She was gasping through her nose. A strip of cloth, probably a robe belt, was tied across her mouth.

'I had to do a little number on her,' Melanie said.

Bodie tipped the shotgun toward Pen. It was resting on the floor, barrel up. Keeping the sweatshirt over her mouth, she gripped the barrel with her other hand and held the weapon upright while Bodie stepped behind the chair.

Joyce's feet were tied to the chair legs. Her nightgown clung to her with blood, but Pen couldn't see any other wounds. All the blood, she thought, had come from the cuts on Joyce's forehead.

If that was all, she ought to recover.

Could've been worse, Pen thought. A lot worse.

She looked at Melanie. Melanie was staring at the shotgun. No, she realized. Not at the shotgun.

At me with my sweatshirt pulled up.

A chill squirmed up her back. She tugged the sweatshirt down. Melanie's gaze lifted to her face.

Pen could hardly believe the hatred in her sister's eyes.

The gaze shifted away from her as Bodie slipped the cloth from Joyce's mouth. 'What're you doing?' she demanded.

'For Godsake,' Bodie muttered. He crouched to untie Joyce's hands.

'Leave her alone.'

Pen realized that Joyce's mouth was stuffed with something. Stepping closer, she shifted the shotgun barrel to her other hand and bent over the woman.

'Don't do that,' Melanie warned.

'Shut up,' Pen said, and dug fingers into Joyce's mouth. She pulled out a sodden rag. A nylon stocking.

Joyce gasped for breath.

'You want her to warn Harrison?'

'Are you all right?' Pen asked.

'Muh . . . my face.'

'Are you hurt anywhere else?'

'Has a nasty bump on the back of her head,' Bodie said.

Pen patted the wadded stocking gently against Joyce's forehead. Lifting the nylon away, she looked at the wounds. The letters AM had been carved into her brow. Holding the cloth to the cuts, she scowled over her shoulder at Melanie. 'What the hell *is* this!'

'You two are such fucking literary types, figure it out.'

'I can't get her hands undone,' Bodie said.

'Why did you *do* it?' Pen blurted. 'God Almighty, Mel . . .'

' "A" for adultery, "M" for murder.'

252

'*Why did you do it!*'

'To get her confession, of course.'

'You idiot! That confession's no good. It's worthless. You *tortured* it out of her.'

'She wouldn't write it. I had to make her.'

'Lying,' Joyce murmured. 'She did this . . . after. Just . . . to hurt me.'

'The confession's no good,' Pen repeated.

'Too bad,' Melanie said. Lunging sideways, she rammed Pen.

'Hey!' Bodie yelled.

Pen's feet tangled. She struck the floor shoulder first and cried out as the shotgun barrel hammered her fingers against the carpet.

Bodie sprang up from his crouch behind Joyce. He shouted, 'NO!' and flung his hands forward to shove Melanie away.

Too late.

The knife (where did *that* come from?) slashed Joyce's throat and a spray of blood whipped across the front of Melanie's blouse as Bodie's hands smashed her shoulders and sent her stumbling away.

She landed on her back.

Pen, getting up, watched Bodie run through the flying blood. He bent over Melanie. 'Give me that!' he yelled. He reached for the knife and drew his hand back fast as Melanie slashed at it. 'Give me that! God! God!'

Melanie squirmed and twisted on the floor, kicking at his shins and slashing at him. Bodie kept yelling and trying to snatch her knife hand.

Pen picked up the shotgun. 'Get out of the way!' she snapped at Bodie.

He looked at her.

Melanie's right leg kicked up, her shoe smashing him in the groin. His eyes bulged. Clutching himself, he doubled over. His knees pounded the floor.

Melanie rolled away from him.

Pen aimed the shotgun at her as she scrambled to her feet. 'Stop!'

Melanie walked slowly toward Pen, hunched over, the knife in her right hand, her eyes almost hidden behind hanging ropes of hair. 'Gonna blow me away, sister? Go ahead. Well, do it. It's you or me.'

Pen backed away from her.

'I'm gonna cut you up. I'm gonna cut up that gorgeous face for you. I'm gonna cut off your precious tits. Then we'll see, won't we? Think Bodie's gonna want you then? Do you? Huh?'

The wall stopped Pen's retreat. She flicked the safety off. 'Just stop.'

'No, no, no, not me.'

Pen pulled the trigger. The shotgun jerked in her hands. Its roar blasted her ears. A circle of ceiling beyond Melanie's head exploded away. White dust and chunks of plaster fell.

Melanie grinned. Taking one more step, she gripped the muzzle with her left hand and pressed it to her chest. 'Go ahead, sister. Try again.'

'Mel . . . for Godsake!'

Glancing past Melanie's shoulder, she saw Bodie on his hands and knees, trying to get up.

The barrel flew upward, thrust high by Melanie. In disbelief, Pen saw her sister duck beneath it and drive the knife at her chest. She lurched sideways. A hot streak burned across the skin under her left breast. She rammed out with an elbow. It caught Melanie in the armpit, knocking her out of the way.

But she still held the shotgun. She wrenched it from Pen and hurled it to the floor.

Pen shoved herself off the wall. She tried to dodge past Melanie, hoping to regain the gun, but Melanie rushed ahead to block her way. And slashed. Pen dropped back as the blade whipped across her belly. It snagged and ripped her loose sweatshirt, but missed her skin. Whirling around, she ran for the bedroom door.

Melanie's feet pounded the carpet close behind her. They stayed behind her as she raced along the corridor.

'You've had it!' Melanie yelled. 'You've had it!'

At the top of the stairs, Pen grabbed the newel post and swung herself around it.

She was three steps down when she was hit. She cried out, more in alarm than pain, as the blade went in. The impact threw her forward. Her feet left the stairs and she flew headlong toward the bottom.

Bodie staggered across the bedroom, each step wracking him with pain as if pliers were squeezing his testicles. He bent over, groaning, and picked up the shotgun. His ears still rang from the blast.

Lurching through the doorway, he swung to the left. The corridor was empty. He heard footsteps on the stairs, but saw no one. The wall blocked his view for a few yards. Then it ended, and he threw himself against the railing of the balcony over the living room.

Melanie, knife raised overhead like a madwoman, was charging down the stairs. Pen was at the bottom, scrambling away on her knees and one hand. Her right forearm, bent at an odd angle, looked broken. The back of her sweatshirt had a slick oval of blood.

'Mel!' Bodie yelled.

She didn't stop. She was halfway down the stairs.

Pen, now on her feet, stumbled toward the foyer, her broken arm flapping.

Bodie jacked a shell into the shotgun chamber.

Melanie, hearing the noise, looked over her shoulder.

'Stop!' he cried out.

He peered down the sighting ramp. The bead at the muzzle's end wavered back and forth across Melanie's neck. He noticed her choker. A memory flashed through his mind of the time in bed when she was naked except for one of those chokers and he started to take it off and she clutched her ears to hold her head on.

His finger eased its pressure on the trigger.

'Just stay put!' he ordered. 'Don't move! Drop the knife!'

Her head turned away.

Bodie shifted his eyes to the right. Pen was at the front door, pulling it open.

Melanie looked back at him, then at the door again.

'Don't!' he shouted.

She raced down the stairs.

Bodie tracked her with the shotgun, knowing that a hit would probably kill her, hating to kill her, wondering if Pen had enough headstart, then swinging the muzzle well ahead of Melanie and firing. The shotgun leapt and kicked his shoulder as the blast slapped his eardrums. The front door, left ajar by Pen, crashed shut as the pellets punched through its bottom.

He ran for the stairway, grimacing each time a foot landed and sent a new shockwave of pain from his testicles.

Melanie reached the front door at the same moment as he started down the stairs.

Running had hurt, but pounding his way down the steps was glaring white agony.

Melanie threw open the door and dashed out.

Bodie worked the pump-action. The spent shell tumbled away.

He leaped down the final three stairs, crying out as his feet struck the floor and pain exploded through his body. He hobbled across the foyer and out the front door.

Melanie, her white blouse a pale bobbing target, was halfway across the dark yard. The dim, running shape of Pen was not far ahead of her.

When Pen reached the closed gate, Melanie would get her. No question.

'Stop!' Bodie shrieked, shouldering the gun.

What if some of the pellets go past her and get Pen?

He aimed at the center of Melanie's back. His finger tightened on the trigger.

Pen was one stride from the gate.

The gate crashed open, smashing her, hurling her aside.

A man charged into the yard, hunched over as if he had just thrown a body-block against the gate. He straightened up abruptly as Melanie, not changing course to fall upon Pen, flew at him.

Harrison.

Harrison had raped Pen.

Bodie held fire.

The man put out both hands to stop Melanie. He yelled, 'Hey!' Then she hit him, driving the knife into his chest as the force of her impact carried him backward to the walkway. Melanie dropped on top of him.

Even from the porch, Bodie heard the thunk of his head striking the concrete.

He ran toward the sprawled shapes.

Harrison, on the bottom, didn't move.

Melanie, on top of him, moved a lot.

Her arm did.

Punching the knife into his body, yanking it out, stabbing him again and again until Bodie stopped her with a quick stroke of the shotgun butt.

He dragged the shotgun beside him as he staggered over to Pen. Letting it fall to the grass, he knelt down next to her. She lay on her back, panting, clutching the wound beneath her breast.

'How bad are you?'

As if it didn't matter, she shook her head. 'What happened?' she gasped.

'Mel . . . I think she killed Harrison. I knocked her out.'

Groaning, Pen struggled to sit up. Bodie pressed her shoulders gently to the ground. 'I think your arm's broken.'

'Tell me about it.'

'Just rest. I'll call the police.'

'No. Help me up.'

'Pen . . .'

'Please.'

He pulled her by the shoulders. When she was sitting, she hooked her left arm around his neck. He clutched her sides, just beneath the armpits, and lifted her. She was very heavy at first, then weightless as her legs took over. 'Okay,' she muttered. Bodie held onto her arm, but found that she needed no support as she led him back to the motionless bodies. 'Would you get her off him?'

Crouching, Bodie pulled gently at Melanie until she rolled away from Harrison. As one of her hands flopped to the ground, she moaned. Her eyes stayed shut.

Pen sank to her knees beside Harrison and stared at him.

Bodie, stepping around Melanie, squatted near his head. The man's eyes were closed, his mouth hanging open. The knife hilt protruded from his chest.

Pen put a hand to his throat.

'She must've stabbed him five or six times,' Bodie said.

'I can't find a pulse.'

'I could've stopped her. I was ready to shoot her, but when she went for him instead of you . . . The man raped you. And he ran down your father.'

'Where's his gun?' Pen asked.

'I didn't see one.'

Leaning over the body, Pen pulled a revolver from the pocket of his jacket. 'I figured he had to have it. I don't know if this'll help much, but . . .' She swung the revolver toward the front of the house and fired twice.

Straddling the body, she put the gun into Harrison's hand and slipped his forefinger through the trigger guard. She pressed his fingertip against the trigger. With the bottom edge of her sweatshirt, she wiped her prints off the rest of the gun.

'What about Joyce?' Bodie asked.

'I don't know.'

'There's no way to make *that* look like self-defense.'

'If we could get rid of the body . . .'

Bodie heard a siren, its distant alarm blaring through the night. 'Too late for anything like that,' he said.

Melanie, sprawled on the grass beside her victim, looked as if she were sleeping.

'Can you think of a story?' Bodie asked Pen.

'Nothing to cover all this. The truth, I guess. It'll have to do.'

'Except for the revolver.'

The siren swelled to a high scream.

Pen stood up.

Bodie, rising, put a hand low on her back. Together, they stepped through the open gate. Pen leaned her head against his shoulder. 'I wish we could go back in time,' she said, 'and change it all.'

'I guess Harrison and Joyce got what they had coming,' Bodie said.

'But Melanie.'

'Yeah.'

'What did we do to her?'

He put his arms around Pen and gently drew her against him. Holding her, he turned slowly until he could see the open gate beyond her head. Melanie was on her hands and knees. Her face lifted. It was a dim patch in the darkness with black pits for eyes.

Staring at us, Bodie knew.

Hating us.

He felt a shiver climb his back.

Would she go for the shotgun?

The siren was a deafening shriek.

She went for the knife.

She tugged it out of Harrison's chest.

Bodie tensed for the attack.

Melanie pushed the knife slowly into Harrison's throat. Clutching it with both hands, she worked its blade back and forth. Her long black hair swayed in front of her face as she rocked above him, putting her weight into the cutting.

'What's wrong?' Pen asked.

'Nothing.' Bodie stroked her head. 'Everything's fine.'

Chapter Twenty-four

'No funny business,' Pen said. She was in bed, naked except for her white shorts, a white bandage beneath her left breast, and a white cast on her arm. The discarded sling lay rumpled on the sheet beside her. 'I am, after all, an invalid.'

'You look valid.' Bodie cupped her breasts and gently thumbed the nipples. Pen squirmed.

'You can validate me later,' she said. 'This is serious business.'

'Of course.'

Bodie's hands went away. Pen raised her head off the pillow. With an open hand, she lifted and flattened her breast and peered over it to see what he was doing. 'Be gentle,' she warned, smiling.

Bodie picked at a corner of the tape with his fingernail. 'Difficult to concentrate,' he said, 'when beholding such a vision of loveliness.'

'Yep. No doubt.'

He pulled the tape slowly, watching the adhesive lift her skin and peel away from it.

'Owooo.'

'Maybe one quick yank.'

'Don't you dare.'

'We should really change this bandage more often than the one on your back. Such scenic surroundings.'

The bandage came off, revealing a four-inch laceration cross-hatched with stitches.

'Yuck,' Pen said.

'Coming along nicely.'

'Easy for you to say. I'm the one looks like the bride of Frankenstein.'

'You look terrific. It gives you character.'

'Sure.'

Bodie unrolled a pad of cotton and gauze, snipped off a section slightly longer than the wound, and taped it into place.

'Good job.' She released her breast and lowered her head to the pillow.

Her fingers had left faint red prints on her creamy skin. Bodie watched them fade.

I'm gonna cut off your tits!

'What's wrong?' Pen asked.

'Melanie. She keeps coming back.'

'Yeah.'

'I wonder how she's doing.'

'I don't know,' Pen muttered. 'At least she probably won't have to stand trial. That would've been tough, nothing going for her except Joyce's confession.'

Bodie put a hand on Pen's belly. He lightly stroked the smooth skin. 'Do you suppose they're treating her okay?'

'It isn't the Hilton. Later on, maybe we can get her moved to a better facility.'

'At least she nailed those two.'

'I wonder if it was worth it.'

The telephone rang. 'I'll get it,' Bodie said. He patted her belly, then stood and hurried toward the kitchen. Suddenly scared. Pen had changed her number. Only the police, the people at Melanie's psychiatric ward, and the hospital had the new one. The call had to mean trouble. He picked up the phone. 'Hello?'

'Is this Penelope Conway's residence?' asked the male voice.

'Yes, it is.'

'May I speak to Miss Conway?'

'Who may I say is calling?'

'This is Dr Herman Gray of the Beverlywood Medical Center. I'm calling about Miss Conway's father.'

Bodie's stomach clenched. 'Just a moment, please.' He let the phone's handset dangle by its cord, and hurried back to the bedroom. Pen was sitting up.

When she saw Bodie, the color left her face.

'It's Dr Gray,' he said.

She clamped her lower lip between her teeth.

Bodie followed her to the kitchen. He stood behind her while she picked up the phone. He put a hand on her bare back. He stared at the bandage over her right shoulder blade.

'This is Pen Conway,' she said.

She listened.

'Oh my God,' she said, and began to cry.

'What the *hell* happened to you?'

'What the hell happened to *you*?' Pen retorted. Then she fell to her knees beside the bed and, weeping, kissed her father.

When her mouth left his, he said, 'Hey, you're getting me wet, babe. Turn off the fountain.'

'God, Dad.' She kissed him again.

His hand came out from beneath the sheets and stroked her hair. 'Sure is good to see you again,' he said. 'Good to see anything, for that matter.'

'How do you feel?'

'Like I was hit by a locomotive.'

'It was a car.'

'So I hear.'

Pen wiped her eyes with her left hand.

'So what's *your* excuse?' Whit asked, glancing at her cast.

'I fell down some stairs.'

'Klutziness must run in the family, huh?' Bodie saw a glint in the old man's eyes. 'Any negligence involved?'

'Just my own.'

'Awwww. We'd have some great personal injury suits, both of us, if only . . .'

'Those are the breaks,' Pen said.

'No pun intended, huh?' Then he said, 'Owooo,' an echo of Pen when Bodie had pulled the tape from her chest.

'Dad, I want you to meet Bodie.' She smiled over her shoulder at him. Tears were shimmering in her eyes.

'I thought Bodie was a town in Wyoming. You don't *look* much like a town.'

'Welcome back, Mr Conway.'

'You banging my daughter?'

'Dad!'

'Hell, I know you are. I can tell by the look of you. You look okay to me.'

'Thanks, sir.'

'Make it Whit.'

'Whit.'

'You drink?'

'I polished off most of the beer in your refrigerator.'

'Make sure you restock it before I come home. Recuperation is thirsty work.'

'Right.'

'Speaking of home, how come you're both here and Joyce isn't?'

'She doesn't know you came out of it,' Pen said. 'Not yet. We'll tell her as soon as we see her.'

'You do that. Tell her to get her sweet buns over here.'

'I will.'

'What about number two daughter?'

'She was here for a few days right after the accident. It looked like you might be the same for a while, so she went back to school. She has her classes . . .'

'Well, that's all right. I'm glad she thought enough to come over.'

'She was awfully upset, Dad.'

A smile drifted over his lips. 'That's good to hear. Melanie . . . we've had our share of troubles since your mother passed away.' He shook his head. 'She doesn't care much for Joyce, I'm afraid.'

'She loves you a lot.'

'Hell, I think I'll go out and pay her a visit once I'm on my feet again.'

Bodie held Pen's hand as they left the hospital. The morning sun was bright and warm, and he watched the way Pen's gleaming hair stirred in the breeze.

There was sorrow in her eyes.

'Are you all right?' he asked.

'I hated lying to him.'

'He doesn't need the truth. Not right now.'

She shook her head. 'It'll really knock the wind out of his sails.'

'Wait a few days.'

'That won't make it any easier.'

'I know.'

'He's in for a world of hurt.'

'When he finds out what his wife and Harrison did to him, he might not be all that upset they're dead.'

'Just a different kind of pain.'

'He wouldn't have had to go through it if he'd stayed in his coma. Better this way, isn't it?'

'Yeah.' A smile tilted her lips. She looked at Bodie. 'A lot better this way.' Her hand tightened in his. 'I'll have to stick around for a while, though. He'll need me.'

'I know.'

'I'm sorry.'

'Summer break is coming up. In the meantime, I'll come every weekend. If you want.'

'Of course I want.'

'Don't let anyone else change those bandages. They're mine.'

'Whatever you say, sir.'

'It'll be a fine summer.'

'We'll go to the beach.'

'Let's go to the beach, now,' Bodie said.

They stopped at a corner and waited for the traffic light to change.

Bodie felt a little sad. He knew he would be leaving Pen in a few days and he knew there would be some hard times ahead for both of them – pain and sorrow and loneliness.

But they were together for the moment. She was with him, a missing part of him that had been found and must never be lost.

The light changed.

The traffic stopped.

Bodie waited on the curb, holding Pen's hand, and looked both ways to be absolutely sure it was safe. Then he stepped off the curb with Pen at his side and they started across.

Chapter Twenty-five

At the intersection of Crescent Heights and Sunset Boulevard, Phil Danson stopped for the red traffic signal. He looked both ways. Not a car was in sight, so he gunned the Jaguar XKE and sped across Sunset.

It gave him a little rush.

A small risk, a small rush.

Keeping the gas pedal to the floor, he shifted and picked up speed. The road up Laurel Canyon was steep and twisting. He took the curves fast, grinning at the way the low car hugged the road. The quick turns pushed him from side to side. If he'd had the safety harness on, he wouldn't have felt the force so much. That's why he had it off.

Ahead of him, a traffic signal turned red. He kept his foot on the accelerator as he approached it.

Not much of a risk. It was two o'clock in the morning, after all, so what were the odds of a car swooping down from one of the sides and nailing him? Slim to none. Phil hoped for a spurt of adrenaline as he shot across the intersection against the red light. He didn't get it.

He crossed the center line.

Oh yes.

His heart quickened, his stomach knotted.

'All *right*,' he gasped.

This is good, this is fine.

Hands slick on the steering wheel, he sped up the downhill lane.

'Bat outa hell!'

He killed the headlights. Enough light came from the street

lamps for him to see the road ahead. Almost. The pavement was a vague runway bordered by dark slopes, curving and twisting upward.

He steered around a bend one-handed as he turned on the radio. 'This is KLFC bringing you mellow sounds from midnight till dawn.'

'Shit on it.' Phil turned the knob and got Bruce Springsteen. 'The Boss!' he yelled, and twisted the volume high.

A ghost of light swept across the darkness ahead. With a whoop, Phil flicked the steering wheel. The Jaguar lurched to the right as the glare of headlights hit his eyes. A horn blasted. A Mustang flew by, very close but missing.

Phil laughed.

He had a green light at Mulholland. He shot beneath it so fast that his tires left the pavement when the road dropped away on the other side.

The road down from the crest was wide and, he knew, often heavily patrolled. He turned on his headlights and slowed down to the speed limit.

The fun was over. He still felt a little light-headed and shaky, and he held onto the good feelings for a while by thinking back to his wild trip to the top and his close one with the Mustang.

It had been bitchin', definitely bitchin'.

When he reached the intersection with Ventura Boulevard, he turned the radio off. He waited out the traffic signal, then made a left and drove to Earl's Body Shop.

He swung into the driveway, stopped in front of the closed double doors of the garage, and honked his horn.

Moments later, one of the doors rolled upward. Earl, the stub of a cigar jutting from a corner of his mouth, waved him in.

Phil pulled the Jaguar forward. Behind him, the door rumbled down. He shut off the engine and climbed out.

Earl squinted at the car through a gray screen of smoke. 'Looks like a beauty,' he said.

'She *is* a beauty,' Phil told him. 'Handles like a dream.'

Earl walked around the car, puffing and nodding. 'You were gonna have this to me last week.'

'Don't sweat it, Earl.'

'I ain't sweatin'. It's only just I told the guy he'd get it, know what I mean?'

'Well, now you've got it.'

'Takes time, the paint job, changin' the serial numbers, all that . . .'

'Takes time,' Phil retorted, 'finding a Jag in mint condition.'

'Thought you had one all lined up.'

'I did. I *had* the baby. Snatched it over in Beverly Hills, but it was raining like shit and some old fart walked right out in front of me and I creamed him. Creamed him real good, and I think some gal saw me nail him so I had to bail out. Who needs that kind of heat? Not me. Hey, this is a better car, anyway. That other one didn't have brakes for shit.'

Blood Games

This book is dedicated
to Mom and Dad
with love and thanks.

I'm proud to be your kid.

Chapter One

'Where *are* we going?' Finley asked. 'To grandmother's house?'

Helen, behind the steering wheel of the rented Wagoneer, grinned over her shoulder and sang, 'Over the river and through the woods . . .'

'Hoping we'll run into the Big Bad Wolf?' Abilene said.

'Finley'd like that,' Cora said from the front seat.

'Gimme a break. I've sworn off guys.'

'Since when?' Abilene asked.

'Since last summer and surfin' Sam, or whatever his name was.'

'You don't even remember his name?' Helen asked.

'He was just another hunk to the Fin-man,' Abilene said.

Finley jammed an elbow into her side. 'Rick. His name was Rick. But I've reformed. I promise to be a good girl.'

'I'll believe that when I see it,' Cora said.

'Where we're going,' Helen explained, 'I don't imagine we'll be running into any fellas.'

'I sure hope this isn't a camping trip,' Vivian said.

'What've you got against fresh air?' Cora asked.

'Fresh air's fine. But I can get it without flying three thousand miles.'

'You sure don't get it living in L.A.'

'Viv's just afraid she'll get her clothes dirty,' Abilene said.

Vivian leaned forward to see past Finley, who was sitting

between them in the back seat, and told Abilene, 'If I wanted to rough it in the great outdoors, I would've joined the Girl Scouts.' Wrinkling her nose, she settled back and muttered, 'This sure has all the earmarks of a camping trip.'

'You just never know,' Helen said, sounding pleased with herself.

'It should've tipped you off,' Abilene said, 'when she told us to bring sleeping bags and grubbies.'

'That could mean anything.'

'It meant we weren't going to a Marriott.' In spite of that, Abilene doubted that they were being taken on a camping trip. A week in the wilds might've been Cora's idea of fun, but this trip was Helen's choice and Helen was neither athletic nor a fan of Mother Nature. She was more inclined toward sedentary, dark pursuits: reading scary novels and true crime books; watching movies that usually featured mad killers using knives, axes and chainsaws to slaughter teenagers. If her choice of adventures involved camping, it was likely to be done in a graveyard.

'I know where we're going,' she said. 'To the Pet Semetary.'

Helen laughed. 'Close, but no prize.'

'*Close?*' Vivian muttered. 'Oh, terrific.'

'Wherever I'm taking you, we'll be coming up on it pretty soon.'

'How soon?' Finley asked.

'According to the odometer, it should be about three more miles.'

'Pull over and let me out, okay? I'll get our arrival for posterity.'

'Oh, great,' Abilene said. 'The epic. Thank God we didn't have to suffer through *that* last night.'

'Gimme a break. You love it.'

'I *hate* some of it.'

'I'd like to see it again,' Helen said. 'Maybe the night before we fly out.'

'My friend.' Finley leaned forward and patted her on the shoulder. 'Now, let me out.'

Helen stopped the car without pulling over. There was no need to leave the road, since it had been devoid of traffic for the entire half hour they'd been on it. While Vivian opened her door and climbed out, Finley twisted around and reached over the seatback. She grabbed her video camcorder, scooted across the seat and got out. Vivian climbed in.

Finley went to the front of the car, stepped from its bumper onto the hood, and walked toward the windshield. The thin metal sank under each footstep and popped up when her weight was gone, making quiet bongey sounds.

'Christ,' Cora muttered.

'Boys will be boys,' Helen said.

Abilene realized that Finley, today more than usual, looked a lot more like a kid than like a twenty-five-year-old woman. She was small and slender. Her brown hair was cut very short. Her outfit masked what she had of a figure and would've been just the thing for a young fellow embarking on a safari; the baggy tan shirt hung loose nearly to the cuffs of her baggy tan shorts, and sported not only shoulder epaulettes but a multitude of deep pockets, flaps and brass buttons.

Of course, most boys probably wouldn't be caught dead wearing hot pink knee socks.

The knee socks and white Reeboks were all that Abilene could see of Finley now that the girl was perched on the roof of the car, calves pressed against the windshield.

'Let's roll, gang!' she called from above.

'You oughta really step on it,' Cora whispered.

'She might fall and break her neck,' Helen said.

'Even worse,' Vivian said, 'she might break her camera. Then there'd really be hell to pay.'

Helen started the car forward. Slowly.

'Turn the wipers on and give her a squirt,' Abilene suggested.

'That'd be cruel,' Vivian said.

Cora, looking over her shoulder, said, 'Abby, you're a genius.'

'Just mean.'

Helen leaned forward slightly. The windshield wipers began to sweep back and forth. Twin streams of water shot up. The blades bumped against Finley's calves. The water soaked her socks. Her legs flew out of the way. 'You bastards!' she cried out.

Helen shut off the blades and fountains, then called out the window, 'Sorry. My mistake.'

'Mistake my butt. I'll get all of you for this. You mess with the Fin-man, you pay.'

'We're trembling!' Abilene called.

'It was your idea, wasn't it?'

'Whose?'

'You! I know it was you, Hickok. You'll die.'

'Oh, quit ranting and film your epic.'

Finley's legs returned to their previous positions against the windshield. Then her head appeared between her knees. Her face was upside down, her short hair blowing in the breeze. Though she said nothing, her lips twitched and writhed ferociously as if she were spitting out obscenities.

'Give her another dose.'

She must've heard that. Her head went away fast.

'Let's just calm down, folks,' she called.

Helen left the wipers alone.

She stayed in the northbound lane, not even crossing the faded paint of the center line to avoid fissures and pits in the pavement. It made for a bumpy ride. Abilene couldn't fault her for being cautious, though. As desolate as the poor ruin of a road seemed to be, an excursion into the downhill lane would probably provoke a vehicle to materialize, speed around a blind curve and smash them. One of life's little magic tricks. Just when you least expect it – wham.

A car could just as easily come racing around a curve on our side, she thought.

She began to wish that Finley wasn't riding on the roof.

Helen stopped the car. 'This must be it,' she said, nodding toward a narrow road that slanted up the hillside to the right.

'You don't know?' Vivian asked.

'Do you think I've been here before? It's just a place I read about. But this is where it ought to be, and it's called The Totem Pole Lodge.'

'Must be it, all right,' Cora said.

At each side of the entrance road stood a totem pole. The old wooden columns depicted forest creatures, demons and beasts, and both had giant birds with outspread wings near their tops. One of the poles, tilted at a sharp angle, looked ready to fall onto any car daring to trespass.

Abilene supposed that the totems had probably once been decorated with bright paint. Now, however, they looked as if they'd been made of driftwood. Or dirty gray bone.

Vandals had carved names, initials, dates, hearts, and even a few swastikas into them. Some of the vandals must've shinnied up them to maim the higher areas. Near the top of the tilted pole, someone had left a hunting knife embedded in the blanched wood of a wing.

A metal sign, bent and rusted, was nailed at eye level to the upright pole. It read, KEEP OUT.

'Why would a lodge have a sign telling people to keep out?' Vivian asked.

'It isn't open to the public,' Helen explained, and turned onto the entry road. The leaning post didn't fall. But as the car nosed upward, Finley's legs kicked away from the windshield. Abilene heard some thumps through the ceiling, and figured she must've tumbled backward. Seconds later, the legs returned.

'I hope Finley kept her camera going,' she said. 'We'll have some interesting views.'

'Spinning tree tops,' Cora said.

'Some of these branches are awfully low.' Helen sounded worried.

'If we have a casualty, can we go home?' Vivian asked.

'You should be tickled,' Cora told her. 'This isn't a camp-out.'

'Right. Instead, we're going to some damn lodge that isn't open to the public. Who, exactly, *is* it open to?'

'Just us,' Helen said. 'I hope. As far as I know, it's been abandoned for about twelve years.'

'Oh, great. Charming. I can see this is gonna be a thrill and a half.'

'That's the whole idea,' Helen said.

'Knowing you, it's probably haunted.'

'I guess we'll find out.'

Just then, the road levelled out. The hood of the car lowered, revealing the area ahead. Abilene leaned a little to the right. Off in the distance, framed on both sides by Finley's pink socks, was The Totem Pole Lodge.

Vivian leaned toward her. Their shoulders touched as they shared the view.

'Utterly delightful,' Vivian muttered.

278

'Great, huh?' Helen sounded as if the lodge fulfilled her best expectations.

'What was this place?' Cora asked.

'Kind of a resort,' Helen said.

'A *last* resort,' Vivian said.

'It was famous for its hot springs. And its cuisine. People came here for cross-country skiing in the winter. It was a hunting lodge in hunting season. The rest of the time, people came for hiking and fishing, that kind of thing. The place was quite popular during its heyday.'

'Looks like shit now,' Cora said.

A fist reached down between Finley's legs and rapped on the windshield. 'Stop the car, okay?'

When it came to a halt, Abilene said, 'This is far enough for me,' and swung open her door. She climbed out. It felt good to be standing up after the long drive. She stretched. She peeled her moist blouse away from her back. She took a deep breath, enjoying the woodsy aromas.

If the lodge could simply pull a quick disappearing act, she thought, this might be a wonderful place.

A bit too hot, but . . .

Finley leaped down off the roof and landed beside her. 'Awesome joint,' she said, aiming her camera at the lodge.

' "With the first glimpse of the building, a sense of insufferable gloom pervaded my spirit." '

'Say what?'

The others climbed out of the car. They all stood motionless, staring at the lodge.

It was a broad, two-story structure with walls of gray stone that looked solid enough to last for a few thousand years and a steep shake roof that sagged near the middle and might not last through the next winter.

Some of the porch roof had already caved in, thanks to a tree branch. The branch, over near the north corner, looked like an arm torn from a giant and rammed down through the top of the porch, hand first. Its jagged stub protruded from the roof. Its lower limbs formed a leafless tangle blocking that end of the porch.

A few of the lodge's upstairs windows were hidden behind closed shutters. Most of the shutters, however, hung open or dangled crooked or were simply gone. At least half of the windows that Abilene could see were broken.

At the center of the porch, straight ahead, the lodge's front door stood open.

'The doorman must've been expecting us,' Abilene said.

'Come on, Hickok, let's you and me go on ahead. The rest of you guys wait till we're there, then come on in and I'll get the big arrival.' Finley started toward the lodge.

Abilene joined her. Twigs and leaves crackled under their shoes.

Though the road was littered with debris from the surrounding forest, enough areas had been swept clear by the wind for Abilene to see patches of gray, cracked pavement. Weeds, wild grass, and even a few saplings grew in the fissures.

She came upon a broken sapling.

'Look at this.'

'So?'

She crouched over it. 'Somebody's been here. Recently, too. The leaves are still green.' She folded a small leaf between her thumb and forefinger. It felt a little springy, but it split. 'I bet it hasn't been dead more than a week.'

'Maybe Bambi stepped on it.'

'Maybe this place isn't as deserted as it looks.'

Finley wrinkled her nose. She nodded. 'Come on.'

They continued toward the lodge. In front of the porch, the road flared out like a T. The lane on the right led past the lodge to a long ramshackle structure that appeared to be some kind of parking barn with empty stalls for at least a dozen vehicles. The other lane had a turn at the far corner of the porch and seemed to lead around toward the rear.

'I guess this is close enough,' Finley said. Halting at the foot of the porch stairs, she faced the road, raised her camera and shouted, 'Action!'

For a moment, Abilene watched the Wagoneer rush forward. But the back of her neck felt crawly. She turned her head and stared at the open door.

All she could see beyond it was shadowy gloom.

We must be out of our minds, she thought, coming to a place like this. Just for the fun of it. Just for adventure.

We must be crazy.

Hell, weren't we always?

Chapter Two
Belmore Girls

It started with Finley and her new, portable video camera.

It started at Belmore University in the east wing, second floor of Hadley Hall, one of the campus's two dormitories for freshman girls. The girls were eighteen, then.

It was the third week of September.

It was a Wednesday night.

Abilene's roommate, Helen Winters, was hunched at her desk, face low over the pages of a Western Civ textbook. Abilene sat at the window, her back to the hot night, hoping to catch a stray breeze while she struggled to make sense of *Othello*. With a sigh, she closed the paperback.

'God, it's hard to think when you're baking.'

Helen dropped a yellow hi-lite pen into the gutter of her book. She turned her chair around. She looked forlorn, miserable. And even more unattractive than usual. Her brown hair, cut in a style resembling a football helmet, was greasy and matted against her scalp. Wet ringlets clung to her face. She had speckles of sweat under her eyes. Dribbles streaked her heavy cheeks. In the crease of one nostril was a white-peaked zit that looked ready to erupt. Her lower lip bulged out so far that it cast a shadow over her chin.

Sullen eyes gazing up at Abilene, she said, 'I hate everything about this place.'

'It's probably just the heat.'

'It's everything.'

'Homesick?'

'That's a good one.'

'I sure am. I wish I was there right now. Mill Valley's great this time of the year. I sure wouldn't be sweating my butt off.'

'Do you want to take a shower with me?'

Abilene felt as if her stomach had been pushed off a cliff. She realized her mouth was hanging open. She shut it. Not knowing what to say, she shrugged.

Helen blew out a long breath that puffed out her cheeks and lips. She rolled her eyes upward. 'Hey, if you don't want to, it's all right.'

'Well . . .'

'You aren't a lesbian, are you?'

Abilene's face went hot. 'No!' she blurted.

'Me, neither.'

'Well, that's good. Not that . . . you know.'

'So how about a shower?'

'Now?'

'Yeah. It'll feel good.'

She grimaced. 'I don't know. I was planning to wait till morning.'

'Please?'

'Geez, Helen.'

'It's just that . . . I really don't want to go alone. There might be some other people there. Strangers.'

'If anyone's there, it'll just be kids from our sector.'

'But I don't know any of them. Not really. And they kind of scare me. If you want to know the truth, I haven't taken a shower since last Thursday night.'

'*Last Thursday?*'

'I just haven't quite worked up the nerve again.'

'Did something happen?'

'Well, that was the night I walked to the movies. I saw a really scary one. It was great. You were asleep when I got back. The place was really quiet. I thought everybody in the whole sector was asleep, so I figured it would be a great time to take my shower. Anyway, I was in there and all of a sudden the lights went off. Somebody *turned* them off. It was pitch black. I couldn't see a thing. I couldn't hear much, either, because of the water. I was sort of spooked, but I figured it was just some creep's idea of a joke. So I went on taking my shower. I was soaping myself, you know? And suddenly there was an extra hand on me.'

'Holy shit,' Abilene muttered.

'The one that wasn't mine . . . it squeezed one of my breasts. I kind of jumped back and slipped and landed on my butt.' She shrugged. Making a sickish smile, she said, 'And that's the true story of why I haven't taken a shower since Thursday night.'

'No wonder.'

'So, will you come with me?'

'Okay. Sure.'

'Great. You're a real friend.'

'Hey, after hearing that, I'm not sure I want to take any more showers alone, myself.' Abilene shoved the chair out of the way with her feet, scooted off the low bookcase and stood up. 'What happened after you fell?' she asked.

'Nothing.'

'Nothing?'

'Well, I sat there for a real long time. But nobody touched me again. Whoever it was just left, I guess. Finally, I worked up enough nerve to get up and leave.'

'God,' Abilene muttered. 'You never got any kind of look at her? She never said anything, or . . . ?'

'For all I know, it might've been a guy.'

'*Jesus.*'

'It probably wasn't,' Helen said, and started to unbutton her blouse.

Abilene took that as her cue to move on. She walked past her bed. Facing her open closet, she stripped to the waist and put on her robe. Then she pulled down her shorts and panties, stepped out of them, and knotted her robe's cloth belt. She didn't realize, until she was done, that it was a pretty dumb way to undress.

Why worry about modesty at a time like this?

From their first night as roommates, less than two weeks ago, they'd maintained unspoken rituals to keep their privacy.

284

They'd jumped at every opportunity to change while the other was away from the room. When that failed, they'd turned their backs to each other. Abilene often stood facing her closet – more to avoid a view of Helen than to prevent Helen from seeing her.

Silly.

If they'd been more open about things, maybe Helen wouldn't have felt compelled to take that shower alone in the middle of the night.

She crouched, scooped up her clothes, and sidestepped past her dresser. She tossed them onto her bed. 'You about ready?'

'Yeah.'

She turned around. Helen had her nightgown on, but her arms weren't in its sleeves. They were busy underneath the loose gown, removing her bra. When they appeared, one was towing the undergarment out through a sleeve.

'You won't tell anyone, will you?' Helen asked.

'About what happened?'

'Yeah. It's . . . you know, kind of embarrassing. There'd be an awful lot of gossip. I'd rather just forget about the whole thing, okay?'

'Fine. I won't tell. We don't know who it was, anyway. It'd just spook people.'

'Thanks.'

They gathered their washcloths, towels, soap and shampoo. Abilene dropped her room key into a pocket. She followed Helen into the corridor, then pulled the door shut and made sure it was locked.

The corridor was filled with music, voices and laughter. On their way to the restroom, they passed several open doors. Girls in the rooms were sprawled on beds, sitting at desks, some studying, while others carried on discussions or watched small televisions. A few were eating snacks and drinking sodas. Abilene nodded and smiled at those who noticed her going by. Though she recognized all of them, she wasn't sure about some of the names.

The restroom was just this side of double doors that separated the east wing of Hadley Hall from the main stairs and west wing.

Abilene entered first. She saw no one. But sounds of rushing water came from the shower room.

'Maybe we should try later,' Helen whispered.

'Don't be ridiculous. Come on.'

Helen grimaced, but followed her past the toilet stalls to the dressing area. Steam was drifting in from the shower room. Voices, too – cheerful, amplified by the tile walls. A couple of robes and towels had been left on the bench.

Abilene slipped out of her sandals, emptied her hands onto the bench, and took off her robe. She rolled it up, set it next to her towel, then picked up her washcloth, soap and shampoo. She looked at Helen just as the girl's large breasts, briefly caught by the hem of the nightgown, came free and dropped, bouncing and swinging. Helen finished dragging the nightgown off her head, gave Abilene a somewhat frantic glance, and deposited the nightgown on the bench.

'Here goes nothing,' she muttered, and gestured for Abilene to go first.

Abilene stepped over the low, tile barrier, and entered the shower room. The steamy air wrapped her.

She raised a hand and said 'Hello' to the two girls who stood under nozzles near the far end. She recognized both of them. 'Cora, right?' she asked the one near the corner.

'Tucson?'

'Abilene. This is my roomy, Helen.'

'Hi,' Helen said from behind her.

'I'm Vivian,' said the other girl. Abilene had never actually met her, but she'd seen her around and knew her name. She supposed that everyone knew her name. Vivian Drake was easily the most beautiful girl in the freshman class: tall and slender with dark auburn hair, emerald eyes, a flawless complexion and a stunning face.

Abilene had stayed clear of her, certain that she must be a conceited bitch.

Now, she said, 'Nice to meet you,' went to the shower right beside Vivian and turned on the water. She stepped out of the way, testing the spray with her hand. When it felt hot, she moved underneath it.

Helen chose the shower on the other side.

'Abilene's a cool name,' Vivian said.

'Thanks.'

'Is that where you were conceived?' Cora asked.

'No, I was named for the song.'

Vivian began to hum it as she soaped her legs.

Abilene began to like her.

'It was my parents' favorite song,' she said. 'It was *their song*, you know? Also, my dad's a western writer.'

'No kidding?' Cora said. 'No wonder you're such a hot-shot in Dalton's class.'

'I'm sure having trouble with Shakespeare.'

'The guy should've tried writing in English.'

'I've got the Cliff Notes for *Othello*,' Vivian said. 'If you want to stop by the room sometime, you can borrow it.'

'Thanks.'

She's actually nice, Abilene thought, and felt a little guilty about prejudging her.

Just because she's gorgeous doesn't mean she's a shit.

But her beauty *was* rather disturbing, and all the more obvious here in the shower room.

Standing next to her, Abilene felt quite plain. She knew she was fairly attractive herself: slender, blonde, with quick blue eyes and an okay face except for a sprinkling of freckles across her nose that she didn't appreciate but boys seemed to find cute.

That's me, she thought. Cute. Ordinary.

Whereas Vivian was an incredible knockout.

Even Cora, hardly a slouch in the looks department, suffered by comparison to the girl showering next to her. She was Vivian's height, but the similarity stopped at that. Her face was wholesome, not striking. Her blonde hair was short and curly, not a long flow of rich, silken tresses. She had broad shoulders, full breasts, wide hips. Though she appeared to be much heavier than her roommate, there was no suggestion of fat. She looked athletic, not regal.

Abilene turned to Helen. The girl's head hung as she slid a bar of soap over one breast.

She wasn't a striking, regal knockout. She wasn't wholesome and athletic. She wasn't even plain but cute. She was homely, fat and dumpy.

Abilene knew she must be feeling like hell.

'Have you got any of your father's books?' Vivian asked.

'Not with me.'

'Does the student bookstore carry them?'

'No, but the Save-More Drugstore has a bunch.' She felt as if she were ignoring Helen. But maybe the girl preferred it that way.

'What's his name?'

'Alex Randolph.'

'Good. I'll pick up something next time I'm in there.' She squirted shampoo into her palm and started rubbing it into her hair. 'So. Helen. What do you think of McMasters?'

'He's okay,' Helen murmured, soaping herself and keeping her head down.

'I hear he was a drill instructor in the Marines.'

'He's a bastard,' Cora said.

'We're all in his eight o'clock,' Vivian told Abilene. She was scrubbing her sudsy hair, froth rolling down the sides of her face. 'How'd you luck out?'

'I'll be taking his course next semester.'

'He's a real bastard,' Cora repeated.

Vivian turned her head. 'He might leave you alone if you'd get there on time.'

'Fat chance.'

Vivian laughed. 'He's decent enough to me and Helen.'

'That's because Helen's got brains and you've got him flustered.' Cora leaned forward and looked at Abilene. 'You should see it. The guy blushes every time he lays his eyes on Viv.'

'He hankers after me,' Vivian said.

Helen burst out laughing, raised her head and turned toward the others. Her mouth was stretched into a wide smile. The laughter shook her shoulders, made her breasts bob and shake.

'Well, he does!' Vivian insisted.

'Hankers!' Helen squealed.

'Don't split a gut,' Cora advised.

'I'm . . . sorry. Oh Jesus! He *hankers* after her!'

And Finley came into the shower room.

At that time, Abilene didn't know her name. If she had known her name, she wouldn't have recognized her anyway; a gorilla mask covered her entire head.

Finley wore a tank top, shorts, and tennis shoes.

At her face, viewfinder to the gorilla's eyehole, rested a portable video camera.

She came bounding into the mist and pranced sideways, sweeping the camera across Helen and Abilene and Vivian and Cora as she rushed by.

At first, Abilene was too surprised and perplexed to realize what was happening. By the time she figured out that the strange apparition was taping them, it was too late to cover herself.

Vivian blurted, 'What the hell?' and whirled toward the wall.

Cora lunged at Finley, reaching out. But Finley, in her tennies, had better traction and sprang clear. Cora skidded. Her feet flew up and she landed on her rump.

Finley backstepped, getting the fall on tape.

'Thanks, hon,' she said in a cheery, muffled voice.

She scampered sideways. Vivian presented her with nothing but her back, hands trying to hide her rear.

Abilene rushed forward. Bent at the waist, arms and legs spread wide like a basketball guard, she blocked Finley's retreat.

The girl slipped to a halt. The big lens of the camera shifted from side to side – from breast to breast – and down.

'You bitch!'

'Time to go!' She feinted to the left. Abilene lurched that way to grab her. She saw her mistake as Finley ducked to the right, but the slick floor didn't allow a quick change of direction.

Sliding and turning, she watched the girl run for the exit and straight into Helen's fist.

Helen, waiting in the middle of the entryway, threw a haymaker that knocked the gorilla head sideways. The camera flew, striking Abilene's right thigh as Finley's back slammed the floor. The girl skidded toward her.

Abilene rubbed her leg. She bent down and picked up the camera.

Then they all gathered around Finley. Helen planted a foot on her belly. Cora pulled off the gorilla head.

The girl grimaced up at them. 'Greetings,' she said. 'Finley's the name. Pleased to make your acquaintance, ladies.'

Chapter Three

The Wagoneer stopped in front of Abilene and Finley. The others climbed out.

Helen's head tilted back and rolled as she surveyed the lodge. Her eyes were wide. Her mouth hung open. She might have been standing for the first time at the feet of the Statute of Liberty, gazing up at the monument with awe and delight.

'Why don't we leave everything in the car,' Cora suggested, 'until we've looked the place over?'

Vivian, nose wrinkled, said, 'Why don't we *not* look the place over and drive back to Burlington instead?'

'Where's your sense of adventure?' Abilene asked.

'It lost out to my sense of self-preservation.'

'No risk, no thrill,' Cora said.

Helen, still gaping at the lodge, said, 'Isn't this place just fabulously *eerie?*'

'I just hope it's fabulously unoccupied,' Abilene said. 'God only knows who might've decided to take up residence in a place like this.'

Helen grinned. 'Yeah.' She sounded tickled by the possibility of encountering a hermit or axe-murderer inside the ruin. 'Let's go in and check it out.'

She hurried up the porch stairs, Cora at her side, Vivian following. Before stepping through the doorway, Vivian looked over her shoulder. 'Coming?'

'I wouldn't miss it,' Finley said and shouldered her camera. 'Go on ahead,' she told Abilene.

Abilene climbed the stairs and strode across the porch. The boards wobbled and squeaked. Even though they'd been strong enough to support Helen, she feared breaking through and was glad to reach the safety of the foyer's marble floor.

The others hadn't ventured off the marble. They stood at its far edge as if the foyer were an island and they weren't ready to get their feet wet. Nobody spoke. Only their heads moved as they looked around. Abilene supposed they were listening, wondering whether the lodge was truly deserted. She halted beside Vivian.

'Bitchin' joint!' Finley yelled.

Abilene flinched. Vivian gasped. Helen twisted around, scowling, pressing a finger to her heavy lips and letting out a long 'Shhhhhhhh.'

A grin spread across Finley's face. Obviously, she had meant to startle them and was pleased by her success. 'Okay,' she mouthed, not making a sound. She came forward ever so slowly on tiptoes, lifting her knees high, setting her feet down gingerly, her lips pursed – a parody of silent sneaking.

She stopped next to Abilene. She turned slowly, panning the room with her camera. Its automatic focus made quiet humming sounds as it adjusted to changing distances. Then she lowered the camera to her side and stood motionless.

All five women looked around and listened.

Other than the quick pounding of her own heartbeat, Abilene heard nothing but sounds from outside: birds chirping and squawking, the sigh of leaves stirred by breezes.

Enough daylight came in for her to see the staircase to her left, an open room beyond it, and the lobby and lounge area to her right. Except for the L-shaped registration desk and the numbered cubby-holes behind it, the huge room was bare.

She supposed that its dark, panelled walls had once been decorated with the heads of deer, with mounted fish and paintings of rustic scenes. There had probably been stuffed raccoons, and such, perched atop the broad wooden rafters. And furniture scattered about. Easy chairs, lamp tables. Maybe even sofas and a rug in front of the broad, stone fireplace. The fireplace, she noticed, was still equipped with andirons, a screen, and a set of fire irons.

Surprising that scavengers hadn't made off with them, sold them as antiques or taken them home.

She wondered what else might've been left behind.

Plenty of time to find out, she thought.

If they wound up spending four whole days here, as planned, they'd get to know this place from top to bottom.

'It's pretty decent,' Cora said, not only breaking the silence but leaving the foyer and walking over the hardwood floor toward the registration desk. 'It's not nearly the shambles I expected. Figured there'd be crap all over the place, from the looks of the outside.'

'Could've been a lot worse,' Vivian admitted. 'It's still pretty creepy, though.'

'It's supposed to be,' Helen informed her.

'I know, I know.'

Cora leaned across the registration desk, stretching over its counter, one leg rising high behind her as she strained to see what was on the other side. She pushed herself away and shook her head.

'Nothing.'

'The more nothing, the better,' Vivian said.

As Cora walked alongside the desk, she glanced down at the front of her white T-shirt and brushed it once, just once, with her open hand. Turning toward the others, she frowned. She plucked at her shirt, pulling it away from her body. She gazed at the taut, slanted cloth.

It didn't look particularly dirty to Abilene – just a trifle dusty – so what could be bothering . . . 'Uh-oh,' she muttered.

'Hey, Viv,' Cora said. 'Guess what? You don't have to worry about soiling your clothes around this place. Not much, anyway.' She brushed her shirt a couple more times, and the traces of dust vanished. 'That counter should've been *filthy*.'

'The maid service must've been by,' Finley said.

'*Somebody*'s been by,' Abilene said. 'From my vast experience with house cleaning, I'd say Cora mopped up less than a week's worth of dust.'

'Should've been twelve years' worth,' Helen pointed out. A corner of her lip curled up.

'If it'd been that dirty, I would've stayed off.'

Abilene turned around, studying the floor. Near the door and windows were some leaves. But not many. And she saw no broken glass, at all, beneath the windows. 'The floor's clean, too,' she said.

Vivian nodded. 'Obviously, this place isn't as abandoned as it looks.'

'The Three Bears must be out for an afternoon stroll,' Finley said.

Spread out and walking abreast, the five women made their way through the room, skirting the occasional support beams. As she neared the fireplace, Abilene saw that it was clean inside. The stones were black with soot, but there were no ashes or chunks of burnt wood.

Several yards past the end of the registration desk, the room branched out to the left.

'Must be the dining area,' Cora said, stepping around the corner.

'This is where it happened,' Helen said.

'Where what happened?' Vivian asked.

Helen grinned and wiggled her eyebrows up and down. 'Later. After dark. I'll tell you all a bedtime story.'

'We might not be here after dark,' Vivian said.

'As long as nobody's around,' Cora said, 'we might as well stay.'

'Somebody *has* been here,' Abilene reminded her.

'That doesn't necessarily mean anyone'll show up while we're around. And whoever it is might be perfectly harmless.'

'Well, we're trespassing.'

'Just doing some innocent exploration. And the door was open, after all. It's not as if we broke in.'

'Besides,' Helen said, 'it wouldn't be fair to quit. This is my choice, and I've always gone along with you guys – whether I wanted to or not. I didn't complain all the time, either,' she added, eyeing Vivian.

'I'm still here,' Vivian pointed out. 'I'm not a quitter.'

'Just a complainer,' Cora said.

'We do have to be realistic,' Abilene said. 'I mean, it's great to have our little adventures, but on the other hand we don't want to get our asses killed. Things *do* happen, you know. And this place looks a little hinky to me. I'm not saying we should call it quits, but we've gotta be damned careful. Someone was here within the past few days. Someone *might* be here right now.'

'Oh, I hope so,' Helen said, leering.

This from the gal, Abilene thought, who is petrified by the idea of taking a shower alone.

Helen hadn't changed much, in that regard, since her encounter with the phantom hand in her freshman year at Belmore.

After the night of Finley's escapade, Helen had taken showers frequently. Not always with Abilene, but always with someone. Often, she'd returned dry, having turned back after discovering the shower room to be deserted. Better to wait than to risk the lights going off, an extra hand touching her in the dark.

Later, during the three years when they all shared a rented house on Summer Street, she hadn't insisted on having a companion in the tub with her. She hadn't even asked. It would've been tight quarters, for one thing. She'd admitted it. And she'd always locked herself in the bathroom.

Even last night at the Wayfarer's Haven in Burlington, Helen had insisted that either Abilene or Finley remain in the room while she bathed. Abilene had stayed behind. Finley had gone ahead without her to have drinks and snacks in the room shared by Cora and Vivian.

So she was a young woman pursued by terror, and yet here she was, putting on a show of bravado about the more immediate threat of running into a stranger in a desolate lodge in the middle of nowhere.

Well, Abilene thought, there are five of us. She damn sure wouldn't be acting this way if she were alone.

But Abilene wondered if any of this was *real* to Helen. The phantom hand in the shower room had been very real. Whenever Helen was in the midst of an adventure, however, she behaved as if she considered the dangers imaginary. As if she were a character in a movie or something, and nothing bad could actually happen to her.

As Abilene entered the kitchen behind Cora and Helen, she realized that Helen wasn't the only one with a carefree attitude about the adventures.

Finley, too, seemed cheerfully reckless.

In Finley's case, however, it was more than empty bravado. The girl was audacious, intrepid to the bone.

Chapter Four
Belmore Girls

'Now let's calm down, everyone,' Finley said as Cora grabbed the front of her tank top and yanked her up.

'No need for violence,' she said as Cora drove her across the room and rammed her back against a wall between two of the showers.

'Is my camera okay?' she asked as Cora clutched her throat. Abilene had picked it up.

She located Cora and Finley in the viewfinder. 'I guess it's all right,' she said.

'Then tape this,' Cora said, and punched Finley in the stomach.

The girl's eyes bugged out. Her mouth sprang open. Her shoulders lurched off the wall as she bent at the waist, her neck thrusting against Cora's hand.

'Hey!' Abilene snapped. 'Don't . . .'

'Quit it!' Vivian cried out. 'For Godsake!'

'Leave her alone,' Abilene said.

Finley, pinned to the wall, wheezed for air. Her face was twisted with pain.

'Let go of her,' Abilene said.

Cora dropped her hand. The girl leaned forward, rump against the wall, and hugged her belly.

'What's the big idea, huh?' Cora asked. 'What are you, a pervert?'

Finley shook her head. She gasped something that sounded like, 'Ontra.'

'What?'

'Let her catch her breath,' Vivian said.

They waited. At last, Finley stopped holding herself, stood up straight, and said, 'Entrepreneur.'

'What?'

'It means she . . .'

'I *know* what it means,' Cora said, casting an annoyed glance at Vivian.

'This guy . . . he offered me two hundred bucks.'

'*To film us taking showers?*'

'Videotape, actually. For his VCR.'

Cora didn't bother to dry. She didn't bother to put on her robe. Stark naked, twisting Finley's arm, she guided the girl out of the shower room and dressing room, past the toilet stalls and sinks, and through the door to the hallway.

Abilene dried herself as fast as possible. Helen, flushed

with excitement, didn't bother to towel off. She struggled to pull the nightgown down her wet body, and finally succeeded. The fabric looked transparent where it clung to her skin. Abilene put on her robe, picked up her toilet articles and lifted the camera. Vivian, who'd also taken time to dry, belted her own robe, then gathered her possessions along with the robe, towel, and other things that Cora had left behind.

The three of them rushed into the corridor.

Helen carried the gorilla mask. It swung from her fist, dripping, like a severed head fresh from the guillotine.

Several other girls stood around, looking perplexed. Some were peering into the room Vivian shared with Cora. It looked as if Cora had caused quite a stir, hustling by with her prisoner.

Those who asked questions were answered with a brusk, 'Never mind' from Vivian. Who shut the door and locked it after Helen and Abilene were inside.

Finley sat on one of the beds, regarding her captors with a quizzical look.

Cora loomed over her, hands on hips. She was shiny and dripping. Her buttocks were red from the fall she'd taken trying to apprehend the girl. Vivian held out her robe. She snatched it away. Muttering 'Thanks,' she shoved her arms through the sleeves.

'I hope this isn't going to get ugly,' Finley said.

'Depends on how you look at death,' Cora told her.

'I must inform you, there's a letter in my safety deposit box with instructions to be opened in the event of my demise.'

'Cut the comedy,' Cora said. 'Who paid you to film us?'

'Actually, he's supposed to pay on delivery. At this point, I don't expect that to happen.'

'What's his name?'

'Darryl Rathbone.'

'Who's he?'

'A senior. He's a Sig.'

'What did he want the film for?'

'I guess he figured it'd be a hit with his frat brothers.'

She shrugged, then frowned as if thinking about something. 'Do you want to know what really happened?'

'That's the idea.'

''Cause there's a little more to it than the two hundred bucks.'

'Tell us everything,' Vivian said. She sounded as if she felt a little sorry for the girl.

'Okay, here's the thing. I'm over at the student union having a Pepsi, and I see him watching me. This is tonight, by the way. I've got my camera along – which is why all this happened in the first place. Anyway, I leave the union and I'm heading back here across the quad when he comes running up behind me and grabs my shoulder. I go, "Does this mean we're going steady?" And he turns me around and goes, "Which dorm are you in?" I tell him, and he gets this big grin. He asks if I know her.' Finley nodded toward Vivian.

'Me?'

'Yeah. He goes, "You know that honey, Vivian Drake?" I say I know who she is. I mean, who doesn't? And then he tells me there's like a pool going at the Sig house. Five hundred bucks, and it goes to the first guy that comes up with videotape of Vivian in the raw.'

Vivian's face went crimson.

'Those bastards,' Cora muttered.

'What a bunch of pigs,' Helen said.

Vivian's face was still bright red, but now her eyes shimmered. Her lips were pressed tightly together, her chin trembling.

'He says I can make him the winner,' Finley continued,

'and he'll give me two hundred. I tell him to get fucked, so then he grabs my camera away and holds it up like he plans to smash it on the concrete. "I'm not asking that much," he goes. "It'll be easy. Just keep your eyes open. Next time she's taking a shower, just walk in and nail her and run. Wear a mask, or something.' So I tell him okay, just so I can get my camera back. He gives it to me. I start to walk off, and he tells me I'd better come through – or else.'

'Or else what?' Cora asked.

'He said he'd put a bounty on me.'

'A bounty?'

'Yeah.'

'What did he mean by that?' Abilene asked.

'He didn't say. But I guess I'll find out. Unless you gals want to do me a big favor and let me have the tape.'

'When hell freezes over,' Cora said.

'Somehow, I thought you might say that.'

Vivian sat down on the other bed. She wiped her eyes with a sleeve of her robe. She sniffed. 'The whole Sig house is in on this?' she asked.

'I guess so.'

'If they've got that pool,' Abilene said, 'somebody else'll be trying to collect. It won't stop till they get you.'

'We could report them,' Helen suggested.

Vivian wrinkled her nose. 'I don't want the *administration* finding out.'

'We've got to do something,' Abilene said.

'Those slimebags,' Cora muttered.

'Do you know what I think we should do?' Finley asked.

'We know,' Cora said. 'Give them your tape.'

Finley shook her head. 'I think we should torpedo the whole damn fraternity.'

'We?' Cora asked.

'Whose side do you think I'm on, anyway?'

'Your own.'

'Yeah,' Abilene said. 'You didn't have to go along with it.'

'He threatened her,' Vivian pointed out.

'That's no excuse.'

'I wasn't *going* to do it, not even after he came up with that bounty crap. But then I got to thinking. You know? I can always use a couple of hundred bucks. Also, I figured somebody else would do it, if I didn't. So why not me? That way, I get the money and Rathbone leaves me alone. And then I sort of got caught up in the whole idea. A challenge, you know? Could I get away with it?'

'Obviously not,' Cora said.

'But I figured it'd be fun to try.' With a somewhat sheepish smile, she added, 'It was. It was a gassaroonie. At least till you guys nailed me.'

'I could tell you were having a good time,' Abilene said.

'Oh, yeah. Haven't you ever done something really outrageous? There's nothing like it. A blast. I do all kinds of stuff just because it's risky. You oughta try it. We *all* oughta try it. And we can start by taking on the Sigs. We've gotta stop 'em in their tracks before somebody collects on the pool.'

Vivian, frowning, gazed at her. 'Have you got any ideas?'

The young man who opened the front door of the fraternity house two hours later looked stunned. As if the last thing he expected to find on the porch at midnight was a group of five freshman co-eds, all wearing fancy, low-cut gowns, all but the girl with the video camera hanging onto beer bottles, mugging and swaying as if they were quite drunk.

'Do y'know who I am?' Vivian asked, slurring her words.

'Uh . . . sure.'

'These're my friends.'

'Yo!' Cora blurted, and raised her bottle as if toasting the guy.

'Pleased to make yer 'quaintance,' Helen said.

'Howdy,' Abilene greeted him, and winked.

Finley, behind them, said nothing as she videotaped the scene.

'What are . . . what's going on?'

'Come t' see the fellas,' Vivian said. 'Hear they're hankerin' t'see *me*.'

'Gonna let ush in?' Helen asked.

'We're gonna give 'em a show,' Vivian said. A roll of one shoulder sent a strap of her gown sliding down her upper arm.

A frat brother appeared behind the guy in the door and looked out. His mouth fell open. 'Holy shit,' he said. 'What gives?'

'We do,' Abilene said, winking as she shook her beer bottle at him.

'They want to come in.'

'For Godsake, who's stopping them? Step right in, ladies.' He pulled his friend out of the doorway. 'Go get the others, Bill. I'll escort these ladies into the parlor.'

Whirling around, Bill dashed to the stairway just beyond the foyer. He sprang up the stairs two and three at a time.

'I'm Doug,' said the other. He held the door wide and swept his arm, gesturing for the girls to enter. 'This is certainly an unexpected surprise.'

'It'll get even bedder,' Vivian said, giving his cheek a brief caress as she staggered by.

'You gals have been partying, huh?'

303

'Just gettin' started,' Cora said.

'Feelin' wild 'n horny,' Helen said.

Abilene halted, facing Doug. With a slanted grin, she said, 'We know you Siggies're wild 'n horny, too.' Doug proved her point by fastening his eyes on her cleavage. 'Yer gonna see a lot more'n that preddy soon.'

He blew through his pursed lips. 'Whew. Can't wait, if I do say so myself.' Abilene walked on.

Looking back, she saw Finley poke her lens into the guy's face. 'I'm the official historian. The tape of tonight's proceeding will be copied by my own self and sent to your esteemed fraternity.'

'Great. Fabulous.'

Doug led them into the 'parlor,' a dimly lighted, plushly furnished room to the left of the foyer. As he scurried about, turning on lamps, the sounds of voices and thudding footfalls came from above.

Abilene heard whoops and yells.

Someone yelled, 'You gotta be shitting me!'

Another voice shouted, 'WHO?'

'Fuckin' A!'

'*Five* of 'em?'

'I be died 'n gone to heaven!'

'Let me at 'em!'

'Bombed? Oh, man!'

Doug laughed and shook his head. 'Sounds as if the guys'll be along any minute. Would you ladies like to be seated and make yourselves comfortable?'

They all glanced around at the sofas and easy chairs, as if considering the offer. Finley panned the room with her camera.

'We can't very well do what we're gonna do,' Vivian said, 'if we're sitting down.'

304

'Sides,' Cora said, 'you guys'll wanta be sittin' for our show.'

Doug pursed his lips again and scrunched up his eyes. He appeared to be in an agony of expectation.

Abilene, standing shoulder to shoulder with her friends, watched a herd of young men stampede down the stairs. They let out whoops and war cries. Only a few were fully dressed. Some wore robes. Many were bare to the waist, some wearing only shorts or pajama bottoms. A few wore nothing but skivvies.

What've we gotten ourselves into here? Abilene wondered.

Her heart slammed so hard that she felt dizzy, and she struggled to catch her breath.

As those at the front of the crowd reached the parlor's entryway, Vivian raised her beer bottle. 'Greetings, fellas!'

A cheer went up.

'Quiet down 'n take your seats,' she announced. 'The show will not begin until you're all seated and we have your undivided attention.'

'You've sure as shit got that,' said a leering thick-neck who looked like a body-builder. He wore black, bikini underwear. He peered at the tops of Abilene's breasts as he sauntered past her.

I'm gonna have a coronary, she thought. I'm gonna drop dead on the floor and they'll gang-bang me while they wait for the paramedics.

Every single one of the Sigs – and Abilene figured there must be more than twenty of them – ogled her and Cora and Finley and Vivian (especially Vivian, of course), and most of them even gawped at Helen, whose massive bosom threatened to pop free of her low-cut dress.

A lot of the guys had red faces. Some looked nervous. Others grinned. Abilene saw plenty of shaking heads. She heard sighs and a few low whistles.

At least they're all strangers, she thought.

She'd seen most of them around campus, but Rush Week hadn't taken place yet so there were no freshmen among them. It was daunting that they were all upper-classmen, but a relief that nobody here was in classes with her.

Turning around, she watched them scurry for easy chairs and crowd onto the sofas, pushing and shoving. Several of them ended up sitting on the floor's plush, burgundy carpet.

Soon, all of them were seated except one. He was a tall, slender guy with short hair and a smirking face. He wore faded blue gym shorts and sandals. He stood in front of an armchair that looked like a throne.

'On behalf of my somewhat astonished brothers,' he said, 'I bid you welcome to the Sig house. I'm Cliff Rogers, President.' With that, he sat down.

Vivian raised her beer bottle toward him. 'Pleased to meet you. I'm Vivian Drake, but I suppose all of you know that.'

Nods, murmurs, grins.

'I'm Cora Evans, Viv's roommate.'

'Abilene Randolph.'

'Helen Winters.'

'Finley here. Virginia Finley.' As she spoke, she swept the audience with her camera.

'We want you all to know our names,' Vivian said. 'Know them and remember them. And remember what we do here tonight.'

'And what, exactly, is that?' Cliff asked.

'First, we collect.'

'Collect?'

She smiled broadly and nodded. 'Five hundred bucks. That's the amount, right?'

'Does anyone know what she's talking about?' Cliff asked, scanning his frat brothers.

They all shook their heads, murmured disclaimers, and tried to act innocent.

'Whoever's keeping the kitty,' Cora said, 'had better run and fetch it.'

'Or the show doesn't go on,' Vivian added. 'The way we see it, a live show with the five of us'll be a lot more fun for you fellas than a plain old videotape of just me.'

'In addition,' Finley announced, 'you'll get a tape of the festivities. To help you remember.'

'You aren't serious,' Cliff said.

'Watch and see,' Vivian said.

'Money first,' Cora said.

Eyes narrow, Cliff regarded the girls. Then he nodded toward a husky guy on one of the sofas. 'Rathbone, go get it.'

A cheer went up.

Rathbone rose to his feet, hitched up his sagging boxer shorts, and strode toward Finley. He jabbed an index finger at her lens. 'You,' he muttered. 'You're meat.'

'I'm trembling,' she said.

Several of the guys booed and jeered.

'Hey Boner, she beat you out?' someone called.

Rathbone flipped his middle finger at his detractors, then hurried from the parlor. Swinging around, Finley taped his exit.

After he was gone, the room fell silent. The girls stood motionless, side by side. The Sigs stared at them, eyes darting about, never settling, focusing briefly on breasts here, faces there, then moving on but coming back a few moments later.

This was a very stupid idea, Abilene thought. Should've just let Finley hand over the shower room tape.

We're out of our minds.

She suddenly ached to whirl around and run for it.

But she stood her ground.

She'd agreed to the plan. It had seemed like madness from the instant it came out of Finley's mouth. But Vivian had fallen for it with vengeful glee. They'd all fallen for it.

Now we're gonna get reamed, Abilene thought.

Rathbone came back into the parlor, stepped in front of the girls, gave Finley a murderous glare, then offered a thick stack of money to Vivian.

She set her beer bottle on the carpet at her feet, and took the money. She counted it. Finished, she smiled. 'Is everybody ready?'

The Sigs went wild, clapping, stomping their feet, shouting and whistling.

'Could we have some music?' Vivian yelled. 'Something lively.'

One of the guys rushed over to the stereo.

Michael Jackson came on, singing 'Bad.'

The girls began.

They danced, writhing sensuously, bobbing their heads with the beat, rolling their shoulders, thrusting out their pelvises. Finley taped the guys as she danced. Abilene, Helen and Cora smiled and waved their beer bottles. Vivian flapped the stack of money in front of her face like a fan.

'Take it off,' Cliff called.

The others started chanting it.

'Take it off, take if off, take it off!'

'Ladies?' Vivian asked.

They nodded.

Vivian switched the bills to her left hand. She slipped her right hand slowly, very slowly, down the top of her gown. Abilene, following suit, reached inside her own gown and caressed her breast. So did Cora. So did Helen.

308

The guys went wild, cheering and hooting.

Vivian's hand came out with a Bic lighter. She kicked over the beer bottle at her feet. Abilene, Cora and Helen upended their bottles. The fluid burbled out, splashing onto the carpet.

A stench of gasoline filled the air.

Fire erupted from Vivian's lighter.

She touched it to the money.

The Sigs went silent.

Shouting, 'Don't ever fuck with us!' Vivian hurled the fiery bills into the air.

Abilene glimpsed them fluttering down toward the fuel-soaked carpet. Most of them seemed to be burning. Most of the Sigs looked as if they'd been kicked in the nuts.

She didn't stick around to watch the outcome.

None of the Sigs pursued them when they fled the house. They must've been too busy – as Finley had predicted – trying to extinguish the fires and maybe save some of the money.

Fire trucks never came.

The fraternity house didn't burn down.

The following week, a new carpet was installed and a rumor went around campus that a drunken Sig had fallen asleep in the parlor while smoking a cigarette.

Finley, as promised, mailed a copy of the videotape to the boys.

Abilene, Helen, Finley, Cora and Vivian stuck together after that, their friendship welded by the madness of that night – welded, too, by determination to protect one another from avenging Sigs.

During the remainder of their undergraduate years at Belmore, they ran into many Sigs. Sigs gave them strange looks. Sigs muttered things, always out of hearing range. Sigs never asked any of them for a date.

And Sigs never, ever fucked with them.

Chapter Five

The kitchen of the Totem Pole Lodge had cupboards, counters, a pantry, large sinks, a walk-in freezer, and empty spaces where Abilene figured refrigerators and stoves had once stood. It also had cobwebs, dust balls, and layers of grime on its counter tops and linoleum floor.

'Looks like the maid missed this place,' Finley said.

'She doesn't do kitchens,' Abilene said.

Vivian twisted a faucet handle. It squeaked. No water came from the spout. 'Great,' she muttered, then gave her dirty hand a disgusted glance. 'I suppose there's no electricity, either.'

'Not likely,' Cora said.

Vivian looked down at her bright yellow sundress, apparently searching for a place to wipe her hand. 'Does anybody have a Kleenex, or something?'

'Use this,' Abilene said. Stepping up close to Vivian, she raised her knee.

'Thanks,' Vivian rubbed her hand on a leg of Abilene's faded, denim cut-offs.

'Should've worn grubbies.'

'She doesn't *believe* in grubbies,' Cora pointed out.

Helen tugged open the door of the walk-in freezer, glanced inside, then shut it quickly.

'Something in there?' Cora asked.

'Not that I could see. Pretty dark.'

As Cora opened it to take a look herself, Abilene wandered over to the sinks. Above them were grimy windows. From the position of the kitchen, to the left of the dining area, she knew that the windows must be facing the rear of the lodge. She was surprised to see that all the glass was intact.

Leaning forward, she peered through one of the panes. She saw the shaded floor of a porch, a wooden railing at its far side, blue sky, tree tops in the distance, and not much else.

'Over here,' Finley said.

Abilene turned away from the window. Finley, off to her right, was standing in front of a door. Shifting the camera to her left hand, she knocked back a bolt. She twisted the knob and jerked. The door stayed put, and she stumbled toward it. Bracing her feet and crouching slightly, she gave the knob another sharp tug. With splintery crackles, it broke free of its jamb and swung at her. Its hinges squawked. Its edge only missed her face because the door's sudden release had sent her staggering backward.

Regaining her balance, she stepped outside. 'Hey, neat!' she called.

Abilene went after her. Surprise at finding the porch high above the ground was forgotten the moment she met the fresh air. She'd been vaguely aware of the kitchen's stuffy heat and musty smells, but hadn't realized just how bad it'd been until leaving it behind. Here, the air smelled rich with fragrances of the forest. The warm breeze felt cool. She untucked her blouse, lifted its front, and felt the breeze caress her belly while she wiped sweat off her face.

Richard Laymon

'I don't think I want to go back in there,' she said.

'Hey, guys!' Finley called. 'Get out here!'

Abilene unfastened a few lower buttons, then looked around as she raised her shirttails and tied them in a half-knot under her breasts.

The porch extended along the entire rear of the lodge. At both ends, stairways led down from the long, second story balcony. The stairways met the porch and descended from there to the ground. Directly in front of her, another set of stairs led downward.

'This *is* something,' Cora said.

'Oh,' Vivian said. 'Great.'

Abilene heard the door from the kitchen grind shut.

'Fantastic,' Helen said.

Abilene didn't know whether they were talking about the fresh air or the scenery.

Now that she had recovered from the stifling atmosphere of the kitchen, it was the view that amazed her.

The rear grounds of the lodge.

She stepped to the edge of the stairway for a better look. Finley was already there, camera to her face. Abilene halted beside her and muttered, 'Weird.'

'I'll say. But neat.'

The lodge cast a heavy shadow halfway across the swath of level land. The far half was bathed in dusty golden light from the late afternoon sun. The end of the field and both its sides were walled by dense forest.

It looked like an oasis.

A picnic area.

A park that had seen better days.

Gazing at it, Abilene felt strange mixtures of excitement, nostalgia and apprehension.

A red brick barbecue stood in the shadow, its chimney almost as high as the porch. A lone picnic table remained near the edifice. There may have been many such tables, once, but only this one remained. It was weathered like driftwood (like the totem poles out front, Abilene thought), and littered with leaves. Weeds climbed its legs.

Off beyond the barbecue was a strip of concrete that resembled a miniature runway – the runway of an airport abandoned long ago. Dandelions grew in its web of cracks. Abilene could see enough of its faint markings, however, to know that it had once been a shuffleboard court.

A ruin, now.

In the days before it was a ruin, in the days before weeds overpowered the trim grass, people had probably played croquet on the part of the field behind the shuffleboard court. Abilene could almost hear the soft clack of colliding wooden balls.

And the ring of a horseshoe clanging into a steel stake.

If they played shuffleboard, she thought, they *had* to play croquet and horseshoes.

It must've been nice. Peaceful, idyllic.

She turned her eyes to the swimming pool. It was way off to her left, far enough from the lodge to be clear of the afternoon shadow, close to the line of woods at the northern side of the lawn. Several flagstone paths converged on it. The pool's stone deck, like the forlorn shuffleboard court, was littered with forest debris and seamed with weeds. From here, the pool looked empty. At one end was a high dive, a low board, and a slide.

'I wonder where the hot springs are,' Helen said.

'I'm sure that's just a regular pool,' Abilene said.

Lowering her camera, Finley started down the stairs. Abilene went with her and heard the others following.

313

Underneath the porch, she found another pool.

'Oh, wow,' Finley said.

'Yeah.' She walked toward it.

The pool, nestled close to the rear of the lodge and entirely sheltered by the porch, was only about six feet wide – seven or eight feet long. Its granite walls were filled to the brim with gently moving water – water that entered from an archway in the wall of the lodge and flowed slowly away down a shallow stone channel at the north side of the pool.

The water looked remarkably clean. Abilene supposed that its constant motion must sweep away leaves and such, and wash them down the channel.

'Fantastic!' Helen blurted when she saw the pool. 'This must be it, huh?' Rushing past Abilene, she knelt at the edge and dipped a hand into the water. 'It's hot!'

'It comes from the lodge?' Cora asked, sounding astonished.

She and Abilene both squatted down and peered through the archway. The opening was the width of a doorway. Above the waterline, it was less than a yard high. In the shadowed gloom beyond it, Abilene could see nothing except a softly undulating surface of water. 'Looks like another pool in there,' she said.

'And a *big* one.'

'They must've built the lodge right on top of the spring,' Helen said.

'Didn't your guidebook tell you that?' Vivian asked.

'It wasn't a guidebook. It was something called, *The Omnibus of Great Unsolved Murders of the Twentieth Century.*'

'Should've known someone was murdered here,' Vivian muttered.

'That's what makes it interesting.'

'So what *is* a hot spring, anyway?' Finley asked.

With a shrug, Helen said, 'Water that's hot and comes up out of the ground.'

Abilene laughed. 'You're a walking encyclopedia.'

'I don't know. I'm not a geologist.'

'Are they something like those geysers at Yellowstone?' Finley asked.

'I don't suppose they shoot up,' Helen said. 'Nobody'd build a lodge on top, if they did.'

'Why don't we go in through here?' Cora suggested, scooting away from the edge of the pool and starting to pull off a shoe.

'We'd get wet, that's why not,' Vivian said.

'So?'

'It'll give you a chance to wash your hand,' Abilene pointed out.

'How do we know the water's clean?'

'It's natural spring water,' Helen said.

'From deep in the bosom of Mother Earth,' Abilene added. 'How can it not be clean?'

Vivian tilted her head sideways as if thinking about it. Then she said, 'Shouldn't we explore the rest of the lodge first?'

'I want to start by going right through there,' Cora said, and pointed at the archway. Barefoot, she stood up and pulled off her T-shirt. Then she reached behind her back and unhooked her bra.

'I think she's serious,' Abilene said, and began taking off her own shoes and socks.

Helen looked around. As if satisfied that no strangers were lurking about, watching, she started to strip.

'Hey, Fin,' Vivian said, 'why don't you and I go around to the front? We can meet them on the other side.'

'I don't think we should split up,' Abilene said.

'*I* don't think we should go wading into this place butt naked,' Vivian said. 'Somebody might be here.'

'Then keep your clothes on,' Cora said, stepping out of her shorts and panties.

'We haven't even got towels. Fin and I could go on to the car and pick up towels for everyone and . . .' She gave up on that suggestion when she glanced at Finley and saw the safari shirt come off.

'Just stay with us,' Cora said. 'What's the fun without a little risk?'

Following Cora's example, Abilene rolled up her shoes and socks inside her clothing. Helen did the same, but she left her bra and panties on. Finley, as usual wearing no bra or panties in the first place, made a bundle of her outfit. She tied it tight with her pink knee socks. 'Can somebody take this for me?' she asked. 'I've got my camera to contend with.'

Abilene held out her arms, and Finley tossed the bundle to her.

Cora, sitting on the edge of the pool, lowered her legs into the water. She looked up at Finley. 'Make sure you keep that thing off,' she said.

Finley grinned. 'Hey, how am I supposed to keep a video history of our adventures if I leave my camera off?'

'You wanta die?'

'Not particularly.'

'Let's have her tape us,' Abilene said. 'She can mail it to the Sigs.'

They all laughed at that. Even Vivian.

'Those poor sons of bitches,' Cora said, scooting forward and standing. The water came halfway up her thighs. 'They never knew what hit 'em.' She stepped forward and gasped as she dropped. When her feet met the bottom, the undersides of her breasts were touching the surface. 'I guess there's a ledge.' She shook her head and grinned while the others laughed.

'Should've gotten *that* on tape,' Finley said.

Leaning forward, Cora reached out and grabbed her bundle of clothes. Abilene stepped down onto the ledge and hopped off it. The water felt like a hot bath. Too hot for a day like this. While she picked up the bundles, Helen and Finley climbed in.

Vivian, still laughing, unbuttoned the front of her sundress, pulled it down and stepped out of it, being careful not to let it touch the granite under her feet.

'You're coming in after all?' Cora asked.

'No risk, no fun.'

'Atta girl.'

She clamped the dress against her side to keep it from falling, and had a tricky time removing her bra. Would've been a lot trickier, Abilene thought, except the flimsy red garment opened in front.

Grinning, they all watched the spectacle of Vivian hopping and teetering as she struggled to take off her shoes, socks and panties with one hand. Done, she allowed the shoes and socks to rest on the granite while she made a roll of her dress and underwear.

She entered the pool, then picked up the sock-stuffed shoes with her free hand. She held the shoes and bundled dress overhead.

'Now don't you dare let them touch,' Abilene warned.

'Yeah,' Finley said. 'Those shoes'll make mincemeat of your dress.'

Cora looked around as if to make sure nothing had been

left behind. Then she turned toward the archway. 'Want to go first?' she asked Helen.

'Oh, that's okay.'

Cora started forward, Vivian close behind her. Helen went after Vivian. Abilene, following her, glanced back. The camera rested on Finley's shoulder. Its tiny red light was off, so she wasn't taping.

'Move it along, Hickok,' she said with a grin.

Abilene turned away.

Cora, the small bundle of clothes perched atop her head and held steady with one hand, waded into the darkness of the lodge.

'Native bearers,' Finley said, 'following the Great White Hunter through unmapped regions of darkest Vermont.'

'Oomgowah,' Abilene said.

'Watch out for water snakes and crocodiles, ladies.'

'Very funny,' Helen said.

'There *might* be snakes,' Abilene said.

'And piranha,' Finley added. 'I think I feel a nibble now.'

The talk, though all in good fun, made Abilene uncomfortably aware of being naked in strange waters. With both hands busy holding the bundles overhead, she felt totally vulnerable. She half expected something squirmy to slide against her. As she followed Helen under the archway, she pressed her thighs together and clenched her buttocks and walked with short steps as if her knees were bound together.

Nobody's yelling, she told herself. Everything's probably fine.

But they aren't talking, either, she realized. All she could hear from inside the lodge was the soft sloshing of water.

Then she was through the archway.

Cora, Vivian and Helen had spread out. They were

wandering about in chest-high water, turning slowly, their heads swiveling and lifting. They looked like a trio of bizarre tourists gaping at a wonder.

Abilene waded forward. She heard Finley moving behind her. Then came the quiet hum of the camera. It sounded very loud in the stillness. But nobody looked around. Nobody objected.

Abilene began wandering about, moving generally toward the pool's far side as she turned and surveyed the place.

It reminded her strongly of indoor swimming pools she'd known in Illinois – at the Y, at the high school – before moving to California after her sophomore year. It had the same dank air, the same acoustics that intensified every sound so that even the soft lapping of the water seemed to echo.

But the pools she'd known had been twice the size of this one. They had never been hot. And they hadn't smelled like this. Instead of a chlorine odor, the air here smelled heavy with sulfur.

She supposed the smell might have been unbearable, but fresh air came in along with daylight from broken windows near the ceiling on two sides of the pool. One row of windows, which she'd noticed from outside while standing under the porch, stretched along the back wall. Another several windows crossed the shorter wall at the north end of the room. Those weren't sheltered by a porch, and narrow strips of sunlight, golden and swirling with dust motes, slanted down from them at sharp angles. The bright strips lighted only one corner of the pool, and the water at that corner glowed like honey.

'Did you get that?' she asked Finley, pointing.

'Yeah. Incredible.'

Their voices, though hushed, resounded off the walls and floors and ceiling.

Helen turned around. She looked very pleased with herself. 'All this was worth the trip, huh?'

'I sure think so,' Abilene said. 'It's fantastic down here.'

'It's pretty darn neat,' Vivian admitted.

'It'll be great at night,' Cora said.

'It'll be *dark* at night,' Vivian said, some of her enthusiasm gone. She tipped back her head and scanned the ceiling. 'If those lights worked . . .'

'It'll be better without them, anyway.'

'It'll be *real* creepy,' Helen said.

While she looked at the lights Vivian had mentioned, Abilene noticed that the ceiling tiles over the pool slanted upward at right angles to a rectangular gap in the center.

She hoped for a better view of the opening, so she made her way forward. As she neared the middle of the pool, currents began to rub the front of her body. The water's temperature seemed to rise. Then she stepped on something that wasn't granite. Iron bars? She lurched back to get away from them, and gazed down through the water.

Set in the floor of the pool, like a trapdoor, were cross-hatched bars a yard long. They covered a square opening. Below them, she saw an orifice surrounded by rough stone. The hole seemed to narrow, farther down. Then darkness obscured its depths.

She tested the strength of the bars with one foot, found them solid, and stepped onto the middle of them. Hot currents climbed her legs, fluttered against her groin and rump, caressed her belly and sides and back. She crouched enough to let the water massage her breasts.

A few moments later, she remembered why she'd come here to the middle of the pool. She tipped back her head. She was directly underneath the gap in the ceiling. It looked like a chimney that ran all the way to the roof. Far up there, she saw a gray smudge of daylight.

'What do you suppose that is?' Finley asked, coming up beside her.

'A vent?'

'Looks like it.'

'I guess you'd need something like that, you build a lodge on top of a hot spring.'

Finley tilted her camera high. 'You'd think snow and crap would fall in.'

'I think it's covered. You can't see sky, just a little light. The sides are probably open. The spring's right here, by the way.'

'Yeah?' Finley looked down.

'Here, stand on it.' Abilene moved aside.

Finley stepped onto the bars, and her eyes widened. 'Hey, now,' she said, 'I might just stay right here.'

'I'm getting out before I melt down to nothing.' Abilene left her there.

Cora, arriving at the far side, tossed her bundle of clothes to the tile floor. She boosted herself onto the edge, stood up and turned around. Feet apart, hands on hips, her skin shiny and dripping, she waited for the others.

And saw Finley, still on the grate, taping her.

'Damn it, Fin!'

'Hey, come on, you look great. Just like Tarzan.'

A corner of her mouth curled up. 'Like Tarzan?'

'Tarzan with tits,' Abilene said.

And Cora began bellowing like the apeman, drumming her chest with both fists, her breasts jumping with each blow, the wild outcry resounding through the room, deafening.

Abilene, aching to plug her ears, hurled her two bundles of

clothes past the edge of the pool. By the time she could poke fingertips into her ears, however, Cora had stopped.

Vivian, cringing, muttered, 'Jesus H. Christ.'

Finley, grinning, gave the side of her camera a fond pat and started forward. 'This is gonna be great.'

'Nobody better ever see it but us,' Cora warned.

'Nobody *ever* sees these tapes but us. You know that.'

'Yeah, but do I believe it?'

Abilene boosted herself out of the pool. She wondered if Finley was videotaping her. Probably. When she turned around, she saw the camera pointed her way, its red light on. 'You want me to hold that for you?' she asked. Crouching, she reached out. Finley waded forward and handed the camera to her.

Abilene reversed it, raised it to her eye, and taped Finley climbing out.

Helen laughed and clapped.

'Real cute, Hickok.'

'The historical record of our adventure wouldn't be complete without you in it,' Abilene said, grinning.

'Yeah yeah yeah.'

'Get this, Abby,' Cora said. She grabbed Finley by the shoulders and hurled her off the edge. The girl flew backward past Helen's side, arms and legs flapping, and smacked the water. Vivian, near the impact site, whirled and ducked away from the huge splash.

'I'd give her a six-point-two,' Abilene said. 'Sloppy entry.'

'Her form really sucked,' Cora said. 'Five-point-nine.'

Finley came up, puffed out a spray, and wiped her face. 'Hardy-har-har-har,' she said.

When she climbed out this time, she quickly dodged past Cora and hurried close to the wall – Abilene taping her.

'Okay, okay,' she said. 'Enough is enough.'

Abilene stopped recording. She held onto the camera while Finley used the sock-bound bundle of clothes to dry her face and arms. Then she handed over the camera.

Vivian, out of the water, stamped her feet and shook her arms. 'Now don't you wish we had towels?' she asked.

'We'll be dry pretty soon,' Cora said. 'Let's just check things out down here.'

'I don't want to go exploring in the raw.'

'Then get dressed.'

'I'm soaking.'

'Then don't.'

'I'm sure not,' Abilene said. She didn't want to get her clothes all wet. And she liked the feel of the air against her skin. Though warm and humid, it seemed almost cool after the heat of the pool.

'Just pretend you're at Hefner's,' Finley said, grinning at Vivian.

Cora wandered toward a recessed area beyond the pool's apron.

Following her, Abilene found a short hallway. Stairs in the center led upward. On each side of the staircase, and just in front of it, were doors with signs that read GENTS and LADIES. 'Must be dressing rooms,' she said.

'Let's take a look,' Cora said, and headed for the door marked LADIES.

'Forget that,' Finley said, and went for the GENTS to the right of the staircase.

'I doubt you'll find one in there,' Cora told her.

'I can always hope.'

'Boy, would he be surprised,' Helen said.

'Boy, would I jump on him.' Hinges squeaked as Finley

thrust open the door. She halted. 'Maybe not,' she muttered.

Except for faint gray light from the doorway, the room was totally dark.

'Must not have any windows,' Abilene said.

'Anybody here?' Finley called.

Abilene cringed. 'Don't do that.'

'Let's go,' Cora said. 'We can always come back when we've got flashlights with us.'

Finley shut the door, and they returned to the pool. They walked alongside it, heading for its south end. There, beyond a broad expanse of empty floor, a U-shaped bar extended out from the far wall. Behind the bar were rows of empty shelves for bottles. Around its front, a dozen swivel stools stood mounted to the floor. The clear space, Abilene thought, must've been for tables and chairs.

'They had a cocktail lounge down here?' she said.

'Neat,' Finley said.

'We'll have to bring our stuff down for Happy Hour,' Cora suggested.

Abilene grabbed the wooden back of a stool. She pushed it sideways. It resisted at first, then turned slowly, groaning on its rusted swivel.

The worn, varnished seat looked clean.

She rubbed a hand across it. Her hand looked pink, unsoiled. With a sinky feeling, she boosted herself onto the stool. The wood was slick under her wet rump.

While others climbed onto stools and Cora went around one side, Abilene looked at the polished granite floor in front of her. No leaves, no debris of any kind, no dirt or moss or mold. The walkway beside the pool also looked spotless. She remembered that, striding along it, she'd felt no grit under her feet.

'This place should not be so clean,' she said.

'It's that maid service,' Finley said.

'I mean it. This is serious.'

'The maid was here all right,' Cora said. 'And she left her mop and bucket.'

Abilene twisted her squawking stool around. Cora, behind the bar, raised a mop. Its thick, gray strands swayed from side to side.

Abilene leaned forward. One elbow on the bar top, she reached for the mophead. She fingered its strands. They were damp.

She met Cora's eyes.

Cora looked worried. 'The bucket's empty,' she said. 'But it's still wet inside.'

'It's humid in here,' Finley pointed out. 'Things probably never get dry.'

'Christ,' Vivian muttered.

'Hey, come on, guys,' Finley said. 'Don't get your balls in an uproar. We *know* somebody cleans the place. We'll just have to remember to leave a tip before we leave.'

'The upstairs wasn't like this,' Abilene told her. 'It was clean, but this is spotless. Someone really . . .'

'And there he is,' Cora said. From the tone of her voice, the look on her face, she wasn't joking.

Abilene swung her stool around in time to glimpse the head and bare shoulders of someone in the pool's archway. Shaggy dark hair, wide eyes, a young and startled face. In the next instant, the stranger vanished, lunging for the outside pool.

Chapter Six

'Oh my God!' Helen gasped.

'Shit!' Vivian blurted.

'Let's get him!' Cora snapped, scrambling over the bar top.

'Are you nuts? We're *naked*!'

Abilene was already dashing for the pool, her feet smacking the granite floor.

'Wait for me, Wild Bill!'

She dived. In midair, she heard Vivian yell, 'Don't go out there!'

She hit the hot water. It smacked the front of her body, stinging. Then it engulfed her. As she darted along beneath the surface, she wondered what the hell she was doing. Did she hope to catch the intruder? Not hardly.

She came up for air, heard others splashing behind her, saw the archway straight ahead. She swam through it and got to her feet. In spite of the porch's shade, the brightness hurt her eyes. Squinting, she spotted the kid.

A lean, tanned teenager in cut-off jeans, shirtless and barefoot, dashing straight across the overgrown rear lawn.

Finley and Cora came up beside Abilene. They were panting for air.

'I'm not going after him,' Abilene said.

'We'd never . . . catch him anyway.'

'And what would we do with him if we did?'

'I could think of something,' Finley gasped.

'I thought you'd sworn off guys.'

'*Is* it a he?' Cora asked.

'I think so,' Abilene said. 'Not sure.' As she spoke, she saw

326

the stranger rush into the forest at the far end of the grounds and disappear.

'What'd he wanta run away for?' Finley said.

'We probably scared the crap out of him.'

'I wonder how long he was there.'

'God only knows,' Abilene muttered.

'Long enough to enjoy the view,' Cora said. 'Vivian's probably thrilled to death.'

'She'll want to leave,' Abilene said.

'We'd better get back inside.' Cora turned around, slipped forward into the water, and swam through the archway. Abilene went next, followed by Finley.

Stroking her way across the inside pool, Abilene saw Vivian and Helen straight ahead. They had abandoned the bar area and returned to the place where they'd left their clothes. Vivian, already in her panties, shot her arms through the shoulder straps of her bra and pulled the flimsy red cups over her breasts and fastened the hooks. Helen was zipping the fly of her Bermuda shorts.

'Did you see him?' Vivian asked.

'Yeah,' Cora said, climbing out. 'He took off into the woods.'

'Was he alone?'

'Yeah.'

'With any luck,' Finley said, 'he's running home to fetch his older brothers.'

'God, this is awful! We've gotta get out of here.'

'Relax,' Cora said. 'I told you, he's gone. Besides, he's just a kid. He couldn't have been much older than sixteen, seventeen. What's he gonna do? There're five of us.'

'He got a free show, that's all,' Finley said. 'It's no big deal.'

'At least he didn't *videotape* us,' Abilene said.

She and Finley climbed from the pool.

'Maybe he's the one who cleans the place,' Helen said, buttoning her blouse.

'Probably is,' Cora agreed. 'And that'd mean we can stop worrying about the damn "maid service." I honestly don't see him as any threat.'

'Except he really might come back with someone,' Vivian said. 'If he is the one who cleans this place, he must live nearby. And if he's as young as you think, I bet he doesn't live alone. What if he tells his parents about us?'

'I've *got* brothers,' Finley said. 'At that kid's age, not one of them would've told Mom or Dad about spying on some naked gals. No way.'

'What would they do?' Helen asked.

'Depends. Joe's the kind of guy who'd keep it to himself and just enjoy the memories. Ray, though – he's more aggressive. He might sneak back, hoping for seconds. He might even bring along some friends. It'd be a big, exciting thing for them, but they wouldn't do anything. Just try to see us again.'

'We don't know anything about this kid,' Vivian said. 'There's no telling what he might do.'

'The way he ran,' Abilene said, 'I don't think he'll be back.'

Cora nodded. 'Let's just go on about our business. We've still gotta check out the rest of the lodge, and it's almost time for Happy Hour.'

'How do you know?' Abilene asked. None of them wore wristwatches.

'My thirst tells me.'

Vivian and Helen, finished dressing, waited while the others got into clothes. Abilene used her blouse to wipe herself dry. Finley put on her baggy shorts and shirt without drying, tucked her knee socks into the deep pockets, and slipped her bare feet into her shoes. Cora didn't bother to dry, either. She put on her T-shirt. It clung as if melting into her skin, but was long enough to hang like a very short dress. She stepped into her shoes and picked up the rest of her clothes.

She started to climb the stairs. Abilene took up the rear, carrying her damp blouse.

At the top of the stairs, they found themselves in a dimly lighted corridor beneath the stairway to the second floor. On the right, the hall led to the rear of the lodge where it met a windowed door to the porch. The far side of the corridor had two shut doors. There were no numbers on them, and Abilene guessed they might open into rooms that had been the living quarters of the lodge's owners. On the other side of the corridor, near its end, was a single door. Picturing the layout of the place, Abilene figured it must lead into the back of the kitchen.

She followed the others out from under the stairway and around it. There, just ahead and to the left, was the front door.

She felt very glad to see it.

Vivian walked straight toward it. As she stepped outside, Cora and Finley wandered into an open room to the right. A parlor or library, Abilene supposed. Much of it was walled with built-in, empty bookshelves. There was a fireplace, smaller than the one in the lobby, on its north side. At the front, some limbs from the huge branch on the porch reached through the shattered window.

Helen gave the room little more than a glance before going out to join Vivian. After a few moments, Abilene followed.

It was good to be outside. It was especially good to see the familiar car parked a few yards from the porch.

Vivian and Helen stood in the sunlight beside the car. They were talking softly. They turned their attention to Abilene as she trotted down the stairs.

'Do you want to leave?' Helen asked her.

Shrugging, she spread her blouse on the hood of the car to dry.

'Vivian does,' Helen said.

'I don't think it's safe.'

'It might not be,' Abilene admitted. 'I don't know.' She looked at Helen. 'I take it you'd rather stay.'

The girl's face twisted as if she were in misery. 'At least for *one* night, you know?'

'What've we got here, a mutiny?' Cora asked, striding out the front door.

'We're just discussing the situation,' Abilene said.

Cora trotted down the porch stairs, Finley close behind her.

'Shouldn't we just climb in the car and drive out of here?' Vivian asked. 'I'm not suggesting that we fly home right away, nothing like that. We could find a nice motel for tonight and maybe spend a few days driving around, exploring.'

'That kid really rattled you,' Cora said.

'This whole place rattles me. It gives me the creeps.'

'It's supposed to,' Helen pointed out. 'That's why I picked it.'

'I think it's neat,' Finley said, climbing onto the hood. She put down her camera, then sat beside Abilene's blouse, lay back, raised her knees and folded her hands under her head. 'We haven't seen the upstairs yet, either,' she added.

'I think we should stay at least tonight,' Helen said.

'It'll be really swift after dark,' Finley said, sounding as if she longed for nightfall.

'What about you?' Cora asked Abilene.

'It's Helen's choice. And we came all the way out here to see this place.' She thought about the lodge for a few moments. It *was* spooky. She didn't care for that aspect, but she realized that she did rather like the mysterious and nostalgic sides of its atmosphere – the wonder it inspired in her of peaceful times that were gone forever. Also, she knew she would hate to leave the hot spring behind. In the cool of the night, the caressing water would feel wonderful. 'I think we should stick around overnight,' she said. 'See how it goes.'

'Right on,' Finley said.

Abilene turned to Vivian, who was not looking happy. 'I know you're worried about that kid. We'll just have to keep our eyes open. If anything happens, we can hightail it.'

'Okay?' Cora asked.

Vivian groaned.

'We've stuck with you,' Helen reminded her. 'Like traipsing all over New York City. Not to mention that time with the Sigs.'

'Low blow,' Finley commented from the hood.

'Yeah,' Cora said. 'It's not like she owes any of us. She's done plenty.'

'We've *all* done plenty,' Abilene added.

'I've just got a bad feeling about this place.'

'We've all had bad feelings about some of the crap we've done,' Cora said. 'But we always stuck together.'

'And had a gas,' Finley said.

'And we're all still alive and kicking,' Helen said.

'Some kicking more than others,' Abilene put in.

Vivian nodded. 'Why don't we at least hoist a couple before we go back in?'

'Now you're talkin',' Finley said.

Cora squinted into the trees to the west. 'Looks to me like the sun's over the yardarm.'

Everyone but Finley went to the rear of the Wagoneer. Helen found the keys in her pocket and opened the tailgate. Cora climbed in, spent a while searching, then shoved the ice chest down past her feet. Abilene picked it up. Moments later, Cora crawled backward dragging the box of plastic glasses, liquor, mixes and snacks.

They carried the ice chest and box to the front of the car.

'Ah-ha!' Finley said. 'Goodies!' She scooted down off the hood and joined them.

Abilene opened the chest. Before leaving the motel that morning, they'd packed it to the brim with ice. Some had melted. But plenty of the ice remained – enough for tonight, at least.

They scooped up cubes with their glasses. Cora opened a bottle of pre-mixed margarita and poured some for each girl.

'To us,' she toasted.

'The daring young maids,' Finley added.

'On our flying trapeze?' Abilene said.

All five touched the rims of their glasses, and drank.

'Isn't this just the greatest?' Helen said.

'I wouldn't go that far,' Vivian said. 'The margarita sure hits the spot, though.'

'We really oughta be imbibing down at the bar,' Cora said.

'Too hot,' Abilene told her.

Finley climbed back onto the hood and sat with her feet on the bumper. Cora, following, looked over her shoulder. 'Do you mind if I sit on your blouse?' she asked Abilene.

'Help yourself,' Abilene said.

Cora dragged the blouse toward the front of the hood, then climbed up and sat on it.

'We oughta get good and polluted,' Vivian said, refilling her glass.

'So we can watch you throw up?' Cora asked.

Helen laughed. 'Just like she did in Hardin's office. Remember?'

'Good ol' Hardass,' Finley muttered.

Chapter Seven
Belmore Girls

Meredith Hardin, Dean of Women at Belmore University, chose the wrong time to throw a fit of shrieking indignation.

It was in May. Almost a full month of classes remained before the end of the semester, the start of summer break. The weather was warm, the air rich with moist and flowery aromas. The girls were restless.

Meredith Hardin also chose the wrong girl to crush.

The girl was Barbara Dixon, Finley's roommate.

Abilene returned to the dorm late from Benedict Park, where she'd spent more than an hour pressed between the trunk of a tree and the body of Robbie Baxter. Her back felt a little sore from the rubbing bark. Her face felt hot and raw from Robbie's whiskers and too much kissing. So did her breasts. Robbie was crazy about them. Since Abilene wouldn't allow him any liberties below her waist, they'd received the brunt of his attention. They'd been caressed, kissed, squeezed and sucked so much that they itched and burned.

Entering the room, she found it crowded with Helen, Finley, Cora and Vivian. 'What's going on?'

'You sure took long enough getting here,' Finley said.

'I was busy.'

'You look it.'

'Who took sandpaper to your mouth?' Cora asked.

Helen, laughing, said, 'Robbie ought to shave better.'

The sound of his name made Abilene's heart pound faster, warmed her and gave her a funny tightness in the throat. 'Yeah. Next time I go to the park with him, maybe I'll take my Lady Schick.'

'Did he pork ya?' Finley asked.

'Screw you. And no, he didn't.'

'What're you waiting for, Hell to freeze over?'

'Keep holding out,' Vivian advised her. 'Once they get it, they act like they own you.'

'I might like that. As long as it's Robbie.'

'Wooooo,' Finley said. 'The babe's hooked.'

'Anyway, what's everyone doing here? Just hanging around to interrogate me about Robbie, or what?'

'Yeah,' Finley said. 'Drop your pants for a cherry check.'

Helen giggled.

'In point of fact,' Cora said, 'we've been trying to conjure up some fun. Too damn dull around here. We haven't had a real blast since we nailed the Goddamn Sigs.'

'And that's ancient history,' Finley pointed out.

'We're trying to come up with an idea that's really *daring*,' Vivian said.

'Like what?' Abilene asked.

'Haven't figured it out, yet. But something to do with Hardass.'

'We want to *get* her,' Vivian said.

'I'm all for that.'

Until coming to Belmore, Abilene had been convinced that people like Meredith Hardin didn't actually exist in real life. The woman seemed too awful to be real – a caricature of prim bitchiness. Finding such types in the movies and on TV, and in the pages of melodramatic novels, her eyes had rolled skyward in disbelief. She'd pitied the poor writers responsible for creating characters so totally, unbelievably excessive in their evil, self-righteous, cold-blooded prudery. There simply *weren't* people like that.

Then she caught the Meredith Hardin show at Freshman Orientation.

The woman stepped up to the lectern and, even before she opened her mouth, the audience of noisy co-eds went silent. This was the Dean of Women. This was Bad News. This was a crone with a cruel face and eyes of ice – all the worse, it seemed to Abilene, because she was neither old nor ugly. She was dressed like a man in a tailored gray suit. Her white blouse was buttoned at the throat. Her face was pallid, her lips nearly as gray as her suit. Her red hair was pulled back tight and bundled into a knot behind her head. She wore no jewelry at all that Abilene could see.

When she began to speak, Abilene was surprised she didn't have a thick German accent.

Abilene could still remember bits and pieces of Hardin's 'welcoming' speech. 'As students at Belmore University, you will *always* conduct yourselves as ladies . . . Loose behavior will *not* be tolerated . . . You will attire yourselves at all times with appropriate modesty ... There will be no gutter language at this university ... The consumption of alcoholic beverages on campus is strictly forbidden ... Any and all infractions of what we deem to be proper and decent behavior shall be dealt with by yours truly. I am fair, but I am strict, as you shall no doubt come to appreciate.'

It might have been funny, but it wasn't.

As the direct result of Hardin's opening remarks, four freshman girls – including Abilene's initial roommate, immediately dropped out of Belmore. In the words of the roomy while she packed, 'There ain't room on this campus for me and that tight-ass cunt.'

'Hey now,' Abilene had said. 'Watch that gutter language.'

The girl had laughed, then added, 'She's probably a dyke, to boot.'

'Oh, don't say that. You're giving a bad name to the entire lesbian community.'

'She'll get you, you know.'

'Maybe I'll get her first.'

'Rotsa ruck.'

During the months following Orientation, Hardin had shown herself to be true to her words. She'd caught Vivian on the way to class wearing a tube top and mini-skirt, fixed her with an outraged glare, and demanded, 'Just *where* do you think you're going, young lady? I'll tell you precisely where you're going – back to your room where you'll change out of that sluttish costume and put on proper attire.' She'd once caught Helen chewing gum. 'Swallow that immediately, young lady. You look like an empty-headed cow masticating its cud.' And she'd once nabbed Abilene dressed in a sleeveless sweatshirt and cut-off jeans. 'This is a university, not a slum.' Abilene had politely explained that she was on her way to play basketball. 'Did you hear me request an excuse? No, I hardly think so. There is no excuse for slovenly attire – nor for backtalk. Am I understood?'

The woman was ridiculous. But a master of intimidation who seemed to revel in her talent for reducing girls to tears.

She'd failed to win tears from Vivian or Abilene, but Helen had wept in humiliation over the bovine reference. And yesterday Hardin had driven Barbara Dixon into mindless, blubbering hysteria.

Finley had found the girl in her room afterward, in such a state that she herself had tears in her eyes while she told the story to the others.

Barbara had been alone at a table in the student union, pouring a dollop of rum into her Pepsi just as Hardin walked in and spotted her. Hardin took the flask. Sniffed it. Said, 'Come with me.'

In her office, she'd raged at Barbara for an hour. She'd called the girl a 'drunken degenerate,' a 'social misfit,' a 'blight on Belmore University,' a 'filthy, booze-sucking slut.' On and on. And worse. She'd phoned Barbara's mother at home. She'd phoned Barbara's father at work. She'd ranted at them and explained that their delinquent daughter would be placed on probation. Finally, she'd concluded her show by emptying the flask onto Barbara's head.

After hearing the story from Finley, the girls had tried to cheer Barbara up. Without success. Today, she'd rented a car, packed all her belongings, and headed for her home in Seattle.

'What'll we do to her?' Abilene asked, sitting down on her bed between Finley and Vivian. 'It's gotta be something good.'

'Get her drunk,' Finley suggested. 'Strip her naked and leave her tied to a tree in the quad.'

'That'd be great,' Cora said.

Helen beamed.

'I don't think she's worth a prison term,' Vivian said.

'Yeah,' Abilene agreed. 'We've gotta come up with something realistic.'

'If it doesn't at least include kidnapping, assault and battery, it's too good for her,' Cora said.

Finley nodded. 'She oughta be gang-banged by a slobbering crowd of escapees from an insane asylum.'

'And that'd be too good for her,' Cora said.

'Yeah,' Abilene said. 'And it'd be cruel to the lunatics.'

'Besides,' Helen pointed out, 'she might enjoy it.'

'Let's get real, gals,' Vivian said. 'Come on. There must be *something* we can do that'll really nail her.'

Abilene nodded. 'Nothing we could go to jail for. Just something that'll piss her off so bad she'll go ape-shit.'

'We can't do that,' Vivian said after they'd finally hit upon a plan.

'*I* will,' Abilene assured her.

'I dare you.'

'*I* dare *you*.'

'Double dare you,' Finley added.

'Double dares go first,' Vivian said.

'You bet.'

The five of them dared and double-dared for a while. Nobody backed out.

'Then it's settled,' Cora finally said. 'Tomorrow we go for it.'

On the ground floor of the administration building that housed Meredith Hardin's office was the campus bookstore, which closed each weekday afternoon at five.

At ten minutes before five on Wednesday, the day after Barbara fled from the campus and her friends plotted conspiracy in Abilene's room, Finley led the bookstore clerk away from the counter to help her locate a textbook. Abilene and Helen rushed behind the counter, ducked into the stockroom, and hid themselves in the maze of file cabinets, shelves and stacked boxes.

A few minutes later, the clerk entered just long enough to turn off the stockroom's lights.

When she was gone, Helen nudged Abilene with her elbow and chuckled softly.

They waited in the darkness. After a while, Abilene removed her flashlight from the sack of food she'd brought along. She crept to the door and eased it open. She glanced around the silent, deserted bookstore. Then she reached down to the outside knob. She tried to twist it. The clerk had left it locked.

She shut the door and went back to Helen. 'Just like I thought,' she whispered. 'They keep it locked. I bet the custodians don't have a key, either. Not for the stockroom. Maybe not even for the bookstore.'

'So we're safe, right?'

'I think so.'

'Can we turn on the lights?'

'That'd be pushing it.'

Sitting cross-legged on the floor, they drank root beer by flashlight. They ate cheeseburgers and french fries. When they were done, they turned off their flashlights. They talked softly and waited.

Waited for ten o'clock.

According to Finley, who spent a lot of time wandering the campus at night, the custodial staff usually finished cleaning the administration building and left it before ten.

At ten, Abilene and Helen would leave the stockroom, sneak out of the bookstore, and open an outside door to let the other girls in.

At five after eight, however, Helen whispered, 'I've gotta go.'

'What?'

'All that root beer.'

'You're kidding.'

'I'm gonna explode.'

'Go in your cup.'

'Abbyyyyyy.'

'I mean it.'

'I can't. I need a toilet.'

'Oh, man. The custodians are probably in the building.'

'Please.'

'Okay. There's probably a john in the hallway. But be careful. If anybody spots you . . .'

'You're coming with me, aren't you?'

Abilene hadn't planned on it. Though she'd consumed as much root beer as Helen, she'd intended to either hold on until ten o'clock or use a cup.

'I don't want to go alone.' The pleading tone of her voice reminded Abilene of Helen's experience in the shower room at the start of the school year: the lights going off, the hand touching her.

'All right, I'll go with you. We'll take our flashlights.'

Abilene led the way. She inched open the door. The bookstore was dark except for a faint glow of lights coming in through the windows along one wall. Stepping out, she turned on her flashlight. As she walked around the counter, she heard the stockroom door bump shut. 'Crap.'

'What?'

'Did you unlock it?'

'Huh? Oh, no.'

'There goes our hideout.' She thought about the A & W bags and cups. No big deal. 'You didn't leave anything, did you? Other than the stuff from the A 'n Dub?'

'No. Did you?'

'Nope. Thank God.'

'They'll know we were in there.'

'They'll know someone was. No way to figure out who, though.'

'Can you get fingerprints off that stuff?'

'You can. But we aren't gonna murder anybody. I'm sure the cops wouldn't go to the trouble.'

'Sure hope not.'

Following the bright beam of her flashlight, Abilene went to the door of the bookstore. Then she shut off the light. She turned the knob and eased the door toward her.

The hallway was dark.

'Fantastic!' she whispered. Leaning into the hall, she looked both ways. The only lights came from the green glow of Exit signs at each end. She stepped out. 'Don't let it lock.'

'Got it.' Helen came into the hallway behind her. 'Maybe the janitors have already left.'

'They might be upstairs, I guess. But you'd think they'd light up the whole building if they were here.'

'Maybe they have Wednesdays off.'

'Or they haven't arrived yet. Come on. Let's make it quick.'

She and Helen hurried through the hallway, checking the doors with their flashlights. Near the center, they came to a door marked LADIES. Abilene pushed it open, and they entered the dark restroom. Helen rushed into the first stall, Abilene into the next.

341

As she shone her light on the toilet, a groan came from Helen.

'What?'

'No t-p,' Helen muttered, and rushed past her to the third stall.

Abilene's stall had a roll of paper. The toilet seat looked clean, but she didn't want to sit on it. Her dispenser of paper seat covers was empty. So, after latching the door and pulling down her pants, she squatted above the seat without touching it.

She was scared, trembling. She couldn't relax enough to go.

From the sounds she heard, Helen was having no such problem.

Then she heard the distant clamor of a closing door.

It sent ice sliding up her back. It sent her urine squirting into the toilet bowl.

'Oh, my God,' Helen murmured.

'Kill your light and be quiet,' Abilene warned. She switched off her own flashlight. But couldn't stop peeing, and neither could Helen. Though the splashing sounded awfully loud, she doubted that it could be heard from the hallway. If someone came into the restroom, though . . . 'Whatever you do,' she gasped, 'don't flush. Stand on the seat when you're done. And make it quick.'

'Do you think they're coming here?' Helen sounded ready to panic.

'Who knows?' She finished. She groped some toilet paper, dried, stood up straight, pulled up her panties and shorts, and climbed onto the seat. One hand held the flashlight. The other held the waistband of her loose shorts. She wished she had a spare hand to press against a wall of the stall; her perch on the seat felt too precarious for comfort.

This isn't such a hot idea, anyway, she thought. If it's the custodial staff, someone's bound to come in.

The restroom was certain to be a place they cleaned, and hiding in the stalls wouldn't do any good at all.

From beside her came a gasp. Then a heavy, thumping splash. 'Shit!'

'Shhhh.'

'Oh, yuck.' Splashing, dripping sounds. 'I stepped in it.'

'Shhhh.'

The restroom door sighed open, and the light came on.

'Go ahead to my office. I'll be along in a minute.'

Hardin!

'Yes, ma'am.'

We're dead, Abilene thought.

Footsteps approached, heels clacking on the tile floor. Abilene held her breath.

Hardin entered the first stall.

The one without toilet paper!

Abilene heard the latch of the door clack into place. Garments rustled. The toilet seat creaked quietly. A long honk of blowing gas resounded through the room. 'Fucking chili,' Hardin muttered.

Abilene, terrified, didn't even come close to laughing. She prayed that Helen felt the same way. If the girl should crack up now . . . but she didn't.

Then came a tinkling sound, another roar of chili thunder.

'Damn bitch,' Hardin said.

The girl she'd sent ahead to her office? Abilene wondered who she was, what she'd done. Must've been something damn serious for Hardin to be nailing her at night. Damn serious, like maybe wearing a short skirt.

This could ruin the whole plan, she thought.

343

And felt like an idiot for worrying about the plan.

You're doomed, and you're worried about the damn plan.

Any second now, Hardin would see that she had entered a stall with no toilet paper. Then, she'd come next door to try her luck.

Make a break for it now? While she's still sitting down, her door latched?

Run like hell?

What about Helen? The move to escape would take her by surprise. She had farther to go than Abilene. And she wasn't nearly so quick on her feet.

Abilene might make it, but Hardin was sure to throw open her door in time to spot Helen.

Then it was too late.

The latch of Hardin's door clattered. A quiet squeak announced the opening of her door.

Footsteps.

Oh God, oh God, no no no!

The sound of the footsteps receded.

Hardin was walking away!

Abilene heard the restroom door swing open. The lights went out. A moment later, the door bumped shut.

She stood motionless, gasping air that was rank with the aroma of used beans and onions. No sound came from Helen's stall.

After a while, she whispered, 'Are you all right?'

'My right foot isn't.'

Abilene laughed. Helen started to laugh.

'Did you hear what she said?' Abilene asked.

'Gutter language.'

'She didn't wipe, either.'

'She didn't flush.'

'Didn't even wash her hands.'

'What a hog!' Helen gasped.

'Thank God she's a hog. That's all that saved us.'

Abilene stepped down from the toilet seat. Flashlight clamped under one arm, she fastened her shorts, opened the door and stepped out of the stall.

A moment later, Helen came out. 'What'm I gonna do about my foot?'

Her right sock, sodden, drooped low around her ankle. Her tennis shoe looked soaked.

'It'll dry. Come on, let's get back to the bookstore.'

'You want to go ahead with it?'

'We've gone this far. We'll just have to make sure she's out of the building by ten.'

Abilene turned on her flashlight. She hurried for the restroom door. Helen followed, one shoe squelching.

Chapter Eight

'I may've puked,' Vivian said, 'but . . .'

'*May've?*' Helen interrupted.

'At least I didn't step in a toilet.'

'Ol' Yeller Foot,' Finley said from the hood of the car, and grinned into her drink.

'Viv was bombed when she blew her supper,' Cora pointed out. 'What's your excuse?'

'It was dark,' Helen said.

'And we were scared out of our wits,' Abilene said. 'I nearly fell in, myself.'

'It was the smell that made me lose it,' Vivian said.

'You shouldn't have been sniffing my shoe,' Helen told her.

'Yeah, well . . .' Vivian chuckled softly and took a sip of her drink.

'That was a hell of a night,' Cora said.

'We were a wild 'n crazy bunch.'

'What do you mean *were*, Hickok? Pass the bottle, huh?'

Abilene picked up the bottle of margarita mixture and wandered around, filling all the glasses. Only a bit remained. She chugged it, then returned the empty bottle to the box.

'Let's knock it off after this round,' Cora said. 'We've still gotta explore the second floor. Don't want to be falling down any stairs.'

'Have to stay sharp,' Finley said, 'in case we run into an ax-murderer.'

Helen took a gulp. 'Besides, this stuff is murdering my diet.'

'Ah, live it up,' Finley told her.

'Yeah,' Abilene said. 'What Frank doesn't know won't hurt him.'

'He'll know if I come back a blimp. He wasn't exactly overjoyed about me coming here in the first place.'

Finley laughed. 'What, was he afraid we'd corrupt you?'

'He thinks the whole thing's crazy. He *knows* you're all crazy.'

'Harris wanted to come along,' Abilene said.

'Should've let him,' Finley said. 'We could use a guy around here.'

'Sorry, I don't share.'

'Spoilsport.'

'He couldn't get away from his job, anyway.'

'God,' Cora said, 'let's not even think about letting guys come along. I mean, the whole idea's to get away and get wild.'

'We'd have to behave,' Helen said, and downed the rest of her drink.

'We'd have to wear clothes,' Cora added.

'Not necessarily,' Finley said.

'And they'd end up trying to run the whole show,' Vivian said. 'They'd be telling us what to do from the get-go. Who needs it?'

Cora nodded, scowling. 'That's for damn sure. And I don't know about Frank and Harris, but I know for sure Tony gets the hots for Viv every time he lays eyes on her.'

'No accounting for taste,' Finley said.

'If he was here, he'd be tripping all over himself staring at Miss Gorgeous.'

'It's you he married,' Abilene reminded her.

'Yeah, but look who he danced with at the reception.'

'You had a broken foot,' Vivian said.

'That's beside the point. Anyway, I just think it'd ruin everything if we let the guys come along on these things. Next thing you know, we'd be dragging along a herd of ankle-biters.'

'Anybody knocked up yet?' Finley asked.

'God forbid,' Cora said.

'Not yet,' Helen said.

'Me neither,' said Abilene.

Vivian shook her head.

'Well, that's something, anyway. We've gotta do this every year. No matter what. Just us. No husbands or loverboys, no kids. They stay home.'

'We oughta take a pledge,' Finley said.

'We don't need no steekin' pledges,' Abilene said. 'We should just be glad we're all here right now, and not worry about the future.'

'We've *gotta* worry about the future,' Cora said. 'Because you wanta know why? Because it's adventures like these that'll keep us from turning into a bunch of old ladies.'

'Speak for yourself,' Abilene said.

'I mean it. You've gotta do something a little nuts every once in a while. Get away from the job and paying bills and going to the grocery store and doing dishes and spending your nights in front of the boob-tube. You know? That stuff wears you down. Pretty soon, you forget what it's like to have fun.'

'I have plenty of fun.'

'Not like this, Hickok.'

'Yeah,' Helen said. 'When was the last time you were really scared?'

'About half an hour ago.'

'See?'

'I don't think you have to be scared to have fun.'

'It's the freedom,' Vivian said. 'That's the important thing. When we're off like this, we can do whatever we want. We don't have to watch ourselves, worry about what anyone might think of us. We've been through so much together. We can really be ourselves.'

'You babes sure get talky when you're looped,' Finley said.

'I'm not looped,' Vivian said.

'She's not looped,' Helen agreed. 'She hasn't puked yet.'

Cora stood on the bumper of the car, and jumped down. She plucked her clinging T-shirt away from her rump. 'Come on, let's stop gabbing and explore the rest of the lodge.'

Finley picked up her camera. She hopped to the ground.

Abilene drained her glass. She set it inside the box, then stepped to the hood of the car. While the others rid themselves of their glasses, she slipped into her blouse. It was dry except for a moist area in the center of its back where Cora's rump had been.

It cut off the pleasant feel of the breeze, making her uncomfortably warm, but she couldn't see herself entering the lodge without wearing it. She even buttoned it shut, as if the blouse would offer her some protection against the creepiness of the place.

Cora came around from the rear of the car with a flashlight.

'Should we all get 'em?' Helen asked.

'Ah, one's plenty. Gotta conserve our batteries.' She strode toward the lodge. Halfway up the porch stairs, she stopped and bent down to tie a shoelace. Her T-shirt slid up, baring her buttocks.

'Are you really going in like that?' Abilene asked.

'Sure. Why not?'

'Don't you feel . . . kind of vulnerable?'

'Just cool and free.'

'She'll be sorry,' Finley said, 'when a mouse runs up her leg.'

'Don't knock it till you've tried it.' She finished tying the lace, picked up her flashlight, and climbed the rest of the stairs.

Helen went after her, Abilene and Vivian following side by side, Finley taking up the rear.

Inside, the lodge seemed a little darker than before. And hotter. There was a sweet, dry aroma of decaying wood that Abilene hadn't noticed earlier. Maybe she noticed it now because of the margaritas; whenever she was a little juiced, her awareness of odors seemed to grow. A very nice side-effect if she happened to be somewhere that smelled good. Not so great, now. The odor was not unpleasant, in itself. But just as a strong scent of flowers sometimes reminded Abilene of funerals, the rotting wood smell sank her mood under sensations of deterioration and ruin.

That's probably the booze, too, she thought.

If she didn't watch herself, it could make her depressed.

And nervous.

Along with feeling gloomy because of the ancient, sad odor, she found herself more nervous than ever about being inside the lodge.

Like the others, she stopped in the foyer. She looked around, half expecting to glimpse the kid – or someone else – lurking in the lobby or hallway or parlor.

Or gazing down at them from the second floor balcony. The balcony, bordered by a wooden railing, extended from the top of the stairs to the far side of the lodge. She thought she might see a face between its balusters, but she didn't.

She saw nobody.

Cora walked to the foot of the stairway and started climbing. The others followed.

'That kid might've come back while we were out front,' Vivian whispered.

'*Anybody here?*' Finley shouted up the stairs.

'Stop it!'

Helen giggled.

At the top of the stairs, they turned to the right and wandered along the narrow balcony. Abilene walked close to its railing. The top rail was constructed of split logs, stripped of bark and varnished. It was dirty, so she kept her hands off it as she gazed over the side, down at the support beams and registration desk and lobby and lounge, the fireplace at the far end.

There wasn't much to see on the walled side of the balcony. Just three doors numbered 20, 22 and 24. Cora tried their knobs. All the doors were locked.

'You'd think somebody would've busted into these rooms by now,' she said, frowning at the last door.

''Tis passing strange,' Abilene said.

'Maybe Vermonters aren't vandals,' Vivian suggested.

'They sure did a job on those totem poles down by the road,' Abilene said. 'Could be, though, that not many people know this lodge is up here.'

'And those who do might be afraid of the place,' Helen said. 'If they live in the area, they know what happened here. They probably stay away, think it's haunted or something.'

'Get real,' Cora told her.

'Well, it's *possible*.'

'Sure didn't stop our friendly Peeping Tom,' Vivian said.

'If this place was in California,' Finley said, 'it'd be a shambles. Every door'd be broken open. There'd be bums living here.'

Cora tried the knob again.

'Why don't you go out and fetch your trusty credit card?' Finley said.

Helen giggled.

'There isn't even a transom for you to climb through,' Abilene said.

Cora gave her a smirk. 'We could always kick it open.'

'Might piss off the ghosts,' Finley said.

Vivian shook her head. 'We're not here to damage the place.'

'Let's keep looking around,' Abilene said. 'I'd be real

surprised if all the guest rooms are locked. Some of them are bound to be open.'

'Might as well find out.'

They returned to the top of the stairway. From there, a corridor led straight to the rear of the building. Its only light came from the windowed door at the far end. Except for the small area brightened by daylight, the length of the corridor was hidden in darkness.

Cora switched on her flashlight.

Abilene watched its beam slide along the floor, the walls. The hardwood floor looked clear. The walls seemed to have no doorways. But the light reached far enough to reveal openings on both sides of the corridor, about halfway down.

They started forward.

The floor creaked under their footsteps.

'Is this spooky enough for you?' Vivian asked.

'Neat,' Helen whispered.

'Hot,' Abilene said. The trapped, stuffy air wrapped her like an old blanket. She felt sweat popping from her skin, trickling down her face and neck, sliding between her breasts and down between her buttocks. It made her blouse cling. It made her panties stick to her rump. And it smelled heavy with the same sweetness of ancient wood that had bothered her in the lobby. There, the odor had been subtle. Here, it clogged her nostrils. She felt as if she were breathing mummy dust. 'Can't wait to get out of here,' she muttered.

'We're having fun,' Finley reminded her.

They halted at the intersection of the corridors. To the right and left, hallways led into total darkness.

Cora's flashlight probed to the left. She followed its beam, and the others went after her.

They came to closed doors on each side of the hallway.

Numbers 26 and 27. Cora tried the knobs, then went on, leading everyone deeper into the suffocating heat. They came to rooms 28 and 29. Neither door was open. Both were locked. The hallway beyond those doors stopped at a wall.

'We'll try the other way,' Cora said.

They turned around, walked back to the center corridor, and crossed it into another tunnel of darkness.

This one'll go on forever, Abilene thought.

This one ran parallel to the balcony, and had to be a third again as long as the hallway they'd just explored.

She was tempted to drop back and wait at the juncture where at least there was light at the end and the air was slightly better. But she didn't want to be alone. And she wanted to be with the others in case they should happen to find something.

So she stayed with them.

She was sticky and dripping. Her clothes felt glued to her skin. She decided that Cora had been smart, after all, to come in wearing nothing but a T-shirt.

When they stopped at the first pair of doors, she lifted the front of her blouse and mopped her face.

The door on the right was numbered 20. Just as she had expected, it was a rear door to the first room on the balcony.

Cora found it locked. The door on the left, 21, also failed to open. She muttered, 'Shit.'

'Is anybody else dying?' Abilene asked.

'Pussy,' Finley said.

'Getting a lot of good footage?'

'Bite me.'

'I don't think we're gonna find any of these unlocked,' Cora said, walking on. She stopped at the next set of doors, 22 and 23. She rattled their knobs.

'Try knocking,' Finley suggested.

'Don't,' Vivian whispered.

Chuckling, Cora rapped on the door of room 23.

A low, husky voice said, 'Who is it?' The voice came from Finley.

'Very cute,' Vivian said. 'You gals are a riot.'

Then from behind the door came a quick scratchy scurrying sound that sent cold prickles up Abilene's spine.

Silence.

'What *was* it?' Helen whispered.

'Let's get out of here,' Vivian said.

'Probably just a rat,' Finley said.

'Oh, shit.'

'It sounded awfully big,' Helen said.

'I *told* you not to knock on the door.'

'Good thing it *is* locked,' Abilene said.

'You know,' Finley said, 'rats are like nuns. They never travel alone.'

'Probably some right here in the hallway.'

'Ouch! What was that?'

'Piranha,' Cora muttered, sounding disgusted. 'You two oughta take your show on the road. Come on, let's check the rest of the doors.'

'Watch your step,' Finley suggested.

'It sounded too big for a rat,' Helen said, as if worried that they had missed her observation the first time around.

'Drop it, huh?' Cora stopped at the final pair of doors. She shone her flashlight on 24. But didn't reach for the knob.

Finley did. The door didn't open. Neither did 25.

'We're in luck,' Abilene said. 'Now, let's go find some fresh air.'

They hurried back to the center corridor and walked to

the light of the door. Cora snapped back a bolt. She twisted the knob and jerked the door. It creaked, crackled, and popped open with a squeal, fanning fresh air into the corridor.

'Careful,' Vivian warned.

Cora kept a foot on the threshold, held onto the jamb, and shoved her other foot against the floor of the balcony as if testing the safety of a frozen river. Satisfied that the floor was stable, she stepped out.

The others followed. Abilene stood motionless for a moment, relishing the soft breeze. She scanned the rear grounds. The entire area was now in shadow. Sunlight didn't even brush the tops of the trees. She looked for the kid, but didn't see him.

Then she went after Finley, who was sneaking along the balcony toward the window of room 23. The window was broken. 'See what made that noise,' Finley said. She leaned forward, peered into the room, then lurched back. 'Oh my God!'

'What?' Helen asked, looking as shocked as Finley.

'It's . . . too horrible!'

Abilene gazed through the window. Resting on its haunches near the center of the room, bushy tail curled in a question mark, sat a gray squirrel munching on a nut.

'What is it?' Helen asked.

Abilene shook her head. 'Don't look. It's hideous!'

Cora kept her distance and watched them, arms folded across her chest, legs tight together, face pale.

Vivian glanced into the room. 'Jesus!' she blurted. 'Thank God it didn't get us!'

Cora and Helen looked at each other. Helen sighed. Cora smirked.

'Yeah, right,' she said. 'Must be something monstrous like a kitten.'

'Close but no cigar,' Finley said.

Cora stepped up to the window, bent forward and peered in. 'Oh, he's darling. Look at those tiny feet. Isn't he cute?' Reaching up through the jagged opening, she released the window's lock.

'What are you doing?' Vivian asked.

'We want to explore a room, don't we?'

'Not that one,' Abilene said. 'The squirrel might be cute, but he probably isn't above biting someone.' As she spoke, she wandered father along the balcony. The window of the next room was also broken. 'We can try here.'

She looked through the shattered glass. The room was bare. She could see its decor. On both sides of the door were enclosures: a closet and a bathroom, she supposed.

'Any visitors?' Finley asked, coming up beside her.

'Looks okay.' She reached in and snapped the lock open. Then she shoved upward on a sash bar. The window didn't budge, so she pounded it with the heels of her hands. It skidded up. When it was open all the way, she swung up a foot and used the sole of her shoe to sweep away the shards of glass littering the inside sill. They clinked and shattered on the floor. And crunched under her shoes when she climbed into the room.

'Why don't you check around before we come in?' Cora said from the window.

'Alone?'

'Don't be a woos,' Finley called.

Abilene walked across the room. On her left was a sliding door. She rolled it open and found a shallow closet with a shelf and clothes bar. Nothing inside. Turning around, she stepped to the other door and opened it.

She saw a tile floor, a sink with a mirror above it, and nothing else but darkness.

'You can come in now, ladies. No boogeyman, rats, or other surprises.'

Chapter Nine
Belmore Girls

After their close brush with Hardin, Helen wanted to wash her foot. Abilene wouldn't let her, fearing that the sound of the faucet might carry through the building. So the girl merely dried her sneaker and sock as best she could with paper towels.

Then they returned to the student bookstore. Abilene twisted the lock button to secure the entrance. They hid among shelves near the back, and waited.

Nearly an hour passed before they heard the distant sound of a door thudding shut.

'Think that was Hardin?' Helen asked.

'Might've been the custodians showing up. Or just her poor victim leaving.' They waited longer. They heard no more sounds from anywhere in the building. At a quarter till ten, Abilene said, 'We'd better go out and scout around, make sure nobody's here.'

She led the way to the door, unlocked it in case they might need to return, then inched it open and looked into the dark hallway. 'Coast is clear,' she whispered, and stepped out.

On her way to the center staircase, she felt terribly exposed and vulnerable. She wanted to run. She walked slowly, instead, listening, setting her feet down softly. At last, she reached the stairs. Helen stayed close behind her as she climbed.

'What if Hardin hasn't left?' Helen whispered.

'Shhhhh.'

From the landing, Abilene could see that the second floor hallway was dark. She continued to the top, and peered around a corner to the right. Hardin's office was the third one down. No light came from under its door or shone through the open glass transom.

Stepping forward, she checked all the offices along the corridor. They were dark.

'Looks like we're in business,' she said.

Helen followed her to the door of Hardin's office.

Abilene tried the knob. 'Locked.'

'What did you expect?'

'I just hope she's not sitting in there, meditating in the dark.'

'Don't say that.'

'Go on down the hall.'

'Huh?'

'Go to the stairs. Get ready to make a run for it.'

'What're you gonna do?'

'Go.'

Helen hurried to the far end of the hall. When she stopped at the head of the stairs, Abilene knocked on Hardin's door.

No harsh voice demanded to know who was there.

Abilene willed herself to hear the slightest sound from inside the office: the creak of a chair, a footstep, breathing, a stir of fabric. She heard nothing. In spite of the silence, she half expected the door to fly open in front of her face, Hardin to reach out and grab her. She ached to bolt.

She wondered what she was doing here in the first place.

Risking expulsion – or worse.

She could've been safe, right now, back at the dorm. Even better, she could've been in the park making out with Robbie.

Instead, she was on this crazy mission. Not really to avenge Barbara, though that was part of it. The real purpose was simply to do something wild for the fun of it.

This is the last time I get myself into something like this, she told herself. I don't care if the others think I'm a chicken. I don't care who dares who.

Madness.

Then she realized that nothing had happened in response to her knock.

She hurried down the hall and joined Helen at the top of the stairs.

'Are you out of your gourd?' Helen asked.

'We both are. But I had to make sure she wasn't there, didn't I? Come on.' They trotted downstairs and stopped at the double doors leading outside. Abilene checked her wristwatch. Five till ten. 'Maybe they're early,' she said. She pushed one of the horizontal bars and eased the door open.

Finley, sitting on a bench in the darkness under an oak tree, raised a hand in greeting. She stood and picked up her video camera. A few strides took her to the end of the bench. Facing the wooded lawn that bordered the campus, she swung an arm overhead.

Moments later, Cora and Vivian appeared on one of the walkways. They were each carrying a grocery sack. They met up with Finley and the three of them, glancing this way and that, hurried to the stoop of the administration building. They rushed up the concrete stairs. The moment they were inside, Abilene pulled the door shut.

'How'd it go?' Cora whispered.

'Hardin showed up.'

'Christ,' Vivian muttered.

'Yeah, we were . . .'

'Tell us later,' Cora said. 'Let's get into her office first. Nobody's in the building, I take it?'

'We don't think so. The custodians never did show up.' Turning to Finley, she said, 'They were supposed to be in and out by ten, remember?'

'I'm not an *expert* on their schedule. But they're in Waller right now.'

Waller Hall was the science building on the other side of the campus.

'As long as they aren't here,' Cora said, and started up the stairs.

'We'd better keep an eye out for them,' Abilene warned.

'How many are there?' Helen asked.

'Just two who come here.'

'That's not so bad,' Cora said.

'It only takes one to spot us and we're dead,' Abilene said.

They stopped in front of Hardin's office door. Cora set her bag on the floor. 'Give me some light.'

Abilene switched on her flashlight and aimed it into the sack. Cora's denim purse was there among bottles and plastic bags of snacks. Crouching, the girl opened it. She took out a credit card.

'This oughta be good,' Finley said.

Card in hand, Cora tried to loid the lock. After a while, she muttered, 'Shit. It always works in the movies.'

'This ain't the movies,' Finley pointed out.

'How'll we get in?' Helen asked.

'Maybe this is our cue to quit,' Vivian suggested.

'No way,' Cora said. 'I had to shell out twenty bucks to get that guy to buy the booze.'

'We could always drink it in the comfort and safety of the dorm,' Abilene said.

'We're gonna get in if I have to kick the fucking door down.'

'One of us might be able to climb in through that,' Finley said, pointing at the open transom above the door.

Cora stared at it. 'Yeah. You're the smallest.'

'You're the jock.'

'Cora's ass might get stuck,' Vivian said.

'Screw you.' With that, Cora put away her credit card and purse. 'Give me a boost.'

Abilene and Helen made stirrups of their hands. They squatted. Cora stepped aboard. They lifted while Vivian and Finley shoved at her rump. Cora pulled herself up by the sill. In seconds, her head and arms were through the gap. She squirmed. The girls thrust her higher. 'Yeeow!'

'What?' Abilene asked.

'My tits. Finley, you bitch, you could've gotten through easy.'

'Me, too,' Vivian said. 'But you're the fearless leader.'

'Everyone let go of me.'

The girls stepped back. Kicking, writhing, groaning, Cora squeezed her torso through the space beneath the window. Then she went motionless, apparently resting before the final assault. Her legs were bent, knees braced against the top of the door, feet up. Her rump did look larger than the gap.

'Here comes the hard part,' Vivian said.

'Screw all of ya,' came Cora's muffled voice.

She kicked her legs, twisted, squirmed, lurched, growled. Her rump made it through the transom. Her shorts didn't. As she fell out of sight behind the door, the gym shorts travelled down to her ankles where they were snagged by a latch at the bottom of the transom and plucked from her disappearing shoes.

Helen giggled.

Inside the office, Cora thudded.

Vivian jumped. She grabbed the shorts, gave them a flip, and freed them.

Muttering a string of curses, Cora opened the door.

'Lost something,' Vivian said, and handed over the shorts.

Cora put them on. She and Vivian picked up the grocery bags, and everyone entered the office. Abilene shut the door after them.

They walked past the secretary's desk, through a doorway into Hardin's office. Abilene shut that door, too. Cora flicked a light switch, and overhead fluorescents blinked on.

'Hey!' Helen protested.

'It's okay,' Cora said, nodding toward the closed blinds.

'Light'll still get through,' Abilene said.

'Not much. Besides, we're on the second floor. Nobody'll notice.'

'And I can't record the event for posterity if we don't have the lights on,' Finley said. She lifted her camera and began to tape.

'That better not fall into the wrong hands,' Cora warned.

'Nobody'll ever see it but us.'

Cora and Vivian set their sacks on Hardin's desk. They removed bags of potato chips and corn chips, a stack of plastic glasses, two bottles of tequila, two cartons of lemonade, and a clear plastic bag full of ice cubes. As they began to prepare drinks, Abilene looked around the office.

In front of the big desk was a single armchair with brown

vinyl upholstery. The hot seat, she thought. Probably where Barbara was sitting when Hardin dumped the rum on her head. Some must've gotten on the carpet. Sure enough, the old gray carpet was stained around the chair. More than a little rum, Abilene guessed, had been spilled there.

A couple of straight-backed chairs stood just inside the door. There were bookshelves against two walls, filing cabinets in one corner. The room reminded her of other campus offices she had seen: cluttered with books, pamphlets, magazines, stacks of paperwork. Only the top of Hardin's desk was tidy, bare except for the telephone, in and out baskets, a Rolodex and a pen set – and the items brought in by Cora and Vivian.

Soon, all five glasses were fully loaded with ice, lemonade and tequila. 'Help yourselves, ladies,' Cora said. She took one, went around to the rear of the desk, sat in a swivel chair and put her feet up.

The others lifted their glasses. They waited while Helen finished breaking into a bag of potato chips. When she finished and picked up the last glass, Cora raised hers and toasted, 'To us.'

'More guts than brains,' Abilene added.

'That's for sure,' Vivian said.

'Daring young maids,' said Finley.

'Can't believe we're doing this,' Helen said.

Then they drank.

Vivian made a face. 'Yuh! This stuff is strong.'

Abilene hadn't watched the preparation of the drinks. From the taste of hers, however, she suspected that her tequila had been flavored by a splash of lemonade.

'Yum yum,' Finley said.

'So Hardass was in here tonight?' Cora asked.

'Yeah,' Abilene said. 'And she nearly caught us.'

While everyone sipped their drinks and munched chips, she told the story of their trip to the restroom.

'You *stepped* in the toilet?' Cora blurted, laughing.

'It was dark,' Helen explained.

'Gross,' said Vivian.

'I wondered what that smell was,' Finley said.

'So anyway . . .' and Abilene went on. They all cracked up when she told of Hardin's fart. 'And she said, "Fuckin' chili." '

'You're making that up,' Vivian protested.

'No lie. That's just what she said. Helen heard her.'

'Yeah, that's what she said.'

'And you should've *smelled* that sucker!'

'Hardin didn't say "fuck". Not Hardin.'

'Did, too.'

'I always knew she was a fraud,' Finley said. 'Nobody can be as uptight as she puts on.'

'She called that gal a bitch, too.'

'Wonder who it was,' Cora said.

'Wonder what Hardin did to her,' Finley said. 'Pretty weird, bringing someone up here at night.'

'Maybe it was her girlfriend,' Helen suggested.

'Yeah, brought her up here to mess around.'

'Come on,' Abilene said. 'She has a house or apartment or something. Why would she bring anyone here? Probably just some poor slob she caught chewing gum.'

'Pour some more,' Cora said.

Finley refilled the glasses. With ice, a lot of tequila, and a dab of lemonade.

Already, Abilene's cheeks were feeling a trifle numb. 'We're gonna get juiced,' she warned.

'That's the point, Hickok.'

'Hickok?' Abilene asked.

'You know, Wild Bill. James Butler. The guy that cleaned up Abilene.'

'He didn't clean up me.'

'You sure know your history,' Vivian said, grinning crookedly at Finley.

'I'm a whizz kid.'

'Speaking of whizz,' Helen said, 'Hardin didn't have any paper in her stall.'

'I figured she was gonna come over to mine,' Abilene said, 'and that'd be it. But she didn't. She didn't wipe.'

'You lie.'

'Or flush,' Helen added.

'Or wash her hands.'

'A real hog.'

'A bitch,' Finley said. 'Maybe she licked herself clean.'

'Disgusting!' Vivian blurted.

'And she wants *us* to be proper young ladies,' Cora said.

'Which we are,' Finley said. She reached into one of the bags and lifted out a stack of magazines. She passed some of them around.

Abilene set down her drink and leafed through the magazine Finley had given her. Its pages featured photographs of naked men. They had oiled, shiny skin. They had bulging muscles. They had big penises.

Helen stepped closer and looked. 'Wow,' she said. 'Wanta trade?'

Helen's magazine showed women posing with their legs spread wide. They were licking their lips, caressing themselves. Many of them had no pubic hair. One had a fingertip buried in her vagina. Some of the photos showed two or three women together, biting and squeezing and licking each other.

'Raunchy stuff,' Vivian commented.

'Terrific,' said Cora. 'Look at the schlong on this guy.' She turned her magazine around and showed them a full-page picture.

'I wouldn't let him near me with a ten-foot pole,' Abilene said.

'That *is* a ten-foot pole,' Finley remarked, laughing. Then she dug into the sack and pulled out some rolls of tape. 'Enough ogling the bods,' she said. 'Let's get to work.'

They filled their glasses again. Laughing, sipping, sharing their discoveries of particularly outlandish photos, making return trips to the desk for chips and refills, they spent the next twenty minutes tearing pages from the magazines and taping them all over Hardin's office. They taped pictures to the sides of the desk, to the chairs, to the door and walls and filing cabinets and bookshelves, to the window blinds. Cora, standing atop the desk, even papered a portion of the ceiling.

'I thing thas enough,' Vivian finally said. She tossed the tattered remains of a magazine onto the desk and turned around slowly, admiring their work.

Turning around did it.

Her face went ashen and slack. She staggered backward, waving her arms. 'Oh my God,' she muttered. Her rump hit the floor. Groaning, she lay down. 'Spinning,' she said.

Helen crouched beside her. 'Are you . . . ?'

'Oh my Gah . . .' Vivian flipped over, thrust herself to her hands and knees, and vomited.

'Gross out!' Finley called, and rushed for her camera.

Before she could lift it off the desk, Cora grabbed it. 'Leave her in peace.'

Vivian finished, and crawled away from the mess she'd made on the carpet.

Abilene patted her back. 'Are you okay?'

She moaned.

'We'd better get out of here.' Abilene and Helen helped the girl to her feet. 'Can you walk?'

'Yeah, yeah. I'm ogay.'

'Let's go.'

They waited for Cora to finish writing something on a sheet of letterhead she'd taken from Hardin's desk.

Then they followed her into the secretary's office, turning off Hardin's lights and closing her door. Leaving behind the grocery sacks, empty glasses and bottles and chip bags, a swollen plastic bag of melting ice cubes, torn magazines, the vast photo gallery of naked men and women, and a puddle of vomit.

To the outside of Hardin's door, Cora taped the note. Abilene lit it with her flashlight. In bold printing, it read, KEEP OUT. THIS MEANS EVERYONE, CUSTODIANS INCLUDED. I WILL NOT HAVE MY SANCTUARY VIOLATED. Scribbled beneath the message was: M. Hardin, Dean of Women.

'Give me that,' Cora said.

Abilene handed the flashlight to her. 'What are you doing?'

'You'll see.' She stepped behind the secretary's desk. She shone the bright beam on the Rolodex. Flipped through the cards. 'Here we are.'

She picked up the phone and tapped in a series of numbers.

'Oh my God,' Vivian mumbled.

'You're not!' Abilene gasped.

Finley started to laugh.

Helen groaned.

'Hello?' Cora said into the phone. Making her voice low and husky. 'Never mind who this is, you tight-ass bitch. I'm calling to give you a friendly warning. Stop eatin' all that fuckin' chili. The more you eat, the more you toot. Bye-bye for now.'

They were on their way downstairs when a door clamored.

Abilene's stomach dropped. Her heart thundered. Vivian clung to her, and she could feel the girl shaking.

They all stood motionless.

Heard footsteps, men talking loudly in Spanish.

Slowly, the sounds faded.

Abilene let out her breath.

Cora crept down the rest of the stairs and peeked into the corridor. The others waited. At last, she waved them to follow.

She held the door open for them and eased it silently shut when they were out.

All the way to the sidewalk at the border of the campus, Abilene glanced around, terrified of being spotted. But she saw no one.

'We dood it,' Finley said.

Afterward, they spent a lot of time laughing about their adventure. And more time worrying. Abilene half expected Hardin to order the entire student body fingerprinted.

But it never happened.

Word never leaked out about what had happened to Hardin's office.

At first, they wondered if the custodians had entered the office in spite of the note. Maybe they couldn't read English. Maybe they simply ignored the message, entered, and cleaned up everything.

But the next afternoon, they saw Hardin in the student union. She sat alone at a table, sipping coffee, glaring at everyone, studying faces.

While she was busy eyeing a trio of laughing jocks, Finley taped her.

'I bet she thinks guys did it,' Helen whispered.

'Thinks gals wouldn't have the nerve,' Cora said.

'What a sexist,' Vivian said.

Still glowering at the boys, Hardin lifted a hand. With her thumb and forefinger, she stroked her thin lower lip.

Abilene grinned. 'I wonder when was the last time she washed her hands.'

Chapter Ten

It was Abilene's idea that they move the Wagoneer to the side of the lodge, where it would be out of sight in case anyone should drive up from the road. Cops, teenagers looking for a place to make out, *anyone* might come along. It just wouldn't be smart to give away their presence by leaving the car out front.

The others agreed. But Cora suggested they unload it first.

'I don't think we should,' Abilene said. 'Why don't we leave everything in the car – use it like a base camp?'

'That's a lot of trouble,' Cora said.

'What if we have to make a quick getaway?'

'You worry too much.'

'We've already had one visitor,' Vivian said.

'If we need to take off fast,' Abilene continued, 'we don't want to be messing around with our luggage.'

'Or leaving it behind,' Vivian said.

'Why don't we keep the car packed and ready to roll? Just take in whatever we really need.'

'Makes sense to me,' Finley said.

'So what do we do,' Cora asked, 'troop back and forth to the car every time we want to change clothes?'

'That's the general idea.'

'Sheesh.' She picked up her bundle of clothes.

After stowing the ice chest and the box of drinks and snacks in the rear of the Wagoneer, they all climbed in. Helen drove to the north end of the lodge. There, the lane of cracked concrete slanted downward.

As Helen steered toward the slope, Cora said, 'Hold it. Everyone's so worried about quick escapes, maybe you oughta go down tail first.'

'Good idea,' Abilene said.

Helen moaned as if she didn't care much for the plan. But she swung away from the slope, drove forward to the edge of the pavement, then slowly backed her way down past the end of the porch, past the corner of the lodge.

'That's good enough,' Cora said.

She set the emergency brake, shifted to Park, and killed the engine.

They had a hard time pushing open their doors. Once they were out, gravity dropped the doors shut.

Vivian tugged hers open again, apparently just to see if she could. From the look on her face, it wasn't easy. 'Oh, yeah,' she muttered. 'This'll be great for speedy getaways. One of us could lose a foot.'

'At least it's hidden,' Abilene said.

They lurched downhill to the rear of the car. Beyond it, Abilene saw the rows of windows that had lighted one corner of the inside pool in such a grand fashion. She could see the ends of both porches. And the north side of the grounds, including the swimming pool with its diving boards and slide. She gazed along the edge of the forest. She saw nobody.

Helen opened the tailgate.

'I don't know about you guys,' Finley said, 'but I gotta take a leak.'

'Me, too,' Abilene said.

'Maybe we should all take care of it,' Vivian suggested.

Helen crawled into the car. She came out with a roll of toilet paper. She tore off strips and handed them around.

Abilene held up a hand as if refusing. 'I'll just use the Hardin method,' she said.

'Hog!'

Laughing, she took the offered paper.

They wandered into the woods, fanned out, and returned to the car when they were done.

'Okay,' Abilene said. 'Let's get to it.'

'And what will we be allowed to take with us?' Cora asked.

'Dinner and the stove,' Helen said.

'The booze,' Finley added.

'Flashlights,' Abilene said. 'And the lantern. It'll be dark before long.'

'If we don't hurry,' Vivian said, 'we'll be *cooking* in the dark.'

Leaning against the side of the car, Cora stepped into her panties and shorts. She joined the others at the rear, tossed her socks and bra toward the back seat, and helped with the unloading.

'Where do we want to make dinner?' Abilene asked.

'In the kitchen?' Finley said.

'Oh, right.'

'This kind of stove isn't safe to use indoors,' Helen pointed out.

'Maybe we should cook out front on the driveway,' Vivian said. 'The back's too exposed, you know? And that's where the kid went.'

'You and the kid,' Cora muttered. 'My God, we just moved the car so it couldn't be seen from the front, and you want to make supper there?'

'I don't think it would hurt to cook inside,' Abilene said. 'With so many broken windows, there isn't much danger of the fumes getting us.'

Finley nodded. 'Yeah. Let's do it civilized indoors.'

They carried the boxes and equipment up the slope and entered the lodge by its front door. The faint light from the windows left the lobby in deep gloom. They put down their loads. Cora crouched over the Coleman lantern. Soon, its gas was hissing loudly, its twin mantles glaring behind the glass chimney. By the stark pale brightness of the lantern, they lit the gas stove and prepared a simple dinner of hot dogs.

They sat on the floor in a circle, sipping margaritas as they ate the franks.

'A good, healthy meal,' Vivian said.

'At least it was easy,' Abilene said. 'Sometimes, I think I spend half my life cooking.'

'The other half doing dishes,' Helen added.

'Doesn't Harris help out?' Cora asked. 'Tony and I take turns with all the chores.'

'Both of you work, though,' Abilene said.

'Going for a Ph.D. isn't work?'

'I'm home a lot. He doesn't get in till about six. I like to have something nice waiting for him.'

'I do all the cooking, too,' Helen said.

'Whatever happened to women's lib?' Cora asked.

'The guys who go in for it are all a bunch of wooses,' Finley said.

'You saying Tony's a woos?'

'Hell, you'd probably beat him up if he gave you any crap about sharing chores.'

'That's a good one,' Abilene said. Tony, a physical education teacher and football coach at the same high school where Cora taught girls' PE and coached basketball, outweighed her by at least fifty pounds. As strong as Cora was, a fight between the two would be no contest.

'He never gives me any trouble,' Cora said. 'He likes to cook.'

'We should've brought him along,' Helen said.

'If you didn't want to spend your life cooking,' Finley told her, 'you shouldn't have gotten married.'

'Don't you eat?' Helen asked.

'Not at home, that's for sure. Hardly ever, anyway. I usually have a big lunch at the studio or on location – whatever. Then I go somewhere for Happy Hour. The places I go, you get all sorts of free food with your drinks. Potato skins, buffalo wings, meatballs, all that good stuff.'

'You have that instead of dinner?' Helen asked, grinning.

'Hey, it's great. And I usually go out with guys a few times a week.'

'Anyone special?' Abilene asked.

Finley grinned. 'They're all special.'

'You know what I mean.'

'I like variety,' she said, and chomped down on her hot dog.

'But wouldn't you like to settle down and get married, have kids?'

'Barf,' she said through her hot dog. 'Who needs it?'

'Right on,' Cora said. 'The beginning of the end.'

'Is not,' Abilene said.

'Are you telling me you *like* being tied down?'

'I'm not "tied down." '

'Yeah, right.'

'My God, Cora, you've got a good job. Tony's a terrific guy . . .'

'He *cooks* for you,' Helen pointed out.

'What's the problem?' Abilene asked.

'It's all a big bore, that's the problem. I mean, don't get me wrong. I love Tony. We get along great. We do stuff on our time off.' She shook her head. 'It just isn't enough. Where's the excitement, you know?'

'That's what we're here for,' Finley told her.

'Exactly.'

'You've just got it too good,' Vivian said. 'You have every-thing a woman could want . . .'

'Except kids,' Abilene put in.

'Oh, spare me. That's just what I'd need. Rug rats.'

'I'm serious,' Vivian went on. 'If you think life's so boring, it's only because you don't have any serious problems.'

'Or serious ambition,' Abilene added.

'Oh, give me a break.'

'Maybe you need some kind of goal in life,' Abilene said.

'What's yours?' Helen asked.

'Yeah, Hickok. Planning to syndicate an advice column?'

'I'm going to finish my Ph.D. and get a job at a nice university somewhere . . .'

'Like Belmore?' Helen asked.

'Anyplace that'll take me. Harris has already agreed that

he'll go wherever I can find a position. And once I've got tenure, I'll have a kid.'

'You've got it all mapped out,' Cora said, sounding a little disgusted.

'I know what I want. And I'm sure not bored with my life.'

'Well, good for you.'

Vivian sighed. 'Geez, Cora, you just don't know how good you've got it.'

'Want to trade?'

'You betcha.'

'Tony'd love that.'

Helen stared at Vivian, frowning. 'Are you kidding? Why on earth would *you* want to trade with anyone? My God, you've gotta be joking.'

'Oh, yeah. I've got the world on a string.' She set down the uneaten remains of her hot dog, and raised her left hand toward Helen. 'What do you think of my lovely ring?'

Her hand was bare.

'What ring?'

'That's the point.'

'You're upset because you're not married?' Helen sounded astonished.

'Wouldn't you be? God, I'm twenty-five.'

'Enjoy your freedom while you've got it,' Cora told her.

'It isn't freedom, it's loneliness.'

'You could take your pick of men,' Helen said. 'I mean, look at you. You're . . . stunning.'

'It's not all it's cracked up to be.'

'I'm gonna start weeping,' Finley said. 'It must be so tough on you, being gorgeous.'

'You'll never know,' Abilene told her.

'You're no cover girl, yourself, Hickok.'

'Guys treat me funny,' Vivian said. 'You've all seen how they act. It's like I'm not a person. Hell, look at the stunt those Sigs pulled.'

'Look at the stunt *we* pulled,' Finley said.

'Man, oh man.' Cora grinned as she shook her head.

'They do act strange around her,' Abilene said.

'They do, and it's . . . I'm tired of it. I'm really tired of it. All I ever attract are weirdos and slick bastards who think they're God's gift to women. All the normal, nice guys just run the other way. They don't even give me a chance. It's like they're scared of me.'

'If it bothers you so much,' Finley said, 'put on a hundred pounds.'

'I've thought about it.'

'Are you kidding?' Abilene said.

'There'd go your career,' Cora said.

'Hey, she could model tents.'

'If you think you've got troubles now,' Helen said, 'just try being a tub.' With a glance at Finley, she added, 'You get stuff like tent jokes. You get people crapping on you from every direction.'

'Geez,' Finley said, 'I didn't mean anything.'

'Yeah. They never do.'

'At least you've got a man, Helen.'

'Yeah, Viv, I sure do. And he never lets up on me. All I ever hear about is how fat and gross I am. If I looked like you . . . I'd be the happiest person in the world.'

'I doubt it.'

'Has anybody ever called you "Porky"? How would you like to have a husband who won't take you out of the house because he's ashamed to be seen with you?' Helen's voice began to tremble. 'How would you like a husband who won't even sleep in the same bed because he says you might roll over and squish him?'

'Jesus H. Christ,' Finley muttered.

Abilene felt sick.

'Does Frank really act that way?' Vivian asked.

'The bastard,' Cora said.

Starting to sob, Helen stammered, 'He . . . he says . . . says I'm repulsive.'

'He's the repulsive one,' Cora snapped. 'Why'd the bastard marry you if he felt that way?'

'I don't know. I wasn't so . . . heavy when we started going together.'

'You were never exactly svelte,' Finley said.

'But I got bigger. After we were married. If you wanta know the truth, I think he was . . . mostly interested in my money.'

'You think he married you because of your inheritance?' Abilene asked.

Helen nodded, sniffed, and wiped her nose. 'He just . . . pretended to love me.'

'You don't know that for sure,' Vivian said.

'No. But . . . he doesn't love me. Not any more. Probably never did. If he loved me, it shouldn't have made any difference when I . . . put on more weight. I think he just got tired of faking it. He *moooos* at me. Like I'm a cow.'

'Bastard,' Cora said.

'You oughta dump him,' Finley suggested.

'Oh, sure.'

'I mean it.'

'Yeah,' Cora said. 'If somebody treated me like that . . .'

'I don't wanta . . . be alone.'

'There are other men,' Abilene told her.

'Oh, sure. Not when you look like me.'

Abilene reached out and rubbed her shoulder. 'Hey, there are plenty of guys out there. They're not all creeps.'

'Only ninety per cent of them,' Vivian said.

'Those aren't such bad odds,' Abilene said. 'That'd mean a hundred out of a thousand are okay.'

'I'll never find anybody,' Helen muttered. 'I'd . . . rather have Frank than no one.'

'There are guys out there,' Abilene repeated. 'All you've got to do is find the right one.'

'Yeah,' Finley said. 'Remember what's-his-face? The poet?'

'Maxwell?'

'Right, Maxwell Charron.'

'Max,' Cora said. 'I wonder what he's up to, these days.'

'He wouldn't even remember me,' Helen said.

'That's ridiculous,' Abilene told her. 'You two were in love. He'd remember you.'

'He dumped me, remember?'

'He didn't dump you. He transferred to USC because his mother was sick.'

'Yeah, but . . . he didn't keep in touch.'

'I bet we could find him,' Cora said.

'What's the use.'

'You never know. Maybe he's available.'

'Whether he is or isn't,' Abilene said, 'the important thing is that there are guys like him around. You don't have to be stuck with Frank forever. It's not a question of him or no one.'

'I don't know,' Helen muttered.

'Do you still love him?'

She nodded. 'That's what makes it . . . so awful.'

'Get skinny,' Finley said.

'Do you think I haven't tried? The more I try, the heavier I get.'

'Then you just aren't trying hard enough,' Finley said. 'All you've gotta do is eat less.'

'Sure. That's all.'

'She's right,' Cora said. 'In spite of all the psychological matters involved, what it comes down to is a simple matter of calorie intake. Eat less, exercise, and you'll lose weight.'

'I know all that.'

'Easier said than done,' Abilene said.

'Right,' Helen said. And leaned forward. And poked her fork into the last hot dog sizzling on the skillet. And, not bothering with a bun, guided the frank toward her mouth.

Abilene grabbed her wrist.

'Hey,' Helen said.

'Do you really want to eat that?'

'Does somebody else want it?'

The others shook their heads.

'Then it'll just go to waste.'

'Eat it,' Finley said, 'and it'll go to *your* waist.'

'Very funny.'

'She's right,' Cora said. 'Look, why don't you let us help you? The flight home isn't for five more days. I'll bet you could lose seven or eight pounds by then.'

Abilene plucked the hot dog off the tines of Helen's fork, bit off its end, and passed it to Finley.

'Real cute,' Helen muttered as Finley took a bite.

'We're helping you,' Finley said with a mouthful. She handed the remaining half of the hot dog to Cora.

'Whether you like it or not,' Cora said, bit, and passed the stub to Vivian.

Vivian popped it into her mouth.

'This is a *vacation*,' Helen protested. 'How'm I supposed to have fun if I'm starving?'

'You won't starve,' Cora told her.

'Besides,' Abilene said. 'It's not really a vacation, it's an adventure.'

'It's *my* adventure. And it *is* a vacation. You don't diet when you're on vacation.'

'*You* do,' Cora said. 'Starting right now.'

'It won't make any difference.'

'Sure it will,' Abilene said. 'If you lose a few pounds, you'll feel a lot better about yourself.'

'It won't even show.'

'Sure it will.'

'It's a start,' Abilene said. 'By the time you step aboard that jet in Burlington, you'll know that you can lose weight. All you've gotta do is keep at it.'

'Pretty soon,' Finley said, 'Frank'll be calling you "slim." '

'I've got an idea,' Vivian said. 'Helen has a point about how losing a few pounds won't show all that much on her.' She faced Helen, narrowed her eyes. 'Is there any reason you have to get back to Portland right away?'

Helen shrugged. 'I don't guess so.'

'Then why don't we change your ticket? You can fly back to L.A. with me. I've got a guest room in my condo. You can spend a couple of weeks – a couple of months – whatever it takes. Stay as long as you want. We'll get that weight off you. By the time Frank sees you again, you'll be looking terrific.'

'That's a great idea!' Cora said.

'I don't know,' Helen muttered.

'Come on. We'll have a great time.'

'You don't want me in the way.'

'You wouldn't be in the way of anything. It'll be fun to have you around. I'll keep my schedule light. We can go to Disneyland, Knotts, do the Universal tour.'

'Don't forget the wax museums,' Finley added. 'I know two of them with terrific Chambers of Horror. She'd love 'em. Hell, I could take her to those.'

'Yeah. Fin's only a half hour drive from my place. We can show you around together.'

'This is sounding better and better,' Abilene said. 'Wish *I* could come along.'

'Do,' Vivian told her.

'Can't. I've got a graduate seminar in Dickens that starts in a couple of weeks. Besides, Harris would start climbing the walls.'

Cora huffed. 'See what I mean about being tied down?'

'Okay. Put it this way. *I'd* start climbing the walls. I'd miss him too much.'

'How about you?' Vivian asked Cora.

'No way. Me in L.A.? Crowds, traffic, smog, earthquakes? Not a chance.'

Finley chuckled. 'She's just afraid Tony might put his foot down.'

'Bull. Tony has nothing to do with it. I'd have to be nuts to spend time in L.A. when I can be home in Aspen.'

'Good point,' Abilene said.

'I don't think I should do it, anyway,' Helen said. 'I mean, I appreciate the offer. I really do. But . . . even if I can lose enough weight to make any difference . . .'

'You can,' Vivian assured her. 'I know you can.'

'It'd take a *long* time.'

'So?' Cora said.

'Frank . . .'

'Screw Frank,' Finley said.

'You're miserable with him, anyway,' Abilene pointed out. 'For Godsake, go with Vivian. It's a great opportunity. Lose some of that weight. Lose it, and then go back to Frank. If he doesn't start treating you right, forget him.'

'Dump his sorry ass,' Finley said.

Helen grimaced. 'I don't know.'

'You don't have to make up your mind right this instant,' Vivian told her. 'Just think about it, okay?'

'And in the meantime,' Cora said, 'we'll see to it that you knock off a few pounds while we're here.'

'I guess . . . it wouldn't hurt to think about it.'

'Great,' Finley said. 'Now. What's for dessert?'

She was seated on the floor between Abilene and Cora. They both struck out. Cora, quicker, hit her first. The two rough, open-handed shoves rocked her from side to side.

'Hey hey hey! Easy on the merchandise! I was just kidding, for Godsake!'

Helen sighed. 'Remember those sundaes they had at the Delight?'

'Oh, they were great,' Finley said.

'Maxwell and I used to go there all the time. You could build your own at the sundae bar, load them up with hot fudge and marshmallow toppings – butterscotch – and a big pile of whipped cream on top – maraschino cherries and nuts.'

'You shouldn't even think about that kind of thing,' Cora told her.

'My weight never bothered Maxwell.'

'That's where you two went the night Wildman got you,' Abilene said.

'Yeah, that's right. We went there after the movies.'

'Wildman,' Finley said.

'What a crud,' said Vivian.

Chapter Eleven
Belmore Girls

They kidnapped Andy 'Wildman' Wilde during their sopho-more year.

They were living in an apartment half a mile from campus. A few times, on the rare occasions when they were all together with free time on their hands, Cora or Finley had suggested adventures: a weekend excursion to the ocean fifty miles west, hitchhiking (though they had cars), and sleeping on the beach; a clandestine overnight stay inside the Belmore Galleria shopping mall.

Abilene, remembering her vow to avoid further adventures, had insisted that hitchhiking to the beach was foolhardy and dangerous. Vivian and Helen had agreed. No one except Finley had been in favor of breaking into the shopping mall.

So they'd agreed, at least for the time being, to forget about spicing up their lives with another adventure.

That was a few weeks before Andy Wilde made the mistake of messing with Helen and her boyfriend, Maxwell Charron.

Maxwell, a poet, was a tall, soft-spoken young man who struck most people as being effeminate. He was generally referred to as Sharon.

Helen, who saw him frequently around campus, figured him for a pansy.

Then, on a beautiful day in early spring, Helen caught him staring at her while she was eating her lunch in the shade of an oak tree. He sat cross-legged on the grass, a notebook on one knee. He gazed at her, looked down, scribbled with his pen, gazed at her some more.

For a while, he didn't realize he was being observed. Then his mouth fell open. He closed his notebook, got to his feet and started to hurry away.

Helen rushed after him. 'Hey!'

He halted. He faced her, grimacing and blushing.

'What were you doing back there?'

'Me? Nothing.'

'Were you sketching me?'

'No. Honest.'

'I mean, it's all right if you were.'

'I wasn't. No.'

'Could I see?'

'No, really. I was only . . .'

'Please?'

With a long sigh, he opened his notebook and handed it to her.

She sits lonely, so alone,

Like me

Outcast

Solemn in her solitude

Lovely

Solitary tulip

In rank weeds

Unloved

Unpicked

Kissed only

By the shy breeze

Caressed only

By my eyes

'You wrote this just now?' Helen asked.

He shrugged and nodded.

'It's about me?'

'Well ... Kind of. I guess you might say you were the inspiration. You looked sort of lonely sitting there.'

'I think it's beautiful,' she said. 'Could I make a copy of it?'

'Well, I'll copy it for you.'

'Would you like to go over to the student union with me? We could have coffee, or something.'

That was how it began. She told Abilene and the others about it, late that night. She showed the poem. She told about their conversation in the student union, and how they'd both cut their afternoon classes and spent hours wandering together, eaten supper at a downtown diner, gone to a movie theater and watched *The Hungry Dead*, then roamed through the parks.

'He's just so fabulously wonderful,' she said. 'He even likes horror movies. Can you believe it? I think he really likes me.'

After that, she saw him every day. She was often out late at night. Abilene had never seen her so happy.

Until the night she came home bloody and crying.

She and Maxwell, returning on foot after enjoying their sundaes at the Delight ice cream parlor, had been halfway across a street when a a Porsche failed to stop for the red light and stunned them with a quick right turn. As it shot by, barely missing them, Maxwell kicked its side and shouted, 'Asshole!'

Brakes screeched.

'Uh-oh,' Maxwell said.

'Let's get out of here!' Pulling his hand, Helen raced for the corner.

She didn't dare look back. But she heard a second squeal of

brakes. Heard a door slam. Heard a shout. 'You're gonna die!' Then quick smacking footfalls on the sidewalk behind her.

The street was empty and quiet. The shops on both sides were closed for the night.

'This way,' Maxwell gasped. He dashed into the street, Helen at his side. They ran up the center line. It seemed like a good idea. Better to be out in the open, under the bright glow of lights, than off to the side where their pursuer might overtake them in the shadows and work his violence in the privacy of an alley or store entryway. And a car was sure to come along, sooner or later. Someone would stop and help.

But the road ahead remained empty. As if everyone in town except Helen and Maxwell and the man giving chase were asleep or dead.

He was gaining on them.

Helen realized that Maxwell was holding back. Staying with her, even though he was capable of running much faster.

'Go!' she gasped. 'It's you he's after.'

'True.'

With that, he halted and turned around.

'Max!'

'Run!' he yelled over his shoulder.

He was still looking over his shoulder at Helen and before she could call out a warning, the man from the Porsche shouldered into his belly. Lifted him off his feet. Drove him backward, rump first. Slammed him down on the pavement.

Maxwell cried out as he skidded.

The assailant, straddling him, punched Maxwell's face. Right fist, left fist, right, left.

It was then that Helen recognized him.

Andy 'Wildman' Wilde.

A senior. A star of the wrestling team.

A skinny, short little guy. But quick and strong.

Quick enough to grab Helen's foot when she tried to kick him in the face. Strong enough to throw it high with just one hand, hurling Helen onto her back.

'Stay out of it, lard-ass!' he warned as she got to her feet.

'Leave him alone!'

'Beat it.' He resumed punching Maxwell.

Helen dived onto him, hugging his head, throwing him sideways to the pavement. So fast that she didn't know what was happening, he slipped out of her hold, rolled her and came down on top of her. He pinned her arms beneath her back. He began to strike her face.

Open handed. Slapping, not punching. Apparently in deference to her sex.

'A fuckin' gentleman,' Cora said as she listened to Helen's story.

'Well then I called him a dickless pip-squeak.'

'Smart move,' Finley said.

'So after that he really slugged me.'

'Nobody came along?' Abilene asked.

Helen shook her head.

'Anyway, he finally just quit and went back to his car.'

'How's Maxwell?' Vivian asked.

'Oh, he was . . .' Her chin shook. She began weeping again. 'His face was awful. All bloody, and . . . He was so much worse than me, but when he crawled over and looked down . . . He started to cry. It was like he didn't even care about himself. He cried and touched my face and kept saying, "Oh, Tulip. Oh, Tulip." ' Helen shuddered with a sob.

* * *

They plotted. They followed Wilde. They kept watch on his apartment.

Each morning, he left his apartment at seven o'clock and jogged to Benedict Park, where he ran on the trails for an hour.

Friday, they were waiting for him.

He stopped running when he came upon Cora crouched in the middle of a narrow stretch of trail above Benedict Creek. She was tying a shoelace. She wore red gym shorts, a pink tank top, sunglasses and a red wig that Vivian had borrowed from the costume room of the theater department. She smiled up at him. 'Oh, hi.'

'Morning,' he said. He started to step around her.

'Say, aren't you Wildman? The wrestler?'

'Sure am,' he said, halting and smiling down at her.

She rose to her feet. 'I've seen some of your matches. You're really great.'

'Thanks. Do you go to Belmore? You don't look familiar.'

'I'm a frosh,' she lied.

He nodded. 'And you've seen me at work, huh?'

'I sure have. I love to watch wrestling. Especially you. You're so quick and strong. You've got a wonderful body.'

His eyes roamed down Cora. 'You've got a great body, yourself.'

'I used to wrestle with my brothers. I always won.' She grinned. 'Think you could take me?'

'It's sure tempting.'

She got down on her hands and knees, looked over her shoulder at him.

'Are you kidding?'

'Do I look like I'm kidding?'

'You asked for it.' He peeled off his T-shirt and draped it

over a bush beside the trail. It blocked Abilene's view. She slipped sideways. Peering around the bush, she watched Wilde sink to his knees beside Cora. He hunched down against her back and hooked his right arm across her belly.

'On the count of three,' Cora said.

'Nobody's ever gonna believe this,' he muttered.

'Let it be our little secret.'

'Man, this has to be the weirdest come-on I've ever seen.'

'Maybe I just like to wrestle.'

'Yeah. Right.'

'Three,' she said, grabbed his wrist and dropped flat, pulling him down on her back.

Abilene darted out, threw herself onto Wilde's back and jammed a pillowcase over his head. As he writhed beneath her, she looped a short length of rope around his neck to keep the pillowcase on. Finley stepped into the trail in front of her, taping. Vivian rushed in from the side, grabbed Wilde's left hand and snapped a metal cuff around his wrist.

'Hey!' he yelled. 'What's . . . Get off! Goddamn it, what the fuck is . . . ?'

'Okay.' Helen's voice.

Abilene rolled clear. She saw Helen on the trail behind Wilde, tugging at the rope she'd looped around his ankles. Vivian, the other cuff in both hands, was stretching Wilde's left arm. His right was still trapped under Cora.

Cora twisted out from under him, bringing the arm with her. Twisting *it* so hard that he cried out in pain.

Dropping a knee onto his back, she shoved the arm up behind him. She held it there while Vivian lunged forward, sank to her knees, and bent his left arm back. She snapped the other cuff around his right wrist.

'Weirdest come-on *you've* ever seen,' Cora said.

'Cunt!'

She punched the side of his head through the pillowcase.

While Finley taped the scene and Helen clutched the rope, the others lifted Wilde to his feet.

'I get it,' he said. 'This is a gag. Right? Who put you up to this? Janke?'

Helen tugged the rope.

His legs leaped out from under him. Hands cuffed behind his back, he couldn't catch himself. He slammed the trail chest-first. His breath huffed out.

'Let's see if you still think it's a gag,' Cora said, 'when you're sucking water at the bottom of the creek.'

'Hey! No. Come on.'

While Helen kept the rope taut, Cora and Vivian and Abilene rolled him off the trail. To the edge of the embankment above Benedict Creek.

'Come on! This isn't . . . !'

They pushed. He yelped with alarm as he began tumbling down the slope. He cried out with pain as bushes and rocks scraped his bare skin.

The girls hurried after him.

He flopped into the creek.

A moment later, the girls jumped in.

Abilene cringed. The water was awfullly cold. But it only came up to her thighs.

She helped Vivian and Cora hold their captive under the surface.

'We'll see how long he can hold his breath,' Cora said.

Helen laughed. 'Half an hour, do you think?'

'Maybe even longer.'

'I wish Maxwell was here to see this.'

'Shhh. No names.'

'Do you think he heard?'

'Doubt it.'

'We'll let you-know-who see the tape,' Finley said.

'Maybe we'd better let him up,' Abilene said.

'Rather not,' Cora said. But she pulled Wilde up by the rope at the back of his neck. He gasped, making whiny sounds. The front of the pillowcase, clinging to his face, puffed out and sank in as he fought for breath. His chest heaved. He had goosebumps. His arms, chest and back were blotchy with red smudges that would soon turn into bruises. His skin was scratched, scuffed, gouged, ridged with pale welts, even tinted in places with grass stains. His blue shorts hung low and crooked below his hips. The waistband of his jockstrap showed.

Cora hooked a forefinger under it, drew it back like a slingshot and let go. The elastic snapped him. He flinched.

Helen laughed.

'Okay, stud,' Cora said. 'Let's go.'

When they tried to lead him upstream, they found that he couldn't walk with the rope hobbling him. Abilene crouched into the water, found the rope around his ankles, loosened it a little, and slid it up to his waist. There, she tightened its slipknot against his spine.

His legs suddenly free, Wilde tried to make a break. He shouldered Vivian aside and rammed Cora with his other shoulder. Helen yanked the rope. He flopped backward and submerged. Abilene plunged a hand down after him and held his face under until Vivian and Cora returned and pulled him up by his arms.

After that, he behaved as they guided him up the creek.

Finley preceded them, wading backward, the camera to her eye.

Soon, they came to the Shady Lane Bridge.

Shady Lane traversed the park. Once, it had apparently been open to traffic. But that was long ago. Now, both ends were blocked by permanent barricades. The road, with its bridge over Benedict Creek, was reserved for pedestrians. It was not heavily traveled, especially on weekdays.

In the shadows under the bridge, they climbed ashore.

Vivian, Cora and Abilene held onto Wilde while Helen pulled the loop up his back. She cinched it tight between his shoulder blades, then drew the rest of the rope out from behind his cuffed hands. She flung its end over a support beam of the bridge, caught it, tugged until the rope pressed into his armpits, then tied it to the slipknot between his shoulders.

'That oughta keep him for a while,' Cora said.

'Why are you *doing* this?' he gasped.

'Because you're such a sweetheart.'

'Don't worry,' Finley told him. 'Somebody'll find you sooner or later.'

'Maybe one of the bums who sleeps under here at night,' Abilene added.

'Come on,' he pleaded. 'You can't leave me here.'

'You know,' Helen said, 'he's gonna start yelling the minute we're gone.'

'We can't gag him,' Abilene said. 'He might suffocate.'

'Wouldn't that be just too bad,' Vivian said.

'Besides, we'd have to take off the pillowcase.'

'I know how to keep him quiet,' Cora said. She yanked down his shorts and jockstrap.

'No! Please!'

She jerked them out from under his feet. He started to fall backward, but the rope stopped him. He cried out as it dug into his armpits. Then he found his balance and stood there. He sniffed. 'Please.' His voice was high, quivering. He was crying.

Cora smiled at Abilene, waved the shorts and jockstrap in front of her, and said, 'Souvenirs. We'll take them home with us.'

'Don't leave me. Please. Please!'

They left him.

'Do you think he'll be all right?' Abilene asked as they walked home.

'Sure,' Cora said. 'I bet he won't be there an hour before somebody finds him.'

'Foul play is suspected in the disappearance of Belmore University senior, Andrew Wilde, a varsity wrestler who vanished Friday morning. A neighbor observed the young man leaving his Oak Street apartment at approximately seven o'clock . . .'

'Uh-oh,' Finley said.

The announcer was Candi Delmar, anchorwoman of the six o'clock news.

It was Sunday evening.

'Holy shit,' Cora said.

They went ahead and ate dinner. Then they trooped to a pay phone three blocks away. Cora tapped in 911. In a rough, husky voice, she said, 'Andrew Wilde? You'll find him under the Shady Lane Bridge.'

According to Candi Delmar on the eleven o'clock news, 'Andrew Wilde, the Belmore University student missing since Friday, was found earlier this evening when an anonymous tip led the police to the Shady Lane Bridge in Benedict Park.

Though suffering from dehydration, exposure and various superficial injuries, the young man was listed in satisfactory condition upon admittance to Queen of Angels hospital.'

'Oh my God, they hospitalized him,' Abilene said.

'Ain't that a shame?' said Finley.

'According to police officials, Wilde was abducted early Friday morning while jogging in the park. His assailants were said to be five males, possibly teens, who knocked him unconscious and stole his wallet before leaving him hand-cuffed beneath the bridge.'

Chapter Twelve

It was after dark when they returned to the Wagoneer with the boxes, ice chest and stove.

'We might as well take out whatever we'll need for the night,' Cora said.

'What're we planning to do?' Abilene asked.

'That's Helen's department,' Cora said.

'So what's on the schedule?' Finley asked.

'I suppose pigging out on nacho chips isn't in the cards?' Abilene was glad to hear Helen joking about her deprivation.

'It'll be easier on you,' Cora said, 'if you don't talk about food.'

'Okay if I think about it?'

'Try not to.'

'Why don't we go down to the hot spring?' Abilene

suggested, handing the ice chest to Cora, who slid it into the rear of the car. 'It's cooler now. The pool'll feel good.'

'Sounds fine to me,' Helen said.

'This time,' Vivian said, 'we can take our suits and towels.'

'Does that mean you want your suitcase?' Cora asked from inside the car.

'Yes.'

'Let's take all the suitcases,' Cora said. 'And the sleeping bags. This running back and forth to the car is gonna get old real quick.'

The others agreed, so she unloaded the luggage and bedrolls.

'Is that everything?' she asked.

'Aren't we taking any food at all?' Helen asked.

'We'll eat in the morning,' Cora said.

'Great,' Helen muttered. 'Anyway, what about the water? Or is that forbidden, too?'

Cora crawled backward, dragging a two-gallon plastic bottle out of the car. She slammed the tail gate shut. 'I wonder if the spring water's okay to drink?'

'You'd think so,' Abilene said. 'But I wouldn't want to drink it.'

'It's hot,' Helen pointed out.

'It's had our butts in it,' Finley warned.

'I'm not gonna drink that stuff,' Vivian said.

They picked up their things and began trudging up the steep driveway.

'There's supposed to be a lake not far from here,' Helen said.

'I'm not about to drink lake water, either,' Vivian told her.

'We've got this,' Cora said, and shook the bottle. 'Plus two more in the car.'

'That should be plenty.'

'We only agreed on one night, people.'

'I'm sure there must be a stream, too,' Helen said.

'We'll have to do some exploring tomorrow,' Cora said. 'I'd like to see that lake.'

'Maybe it's got a Boy Scout camp,' Finley said.

'You've reformed, remember?'

'Maybe that kid was a scout,' Abilene said as she climbed the front porch stairs.

Vivian groaned. 'Did you have to mention him?'

'Probably with the Beaver Patrol,' Finley said.

Helen giggled.

'All right!' Finley blurted. 'Starving hasn't dimmed your sense of humor.'

Nudging open the front door, Abilene was greeted by the glare of the Coleman lantern atop the registration desk. She squinted against its brightness, then turned away and watched the others come in.

'Where'll we want to sleep?' she asked.

'How about a Holiday Inn?' Vivian suggested.

'We can worry about that later,' Cora said, letting her sleeping bag drop out from under her right arm. She set down her suitcase and the water bottle.

'Just leave our things here?' Abilene asked.

'Might as well. I don't think we'll be sacking out downstairs, do you?'

'I'm certainly not going to sleep down there,' Vivian said.

'Too hot and damp,' Abilene said.

There in the lobby, they opened their suitcases. Abilene took out her towel. She didn't much want to wear her swimsuit in the pool, but she saw that Vivian and Helen had theirs, so she found her bikini before shutting the suitcase.

'Should we change here?' Helen asked.

'I'm not going anywhere without my duds,' Vivian said, rolling her suit inside her towel.

'Wary of visitors,' Finley said.

'You're darn right.'

Cora lifted the lantern down from the registration desk. The others turned on their flashlights. They followed her to the doorway behind the staircase, and down the narrow flight of stairs to the pool area.

At the bottom, Finley shone her light on the door marked GENTS. 'Anybody in . . .' She paused as her voice resounded through the darkness. Speaking softly, she said, 'Anybody in the mood for a john inspection?'

'Feel free,' Cora told her. 'I'm going in the water.'

'Hickok? There're probably lockers. Maybe we'll find something interesting.'

'Not me. Maybe tomorrow.'

'I'm sure not going in there at night,' Helen said.

Probably afraid there might be a shower room, Abilene thought. Probably remembering that phantom hand from when she was a freshman.

Vivian had kept on walking.

'Some other time,' Finley said.

They continued forward to the edge of the pool. There, Cora set down the lantern. In spite of its bright glow, it left both ends of the pool in darkness and failed to illuminate the far side. The beams of their flashlights searched those areas, sliding along the water's surface, sweeping across the archway that led outside, shining on the empty expanse of floor beyond the right end of the pool, the stools and bar, probing every dark corner.

'Nobody here but us chickens,' Finley said.

'Unless behind the bar,' Abilene muttered.

Cora already had her T-shirt off. Balancing on one foot, she tugged off a shoe. 'If it worries you, go look.'

'Me?'

'Maybe somebody should,' Helen said, shining her light on the distant bar.

'I'm not going over there alone.'

'Gobble-gobble-gobble.'

'You check it out, Finley. You're such a fearless explorer.'

'Ah, Hickok, what a pussy.' Laughing softly, shaking her head, she strode quickly alongside the pool. She left the lantern's brightness behind. Abilene and Helen kept their flashlights on her back.

In unison, they flinched at the noise of a heavy splash.

Abilene whirled around. She saw Cora, long and pale, gliding beneath the water.

Vivian stood motionless beside the pool, gazing toward Finley.

Abilene turned again, and picked up Finley with her flashlight just as the girl stepped behind the bar.

'Hey. What the . . . ?' Finley crouched, disappeared.

'What are you doing?' Abilene called.

No answer.

'She's just screwing around,' Vivian said.

'I know. But I wish . . .'

A sudden harsh clamor made Abilene jump, Helen yelp, Vivian gasp 'Damn!'

Abilene, shaken, yelled, 'You bitch!'

Finley stood up behind the bar. 'That was just me kicking the bucket.'

'You're a riot.'

'I know, I know.' She made a little bow, then stepped around the bar and walked toward them. She tossed her flashlight into the air. It tumbled high, its beam somersaulting. She caught it and switched it off.

'One of these days,' Helen said, 'you're gonna be sorry.'

'Hope I didn't upset anyone.' Joining them, she started to unbutton her safari shirt.

'Where's Cora?' Vivian asked.

They turned to the pool. Abilene saw no one swimming. She heard no sounds except a soft lapping of the water. She saw nothing gliding beneath the surface.

'Don't tell me she's starting to play games.'

'Oh, man,' Helen murmured.

The beams of four flashlights began criss-crossing the water.

'Hey, Cora!' Finley yelled. 'You're making the babes nervous!'

Something pale moved in the archway.

All the lights hit Cora at once. Wincing, she squinted and ducked her head. 'Gimme a break.'

They lowered their lights.

'It's really neat outside. Come on.' She started to turn around.

'Just wait for us,' Vivian said. She sounded upset. 'You shouldn't have gone out there alone.'

'I'm a big girl.'

'Just wait for us,' Vivian repeated.

'Okay, okay.'

The idea of venturing to the outside pool changed Abilene's mind about wearing a suit.

Finley finished undressing, entered the pool, swam to its far side and waited near Cora while the others put on their swimsuits.

'I'm taking my flashlight,' Helen said.

'Me, too,' Abilene told her.

'What about the lantern?' Helen asked.

Vivian grimaced. 'No. Leave it here.'

'It'd ruin the view,' Cora said from the archway.

'It'd light us up like . . .'

'Sitting ducks?' Finley suggested.

'That's right,' Vivian said.

Finley, laughing, waded after Cora. The two of them vanished through the archway as Abilene, Vivian and Helen jumped into the pool.

The hot water felt wonderful sliding against Abilene. She made her way to the center of the pool, found the barred opening, and stepped on top of it. She lingered there, savoring the soft rub of the currents that rolled up from below. Raising the flashlight overhead, she squatted so the water covered her to the neck.

Then she realized that Vivian and Helen were already outside. She was alone. As she looked around at the bright lantern and the darkness beyond its glow, she felt a crawly sensation on the back of her neck.

She waded quickly to the archway and hurried through it.

The others were all in the smaller pool, sitting on the submerged ledges along two of its sides. Helen and Finley sat at the south end. Facing them across the water were Vivian and Cora.

'Isn't it terrific out here?' Cora asked.

'Nice,' Abilene said. She waded over to the north end, put her flashlight on the edge, then sank down and sat beside Cora.

'Fresh air.'

The air was warm, but cooler than inside. Its sulphur odor

was not so strong, and Abilene could smell the sweet aromas of the forest.

Directly overhead was the porch. From its edge all the way to the treetops at the far end of the lodge's grounds, the night sky was sprinkled with stars. There were no clouds that Abilene could see.

The high, full moon cast its brightness down on the woods, the field, the ruin of the swimming pool, the brick barbecue and the old picnic table. It lit the area under the porch, as well.

It glinted silver on the rippled surface of the hot pool.

It shone on the girls, gleaming on their hair, painting their skin with its milky glow, leaving black shadows where it couldn't reach.

Nobody looks quite right, Abilene thought.

Faces pale on one side, dark on the other. Faces that seemed to have holes instead of eyes. She supposed she must look just as strange.

'Look at all those stars,' Cora said.

'I know *I'm* thrilled,' Finley said.

'Bet you don't see stars like this in L.A.'

'Maybe we should go back inside,' Vivian suggested.

'It's much nicer out here.'

'We're so exposed.'

'With moonlight like this,' Abilene said, 'I could probably read a book by it.'

'*Anybody* could be out there. Watching us.'

'Still worried about that kid,' Cora said.

'Maybe he'll come over and join us,' Finley said. 'If he does, I call firsties.'

Abilene realized that they all had their heads turned, were gazing out at the moonlit grounds as if expecting someone to creep out of the forest.

'What if someone *does* come along?' Helen asked, her voice hushed.

'Stop it,' Vivian said.

'We'll just let Finley keep him busy,' Abilene said, 'while the rest of us skedaddle.'

'My pleasure.'

'Nobody's gonna come along,' Cora said. 'Why don't you all just settle down and enjoy yourselves. Helen, you've got a story to tell us, don't you? About the murders?'

'Maybe this isn't the best time to tell it.'

'I'll second that,' Vivian said.

'This is the perfect time for it. Just pretend we're sitting around a campfire.'

'This *is* like sitting around a campfire,' Abilene said. 'You know? Supper's over. Nothing else to do before bedtime. It's warm and cozy. We're all gathered here, surrounded by the dark.'

'Campfires are bright and cheerful,' Helen pointed out.

'Finley's bright and cheerful. She can get in the middle and make crackling sounds.'

'Cracks is more like it,' Cora said.

'I'm hot enough. I just *might* burst into flame.'

'People do, you know,' Helen said. 'Sometimes, they just burn up for no apparent reason. I've read accounts of that happening. I read where some guy went up in smoke, and it happened so fast that his clothes didn't even get burnt. All they found were ashes and charred bones inside his clothes.'

'They were probably flame retardant,' Abilene said.

'Maybe the guy was a vampire,' Finley suggested. 'We made this movie where a guy – one of your basic Dracula types – just crumpled to crap right inside his duds.'

'*Night Fang*,' Helen said.

'Yeah, that's the one.'

'You were script supervisor?' Abilene asked.

'Right. It was my last big epic before I moved up to assistant director.'

'I saw it,' Helen said. 'The sunlight got him. But that's different from spontaneous combustion.'

'I feel like *I'm* gonna spontaneously combust.' Finley stood, turned around, and climbed onto the submerged shelf. She sat on the edge of the pool and crossed her legs. And sighed. 'Ahhh. This is much better.'

'Are you sure you want to be sitting up there?' Vivian asked.

'Yep.' She stretched, folding her hands behind her head, arching her back, twisting slightly from side to side. 'Nice breeze.'

'You really do stick out,' Helen said.

'Do I? Thanks.' Lowering her arms, she gazed down as if inspecting her breasts. 'Not as much as I'd like, actually.'

Helen chuckled. 'Not them. You.'

'You are awfully visible,' Abilene said. 'You look like a snowman up there.'

'Gee, I should've brought my camouflage makeup.'

'You stick out like a sore thumb,' Helen told her.

'Why don't you get back in,' Vivian said, 'before somebody sees you?'

'Nobody's gonna see her,' Cora said.

'Ah, the voice of reason. You'd think we were in a war zone, the way these babes are carrying on. We're in the middle of nowhere. Wishful thinking aside, that kid showing up was a fluke. There's probably nobody but us around for *miles*.'

'That's telling 'em,' Cora said.

'It's not true, though,' Helen said. 'There really are people who live in these hills.'

'The dreaded Hill People,' Finley said. 'Who prowl the woods by night.'

'I'm not joking. I read about them.'

'Are these the same people who spontaneously combust?' Finley asked.

'These are the same people who invaded the Totem Pole Lodge twelve years ago and slaughtered everyone.'

'All *right*!' Finley pumped a fist beside her face. 'We get to hear the story, after all.'

'Lucky us,' Vivian muttered.

'I guess so,' Helen said. 'Since Fin wants to insist nobody's around for miles. The fact is, half a dozen families live within a few miles of here. Or did, anyway. I don't know if they're still around. But back at the time of the murders, there were the Sloanes, the Hacketts, the Johnsons . . .'

'The Hatfields and McCoys,' Abilene interrupted.

Finley laughed. 'You've got your geography screwed up, Hickok.'

'Well, it was never my strong suit.'

'Let's shut up and listen,' Cora said.

'Anyway, there were these families. They lived near here and they *were* hill people. They lived in shacks. They didn't have much to do with the outside world. They hunted and fished and kept to themselves.'

'Probably some terrific banjo players,' Abilene said.

'Apparently, there was a lot of inbreeding.'

'Halfwits and harelips,' Cora said.

'I thought we were supposed to shut up and listen,' Finley reminded her.

'And don't you forget it,' Cora said.

'*I* was behaving.' Finley leaned back and braced herself up with stiff arms. 'Go on, Helen.'

'Well, Cora's right. The inbreeding did result in some abnormalities. The book didn't go into much detail about it, just that some of them were retarded and some looked kind of freakish. But they minded their own business, and generally tried to keep their distance from the lodge. They were in the woods all around here, though. So when guests from the lodge would go out fishing or hunting, sometimes they'd spot one or two off in the distance. They used to make jokes about bagging one. How they could have the head stuffed, and hang it up in the lodge along with the other trophies.'

'These lodge guests sound like charming people,' Abilene said.

'Hunters are all like that,' Vivian said. 'Macho bastards.'

'You've known some?' Abilene asked.

'Hell, my father was one.'

'I thought he was a neurosurgeon.'

'He was that, too.'

'I thought doctors only played golf.'

'My dad played Daniel Boone. He made me help him dress out a deer when I was ten years old.'

'What did you dress it in?' Finley asked.

'A Tipton shirt,' Cora said, and laughed.

'I didn't dress it in anything. I had to cut off its head and gut it and . . .'

'Jesus,' Helen muttered.

'I can't picture you doing something like that,' Abilene said.

'Well, I puked all over it.'

'*That* I can picture.'

'He would've fit right in with a crowd of guys who think it'd be laughs to plug a hillbilly. He and his pals were all a bunch of gun-toting assholes.'

'Guys and their guns,' Finley said.

'Anyway,' Helen went on, 'they *did* end up shooting one of those people.'

Chapter Thirteen

'It wasn't on purpose, though,' Helen said. 'Three guys from the lodge were out deer hunting. They were over near that lake I mentioned. Something moved in the trees, and they opened fire. Then they went over to it, and what they found instead of a deer was a teenaged girl. Only she wasn't dead. She was hit in the shoulder, is all.'

'Not only assholes,' Finley said, 'but lousy shots.'

'It's not funny,' Vivian muttered.

'One of the hunters wanted to take the girl back to the lodge and get her to a hospital. At least that's what he claims, and there was nobody left to refute him. Henderson. He told the whole story to the police later. He said the girl would've been all right if they'd gotten her some medical attention. But the other two were against it. They said there'd be hell to pay if it got out about them shooting her.'

'It was an accident, wasn't it?' Abilene said.

'Sure. And they figured they'd be all right with the authorities. What worried them was the girl's family.'

'Her kinfolks,' Finley said.

'Right. When something happens to blood relatives, people around here go nuts. They believe in an eye for an eye. They wouldn't rest until they'd gotten their revenge, and they wouldn't be very picky about who they nailed. The hunters were here with their families. Henderson had a wife and two little daughters back at the lodge, and the other two guys told him that nobody'd be safe. Especially daughters. But everything would be all right if the girl they shot could just disappear. That way, nobody would blame people from the lodge. Maybe she just got lost, or ran afoul of some wild animals. One of the other families might even get blamed. Apparently, there was bad blood between some of the clans, and the hunters knew about it.'

'So they're discussing all this,' Cora asked, 'while the poor kid is lying there bleeding?'

'I guess so.'

'What a bunch of bastards.'

'They were hunters,' Vivian said. 'What do you expect?'

'A little decency.'

'Fat chance.'

'The girl couldn't hear them anyway. She was a deaf mute.'

'Terrific,' Vivian muttered.

'Henderson says he told the guys they were talking about cold-blooded murder, and how this eye-for-an-eye stuff was no excuse to kill an innocent kid. She couldn't exactly tell on them.'

'She could point them out,' Abilene said.

'And grunt.'

'You're seriously disturbed, Finley.'

'They told Henderson she had to be eliminated, but he didn't listen. He knelt down and opened her shirt so he could get at the wound. He started to cut off one of her sleeves to use as a bandage, and that's when one of the other guys clobbered him. Hit him in the head with a rifle butt. He says it knocked him out cold, so he didn't have anything to do with what happened next.'

'There's a likely story,' Finley said.

'That's what the cops thought. But they didn't have any evidence against him, so he was never prosecuted. They never found the body. They never found out who she was. They never even found evidence that the murder had taken place, at all. Henderson's story was all they had to go on. So he was never even arrested.'

'But Henderson said they killed her?' Abilene asked.

'Yeah. And they raped her, too.'

'Jesus,' Cora muttered.

'Henderson was pretty sure they did. When he came to, his buddies were both naked. So was the girl. And the girl was dead by then. Her throat had been slashed. And the guys were busy opening her up and stuffing rocks into her. You know, so she'd sink.'

Vivian groaned. 'I knew I didn't want to hear this.'

'I'm surprised they didn't kill Henderson,' Abilene said.

'It's only his word,' Cora said, 'that he didn't go along with the whole thing. He might've had at her, just like his two buddies. Maybe he was even the one who killed her.'

'What he claimed,' Helen explained, 'was that he was afraid they *would* kill him. Guys get shot all the time in hunting accidents. So Henderson acted as if he'd had a change of heart and approved of what they'd done. They were still afraid he might turn them in, though. So they had him shoot her. That way, if the cops found her body, there might be ballistics evidence that Henderson's rifle had been used on the girl.'

'Pretty smart,' Abilene said. 'Or smart of Henderson, making that part of his story.'

'Well, that was when they stopped being smart. Their idea was to swim out into the lake with the body and let it go. They figured the rocks would sink it, and it'd never be found. But one of them went down to the shore for a look around. They were on the far side of the lake, but apparently it isn't very large. And the guy who went to scout around noticed some people from the lodge swimming off the dock on the other side. They were afraid they might be seen. So what they decided was to hide the body and come back after dark to take care of sinking it. They covered it with some bushes, then went back to the lodge.

'Henderson made up a story about falling down and hitting his head on a rock. He told his family he was still feeling dizzy and sick, and that he thought he'd better check into a hospital. So they all packed up and left. They drove into town. They found an emergency room, and he was being examined right at about the same time that everyone back at the lodge was sitting down in the dining room for supper.

'Nobody at the lodge was alive the next day when a fellow and his wife showed up to register.'

'My God,' Cora said.

'There were twenty-eight bodies, including the owner and his wife and three kids.'

'What *happened*?' Abilene asked.

'Somebody found the girl, obviously,' Finley said. 'And got pissed.'

'I mean, how the hell do you kill twenty-eight people?'

'Well, there was poison in the Mulligan Stew. Apparently, no one died from the poison, though. Not everyone ate it, for one thing. A lot of the kids were served hot dogs and hamburgers. Mostly just adults ate the stew. The thing is, though, that the killers didn't wait around long enough for the poison to kill anyone. Maybe they just kept watch until people started getting sick so there wouldn't be much of a fight. Then they stormed the place. With guns and knives and hatchets and axes.'

'They killed most of the people right there in the dining room. But some got away, at least for a while. Bodies were found all over the place: behind the registration desk, on the stairs, a few in the upstairs hall. A headless body was even found in there,' she said, nodding toward the archway entrance to the inside pool.

Vivian grimaced. 'In the *water*?'

'Floating.'

Abilene's skin suddenly felt crawly. 'Oh, yuck.'

Vivian was already on her feet, turning around and climbing out.

'Thanks for telling us,' Abilene said.

'Oh, calm down,' Cora said. 'This was twelve years ago, for Godsake. It's not like we got any *on* us.'

'Even so . . .' Abilene muttered. The hot water caressing her skin suddenly seemed thick and foul. She saw Vivian standing on the concrete, arms lifted away from her body, head down – inspecting her body as if she expected to find something hideous clinging to her skin.

Abilene was tempted to follow her example. But Helen and Cora were still in the water. And it was ridiculous to think that the pool could still be tainted after all these years. Besides, she'd already spent a lot of time in it. The harm was already done.

'This,' she said, 'is like eating an apple and being told later that it had a worm in it.'

'You're grossing me out, Hickok.'

'You mean you aren't *already* grossed out?'

'So the pool had a stiff in it. Big deal.'

'I knew we shouldn't have come to this place,' Vivian said.

'Pussies,' Finley said.

'It's ancient history,' Cora pointed out. 'I don't know why anybody's getting upset.'

'I need a shower,' Vivian said.

'Good luck,' Finley told her.

'Why don't you just sit down and relax,' Cora said. 'I want to hear the rest of Helen's story.'

'You mean there's more?' Vivian asked. She didn't sound pleased.

'Well, that's just about it. Guess I should've left out the part about the body in the pool.'

'Wish you had,' Abilene said.

'Ignorance is bliss, Hickok. That must be how come you're always smiling.'

'Take a leap.'

'Maybe I shouldn't tell the rest,' Helen said to Cora.

'Go on. If anybody doesn't want to hear it, they can cover their ears.'

'I imagine we've already heard the worst,' Abilene said.

Without saying a word, Vivian sat down on the pool's rim and crossed her legs. She began to flick her hands against her thighs as if brushing off ants.

'Anyway,' Helen said, 'bodies were found all over the place.'

'So we understand,' Abilene muttered.

'A few had been shot. But most of the wounds were in the legs, as if the attackers only used the guns to cripple them. The actual killings were done with sharp instruments. All the bodies were found with their bellies split open. Just like the girl the hunters killed. But it didn't stop with that. They were mutilated and dismembered in all sorts of awful ways. Eyes

411

were gouged out. Heads were split apart down the middle, or cut off at the neck. Arms and legs were chopped off. Same with the genitals of all the guys.'

'Oh, for Godsake,' Vivian muttered.

'There were women whose breasts had been . . .'

'I don't want to hear this!' Vivian clapped her open hands against her ears. 'Just quit it! You don't have to rub our noses in it. Christ.'

'Okay, well . . .'

'What about the women?' Cora asked. 'Had they been raped?'

Helen, casting a glance at Vivian, nodded. 'And then some,' she said.

'The cops never got anyone for it?' Abilene asked.

'They figured it must've been the girl's family. Or maybe more than one family was involved. I mean, there were an awful lot of assailants. They'd tracked blood all over the place. The cops think there must've been anywhere from twelve to fifteen of them. Including women and children.'

'Some of the killers were kids?'

'A real family affair,' Finley said.

'The problem was, the cops didn't know the identity of the girl who'd been killed by the hunters. So they didn't know who to go after. They went around questioning the locals, but they never came up with anything. So the massacre at the Totem Pole Lodge was never solved.'

'If there were bloody footprints everywhere,' Abilene said, 'there must've been fingerprints, too. All they would've had to do is round up all the people in the area and try to come up with matches.'

'I guess they didn't do that,' Helen said.

'When it comes right down to it,' Cora said, 'maybe they

didn't *want* to find the culprits. The cops must've been local people. Maybe they had a pretty good idea who did it, but they just decided to let it go.'

'Afraid they'd stir up more trouble,' Finley suggested.

'That doesn't seem likely,' Abilene said. 'We're talking about a major atrocity. Cops aren't gonna just look the other way.'

'Who knows? Once they heard Henderson's story, maybe that's exactly what they did.'

'I don't know,' Helen said. 'I just know that they never arrested anyone. And the lodge was closed down, right after the killings, and never reopened. Apparently, some bank owns the place. They've tried to sell it off, but everybody around the area knows what happened here. Potential buyers find out pretty quick, too. Once they hear about the massacre, they won't have anything to do with the place. On top of all that, the book says that the lodge is supposed to be haunted.'

'Surprise surprise,' Finley said.

'People who've come near it at night have sometimes seen lights inside. And heard strange noises.'

'This place is no more haunted than I am,' Cora said. 'The locals probably made up all that garbage just to keep people away from the place.'

'Hey,' Finley said. 'That kid this afternoon? Maybe he took *us* for spooks.'

'Yeah,' Abilene said. 'We might be contributing to the legend.'

'Improving on it,' Finley added. 'Ghosts of bare-ass babes.'

'Joke about it,' Vivian said. 'For all we know, he might be part of the bunch that murdered all those people.'

'He would've made a hell of a killer,' Finley said. 'What'd he do, brain 'em with his bottle?'

'He couldn't have been older than four or five back then,' Abilene said. 'Unless he's older than he looked.'

'I don't mean he was necessarily in on it. But his family might've been. Maybe the girl was his sister, or something. What if they have him come over to check on the place, and he's supposed to let them know if anyone's here?'

'Maybe they've got us surrounded.' Finley swiveled her head, making a show of scanning the moonlit grounds.

'We didn't do anything.' Helen sounded nervous.

'We've *done* plenty,' Abilene said. 'But nothing to them.'

'They've gotta be maniacs,' Vivian said, 'to've killed all those people like that. Who knows what it might take to set them off? Suppose it's enough that we're staying here?'

'We're at the lodge, so we're fair game?'

Cora sighed. 'Come on, gals. You're letting your imaginations run wild. Before you know it, you're gonna get yourselves so worked up you'll want to pack up and get out.'

'Which is what I've wanted to do from the start,' Vivian reminded her. 'But now that we know what happened here . . . Those maniacs probably still live in the same place. Somewhere nearby. And maybe they *do* know we're here. And maybe they don't like it.'

'Maybe they enjoyed the last chop-fest so much that they're eager for another.'

Cora let out a loud sigh. 'You're not helping matters, Finley.'

'Hey, I'm on your side.'

'Then quit horsing around.'

'I don't think we should stay,' Vivian said.

'See? What'd I tell you?'

Turning toward Vivian, Helen said, 'We already agreed to give it at least one night.'

'That was before you told us what'd happened here.'

'I don't see how it really changes anything,' Cora said.

'Besides,' Helen said, 'I *did* tell you there'd been murders.'

'You didn't say there'd been twenty-eight.'

'Twenty-nine,' Finley corrected. 'Don't forget the gal the hunters killed. Or maybe she shouldn't count, since she didn't get trashed in the lodge.'

'The place was a *slaughter house*. I'm not gonna be able to sleep a wink, knowing I'm in a place where all those people were killed . . . mutilated.'

'Good,' Finley said. 'If you can't sleep, you can be our official lookout.'

'What do you think, Abby?' Vivian asked.

She shrugged. 'Even if I'm on your side, it'd still be three against two for staying. I've got to admit, though, the place has lost some of its charm. I might be in favour of leaving if we had somewhere to go. But the nearest town is – what – forty miles away? On these roads, it'd probably take us a couple of hours to get there. And we don't even know if it has a motel. We could end up spending a very long, miserable night. And I'm tired already.' Even as she mentioned it, she yawned.

'So you don't want to go?'

She finished her yawn, then said, 'If I thought there was any real danger . . .'

'Hey,' Cora said, 'I wouldn't stay, either, if I thought someone might show up and attack us.'

'None of us would,' Helen said.

'Finley might,' Abilene said.

'Just if I can get it on tape.'

'So that's it, then, huh? We're going to stay? In spite of everything?'

'It's *supposed* to be creepy,' Helen reminded her.

'It's that, all right,' Abilene said.

'Should we go back in, now?' Helen asked. 'I'm starting to prune.'

'You oughta climb out and cool off,' Finley suggested.

'Just ignore the audience in the woods.'

'Thanks anyway. Is everyone else ready?'

'I've had enough,' Abilene said, and yawned again.

'We keeping you up, Hickok?'

'I am starting to get awfully groggy.'

'It's the hot water,' Cora told her. 'I'm feeling about ready to hit the sack, myself.'

'Why don't you all get out?' Vivian suggested. 'We can walk around to the front. It'll give you a chance to dry off and get cool. Besides, I'm not stepping foot in that water again.'

'I don't want to walk,' Helen said. 'I'm not wearing any shoes.'

'I'm not wearing anything,' Cora said.

Abilene laughed. 'Since when does that bother you?'

'Since she heard about the wild hillbilly clan,' Finley said.

'Anyway, all our stuff's in there.'

Vivian rose to her feet. She picked up Abilene's flashlight. 'If I have to walk alone, I will.'

'That's all right,' Finley said. 'I'll go with her.'

'You scared of the water, too?' Cora asked.

'Oh, sure. I just don't need to get wet again.' She uncrossed her legs, stood up, and brushed off her rump. 'You guys go on through the pool. We'll circle around and meet you.'

'You're naked,' Helen pointed out.

She looked down at herself. 'Yep.'

'Be careful,' Abilene said.

Finley, striding alongside the pool with Helen's flashlight

in her hand, said, 'Never fear, the Fin-man's here.' To Vivian, she said, 'Let's keep the lights off unless we need them.'

Abilene was glad to hear it. In spite of Finley's carefree façade, she wasn't reckless.

'Ta ta for now,' Finley said. She and Vivian began walking away, staying on the granite beneath the porch, heading towards the north end of the lodge.

Cora stood up and turned around. 'Watch your tails,' she called.

Finley gave her rump a jaunty swish.

In a low voice, Abilene said, 'Let's keep an eye on them for a minute.'

'Intended to,' Cora told her.

'Viv's really spooked,' she whispered.

'You're telling me.'

'Maybe we should leave tonight.'

'She'll be okay.'

'I sure didn't think it'd upset her so much,' Helen said, coming up behind them.

'It was a pretty awful story.'

Finley and Vivian disappeared around the corner.

'I hope they'll be all right,' Abilene said.

'Let's get on in.' Cora, turning around in the chest-high water, waded past Helen and halted facing the archway. 'When did the lantern go out?'

'Oh, my God,' Helen said.

Abilene followed Helen. They stopped at Cora's back.

Beyond the archway was darkness.

'It probably just ran out of fuel,' Cora said. She didn't sound troubled.

'God, why did we give them *both* the flashlights?' Helen sounded greatly troubled.

'No big deal.'

'Maybe we should go around,' Abilene said.

Cora didn't answer. She slipped through the archway and vanished.

Helen and Abilene followed.

Chapter Fourteen

The windows high in the wall at the far end of the pool glowed dimly with gray light from outside. Turning around, Abilene looked up at the row of windows sheltered by the porch. They were barely less dark than the blackness surrounding her.

The half-circle of the archway was like the mouth of a tunnel, but the moonlit night beyond it was where she had already been, not where she was going.

Abilene turned away from it. She waded slowly forward.

She couldn't see Cora or Helen. She couldn't see anything at all except for the murky strip of windows way off to her right.

She could hear the others, though. The sounds of their breathing, along with her own. And the slurpy sounds of their wading. They seemed to be in front of her. But not very close. They had continued across the pool while she had paused to look around.

'Abby?' Helen's hushed voice was high and shaky.

'Right behind you.'

'I don't like this.'

'Me neither.'

'I can't see a thing.'

'Shhhh.' From Cora?

'What?'

'I thought I heard something.'

'Oh, Jesus,' Abilene murmured.

Then yelped as she bumped something and arms clamped around her.

'Is that you?' Helen gasped, her breath hot on Abilene's face.

'Of course it's me! Jesus! You almost gave me a heart attack.'

'I'm sorry.' The clench loosened, went away. She felt hands grip her upper arms. 'Stay with . . .'

'Shhhh.'

They went silent, stood motionless.

'Somebody's in here,' Cora whispered.

Helen made a whimpery sound. Her fingers dug into Abilene's arms.

And Abilene heard it, too. A single, soft flop of water somewhere in the blackness to her left.

Her bowels squirmed. Shivers scurried up her back. In spite of the water's heat, she felt her skin go stiff with goosebumps.

Cora's calm, quiet voice said, 'Let's just get out of the pool.' The words were followed by a flurry of lapping, splashing sounds from her direction.

Abilene clutched Helen's wrists and forced her hands away.

'Don't leave me!'

'Come on!' Clinging to one wrist, Abilene lunged past Helen. Pulled her around. Towed her. The sounds of their own rush through the water masked whatever noise the intruder might be making.

Making as he hurried closer to them in the darkness.

The water felt like a strong, hot wind thrusting against Abilene, trying to slow her down.

She wished she could let go of Helen. She could slip beneath the surface and swim silently to the other side. But she kept her grip on the wrist of the terrified, whimpering girl, and kept trudging forward.

'What's going on?' Cora didn't sound so calm, now.

'We're coming.'

'Hurry.'

'*Jesus!*'

'I'm right here,' Cora said. Straight ahead. Close.

'Are you out?'

'Yes.'

Helen squealed, 'Yeeahhh!'

'It's me. Just me.' Cora.

Helen jerked her hand free. Abilene heard water suck and splash and drip. She reached out to the side and felt a slick, bare leg. Though she could see nothing, she pictured Helen scrambling out of the pool, being helped by Cora.

Nobody in here now but me and him.

Abilene flung herself forward. Her hands slapped the rim of the pool. Kicking at the water, she boosted herself up. She expected a hand to grab one of her ankles and jerk her down. Then her knees met the cool hardness of the pool's edge. She scurried through the darkness, hands and knees sliding. From off to the side came sounds of slapping feet.

'Where are you?' A whisper. Cora.

'Over here.' She stopped. 'Helen with you?'

'Yeah. Don't move. Quiet.'

Silently, Abilene got to her feet. She put out her hands and crept forward. She thought the stairway should be straight ahead of her, but it wasn't. Instead, she met a wall. Turning around, she leaned back against it. The wall felt cool and slippery against her wet skin.

She was breathless, her heart slamming. She struggled to stop gasping.

The only sounds she heard were her own heartbeat, her own breathing, and the faint lapping sounds of water. Nothing from her friends. Nothing from anyone moving about in the pool.

That doesn't mean he's gone, she thought. He might be swimming under water. Coming closer. Or standing motionless, listening and waiting.

She gazed into the blackness. She couldn't see the pool. Nothing at all was visible except the gloom of the high windows and the pale archway. She realized that the archway with its curved top and vertical sides was shaped like a headstone.

A headstone. A marker for the grave of the headless body found in the pool twelve years ago.

She imagined the body floating there now. And wondered if *that* was what they'd heard. Not an intruder at all, but the decapitated corpse of . . .

Bull.

There's no damn stiff in the pool.

Maybe there's no one at all, she told herself. Maybe what we heard was nothing. Maybe currents from the hot spring had simply disturbed the surface and made those splashy sounds.

Abilene's heart lurched as she heard a quiet, groaning creak.

Someone stepping on a floorboard?

That didn't make sense. The pool's apron was granite, not . . . the stairs.

A beam of light, angling downward, swirled through the darkness just to her right. It cast a bright disk on the floor. Scooted about. Settled on the extinguished lantern.

A second beam started flitting around.

Two people with flashlights?

And Abilene almost laughed as she remembered Finley and Vivian.

What if it's not them?

'Who turned out the lights down here?'

It was them, all right.

'Get down here quick!' Cora called.

Abilene turned her head. Though the flashlight beams were on her other side, they provided enough brightness for her to make out the dim shapes of Cora and Helen. The two stood only a few feet to her left, just in front of the wall, Helen hanging onto Cora's arm.

She gave the pool area a quick scan, saw no one, then watched as Cora pulled away from Helen.

'Do you think it was a false alarm?' Abilene asked.

'I don't know.' Cora watched the water as she hurried toward Abilene. Helen, right behind her, kept a hand on Cora's shoulder.

'What's going on?' Finley asked. She was still out of sight, but the light beams were jumping around and Abilene heard feet thumping down the stairs.

'Is everything all right?' Vivian asked.

Abilene rounded the corner just as Finley and Vivian, side by side, stepped off the bottom of the stairway.

Cora rushed toward them, leaving Helen behind. 'What took you guys so long?'

'I thought we were pretty snappy about it. Why's the lantern out?'

'Somebody's here.'

'Holy shit. Someone's here *now*?'

'Think so.'

'Oh my God,' Vivian said.

Cora snatched the flashlight from Finley's hand and swung around. Rushing toward the pool, she flicked the beam to the right and left, making sure nobody had followed them out.

Abilene went after her. She heard the others approaching as Cora began to sweep the light over the water's surface.

She saw cut-off jeans.

With a gasp, she lurched backward. Collided with someone. Dry hands grabbed her sides. She felt skin against her back. Bare breasts. Finley.

Then she saw that the cut-off jeans were empty.

Nobody in them.

Another flashlight joined Cora's. Both beams searched the water.

As Finley stepped around to her side, Abilene saw that the pool was littered with floating and submerged garments. The cut-offs that had given her such a fright were her own, sinking toward the bottom. Finley's safari shirt drifted nearby. Deep beneath the water were Vivian's sundress, Cora's shorts, Helen's blouse and her own. Cora's T-shirt, puffed with air, bobbed on the surface like a Portuguese man-of-war beside a floating bra. Panties hung suspended like flimsy, limp rags. Finley's tan shorts lay at the bottom, along with several shoes and socks, towels and the three flashlights that they hadn't taken with them when they entered the pool.

Except for the lantern, everything they'd left behind now seemed to be in the water.

The flashlights searched the rest of the pool. Farther away, the beams weren't powerful enough to penetrate the depths.

They lit little more than the surface as they skimmed the middle, darted into the corners, and swept along the far side.

They criss-crossed again and again.

'If he's still in here,' Cora whispered, 'he must be holding his breath.'

'He might be anywhere,' Abilene said.

Vivian turned, swinging her light toward the open space and bar beyond the end of the pool.

'Want me to check back there?' Finley offered.

'No,' Vivian said.

'We stay together,' Cora said.

Vivian, stepping back away from the edge of the pool, turned completely around as if to make sure nobody was sneaking up on them.

'He didn't go up the stairs,' Finley said. 'We would've run into him. Might've ducked into one of the dressing rooms, though.'

'I don't think he left the pool. Not over here, anyway.'

'Yeah,' Cora said. 'We'd have heard him.'

Both flashlights returned their beams to the water.

'Maybe he snuck out through there,' Cora said, pointing her light at the archway to the outer pool.

'We'd better check behind the bar,' Abilene said.

Cora and Vivian led the way, continuing to play the beams of their flashlights over the water. The others followed close behind them. When they reached the bar, Cora knelt on one of the stools. She stretched over the counter top and shone her light down behind it.

'Not here.'

'So he's either still in the water,' Abilene said, 'or he's gone.'

Cora climbed off the stool.

For a while, they all stood motionless at the end of the

pool. They listened and watched as Cora and Vivian swept the surface again and again with their flashlights.

'I think he's gone,' Finley said.

'Guess so,' Cora finally agreed.

'Are we *still* planning to spend the night?' Vivian asked.

Cora let out a sigh. 'No. I think this does it for me.'

'Same here,' Helen said.

Abilene felt almost giddy with relief.

'Let's get our stuff and hit the road,' Cora said.

They started to walk back along the side of the pool.

'It was probably that kid,' Finley said. 'He must've come back, after all.'

'Why'd he want to throw our things in the water?' Abilene asked.

'Pissed off at us?' Finley said.

'Maybe to scare us away,' Cora suggested.

'Glad it worked,' Vivian said. 'I might've done it, myself, if I'd thought of it.'

'God,' Helen muttered. 'How creepy. He must've been sneaking around in here while we were right outside.'

'I wonder where he came from,' Abilene said.

'He couldn've been in here all along,' Cora pointed out. 'Even before we came down, you know? Maybe he was in the water and we just didn't spot him.'

'Wonderful,' Vivian said. 'Watching us undress.'

'Nothing he hadn't seen already,' Finley told her.

They lined up along the rim of the pool. Cora and Vivian aimed their lights into the water. Everything except the air-bloated T-shirt had sunk.

'There's no point in all of us getting wet,' she said.

'We're the dry ones,' Finley remarked, and clapped a hand onto Vivian's shoulder.

'Yeah. *I'm* not going in.'

'We'll hold the lights,' Finley said, 'while you three bring up the stuff.'

Helen moaned. 'Don't let anybody sneak up on us.'

'Just hurry,' Vivian urged.

'Maybe we should light the lantern first,' Abilene suggested.

Cora crouched, picked it up and shook it. Fuel sloshed in its tank. 'Didn't run out,' she muttered. She twisted a knob at its base. There was a brief hissing sound, then silence. 'He shut it off.'

'Figures,' Finley said.

'The matches are upstairs.'

'We could go get them,' Abilene said. 'It'd be a lot better if we had some decent light.'

'Geez,' Helen said, 'I hope he didn't bother the stuff up there.'

'Didn't look like it,' Vivian told her.

Cora set down the lantern. 'Let's just get this over with. Shouldn't take more than a couple of minutes.'

She stood, stepped over to the pool and jumped in.

Abilene considered going after the matches herself. Finley would probably be glad to accompany her. But the thought that someone might be up there changed her mind.

She sat on the edge, lowered her legs into the water, and hesitated. She scanned the pool. The flashlights brightened only the small area surrounding Cora, who had already grabbed her T-shirt. The rest of the pool was shrouded in darkness. A beam shone on Cora's gleaming buttocks as she curled forward, kicked and plunged.

Abilene pushed off. She dropped, the heat rushing up her body. Peering down through the clear water, she saw towels and flashlights, shoes and a few garments near her feet. She ducked under and started to grab for them.

A heavy splash thudded in her ears. Currents buffeted her. Helen coming in.

Struggling to keep herself close to the bottom, she snatched up a towel, a flashlight, three socks and a pair of panties. She sprang to the surface. Cora was already turning away, having deposited a heap of sodden clothes in front of Vivian.

Abilene set her load onto the edge, then waded past Helen's submerged body. She spotted her cut-offs. They were down near the bottom, quite a distance from the side of the pool, barely visible in the murky light. She dove. Swimming toward them underwater, she glided past Finley's shirt. She grabbed it, continued on her way, and finally snatched up her jeans. She was about to rise with them when something ahead caught her attention. She could hardly see it through the gloom of the poorly lighted water. But it seemed to be fabric undulating near the bottom, very close to the bars of the grate that covered the hot spring.

Had she strayed *that* far from the poolside?

She suddenly felt very alone and vulnerable. She ached to turn back. But the thing near the grate was probably clothing. And she was almost close enough to grab it.

Though her lungs were starting to burn, she swam forward and reached down. Her fingers snagged fabric. She clenched it, kicked to the surface and stood up. Gasping for air, she twisted around.

She was alone in the middle of the pool, surrounded by darkness. Neither of the flashlights were on her; they were aimed down at Cora and Helen.

'Hey!' she called.

A beam darted about, then found her.

'Thanks.'

As she waded toward her friends, she lifted her hand out of the water to see what she had retrieved. Helen's plaid, Bermuda shorts. She had snagged them only by one leg, and they hung upside down.

She gathered them in against her belly. Holding them there along with her shorts and Finley's shirt, she trudged through the chest deep water. She took only a few steps before the light abandoned her. She almost called out to complain, but decided not to bother. She would be with the others soon.

It was slow going, though. She thought about the darkness at her back. The nape of her neck tingled. A few times, she glanced over her shoulder, but saw nothing.

She gasped when something brushed her thigh. Goose-bumps scurried up her skin.

Telling herself it was probably just an article of clothing, she reached down. Her fingers hooked a strap, and she lifted a bra out of the water. From the size of the thing, it had to be Helen's.

Ahead of her, Helen flung some things at Finley's feet, then boosted herself out of the water.

Exactly what I'm going to do, she thought. Get out. I've had enough of this.

She was nearly to the side when Cora emerged with Vivian's wadded sundress clutched to her chest.

'I'm done,' Abilene said.

'I think we've about got it all,' Cora told her.

'I don't see anything else,' Finley said, peering down from the rim and sweeping her light through the water.

Abilene and Cora reached the side at the same time.

As Cora climbed out, Abilene tossed the bra and Bermuda shorts to Helen.

'Thanks,' she said, catching them.

Finley was looking the other way when Abilene tossed the safari shirt to her. The shirt hit her belly with a sodden smacking sound and clung there long enough for her to bring up an arm and clamp it. 'Thanks for getting me all wet, Hickok.'

'Welcome.' She flung her cut-offs onto the granite, then boosted herself from the pool.

Helen, still in her swimsuit, was stepping into her shorts. She hadn't even bothered to wring them.

'We can get dressed upstairs,' Abilene told her. 'Let's just get out of here.'

'Yeah,' Cora said. 'The sooner the better.'

After that, everyone began crouching and squatting, gathering up the things that had been recovered from the pool, not bothering to separate their belongings from those of others, just grabbing as fast as they could, then rolling clothes and shoes and flashlights inside towels.

Cora, a bundle pressed against her side, picked up the lantern. 'Okay,' she said. 'We got it all?'

Helen, the last to finish, clutched a lumpy rolled towel to her chest and rose from her crouch. 'I'm done,' she muttered.

As they started for the stairs, Finley turned around. Abilene, beside her, also looked back. The light swept over the pool's apron. Where they'd been, the granite was wet and shiny. If anything had been left behind, Abilene didn't see it.

She and Finley turned and followed the others up the stairs. At the top, Abilene stepped into the corridor and closed the door. The snap of its latch sounded wonderful to her. She felt as if she had shut away whatever danger lurked in the pool area.

And we'll be out of here in a few minutes, she told herself.

She no longer cared about whether they would have any luck finding a motel. Being far from this place would be enough.

Just a few more minutes.

She felt even better once the lantern was lit, the glare of its mantels filling the lobby with brightness.

The suitcases, bedrolls, video camera and water container didn't appear to have been disturbed.

She pulled off her bikini, dropped it onto the wet towel, and used a blouse from her suitcase to mop herself dry. She stepped into panties, then put on a bra. The dry garments felt wonderful.

'You should get out of those wet things,' she advised Helen.

Helen, still in her swimsuit and Bermudas, shook her head and finished buttoning a blouse from her suitcase.

'You'll be sorry,' Finley said. She wore a fresh pair of baggy tan shorts that were much the same as those that had been rescued from the pool. Adding, 'You'll itch,' she slipped into a big, tan safari shirt identical to her wet one.

Abilene drew a short, denim skirt up her legs and fastened it. She dug her moccasins out of the corners of her suitcase and slipped her feet into them.

While she put on a blouse, she watched Vivian, dressed in a knit pullover and matching white shorts as if prepared to hit the tennis courts, hop on one foot as she struggled to get into a sock.

Cora, already dressed in a tank top and glossy red shorts, squatted down and shut her suitcase.

Abilene closed her own case and latched it.

She glanced about at the wet bundles, the suitcases and bedrolls, camera, water container and lantern. 'Can we take all this out in one trip?'

'Sure as hell try,' Cora said.

'Maybe if we consolidate the wet stuff . . .'

'Yeah.'

They'd brought five dripping towels, loaded with clothing and shoes and flashlights, up from the pool area. Working together, Abilene and Cora quickly combined the bundles until everything was gathered inside two towels. They knotted corners together, forming a pair of makeshift sacks.

By the time they were done, the others were ready to go. Cora and Abilene each clamped their bedrolls under one arm, picked up their suitcases with the same hand and a wet load with the other. Finley, Helen and Vivian also managed their sleeping bags and suitcases with one arm, leaving hands free to carry the video camera, water and lantern.

Vivian, holding the lantern by its wire loop, led the way to the door. She opened it. She waited until everyone was outside, then shut the door.

'And so we bid this damn place a fond farewell,' she said, and followed them down the porch stairs.

'Farewell, farewell,' Abilene said. She felt great.

They hurried over the paved area to the north corner of the lodge, then stepped down the slope and walked down alongside the Wagoneer to its rear.

Helen, halting at its tailgate, set down her suitcase and bedroll. She shoved a hand deep into the right front pocket of her Bermuda shorts.

'Oh my God,' she muttered.

'What?' Cora asked.

Shaking her head, she dug into the left front pocket. Then she patted both seat pockets. Hands clasped against her huge buttocks, she straightened her back and gazed straight ahead.

Abilene felt her stomach go cold and tight.

'Don't tell me,' Vivian pleaded.

Cora groaned. 'You've lost the keys?'

The sound that came from Helen was like a low, husky laugh. But it wasn't laughter. Lowering her head, she pressed her hands against her face and wept.

Chapter Fifteen

'Are you sure the keys were in your pocket?' Cora asked.

Helen's head bobbed up and down as she sobbed.

'Oh, man,' Finley said.

Vivian lowered her suitcase and sat on its edge. She put the lantern down beside her. Though it came to rest at a sharp angle, it didn't fall over. She hugged her sleeping bag.

'I'm . . . sorry,' Helen gasped.

Abilene crouched and set down her load. Then she gently squeezed Helen's shoulders. 'It's all right,' she said.

Sure it is, she thought. Jesus. What if we can't find them?

Cora let her wet bundle and sleeping bag drop to the pavement, then set down her suitcase. 'When did you have the keys last?' she asked.

'When we . . . took out our . . . suitcases and stuff.'

'That was just before we went down to the pool.'

Helen nodded.

'And you're sure you put them back into your pocket?'

'*Yes!*' She slapped her right front pocket three times hard as if to punish it – and her thigh.

'Take it easy,' Abilene said, and rubbed the girl's heaving shoulders.

'Are you sure you didn't put them somewhere else? In your purse, maybe? Or your suitcase?'

'I know where I put them.'

'I *saw* Helen stick them in her pocket,' Vivian said. 'The right front. The first place she checked.'

'And you changed into your suit when we were down by the pool?'

'We all did,' Abilene pointed out, wishing Cora would quit the interrogation.

'Those of us who wore 'em,' Finley said. She had put down her own things, but still held her video camera.

'Were the keys in your pocket when you put your shorts back on?'

'I don't know.'

'Obviously, they weren't,' Finley said. She sounded a little annoyed. 'I've kept a sharp eye on Helen, and she didn't do a single hand-stand after she got out of the water.'

Helen let out a choking snort, as if a sob had blocked the way of a laugh. Turning around, she snuffled and wiped her eyes with the backs of her hands.

'They must've fallen out in the pool,' Abilene said. 'Either when the guy threw . . .'

'Maybe he took them as a souvenir,' Finley suggested.

'Or to keep us from leaving,' Vivian muttered.

Helen moaned.

'They probably just fell out of the pocket,' Abilene said. 'I'm the one who found Helen's shorts. When I was way out toward the middle of the pool? The keys could've fallen out when I picked them up.'

'I don't know,' Cora said.

'They way I grabbed them . . . they came out upside-down.'

'Good going, Hickok.'

'How could the shorts get way out there with the keys in the pocket?' Cora asked. 'They would've sunk as soon as they hit the water.' To Helen, she said, 'You had your house keys and things in the same case, didn't you?'

'Yeah.'

'They would've sunk the shorts.'

'Not necessarily,' Abilene said. 'If some air got trapped in the pants, they might've floated for a while. Just like your T-shirt.'

'Maybe the guy gave them a toss,' Finley said.

'We would've heard splashes,' Cora told her, 'if he'd thrown stuff.'

'I don't know why you're arguing,' Abilene said. 'The fact is, I found the shorts in the middle of the pool and the keys were gone when Helen put them back on. So unless the bastard stole the keys, they've gotta be down at the bottom of the pool right now.'

Cora lowered her head. She let out a sigh that was louder than the hiss of the lantern.

'Fun 'n games,' Finley said.

Cora said, 'Shit.'

Helen sniffed loudly, then said, 'If someone'll come with me, I'll look for them.'

Vivian, still sitting on her suitcase, muttered, 'We could've been gone by now.'

'I mean it. I'll find them. It was my fault. I just don't want to go alone.'

'You can't go alone,' Abilene said, but couldn't force herself to volunteer. Stepping up the slope, she tried the handle of the car's rear door. The latch released. She tugged the door open slightly, then let it drop shut. 'Well, we're not locked out of the car. Anybody know how to hot-wire one of these things?'

'Television stuff,' Cora said.

'Like getting into locked rooms with credit cards,' Finley added.

'What are we gonna do?' Vivian asked. She sounded as if she might start crying.

'I already said I'd . . .'

'We're not going back in there,' Cora snapped, stunning Abilene with her vehemence. 'I'm not. You're not. None of us are. Not tonight.'

'Wow.' From Finley.

'What's your problem?'

'Nothing. Just . . . I'm surprised, that's all. I figured you'd be all gung-ho to go for the keys.'

'Well, I'm not. Okay? Do you have a problem with that?'

'Me? No. Huh-uh. I don't want to go down there, either.'

'Neither do I,' Abilene admitted. 'But if we don't, it means we're stuck here.'

'I'm aware of that.'

'Calm down, will you? We're *all* scared. It's nothing to be ashamed of.'

'I'm not ashamed of anything.'

'Well, just calm down.'

'All the shit we've been through together,' Finley said, 'we shouldn't let a little thing like this throw us. We heard a creepy story, and some rat-ass teenager fucked us over. That's really all that's happened, right? Nobody's been hurt. We're all just a bit spooked. So why don't we just make the best of it?'

'And do what?' Cora asked.

'Well, I don't think any of us want to go back inside the lodge tonight. So why don't we find a nice, hidden place in the woods somewhere? We'll sack out till morning. Then, when it's broad daylight, we'll go back down to the pool and find the keys and get our asses out of here.'

'Spend the night?' Vivian didn't sound thrilled by the idea.

'Sounds good to me,' Abilene said. 'The only other choice, if we don't go after the keys, is to hike out. I can't see the point of that. We're out in the middle of nowhere.'

'Besides,' Finley said, 'we'd have to leave our stuff here. Which means we'd need to come back for it, sooner or later.'

'Let's stay,' Cora said.

Helen nodded.

'First thing in the morning, we'll go back down to the pool.'

'We can throw everything in the car,' Abilene said, 'and just take our sleeping bags. And whatever else we'll need for the night. Toothbrushes, the water . . .'

'Let's do it,' Cora said.

Spreading out behind the car, they opened their luggage. Abilene took out her toilet kit, then shut the case.

Cora climbed into the car and knelt on the back seat. Abilene kept the door open by leaning back against it, her legs braced. The others passed suitcases to Cora, and she stowed them in the rear. She placed the wet, loaded towels on the floor in front of the seat. 'Is that it? What about your camera, Fin?'

'I'll keep it, thanks. I'm not about to leave it in an unlocked car.'

'You'll leave your purse, but not your camera?'

'Maybe we ought to take our purses,' Abilene said.

'Shouldn't have left them here in the first place with the car unlocked.'

436

'Good thing we did,' Cora said. 'They might've ended up in the pool.'

'Well, I think we'd better keep them with us from now on. If we lose our money and credit cards, we'll really be up the creek.'

Cora hunted around, and finally handed out the purses. She was holding a roll of toilet paper when she climbed from the car. She tossed it to Helen. Abilene stepped clear of the door, and it fell shut with a solid thud.

After gathering their things, they trudged uphill past the side of the car. Vivian, holding the lantern, halted. 'Where to?' she asked.

'First off,' Cora said, 'let's kill the light.' She reached out and twisted the knob at its base. The hiss went silent. The brightness faded until the only light came from the hot mantles. They looked like a pair of small, net sacks, glowing white then dimming to red.

'If we're not going to use the lantern,' Finley said, 'why don't we leave it in the car?'

'We might need it later,' Cora told her.

'You've got the matches?'

She patted her belly. She had no pockets, so Abilene supposed she must've tucked the matchbook under the elastic of her shorts. It was out of sight under the hanging front of her tank top.

Turning to Finley, Cora said, 'This is your idea. You want to lead the way?'

'Sure.'

Cora offered her a flashlight. Finley accepted it, said, 'You take this,' and handed the video camera to Cora. 'Be careful with it.' Then she started walking. She kept the flashlight off.

They followed her along the pavement that stretched in front of the porch. Where it met the main driveway, she headed to the right. Away from the lodge.

'Just in case anyone's watching,' she explained, 'we'll make it look like we're actually taking off.'

Abilene turned around. As she walked backward, she gazed at the lodge. With the moon out of sight behind it, the building was masked in black shadow. Someone might be watching – from the porch, from the doorway, from a window, from anywhere. But she saw only darkness.

She faced the front again. Soon, the driveway began sloping downward. Gravity pushed at her back as if it wanted to send her running for the bottom. She shortened her strides. Her legs trembled, but she supposed that the shakiness had more to do with her fears than with the exertion of trying to control her descent.

'Are we going all the way to the road?' Helen asked.

Finley looked back. They all did. The lodge was out of sight. Abilene could see nothing except the dim, rising lane of the driveway, a few patches of sky through the tree tops, and the dark woods on both sides.

'This is good enough,' Finley said. She strode to the right and stepped off the driveway. Her sneakers crunched dead leaves and twigs on the forest floor. She ducked under a low branch. Cora went after her, followed by Vivian. Abilene cast a final glance up the deserted lane, saw nobody, and followed Helen into the trees.

Ahead, she glimpsed a flashlight beam. It dug a bright tunnel through the darkness to the right, then slipped aside and disappeared.

They trudged along in single file, traversing the hillside, Finley leading them around brambles, boulders and massive trunks that loomed in their way. Nobody spoke. Abilene stayed close to the gray smudge of Helen's back.

There was no breeze. The heavy, sweet air felt nearly as hot as the water in the pool. It had to be much cooler, but it sure didn't feel that way. She was sweating. Dribbles tickled her face and neck, her chest and sides. The back of her blouse and the seat of her panties were wet and clinging.

In spite of the heat, she trembled.

She supposed she ought to feel safe, surrounded by the woods. After all, the chances of being found in here were remote.

Unless the guy had somehow followed them.

Awfully unlikely.

But if he *had* followed them, he could be close enough to reach out of the darkness and grab her.

Would've heard him coming, she told herself. No one could possibly tromp through all this without making noise.

The thought didn't reassure her. She was scared. She supposed the others were scared, too.

It's my fault we're here, she thought. God, how stupid, picking up the shorts like that. The damn keys were probably right inside the pocket till I did that.

If only I'd taken my time. If only I'd been more careful.

It's little mistakes like that . . .

We'd be safe in the car right now, tooling along the road, a nice wind coming in through the open windows. Out of here. Gone.

Never should've come here in the first place.

Helen must be nuts, bringing us to an abandoned lodge in the middle of nowhere.

We were just as nuts, going along with it.

I could've been home right now with Harris. Watching some TV, having some popcorn and a Pepsi.

It wouldn't be this damn hot, either. And if it was, we'd have the fan going, a nice breeze blowing against us.

Nobody put a gun to my head, she reminded herself.

They'd always had great times with their adventures. They'd done stuff that was a lot more crazy than coming to an old lodge. Though Abilene regretted some of the things they'd done, nobody had ever gotten hurt and they'd always gotten away with their stunts, no matter how wild and dangerous.

We'll get away with this, too, she thought.

This time tomorrow, we'll be in a nice motel.

If we find the damn keys.

If we don't, we'll hike out.

Either way, we'll be gone from this place.

Abilene suddenly realized that she was walking uphill. 'Hey!' she called in a loud whisper. 'What're we doing?'

Finley halted. The others continued toward her. As Abilene approached, she noticed that neither flashlight was on.

'We're going uphill,' she whispered.

'Yeah,' Finley said. 'I know. Have you ever tried sleeping on a slope?'

'But we're heading back toward the lodge.'

'Where the ground is level. Don't worry, we'll stay in the trees. As long as we keep quiet and don't use our lights, nobody'll be the wiser.'

'I don't want to get any closer to the lodge.'

'We're almost to the top of the hill. Just a little bit farther, then we'll find a good place to sack out.' Without waiting for approval or more objections, Finley resumed her trek up the slope.

Cora followed. Vivian shook her head and Helen shrugged.

'We should be going the *other* way,' Abilene muttered.

440

'I knew this'd turn into a goddamn campout,' Vivian said, and started after Cora.

'At least we won't have so far to walk in the morning,' Helen said.

'We keep this up, we might as well sleep on the front lawn.'

'The whole thing was a big mistake. I wish we hadn't come here.' With that, Helen turned around and hurried to catch up with Vivian.

Abilene stayed close behind her.

This is what we get, she thought, for letting Finley take the lead.

Before she could get too annoyed, however, she found that the group had come to a halt.

'Are we close enough for you?' she asked.

'It's nice right here, don't you think?'

Abilene looked around. They were in a small clearing surrounded by a wall of trees and low bushes. There appeared to be barely enough room for the sleeping bags. Peering into the darkness, she could see no trace of the lodge. 'I guess it's okay,' she whispered.

'Okay? It's perfect. Perfecto.'

In silence, they set down their things. They opened the sleeping bags and spent a while arranging them. Three could fit side by side. Two fit crosswise.

Finley's bag was in the middle between Abilene's and Helen's. She dropped down on it and crossed her legs. 'Great, huh? Now, if we just had some margaritas and chips.'

'Feel free to go back for them,' Abilene said. 'I'm sure we're not far from the car.'

'Did *anybody* bring food?' Helen asked.

'We should've,' Finley said.

'But we didn't,' Abilene said.

'Geez.'

'You're trying to lose weight,' Cora reminded her.

'That was before.'

'You can survive till morning,' Vivian said.

Helen sighed. 'Yeah. Sure.'

'Just forget about it,' Cora said. 'Let's brush our teeth and get some sleep.'

'And take a leak,' Abilene added.

'Not necessarily in that order,' Finley said.

They gathered their toothbrushes, paste, the big plastic water bottle and the roll of toilet paper. Helen passed the roll around, and they each tore off some paper.

'We go *that* way,' Abilene said, pointing back the way they'd come.

They crept into the trees. A short distance from the clearing, they crowded together in a circle to share the water while they brushed their teeth.

Then they separated. Glad that she'd changed into a skirt instead of shorts, Abilene slipped out of her panties. Poor Helen, she recalled, was still in her swimsuit. Everything would have to come off. While she squatted close to the ground, she heard the others nearby: footsteps mashing forest debris, muttered curses, splashing sounds.

Done, she backed away and stepped into her panties. She didn't go looking for the others. Instead, she made her way to the clearing. Cora and Finley were already there. As she was putting her toothpaste and brush into her toilet kit, Vivian returned.

Abilene sat on her sleeping bag. She was pulling off her moccasins when Helen came slouching out of the trees.

'What a pain,' Helen muttered. She carried her swimsuit

and Bermudas in one hand. She wore only her blouse and shoes. The blouse hung open, its front bouncing and swaying with the motions of her loose breasts.

'The Tipton girl,' Finley said.

In spite of Helen's miserable appearance, Abilene found herself grinning. Helen really did look like some kind of bizarre parody of the Tipton shirt commercial that, during the past year, had made Vivian something of a national celebrity.

In the commercial, Vivian strides languidly across a veranda, leans her shoulder against a pillar and gazes out at swaying palm trees, combers rolling in toward a deserted beach. A breeze caresses her thick, auburn hair and stirs the front of her white Tipton dress shirt. It is a man's shirt, too large for her. Its sleeves are rolled partway up her forearms. Its tails drape her buttocks and thighs. She seems to wear nothing except the shirt. Only a single, closed button prevents it from blowing open.

The camera slowly circles her as she enjoys the tropical scenery. Then a sleek, handsome man, dressed only in slacks, crosses the veranda. He wraps his arms around her, kisses the side of her neck. The voice of the announcer says, 'Men prefer Tipton shirts.'

'Men prefer Tipton shirts,' Finley said.

'This is J.C. Penny's,' Helen muttered. 'And it's wet.' She dropped onto her sleeping bag. 'Everything's wet.'

'You should've changed when you had the chance,' Cora told her.

'Your stuff would've gotten soaked, anyway,' Abilene said. 'Unless you don't sweat.'

'Hotter than a huncher,' Finley said.

Vivian shook her head. 'We could've been in an air-conditioned motel room right now.'

'Tomorrow night,' Abilene said.

'If we can find the keys.'

'We'll find them,' Cora said, and lay down on top of her sleeping bag.

Finley stretched out on hers, too. 'Let's all go to sleep, kiddies. The sooner we fall asleep, the sooner morning will come. Maybe Santa will leave us a nice set of car keys under the tree.'

'I don't care where he leaves them,' Abilene said, 'as long as we find them and get out of here.'

Vivian sank down beside Cora, rolled over, and rested her face on her crossed arms.

Abilene was about to lie down, but remained sitting, curious, when she saw Helen take off her blouse. Pale in the darkness, Helen leaned forward. She spread her blouse, swimsuit and Bermuda shorts over the top of her sleeping bag. Then she got to her hands and knees. She pulled down the zipper at the side of her bag and struggled to crawl inside.

Finley, also watching, said, 'You've gotta be kidding.'

'You'll cook in there,' Abilene added.

'Leave her alone,' Vivian murmured.

Abilene heard a rip-like sound of the zipper sliding up.

'Maybe she's planning to sweat the pounds away,' Finley said.

'Ha ha, very funny,' came Helen's muffled voice.

Abilene eased down onto her bag. Its slick fabric felt cool through her blouse and against the backs of her bare legs. She folded her hands under her head. Her hair was tangled and wet. But lying down felt very good. The thickness of the sleeping bag cushioned her from the ground. If there were twigs or rocks beneath her, she couldn't feel them. She stretched, and sighed softly.

The branches overhead were motionless. Beyond them, she could see pieces of sky and a few tiny dots of starlight.

She closed her eyes.

She heard birds singing, squawking, and the distant, lonely sound of an owl calling *whooo*. Insects chittered and hummed. She realized she hadn't been bothered by mosquitos. That, at least, was something to be grateful about. So long as mosquitos didn't assault her, she would be able to sleep on top of her bag.

There were other sounds. Flutters. Furtive scurryings. Papery rustling sounds. Sometimes, soft thumps that she supposed must be something – twigs or pine cones – dropping out of the trees.

She heard nothing that sounded like a person creeping through the woods. But that, she realized, was what she was listening for.

Nobody will find us here, she told herself.

In the morning, we'll find the keys.

Please, let us find the keys.

If only I'd been more careful picking up the shorts.

In her mind, she was swimming underwater. Reaching for the plaid Bermudas. This time I'll do it right, she thought. Grab them by the waist.

As she reached down through the murky water, she saw the crossbars covering the top of the spring.

So very close to the shorts.

Oh, my God.

If the keys dropped through the bars . . .

It was a long time before she fell asleep.

When she woke up in the morning, Helen was gone.

Chapter Sixteen
Belmore Girls

It was their junior year at Belmore.

It was Thursday, 30 October.

The girls, scattered about the living room of their apartment, had the television on. Abilene, slumped on the sofa with her feet resting on the coffee table, watched the eleven o'clock news anchored by Candi Delmar while Vivian fiddled with hair curlers, Finley studied *TV Guide*, Cora skimmed a chapter in her physiology textbook, and Helen munched nacho-flavored tortilla chips.

'Parents,' Candi reported, 'are being encouraged to take advantage of various community activities, such as Halloween parties being hosted at local recreation centers, which provide a safe alternative to the traditional trick-or-treating.'

'Oh, what fun,' Abilene muttered. 'Next thing you know, they're gonna *outlaw* trick-or-treating.'

'For those who do intend to allow their children to go from door to door, however, we at Newscene urge that several simple precautions be followed. Naturally, small children should always be accompanied by an adult. Make sure their costumes are made of flame-resistant fabrics and light in color so that they will be plainly visible to motorists. Masks should not restrict the child's vision. Finally, take special care to inspect all the treats before you allow them to be eaten by your young ones. Be on the lookout for any signs of tampering, especially with such items as home-baked goods and fruit.'

'The ol' razor blade in the apple gag,' Finley said, looking up from the *TV Guide*.

'Ouch,' Helen said.

'. . . foreign objects in your child's treats, you should immediately alert the police.'

'Who would *do* something like that?' Helen asked.

'A lot of sick bastards in this world,' Abilene said.

'. . . these simple guidelines and have a safe and sane Halloween.'

Cora shut her textbook. 'Halloween was never intended to be safe and sane. The whole idea's to get wild.'

'I used to get scared silly,' Helen said. 'You know? You go up to some creepy old house and ring the doorbell? You never know who's gonna open the door.'

'Or *what*,' Finley added.

'Oooo, I get goosebumps just thinking about it. I think it was my favorite holiday, besides Christmas.'

'Once I got too old for trick-or-treating,' Abilene said, 'we'd always stay home and fix up the house. To make it look spooky. I'd hand out the goodies, but Dad'd pull stuff. Come to the door in a vampire outfit, or something. I remember this one time, he rigged up an overcoat so it covered his head. Then he hid on the porch and snuck up on the kids. Scared the hell out of them. Some of 'em actually ran off screaming. And Dad would end up laughing like crazy and Mom'd yell at him. He'd say, "Don't be a stick-in-the-mud. They *love* it." ' Abilene shook her head. 'It was so neat. He'll probably be up to his same old tricks tomorrow night.' She felt her throat tighten. 'God, I'm making myself homesick.'

'We oughta do something,' Finley said.

'Yeah,' Abilene said. 'Last year was a drag. We bought all that stuff and nobody showed up.'

'A few did,' Vivian pointed out.

'Six or seven. Might as well not have *been* a Halloween.'

Cora grinned. 'We could crash the Sig party. They're having that Midnight Sabat thing.'

'You got a death wish?' Abilene asked.

'Why don't we go out trick-or-treating?' Finley suggested.

'I think we're a little old for that,' Vivian said, pinning a final curler into her hair.

'We could go to the movies,' Helen said. 'They're having a special all-night Shock Festival at the Elsinore.'

'That sounds pretty lame,' Finley said.

'Yeah,' Abilene said. 'We can go to movies any time.'

'Helen *does*,' Cora pointed out.

'It doesn't have to be actual trick-or-treating,' Abilene said. 'But it'd be neat to get out into the streets. Put together some costumes. Get a look at the kids.'

'See if any are even out there,' Cora said. 'Maybe they'll all be off having a safe and sane time taking advantage of community activities.'

'If they are,' Abilene said, 'I pity them. Anyway, how about it? We don't actually have to go around ringing doorbells. What we could do is buy a bunch of candy and take it with us, and hand it out to the kids we see.'

'I'll wear my gorilla mask,' Finley said.

'Newscene wouldn't approve,' Cora told her. 'It restricts your vision.'

'Screw Newscene.'

Finley wore her gorilla mask and a suit of green, mechanic's coveralls that she found after cutting her afternoon classes and searching thrift shops in the seamier area of town. She announced that she would be going out as a grease monkey.

Cora, averse to dressing up, gave in to pressure from the others and wore her varsity cheerleader costume from high school. It consisted of a white pullover sweater with a large M in front, a short white pleated skirt, white crew socks and sneakers.

Vivian borrowed a costume from the wardrobe room of the theater arts department. She would be going out as a witch, complete with pointed hat and a flowing black gown. She used makeup to construct a nasty, bulbous wen for the tip of her nose. She didn't want to carry a broom but Finley talked her into it.

Abilene prepared her costume in secret. She cut out a foot-long crescent in cardboard, taped it securely to the pendant of a chain necklace, covered the cardboard with aluminium foil and attached the Schick label from a pack of injector blades. She scissored a big hole under one arm of an old sweatshirt. While the others were in the living room, she dressed herself in Reeboks, corduroy pants and the maimed sweatshirt. She dropped the chain over her head so that the shiny crescent hung across her chest. Then she joined the rest of them.

'What the hell are you supposed to be?' Cora asked, seeming to frown and smile at the same time.

Abilene grinned. She raised her right arm and waved it up and down, showing her exposed armpit.

'An ad for Ban deodorant,' suggested Finley, who was tossing her gorilla head from hand to hand.

'Beeeeep. Wrong.' She tapped the dangling crescent.

'Moon something,' Helen guessed. 'A silver moon.'

'You're a Moonie,' Cora said.

'Beeeeep. Wrong.'

'A lunatic,' Finley said.

'I get it,' Vivian said. Shaking her head, she rolled her eyes upward. 'I'll give you gals a couple of hints. One, it's *really* dumb.'

'That narrows things down,' Cora said.

'Two, Abilene's an English major.'

'Got it,' Finley said. 'She's *Huckleberry Armpit*.'

In unison, Vivian and Abilene said, 'Beeeep. Wrong.'

'Give up?' Abilene asked. 'Tell 'em, Viv.'

'She's "The Pit and the Pendulum," you weenies.'

The revelation was greeted with groans, chuckles, smirks and shaking heads.

'Nobody's gonna *get* that,' Cora said.

'So what? I think it's pretty neat. That's all that counts.'

'You're so weird, sometimes,' Helen said.

'Me? What are *you* supposed to be?'

Helen, standing there among a grease monkey, a cheer-leader, a 'Pit and the Pendulum' and a witch, seemed to be dressed as nothing more than Helen. She wore sneakers, brown corduroy pants and a white blouse. Clutched against her stomach was a wadded white sheet.

'A laundry woman?' Abilene suggested.

'Hardly.' Helen shook open her sheet. When she draped it over her head, Abilene saw that holes had been cut for her eyes and mouth.

'Caspar the Friendly Ghost,' Finley said.

Helen raised her arms and went, 'Woooooo.'

'And you say *I'm* weird.'

'I always used to go as a ghost,' Helen explained.

'Always?'

'Every Halloween. But you've gotta get the full effect.' Pressing the sheet to her face so she could see out the eyeholes, she drifted over to the sofa. She picked up a short length of

450

rope with a hangman's noose at one end. She dropped the loop over her head like a necklace, positioning the thick row of coils in the center of her chest. The weight of the noose, Abilene realized, was intended to hold the outfit in place.

'Pretty decent,' she said.

'*She* won't have to worry about getting hit by a car,' Cora said.

'True,' said Abilene. 'Not a ghost of a chance.'

'Groan,' Finley remarked. She put on her gorilla head. Bending over the sofa, she picked up her video camera. She taped the others while they gathered flashlights and several plastic sacks loaded with candy they'd purchased that day at a nearby convenience store. Then she led the way, walking backward through the doorway, the camera at her shoulder, recording the procession as it paraded along the corridor.

Lowering the camera, she trotted downstairs. They followed her into the night.

' "The sky, it was ashen and sober," ' Abilene intoned. ' "The leaves, they were crisped and seer. 'Twas night in the lonesome October of my most immemorial year." '

'Say what?' asked Finley in a muffled voice.

'A perfect Allhallows Eve,' Abilene said. The wind in the tree tops sounded like cars rushing by on a freeway. It made shadows tremble and shake on the pavement of the road and sidewalk. It tumbled leaves through the air. It billowed Helen's sheet and flapped Vivian's witch gown and lifted Cora's pleated skirt. It tossed Abilene's pendulum from side to side. It licked her bare armpit, eased inside her sweatshirt's gaping hole and slid its chilly tongue over her breast. Though it gave her gooseflesh, she rather liked the feel of it.

Stopping at a corner, Finley asked, 'Which way?'

'Let's not get any closer to campus,' Vivian said.

451

Campus was several blocks straight ahead.

Abilene glanced to the left. That direction would lead downtown. To the right, however, the street passed between rows of family houses. Cars were parked along both sides and in driveways. Lights glowed on porches. Windows were bright. She saw jack-o'-lanterns in front of many nearby homes. And as she watched, a group of kids hurried toward the sidewalk from a house midway down the block.

'This way,' Abilene said.

They went to the right.

The kids were heading in their direction. Four little tykes, accompanied by a couple of women who waited on the sidewalk while they made forays to each house.

'I hope these mothers don't think we're nuts,' Vivian said.

Approaching them, Abilene suddenly found herself feeling very self-conscious about her armpit. She wished she'd worn a more conventional costume. Or a jacket.

The kids came scampering back to the sidewalk. The boys were Batman and a Freddie Krueger. One girl was a ballerina. The other, in high heels, fishnet stockings, a black leather miniskirt and silky silver blouse, wore a great deal of makeup and a shaggy red wig. Abilene supposed she was meant to be a rock star, but she looked like a six-year-old hooker.

What kind of mother would let her go out looking like that?

Neither woman looked particularly weird.

'Happy Halloween,' Finley said.

'Yikes, an ape!' said one of the women.

'He's not a *real* ape,' Batman pointed out.

'We're the Merry Halloween Team,' Finley said. 'And we bear gifts of goodies for all the little boys and girls.'

A snort of laughter came from under Helen's sheet.

Finley clapped Cora on the back. 'This is Cheery the Cheerleader. Cheery, give the kids some candy.'

The children gathered around Cora. She reached into her sack, pulled out a handful of miniature Three Musketeers bars, and dropped one into each bag.

Receiving his treat, Freddie Krueger said, 'Unpleasant dreams,' and let out an evil laugh.

The ballerina shyly murmured, 'Thank you.'

'Thank you very much,' said Batman.

The hooker muttered a petulant 'Thanks' and stepped right over to Abilene. 'What're you?' she asked in her snotty little voice.

'I'm the Razor Lady,' Abilene told her, tapping the edge of her foil-wrapped crescent. 'I sneak around in the night and cut out the tongues of obnoxious little children.'

'You are not. Sides, that's too big to go in a mouth.'

'I make it fit,' Abilene said.

Helen started giggling inside her sheet.

Vivian cackled in a very witchlike manner.

'Come along, kids,' said one of the women. If she'd caught Abilene's remarks, apparently they hadn't bothered her.

Abilene and the others stepped aside to let the group pass, then continued along the sidewalk.

'Geez, Hickok.'

'She was a little creep.'

'Can't take you anywhere.'

At the end of the block, they spotted several small clusters of trick-or-treaters in both directions. Since going to the left would lead them toward campus, they headed to the right.

They met a pirate, a princess and a tiny little girl in a Snow White costume accompanied by a young man and woman who seemed to enjoy the encounter more than the kids.

'The Merry Halloween Team?' asked the man after hearing Finley's spiel.

'This is really neat,' said the woman. 'What a nice idea.'

'We're just out to have some fun,' Cora told them.

'Monkeying around,' said Finley.

'Wooooooo,' said Helen.

'And look at you,' the man said, smiling at Abilene – eyeing her armpit.

'She's the Razor Lady,' Finley said. 'She sneaks around and slices off the tongues of obnoxious children.'

'Really?' asked the woman.

The man, frowning, shook his head. 'I would've guessed you might be "The Pit and the Pendulum." '

Abilene burst out laughing. 'You're right! Fantastic!'

'Obscure, but clever,' the man said.

'You've made her night,' Vivian told him.

'Give *them* some candy,' Abilene said.

Cora gave a couple of Three Musketeers bars to each of the adults, then dropped a few more into the bags of the kids.

On their way again, Vivian said, 'Nice people.'

'Smart, too,' said Abilene.

Next, they met up with a flock of eight or nine yelling, laughing kids being shepherded by three teenaged girls. While Cora handed out candy, a kid wearing a plastic Rambo chest looked Vivian in the eyes and grumbled, 'I'm your worst nightmare.' A vampire pranced around Helen chanting, 'Fatty ghost, fatty ghost!' Minnie Mouse, as high as Abilene's waist, reached up and tugged the front of her sweatshirt and said, 'I'm Susan and I'm four.'

'Hi, Susan. I'm Abilene.'

'That's a pretty name.'

'Why, thank you.'

'I'm four.'

'Are you getting lots of candy?'

'Oh yes. Lots and lots.'

The prancing, chanting vampire yelped and went down. He fell flat on the sidewalk and started to cry.

Once they'd left the bunch behind, Abilene asked Helen if she'd tripped him.

'Who you mean? "Fatty ghost, fatty ghost"? Naw. He was just a klutz, the little asshole.'

'Have you noticed how some of these kids are such jerks?' Vivian asked.

'Did you see that little shit grab for my camera?' Finley asked. Abilene hadn't noticed.

'Gives abortion a good name.'

'Most of them are okay,' Abilene said.

'Here come some big ones,' Cora announced.

'Ohhh, boy,' Helen muttered.

'Hey, that guy's not bad lookin',' Finley said. 'The blond?'

'Keep your panties on,' Cora told her.

'How can she?' Abilene said. 'She never wears 'em.'

Finley popped open a couple of snaps at the top of her coveralls. Apparently, she didn't want this group to make the same mistake as Batman regarding her gender.

'Give it a break,' Vivian muttered.

'Awfully hot in this thing.'

The four boys, who looked old enough to be high school seniors, were just leaving the sidewalk, ready to head for a house, when one of them noticed the approaching girls. He said something to his buddies.

They returned to the sidewalk.

They shambled forward like drunks, weaving and dragging their feet.

'*Night of the Living Dead*,' Helen said.

Abilene realized she was right. They weren't drunk; they were supposed to be zombies.

The blond-haired guy who'd caught Finley's fancy wore a business suit. A sleeve of his jacket was missing. His necktie hung loose. The hilt of a knife protruded from the chest of his bloody sport shirt.

A stocky guy shuffling along beside him wore Bermuda shorts and a T-shirt. He must be freezing, Abilene thought. His face was dark with blood. A meat cleaver was buried in the top of his head.

One was dressed in a plaid bathrobe over pale blue pajamas. His fidelity to the outfit, however, had been compromised by his footwear: sneakers instead of slippers. Neither he nor the fourth member of the group, dressed in a baseball uniform, had attached phoney weapons to their bodies or smeared themselves with fake blood. Probably didn't want to ruin their clothes, Abilene thought. But the pajama boy carried a rubber foot, which he pretended to munch as he approached. The baseball player staggered along swinging a bat with one hand. He looked as if he might like to bash in some heads with it.

All four of the zombies had plastic shopping bags for their goodies.

'Don't anybody get cute,' Vivian warned. 'These guys could be trouble.'

Finley walked right up to them. 'Greetings. You guys look dead on your feet.'

The one with the cleaver in his head moaned and swayed.

The baseball player raised his Louisville Slugger overhead and said, 'Trick or treat.'

'Just so happens,' Finley said, 'we come bearing gifts.

Cheery the Cheerleader has some Three Musketeers for you fellows.'

'We just eat flesh,' explained the pajama boy. He stuck the big toe of the rubber foot into his mouth and gnawed on it. He moaned with pleasure.

'The really good part,' Finley said, 'must be the jam.'

He laughed. So did Finley's favorite in the torn suit. The one with the cleaver looked at Abilene and stopped swaying.

Vivian groaned.

Cora reached into her sack and took out a handful of candy bars. As she dropped them into the zombies' bags, the one in the torn jacket asked in a very normal pleasant voice, 'Are you gals on your way to a party, or something?'

'We're just going around spreading Halloween cheer,' Finley said.

'You're from the university.'

'We've been known to frequent its ivy halls.'

'Same here.'

The news surprised Abilene. Obviously, the boys were older than they looked.

'First year?' Cora asked.

'It shows,' said the one with the rubber foot.

'Aren't you kind of old to be trick-or-treating?'

'Why should little kids be the only ones having fun?'

'Our sentiments, too,' Finley said, and plucked off her gorilla head. Smiling, she rubbed her mussed, shaggy hair. 'I'm Finley,' she said.

'I'm Bill,' said the one in the suit. 'These three cretins are Gary, Chuck and my roomy, Harris.'

Gary was the pajama boy with the foot. Chuck was the baseball player. Harris was the guy wearing the plastic meat cleaver.

'We oughta get going,' Abilene said.

'I've seen you around,' Harris said, looking into Abilene's eyes.

'That's Hickok.'

Thanks a heap, she thought.

Harris frowned. 'I thought it was Abilene.'

Chapter Seventeen
Belmore Girls

Abilene felt heat rush to her face.

Christ, how does he know my *name*?

'Whoooa,' said Finley. 'He knows ya! Do you know him?'

She shook her head.

'I've just seen you around,' he said. 'That's all.'

Bill suddenly looked startled. 'Hey! She's the one in the year-book!'

'She is not! Shut up!'

'Oh, wow.'

'He doesn't know what he's talking about,' Harris said, his bloody face grimacing. 'Come on. We've gotta get going.' He didn't wait for the others. Forgetting his zombie walk, he hurried past Abilene with his face turned away.

'Geez, Harris!' Bill called, and rushed after him.

As the other two followed, Chuck the baseball player grinned at Abilene. 'That guy's got a major-league crush on you.'

'No kidding,' she muttered.

She looked back in time to see Harris throw a punch into Bill's shoulder.

'Curiouser and curiouser,' Finley said.

'Maybe you oughta go after him,' Cora said.

'Give me a break.'

'He was pretty cute under all that blood,' Vivian said.

'Yeah, sure thing.'

'He must've gotten your name from the yearbook,' Helen said.

'Freshmen don't even *have* yearbooks yet.'

'Wouldn't be hard to get your hands on one,' Cora told her.

'I'd be flattered,' Helen said.

'Well, I'm not.'

She looked over her shoulder. The boys were half a block away. They weren't walking like zombies. Harris seemed to be the center of attention. He'd taken the meat cleaver off his head. He was shaking it at the others, who shoved him and slapped his back and pointed toward Abilene.

Really giving him the business, she thought.

The poor guy was probably embarrassed half to death.

Serves him right.

He looks at pictures of me in the *yearbook*?

Turning away, she muttered, 'What a creep.'

'Just in love,' Finley said.

'Take a leap.'

'Cut it out,' Cora said. 'Here come some more kids.'

Abilene felt hot and shaky inside. In spite of the chilly wind, her skin seemed to be on fire. Sweat dribbled down her sides.

A major-league crush.

I don't even know the guy.

He knows my name. He looks at my picture.

God, what else does he do? Follow me around?

A freshman, no less.

A moron going around wearing a toy meat cleaver like a hat and fake blood all over his face.

He had nice eyes, though.

A woman and two kids – another Freddie Krueger and a pirate – distracted Abilene from her thoughts about the zombie. Cora handed out candy bars. After the mother led her children away, Cora folded her empty bag and shoved it into Vivian's. 'That's it for me,' she said. 'Your turn to do the honors.'

'Oh, okay.'

'How long are we planning to keep at this?' Abilene asked.

'Aren't you having fun?' Finley asked. 'Not every night you bump into a secret admirer.'

'Don't remind me.'

'Maybe they'll come back,' Helen said.

'Oh, please.'

Abilene found herself keeping watch, half-expecting the zombies to show up again, hoping they wouldn't, but surprised and annoyed at herself when, some time later, she glimpsed a group of guys in the distance and felt a tremor of excitement. Which turned into disappointment when they approached and she saw they were a vampire, a hobo, a soldier and a Frankenstein monster. They were also younger than the zombies. And creeps. They blocked the sidewalk. The soldier raised his M-16 and ordered, 'Halt.'

'Oh, this is terrific,' Finley said. Ignoring the soldier's command, she stepped onto a neatly trimmed lawn, shouldered her video camera, and began to tape the episode by the light of the full moon and streetlamps.

'What's she doing?' asked the hobo.

'Forget her,' said the Frankenstein monster. 'Look at these babes.'

'I vahnt to suck your blood,' said the vampire, leaning close to Vivian and wiggling his eyebrows.

'Have a Three Musketeers bar,' Vivian said. She reached into her bag.

'Zee blood is zee life.' His head darted toward the side of Vivian's neck. She shoved him away. The soldier opened up, his M-16 clacking, spitting out bursts of water that splashed Vivian's face.

'Cut it out,' Cora warned.

'Oh yeah?' He swung the muzzle of the automatic squirt-gun toward her.

'You shoot me with that, I'll shove it up your wahzoo.'

'Oooo, I'm trembling. I'm shaking.'

Cora took a step toward him, and he backed away.

The Frankenstein monster, meanwhile, had wandered over to Helen's side. 'Look at this,' he said. 'This babe's dressed up as a sheet.'

'I'm a ghost,' Helen said.

'No such thing as ghosts.' He lifted the sheet. 'It's not a ghost, it's a blimp!'

Abilene muttered, 'Fuck you, Charlie,' and shoved him off the sidewalk. He staggered backward, tripped on a lawn sprinkler and fell on his rump. The soldier opened fire on Abilene. Cold spurts of water hit her forehead, her eyes, her cheeks. Then the kid squirted her bare armpit and swept his weapon sideways. Her sweatshirt went cold and wet against her breasts.

She heard laughter.

Cora lunged forward. She ripped the M-16 out of the soldier's hands and shoved its muzzle against his crotch.

'Ow!'

Tat-tat-tat-tat-tat.

The vampire rushed Cora. Vivian slipped the broom handle between his feet. He yelped, stumbled past Cora and slammed the lawn at Finley's feet.

The hobo whirled and ran.

The Frankenstein monster scurried up and went after him.

The soldier swatted the plastic gun barrel away. Clutching his sodden crotch, he staggered backward, blurting, 'Leave me alone,' as Cora pursued him. 'Leave me . . .' She stuck the muzzle into his mouth and pulled the trigger. He coughed as water flooded his mouth.

The vampire fled, his black cape fluttering behind him.

Cora shoved the M-16 into the hands of the choking, spluttering soldier. 'Next time,' she said, 'be nice to people.'

The soldier twisted around and raced after his friends.

'Good show!' Finley called out. 'Bravo!' Lowering her camera, she came back to the sidewalk.

'You were sure a lot of help,' Abilene said.

'Didn't look to me as if you guys needed any assistance. Sure gave *them* a Halloween to remember.'

'Dirty rats,' Helen muttered.

'Kind of fun, actually,' Cora said.

'He didn't shoot *you*,' Vivian pointed out.

'I sure shot him, though.' She laughed. 'Poor kid.'

'Poor kid, my butt,' Abilene muttered. 'He soaked me.' Bending over, she swung her pendulum out of the way and lifted the lower part of her sweatshirt. She dried her face with it, then wiped her wet armpit and rubbed her breasts. Deciding she would prefer to have the chilly dampness against her back, she pulled her arms inside and twisted the sweatshirt around before struggling into its sleeves. That did feel better.

Finley grinned at her. 'Now you're "The *Other* Pit and the Pendulum." '

'A sequel,' Vivian said.

'Are we about ready to call it quits?' she asked.

'You don't want to disappoint all the children who haven't yet had the opportunity to enjoy the Merry Halloween Team, do you?' Finley asked.

'I could live with it.'

'Most of the little ones ought to be heading for home before much longer,' Cora said. 'Why don't we stick it out for a while?'

'Those creeps'll probably come back and egg us.'

'They wouldn't dare,' Finley said.

'Let's give it a few more minutes,' Cora said, and started walking.

As everyone followed, Helen laughed through her sheet. 'Yeah, just a few more minutes. That'll give us a chance to run into some *real* trouble.'

'We should've gone to your all-night Shock Festival at the Elsinore.'

'We'd gone to the movies, Hickok, you wouldn't have met the love of your life.'

'You and the horse you rode in on.'

Abilene discovered that, by walking with her spine arched and her shoulders back, she was able to keep the wet fabric from touching her skin.

They continued along the street, pausing each time they met kids. Block after block, Vivian handed out candy bars. When her bag was empty, Helen took over.

Though they came upon teenagers as well as little kids, nobody gave them much trouble. A few smart-alecks, but most of the trick-or-treaters were nice and none assaulted them with squirtguns or other weapons. Abilene found herself enjoying the encounters and was a little disappointed when she realized that they'd walked a full block without meeting any more kids.

'I guess they've mostly gone home,' she said.

'I'm getting low, anyway,' Helen said, and shook her sack. She was carrying the last of the candy. 'Should we start back?'

'Let's try one more block,' Abilene suggested.

Cora grinned back at her. 'You're the one who wanted to quit.'

'That's when I was wet.'

They crossed a street. And Abilene saw, near the far end of the block, a group of three small kids run from a lighted porch, laughing, their treat bags bouncing and swinging. The children joined a woman waiting on the sidewalk. They hurried ahead of her and scampered toward the next house.

'Hey, one's a ghost,' Helen said. She sounded very pleased.

Soon, they were close enough for Abilene to see that the other two were dressed as a kitten and a gremlin. From their size, she guessed that they were no older than five or six.

They were off at a house when Finley strode up to the woman and announced, 'Hi! We're the Merry Halloween Team!'

The woman laughed and shook her head. She had red hair and freckles. She didn't look old enough to have three kids.

Maybe just one is hers, Abilene thought.

'We've been going around giving stuff to the kids,' Helen said.

'Hey, that's a great idea. Sort of like trick-or-treating in reverse.'

'Just an excuse to get out and see what's happening,' Abilene told her.

The ghost, kitten and gremlin came running across the lawn. They slowed down near the sidewalk. Then stopped on the grass. And stared.

'It's all right, kids. This is the Merry Halloween Team.'

'With treats!' Helen said. She bent over and reached into her sack. 'It's so nice to meet a fellow ghost,' she said, smiling at the spook.

'I'm not really a ghost. I'm Heather.'

'Nice to meet you, Heather. I'm Helen. But I'm a *real* ghost.'

'Oh, I bet you aren't really. There's no such thing. Is there, Mommy?'

'If she says she's a ghost, I guess she is.'

'But I'm a very friendly ghost,' Helen explained, and dropped a couple of Three Musketeer bars into Heather's bag.

The girl said, 'Thank you very much.'

'You're a very pretty kitty,' Helen said as she gave treats to the kitten.

'Meeeeooooow.'

Abilene grinned. 'They're really cute kids.'

'I'm Gizmo,' said the gremlin.

'Here you go, Gizmo.'

The candy bars no sooner hit the bottom of Gizmo's bag than all three girls rushed on down the sidewalk.

'Don't run,' the mother called. Then, 'Thanks a lot. Happy Halloween.'

'You, too,' Finley said.

The mother hurried after the girls. 'Wait,' she called. 'Forget that place.' Over her shoulder, she said, 'I told them, only houses with lighted porches or pumpkins.'

The girls were running toward a dark porch.

'You heard me,' she called.

'Oh, Mom.'

'Probably no one's home, anyway,' Finley said.

The mother shrugged.

The kids went ahead and climbed the porch. The kitten rang the doorbell.

'Should we start back?' Vivian asked.

'Might as well,' Helen said. 'We're almost out of candy.'

They walked toward the waiting mother. She nodded a greeting, then returned her attention to the girls.

Light spilled onto the porch as the door swung open.

A tall, thin man loomed over the girls.

In unison, they chanted, 'Trick or treat, smell my feet, give me something good to eat!'

'Scat!' the man snapped. 'Get outa here, ya little snots!' He slammed the door. It crashed shut with such a clap that all three girls jumped.

Even Abilene flinched. 'Jesus!' she gasped.

The girls ran. At the sidewalk, Heather wrapped her sheeted arms around her mother's waist. The kitten was crying, wiping her eyes with small, furry paws. 'I wanna go *home*,' whined Gizmo.

'I wanna *kill* the son of a bitch,' Cora muttered.

'You and me both,' Abilene said. 'Doing that to little kids.'

'Let's have a word with him,' Vivian said. She strode across the lawn, heading for the porch, her black gown flapping in the wind. Then Cora was at her side. Finley rushed after them. Helen and Abilene followed.

Glancing back, Abilene saw the mother hurrying away down the sidewalk, the three girls clustered close around her.

The dirty bastard, she thought. Her throat felt tight.

The little kids had been out having a wonderful time. It

had been ruined, now. They'd been scared half to death. For the rest of their lives, they would probably always remember tonight and the horrible man who'd yelled at them. Halloween would never be quite the same for them. It would always be tainted.

Thanks to one thoughtless, selfish bastard.

She trotted up the porch stairs as Vivian jabbed the doorbell button. She heard the bell jangling inside the house. Again and again.

The door swung open.

The man standing in the lighted foyer was not an old grouch. He was young, probably no older than thirty. He looked perfectly normal in his plaid shirt and jeans, his short hair neatly combed. But his eyes were narrow, his lips twisted with a sneer.

'What the hell do *you* want?'

'What the hell is the *matter* with you?' Vivian demanded. 'We saw what you did to those little kids. There's no excuse for that kind of behavior.'

'It's Halloween, for Godsake,' Cora said.

'They were just trying to have fun,' Abilene said.

'Shouldn't have rung my bell, should they?'

'If you don't like it, you shouldn't have opened the door,' Abilene told him. 'Why'd you have to scare them like that!'

'It was really shitty,' Finley said.

'Awwww, I'm so sorry.'

'You should be,' Helen said.

Leaning forward, he raised his upper lip high enough to bare his gums. He turned his head slowly as if inspecting a group of repulsive but somewhat amusing lepers. 'Get out of here. Fuck off.'

With that, he slammed the door.

* * *

At a twenty-four hour convenience store several blocks away, they bought a dozen eggs, a can of shaving cream, and a pair of rubber dish-washing gloves. As the clerk loaded the items into a paper bag, Cora helped herself to a couple of free matchbooks.

On their way back to the man's house, they found a pile of dog waste in the grass beside a tree.

'Allow me,' Finley said.

Cora emptied the bag. Finley put on the rubber gloves, picked up the rank, gooey pile, and dropped it into the bag. She tossed the gloves in after it.

They arrived at the house.

Its porch was still dark, but faint light glowed through the living room curtains.

Cora took the bag from Finley. Helen, Vivian, Finley and Abilene crouched down beyond a corner of the porch. From there, they watched Cora through slats in the railing.

Abilene trembled. She gritted her teeth to stop her chin from shaking as Cora climbed the stairs.

Crazy, she thought. This guy might be dangerous.

But he'd asked for it. And he's gonna get it.

Cora slid the welcome mat out of the way. She placed the bag just in front of the door. Squatting, she struck a match. She touched its flame to the crumpled paper. As fire crawled over the bag, she sprang up, poked the doorbell a couple of times, and rushed down the stairs.

Reaching the middle of the lawn, she whirled around in time to see the man throw open his door.

'Shit!'

He leaped over the threshold and stomped the blazing bag. Embers flew. Abilene heard a soft splat. His ankle, bare above the top of his house slipper, went dark.

'Yeeeuug!'

But he kept stomping until the fire was out. Then he lifted his foot and looked at it. Then he looked at Cora.

'Trick or treat!' Cora called.

'Cunt!' He lurched across the porch, gasped when his clotted slipper skated sideways, but kept his balance and raced down the stairs.

Cora took off.

The man dashed after her.

He was hot on her tail by the time she reached the sidewalk. There, she ducked her head and sprinted. The guy went after her. A moment later, they were both out of sight.

'Man, was he ever pissed,' Finley said.

'What if he catches her?' Helen asked.

'He won't,' Finley said.

'Come on.' Abilene rose from her crouch. She led the way along the front of the porch and up the stairs toward the open door. Her legs felt weak and shaky. Her heart pounded.

'I sure hope nobody else is here,' Vivian whispered.

'Who would live with a jerk like that?' Abilene said.

'Another jerk, maybe,' Helen suggested.

Careful to avoid the charred remains and brown smears, Abilene stepped onto the threshold. She leaned forward. To the right of the tile foyer was the living room. From where she stood, she couldn't see much of it.

She heard nothing except her own heartbeat.

'Let's do it and get out,' Vivian whispered.

Nodding, Abilene shook the can of shaving cream and pried off its lid. She crept across the foyer and stepped onto the carpet. The television was off. The only light came from a single lamp at one end of the sofa. Its dim bulb left deep shadows in the corners of the room.

'Nobody here,' Finley said.

'I guess . . .'

An egg came from behind, dropped just in front of Abilene's face and shattered on the carpet at her feet.

'Watch it.'

Finley laughed.

Another egg sailed by. This one smashed against the wall above the TV set. Its viscous contents splattered and dribbled. Turning around, Abilene watched Finley and Vivian pluck more eggs from the carton in Helen's hand and hurl them. The missiles exploded, splashing yellow glop against walls, the ceiling, a lamp table, a rocking chair barely visible in one corner.

Abilene hurried over to the coffee table. A glass half full of soda was there. With a quick squirt, she gave the soda a frothy head of shaving cream. Eggs exploding all around her, she drew curlicues of suds on the table top. Then she went to the sofa. Its upholstery was covered with something that looked like an old bedspread, so she figured the shaving cream wouldn't do any real damage. She started at the lighted end of the sofa and made her way down its length, leaving thick, fluffy designs along its cushions.

She kept her eyes on the job.

Until she came to the far end of the sofa.

In the gloom between Abilene and the wall, some five feet away, she saw a chair. She'd noticed the chair earlier. Hidden in a dark corner as it was, however, she hadn't realized it was a wheelchair. Nor had she noticed that it wasn't empty.

Something was in the chair.

A bundle of blankets topped with a small, gray orb that almost resembled a head.

Her heart gave an awful lurch.

She stared at the thing. It didn't move. It didn't make a

sound. The head really didn't look much like a head, at all, more like a shriveled grapefruit perched on a stalk above the blankets. But it seemed to have a face.

A dummy? A mannequin? Maybe one of those inflatable sex dolls.

'Hey,' she gasped. 'Over here.'

'What is it?' Finley came up beside her. 'What *is* it?'

'I don't know.'

'We've gotta get out of here,' Vivian said, hurrying over with Helen to see what they'd found.

Finley pulled a flashlight out of a pocket of her coveralls. She switched it on. She aimed it at the thing in the wheelchair.

The small head was hairless, the color of wet, dead leaves. Its face looked like something that a careless child might've formed out of papier-mache: lumpy, ragged flesh; eyes holes poked by fingertips; a couple of quick pinches to make the nose; a slit for a mouth; a tiny knob of chin.

'It . . . it isn't a corpse, is it?' Helen whispered.

'Christ, no,' Finley said. 'It's just a dummy. A *homemade* dummy, at that.'

'It's hideous,' Vivian muttered.

'Maybe that bastard has some Halloween spirit, after all,' Finley said. 'Hold the flashlight. I've gotta get this.'

She gave the light to Abilene.

Then she raised her video camera, turned around for a slow pan of the trashed living room, and pointed her lens at the ghastly thing in the chair. 'Say cheese,' she said.

It said, 'Cheese.'

The slash of its mouth spread open and it said, 'Cheese,' the word rolling out slow and deep like a voice on a record player at low speed. A tinny, scratchy voice. A voice that resounded as if spoken in an echo chamber.

Finley gasped, 'Fuck!'

Helen made a high, whiny noise.

Vivian gagged.

Abilene wet her pants.

The four girls didn't stop running until they reached the convenience store. Cora, as planned, was waiting outside its door.

'I got away from that bastard quicker than ... What's the matter with *you* guys?'

She was answered with shaking heads as the girls struggled for breath.

Helen removed the noose from around her neck, and pulled off the sheet. Crumpling it, she slumped against the store wall.

'He didn't catch *you*, did he?'

Vivian shook her head. She was bent over, hands on knees.

'In his house,' Abilene gasped. 'He had ... a guy. Someone. In a wheelchair.'

'It didn't look *human*,' Finley blurted.

'Like a dummy. Something. Horrible.'

'Its face,' Vivian murmured.

'What was *wrong* with him?' Abilene gasped.

'What was *right* with him?'

'Never ... seen anything like it,' Vivian said. 'God. I'm gonna have nightmares forever.'

Abilene met Cora's eyes. 'You're really lucky. You didn't see him.'

'Oh, come on. He couldn't have been that bad.'

'Oh, yeah?' Finley asked.

Back at their apartment, Finley inserted the tape cassette in the VCR. She fast-forwarded past the skirmish with the four teenagers.

Then the living room of the house was on the television screen. Eggs splattered everywhere. Thick curls of shaving cream on the coffee table, the sofa.

'Boy,' Cora said, 'you done good.'

Abilene couldn't watch the rest. She stood very still, itchy in her damp corduroys, and watched Cora.

Cora's eyes went wide. 'Holy shit,' she said.

When the thing said, 'Cheese,' the color left her face.

Finley shut off the tape.

'Maybe that's why the man was such a creep,' Vivian said. 'I mean, he lives with that. Takes care of it. Maybe it's . . . one of his parents, or something.'

'We shouldn't have trashed the place,' Abilene muttered. 'Oh God. How could we?'

'We didn't know,' Finley said. 'I'm gonna tape over that part. I never wanta see that thing again. I don't even wanta *think* about it.'

Chapter Eighteen

A tickle on her shin roused Abilene from sleep. A moment later, she felt the tickle moving. She bolted upright, saw a spider scurrying toward her knee, and whisked it off. Squirmy with gooseflesh, she inspected her legs and arms. Nothing else seemed to be on her. Except for a film of dew, which made her skin feel clammy and had dampened the front of her blouse and skirt.

She stretched and yawned. The morning air was pleasantly warm, not yet hot. Though no sunlight was on her, she saw paths of dusty gold slanting down through the trees.

Probably no later than seven o'clock, she supposed.

She'd slept very well. It looked like a beautiful morning, and she felt wonderful until she remembered the task that awaited her and the others: returning to the pool and searching for the keys.

Won't be so bad in daylight, she told herself.

Then we'll be out of here.

If we find them.

Ought to wake up the rest of them and get it over with.

On the sleeping bag next to Abilene, Finley continued to sleep. Helen's bag was flat against the ground. She'd crawled into it last night, in spite of the heat.

But she wasn't in there now.

Abilene scanned the clearing. Cora and Vivian continued to sleep. There was no sign of Helen.

With a flutter of worry, Abilene decided that she must've gone off. To take a pee, or something.

Her blouse and Bermuda shorts were still spread out on top of her sleeping bag. But her swimsuit was missing. So were her shoes.

She must've taken the suit with her, Abilene thought, to put on after she finished.

She'll be back in a minute.

Abilene waited, sitting motionless, listening. The forest was noisy with birds. There were rustling sounds. Buzzes and hums of insects. But no heavy, crunching sounds. Nothing that might indicate a person moving about.

How far did she go, anyway?

Helen was really too timid to go wandering off alone.

Wasn't she?

It passed through Abilene's mind that someone might've found the encampment and taken her. But that seemed very unlikely. Why would anyone just grab Helen? And how could that happen without a struggle that would've disturbed the rest of them? Besides, nobody abducting her would've bothered to take her swimsuit and shoes.

No, she'd gotten up and left of her own free will.

In her swimsuit.

Good God!

No, she wouldn't. She wouldn't dare go back to the lodge by herself. To go swimming and look for the keys.

She'd offered to go in and search for them last night. Not alone though.

But what if she woke up just a while ago? Already daylight. Everyone else still sleeping. And she'd decided to go ahead and find the keys and return and surprise everyone.

Any minute, she might come tromping through the woods, all wet and grinning, holding up the key case, saying, 'Look what I found.'

She might be in the pool right now.

Maybe not alone. Maybe struggling, this very moment, with the guy who'd thrown their things in the water last night.

Sick with worry, Abilene shook Finley awake. As the girl groaned and mumbled, she twisted around and shook Cora.

'Wake up. Quick. Everyone. Helen's gone.'

'Huh?' Finley murmured. 'Whuh?'

'She's gone! I think she went to find the keys.'

Abilene slipped into her moccasins as the others stirred and sat up.

'Holy shit,' Cora said.

'We've gotta go after her. Quick.'

'Helen's *gone*?' Vivian asked.

'When did she leave?' Finley asked.

'I don't know! I don't know! I just woke up. She wasn't here. She took her swimsuit.'

'She *must've* gone to the pool,' Cora said.

On her feet, Abilene turned slowly and scanned the woods. When she turned toward the east, she saw the lodge. It had been out of sight, last night, only because of the darkness. Now, bits of it were visible beyond the trees. It was no more than a hundred yards away.

'My God,' Abilene said, 'it's right there. She must've gotten up and seen how close we were.'

'I can't believe she'd go without us,' Vivian said.

'She sure went somewhere,' Finley said.

Cora called, 'Helen! Helen!'

No answer came.

Abilene rushed into the trees. As she dodged trunks and ducked under low limbs, she heard the others following. Soon, she left the trees behind. She raced through the high grass and weeds of the field. Vision jarring, she scanned the length of the lodge, its windows and porch and doors, the driveway and garage area off to the right. No Helen. No one at all.

Straight ahead, the front of the Wagoneer came into view.

She ran toward the car. The springy foliage gave way to concrete that smacked her feet through her moccasins. Abruptly, she slowed, knowing that if she took the slope at full speed, she would probably tumble headlong. With short strides, she hurried down alongside the car.

And stopped behind it. There, resting on the pavement, was a cardboard box. One that they'd left in the car last night.

The box contained packages of cookies, potato chips, crackers and cheese puffs.

Cora, halting beside her, looked at the box. 'This explains plenty.'

Finley, huffing, said, 'What'd she do? Stop by for a snack?'

'Looks that way,' Cora said.

'Someone else might've done it,' Abilene suggested.

'Must've been Helen,' Vivian said. 'God, we should've just let her eat what she wanted.'

'If she came here for food,' Finley said, 'where is she now?'

'I still think she went to find the keys,' Abilene said. 'I mean, why the swimming suit?' Without waiting for a response, she made her way down the steep pavement. At the bottom, she scanned the rear grounds. Seeing no one, she peered around the corner of the lodge.

Near the edge of the outside pool were Helen's sneakers. Propped up between them was an open plastic bag.

She stepped over the flowing water of the drain channel, then followed it to the small pool.

The bag was a package of taco-flavored tortilla chips. It was half empty.

Squatting, she gazed through the archway. The interior pool was murky with shadowed light. A pale mist hung above the water.

'Is she in there?' Vivian asked.

'I don't see her.' And all that Abilene could hear was the soft, hollow sound of lapping ripples. 'Helen!' she yelled. She stood, kicked off her moccasins, then leaped off the edge. The hot water tossed her skirt up, clutched her body, splashed her hair and face. Pushing her skirt down, she trudged toward the opening. Her heart thudded painfully. Her bowels felt cramped.

She didn't want to go in there.

What if Helen's dead? Floating face down . . . ?

Behind her, someone plunged into the water. She looked back and saw Cora. Still in her tank top. Hadn't bothered to undress for this.

Her eyes were wide and scared. Her face was pale.

Let her go first?

No. Helen's *my* responsibility. She wasn't sure why she felt that way but, ever since that first week at Belmore, Abilene had seen herself not only as Helen's friend but also as her protector.

She took one more step, passing through the archway. Then she stopped.

She swept her eyes over the surface of the pool. And saw only water below the gently swirling veils of mist. No floating body. No dark form suspended beneath the surface. Gazing through the white vapors, she scanned the walkway at the far side of the pool. Then the clear area off to the left. And the stools, and the bar.

'Nothing,' she said. Her voice reverberated through the silence.

'She isn't here,' Cora called back. 'Nobody's here.'

'Where *is* she?' Abilene whispered, moving away from the entrance.

'God only knows. She must've been here, though. She must've come for the keys, just like you figured.'

'Are you coming back?' Finley asked. 'What are you doing?'

Cora turned toward the opening. 'We'll scout around for a minute. Are you two staying there?'

'I guess so. Vivian's still nervous about getting in the water.'

'I will if I have to,' Vivian said in a quiet voice as if speaking only to Finley.

'That's all right,' Cora said. 'Just stay put.' To Abilene, she said, 'We oughta see if the keys are still here. They shouldn't be too hard to find if they fell out of her pocket.'

'She might've already fished them out.'

'Yeah, but maybe she didn't. Who knows? We're here. We might as well look.'

'Okay. Over this way.'

Abilene in the lead, they pushed through the water toward the center of the pool.

The mist parted around them like smoke stirred and tattered by the mild breeze of their movements.

Peering down through the water, Abilene soon located the dark, barred mouth of the hot spring. As she stepped closer to it, she felt the hot currents roll against her legs and rub her panties. 'I picked up the shorts right near here,' she whispered.

'Oh, great. What if the keys fell through?'

'I know. I already thought of that.' She took a long stride to the other side of the bars. 'Right here,' she said. She pressed the front of her skirt against her thighs, bent over, and lowered her face into the water. Her legs looked distorted: strangely white, bent at odd angles, undulating as if their bones had turned to squirmy soft rubber.

She could see the pale floor of the pool just fine.

She couldn't see a key case. Not between her feet, or for a yard in front of her feet, or off to either side. Coming up for air, she glanced over her left shoulder and found Cora hunched down with her face in the water.

She pivoted to the right, ducked under again, and searched a different section of the bottom.

Still no luck.

For a long time, she and Cora hunted in the area surrounding the spring. They even searched the darkness below the crossed bars, diving down and grabbing hold, peering into the mouth of the pit. If the keys were there, however, they were out of sight and beyond reach.

They fanned out and continued looking. Later, Abilene made her way gradually toward the side of the pool, thinking that the keys might've dropped out of the pocket while she was returning with the shorts. She reached the wall without finding them. Standing there, she checked the granite in hopes of spotting wet footprints left by Helen.

The granite was wet all right. Puddled. And there were countless footprints. After a moment of confusion and excitement and fear, she realized that she was looking at the water they'd all left on the pool's apron last night. It simply hadn't dried.

Out of breath, Cora asked, 'Anything?'

'She might've climbed out over here, but I can't tell for sure. It's still all wet from us.'

'But where the hell are the keys? Maybe we oughta get the other two in here for some help.'

'Why bother? The keys just aren't here. Either Helen already found them or they went down the hot spring.'

'We'd better keep looking.'

'We should be looking for Helen, not the keys. If she hasn't got them . . . we can't leave, anyway, until we find her.'

'Helen!' Cora shouted. 'Helen!'

In the silence that followed the boom of her voice, Finley called from outside, 'Did you find her?'

'No, damn it!'

'Find the keys?' Finley asked.

'No!'

'Why don't you come on out?' Vivian called.

'We're on our way,' Abilene answered. To Cora, she said,

'Hey, for all we know, Helen might be back at the sleeping bags and wondering what happened to *us*.'

'Fat chance.'

Abilene didn't believe it, either.

It was about as likely, she thought, as waking up and discovering that Helen's disappearance had been nothing but a bad dream.

They made their way slowly back through the pool, studying its bottom. Then they passed under the archway. Abilene felt guilty about quitting the search, but it was good to be in the sunlight again and very good to see Finley and Vivian. She climbed out. The morning air felt cool after the heat of the water.

'Helen might've already found the keys,' she said.

'Unless they fell down through the grate,' Cora added.

'Maybe the guy took them,' Finley said.

'Anything's possible,' Abilene said.

'They might even still be in the pool,' Cora explained, 'and we just couldn't find them. Maybe later we should all go in and do a really thorough search.'

'The main thing's finding Helen,' Vivian said. 'We can get by without the keys, if we have to. We can walk out. But . . . God, where is she?'

'Somebody must've grabbed her,' Finley said.

Though Abilene had already suspected as much, the words struck her like a blow. 'There's gotta be some other explanation.'

'Like what? She left her shoes here. And the chips. Obviously, she went in the water to look for the keys. But she didn't come out.'

'How could she go *in* there?' Vivian sounded as if she might start crying. 'Was she out of her mind?'

'Took a lot of guts,' Cora muttered.

'I'm sure she thought she'd let us down,' Abilene said. 'Wanted to make things right.'

'But God!'

'The thing is,' Finley said, 'her shoes are still here. And the chips. So she didn't come out this way. Unless she was *taken* out by someone.'

'No footprints,' Abilene said.

'She could've been taken out this way,' Finley said. 'The sun's pretty damn hot. Footprints wouldn't have lasted all that long.' Turning around, she gazed across the field. 'Maybe took her into the woods. If it was that kid we saw yesterday.'

'I'm not sure he was big enough to handle Helen,' Cora said.

'Maybe he wasn't alone.'

'Look,' Vivian said. 'Suppose she was in the pool and someone came in from here? She might've climbed out the other side and run upstairs to get away from him. She could be hiding somewhere in the lodge. Maybe she even heard us calling, but she was afraid to answer.'

'It *was* all wet over there,' Abilene said. 'It was still wet from last night, but she might've gone out that way.'

'She's gotta be somewhere,' Cora said.

'We'd better search the lodge,' Abilene said, feeling a renewal of hope. 'Start there, at least.'

'Come on.'

With Cora in the lead, they returned to the car. She tugged open a rear door and Abilene braced it wide while she climbed in, crawled over the seat back and came out with a tire iron in her hand. Abilene let the door drop shut. Cora smacked the rod against her palm. 'Just in case,' she muttered.

'We'd better take flashlights, too,' Abilene said. 'I'll go get 'em.' Without waiting for a response, she trotted up the remains of the slope. When the pavement leveled out, she broke into a run. Her moccasins pounded the concrete. Then she was in the deep grass and weeds of the front lawn, racing toward the section of the woods where they'd spent the night.

It felt good to be moving fast, making her own breeze, a breeze that cooled her wet skin and clothes, that slipped through her hair and caressed her hot scalp. If only there was nothing else. Just the running, the feel of the air, the sweet mixture of aromas, the strong quickness of her body. Like being a kid on a summer holiday. Savoring all the wonderful sensations, free and excited.

Just that, and no dread.

None of this numbing, gnawing fear that Helen might be gone forever.

She'll be all right, Abilene told herself. We'll find her. Or she'll just show up.

Nearing the edge of the woods, Abilene suddenly *knew* that Helen was sitting on the porch steps of the lodge. Watching her. Wondering why she was in such a hurry. Any moment, Helen would call out, 'What's going on?' Abilene would turn around, and call, 'Where the hell have *you* been?' and run to her, overwhelmed with relief and joy.

She looked over her shoulder.

The porch steps were gray, sunless, deserted.

Abilene's throat thickened. Plunging into the forest, she didn't dare to hope that she would find Helen waiting with the sleeping bags.

How could this have happened?

If only we'd gone back to find the keys last night.

How could Helen have gone there alone?

It was daylight. Daylight can trick us into thinking we're safe. The spooks that haunt the night have gone back to their dark lairs. So we think.

And if they haven't, at least we figure we can see them coming. And get away.

Helen must've been possessed by that false confidence that comes with the morning light. Figured she'd do her good deed for the day. Save us the trouble of returning to the pool.

Why'd you have to do it!

Abilene burst into the clearing. She staggered to a halt on top of her own sleeping bag.

No Helen. Of course not.

The sight of the girl's baggy, plaid Bermudas ripped Abilene's heart. Tears flooded her eyes. She gasped out painful, breathless sobs. With wet fists, she rubbed her eyes. But new tears came, blurring her vision.

No time for this!

We'll find you, Helen. We'll find you. You'll be all right.

Dropping to her knees, she scurried over the sleeping bags. She grabbed the flashlights, then the water bottle. Her mouth was parched. She wanted to drink, but doubted that she would be able to swallow. Out of breath, panting and sobbing at the same time, she figured she would choke.

Blinking to clear her eyes, she glanced around the encampment wondering if there was anything else she should take.

The lantern?

No. The flashlights would be good enough for now. Besides, she didn't know how she might manage it along with the big plastic water bottle and the two flashlights.

Finley's camera? Why bother?

She scurried to her feet and rushed into the trees. As she made her way through the woods, another fantasy forced itself into her mind. She would break out of the trees and see the others waiting in front of the lodge. And Helen would be standing there among them. Fat and homely in her black swimsuit. Smiling and beautiful. Waving. Calling, 'What took you so long?'

Abilene knew it wouldn't happen.

But it might.

She trotted out of the trees, the water bottle sloshing at her side, and gasped when she saw her friends standing in front of the lodge just as she'd imagined them. Vivian, all in white as if ready to prance onto a tennis court. Cora, as if dressed for a game of basketball in her tank top and shorts. Finley, looking like a tomboy in her safari suit. Helen, doughy white, bulging out of her black swimsuit – smiling, waving.

Then they were crouching over Abilene.

She was on her back, looking up at them.

At Finley and Vivian and Cora.

Cora, bare to the waist, was patting Abilene's cheeks and brow with the moist rag of her tank top.

'Are you okay?' Finley asked.

'Where's Helen?'

'We'll find her,' Cora said.

'But she was *with* you.'

'If only,' Vivian muttered.

'I *saw* her.'

'You passed out, kiddo,' Finley said, and gently squeezed her shoulder.

'I what?'

'Fainted. What do you think you're doing on the ground?'

'You . . . She wasn't with you?'

From the looks on their faces, Abilene knew the answer.

'You'd better drink some water,' Cora said. 'You're probably dehydrated.'

'You gave us an awful scare,' Vivian said. 'How are you feeling?'

'I . . . thought she was with you.'

Chapter Nineteen

Cora helped her sit up. Vivian uncapped the water bottle and handed it to her, but Abilene only rested it on her lap, still too breathless to drink.

Looking concerned, Vivian asked Cora, 'Do you think it might be heat stroke or something?'

'I doubt it. Like I said, probably just dehydration. And tension.'

'What's to be tense about?' Finley muttered.

'Her eyes are all bloodshot. What's that a symptom of?'

'I've . . . been crying.'

'Oh,' Vivian said. Suddenly her chin began to shake. The corners of her mouth turned down and tears shimmered in her green eyes.

Looking embarrassed, Finley patted her on the back and murmured, 'Hey hey hey. Come on.' To Abilene, she said, 'Now look what you've started.'

'Drink some of that water,' Cora said.

Abilene took a deep breath, then lifted the bottle and filled her mouth with warm water.

'We oughta get you into the shade. Let you rest a while.'

After swallowing, she said, 'We've gotta find Helen.'

'We will. We will.'

'We already checked in the lodge,' Finley said.

'Not much of a search,' Cora added, 'but at least we went in for a quick look around and called her name a few times. She *might* be in there, but . . .'

'We can take a better look later,' Finley said.

'Come on, let's get you to your feet.'

Finley took the water bottle, capped it, and picked up the two flashlights. Cora shook open her tank top and pulled it down over her head. Then she and Vivian clutched Abilene by the arms and helped her up. She felt light-headed. Her heart was pounding rapidly. She was weak and shaky all over. But the girls held onto her, guiding her toward the lodge.

They lowered her onto the steps of the porch. Cora picked up her tire iron, which she'd left on the top step. Then they all sat down in the shade.

'How you doing?' Finley asked.

'I'll be fine if Helen shows up.' Leaning forward, she braced her elbows on her knees and rubbed her face. 'You didn't find . . . anything . . . inside?'

'Some wet places. You know, in the hall and lobby. Just places where we dripped last night bringing the stuff up from the pool.'

'I took a quick look around upstairs.' Cora shook her head. 'I don't think she's in the lodge.'

'If she is,' Finley added, 'she couldn't answer when we called.'

Couldn't answer. Because she wasn't there? Or because she was unconscious or dead?

Not dead. No. Jesus!

'Maybe . . . she's being held captive. In one of the rooms. Maybe she's gagged, or something.'

'It's possible,' Cora said. 'But what we think is that she was taken into the woods. Probably out behind the lodge, somewhere. We were just talking about it when you came along and . . . passed out.'

'It's only a theory,' Vivian muttered.

'We know she didn't go off on her own,' Finley said. 'Not without her shoes. So somebody *had* to take her. It was probably that kid. Maybe with some friends. But whoever it was, he had to know about the rest of us. And he'd know that the lodge is the first place we'd come looking for her. So if he didn't want to deal with the rest of us, he'd hurry and get her away from here.'

'Into the woods,' Cora said.

'She might've . . . just gone along with him,' Vivian suggested. 'You know? There's no reason, really, to think that he forced her. Or hurt her. Maybe she went willingly. Maybe he's a nice kid and they got talking, and she just . . . went *with* him somewhere.'

'She would've put on her shoes,' Finley said.

'Not necessarily. I mean, if it wasn't something like that, then . . .' Vivian hesitated. Voice trembling, she went on. 'Then she isn't going to be all right. She's probably . . . she's probably already been raped. She might even be . . .'

'Cut it out,' Cora broke in. 'Let's not go off the deep end. We don't know what happened. Maybe nothing, and she'll just turn up.'

'Here's the thing,' Finley said, a sudden eagerness in her voice. 'Look, we're assuming she was attacked. That's really the most logical explanation. Nothing else makes much sense. Somebody got to her while she was down in the pool. And I know how bad all this looks. But if the guy'd only wanted to rape her or kill her, he could've done that right at the pool.

And left her there. But he didn't. He took her away instead. Would've been a lot easier just to leave her, even if there was a whole bunch of guys. So what I think is that he – they – plan to hang onto her.'

'Keep her prisoner,' Abilene said, now understanding why Finley sounded excited about the idea.

'Which means she's probably alive,' Cora said.

'You got it.'

'God, I hope you're right,' Vivian said.

'It makes sense, doesn't it?'

'All we've gotta do is find her. And nail the bastard that grabbed her.'

'Bastards,' Finley corrected her. 'I think it's gotta be more than one.'

Cora put a hand on Abilene's back. 'How are you feeling?'

'A lot better. Let's get going.'

They left the flashlights on the porch stairs and headed for the corner of the lodge. Finley carried the water bottle. Cora carried the tire iron.

Stopping on the slope beside the Wagoneer, Cora suggested they find something to eat. Abilene climbed in. Reaching over the seatback, she opened the cooler. She grabbed a pack of hot dogs and crawled out. Finley had already taken a bag of potato chips from the box that Helen had left on the driveway. The bag was clamped between her knees as she lifted the box onto the roof of the car.

'Anybody wanta change before we take off?' Cora asked.

Abilene considered it. A change into dry clothes would feel good. Sneakers would be much better than moccasins for hiking through the woods. They were probably still wet though.

'Let's just go,' Finley said. 'Whatever we put on is gonna be soaking before long anyway.'

Vivian nodded.

They hurried down the steep driveway. At the rear corner of the lodge, they followed Cora to the small, outside pool.

Helen's sneakers and the bag of chips were still there. Abilene noticed that the granite, where she and Cora had climbed out dripping, was completely dry.

'Okay,' Cora said. 'We figure they started here. Why don't we spread out and head across the field?'

'Just a second,' Abilene said. 'There might be some kind of signs.' The others waited while she walked along the stone slabs, studying the ground cover beyond the edge, looking for trampled weeds, mashed grass. 'I don't see anything,' she said as she came back. 'But maybe they stayed on the cobblestones.'

'Well, let's keep our eyes open. At least we saw where the kid went yesterday.'

They each took a drink from Finley's bottle. Then they fanned out, stepped off the granite and made their way slowly across the field. Cora, at the right end of the line, circled around the far side of the brick fireplace. Abilene, in the middle, strode along one of the cobblestone walkways.

The sun, high above the trees ahead, glared in her eyes. She wished she had a hat or sunglasses, but she rarely wore them and they were back in the car. So she squinted and kept a hand at her brow to shield her eyes.

Near the far end of the grounds, they converged on the old swimming pool. Its bottom was swampy with stagnant rain water that looked like brown muck, thick with decayed leaves and branches. It smelled rank. It buzzed with mosquitos and flies.

Helen wasn't down there.

But something was.

Directly beneath the high dive, four small furry legs protruded from the soupy water. The instant Abilene realized what she was seeing, she averted her eyes. She didn't want a *good* look at it.

Finley pointed. 'Hey. A critter. Toes up.'

Vivian covered her mouth and turned away fast.

'Probably a raccoon,' Cora said.

'Should we fish it out and take it along for lunch?'

Cora and Abilene stared at her.

Finley shrugged. 'Guess not.'

Walking away from the pool, Abilene realized that she'd been holding her breath. She inhaled. The air was fresh and sweet. But the smell of rot and the image of the dead animal seemed to be stuck inside her head. A raccoon? It might've been a dog. She wondered if it had jumped into the pool on purpose. Maybe it saw something appetizing down there, leaped in, and found itself trapped. Or it might've been careless, gotten too close and fallen off the edge. Maybe someone had killed it, then thrown it in.

Could've been Helen down there, she thought.

But it wasn't.

Finley has to be right: Helen wasn't killed. For whatever reason, she was taken prisoner. Abducted. Led away.

Why?

As Abilene wondered about it, Cora led them to the border of the forest at about the same place where the kid had rushed in yesterday afternoon. She was glad to get out of the sunlight. But the hot air felt motionless and moist.

Cora stepped around a clump of bushes and halted. 'A trail,' she muttered.

'All right!' Finley said.

The footpath was barely visible, a narrow strip of matted

leaves and undergrowth winding away from them. It didn't look as if it had been heavily used. It might've been made by a lone person trampling over the same area every once in a while. A couple of times a day. Maybe only a few times each week.

'This must be the path the kid takes,' Cora said.

'I'd bet on it,' Finley said.

Abilene wondered why they hadn't found a similar track leading across the field from here to the lodge. Maybe once clear of the forest, however, the kid altered his route often enough to avoid making a trail.

Single file, Cora going first, they began to follow the path.

Helen might've walked over this same ground just a couple of hours ago, Abilene thought. It was probably the way Finley suggested: more than just the kid taking her away. He and some friends. One guy just couldn't have handled someone as big as Helen. Not the kid, anyway. He'd been fairly small and thin. So he must've had help. Even if there'd been several attackers, however, it didn't seem likely that they would've carried Helen away. They took her, but didn't hurt her. Didn't hurt her so much, at least, that she wouldn't be able to walk under her own power.

Could've been just one guy, Abilene thought. If he had a gun. Threatened to shoot her if she didn't cooperate.

'I hope he doesn't have a gun,' she said.

Finley glanced back at her. 'That'd sure be the pits, huh?'

'Gun or not,' Cora said, 'we're gonna have to take him by surprise. Sneak up on him. So maybe we'd better keep quiet for a while.'

'They've got an awfully big head-start,' Finley pointed out.

'Yeah,' Cora said. 'And they might've stopped anywhere. For all we know, they're ten feet away from us right now.'

'Do you think we should try calling out?' Vivian asked.

Cora and Finley, in unison, said, 'No.'

After that, they stopped talking. Abilene, at the rear, listened for sounds of voices or movement in the woods around her. She peered through breaks in the trees. For a while, she held onto hopes of spotting Helen off in the shadows. Then she began to hope that she wouldn't. If Helen were out here, she might be on the ground. Sprawled motionless. Left behind. Discarded like trash.

Afraid to keep looking, Abilene turned her eyes to those in front of her.

Cora's head kept swiveling. Her short hair, the color of dry hay on top, was dark around her ears and neck where it clung to her skin in wet points and curls. Her tank top was sodden. Her tanned shoulders looked greasy with sweat. The seat of her red shorts looked molded to her buttocks.

By comparison, Vivian appeared almost cool in her white knit shirt and shorts. But the back of her shirt was pasted to her skin. It took on the contours of her shoulder blades and rib cage. Abilene could see the straps of her bra through the thin fabric.

Finley, just in front of Abilene, wore her baggy shirt with its tails hanging out. It looked dark as rawhide down to her hips. There, where the shirt overlapped her shorts, it was still dry and its usual tan color.

We'll be lucky if we don't all collapse, Abilene thought.

Though her head seemed clear, she felt hot and filthy and miserable.

She wished she'd worn socks. She didn't like the slimy feel of her moccasins against the bottoms of her feet.

Her denim skirt was damp and thick and heavy, but at least it was very short and air came up from below. Her panties, bra and blouse were wet and clinging. After a while, she asked the others to wait. She clamped the cool, wet pack of hot dogs between her thighs, peeled off her blouse and removed her bra. It felt good to be free of the hot, confining straps and cups. She folded the bra, tucked it under the waistband of her skirt, then struggled back into her blouse. As she fastened a couple of its buttons, Finley set down the water bottle and bag of chips. She pulled the pack of hot dogs from between Abilene's legs.

'Let's go ahead and eat these suckers,' she said. 'I'm starving.'

'Just a short break,' Cora said.

Finley peeled open the plastic wrapper. She slipped out a wiener, poked it into her mouth, and held the package while the others helped themselves. 'Gourmet breakfast,' she said, her words garbled, the end of the frank bobbing and wiggling.

Abilene took a bite of the hot dog she'd taken. It was warm, moist, mushy. It tasted okay, but she suddenly felt sick as she remembered dinner last night. The sizzling dogs had tasted wonderful, then. Helen had wanted the last one. They hadn't allowed her to eat it. They'd passed it around, instead, 'helping' Helen with her diet.

Abilene's throat went tight.

God, she wished they'd let her have it. It might've been the last hot dog she would ever get a chance to eat.

She's all right. She's gotta be all right.

Abilene had a very hard time swallowing, but she managed to finish her hot dog, washing it down with a lot of water. Finley offered her another.

'No thanks.'

'Go ahead. Two each, then we can toss the package.'

'Maybe we should save a couple for Helen.'

Finley looked as if she felt a sudden pain. She caught her

lower lip between her teeth and nodded. Cora, about to bite into her second hot dog, slipped it back into the wrapper in Finley's hand.

Nobody ate a second one.

Finley shook some juice out of the pack, then folded it carefully and slipped it into a deep pocket of her shorts.

They all drank some more water, then resumed their trek through the woods.

Soon, they came to a split in the trail. One path veered off to the right and the other continued straight ahead.

'Now what?' Vivian asked.

'Flip a coin?' Finley suggested.

'We can come back to this if we don't find anything,' Cora said.

They stuck to the original path and soon came to a lake. An old, weathered dock reached out from its shore. Off the end of the dock was a diving platform that floated at such an angle that one corner dipped into the water. Apparently, one of the drums buoying it up had sprung a leak.

Abilene supposed this must be the lake Helen had told them about. Somewhere near its shores, the hunters had killed that girl.

The lake was bigger than she'd pictured it. Maybe a quarter of a mile wide and twice that long. She saw no boats on its surface. No other docks. No dwellings along its shores. No people. In spite of its blue, glinting surface and the lush beauty of the forest surrounding it, the lake seemed forbidding. An alien, ominous place.

Abilene rubbed her arms and the nape of her neck. Her hot skin, slick with sweat, was pebbled with goosebumps.

'Sure looks deserted,' Vivian whispered, as if afraid to raise her voice in the stillness.

'Doesn't anybody *live* around here?' Finley said.

'Creepy,' Vivian muttered.

'It's like the whole lake's been abandoned,' Abilene said, still rubbing the achy skin on the back of her neck.

'There might be houses we just can't see from here,' Cora said. 'Hidden off in the trees. I'd bet on it.'

Leaving the shelter of the forest's edge, they made their way down to the foot of the dock.

Just to the left, Abilene saw what looked like the remains of a beach. The small area sloped down gently to the shore. It had probably been cleared by workers from the lodge, sand carted in to create a nice little beach for the guests. Now, weeds and bushes grew there and the sand was littered with driftwood.

At the far side of the beach area was an overturned canoe. The wooden hull was bashed in as if someone had stomped through it with a boot. The canoe's green paint was flaking. Painted in white near its bow, faded but still legible, were upside-down letters that read Totem Pole Lodge and a large number 3.

Abilene walked over to the canoe, dropped down to all fours and peered underneath it. Nothing but weeds and sand. Getting to her feet, she said, 'Just wanted to make sure.' She brushed sand off her hands and knees.

'I think we should circle the lake,' Cora said.

'That'll take hours,' Vivian protested.

'You got an appointment or something?' Finley said.

'Maybe whoever took Helen lives along the shore,' Cora explained. '*Somebody* must. This lake can't be as deserted as it looks.'

'The kid we saw has to live somewhere,' Abilene said. 'And the trail led here.'

'One did, anyway,' Finley said.

'You think he'd take her home?' Vivian said.

'Who knows?' Cora said. 'He took her someplace, didn't he?'

'Somebody did,' Finley said. 'Probably.'

'So why not back to his cabin or shack or wherever the hell it is he came from?' Cora asked. 'And what are our alternatives, anyway? Wander around in the woods all day? Go back to the lodge and hope for the best?'

'If we could just get some help . . .' Vivian muttered.

'By the time we could get help,' Cora said, 'it might be way too late for Helen.'

'I think we're her only chance,' Abilene said.

'We'll find her,' Finley said. 'And if she isn't a hundred per cent fine, God help the bastards that did it.'

Chapter Twenty

In case someone might be watching, they walked away from the lake and entered the woods. They didn't go far, however, before turning north. Through breaks in the trees, they kept track of the lake and stayed roughly parallel to its shoreline.

Here, there was no path. They tromped through undergrowth, ducked under low branches, circled around brambles and dead-falls and boulders that sometimes blocked their way, climbed down and up the sides of shallow slopes.

Near the north end of the lake, they were stopped by an

inlet. It was twenty or thirty feet across at the mouth, but from there the glassy water reached westward at least a hundred yards before it vanished under a field of reeds and lily pads.

'Great,' Vivian muttered. 'Now what?'

'Simple,' Cora said. 'We either cross here or go around.'

'Going around would be a bitch,' Finley said. 'Let's take a dip.'

'Might be nice,' Abilene said.

They made their way to the right, walking along the top of a fallen trunk, then hopping down and climbing out on a low clump of rocks where the inlet joined the lake. Abilene sat on a boulder and struggled to catch her breath.

Cora, hands on hips, stood at the edge of the outcropping and peered down. 'Doesn't look very deep,' she said, and jumped.

Her splash showered Finley and Vivian.

'Hey, feels good,' Finley said.

Abilene got to her feet.

'Deeper than it looked,' Cora said. The water covered her to the neck. She dipped her head in, apparently just to get it wet, then swept a hand over her matted hair and began gliding toward the other side.

Halfway across, the water level began to lower. It uncovered her shoulders, descended her back. When it reached her waist, she turned around. 'A piece of cake,' she said. 'And it's nice and cool.' Instead of continuing to the other side, she squatted and dunked her head again.

Finley leaped in, waving the plastic bottle and bag of chips overhead.

Vivian looked down at her white Reeboks. She crouched, untied the lace of her right shoe, hesitated, apparently changed her mind about removing her shoes, then retied the lace and stepped off the rock.

Abilene, afraid she might lose her moccasins in the water, took them off. Clutching them tightly in one hand, she jumped. The water swarmed up her body. She gasped at the unexpected chill of it. Her bare feet met slippery rocks on the bottom. They slid out from under her, but she grabbed a breath of air before her head plunged into the cold.

Once submerged, she was in no hurry to rise.

The water felt incredibly wonderful. She imagined steam rising off her skin.

But there was no time to waste, so she swam forward underwater, surfaced just behind Vivian, and saw that Cora was already climbing out.

As Finley and Vivian boosted themselves onto the rocks, she dropped into the coldness one more time. Then she scurried up the outcropping. She shook water out of her moccasins, slipped into them, and followed the others back into the shadows of the forest.

The water on her skin and clothes was like a cool shield against the heat. Making her way through the woods beyond the northern end of the lake, she felt refreshed and strong, and even found herself strangely optimistic about Helen.

Maybe they'd blown her disappearance out of all proportion. Maybe there was a simple, innocent explanation. She'd just gone wandering off. Thought she'd do some exploring. Come back later and pick up her shoes. Maybe she'd stretched out in the shade somewhere and fallen asleep. It was possible. She might've been too nervous – or hungry – to get much sleep last night. But in the light of day, and after eating half a bag of tortilla chips, drowsiness could've overcome her.

She might be wandering around the lodge right now,

looking for them, worried sick, thinking *they* were the ones who'd disappeared.

Abilene considered mentioning this to the others, but decided to keep quiet. They would only point out flaws in her reasoning and depress her again.

As she followed them across a bright pasture, the sunlight baked the last of the lingering coolness out of her wet clothes and skin. Hot and sweaty, she realized her hopeful scenario about Helen was probably ridiculous. Nothing more than wishful thinking. She tried to hold onto it, but just couldn't.

Helen didn't wander off and fall asleep. She was grabbed and taken away.

We might never find her.

We might never see her again.

What'll we tell Tony? The hell with Tony. He gave her all kinds of crap. He'll probably be glad to be rid of her, the bastard. *We're* the ones who care about her. We're the ones who love her.

What'll we do if . . . ?

Cora suddenly leaped sideways and crouched against a tree. She raised a hand to warn the others. They rushed up behind her. Huddling near her back, they peered around the trunk.

At first, Abilene saw only more trees and rocks and bushes in the gloom ahead. Then she noticed some sort of platform surrounded by a railing of split wood. A rocking chair sat empty on the platform. Wooden stairs led down to a sloping ground. A porch? That's what it was all right. And now that Abilene recognized it, she was able to make out the vague shape of the log cabin that hovered in the shadows behind it.

The bark of the cabin's walls blended in with the trunks of the nearby trees. Its roof – if it had a roof – was hidden under a canopy of branches and leaves. The cabin seemed almost to be a natural part of the forest. As if it hadn't been built by humans. As if it had simply grown there.

'I don't see anyone,' Cora whispered. 'Let's check it out.'

Abilene half expected her to stride straight over to the cabin, but she didn't. Instead, crouching low, she rushed forward about fifteen feet and ducked behind another tree. The others followed.

From there, Abilene could see a couple of old sheds behind the cabin. They were surrounded by a lush, sunlit garden. In front of the cabin, some distance beyond the end of its porch, was a long-handled water pump. The ground sloped down about fifty feet to the lake. A weathered rowboat, moored to the shore by a block of concrete serving as an anchor, floated under the droopy limbs of a willow. Its oars lay across the bow and center bench seats.

'What do you think?' Abilene whispered.

'Sure looks like someone lives here,' Vivian said.

'It's like a place out of one of those damn slasher movies Helen's so crazy about,' Finley said. 'Where the crazy guy with the machete hangs out.'

'Hope she's in there appreciating it,' Cora said.

'Let's find out,' said Finley. She set down the water bottle and chips, studied the ground for a moment, then picked up a chunk of rock the size of a hardball.

Abilene's stomach seemed to drop.

Cora had been lugging around the tire iron all morning, and Abilene had seen that merely as a sensible precaution. But now, Finley had found herself a weapon.

We aren't just searching anymore, she realized.

Jesus.

This *might* be where Helen is. We might be about to find

501

her. And we might be about to face whoever took her. A minute from now, we could be fighting for her life – and for ours.

Suddenly trembling, she glanced around the base of the tree. She spotted a rock half-hidden under the matted leaves and grabbed it. The chip of granite was as large as her hand, shaped roughly like the head of a hatchet.

Vivian picked up a broken limb. It was two inches thick and nearly a yard long.

'Everyone ready?' Cora asked.

'Let's rock 'n roll,' Finley said.

They stepped out from behind the tree. Abilene was relieved to see that Cora, leading the way, wasn't heading for the front of the cabin. The plan, apparently, was to circle around its rear and check things out before going in.

The wall of the cabin had a single window. It was open, but Abilene could see nothing through its rusty screen or the glass panes at the top.

She kept her eyes on it, fearing that a face might suddenly loom out of the darkness and push against the screen.

Finley, hunched over, broke away from the line and took one step toward the window before Abilene clutched the damp collar of her shirt. Finley glanced back at her. Abilene shook her head. Frowning, Finley shrugged. But she said nothing, and resumed her position behind Vivian.

They passed the rear corner of the cabin.

There were two windows, one on either side of the back door. Wooden stairs descended from the door to a path which led through the center of the garden and into the woods. Scanning the area, Abilene saw no one.

She watched the door and windows, only turning away from them when Cora halted in front of the first shed. It looked to Abilene like an outhouse. Its flimsy door had no handle and was latched shut by a hook and eye.

Cora reached for the hook.

My God, Abilene thought, does she think *Helen's* in there?

Cora flicked up the hook. The door swung open, groaning on its ancient hinges. The draft of its opening swept out a miasma of hot, foul air.

Nothing inside but a bench with a hole in it, and a swarm of buzzing flies.

While the others stepped away from the foul aromas, Cora closed the door and hooked it shut.

They followed a path through the garden to the other shed. It was three times the size of the outhouse – a more likely place for keeping a prisoner. Abilene could picture Helen inside, sprawled on the dirt floor, bound with ropes, a gag in her mouth.

But Cora opened the door and nobody was there.

Peering into the gloom, Abilene saw shovels, rakes, hoes, a scythe, fishing gear and an ax. Shelves laden with bottles and jars.

'Jeez,' Finley whispered, 'we can sure improve on our weaponry.'

They stepped into the shed. The hot, heavy air smelled sweet and musty.

Finley dropped her rock and picked up the ax.

'I don't know if you should do that,' Vivian whispered.

'Christ on a crutch,' Cora gasped. She took a jar down from a shelf and looked at it more closely. 'Chicken heads.'

'What?'

They gathered around her.

In the dim light from the doorway, Abilene saw that the heads of at least half a dozen chickens were drifting about in the jar's murky yellow fluid. She glimpsed their tiny black eyes, their open beaks. Then she looked away fast.

Vivian gagged.

'Why would anyone want to save chicken heads?' Cora asked.

'Appetizers?' Finley suggested.

Cora replaced the jar on its shelf. She lifted down another and held it toward the light. 'Oh my God.'

Abilene took a quick look.

The things suspended inside the bottle looked back at her. Eyeballs.

'Holy shit,' Finley said.

'They probably aren't human,' Cora whispered. 'Maybe from pigs or . . .'

The crash of an explosion slammed Abilene's ears. She jumped. They all jumped. Cora dropped the jar. Ears stunned by the blast, Abilene didn't hear the jar shatter. But it did. Warm liquid splashed her ankles. Eyeballs rolled.

The door of the shed slammed shut.

Chapter Twenty-one

The explosion must've been a gunshot. From the noise of it, Abilene figured it had been fired from only a few feet away. During the moment between the blast and the door flying shut, however, she'd seen none of her friends react as if hit.

'Is everybody okay?' she whispered.

'Just fine,' Finley muttered.

'What *was* that?' Cora asked.

'Sounded like a shotgun,' Vivian said.

'We're in deep shit,' Finley said.

Abilene flinched as something – probably the butt of the shotgun – crashed against the door.

'Whatcha doin' in there?' called a high, scratchy voice. It sounded as if it came from someone old, but Abilene couldn't tell whether it belonged to a man or a woman.

'We aren't doing anything,' Cora answered. 'We were just looking around.'

'Snoopin'!' He – or she – struck the door again. 'I don't abide no snoopers!'

'We're sorry,' Cora said. 'We didn't mean any harm. We're looking for someone.'

'Y'found someone. Me!'

Abilene turned around slowly to look at the door. She stepped on an eye. It popped and squished under the soft sole of her moccasin. She groaned.

'Who are you?' Finley asked.

'Who y'lookin for?'

'A friend of ours,' Cora said. 'Her name's Helen.'

'Ain't me.'

'She's twenty-five,' Cora said. 'Dark-haired, pretty husky.'

'A fatty?'

'Have you seen her?'

'Ain't in there.'

'Do you know where she is?'

Silence.

'Gonna letcha out. I got my over-'n-under here, so come out easy 'r I'll blow y'innards out her backside.'

'For Godsake,' Vivian whispered, 'drop the ax, Fin.'

'We'd better all empty out hands,' Cora said.

Abilene let her rock fall. It clinked against some glass in the darkness. She heard soft thuds as the others discarded their weapons.

The door swung wide. Abilene squinted into the brightness.

Standing just outside the shed, aiming a shotgun at her belly, was a short, skinny man – or woman. Abilene still couldn't tell which. The person had wild gray hair. The wrinkled, leathery face bristled with stubble, but Abilene had seen old women who had similar whiskers.

'C'mon out.'

Finley raised her hands overhead and stepped through the doorway. Abilene did the same, followed by Vivian and Cora. Just in front of the shed, they spread out. They stood abreast, their arms high.

A quick look around satisfied Abilene that their captor was alone.

One is all it takes, she thought. One lunatic with a shotgun.

And the person in front of her *did* look like a lunatic.

Both earlobes were adorned with small tufts of bright red and yellow feathers. Not earrings, but fishing jigs. Flies. Fixed to the ears by tiny, barbed hooks. From a rawhide thong around the stranger's neck dangled a pendant of dry, white bone. It looked like the skull of a rodent. The leather strip passed through the skull's earholes. The jaw hung open, showing a snout packed with sharp little teeth.

The skull rested against tawny skin between the edges of a rawhide vest. The vest, loosely tied with a couple of thongs, was open a couple of inches all the way down its front but revealed no hint of cleavage. Low on the stranger's hips hung ragged jeans with their legs cut off, their sides slit nearly to the waistband. Cinched around the waist of the jeans was a belt that held a hunting knife in a wide leather scabbard. The knife had a staghorn handle. Its blade reached halfway down the side of the stranger's thigh.

Both feet were bare and filthy. The small toe of one foot was missing.

While Abilene inspected this peculiar person, he or she slowly swept the shotgun down the line, pale blue eyes studying all of them.

'Yer a handsome pack, gals.'

'Do you know where Helen is?' Cora asked.

A smile. Brown teeth and gaps. Then the pale eyes fixed on Vivian. 'What kinda shoes y' got there?'

'They're Reeboks.'

'Land, ain't they somethin'? Give 'em t'old Batty.'

Bending down slightly, Vivian lifted a foot off the ground. She crossed it over her knee. Cora grabbed her shoulder and held her steady while she pulled off the shoe, tossed it toward Batty, then switched legs and removed the other. An underhand throw landed it on the ground in front of Batty's feet.

'I getta keep 'em.'

Vivian said nothing.

Cora said, 'You're the one with the shotgun.'

'Ain't no thief.' Batty braced the shotgun with one arm, crouched and picked up the shoes. 'I don't work free. Got my pay here. Y'lookin' for Helen, old Batty's gonna point y'where to look.'

'You know where she is?' Cora asked.

Batty answered with a wink, then shouldered the shotgun, turned around, and strode toward the back door of the cabin.

Nobody else moved.

They looked at each other. Abilene saw surprise and confusion on their faces.

She looked again toward Batty. Without so much as a glance back, the old weirdo climbed the stairs and swung open the screen door and vanished into the cabin.

'Jesus H. Christ,' Finley muttered. 'What was *that*?'

'Batty,' Abilene said.

'Appropriately named.'

Vivian stayed on her feet, but sagged as if she'd lost the strength to hold herself upright. 'God,' she said. She bent over and grabbed her knees.

'I guess we're free to leave,' Cora said. 'But maybe we'd better go inside and see what he has to say.'

'He?' Abilene asked.

'Whatever.'

'I don't think he's got Helen,' Vivian said, still holding her knees.

'But he's got your shoes,' Cora told her.

'He's welcome to them.'

'She,' Finley said. 'It.'

'Sounded like Batty considered them payment for services,' Abilene said. 'I think he's planning to help us find her.'

'I think Batty's batty,' Finley said. 'Probably doesn't know shit.'

'There's only one way to find out.'

'What else have we got to go on?' Cora asked. 'Hell, he lives here. Even if he hasn't seen Helen, he might have some ideas about who took her.'

'Besides,' Abilene said, 'if nothing else, this'll give us a chance to check out the cabin.'

'Enter the lair,' Finley said, grinning slightly.

'It isn't as if he's forcing us.'

'Yeah,' Cora said. 'He had us and walked away.'

Vivian stood up straight. She shook her head. She said,

'Let's do it. What's the worst that can happen?' With that, she walked toward the back of the cabin.

The others followed.

Finley, striding along beside Abilene, said, 'What's the worst that can happen? Let's see. We might all end up in jars.'

At the top of the stairs, Vivian rapped on the door.

'Come into my parlor,' whispered Finley.

'Can it,' Abilene said.

Vivian pulled open the door. She stepped over the threshold and paused, an arm stretched back to hold the door open for the rest of them.

Entering, Abilene found herself in a long, narrow kitchen. She saw cupboards, a black iron stove, a small pump over the sink that looked like a smaller version of the pump she'd seen outside. No refrigerator, not even an old icebox. A gas lamp hung suspended from the ceiling, and another rested atop a small wooden table in one corner.

'Batty?' Vivian called.

'Waitin' for ya.'

They stepped through a doorway into the main room of the cabin. It wasn't as brightly lit as the kitchen, its few windows apparently hidden from the sun by overhanging trees. In the center of the room, Batty was leaning over a table, spreading out a leathery scroll.

Vivian's Reeboks looked enormous on the lunatic's small feet.

'Come over and sit.'

On her way to the table, Abilene took a quick look around. Except for the kitchen, this seemed to be the only room. A bed along the right wall was neatly covered with a quilt. The shotgun was propped against the wall near its head. At the foot of the bed was a steamer trunk, lid shut. In the room's far corner was a pot-bellied stove. There were a few chairs scattered about: straight cane-backs and one rocker. She spotted a few gas lamps on small tables. Every wall had shelves laden with bulky old tomes and an odd assortment of nick-nacks: wax figures, candles, crucifixes, pictures of saints, bones and feathers, stuffed birds and squirrels, bowls, every size and shape of clear glass jar – from which Abilene quickly averted her eyes.

Only to notice a stuffed bat, wings outspread, nailed above the front door.

From the general size and shape of the creature's ugly head with its stubby snout and pointed teeth, she realized that Batty's necklace ornament must be the skull of a bat.

Charming, she thought.

I'm in a madhouse.

Clearly, Helen wasn't here.

Unless in that trunk . . .

She glanced again at the trunk beyond the foot of the bed and decided it wasn't large enough for Helen. Not unless . . .

'Are you some kind of a witch?' Finley asked.

'Some say so.' Cackle. 'Some say I'm batty.'

'What do *you* say?'

'Old Batty sees the unseen, knows the unknown. Sit sit sit.'

They pulled out chairs, and sat around the table. Most of its top was covered by the mat that Batty'd been unrolling when they came in. It looked like tanned animal hide, stained dark brown. A wiggly oval outline about the size of a football was faintly visible near the center.

The wood of the table showed through a hole near one end of the outline.

Coming up behind Abilene, Batty poked the hole with the point of his knife.

510

'Batty's place.'

'This is a map?' Cora asked.

'Oughta be.'

Cora reached out and touched an edge of the oval. 'And this is the lake?'

Batty, scurrying away, didn't answer.

'You're going to show us where Helen is?'

Batty came back from a shelf, cupping an earthenware bowl.

Off in a corner, something creaked. Abilene flinched. She shot her eyes in the direction of the sound, and saw the rocking chair teetering. For just a moment, her mind was stunned by a memory of the hideous deformity they'd encountered one Halloween night a few years ago. In a chair in a corner. Unseen at first. Just like now.

Then she saw the snow-white cat crouching on the seat of the rocker.

She let out a shaky sigh of relief.

The others, as startled as she by the unexpected disturbance, also seemed glad to find nothing worse than a cat in the chair.

'Amos,' Batty informed her guests.

The cat switched its tail.

'Figures,' Finley said. 'A witch, a cat.' Smirking at Batty, she asked, 'Do you *know* where Helen is? Have you seen her? Or are you just planning to *divine* for us?'

Abilene grimaced. Was Finley nuts? How could she talk this way to a lunatic?

'I'll know,' Batty said, and placed the bowl on top of the map.

'If this is gonna involve chicken heads . . .'

'*Can* it!' Abilene whispered. 'Okay? Just cut it out.'

511

Finley tilted one corner of her mouth and rolled her eyes upward.

Vivian seemed to be in her own mind, ignoring the exchange, gazing across the table with narrowed eyes. Her lips were stretched back, baring her teeth.

Cora looked intense. As if she were scrutinizing Batty, wary but fascinated.

Abilene flinched as Batty reached around from behind and slapped the huge knife on the table in front of her.

'Part y'flesh and give.'

Abilene twisted her head sideways and stared up at the wizened, whiskered face.

'What?'

'In the vessel.'

'I don't get it.'

Finley grinned. 'I think you're supposed to cut yourself and bleed in the bowl. That right, Batty?'

'All ya.'

'Whoa, boy. I knew this'd get queer.'

'It's the way.'

'Might be *your* way. That's why they call you Batty.'

'Shut up!' Cora snapped.

Finley flinched as if stunned by the loud rebuke. Face red, voice soft, she said, 'You don't believe in this stuff, do you?'

'It's worth a try.'

'This androgynous loonytune wants us to cut ourselves.'

'Stop it, Fin,' Vivian said gently. 'I think we should do what Batty asks. If it helps us find Helen, that's all that really matters.'

'I want to find her as much as anyone. But going along with this crazy . . .'

Abilene snatched up the knife and slashed the edge of her left hand.

Finley gasped, 'Shit!'

Abilene stretched out her arm in time for the blood to spill into the bowl. The wound stung, but didn't hurt as much as she'd expected. She watched the bright streamer of blood fall, heard quiet, plopping splashes.

A hand squeezed her shoulder. Batty's hand.

'Yer a shiny soul.'

She passed the knife to Finley, who sat to her right.

'I'm sure,' Finley muttered. She glanced at the others. She scowled at Abilene's bleeding hand. Muttering, 'We'll probably end up with gangrene and lose our arms,' she sliced herself. She reached out, and her hand joined Abilene's above the bowl.

She passed the knife to Cora. Without a moment's hesitation, Cora gashed her hand and put it over the bowl. She gave the knife to Vivian.

Vivian inspected her left arm as if searching for the best place to cut it. Then she settled, like the others, for the edge of her hand. As she slid the blade against it, her lips pursed and she murmured, 'Ooooo.'

There was silence as they all sat around the table, their left arms outstretched, their blood splashing into the bowl.

Finley broke the silence.

'Can't wait to see what comes next.'

'Nuff,' Batty said.

They pulled in their arms.

'I don't suppose you provide bandages,' Finley said.

Batty didn't answer.

Abilene pressed her cut against her skirt. Blood seeped through the denim, hot against her thigh. Finley grabbed a handful of shirttail and clutched it to her wound. Cora's hands were out of sight beneath the table, so Abilene couldn't see what she was doing, but Vivian kept her arm far to the side and bent down low. She pulled off her right sock, then wrapped it around her left hand.

Batty stepped to the corner of the table between Abilene and Vivian, picked up the knife, then reached out and slid the bowl in front of Abilene.

'Drink.'

'Oh boy.' From Finley.

Abilene stared down at the bright red fluid. She felt as if her brain was shrinking and going numb. Her cheeks tingled. Saliva flooded her mouth, the way it sometimes did when she was on the verge of vomiting.

'It's only blood, she told herself. Nothing to freak out about.

She'd tasted blood before. Licking or sucking on tiny wounds after hurting herself. It wasn't awful.

But it was only my own.

So what? This is just mine and Finley's and Cora's and Vivian's. They're like family. They're like *part* of me.

And it's for Helen.

Gulping her saliva down, she lifted the bowl with her uninjured hand. She tilted it to her mouth, shut her eyes to avoid looking at the crimson fluid, and sipped. It rolled in, warm against her gums and tongue, thicker than she'd expected. Her throat squeezed shut. She forced herself to swallow.

She was about to lower the bowl when Batty said, 'More.'

Quickly, she tipped the bowl for another drink. Too quickly. Too carelessly. Her trembling hand, not quite in control of the heavy bowl, flooded her mouth with blood. She gulped it down. She gagged. Her eyes brimmed with tears. But she didn't vomit.

She passed the bowl to Finley.

'This gonna turn us into vampires?' Finley quipped.

'Just drink some,' Cora said.

Finley raised the bowl close to her face. 'Through the teeth and over the gums, watch out, stomach – here it comes.' She drank. She took two big gulps. As she swallowed, she had a frantic look in her eyes. A look that made Abilene think she might suddenly hurl the bowl away and scream.

Then Finley finished. She had a mustache like a kid who'd just polished off a glass of milk. But this mustache was red. She gave the bowl to Cora, and wiped her mouth with the back of her hand.

Cora took two sips of blood in the same way she had slit her hand – fast and determined. Then she sat very rigid for a moment. She shuddered. She passed the bowl to Vivian. She rubbed the shiny crimson from her lips.

Vivian stared into the bowl. Her face looked unnaturally pale and slack. 'I don't know if I can,' she muttered.

'It's not so bad,' Abilene said.

'Zee blood is zee life,' Finley said.

'Just don't think about it,' Cora advised her. 'A couple of sips and you'll be done.'

'It'll put hair on your chest,' Finley added.

'Just what I need.' Vivian managed a sickly smile. Then she took a deep breath, sighed, raised the bowl to her mouth and drank. She swallowed twice. Lowering the bowl, she gasped as if she'd finally come up for air after nearly drowning. Blood dribbled down her chin. Before she could wipe it away, a drop fell onto the front of her white, knit shirt.

Batty stepped up between Vivian and Abilene, lifted the bowl and drank. Gulp after gulp. Swallowing. Seeming to relish the taste. Then, lips tight, cheeks bulging, the old lunatic removed the bat-skull necklace. Held it high by its leather thong.

Head tipped back, Batty opened wide and lowered the dangling skull. It went in white. It came out red. Batty's lips wrapped around the base of the skull. Sucked off some of the excess blood before swallowing the mouthful and easing the necklace away.

Like a pendulum, it swung across the leather map. Back and forth. Slowing down. Beginning to drift in lazy circles.

A drop of blood gathered on the hanging jaw. Bloomed. Fell. And splashed the map midway between Cora and the edge of the lake.

'Ah!'

The single red bead was all that fell before Batty slipped the necklace back on. The skull made a smudge on the skin of the old lunatic's chest.

Batty aimed a finger at the spot of blood on the map.

'That's where you think Helen is?' Cora asked.

'Ghost Lodge.'

'*The Totem Pole Lodge?*'

'Call it whatcha want.'

Stunned, Abilene stared at the dot of blood. Its position, in relationship to the outline of the lake and the hole marking Batty's cabin, actually did seem to be in the vicinity of the Totem Pole Lodge.

Finley murmured, 'Holy shit.'

Vivian gazed at the spot. Her head shook slowly from side to side.

Looking up at Batty, astonishment in her eyes, Cora said, 'That's where we *were*. That's where she disappeared.'

'She's there.'

'Is she all right?' Abilene asked.

'Can't say.'

'Do you *know*?'

Not answering, Batty picked up the bowl and set it on the hardwood floor beside the table. A creak sounded in a far corner of the room. Abilene turned her eyes to the rocking chair. The cat was gone.

Vivian groaned. She was looking down. Abilene followed her gaze and found Amos hunched over the bowl. Tail twitching, the cat lapped away at the remaining slick of blood.

'Y'ain't from these parts,' Batty said. 'Don't know better. Get y'Helen 'n get back where y'come from. 'N praise the Lord it's old Batty y'run into. Some folks nearby, they'duz soon kill y'dead as spit on y'feet. Now scat.'

Chapter Twenty-two

Batty followed them through the kitchen door and down the back stairs.

'I left something of mine in your shed,' Cora said.

'Fetch it.'

'Watch what you step in,' Finley warned.

They waited while Cora hurried into the shed. She came out with her tire iron.

Seeing it, Batty cackled. 'That spose t'hurt someone?'

'She just carries it around in case of a flat,' Finley said.

The mention of a flat tire triggered a thought in Abilene. She'd seen no evidence of a driveway or road, much less a car, since leaving the lodge. But she asked, anyway. 'You don't have a car, do you?'

Batty answered with a snort.

'What about a telephone?'

'Who'd old Batty wanta call?'

'Are there any homes nearby with cars or telephones?'

'Y'find any home 'round this neck a the woods, y'd best run from it. Now get on back 'n find Helen, 'fore y'all get got.'

Batty stood watching while they turned away and walked around the corner of her cabin.

Vivian glanced back as if afraid the old creature might be pursuing them. 'God, is it good to get away from *there*.'

'Too bad Helen wasn't with us,' Finley said. 'She would've loved all that.' Leading the way, she returned to the tree where she'd left the water bottle and chips. She picked them up, then looked back at the cabin. 'Should we go the rest of the way around the lake, or what?'

'Maybe we'd better head back the way we came,' Cora said. 'It'll be quicker. If Helen's really at the lodge . . .'

'Besides,' Abilene said, 'I didn't much care for what Batty had to say about her neighbors.'

'What do you expect from a loony?'

'I just want to get back to the lodge,' Vivian said. 'If we keep going around the lake, there's no telling who we might run into. I sure don't like the idea of meeting up with any more weirdos.'

'Yeah,' Abilene said. 'Batty was more than enough.'

'And it'd be a lot farther, that way,' Vivian pointed out. 'I don't have any shoes.'

'We're lucky that's all he wanted,' Cora said.

'She, it,' added Finley.

'We need to look after our cuts, too,' Abilene said.

'I've got a first aid kit in my suitcase,' Cora said.

'Is it settled, then?' Vivian asked.

'I don't hear any objections,' Cora said. 'So I guess we'll go back the way we came.'

'And let's be quick about it,' Finley said. 'Before we get got.'

They started hiking away from the cabin, heading for the north end of the lake. As she walked along, Abilene inspected her cut. The short slit, caked with a thread of thickened blood, was no longer leaking. The edge of her hand was stained as if she'd rubbed it against a rusty sheet of metal. It felt stiff and sore. The patch of blood on her skirt was tacky when it touched her thigh. Lifting the skirt, she saw a ruddy stain on her skin.

Now that she was away from Batty, she found it hard to believe that they had actually entered the cabin at all, much less cut themselves with the maniac's knife *and drunk their own blood*.

'That was about the craziest damn thing we've ever done,' she said.

Cora smiled back at her. 'Seemed like a good idea at the time.'

'Speak for yourself,' Finley said. 'It *never* seemed like a good idea to me.'

'You didn't have to go along with it,' Abilene said.

'Didn't want to be the party-pooper. Besides, it might've ruined the spell. Such as it was.' After a few moments, she said, 'Hey, if it turns out the old bat was full of shit, does Vivian get her shoes back?'

'That's only fair,' Vivian said. 'Will you collect the refund for me?'

Abilene smiled, surprised to find Vivian joining in the banter.

Cora abruptly halted and turned around, frowning.

'What?' Vivian asked.

'This talk of going back makes me think. While we were there, we should've asked Batty where to find the car keys.'

'Oh, let's go back right away,' Finley said.

'She'd want somebody else's shoes,' Vivian said.

'He, it.'

'He/she/it's got Viv's,' Abilene pointed out. 'We'd have to give up something else.'

'Like our duds,' Finley said. 'Old Batty could sure use a decent wardrobe.'

'Yours,' Abilene told her. 'The fit'd be just right.'

'Gimme a break.'

'Maybe arrange a trade,' Vivian said. 'Fin'd look great in that vest, wouldn't she?'

'You got blood on your polo shirt,' Finley pointed out. 'Never gonna come out.'

'So?'

Finley shrugged. 'Just hoping to ruin this giddy mood of yours. You're really annoying when you're cheerful.'

We're *all* acting incredibly cheerful, Abilene realized. It seemed strange until she thought about it. They'd just gone through some bizarre, rather harrowing experiences, and come out of them unscathed. It was the nervous, heady feeling of exhilaration that comes from knowing the crisis is over and everything is okay once again.

Like after an earthquake.

But the crisis isn't over, she reminded herself. Everything isn't okay. We're safe from Batty, but Helen's still missing.

Maybe we *will* find her at the lodge.

Following the others as they continued their journey around the end of the lake, Abilene thought how great it would be if Batty had been right about Helen's location.

There all the time. Never *was* abducted.

It was what Abilene had really hoped all along.

But don't count on it, she warned herself. Helen might be anywhere. You can't rely on the hocus-pocus of some freaky old hermit.

You can't rely on it, but you can't discount it, either.

Abilene considered herself to have an open mind. Maybe too open. Harris sometimes accused her of being gullible. But she couldn't help what she believed.

Among other things, she accepted the possibility that mysterious forces might be at work in the universe. There was plenty of circumstantial evidence to support the notion of God, for instance. The same with such matters as telepathy, visitors from outer space, reincarnation, ghosts, and various forms of fortune-telling. Some of these things were undoubtedly hogwash. But she suspected that not *all* of them were.

So why not a Batty able to 'see' where Helen is?

Maybe hogwash. But maybe not.

Batty'd had no control over just where the drop of blood would land when it fell from that awful pendulum. But it had struck the map almost exactly in the location of the lodge.

Even if Batty somehow knew that's where we'd come from, Abilene thought, why did the blood fall at that particular place?

Maybe just coincidence.

Coincidence. A nice catch-all for cynics. It could be used to explain away a whole array of mysteries.

Maybe *that's* the real hogwash, Abilene thought. Maybe there's no such thing as coincidence. Nothing is accidental, nothing random. Maybe *everything* is part of a pattern.

In some ways that seemed to make a lot more sense than the idea that events were ruled by chance.

Chance could obviously play a part in things. But as certain as Abilene felt that chance was a factor, she was even more certain that it was a minor player. A wild card.

Cause and effect ran the game.

Some of those causes, some of those effects, were just too subtle or disguised or mysterious to be recognized.

So maybe it was chance, coincidence, that the drop of blood fell on the map just where it did. Or maybe Batty's bizarre little ritual somehow *caused* it to land there.

We'll never know, Abilene thought.

If we find Helen there . . .

We still won't know for sure. Finley would say it was a mere coincidence. Cora was too matter-of-fact to care one way or the other. She would just be glad that Helen was back in the fold, and not concern herself with Batty's hand in the matter. Vivian would probably be just as astonished and perplexed as Abilene.

Helen was the only one who would truly believe, without any doubt, in Batty's power.

It really *is* a shame she wasn't with us, Abilene thought. Finley was right about that. Helen would've been scared witless, but she sure would've loved it.

'When we find Helen,' she said, 'we really oughta take her back and introduce her to Batty.'

'*If* we find her,' Finley said, glancing back.

Vivian looked over her shoulder, frowning. 'I sure wish Batty'd told us whether she's all right.'

'Bat-brain doesn't know shit, anyway. It was a waste of time. And blood.'

'I don't know,' Vivian said.

Then they came to the mouth of the inlet. As Cora hurried over the rocks, apparently eager to jump in, Finley said, 'Wait. Why don't I fill up the bottle before you go in and mess up the water?' She shook the plastic container. Only a couple of inches of water remained, sloshing about its bottom.

'That'll be enough to last us till we get to the lodge,' Cora said.

'Yeah,' Vivian said. 'Don't ruin it.'

'We can always come back if we run out,' Cora explained.

'This stuff looks fine to me,' Finley said.

'Why bother?' Abilene said. 'We've got two more bottles in the car.'

With a grin, Finley said, 'But they aren't filled with clear, sparkling Vermont *lake* water.'

'God knows what's in that stuff,' Vivian said.

'Woosies.'

Cora jumped.

The rest of them followed her into the water. Once again, Abilene was stunned by its sudden chill. She submerged herself completely, then surfaced. Cora and Finley were continuing toward the other side, but Vivian had halted, unwrapped her hand, and was using a clean part of the sock to work on the bloodstain marring her shirt.

Seemed like a good idea. After switching the moccasins to her injured left hand, Abilene reached across with her right and rubbed the bloody area of her skirt briskly against her thigh. Probably wouldn't do a lot of good. But she was bound to get out the worst of it.

'Any luck?' she asked Vivian.

Vivian dropped her hand. The pink of her skin showed through the clinging fabric. The bloodstain was faint, but still visible.

523

'Better,' Abilene said.

'I guess the shirt's ruined. Doesn't really matter, though.'

'Don't you get a free supply from Tipton?' Finley asked.

Vivian turned around. Finley had already climbed onto the rocks at the far side. 'Sure do. If I had any with me, I'd give one to you.'

Finley smiled down at the darkly stained tail she'd used to wrap her hand. 'Gives my shirt character, don't you think?'

'A red badge of courage,' Abilene said.

'A red badge of lunacy,' Finley corrected.

Following Vivian to the other side, Abilene said, 'If this was a war, we could all get Purple Hearts.'

'Not sure they give 'em for self-inflicted wounds,' Cora said.

They climbed out. Abilene slipped into her moccasins.

'I guess our little communion does make us blood sisters, though,' Cora added.

'Whoopee,' Finley said.

'It wasn't actually so bad,' Vivian said. 'I mean, it was only *our* blood. I thought about that. I figured it wasn't any worse than if it'd just been my own.'

'I thought about that, too,' Cora admitted.

'Yeah,' Finley said. 'Could've been worse.'

Vivian nodded. 'If Batty's blood had been in there, I know I couldn't have drunk it. Not a chance.'

'In a way it's kind of neat,' Abilene said.

'Oh yeah,' Finley said.

'I mean, we all have each other's blood inside us right now. We're digesting it. It'll become part of us.'

'You're weird as hell, Hickok.'

Cora started to walk away but Vivian asked her to wait. With Abilene holding her steady, Vivian balanced on one leg and struggled to get the wet sock onto her foot. The bottom of her foot looked ruddy, but there were no cuts or scrapes that Abilene could see. At least the sock would now give it a little protection.

'If you have any trouble you can borrow my moccasins for a while.'

'It's not bad.'

'All set?' Cora asked.

'Yep.'

They followed Cora across the rocks, over the top of a fallen log, then along the shoreline to the place where they'd first come upon the inlet that morning. From there, they journeyed through the woods, keeping the lake in sight.

Abilene was surprised at how quickly they came upon the path to the lodge. She supposed that she shouldn't be surprised; return trips, she had noticed even as a child, always seemed faster than the trips going out.

With a glance to her left, she saw the old dock and the strangely tilted diving platform beyond its end.

'Anybody wanta go down to the beach and take a snack break?' Finley asked, waving the bag of chips.

'Let's just get on to the lodge,' Vivian said.

'You mean I traipsed all over creation with this for nothing?'

'Eat some yourself,' Abilene suggested.

Finley didn't bother, but she did open the water bottle. They all took drinks from it before resuming their trek.

Soon, they stepped out of the woods at the far end of the lodge's grounds. Abilene felt her heart quicken as she started across the field. She squinted through the bright sunlight, scanning the back of the lodge, half expecting to spot Helen. Maybe by the outer pool. Maybe watching from one of the high balconies. But she saw no one.

Though the field seemed fairly level all the way to the rear of the lodge, Abilene realized that it had a slight upward grade. She was too low, for a while, to see the granite walkway or pool.

But as she neared them, the ground rose.

Helen's shoes were still there, the open bag of chips propped up between them like before.

Abilene felt her excitement wither.

'She hasn't been back for her shoes,' Cora pointed out.

Nobody else said anything.

They trudged the final distance. The sun was high enough, now, for the balcony of the lower porch to cast a shadow across half the width of the walkway and pool. They stepped into the shade and leaned back against the wall of the lodge.

The granite wall felt wonderfully cool through Abilene's blouse. Huffing for air, she lifted the front of her blouse and wiped her face.

Nobody spoke.

Cora alone didn't appear to be winded. But she, like the others, was flushed and dripping.

Vivian bent over and clutched her knees.

After a while, Finley sat down.

Whether or not they believed in Batty's power, Abilene guessed that they had all approached the lodge with hopes of being met by Helen. Now, they felt only let down and exhausted.

'This isn't accomplishing anything,' Cora finally said. 'We'd better look for her.'

'Let's go back to the car first,' Vivian suggested. 'I want to get some shoes on.'

'And we can take care of our cuts,' Abilene reminded them.

Nobody made a move to leave.

Maybe we're scared, Abilene thought. Afraid to start searching. As long as we haven't searched, there's still a chance of finding her. But if we look everywhere and don't turn her up . . .

'Why don't we just rest for a while?' Finley said. 'I'm really bushed.'

Chapter Twenty-three

Finally, they left the shade and climbed the driveway to the car. Vivian crawled inside. With instructions from Cora she was able to locate the first-aid kit. She handed it out, then retrieved a pair of socks and blue Nikes from her own luggage.

'Our stuff's still wet,' she informed the others. 'Why don't we set everything out in the sunlight?'

The suggestion seemed to Abilene like a delaying tactic. And she was all for it.

Vivian got into her socks and shoes while the others took turns applying antiseptic and bandages to the wounds on their hands. After Vivian had patched her cut, they unloaded all the garments, shoes and towels, and the flashlights that had been thrown into the pool last night. Finley tested the flashlights.

'Dead,' she announced, and tossed them back inside the car.

They carried the other things to the top of the driveway, spread them around on the pavement, and weighted them down with shoes.

When the clothing and towels were secure, Finley suggested they get the rest of their things from the campsite.

Once we've done that, Abilene thought, we won't have any excuses left. We'll *have* to search the lodge.

But maybe Helen will be waiting at the campsite.

Sure.

She couldn't even begin to believe it.

As they walked through the overgrown lawn toward the edge of the forest, Abilene realized that nobody had called out for Helen. We've been back for half an hour – maybe a lot longer – and we haven't once shouted out her name.

Probably, she supposed, for the same reason we've procrastinated like this about searching the lodge.

Holding onto our hope for as long as we can.

They entered the trees. When they came upon the clearing, it looked just the same as when Abilene had left it early that morning.

The sight of Helen's blouse and plaid Bermuda shorts again brought tears to her eyes.

'At least nobody swiped my camera,' Finley muttered. She sounded as if she didn't care at all.

They rolled their own sleeping bags. When they finished, Helen's bag was still on the ground, her purse beside it, her abandoned shorts and blouse spread across its cover.

'I'll do it,' Abilene said. She knelt and picked up the clothes. They were dry. She wrapped them around the purse, then rolled the sleeping bag.

Helen's 'effects.'

They aren't her *effects*, Abilene told herself. They're her *stuff*, not her effects. Christ!

She carried them, along with her own sleeping bag, toilet

kit and purse, out of the forest and across the sunny yard to the driveway.

Cora set down the lantern.

Everything else – including Finley's camera – was stowed without comment in the rear of the Wagoneer.

As if we're getting ready to drive away, Abilene thought.

If only . . .

The car door dropped shut with a crash.

They all looked at each other.

'Okay,' Cora said. 'Let's get on with it.'

They walked alongside the porch and climbed the stairs. Finley and Abilene picked up the flashlights. Cora switched the tire iron to her left hand. With her right, she opened the door.

'Helen!' she called into the stillness.

No answer came.

They entered the lodge.

Cora went straight to the registration desk and leaned over its counter, just as she'd done yesterday when they first arrived.

Abilene's gaze roamed to the top of the stairway, lingered on the dark opening of the corridor at its top, then swept along the balcony. No sign of anyone. The doors beyond the railing were shut.

Cora in the lead, they made their way through the lobby and rounded the corner into the dining area.

It looked much the same as when Abilene had last seen it. Nothing had changed about the empty room except, perhaps, the angles of light coming in through the windows.

The last time she'd been here, though, she hadn't known about the slaughter.

Thanks to Helen's story, she couldn't help but picture a

long table surrounded by guests. Men, women and children choking with poison. Gagging. Yelling. Shoving themselves away from the table in panic as they were suddenly stormed by a savage tribe. Fleeing, only to be cut down.

The images stayed with her as she stepped through the kitchen door. Here, a wild denizen of the woods (she pictured Batty) had snuck poison into the Mulligan stew.

'I guess we'd better check that,' Cora said, nodding toward the door of the walk-in freezer.

Finley opened it and shone her light inside.

No Helen. The floor was bare. Pipes stretched along the walls and across the ceiling. From a center beam dangled meat hooks. The walls had empty shelves.

'Just as well she isn't in here,' Cora said.

Finley shut the door. They wandered about the kitchen, checked inside the pantry and pulled open a few of the lower cupboards. Abilene yanked open the back door, leaned out, and glanced up and down the balcony. Briefly, she scanned the rear grounds. Then she met up with the others and they made their way through the dining area to the lobby.

They paused at the foot of the stairway.

'Let's save upstairs for last,' Cora suggested. 'We'll have to bust open all the doors.'

They stepped across the corridor. A glance was all it took to satisfy themselves that the room was empty. They left it behind and followed the corridor to the first door.

Finley and Abilene trained their flashlights on it. Cora tried the knob, then rammed the wedge end of the tire tool into the crack between the door and frame. She strained at the bar. The wood groaned and crackled. She dug the wedge in deeper, pried some more, then withdrew it. 'Stand back,' she muttered. She stepped to the other side of the corridor, then dashed at the door. Just in front of it, she cocked her knee up and shot her foot forward. The blow crashed the door open and her momentum threw her stumbling into the room.

The others followed her inside. Light from a single, broken window revealed a floor thick with dust and littered with leaves. The broken pane was shrouded with spider webs.

There was no furniture. A couple of doors at the far end of the room probably enclosed a closet and toilet, but Abilene saw no footprints other than Cora's in the layer of filth coating the floor.

'Nobody's been in here for years,' she said.

They didn't bother to approach the doors. Instead, they returned to the hallway.

As Cora pulled the door shut, a faint '*Eeeeowww*' froze them all.

They stood motionless. Abilene realized she was holding her breath.

Could Helen have made such a sound? Maybe. If her mouth was gagged, or she was moaning in agony, or . . .

'*Weeeeowwww.*'

'Sounds like a cat,' Vivian whispered.

Finley switched her flashlight on. She turned slowly, sweeping its beam along the floor and walls of the corridor in the direction of the lobby.

When the sound came again, her light jumped to the door beneath the staircase.

'Came from there,' she said. 'I think.'

'I think so, too,' Cora said.

Staying close together, they went to the door. Finley opened it. She and Abilene aimed their flashlights down the stairway.

The brightness caught the cat's eyes in just such a way as to make them shine like clear, glowing, yellow marbles.

A white cat.

Crouched at the foot of the stairs.

It seemed to be gazing up at them, waiting for them.

The fur of its muzzle was wet and red.

Abilene's skin went crawly.

'Is it Amos?' Vivian whispered.

'Batty?' Cora called. 'Batty? You down here?'

The cat twitched its tail.

No response from Batty.

Maybe the cat had come to the lodge by itself.

From where they stood at the top of the stairs, only a small portion of the pool was visible. Abilene could see nobody in the water. The stretch of granite where they'd climbed out last night was dry.

'How the hell did it get down here?' Finley asked.

'A window?' Abilene suggested.

'They're awfully high.'

'It obviously didn't swim in,' Abilene said. The white fur wasn't wet. And if the cat *had* come in through the archway, the water would've washed the blood from its face.

The blood, she realized, looked very red and wet.

Her stomach seemed to drop.

It's *got* to be our blood, she told herself. The leftovers from Batty's bowl. It's got to be.

But she knew it wasn't.

She started down the stairs. The cat watched her, waited. When she was halfway to the bottom, it rose and casually strolled away to the left.

To the door marked Gents.

The door was open. Just a few inches.

Abilene felt as if her breath had been kicked out.

'God, the door's open!' she gasped.

The cat slipped through the gap.

'Wait for us!' Cora snapped.

Abilene stopped at the door. She gasped for air. Her heart thudded hard and fast.

'Helen?' she called into the dark gap.

'*Eeeeeoww.*'

The others clustered behind her.

'Oh Jesus, I'm scared,' Vivian whispered.

Abilene shoved the door open wide. It groaned on its hinges. No window. Total blackness. She raised her flashlight, and its beam pushed a funnel of brightness through the dark. All she saw was a bench just to the left, a high bank of lockers in front of it.

She stepped forward. Hot, stale air wrapped around her. It smelled ancient, foul. It clogged her nostrils and seemed to coat the lining of her windpipe.

Finley brushed against her side. Both flashlights darted about. 'Smells like somebody took a dump in here,' she muttered.

'Where's the fucking cat?' Cora said.

Finley stepped sideways, and Abilene followed her past the end of the lockers. Clear floor. A couple of sinks, two urinals. Against the back wall was a toilet stall, its door hanging open and nobody inside. The stall was enclosed on its far side by a wall that extended outward to within a few feet of another bench.

'Showers are probably in there,' Finley said, and pointed her light at a wide entryway facing the lockers.

Showers.

Oh God, Abilene thought.

Helen can't be in there. Can't be! She's terrified of shower rooms.

Fighting for air that was thick and rank, Abilene followed Finley. They stopped in front of the opening, Cora and Vivian at their backs. They searched it with their flashlights.

It *was* a shower room.

Nozzles high on the walls.

Helen on the floor.

Sprawled on her back, arms at her sides, legs spread, swimsuit gone, the handle of a knife standing upright from the gory mound of her belly, her head turned, her open eyes greeting her friends with a blank stare.

The white cat, near her hip, lapped at the lake of blood.

Chapter Twenty-four
Belmore Girls

'Virginia Finley, but everybody calls me Finley. The reason I'm calling, I'm a student at Belmore University, and I'd really like your permission to make a film of one of your stories . . . The one in *The Book of the Dead* . . . Right, that's the one. A friend of mine read it and it really grossed her out. Anyway, I've read it a few times now and I think it'd make a neat little film. The thing is, I need to come up with a showpiece, sort of, to submit for acceptance into a film program down there in Los Angeles. I think "Mess Hall" would be perfect. I've got a friend who's already agreed to write the script.' Grinning across the room at Abilene, Finley added, 'She's the daughter of Alex Randolph ... You think so? I'll have to tell her. Anyway, she'd do the script and we'd shoot the film out here on video tape. If it's okay with you ... Yeah, just the rights to make this production of it for amateur purposes only. I'd pay you a whopping one dollar ... Great ... You can count on it. I'll make you a copy myself and sent it to you as soon as it's finished ... Yeah, I'll send along a contract tomorrow. If there's anything you don't like about it, just let me know. And, you know, sometimes things happen with these student productions. If the right person likes it ... Yeah, you and me both. Anyway, you'd get a percentage of any deal that might come up for a feature film, television, whatever ... Right, fabulous wealth ... Thanks, I'll need it. And thanks very much for letting me do this. I really appreciate it.' She nodded, smiling. 'Okay. And I'll get the contract to you right away ... Bye-bye for now.'

Finley hung up. She took a deep breath, and let it out loudly.

'That wasn't so bad, was it?' Abilene asked.

'He was really friendly and cheerful.'

'See? What'd I tell you? Can't judge a guy by the kind of stories he writes.'

'Geez, but "Mess Hall"? I figured he'd *have* to be some kind of sleezy creepoid. By the way, he said he's read all your dad's books and thinks he's great.'

'The man's got taste.'

'Anyway, he sounded pretty enthusiastic about the project. He gave the go-ahead, so you'd better get cracking. How long before you can come up with the script?'

* * *

Finley had made the call on Monday. By Tuesday afternoon Abilene had finished the term paper for her Chaucer seminar and was ready to start on the script. That night, cast and crew 'took a meeting' in the student union.

Finley had already scouted locations. She gave her ideas about how the story should be revised and who should play which characters. Vivian, being a theater major who had already played major roles in several campus productions, was offered the lead.

'I think Abilene should play Jean,' she said. 'It opens with a love scene. Abilene and Harris would be perfect for that.'

Harris blushed.

'But you're the actor around here,' Abilene pointed out. 'You should have the main role.'

'It'd be more fun to play one of the zombies anyway.'

'Same here,' Helen said. 'I've always wanted to be a zombie.'

Abilene laughed. 'It'd be a big stretch after all those Halloweens as a ghost.'

'I can handle it.'

'So,' Vivian said, 'how about Abilene as the main gal?'

'Fine with me,' Finley said. 'Hickok's got that great, vulnerable look. Make a terrific victim.'

'Oh thanks.'

She and Harris agreed to take the roles of Jean and Paul, the lovers. Vivian, Cora and Helen would be the zombies.

'And you'll be The Reaper,' Finley told Tony, a handsome, powerfully built young man who'd been going with Cora for the past few months.

'Now hold it just a second,' Cora said. 'I'm not so sure I like the idea of my guy getting to mess around with Abilene.'

'He doesn't mess around with her,' Finley pointed out, 'he *tortures* her.'

'He might just enjoy it too much,' she said, giving Tony an amused scowl.

Harris grinned at him. 'Better not.'

'What'll she be wearing?' Cora asked.

'Not a whole lot.'

'That's what you think,' Abilene said.

'Well,' Finley said, 'we don't need actual nudity, but it's gotta look real, you know. This guy is a sex maniac, a psychopath. So . . .'

'I'll work it out in the script,' Abilene told her.

'Can you have it done by Friday?'

'Sure. No problem.'

'Great. Then we can go out on location first thing Saturday and get it done.'

'Problem,' Tony said. 'I've got a track meet on Saturday. Sorry.'

'What about the weekend after?' Finley asked.

'That's getting awfully close to finals,' Abilene said.

Tony held up his hands. 'Hey, look, I don't want to screw things up for you gals. I'm no actor, anyway. Maybe you oughta find someone else for my part. That'd be fine with me. In fact, I'd prefer it. Honestly. Why don't you just go ahead without me? Okay?'

Looking concerned, Finley asked, 'Are you sure? I mean, we'd really like you to be in it.'

'Maybe you should find someone else. Really.'

'I guess we could,' Finley said.

'There are some guys in the drama department,' Vivian said. 'I could ask around and . . .'

'They're such a bunch of weenies,' Finley complained.

'Not all of them. What about Jack Baxter?'

'Baxter?' Abilene asked. 'The guy who played Stanley in *Streetcar*?'

'He's such a Neanderthal,' Finley said. 'What I had in mind was someone more . . . clean-cut, handsome. You know, a Ted Bundy type.'

'*I'm* a Ted Bundy type?' Tony asked. 'Gee, thanks.'

'I'm not particularly thrilled,' Abilene said, 'about the idea of playing victim for a guy like Baxter.'

Vivian shrugged. 'Oh, he's not so bad. And I think he'd be awfully good in the role.'

'Typecasting,' Abilene said.

'Well,' Finley said, 'why don't you check with him, Viv? See if he's interested. And if he's *available* for this weekend.'

'I don't know about this,' Abilene said as she walked with Harris into the secluded clearing near Shady Lane Bridge that Finley had chosen for the opening scene. She wondered if she sounded nervous enough. She certainly *felt* nervous. The idea of making out with Harris in front of her friends was bad enough, but Baxter had joined the troupe.

'What don't you know about?' Harris asked. Stopping, he faced Abilene and took hold of both her hands.

She glanced about. 'It's so . . . deserted around here.'

Sure. Deserted. Finley with the video camera at her eye, taping, while Cora and Vivian and Helen watched from the shadows beneath a nearby tree and Harris fooled with the trick knife Vivian had borrowed from the prop room. At least he's not staring at me, she thought.

'It's supposed to be deserted,' Harris said. 'That's the whole idea.'

'I know, but . . . Maybe we should go back to my apartment.'

'So your damn roomy can listen through the wall and make noises?'

Smiling slightly at that, Abilene said, 'She won't be there. She's going to a matinee this afternoon. We'd have the place all to ourselves.'

'I like it here.' Harris pulled her gently into his arms. He nibbled the side of her neck. That hadn't been in the script. It made her shiver and squirm. 'So much nicer,' he muttered, 'than some stuffy old room.'

'Somebody might come along.'

'You worry too much.' Nuzzling the side of her neck again, he untucked the back of her blouse and slipped his hands up beneath it.

'No,' she said, and gently pushed him away. 'I mean it. Not here.'

Harris frowned. 'What's the matter with you?'

'I don't know. It's just . . . I guess I'm worried about The Reaper.'

'The *Reaper*? Oh, for Godsake. Everybody's got Reaperitis. It's broad daylight. Besides, he's in *Portland*.'

'That's only a half-hour drive.'

Harris sighed. 'Shit. Okay. Forget it.' With that, he whirled around and began to walk off in a huff. Finley sidestepped, keeping the camera on him.

'No, wait!' Finley swung the camera toward Abilene. 'Don't be this way. Please. I . . .' Shaking her head, she hurried after him. She caught him by the shoulder. As he turned to face her, she flung her arms around him. She hugged him hard, kissed him.

He seemed rigid at first, his mouth tight, as if holding onto his anger.

You're pretty good at this acting stuff, she thought.

Then his lips parted. He wrapped his arms around her, caressed her back. Writhing slightly against her, he eased his tongue into her mouth. Abilene sucked it in deep. He rubbed her buttocks, and then his hands moved slowly upward beneath her blouse. They roamed her back with gentle caresses.

For just a while, Abilene forgot about everyone else, forgot the camera and audience. There was only Harris. The familiar feel of him, the closeness and desire. But when his hands passed over the back strap of her bra rather than pausing to unfasten its catches, the illusion fell apart. Embarrassed, she felt her face go hot.

Here we are, doing this in front of everyone. On tape, *for Godsake. Total strangers will be seeing all this.*

Beneath the blouse, a fingertip prodded her shoulder.

Harris, at least, still had his mind on business.

Abilene concentrated, trying to remember what came next. Then she eased her mouth away from his and smiled up at him. 'It's pretty nice here, after all,' she said.

'I love you so much, Abilene.'

'Cut cut cut,' Finley said.

Laughter and applause from the sidelines.

'Woops,' said Harris.

Abilene gently slapped his chest. 'Dope.' She looked over her shoulder and mugged at her friends. Then she glanced at Baxter. No smile there. He was staring at her.

'Okay, okay,' Finley said. 'Nothing a little editing won't cure. We'll take it up with a close on Harris. "I love you so much, *Jean*." Got it?'

'Hope so.'

'You're doing fine, both of you,' Vivian told them.

'Really into the scene,' Cora said.

'They've had so much practice,' said Helen.

'Hey, let's have silence on the set. Ready? Action.'

'I love you so much, Jean.'

Abilene, gazing into his eyes, reached up and touched his cheeks. 'And I love you,' she said. Her fingertips wandered down his face, his jaw and neck. Slowly, she unbuttoned his shirt. She spread it open. While she caressed his bare chest, Harris undid the buttons of her blouse.

It's no big deal, she told herself as her face again burned with embarrassment.

Harris spread her blouse wide, and she immediately pressed herself against him. It felt strange to have the stiff cups of the bra in the way, keeping her breasts from the warmth and smoothness of his chest. But this was show business, not the real thing.

Show business, with Baxter probably leering at me.

Abilene decided to get on with it. She kissed Harris's neck, his chest, his belly. Kneeling on the carpet of leaves and twigs, she tugged open his belt buckle. She unbuttoned the waist of his jeans. As she slid the zipper down, Harris sank to his knees in front of her.

He drew her close against him and their mouths joined as his hands moved feverishly up and down her back. Abilene felt a solid thickness against her belly.

You *are* into this, she thought. Hope you don't pop out of your skivvies.

Breaking away from him, she lowered herself to the ground. She felt terribly exposed, lying there with her blouse open. As she raised her knees, her skirt slid down, baring her thighs.

Damn!

Then Harris was on top of her, shielding her body from the camera and the watching eyes.

She wrapped her arms around him. She kissed him. She moaned as he squirmed, and sucked in a quick breath when he thrust as if entering her. He went motionless then, the same way he did when it was real and he wanted to do nothing for a few moments but savor the joining.

She could feel him pressed against her, only their underwear in the way.

He began to move up and down, going away and coming back, prodding her, rubbing her. She pushed up to meet his thrusts. She writhed and gasped.

Let's not get carried away!

My God!

Isn't supposed to be . . .

'Looks to me like fornication in the park.' Baxter's voice. Words from the script.

Harris seemed to freeze on top of her. Then he twisted his head around. They both looked up at Baxter, who was standing near their feet, grinning down at them. One hand was out of sight behind his back.

'Don't you know it's against the law?' he asked. 'Not to mention poor taste.'

'We didn't mean any harm,' Harris said, sounding sheepish and scared.

'What if some children had wandered by?' Baxter asked.

'I'm sorry,' Abilene said. 'We'll leave.'

She relaxed her hold on Harris. As he rose to his hands and knees, she gave her skirt a quick tug to cover her thighs. She was closing her blouse when Baxter grabbed Harris by the hair and yanked his head back.

The look of pain that flashed through Harris's eyes wasn't fake.

'Hey!' she snapped. Not in the script.

Baxter's other arm swept around. The knife slashed Harris's throat, its hollow blade squirting out a bright red stripe.

'Great!' Finley blurted. 'Fantastic!'

She lowered the camera. Baxter released Harris's hair and stepped away. Harris, rubbing his scalp, gave the guy an annoyed glance. 'You were a bit rough, don't you think?'

'Sorry about that, dude. Going for the realism.'

'From now on,' Abilene said, 'take it easy. Are you okay?' she asked Harris.

He nodded. As he got to his feet, Vivian came over and gave him a towel. He thanked her, and wiped the red fluid from his throat and chest.

'Now for the fun part,' Helen said, approaching with a paper cup full of the stuff.

Cora laughed. 'I think they just finished the fun part.'

'You're right about that,' Harris said. With a blush and a smile, he pulled his zipper up. He turned to Finley. 'Are you sure it turned out all right? Maybe we need to do another take.'

'Or several,' Abilene added from the ground.

'Hate to disappoint you,' Finley said. 'It was fabulous. Gonna look like you were really doing it.'

Almost felt that way, too, Abilene thought.

Smiling down at her, Vivian said, 'You can always come back tonight and do a take without us.'

From the look that came into Harris's eyes, Abilene knew he liked the idea. So did she.

'Okay,' Finley said. 'Time for some wet work.'

Helen, the cup of stage blood in hand, knelt between Abilene's legs and ducked low. Finley crouched behind her and aimed the camera at Abilene. The red light appeared.

'Action.'

Helen hurled the fake blood. It splashed warm against Abilene's face.

She was alone with Baxter. The blood felt like a sticky mask. Though it had dried somewhat during the hike back through the park, it still dribbled. It tickled her face and neck. It made her itch. She ached to rub it, but kept her hands away and reluctantly started to unbutton her blouse for the next scene.

Baxter looked. She pulled the blouse shut.

He didn't say anything.

Just as well. She was still angry about the rough way he'd treated Harris.

They waited, watching the others walk toward the parking lot. A few cars had come along after their arrival earlier that morning, but none was parked very close to the one they intended to use for the upcoming scene. Shouldn't be a problem.

Finley stopped beside it. The rest of the group stepped back to stay clear of the shot. Camera to her face, Finley wandered about as if trying to find just the right angle. Then she called, 'Let's go for it!'

'Just take it easy,' Abilene told Baxter.

'No sweat.'

He ducked, shoved his shoulder into her belly and clamped an arm across the backs of her thighs. Below the hem of her skirt.

This sucks so bad, she thought.

The crap I do for you, Finley.

As he lifted her, she bowed forward. The shoulder pushed into her. She dropped against his back. Turning toward the parking lot, he began to trot. The rough motions bounced her. She felt as if her breath were being punched out with each of his strides.

She could see nothing but the back of his white T-shirt.

She could feel the heat of his body through it.

She wanted to brace herself up, at least enough to stop her breasts from pushing against him. But she was supposed to be limp. If she struggled, Finley might want to do the scene over again. So she let her arms hang and sway. She shut her eyes. She wished she'd never agreed to be part of all this.

Would've been fine if Tony'd played The Reaper. But this jerk!

He stopped abruptly and bent forward, throwing Abilene off his shoulder. She gasped as she fell. Her back slammed into a flat sheet of metal and she knew he had unloaded her onto the hood of Finley's car.

He could've been more *gentle* about it!

But at least her head didn't bang.

She heard quick footfalls on the pavement, rushing away from her.

Remembering the script, she opened her eyes. She saw the clear, pale sky. She raised her head. Her arms were outstretched across the hood, her blouse wide open, her legs hanging over the front of the car.

She heard a door swing open.

As she struggled to sit up, Baxter returned. He swung his fist down like a hammer.

Shit!

But he pulled the punch, surprising her. His hand smacked softly against her belly. She whooshed out her breath and bucked as if really hurt, then sagged on the hood, wheezing. Baxter gathered her arms in front of her waist. He snapped handcuffs around her wrists.

Then he pulled a rag from his pocket and wiped her face. 'All pretty again,' he said, smiling down at her. The cloth rubbed her neck and collar bones and the top of her left breast. She didn't like being touched by him, but it felt good to have the itchy fluid removed.

Grabbing the front of her blouse, he dragged her off the hood. She was hardly able to stay on her feet as he rushed her alongside the car. He shoved her onto the passenger seat, picked up her legs and flung them in, then slammed the door.

He hurried around to the other side. He climbed in behind the wheel, started the engine, and shot the car backward. The tires squealed as he skidded into a tight turn. He sped toward the parking lot exit.

After a glance at the rearview mirror, he slowed the car. He turned it around and drove back to where the others were waiting.

Finley grinned through the passenger window. 'That was great, guys. Let's head for the Mess Hall.'

Finley led the way with Cora, Vivian and Baxter in her car. Abilene and Helen travelled in Harris's car. They left the town of Belmore behind, heading eastward into the wooded hills.

'Where's she taking us?' Harris asked.

'It's only about a half-hour drive,' Abilene said. 'Some place she found that's really off the beaten track. Figured we shouldn't do the nasty scene in the park.'

'We're lucky we got through *our* scene without visitors,' Harris said.

'Would've been even *more* embarrassing.'

'It was pretty strange, doing that in front of an audience.'

'You both sure seemed to enjoy it, though,' Helen said from the back seat.

Harris smiled over his shoulder at her. 'I can think of worse ways to spend a Saturday morning.'

Soon, they followed Finley's car onto a dirt road that twisted through the woods. Harris slowed down to stay out of her dust cloud. The car lurched and bounced. Branches squeaked against its sides.

'Hope we're almost there,' Harris said.

Abilene nodded, but she was in no hurry to reach their destination.

Five minutes later, the road dead-ended. Harris stopped short, apparently waiting for the dust to settle a bit. Up ahead, the doors of Finley's car swung open. Cora and Vivian climbed out of the back seat. During the trip, they'd changed into their zombie costumes.

Along with Helen, they were supposed to be earlier victims who'd been tortured and murdered by The Reaper, then left behind as meals for the woodland creatures. They were to show up for revenge just in the nick of time to save Abilene's character. But in the story, there were six of them and they were a mess. The Reaper had mutilated them: scalped one, skinned another. He'd gouged eyes, cut off noses and breasts. Mother Nature's scavengers had then gotten to the girls: ants, maggots, coyotes, birds. By the time the zombies came staggering to the rescue, some were missing limbs and all were filthy, ruined cadavers in various stages of decay. They were all naked, too.

Finley had known when she chose the story that such things couldn't appear in her film. First, she didn't have the time or resources for any elaborate special effects. Second, nudity was out. There was no choice but to have zombies that looked much too healthy and wore clothes.

The girls had been left to their own devices about what to wear.

Vivian wore an old sundress, ripped here and there with a razor blade, its skirt half torn off. Cora wore panties (two pairs, actually), and a tattered T-shirt. The garments of both girls were filthy with dirt and large amounts of stage blood that had been applied last night and now looked stiff and brown.

'Maybe I'd better change,' Helen said as Harris pulled the car forward. He parked, and Helen stayed inside while he and Abilene climbed out.

'You gals look pretty good for a couple of stiffs,' Harris said.

Cora smirked at him. 'We sure look better than you and your pals did, that Halloween.'

Abilene smiled as his face turned red. 'Talk about embarrassing moments,' he muttered. 'Jeez. I wanted to crawl into a hole and die.'

Abilene laughed. 'Oh, you were so cute.' Suddenly, she remembered what they'd found in the man's house later that night. The thing in the wheelchair.

What had been *wrong* with him?

God, don't think about him!

As Finley and Vivian came back from the trunk of the car with a couple of make-up kits, Helen joined the group. She wore a blouse and jeans. Yesterday, they'd been white. Today, they looked as if they'd been used to mop up the floor of a slaughterhouse. The legs of the jeans were torn. Half the blouse was ripped away, including most of its left sleeve. The remnant of that sleeve was empty, Helen's arm hidden inside the blouse. With the proper camera angles to keep the bulge out of sight, she ought to look as if she'd lost the arm.

For the next few minutes, Finley and Baxter helped the girls apply make-up. It consisted mostly of the stage blood, which was smeared over nearly every visible inch of their skin. For the sake of variety, Vivian's face was spared the red goo. A gray substance was applied to her face by Finley, who then added a few colorful purple contusions. For a final touch, they mussed their hair.

Then everyone followed Finley along a footpath to a sunlit clearing. It looked perfect.

'How did you ever find this?' Abilene asked.

'Wasn't easy. I was out here with Brian last year.' Grinning, she added, 'We had a little picnic. Right under that tree. Just like the one in the story, huh? I remembered the limb. We swung on it.'

'It's perfect,' Baxter said.

Ten minutes later, Abilene was hanging from it by a rope tied to her wrists. The rope was long enough to let her feet touch the ground, but it stretched her arms overhead. Higher than she appreciated, but she didn't complain.

Better to suffer with it than risk having to go through anything a second time. Once had been more than enough, being carted into the clearing on Baxter's shoulder, thrown against the trunk and punched again in the stomach so she wouldn't resist while he took off the handcuffs, bound her with the rope and suspended her under the limb.

Now, standing just in front of her, Baxter pulled the knife from his belt.

'No,' she gasped. 'Please.'

He smiled. 'I knew you'd get around to begging.'

'I never did anything to you.'

'But you're about to do something *for* me. Oh, yes.' With the flat of the plastic blade, he caressed her cheek.

On cue, Helen let out a coyote howl. She did a good job of it. The plaintive cry seemed to come from far away.

Baxter slid the blade under Abilene's chin and up to her other cheek. 'That's my friend,' he said. His voice was slow and lazy. He sounded a bit amused. He had a languid look in his eyes as he watched the movements of his knife. 'We've got an arrangement. I leave a meal for him and his forest friends, and they do the clean-up for me. None of this "shallow grave" nonsense.' The point of the knife eased down the side of her neck. It nudged the blouse away and stroked along her collar bone. 'I just leave you here, tomorrow you'll be gone. They'll come like the good, hungry troops they are, and leave the area nice and tidy.' The knife went lower. Its point scraped lightly over the slope of her breast, traced the edge of the bra cup. 'No fuss, no bother.'

'Please! Please don't.'

'Please!' he mimicked her. 'Please don't.'

He drew the knife sideways, pushing harder, and Abilene felt fluid squirt from its tip as he sliced her across the chest. She flinched rigid and cried out, 'Yeeeah!'

Laughing, he took the knife away. He licked the blood from its blade.

'You bastard!'

'Is that any way to talk?'

'HELP!' she shouted. 'HELP! PLEASE, HELP ME!'

'Nobody's going to hear you but the coyotes.'

'You can't *do* this!'

'Sure I can. Done it plenty of times before.'

'Please! I'll do anything!'

'I know just what you'll do. Scream, twitch, cry, kick, beg, drool . . . bleed. Not necessarily in that order, of course.'

Bending over, he kissed her chest.

Not in the script.

What the hell's going on?

He licked, his tongue sliding and flicking at the bare skin where he'd 'cut' her. Licking up the fake blood.

Why isn't Finley stopping this?

Probably figures it looks good.

'Don't!' Not in the script, either. But in character. Finley kept taping.

He'll quit in a second, she told herself. Hang in. It's almost time for the zombies to show up and that'll be the end of him messing with me.

Baxter licked his way up Abilene's neck. She turned her face away as he tried to kiss her. His mouth found her cheek. He was breathing hard, moaning.

Christ!

One of his arms went around her back, underneath her blouse. It pressed her hard against him and she felt the warm fluid squirting against her spine. His mouth got to her lips.

'No!'

He kissed her hard, and now she couldn't call out and make it all stop.

She strained against the rope. Squirming, she tried to get her mouth away from his.

Somebody make him quit!

A hand clutched her right breast. Fingertips pushed under the cup of the bra, tugged. The strap dug into her shoulder, snapped. Her breast was bare under his rubbing, squeezing hand.

She drove a knee up.

It pounded against him. He grunted but didn't let go.

Where the hell is Harris?

With a quick twist sideways, she freed her mouth. 'Stop it!'

He didn't stop. His other hand, knife gone, went down her back and rump. It scratched her skirt up. It rubbed her buttocks for just a moment, then hooked the panties down and he yelped with surprise and pain as Helen clutched his face with a bloody hand and yanked him backward.

He flopped onto the ground.

All three zombies went at him.

It was nothing like the script.

Sobbing and gasping, she watched the zombies pound Baxter.

Cora, sitting on his chest, punched him in the face. Vivian stomped on his legs. Helen kicked him in the side.

They weren't pretending.

Neither was Baxter. He bucked and twisted. He flung up arms, trying to shield his face. He grunted. He cried out. Real blood poured from his nostrils. He began to beg. 'Stop! Please! Leave me alone! Don't! I'm sorry. I'm *sorry*!'

Finley taped it all.

Harris came rushing into the clearing. Where had *he* been?

One look at Abilene and he stopped abruptly. Confusion on his face. Then fury.

He took a step forward.

And halted and watched as one-armed Helen lurched forward between Baxter's legs and kicked him in the groin.

Baxter didn't respond.

He just lay there, silent and limp.

'Cut,' Finley said. Voice grim.

'What the hell happened here!' Harris blurted. Not waiting for an answer, he ran over to Abilene. As he approached her, the zombies stood over Baxter and stared down at him.

'Things got out of hand,' Finley muttered.

'Jesus.' He pulled Abilene's blouse shut. His arms went around her and he drew her gently against him. 'Are you all right?'

'Where *were* you?' she sobbed.

'I didn't want to watch what he . . . Did he hurt you?'

She shook her head. 'Could you get me down from here?'

He reached for one of her bound wrists.

'Hold it,' Finley said. 'Let one of the zombies do it. Then we'll have an ending.'

'Screw your damn film!'

'It's okay,' Abilene said. 'Let . . . it's okay.'

He backed away. Finley gave Vivian a real knife similar to the fake one.

Finley taping, Vivian staggered forward in good zombie fashion but with a strange, frantic look in her green eyes. She sawed through the rope. Abilene lowered her arms. Her panties were down around her knees. She bent over and pulled them up. Then she whirled around and ran for the trees, the loose end of the rope dragging along the ground beside her.

'That's it,' Finley called.

When Abilene returned, the girls gathered around her while Harris untied her wrists.

'I'm really sorry,' Finley said. 'It just didn't hit me what he was doing. I knew he wasn't sticking to the script, but . . .'

'I should've been here,' Harris said. He sounded miserable.

'I just wish we would've nailed him sooner,' Cora said. 'I don't think any of us realized . . .'

'It wasn't till you kneed him,' Helen said.

'Yeah,' Vivian said. 'I didn't know what was going on. God, I'm sorry.'

'It's all my fault,' Finley said. 'I should've stopped things when he started licking off the blood. He wasn't supposed to do that. But it seemed right for The Reaper, you know? It all seemed right for The Reaper, and you were reacting like a good victim even though . . .' She shook her head. 'Shit.'

Abilene rubbed her sore wrists, then fastened the buttons

of her blouse. 'It's okay. It's over. I just don't want my breast ending up in your movie.'

'It won't. I promise.'

'And you owe me a new bra.'

Just for an instant, a smile tipped up a corner of Finley's mouth. Then she was looking grim again, nodding.

They all turned their attention to Baxter as he groaned. He shook his head, grimaced, rolled onto his side, clutched his groin and drew his knees up.

'What'll we do with him?' Abilene asked.

Harris took a step toward him, but Abilene grabbed his shoulder. 'Don't. He's had enough.'

'We oughta get a final shot of him,' Finley said. 'Gotta mess him up first, though.'

Vivian and Helen went to the edge of the clearing. As they came back with jars of blood, Cora nudged Baxter with her foot. 'Roll over and play dead.'

Wincing and moaning, he eased down onto his back. Cora bent over and tore his shirt open. Then Vivian and Helen doused him all over with the crimson fluid. It mixed with the real blood on his face. The real blood looked brighter.

'Okay,' Finley said. 'Get down around him and act like you're ripping him apart. Don't move a muscle, Baxter. The mood my pals are in, they just might get carried away. That happens, you know.'

Helen, Vivian and Cora knelt over Baxter. While Finley taped, they pretended to tear at him with their fingernails and teeth. He didn't move at all.

'That's a wrap,' Finley said.

The zombies got to their feet and stepped away from him.

He remained on his back. His eyes found Abilene. 'I'm sorry,' he said.

'I'll bet,' she muttered.

'I mean it. I never . . . I just couldn't stop myself. I never planned to do any of that. It . . . just happened.' He turned his face away. 'I'm sorry. I'm so sorry.'

'You'll have plenty of time to think about it,' Finley said, 'while you're walking back to town. Come on, let's get out of here.'

'We aren't gonna leave him,' Abilene said.

'He's not going back in *my* car.'

'Then we'll drive him,' she said, and looked at Harris. He was frowning at her. 'Hey, I'm the one he messed with. And I didn't appreciate it one bit. But we all got him into this, and maybe it's not completely his fault. *You* got carried away in the love scene. We both did. I'm not so sure we should blame him for losing it. I mean, I wish it hadn't happened but . . . it was this damn story. We never should've asked *any* guy to play The Reaper.'

'Would've been okay,' Finley said, 'if Tony . . .'

'Tony didn't have any track meet today,' Cora said.

'What?' Finley blurted.

'He lied about it. He just didn't want to play The Reaper. He said, "I can't do that stuff to Abilene or to anyone else. Not even pretending." It's like he knew what might happen.'

'He wouldn't have done that stuff to her,' Vivian said.

'Maybe he was afraid he might. I don't know.'

'I know one thing,' Abilene said. 'He's smarter than the rest of us; he stayed out of it.'

' "A nifty little film. Though I realize you were limited as far as special effects, you managed to carry off the story quite effectively. The cast was great. Very convincing portrayals all around. My regards to everyone involved. I wish you success with your film, and I should think you'll have a great future in the cinema. Sincerely, Dick." How do you like *them* apples?' Finley asked, grinning up from the letter.

Abilene sneered. 'Convincing portrayals, huh?'

'They should've been,' Cora said. 'Nobody in the whole damn film was acting. You and Harris were really making out, Baxter tried to *rape* you, and we zombies kicked his ass in earnest.'

'Turned into *cinéma vérité*,' Finley said. 'Hope the Institute appreciates it as much as the author.'

'I'm a connoisseur of such things,' Helen said, 'and I think it was fabulous. Especially that one-armed zombie.'

'You did a great job pulling Baxter off me,' Abilene admitted.

Helen beamed at her. 'Pretty good for a fatty, huh? And a dead one, to boot.'

Chapter Twenty-five

Nobody screamed. Nobody fled. Nobody spoke or wept.

They all stood there, staring at the body.

Abilene supposed it came as no surprise to any of them that Helen had been murdered. It was what they had all suspected, dreaded, tried to deny all morning during their search for her. They'd clung to feeble hopes, but they'd known they would probably never find her alive.

Now it was over. There was no more room for hope or denial.

Someone had brought Helen into the shower room and butchered her.

It occurred to Abilene that she ought to be afraid. The killer might be nearby, might come for the rest of them. But she felt no fear. She felt only tired and dazed and numb.

She sank to the floor of the shower room. Slumping back against a wall, she raised her knees and hugged them tight. She was vaguely aware of the white cat scooting by, fleeing as Cora and Finley walked slowly toward Helen's body.

Cora crouched. Her hand went to Helen's neck. Searching for a pulse beat, though there could be no doubt that Helen was dead. A few moments later, she straightened up.

Finley, bending over, reached for the knife.

'No,' Cora whispered. 'Don't touch it. We shouldn't . . . disturb anything.'

They both stepped backward away from the body. They turned around.

'We'd better get out of here,' Cora said. 'Whoever . . .' She halted in mid-stride. The tire iron dropped from her hand and clamored on the floor. She stood motionless as if frozen stiff. Then, hunching over slightly, she squeezed her arms against her chest, buried her chin against her crossed wrists and shuddered.

Finley put an arm around her.

Turning her head, Abilene saw Vivian standing rigid, fists pressed tight against her thighs.

Finley's flashlight, in the hand she wasn't using to hold Cora, shone its beam near Vivian's feet. Abilene's flashlight, on the floor beside her, made a bright path across the floor to Helen.

Helen seemed to be watching her.

Just look at me, Abby. Look what happened to me.

Wanting her to do something about it. Make it all right. Make it go away.

Too late for any of that. Way too late.

Abilene felt a hand stroking her hair. Raising her head, she saw Vivian beside her. She picked up the flashlight. As she stood, Cora came unfrozen and bent down like a palsied old woman to retrieve the tire iron she'd dropped. Finley kept an arm around her and, together, they staggered out of the shower room.

Vivian took Abilene's hand, squeezed it.

They got as far as the threshold. Abilene stopped and looked back. She couldn't see Helen. Only darkness.

'We can't leave her alone in here.'

'It doesn't matter,' Vivian murmured.

'She's . . . scared of shower rooms.'

Finley came back. Her light made Abilene squint and look away. 'Helen isn't scared of them any more. Nothing can scare her now. Okay? We need to get out of here.'

In silence, they returned to the car. It seemed like the only place to go. It was a rental car, but it was theirs. It was loaded with their things. It gleamed in the sunlight. It felt to Abilene like a sanctuary. They were safe here. Nothing could get them.

Cora sat on the rear bumper and lowered her head. Abilene sat beside her and watched Vivian lie down on the sloping pavement and fold her hands under her head and stare at the sky.

Finley stayed on her feet. She paced around, taking deep breaths. Then she stopped and reached into a pocket of her shorts and pulled out the package of hot dogs. She raised it in front of her face. 'Anybody want one?' she asked.

Nobody answered.

'Helen won't be . . .'

With such sudden violence that Abilene flinched, Finley hurled the package down. It smacked the pavement, wieners blasting apart, juice and pink mush exploding from the wrapper. She stared down at the mess. Then her face turned scarlet and crumpled, eyes squeezing shut, mouth stretching as if invisible fingers wrenched her lips. Abilene leaped up. She rushed to Finley, bursting into tears herself as she hugged her stricken friend.

Some time later, she realized that Cora had her arms around them both. Then Vivian was with them, embracing them, crying. They all were crying. Huddled together, hot arms around quaking backs, faces dripping sweat and tears as they gasped and sobbed and sniffled and whimpered and blubbered.

'Sounds . . . like a fuckin' barnyard,' Finley cracked after a while.

Abilene laughed once and choked. Her face was tight against the side of Finley's head. She eased back. Finley's hair, sticking to her itchy wet cheek, pulled away. She met the girl's eyes and saw such misery there that she murmured, 'Aw, Fin,' and stroked her face with both hands and kissed her eyes.

'Break it up, you guys,' Cora whispered. She rubbed the back of Abilene's head, kissed her ear, pressed her lips briefly against Finley's cheek, then backed away.

'Gettin' awful smoochy around here,' Finley muttered.

'Don't worry,' Vivian said, her voice high and shaky. 'I'm not about to . . .'

With a quick turn of her head, Finley kissed her full on the lips. Vivian didn't pull away. As she caressed Finley's hair, Abilene pressed her mouth to Vivian's wet cheek. It slid, and Vivian's lips were there against hers, soft and comforting.

'Come up for air, guys,' Finley said.

They parted. Abilene gave Finley a gentle punch on the shoulder. She felt exhausted, drained.

Everyone stood around, sniffing and sighing, wiping sweat and tears and slobber from their faces.

The pack of hot dogs, dashed at Finley's feet, had been trampled flat.

Cora was the first to start picking up clothes and towels and shoes that they had set out on the pavement to dry. The rest of them joined in.

It's something to do, Abilene thought.

Before we do what?

The clothes she gathered were stiff and dry. She took off her filthy, damp blouse, used one of the towels to rub herself dry, then put on the blouse she'd worn yesterday. She was about to button it when she noticed her wadded bra under the waistband of her skirt. She'd forgotten about putting the bra there. She tugged it out. The bunched fabric had been pressed tight against her low belly, leaving the skin marked with a pattern of seams and folds and wrinkles. She loosened the belt of her skirt and slipped a hand under the waistband.

Rubbing the irritated skin, she watched Finley change blouses. Yesterday's looked the same as the one she removed, but its tan fabric wasn't dark with moisture and didn't have blood all over it from her cut hand.

Though Vivian's white knit shirt and shorts were filthy, she didn't change.

Neither did Cora. They were both busy carrying things to the car.

Abilene buttoned her blouse, then slipped off her moccasins and sat on the pavement and pulled on her socks and sneakers.

She picked up the moccasins, some scattered garments and

towels, and took them to the car. Cora, inside, dumped them behind the back seat.

'Is that it?' Cora asked.

Abilene thought of Helen's shoes at the edge of the outside hot pool. She decided not to mention them.

Vivian came along with her arms full. 'Nothing else.' Abilene took the load from her and handed it in to Cora.

She handed out their purses. 'You want your camera, Finley?'

'What are we doing?'

'What do you think? Getting away from this damn place.'

'I'd better take it, then.'

Cora crawled out with the video camera and gave it to Finley.

Vivian let the door drop shut.

'Maybe we'll be able to hitch a ride,' Cora said, 'once we get down to the main road.'

'Are we just going to leave her?' Abilene asked.

'We can't take her with us,' Vivian said.

'We could bring her outside. It doesn't seem right to leave her down there.'

'It's a crime scene,' Cora said. 'We might screw up evidence for the cops if we move her.'

She was right. And Abilene felt too dazed and weary to care much one way or the other.

They were silent for a while as they walked past the front of the lodge and headed down the long driveway toward the road.

Then Finley said, 'Do you think Batty had anything to do with it? He knew where Helen was.'

None of the 'he, she, it' business.

'He couldn't control where the blood dropped,' Cora said.

'Pretty damn weird,' Abilene said, 'how the cat led us to her. It had to be Amos. Almost as if Batty sent it along . . . like a guide, or something.'

Cora shook her head. 'It smelled the blood, that's all.'

'Fuckin' beast,' Finley said.

'I hope we didn't shut it up in there with her,' Vivian said.

'It was long gone,' Cora told her.

'Are you sure?'

'I'm not sure of a damn thing,' she muttered. 'You wanta go back and check?'

'You don't have to get huffy.'

'I think it was gone,' Finley said. 'I checked around on the way out. Unless it was hiding pretty good . . .'

'Who gives a rat's ass about the cat, anyway?'

'I don't think it's the cat we're worried about,' Abilene said.

'Well then, what the . . . ?' She suddenly looked sick. She stopped and turned around and scowled up the driveway toward the lodge.

Abilene looked, too. The lodge was out of sight beyond the slope.

'Come on, guys,' Finley said. 'It's probably not in there.'

'Maybe we should go back and make sure,' Cora said.

They all knew Helen's story about the cat woman. The woman's name was Maggie and she had lived with a houseful of cats a few blocks from Helen's childhood home. 'She was so husky she made me look positively svelte,' Helen had explained. 'But she was a real spook, a refugee from the funny farm. Anyway, she ended up croaking. Her body wasn't found for a really long time. She was dead in that house with all those cats. And they couldn't get out. When the cops finally went in, she was nothing but bones. The cats had licked her clean, and all of them were fat and sassy. Except for one. This big tomcat, they found it dead inside Maggie's ribcage. Apparently, it had crawled in there and choked to death eating her heart. It was wedged in so tight that they couldn't get it out, so Maggie's skeleton was finally buried with the cat's corpse still in her chest.' Finley had said that was bullshit. Helen, grinning, had said, 'Cross my heart and hope to die.'

And now, staring up the driveway, Abilene supposed that everyone was probably thinking about Helen's cat-woman story.

'Should we go back?' she asked.

'I really hate to think she might be shut up in there with the cat,' Cora said.

'We don't want to run into the killer,' Vivian said.

'He's probably not around. And even if he is, he wouldn't try to take on all of us. He's already had plenty of chances. He only got Helen because she was by herself.'

'It must've been that kid,' Vivian said. 'God, we should've gotten out of there yesterday.'

'If I hadn't lost the keys . . .' Abilene muttered.

'They wouldn't have *gotten* lost if we'd left as soon as we spotted him.'

'Everything'd be fine if we'd stayed together,' Cora told her. 'Helen shouldn't have gone off by herself.'

'But she did,' Abilene muttered. 'All she wanted to do was help.' Her throat tightened and tears came to her eyes. 'She just wanted to find the keys.' Vivian put an arm around her.

Finley looked at her strangely. Glaring. As if betrayed and outraged that Abilene was starting to fall apart again.

But that wasn't it.

She kept on glaring as Cora said, 'Maybe we'd better forget about going back. The cat's probably not in . . .'

'Fuck the cat,' Finley said. 'Let's go back and waste the bastard that killed her.'

They stared at Finley.

They stared at each other.

Abilene wiped her eyes. 'You're kidding, right?'

'She was *one* of us. Shit, look what we did to Wildman after he hurt her. All he did was punch her a little. And somebody *murders* Helen and here we are, walking away.'

'This is different,' Cora said.

'Fuckin'-A-right, it's different. This guy *killed* Helen. He made her *dead*. He grabbed her and took her into that room and cut off her suit and put her through all kinds of hell. Can you imagine? Think about it. I mean, Helen was always a scared kid and a guy did that to her. God knows what he must've done before he killed her. Can you imagine what it must've been *like*? And we're just gonna walk away?'

'That's the idea,' Cora said. Turning around, she continued down the driveway.

Finley hurried after her, Abilene and Vivian following.

'You always talked big about taking risks!' Finley blurted.

'Helen's dead, you idiot! It isn't a game anymore.' She scowled over her shoulder. 'This isn't Wildman. This isn't what's-his-face getting carried away pretending he's The Reaper. This is real. The guy's a killer. You want to go back to the lodge and nail the bastard. So do I. I'd love to make him pay. But I don't want to see *you* get your guts ripped out. Or Abilene or Vivian. Do you? We've lost Helen, for Godsake. We aren't gonna lose anyone else. Not while I'm around. We'll get out of here and we'll let the cops take care of it.'

'The cops won't take care of shit!'

'They wouldn't do it right,' Vivian said. Abilene looked at her, stunned. Vivian, of all people, was taking Finley's side?

She *couldn't* want to go back. Not Vivian. 'Even if they catch the guy and he gets convicted and everything, he'd only end up in prison.'

Cora gave Vivian an odd look as if she couldn't believe her ears, either. 'Have you lost your mind?'

'I've lost Helen.'

'Hunting down the killer won't change that. She'll still be dead. And maybe some of us'll be dead, too.'

They came to the bottom of the driveway. Cora, stopping, looked up and down the road. 'The nearest town's that way, isn't it?' she asked, nodding to the left.

'I think so,' Vivian said. 'That's the way we came. I don't know what's in the other direction.'

'We should've grabbed the map,' Cora said, and headed to the left.

'Just a second,' Abilene said.

'What?'

'Maybe we'd better think about this.'

'We're not sure what's the other way . . .'

'That's not what I mean.'

'*You* want to go back, too?'

'I didn't say that.'

Frowning, Cora folded her arms and leaned back against one of the old totem poles. 'Okay,' she said. 'What *are* you saying?'

'Just . . . I don't want him to get away with it.'

'Right on, Hickok.'

'I don't know about killing him, either. He sure deserves it, but . . . maybe we don't want that on our consciences.'

'I could live with it,' Finley said.

'The thing is, the cops might never even get their hands on the guy. I mean, *twenty-eight* people were slaughtered at the

565

lodge and the killers got away with it. So what are the chances of the cops nailing whoever murdered Helen?'

'Slim to none,' Finley said.

'If the cops can't get him,' Cora said, 'what makes you think we can?'

'He'll come to us. He'll come *for* us. So far, he's stayed away because we've all been together. It's like you said, he doesn't want to take on all of us.'

'Which means it's probably just one guy,' Vivian added.

'But if he finds one of us alone . . .'

Cora nodded. 'And the rest of us are out of sight.'

'Right. We put out the bait. When he goes for it, we jump him.'

'It's still awfully risky,' Cora said.

'We've taken plenty of risks before. And I know, I know, it was never like this. But . . . what he did to Helen. We've always taken care of each other and we let her down, but the least we can do is make sure the bastard pays the price.'

Cora looked at the others. 'You all want to do this?'

Vivian nodded.

Finley said, 'Fuckin'-A.'

'I'll go along with it on one condition,' Cora told them. 'I'm the bait.'

'You got it,' Finley said. 'And I'm gonna *get* it.' With that, she set her camera on the ground and stepped to the other side of the driveway entrance. There, she wrapped her arms and legs around the leaning totem pole and began to shinny up it. The post wobbled a bit.

'What're you doing?' Vivian asked.

'Trying not to fall.'

Watching, Abilene half expected Finley's weight to uproot

the pole and send it slamming to earth. 'We'll end up with another casualty before we even get started,' she muttered.

'If she gets crunched,' Cora said, 'we can use *her* as the bait.'

'You guys are a laugh riot,' Finley called down. Then, reaching overhead, she stretched her right arm toward an outspread wing of the strange, birdlike creature at the very top of the pole. She grabbed the hilt of the hunting knife that someone had embedded there. She worked the knife up and down. She jerked on it. The post shuddered.

Then the blade seemed to leap from the old, weathered wood. It came out with such a sudden release that Finley's arm shot back. She yelled, 'Aw, shit!' as she slid sideways. She dropped the knife and hugged the post.

The others rushed forward. Cora rammed her back against the totem pole to brace it. Abilene and Vivian positioned themselves under Finley to catch her.

Finley dangled by her arms.

Abilene and Vivian reached high and grabbed her feet.

'I'm okay. Just let go.'

They did as she asked. She kicked and swayed, and finally wrapped her legs around the post. Then she began to work her way slowly downward, clinging to its underside.

'Watch my face,' Cora warned as the shoes neared her.

'Can't even see it.'

'You're low enough.'

'Okay, okay.' Finley's legs released the pole. She swept back and forth like a pendulum until Abilene caught her around the thighs. Once she was steady, Abilene stepped away. Finley let go and dropped to the ground. Her face was red, shiny with sweat. 'Thanks, guys.'

'Dork,' Abilene said.

'Yeah, but I'm a dork with a weapon.' She hunted around for a moment, found the knife and picked it up.

'Everybody better stand back,' Cora said.

They stepped clear of the totem pole, and Cora lurched out from under it. Without her back to support it, the pole stayed put.

'Could've saved your energy,' Finley told her.

Cora shrugged. 'You never know.'

'Anyway, thanks. I could've got turned into mashed potatoes.'

'No sweat.'

With her empty hand, Finley brushed dirt and flakes of wood off the front of her clothes. Then she held up the knife. 'It was worth some trouble, huh?'

The grimy blade, specked with rust, was at least eight inches long.

'Quite a toad-sticker,' Vivian said.

Cora walked back to the other totem pole. She'd dropped her tire iron there before rushing to Finley's rescue. She picked it up. 'If we're really going through with this,' she said, 'we'd better lay our hands on some more weapons.'

'There's a fireplace poker in the lodge,' Abilene said.

'I know where there's a shotgun,' Finley said.

Vivian's eyes widened. 'Where?'

Finley gave her a mysterious look, but didn't answer.

A shotgun? That'd be perfect, Abilene thought. But they sure hadn't brought one along with them, and she hadn't seen one in the lodge. Somehow, though, she seemed to remember seeing one recently.

She remembered. She muttered. 'Oh, Jesus.'

Cora groaned. Apparently, she now realized where the shotgun was.

Vivian gazed at the others, puzzled.

'Batty,' Finley said.

Vivian bared her upper teeth. 'We don't want to go back there.'

'The old buzzard had an ax in the shed, too. And a sickle. All sorts of neat shit. We could come back loaded for bear.'

Cora nodded. 'If we had that over-and-under, we could blow the asshole's head off. We wouldn't even have to get our hands dirty. There'd be no contest. Even if it turns out there's more than one of 'em, we'd be okay.'

'Batty isn't about to give us any of those things,' Vivian pointed out.

'We might be able to work a trade,' Abilene suggested.

'Not a chance,' Vivian said. 'Someone like that doesn't part with a shotgun.'

'So . . . we're talking about stealing the stuff?'

'You got it, Hickok.'

'Oh, man.'

Nose wrinkled, Vivian nodded in agreement. 'That's getting heavy.'

'*Heavy?*' Finley blurted. 'You've gotta be kidding me! We're gonna blow away the fucker who killed Helen and you're worried about *swiping* a few things from some crazy old fart of indeterminate gender who may or may not have *done* it?'

Vivian didn't seem fazed by the outburst. 'I don't think it's a good idea,' she said, her voice firm. 'I'm sure Batty didn't have anything to do with it. And we don't want to turn someone like that against us.'

'Scared he'll hex us?'

Chapter Twenty-six

Back at the Wagoneer, they ate potato chips along with sandwiches of roast beef and sharp cheddar while they discussed plans for the raid against Batty.

Their first idea was to wait for nightfall, sneak up on the cabin in the dark, and subdue the old lunatic by force.

'Catch him while he's sleeping,' Cora said.

'But what if he's *not* asleep?' Vivian asked. 'We've gotta take him by surprise or one of us might get shot.'

'Listen at a window for snoring,' Finley suggested.

'We need to use our heads,' Abilene said. 'You know? We're not commandos. Making a night attack on someone who's armed . . . It just seems out of our league.'

'So what've you got in mind, Hickok?'

'I'm not sure. But we've never done anything like that. The other times . . . we were always tricky about it. That was how we managed to succeed against Wildman and the Sigs and even that guy on Halloween. We didn't just attack. We were clever about it.'

Cora's eyes narrowed. She nodded slowly as she chewed on a mouthful of sandwich. 'You're right,' she said, her voice coming out muffled. 'Let's think up a fake-out.'

'Going back in broad daylight would be a good start,' Vivian said. 'Walk right up to the cabin and knock on the door.'

'Light a bag of shit on fire,' Finley suggested.

'Let's try to do better than that,' Abilene said.

They were exhausted by the time they reached the lake.

'Take five,' Cora said.

She wandered down to the water as the others sank to the ground. Finley leaned back against Helen's sleeping bag and folded her hands behind her head. Vivian lay down, gasping. Abilene crossed her legs. She lifted the front of her blouse and wiped her face.

Though gray clouds dimmed the sky, the air felt heavy and moist. Even the breeze blowing in from the lake gave little relief from the humid heat.

Cora dropped the tire iron, pulled off her shoes and socks, and waded into the water. It probably felt wonderful, but Abilene didn't have the energy to follow her example. The earlier hiking and all the emotional strains of the morning had sapped too much of her strength. Besides, she would get a chance to cool off when they crossed the inlet.

If I can make it that far, she thought. Carrying the water bottle, she supposed, didn't make things any easier. But at least they'd been smart enough not to bring along a full one. Before setting out, they'd merely added some water to the nearly empty bottle that they'd taken along on the first trip to Batty's.

She twisted off the cap. She drank a bit. Lowering the bottle, she watched Cora duck beneath the surface. A few moments later, the girl came up and rolled onto her back and floated motionless beside the ramshackle dock.

Abilene turned her eyes to the beach and stared at the canoe. If we could just take that to Batty's place, she thought. So much easier than walking. If it had paddles. And if it didn't have that gaping hole in the bottom.

Oh well.

When Cora came out of the water, Abilene knew that the rest period was about over. She took a few more swigs from the bottle, then struggled to her feet. Vivian and Finley stood up while Cora got into her socks and shoes. Vivian accepted the bottle in silence, gulped some water, and passed it to Finley.

'Hotter than a huncher out here,' Finley muttered before tilting the bottle to her mouth.

'You gals should've taken a dip,' Cora said.

'It's gonna rain before long, anyway,' Vivian said.

'Think so?' Abilene asked.

Nodding, Vivian sniffed the breeze. 'I'd bet on it.'

'Hope you're right.'

'Let it come,' Finley said. 'The sooner, the better.'

The rain didn't come and the air seemed hotter, muggier than ever as they made their way through the forest. Abilene felt as if she were hiking through a sauna. After a while, Cora peeled off her tank top. Finley took off her shirt.

Why not? Abilene thought. Nobody around to see us, anyway.

She removed her own blouse and tucked it under the waistband at the back of her skirt.

Seeing that the others had stripped down, Vivian pulled off her polo shirt. She balled it up and mopped her face. After a few strides, she took off her bra. She stuffed it into a pocket of her shorts but kept the shirt in her hand as if ready to put it on quickly at the first sign of intruders. Her head turned constantly from side to side. Obviously, she was worried about being seen.

So was Abilene. Though she told herself that there was probably no one nearby, it made her uneasy to be topless outside in broad daylight. She was uncomfortably aware of her naked breasts, how the air felt against their dripping skin and how they jiggled. She was tempted to put her blouse back on. Better to feel exposed and vulnerable, however, than stifled inside the garment.

As they approached the mouth of the inlet, where they would be in plain sight from the lake's opposite shore, Vivian pulled the polo shirt down over her head. Abilene slipped into her blouse and immediately regretted the way it clung to her skin and trapped the heat. Neither Cora nor Finley bothered to cover themselves.

'Somebody might see you,' Vivian warned.

'As if I care,' Finley said.

'It might make somebody come after us.'

'If it's the guy that got Helen, let him come. I'd like to meet him and get it over with.'

'We don't want to meet him before we've got the gun,' Cora said.

'The four of us could take him.'

Abilene wished they would stop standing there in plain sight. *Anyone* might be watching. And getting ideas.

'Either put on your shirts or get in the water,' she said.

'You worry too much, Hickok.'

'It's bad enough we've got Helen's killer to deal with. God only knows who might be out there getting an eyeful and thinking he might like a crack at us.'

'Just let 'em try,' Finley said.

Then she followed Cora into the water. Cora swam for the other side while Finley waded across, holding the sleeping bag overhead.

Vivian jumped in.

Abilene paused on the outcropping.

She scanned the gray, ruffled lake and its shoreline. She saw no one.

The breeze was stronger here. It felt a little cooler than

573

before. Though she wanted to feel it on her skin, she held her blouse shut as she squinted in the direction of Batty's cabin.

She couldn't see it, but she did spot a willow that might be the one concealing the rowboat.

Not very far away.

Batty would have a clear view of them.

'You coming or what?' Finley called from the other side of the inlet.

She and Cora were already out, shiny and dripping and staring at her. Vivian was boosting herself onto the slab of rock at Finley's feet.

Abilene leaped. She gasped as the cold water rushed up her body. Dunking her head, she savored the chill. Then she made her way to the other side, set the plastic bottle on the ledge and climbed up.

Just as she'd expected, the chill stayed with her. The breeze felt wintery against her wet skin. She shivered. But she knew the sensation wouldn't last long.

She walked over the rocks, following the others into the woods. Her sodden feet made squelching sounds inside her sneakers, and she was struck by the memory of Helen, long ago, squelching across the restroom floor after stepping into the toilet. Ol' Yellow Foot. She smiled. Then she saw Helen sprawled on the shower room floor, dead, and a clump of ice seemed to form in her stomach.

She's in the shower room right now, in the blackness, all alone.

Though the heat had already melted away the last traces of chill from Abilene's skin, she crawled with goosebumps. She rubbed her pebbly forearms and thighs.

It's not Helen in the shower room, she told herself. Just her body. Her spirit isn't there. Her soul's free, doing whatever it is that souls do.

If souls exist.

They've got to. You can't just die and that's it . . .

No. Abilene had long ago decided that death was a change, not an end. You leave your body behind, but something goes on. Though raised as a Protestant, she didn't much care for the concepts of heaven and hell. She rather liked the idea of reincarnation.

If you don't come back, maybe you become part of the universe.

Or maybe you stay a soul and go exploring.

Maybe anything. No way to know. Not until you go toes up.

It'd be nice if Helen could tell us what's next.

When all this is over, she thought, maybe we could hold a seance or something. If we can manage to find a medium who isn't a fake.

Batty.

'Hold up a minute,' Abilene said. The others halted. Joining them, she said, 'I just had an idea. Instead of just bullshitting Batty to get him off guard, why don't we see if he'll . . . run a seance. You know? Maybe we can get in touch with Helen.'

'You gotta be kidding,' Finley said.

'It's worth a try. Seriously. If Batty does that kind of stuff . . . It wouldn't hurt to ask.'

'You don't really believe . . .' Cora began.

'I don't know what I believe. But what if we *can* . . . communicate with Helen? I know it sounds crazy, but Batty did tell us where we'd find her. Maybe he does have some kind of special powers. If he can get in touch with Helen, we might be able to find out some things. Like who killed her.'

'And where the keys are,' Vivian added.

'You too?' Cora asked.

'I don't see any harm in trying. You never know.'

Finley shook her head and rolled her eyes upward. 'The heat's gotten to both of you.'

'I know it sounds crazy,' Abilene said. Her throat suddenly going tight, she blurted, 'I just want to find out if she's all right.'

Finley grimaced.

Cora stared grimly at Abilene.

'I *know* she's dead, okay?'

'I think Helen would want us to try it,' Vivian said. 'If she were here, she'd be all for it. Hell, she'd love the idea of sitting around with a witch or whatever Batty is and trying to call up spirits of the dead.'

A corner of Finley's mouth curled up and she nodded. 'Yeah. Crap like that would make her day.'

'We'll see,' Cora said. 'But I've had enough blood to drink for one day.'

'Yeah,' Finley said. 'If it starts getting too weird . . .'

'We'll just play it by ear,' Abilene said.

'Batty might not agree to do it anyway,' Vivian pointed out.

They made their way around the northern end of the lake. As they neared Batty's cabin, Cora and Finley put their shirts back on and Abilene buttoned her blouse. She wondered how her hair looked, and smiled. It's like approaching the home of relatives after a long drive, she thought. A few blocks away, you brush your hair, freshen your lipstick. But this wasn't a relative. This was a crazy hermit about to be visited by four young women planning to rob him.

We can't steal his stuff if he gets in touch with Helen for us. It wouldn't be right.

We've gotta have that shotgun.

It won't be exactly stealing if we bring the stuff back when we're finished.

Forced borrowing.

'Batty!' Cora shouted. 'It's us again! Hello?'

Startled from her thoughts, Abilene gazed past the others. She saw only more trees in the gloom ahead, and wondered why Cora had called out. Down the shore to the right, however, she spotted the rowboat rocking and bobbing on the choppy water. She looked again into the trees. This time, she was able to make out the vague shape of the cabin.

Her stomach knotted.

Oh Christ, we're here.

Heart thudding, she took a deep breath and followed the others toward the porch.

'Hello!' Cora called again. 'Batty! It's us!'

'We've got something for you,' Finley added, hoisting Helen's sleeping bag overhead.

The screen door swung open. Batty stepped onto the porch, the shotgun cradled in his arms. *Her* arms, Abilene thought. The old lunatic looked uglier and wilder than she remembered. And somehow, now, more like a woman than like a man.

Batty studied them with squinted eyes. 'Find y'friend?'

'We did,' Cora answered. 'She's dead.'

'Can't help that. Get away from here.'

'We brought this for you,' Finley said, and dangled the sleeping bag by its draw-cord.

'Got no use for it.'

'What *do* you have a use for?' Cora asked.

Batty just stared at her.

'We'd like you to do a seance for us.' The pale blue eyes

shifted to Abilene. 'We want you to contact the spirit of our friend. Do you do that kind of thing?'

'Mebbie.'

'We'll give you whatever you want. If we've got it, it's yours.'

'Anythin'?'

'Within reason.'

'Get on in here.' Batty turned away and entered the cabin. The screen door banged shut.

Cora in the lead, they climbed the creaking plank stairs and crossed the porch. She held the door open, then followed them inside.

Amos, on the rocker, raised its head off its paws and gazed at them. The white fur of its face was clean.

Maybe some other cat . . . No, it had been Amos. Lapping up Helen's blood.

Beast.

But at least it's here, Abilene told herself. It didn't get trapped inside the changing room with Helen, after all. Thank God for that.

'Sit,' Batty said, using the shotgun to gesture toward the table.

Each went to the same chair she'd occupied that morning, and sat down.

Batty propped the shotgun against the wall near the head of the bed. 'Ain't simple, y'know, callin' up dead folk.'

'But you can do it?' Abilene asked.

'Done it plenty. Y' friend got herself killed, did she?'

'She was murdered with a knife,' Cora said.

'Figgers.'

'What's that supposed to mean?' Finley asked.

'Y' don't dally 'round the ghost lodge 'less y'aim to get

y'guts spilled out.' Batty pulled the big knife from its scabbard, stepped between Cora and Vivian, and swept the blade down, ramming its point deep into the center of the table. 'Gotta fetch some items.'

'So you'll do it?' Abilene asked.

'Gimme what I want, I'll call her up.'

'What do you want?'

'Jest a finger.'

'A *finger*?' Abilene gasped.

'Jest a one. Don't matter which, 'r who gives. Want her whole, though, right off at the first joint. There's the knife right there.' With that, Batty hobbled out of the room.

Finley met Abilene's eyes. 'Play it by ear, huh?'

The back door clapped shut.

'I didn't expect anything like this,' Abilene muttered.

'Wants to put it in a jar, no doubt.'

A grim smile formed on Cora's face. 'So. Anyone want to donate?'

'Here's your big chance, Hickok. This was your idea.'

'Don't be ridiculous,' Vivian told her.

Reaching out, Abilene clutched the knife handle. She tugged at it, working the blade back and forth until its tip jumped from the wood.

'Hey!' Finley gasped. 'You're not . . .'

'Now we've both got knives,' Abilene said.

Finley looked relieved.

'I may be gullible, but I'm not crazy.'

Cora shoved back her chair, rushed across the floor, and grabbed the shotgun. As she whirled around, the others sprang from their seats.

'Let's get!' Finley blurted.

Cora shook her head. 'We've got some business to finish.'

She shouldered the weapon and aimed its long barrels toward the kitchen entryway. With a glance down at the breech, she muttered, 'Wonder if it's loaded.'

'I'm sure it is,' Vivian said.

'We oughta get more shells before we . . .'

A screen door bammed shut. After a few unsteady shuffling sounds, Batty stepped into the living room and halted. Cupped in her hands – or his – was a human skull. A skull with bulging eyes. Abilene wondered if they'd come from the jar Cora had dropped in the shed. She imagined Batty scurrying around, crouching and picking up a couple and stuffing them into the sockets.

'Come in here and sit down,' Cora said. She nodded toward the table.

'What's this foolishness?'

'Do it!'

Batty carried the bug-eyed skull to the table, set it down, then sank onto one of the chairs.

'For starters, take off the shoes.'

'No,' Vivian said. 'They were fair payment. We don't take them.'

'Suit yourself.' Squinting down the sight ramp at Batty, Cora asked, 'Where do you keep your extra ammunition?'

'Yonder.' A nod at the shelves.

'I'll get the ax,' Vivian said. As she bolted from the room, Abilene and Finley scanned the shelves.

'I see 'em.' Finley rushed across the floor, reached up, and plucked a small red box from between a black candle and a bowl. It was the same bowl, Abilene realized, that they'd used for the bleeding ritual.

'Y'gonna rue the day y'tampered with old Batty.'

'Screw you,' Finley said. She flipped open the flimsy lid

and dug into the box. Her hand came out full of shotgun shells. She dumped them into a pocket of her shorts, then tossed the empty box aside.

'That's all?' Cora asked.

'Y'take my over 'n under, I'm gonna call down a curse on all y'heads. It'll be my killin' curse.'

'Curse away, bat brain,' Finley said.

'We're only going to borrow it,' Abilene said. 'This, too,' she added, raising Batty's knife. 'We need to have some weapons. But we'll bring everything back to you. I promise.'

The way Batty looked at her, she wished she'd kept her mouth shut. 'Doubt it. But I'll get'm back. I'll pick 'em up my own self outa y'dead hands.'

'Not if you're dead first, gonzo,' Finley said. 'Hey, Cora, go ahead and blow his fucking head off. Or hers. Or whatever. We don't want that curse on us, do we?'

Abilene couldn't tell whether or not she was serious.

Cora kept the shotgun trained on Batty's face, but didn't pull the trigger.

Vivian hurried back into the room. An ax rested over one shoulder. 'We ready to go?'

'Find something we can use to tie Batty up,' Cora said.

'Right here,' Finley said. She stepped up close to the side of the chair. 'Get your arms up. Good. Keep them that way. Touch me and you'll be sorry.' Crouching, Finley unbuckled Batty's belt and pulled it from the few remaining loops of the faded, cut-off jeans. The knife scabbard dropped to the floor. She tossed it to Abilene.

Abilene sheathed the knife and slid it under the waistband of her skirt. It went under the side of her panties, too, but she decided that was all right. The leather case felt smooth and soft like doe skin.

581

Finley was standing upright now, frowning at Batty, the belt in her hands.

'What's the problem?' Cora asked.

'Just trying to figure out the best way to . . .'

Abilene glimpsed a flying streak of white. Amos. 'Look out!'

Cora yelped, staggered forward under the impact and twisted around. The cat had hit her just above the waist. It clawed its way up her back, ripping cloth and skin.

Before the others could move to help her, Batty's upraised right hand darted sideways, clutched the front of Finley's shirt, and yanked. Buttons popped away. A quick stumble, and Finley dropped across Batty's thighs.

Like a kid about to be spanked.

Cora dropped the shotgun, tucked, and jumped. In midair, she flipped herself heels over head. The cat rode her down. Her back slammed it against the floor.

Batty's left hand clenched the nape of Finley's neck. The right snatched her shirt halfway up her back, then reached for the hilt of the knife at her hip.

Cora rolled. Vivian rushed the stunned cat and raised her ax.

Batty jerked out the knife. Brought it up over Finley's squirming, bucking body.

With both hands, Abilene grabbed Batty's forearm. She wrenched it backward and down, unaware of Batty turning, stretching out her other arm. Suddenly, something was coming at her face. She looked up just in time to see an eyeball leap from its socket. The other seemed to watch her. She turned her face away an instant before the skull struck her. Its brow pounded her cheekbone. But she kept her grip on Batty's arm as she staggered back. And heard a *crack* like a snapping branch. Batty wailed. The knife fell to the floor. Abilene released the arm.

Staggering back, she saw Vivian double over and vomit. Cora was struggling to free the ax from the floor. As she pumped its handle, Amos wobbled.

Abilene's stomach turned. She fell to her knees, heaving.

When she finished and lifted her head, she saw Finley shoving Batty's legs into the air. The chair tipped backward and crashed down. Batty spilled out of it, did an awkward somersault, hit the floor knees first, and flopped down flat.

Finley kicked the chair. It tumbled and skidded. Cora leaped out of its way. The chair stopped abruptly when a corner of its seat met the dead cat.

Finley picked up her knife. Clamping it between her teeth, she turned Batty over. As the body rolled, the skinny arm swung the wrong way from its elbow.

Abilene groaned.

I did that, she thought. Oh, Jesus.

Finley dropped onto Batty's stomach and took the knife from between her teeth. Breathless, she gasped, 'Told you not to touch me, you bastard.'

'Leave her alone,' Abilene said.

'Him,' Finley corrected. 'See?' She reached behind her and flapped aside a leg of the split cut-offs. 'Felt it when he had me down.' She leaned over and pressed the blade to his throat. 'Dirty old shit. *You* killed Helen, didn't you? Didn't you!'

'Fin,' Abilene said quietly.

She looked up, her eyes red and wild. 'He did it.'

'Even if it was him . . .'

'Weren't,' Batty gasped. He was panting for air, wincing. Abilene saw no fear in his eyes. They seemed sly and full of hate. 'I purely aim t'kill *you*, though. Ever' one a ya. Get me plenty a fresh items for m'stock.'

His lips peeled back, forming a nasty grin of gaps and brown stumps. Finley pressed the blade harder against his throat. Ignoring it, he reached up with his left hand. Reached inside Finley's drooping, open shirt. She sucked a quick breath.

'I'll cut me this one right off.'

'*Uhhhhhh!*' She lurched backward, slashed his forearm and leaped off him, gasping and frantically rubbing the front of her shirt against her breast.

Batty laughed. Quick, nasal beeps that sounded like a honking car.

'You're fuckin' *nuts!*' Finley shouted.

Batty laughed harder. He lay flat on his back only a couple of yards from his chopped cat, laughing. One arm broken, the other pouring blood, and he was shaking with laughter.

Finley was first out the door. Vivian followed her with the ax. Cora backed away, keeping the shotgun aimed at Batty. 'Let's go,' she said.

'I'm coming.' Abilene picked up Helen's sleeping bag. No way would she leave a possession of Helen's with this lunatic. Sidestepping toward the door, she said, 'I'm sorry about your arm. But you shouldn't have tried to stab . . .'

'I'll . . . have *yers!*' Batty squealed between honks of hilarity. Abilene rushed for the door.

Chapter Twenty-seven

She found the others down at the lake, Finley bending over the knee-deep water and washing her breast, Vivian washing splatters of cat blood off her thighs, Cora picking up the block of concrete that served as the anchor for Batty's rowboat. The ax and shotgun were already stowed in the craft.

'We're taking his boat?' Abilene asked.

'You got it.' Cora dropped the anchor into the bow. 'In in in! I'll row.' She held the boat steady while Vivian climbed aboard and made her way, crouching low, toward the stern.

As Finley lunged over its gunwale and the boat tipped wildly for a moment, Abilene waded into the lake. The back of Cora's tank top was bloody and torn. Above its low neckline and around the right shoulder strap, her bare skin was furrowed with claw marks.

Abilene tossed the sleeping bag aboard. It rolled under the center seat. 'I'll hold on,' she said. 'You climb in.' As Cora moved out of her way, she grabbed the prow.

Twisting her head around, she gazed back at the cabin. No sign of Batty. Nor could she hear the crazy laughter.

He won't come after us, she told herself. Not with a broken arm. Not with that gash.

Not right now, anyway.

She realized they had left their water bottle in the cabin.

It's okay. We've got two more back at the car. Sure not going back in for it.

Just stay where you are, Batty. Don't come after us.

Returning her attention to the boat, she saw Cora already seated in the center and busy fitting an oar into the metal U of its oarlock. Finley, behind Cora, sat cross-legged on the bottom of the boat and now had the shotgun. She held it straight up, the barrels rising like a mast above her head.

Cora got the other oar into position.

Abilene leaned against the prow and pushed. The boat began gliding away, stern first, and she sloshed after it, guiding it farther from shore until the water climbed to her waist. Then she boosted herself up, kicked high enough to hook a calf over the gunwale, squirmed and twisted until she dropped aboard.

She lay on her back, struggling to catch her breath. Beyond her upraised knees, Cora was rowing with a single oar to turn the boat around. Then both oars were in motion, Cora leaning forward to dip them in, coming back toward Abilene as she drew their blades through the water, and starting over again.

Abilene lifted a hand to her face. Gently, she fingered the lump of soreness beneath her right eye. Her cheekbone felt as if a golf ball were growing out of it.

I got him better than he got me, she thought. Still, she wished she hadn't broken his arm. She had never hurt anyone like that before and the memory of it sickened her.

He was going to stab Finley, she reminded herself.

Besides, it was an accident. I only broke it because he bashed me with that skull and I started to fall.

The boat dropped abruptly, then rebounded off the water, its wooden ribs pounding against her. Enough of this, Abilene thought. Rising, she scooted across the bottom until her back met the edge of the bow seat. She clutched the gunwales, pushed herself up, and sat on the narrow bench.

The slate gray lake was choppy, but didn't look nearly as rough as it had felt when she was lying on the bottom of the boat. The fresh breeze felt good.

Leaning sideways, she looked past Cora's back. Finley met her eyes and nodded. Vivian was twisted around, gazing toward shore.

The limbs of the willow, hanging out over the lake, blew like green streamers.

We really haven't gone very far, Abilene thought. Maybe a hundred feet.

And then she saw Batty come prancing down the slope stark naked. 'Oh, my God,' she murmured. The broken arm swung from its elbow like a dead thing. The other arm, bound with a red rag, was upraised and shaking a pale club that had a knob at both ends.

A bone?

Batty's long gray hair blew like the willow limbs.

Her breasts bounced and flopped like loose sacks of pudding.

His erection was a rigid, jerking spike.

Abilene's mind reeled.

Vivian pointed, swiveled her head and said something to Finley.

Finley got to her knees and turned around and shouldered the shotgun.

'Don't you shoot,' Cora warned, still rowing.

Batty stopped at the water's edge. And began to dance. Hopping from foot to foot, shaking the bone at the gray sky then bowing to dip it into the lake before thrusting it again overhead.

Finley looked over her shoulder. Abilene expected a remark about hermaphrodites until she caught the strangeness in her friend's eyes.

Too freaked out to crack wise.

This was the thing that had grabbed her breast. A lecherous

old coot but also a hag, mad and sly, a drinker of blood, a collector of body parts, a conjurer.

Freaks me out, too, Abilene thought, and I'm not the one who got groped.

Finley turned away.

Batty was still dancing, twirling and leaping, sweeping the bone from the water to the sky.

A heavy blast slammed Abilene's ears. The shotgun leaped beside Vivian's shoulder. Vivian jumped as if her boat seat had turned into a cattle prod. Then she grabbed the barrels and shoved them up. Her face red and twisted, she glared back at Finley.

She said nothing.

But Cora shouted, 'Damn it!'

On the shore, Batty shook the bone and hopped with both feet, broken arm and breasts and penis bouncing up and down.

Abilene found herself wishing Finley hadn't missed.

Finley yanked the barrels from Vivian's grip, but she didn't take aim again. Holding the shotgun upright, she scowled back at Cora. 'The fuck's putting a curse on us!' she called.

'Since when are you scared of shit like that?' Cora asked.

'Since today.'

'Don't worry. The creep can't hurt us now.'

'Should've cut its throat when I had the chance.'

Batty still capered about the shore, bobbing and spinning and leaping. But indistinct now. A pale, blurry shape in the distance. *In the darkness*.

Abilene tipped back her head.

A low, black mass of thunderheads was rushing in from the hills behind Batty. As if it carried winds of its own, the advancing range of clouds roughed up the water in its path.

'Oh shit!' Cora yelled, and started rowing faster.

A blinding dagger of light gashed the nearest black cloud, splitting it with a noise like ripping fabric. Then came an explosion that shook the air. Abilene felt the concussion all the way to her heart.

Batty vanished behind a curtain of rain.

Cora rowed furiously as if trying to outrace the approaching storm.

'Should we head for shore?' Abilene called.

'We'll make it!' Cora shouted.

Twisting around, Abilene peered forward and saw that they were heading straight for the old dock at the far side of the lake. But they weren't even halfway there.

Rain suddenly poured down, drenching her.

The boat pitched. She turned back toward the others and grabbed the gunwales. Cora's hair was matted flat. Raindrops splashed off her bare shoulders, rinsed the blood from her skin, exposed the raw scratches. Finley was facing forward. She'd put down the shotgun. With outstretched arms, she clung to the sides of the tossing boat. Her head and shoulders jerked from side to side. Vivian, abandoning her seat at the stern, lowered herself behind Finley then reached out and held on.

The boat rocked and bounced. Abilene flinched as a wave broke over the bow, slopping her rump with water much colder than the rain.

Lightning cracked the sky. Thunder roared. The rain came down even harder than before.

A sudden lurch nearly threw Abilene overboard. With a gasp of alarm, she hunched down to lower her center of gravity.

The bottom of the boat was awash with water, a puddle erupting with tiny splashes of raindrops as it slopped from side to side, forward and back, sometimes rolling over the white toes of her sneakers. Willow leaves floated on its surface. So did a few dead worms.

Not enough water to worry about, she told herself. It'd take a lot more than this to sink us.

Shouldn't have taken the boat, damn it.

Stepped right into Batty's trap.

Come on, give it a break, she thought. Batty didn't do this. It's a storm. Storms happen. Even before we got to Batty's place, Viv had said it was going to rain.

Man, she was right!

But what was that fuckin' dance Batty was doing? Sure looked like some kind of ritual. A rain dance?

Bull. Batty didn't do this.

The seat dropped abruptly out from under Abilene. She clenched the gunwales. The bench smacked her rear and she felt as if a bucketful of water had been hurled at her. It splashed high up her back but most of it hit her skirt. Some, spilling beneath her, licked between her buttocks with an icy tongue that made her gasp.

'We're taking in an awful lot of water!' Finley yelled.

'Tell me about it!' Abilene called to her.

The puddle, now, was ankle deep. She knew it must be worse at the other end of the boat.

Sitting up, she leaned sideways to see past Cora. Finley sat on the bottom, knees up. Vivian had her legs wrapped around Finley's hips as if they were riding a Matterhorn bobsled at Disneyland. The water surrounding them was high enough to slosh over the tops of Vivian's thighs.

'Start bailing!' Cora shouted.

'With what?' Finley called.

'Try your hands!'

'Oh, that'll help a lot!' In spite of her remark, Finley apparently decided to give it a try. With both hands, she scooped up water from between her legs and hurled it over the side. Much of it blew back into her face.

Thinking that Batty might keep some kind of container aboard, Abilene slid to her knees and managed to turn herself around. Ducking, she peered under the narrow bench. The concrete anchor was there, piled with rope. But nothing that might be helpful for bailing.

It'll help, she realized, getting rid of the anchor.

She reached under the seat with both hands and started to drag the heavy block toward her. As it skidded closer, a wave dumped water over the back of her head. She blinked her eyes clear and tugged the anchor out against her knees.

The rope was knotted to a rusty steel eye embedded in the concrete.

Hanging onto the rope as if it were the reins of a bucking bronco, she straightened up. She drew Batty's knife from the scabbard at her hip and slashed through the taut rope. The instant it gave way, she was thrown backward. She grabbed the gunwale and managed to stay on her knees.

Trying to sheath the knife, she missed its scabbard and poked her hip bone. 'Damn it!' She dropped the knife into the puddle by her knee, then clutched the anchor with both hands. She lifted it, twisted sideways, and dropped it over the side. It thumped the water and flung up a cold geyser.

Good show, she told herself. She wondered if any of the others had witnessed her exploit, but decided it didn't matter. The anchor was gone. She'd accomplished something that should help to keep them afloat. At least for a while.

Still on her knees, she leaned forward until the edge of the seat pushed against her ribs. She reached out with both arms, and hung on.

All she could see was darkness and pouring rain and leaping, churning waves capped with froth.

Are we even going in the right direction?

As the boat plummeted, she shut her eyes and mouth. The edge of the seat jammed her chest. Water flew into her face. Then the boat started to rise, so she blinked and squinted.

A flash of lightning streaked down through the clouds ahead. In its stark glare, she glimpsed something on the surface of the lake.

A thrill surged through her.

'The raft!' she yelled through a crash of thunder.

Doubting that anyone had heard her, she pushed away from the seat, turned around, and sat in the sloshing swamp at the bottom of the boat. She felt the knife under her rump.

Good. Wouldn't want to lose it.

Cora was still rowing like a madwoman.

Cupping her hands to her mouth, Abilene shouted, 'The diving raft! Dead ahead!'

Cora glanced around.

Abilene gave her a thumbs up, and yelled, 'Almost there! Fifty, sixty feet!'

Nodding, Cora turned away.

Abilene rolled a bit, reached down, and pulled the knife out from under her.

She realized she was grinning.

We're gonna make it!

Another wave came down, washing over her back, but she didn't mind. She reached under the side of her skirt and plucked the scabbard out. Carefully, her jerking hands guided the blade into the leather slot. She slid the blade home, leaned against the port side of the pitching boat and pushed the sheathed knife down the waistband at her hip.

Only then did she realize she was sitting in water up to her belly.

If it's this high here . . .

She pushed herself onto the seat. Cora still pulled at the oars, but the boat resembled a kid's wading pool, water nearly to its brim. Finley and Vivian were both on their knees, wildly hurling away handsful while more water splashed in over the sides.

Abilene twisted around. No lightning at the moment, but she could see the diving raft through the downpour.

Twenty feet away? Thirty?

She turned back to Cora. 'We aren't gonna make it!'

Cora kept straining at the oars as if she hadn't heard.

We'll have to swim for it, Abilene thought. Shit!

She knew they were all capable of swimming such a short distance, even in such rough water. But if it came to that, they'd lose the shotgun and ax.

If we could dump some excess baggage . . .

She tugged her shoes off. Reaching down behind the seat, she pulled the anchor rope. She found its end, drew it around her waist, and knotted it. 'Hang in!' she shouted, then threw herself overboard.

She plunged head first into the lake, thrashed to the surface and trod water for a moment to get her bearings. She was beside the boat, close to its bow. Turning, she spotted the raft. She swam for it. The waves shoved her upward, dropped her, tipped her from side to side. Then the slack of the rope gave out.

The line tugged at her waist, pressed into her groin. She felt as if she'd been yanked to a dead halt. But she kept on jabbing out her arms and drawing them back, kept on kicking in spite of the taut rope wedged between her legs.

She raised her head. The near end of the raft appeared to be no more than ten or twelve feet away.

She switched to the breast stroke and saw the distance close a bit.

We're not stopped dead, she thought.

The boat seemed to be moving along sluggishly behind her.

She watched the raft as she struggled toward it. The platform was high out of the water, pitching about on the churning lake. She supposed it must be anchored to the bottom with chains. The corner on the right was higher than the lefthand one, tipped upward somewhat because of the sunken oil drum kitty-corner from it.

Attached to the right side of the raft was a wooden ladder.

Abilene swam for it, towing the boat.

The boat seemed to be moving along better, now, the rope no longer straining at her waist or digging into her groin.

She swam alongside the raft, reached out and grabbed a rung of the ladder.

Clinging to it, she looked back. Cora still sat in its center, tugging at the oars. Only the gunwales remained above the water line, and every wave flung more water into the nearly submerged craft.

Finley and Vivian weren't aboard.

They were stretched out side by side behind the boat, holding onto its stern, kicking.

They'd been pushing it along while Abilene towed it by the rope.

Glancing over her shoulder, Cora shouted, 'Tie it up!'

Chapter Twenty-eight
Belmore Girls

'To us,' Cora toasted.

'Hear hear,' said the others. They clinked their champagne glasses and drank.

It was a warm June evening three days after graduation. It was to be their last night together in their rented apartment on Spring Street.

Tomorrow, Abilene and Harris would be heading north to Portland where they intended to share an apartment while she embarked on her graduate studies in English literature. Helen would be going home to Coos Bay, where she planned to stay with her parents through the summer. Cora and Tony would embark for Denver to pursue teaching credentials. Vivian and Finley would be travelling together to Los Angeles, Vivian to seek out jobs as an actress and model, Finley to study film-making at the Institute for Creative Cinema which had accepted her application on the strength of her 'Mess Hall' videotape.

As Abilene sipped her champagne, she felt a lump in her throat. She was glad to be moving on, excited by what lay ahead. But God, she would miss her friends.

'We've *got* to stay in touch,' she said.

'Yeah,' Helen said. 'You're the best friends I've ever had. I don't know what I'm gonna do . . .' Her voice broke.

Abilene squeezed her shoulder. 'You'll do fine.'

'I'll miss you all so much.'

'Hey, let's not get all weepy,' Finley said. 'This ain't a wake, for Christsake.'

'I know, I know, but . . .'

'Here's to all the great times we've had,' Cora said, hoisting her glass again.

'They're all over,' Helen muttered. 'We'll probably never see each other again.'

'Sure we will,' Abilene told her. 'Hell, you're gonna come to my wedding, aren't you?'

'Hickok, you're such an optimist.'

'We'll get married one of these days. And all of you'd better show up.'

'There'll be plenty of chances to get together,' Cora said, nodding at Helen.

'It won't be the same.'

'Everything changes,' Abilene said.

From the hurt look on Helen's face, that wasn't what she wanted to hear.

'I mean, that's life. But the changes don't have to be bad. There's no law that says we can't visit each other from time to time and . . .'

'I've got an idea,' Vivian said. She'd been sitting in silence, staring into her drink.

'Hold it,' Finley said. 'We'd better jot this down for posterity. Better yet . . .' She hopped up from her cushion on the floor, hurried across the room, and snatched her video camera off the dining table.

'Give it a break,' Cora protested.

'No, come on,' Vivian said. 'We aren't dressed.'

'Sure you are. Unlike the *first* time I taped you.'

'You've gotten rid of that, haven't you?' Abilene asked.

'Surely you jest.' She raised the viewfinder to her eye and started taping. 'Just act natural, babes. You look great. What was your big idea, Viv?'

Vivian, in a sheer black nightgown, frowned at the lens and covered her breasts with the arm that wasn't busy holding her champagne glass.

'Don't worry. Nobody'll ever see it but us.'

'So you say,' Cora remarked. She wore only an oversized T-shirt.

Helen, sitting on a sofa and dressed in a low-cut nightie, reached out and grabbed a corduroy pillow and clutched it to her chest.

At least I'm okay, Abilene thought. She was wearing pajamas. They belonged to Harris. The morning after her first night with him, she'd worn the bottoms and he'd worn the top while she made instant coffee in the motel room. By the time they'd gotten around to drinking the coffee, it had been cold.

Later, she'd packed the pajamas in her overnight bag and he'd laughed. She'd had them ever since.

Finley, wandering about the room and taping everyone from different angles, said, 'One of these days, we'll get together and watch all this stuff and have a few laughs.'

'Sure,' Helen muttered.

'Which brings us to my idea,' Vivian said. 'Remember? My idea?'

Finley zoomed in on her. 'Spit it out.'

'Well . . .'

Finley turned the camera away to catch Cora.

Cora, on her knees, scurried about the floor and poured more champagne into all the glasses.

Vivian waited until hers was full. She took a drink, then said, 'Anyway. You know that play, *Same Time Next Year*?'

'A movie,' Finley corrected, swinging the camera toward Vivian.

597

'It was a play first.'

'I haven't seen it,' Helen said.

'You wouldn't have liked it,' Abilene told her. 'Nobody gets chopped up.'

Helen almost smiled.

'Anyway,' Vivian continued, 'it's about this man and woman who fall in love. They can't marry each other, so they meet at a certain place once each year.'

'Hence the title,' Finley said.

'No matter what's going on in their regular lives, they always show up and spend this one weekend together. Anyway, here's the thing. *We* could do something like that.'

A smile spread across Helen's face. 'Hey, that'd be neat.'

'That's a *great* idea!' Cora blurted.

'Yeah!' Abilene said. 'We'd have to really *do* it, though.'

'Yeah,' Cora agreed. 'No matter what. Jobs, families. Nothing can get in the way. Once a year, we meet somewhere. Just the five of us.'

'Right,' Vivian said. 'No husbands, no loverboys, none of that.'

'They'd put a cramp in our style,' Cora said.

Helen laughed.

'We'll watch all the old tapes of our adventures,' Finley said.

'Whoa!' Abilene gasped. 'In that case, no husbands for sure!'

'And we'll have *new* adventures,' Finley added. 'New and daring exploits.'

Cora smirked. 'Like what?'

'I don't know. We'll think of things.'

'I know,' Abilene said. 'We can take turns thinking up exploits. Each year, it'll be someone else's turn to arrange the whole thing. We'll all agree on whatever weekend . . .'

'What kind of adventure can you have over a weekend?' Finley complained. 'Maybe we should try for a whole week.'

'A week it is,' Cora said.

'This is great,' Helen said. She polished off her champagne, tossed her pillow aside and leaned toward Cora with her glass. Cora crawled over and filled her up. 'All of a sudden, it's like everything isn't over anymore. You know? This is great.'

'Who goes first?' Cora asked, and raised the bottle to her mouth.

'The whole thing's Vivian's idea,' Abilene pointed out.

Vivian, smiling pleasantly, eased backward. She stretched out on the floor, glass resting on her belly, and crossed her feet at the ankles. 'So I get to go first?'

'Right,' Abilene said.

'We'll all do whatever I want?'

'Within reason.'

'Fuck that,' Finley said. 'A choice oughta be a choice. It's her adventure. We all have to do *whatever* she wants, whether we like it or not.'

'A heavy responsibility,' Vivian said, smiling at the ceiling.

Cora popped a cork from a fresh bottle. It shot past Helen's face. 'Be careful. You'll put someone's eye out.' She shut one eye and started giggling.

'I don't know,' Vivian said.

'You've got all year to think about it,' Abilene told her.

'And please,' Finley said, 'try to come up with something that won't bore us all to death.'

Chapter Twenty-nine
Vivian's Choice

A year and two weeks after graduation from Belmore University, on the fifth night after their arrival in New York City, they stepped out of the Dunsinane Theater on Bleecker Street after a performance of *Mother Courage*.

Vivian led them to the left.

'Are you sure we shouldn't be going the other way?' Cora asked. 'This doesn't seem right.'

'It's not,' Finley said. 'It's left.'

'I don't want to get lost again,' Helen said. 'My feet won't take it.'

'The subway entrance is just a couple of blocks from here.'

'I sure hope so.'

It seemed to Abilene that Helen had spent most of the week complaining about her feet. With good reason, she supposed. Vivian had taken them *everywhere*.

They'd roamed Macy's, Saks, Bloomingdale's, F.A.O. Schwartz, and countless other stores. They'd gone to the Trump Tower and the Metropolitan Museum of Art.

They'd explored Grand Central Station, astonished by the underground world of shops and tunnels that seemed to go on forever, but appalled by the squalor, unnerved by the filthy beggars who seemed to lurk everywhere, and finally so overwhelmed by the smell of the place that they had rushed for fresh air.

They'd explored Central Park.

They'd taken the NBC tour at Rockefeller Plaza and later gone to the top of the Empire State Building.

They'd spent a day at Coney Island, not only trying out some of the rides but hiking far along the beach and spending a long time on a pier where they were fascinated by the assortment of people fishing, throwing out crab traps baited with Kentucky Colonel, cooking meat on grills they'd apparently brought from home, and hawking their barbecued specialities along with such things as ice cream, sodas, beer, hard liquor (in tiny 'airline' bottles kept out of sight under a table) and firecrackers.

Except for subway rides to such distant places as Coney Island, the Battery and Greenwich Village, they'd walked everywhere they went. Throughout, Finley carried her video camera (at least during daylight hours), Vivian and Cora seemed tireless and Helen complained about her sore feet and Abilene didn't complain but sat down every chance she got.

Nightfall had provided some relief, but not much.

They often hiked around the Times Square area for blocks in search of a 'neat place to eat' before deciding on Nathan's or Sbarro or a Mama Leone's or Houlihans.

Then they'd be off, on foot, for the theater district. The plays had been great; you could sit down for a couple of hours.

Then they'd be up again. And wandering 42nd Street to look again at the gawdy display windows and street artists and musicians and break-dancers and tourists and beggars and cripples and cops on horseback and guys peddling wrist-watches.

At last, they would head back for the Hilton, stopping along the way at a small grocery market to pick up sodas, beer and snacks. Finally, they would arrive at their suite, get out of their shoes, get into their nightclothes, and gather in one or the other of the connecting rooms to sit around and drink and eat and chat and moan and laugh for a while before calling it a night.

Today had been the worst, Abilene thought as she walked with the others along MacDougal Street.

After sleeping in late, they'd taken a subway to the Battery, gone over to the Statue of Liberty and stood in line for two hours before entering the statue. Abilene supposed that the climb to the top was the most tiring – and scary – part of their Big Apple adventure. After making their way up flight after flight of 'normal' stairs, they'd come to a circular staircase so steep and narrow that she had almost chickened out. Though Helen had muttered, 'Oh my God,' at the base of the twisting iron stairs, she'd gone ahead and started up, Abilene behind her. The single-file line moved slowly upward. There were long pauses. The air was hot and stuffy. Abilene felt as if she were suffocating. She gasped for breath and blinked sweat from her eyes and wished she could turn back. There was no way to turn back. What happens to people who pass out trying this? She wondered. Is there a rescue team, or what?

The iron railings, because of their steep angle, were so low at her sides that it seemed quite possible to tumble over one. Again and again, she imagined herself going dizzy, rolling over the lefthand rail, and plummeting straight down the center opening.

If Helen can make it, I can, she kept telling herself. And at last she followed Helen into the crown. It had no openings. It had no fresh air. It was even hotter, stuffier than the stairway. All she wanted was out. Nudged on by those behind her, she filed past the tiny windows. Glanced through glass so dirty or scratched that it made a foggy blur of the harbor and the New York skyline. Kept on moving and started downward.

The very best thing about the Statue of Liberty, she found, was escaping from it.

While they rested in the park, Abilene had looked into Finley's camera and said, 'Now I know all about those "tired, huddled masses yearning to breathe free." They're the poor slobs climbing to the top.'

After the ferry ride back to the Battery, Vivian had suggested they walk over to the World Trade Center. 'It's only a few blocks from here.'

'Kiss my sweaty butt,' Helen had told her.

'Thank you,' Abilene had said.

Skipping the World Trade Center, they'd taken the subway back into mid-town, gotten off at the wrong stop, and hiked for an hour before reaching the Hilton.

A brief rest, a change of clothes, and they'd soon been off again. This time, to Greenwich Village for dinner and the Brecht play.

They'd gotten off the subway at the Houston Street station.

Then they'd gone exploring, wandering up and down narrow streets, going into clothes stores and bookshops, walking past sidewalk cafes, scanning menus in restaurant windows. Somehow, they'd found themselves across the street from a park. After checking her guidebook, Vivian had identified it as Washington Square.

Joining a crowd at one end of the park, they'd spent a while watching a young man juggle machetes while riding a unicycle.

Then they'd gone back to the maze of streets where they'd seen so many restaurants. Some of the eating places looked too crowded, others too formal, none just right. So they'd kept on walking, discovering streets they'd missed before, always on the lookout for a 'neat place' to have dinner.

Helen was the one who found it.

'My God!' she'd gasped. 'We've gotta eat here! We've gotta!'

It was an Italian restaurant called 'Grandpa's.' In the window near its entrance was taped a newspaper clipping: an article about the restaurant with a photograph of its owner.

Its owner was Al Lewis, 'Grandpa Munster' from the old TV show.

So in they'd gone, and Al Lewis had greeted them at the door. He wasn't in costume. He wore trousers, a plaid shirt and a ball cap instead of his Munster outfit. But Helen had seemed no less excited about meeting him. She'd blushed and searched her purse for paper and shyly asked for his autograph.

All through dinner, she'd stared at him.

On their way out, Vivian stopped and asked him directions to the Dunsinane theater. While he'd explained how to get there, Helen had watched him in awestruck silence.

'That was so great,' she'd said when they were outside.

'The high point of the trip, huh?'

'Pretty near.'

'Better than the Statue of Liberty?'

She'd rolled her eyes upward and groaned.

Mother Courage, with actors wandering into the audience and shouting in people's faces, had seemed nearly as unnerving to Abilene as the winding staircase in the Statue. She was glad when it ended.

'So where *is* the subway station?' Helen asked.

Finley grinned back at her. 'It must've moved.'

'It's gotta be around here someplace.' Vivian stopped at a

corner, glanced at the street sign, and raised her guidebook close to her face.

Abilene looked up at the sign and found herself grinning. 'Hey, it's Mulberry Street. And to think that I saw it.'

'I don't see it,' Vivian murmured.

'What?' Cora asked.

'Mulberry Street.'

'And to think that I saw it,' Abilene repeated.

'What are you talking about, Hickok?'

'Mulberry Street. Dr Seuss.'

'Give us a break.'

'I can't find it on the map,' Vivian said.

'It's gotta be on the map,' Abilene told her. 'It's famous.'

'You try and find it.'

Vivian handed the guide book to Abilene. In the center of one page was a small map of Greenwich Village. She squinted at it under the streetlight. 'Well, there's MacDougal.'

'But we're on Mulberry. Where the hell is Mulberry Street?'

She kept looking at the map. Streets went every which way, going off at odd angles, ending, resuming elsewhere. She found no Mulberry Street. Finally, she shook her head. 'I sure don't see it.'

'Look for Broome,' Cora suggested. 'We're at Broome and Mulberry.'

She studied the map, searching for Broome. 'It's not here either.'

'Oh man,' Helen moaned.

Vivian grimaced. 'I think we might've gotten off the map.'

'Then where the hell are we?' Abilene flipped the page over and found a small map of the East Village. 'Could we be in the East Village?' she asked.

'You got me.'

'Jesus,' Helen said.

'These street names don't look very familiar,' she said, and a drop of water hit the page. She lifted her face and a cool drop splashed her forehead. 'I hate to mention it, folks. I think it's starting to rain.'

'I was hoping that was just a little bird shitting on my head,' Finley said.

'Just some drizzle,' Cora said. 'It won't kill us. Let's keep walking. We're bound to come to a main road before long. If we can't find a subway station, we'll get a taxi.'

Abilene handed the guidebook back to Vivian. 'So which should we take?' she asked. 'Mulberry or Broome?'

'Either way, we're lost,' Helen said.

'Mulberry hasn't gotten us anywhere,' Cora said. 'Let's try Broome.'

As they crossed the road, the raindrops began to fall more rapidly. By the time they reached the other side, the drizzle had turned into a shower.

Walking backward at the head of the group, Finley stretched out her arms and said, 'Could be worse.'

'Yeah?' Abilene asked. 'We're lost and it's pouring.'

'And my feet are killing me,' Helen said.

'At least we haven't been mugged.'

'The night's still young,' Abilene told her.

Finley laughed and whirled around.

'Where are all those damn taxis when you need them?' Cora said.

A few cars were passing on the street, headlights glaring on the slick pavement, tires swishing. There didn't seem to be a cab among them. Nor were there any shops or restaurants in sight where they might take shelter and ask directions – or phone for a cab. There were only apartment buildings with dark entryways.

'I don't like this,' Helen said.

'Where *is* everyone?' Abilene said.

'Staying out of the rain,' Finley called back.

'We're bound to find a taxi sooner or later,' Vivian said. 'Or a subway station.'

As they walked past a recessed entryway, a derelict wrapped in a blanket raised his head and yelled, 'Hey!' Abilene's stomach lurched. She hurried past him and looked back. He was out of sight.

'Wanta ask *him* for directions?' Finley asked.

Cora elbowed her and she laughed.

'This is getting a little too hairy for me,' Abilene said.

'Just consider it an adventure. That's what we're here for, right? Adventure!'

'Getting lost wasn't what I had in mind,' Vivian said.

'Hell, it's our last night in the Big Apple. At least it'll be a memorable one.'

'If we live through it,' Helen said.

'At least you can die happy,' Finley told her. 'You met Grandpa Munster.'

'Uh-oh,' Vivian said. 'Here comes someone.'

Walking up the sidewalk toward them was a slim man dressed in jeans. His shirt was off. He walked briskly, swinging his shirt beside him.

At least he's not staggering, Abilene thought.

'Everyone just stay calm,' Cora advised. 'If he tries anything, I'll handle it.'

As he neared them, he slowed his pace. He was a young man, rather handsome. 'Are you ladies all right?' he asked.

'We're not sure where we are,' Vivian told him.

Nodding and frowning, he stopped in front of her. His long hair was pulled back in a pony tail. His wet torso gleamed in the streetlight, and Abilene could see raindrops splashing off his shoulders. 'I wondered about that,' he said. 'If you knew where you were, you wouldn't be here. This isn't the best of neighborhoods, you know. You're heading straight into the Bowery.'

'Oh dandy,' Finley said.

'We're trying to get back to our hotel,' Vivian explained.

'Where are you staying?'

'The Hilton.'

'You aren't going to get there this way.'

'We've been looking for a subway station.'

'You won't find one around here. I guess the best bet'd be Canal and Broadway.'

'Where the hell is that?' Cora asked.

'Not far, but . . . maybe I'd better take you, make sure you get there in one piece.'

'That bad?' Cora asked.

'I get scared and I live here. And I'm not a pretty young woman.'

'We don't want to take you out of your way,' Vivian told him.

'That's okay. I was just on my way home anyway. My conscience'd bother me if I let you go on by yourselves.'

'It's mighty nice of you,' Vivian said.

I hope that's what it is, Abilene thought. No telling what he might really be up to.

He's probably just a decent guy who wants to help, she told herself.

But you never know. This is New York.

'I'm Wayne, by the way.' Cracking a smile, he added, 'I'll be your tour guide for this evening's festivities.'

They introduced themselves, and he nodded a pleasant greeting to each of them.

'First on the agenda, let's get you turned around so you're heading out of harm's way.' They parted to let him through, then accompanied him back up Broome Street.

Vivian and Cora walked at his sides, the others following close behind. His wet pony tail hung swaying at the nape of his neck. His jeans hugged his hips so low that the crevice of his buttocks showed and Abilene had doubts that he was wearing underpants.

Finley's kind of guy, she thought.

'How'd you manage to end up on the Lower East Side?' he asked, looking over his shoulder. Probably so everyone could hear, but his question seemed directed at Helen.

'We thought we were in Greenwich Village,' she answered.

He smiled. 'That might be where you started.'

'Map-girl blew it,' Finley told him.

'I guess you're tourists.'

Cora laughed.

'Obviously,' Vivian said.

'Where you from?'

As they walked along, they told Wayne where they were currently living, how they'd gone to college together and come to New York City as an excuse for a get-together.

'We're planning to meet somewhere every year,' Helen explained. 'This year, it was Vivian's turn to pick. She's into acting, so obviously she chose New York. We've been to . . . what? Five shows? The others were, you know, downtown, but tonight we came out to the Village. It seems like all we've done is go to plays and walk.'

Abilene grinned at her. She'd rarely found Helen so talkative with a stranger.

'Next year, it'll be Cora's turn to pick.'

'You won't be seeing us back here,' Cora said. 'That's a guarantee.'

'You don't like New York?' Wayne asked her.

'It's an armpit.'

'Come on,' Vivian protested. 'It's great!'

'Great if you like traffic and crowds and honking horns and jackhammers, weirdos and winos everywhere.'

Mention of the wino made Abilene realize they'd already walked past the derelict who'd called out from the entryway their first time by. She hadn't even noticed. It does help, she decided, having an escort. She found that she didn't even mind the rain so much, now that Wayne was leading them back to civilization.

'And have you ever tried to breathe the air in Grand Central Station? It smells like exhaust.'

'At least,' Finley added.

'I think New York's terrific,' Helen said. 'I've loved every minute.'

That's a hoot, Abilene thought.

She must really like this guy.

While they descended the stairway to the subway station, Wayne put on his shirt. At long last, Abilene thought. Though she had appreciated being escorted back to civilization, and Wayne seemed like a nice enough fellow, she'd found it odd that he had kept his shirt off while walking along with the five of them. Particularly because of the way his jeans hung so low. Was he deliberately showing off his body to them?

As he slipped into his shirt, Finley leaned close to Abilene and whispered, 'Aw, shucks.'

Helen, two stairs below them, looked back and gave Finley a chiding glance.

They gathered around Wayne at the bottom of the stairway. Vivian extended a hand to him and said, 'Thanks so much. I don't know what we would've done without you.'

Smiling, he squeezed her hand. 'My pleasure. It's not every night I get to help out damsels in distress. I think I'd better stick with you for a while, though. You get some pretty strange customers on the subway, especially at this hour.'

'That's very nice of you, but . . .'

'We'll be fine,' Cora interrupted. By the look in her eyes, Abilene could see that she was suspicious of the offer. 'But thanks so much for getting us here.'

'I'll stay with you. At least till we get to your stop. Just in case. I really don't mind.'

'It's not necessary,' Cora said.

'It sounds like a good idea to me,' Helen said. She looked at the others for support. 'You know? You hear about stuff happening on the subways, and it's after midnight, and . . . if Wayne thinks he should stay with us for a while, I'm all for it.'

'I'm only concerned about your safety, ladies.'

'But you've already done so much,' Vivian protested. 'We can't ask you to ride all the way back with us.'

'I insist. Really.'

'Besides,' Finley said, 'it'll give him a break from the rain. *I* sure wouldn't want to rush right back out there.'

'Oh, I like the rain. But I don't like the idea of you girls riding alone at this time of night.'

'Let us at least buy your tokens,' Vivian said.

He laughed softly. 'Fine. If you like.'

Vivian, keeper of the tokens, searched her purse for those she'd bought for the return trip. She passed them around. As

Wayne followed her to the glass-enclosed booth, Cora shook her head.

'I know,' Abilene said.

'What's the problem?' Helen asked. 'He's just being nice.'

'Maybe too nice,' Abilene said.

'You worry too much, Hickok.'

She frowned at Finley. 'We don't know anything about this guy.'

'He's got a nice bod on him.'

'We'd be lost in the Bowery if it weren't for him,' Helen pointed out.

'Right,' Cora muttered.

They followed Vivian and Wayne to the turnstiles, dropped their tokens into slots, and passed through.

On the station platform, Abilene decided that having Wayne along might not be such a bad idea after all. A wino wrapped in a filthy coat was curled up on a bench, apparently asleep, a couple of over-stuffed bags at his feet. He wore mismatched tennis shoes and no socks. Near the far end of the platform three black teenagers were whispering and casting glances in their direction. She wondered if they had screwdrivers with sharpened points. She wondered if Wayne had any kind of weapon. She wondered if she would be worrying about such things if the three young men had been white.

Soon, a train came roaring into the station. They boarded it.

The wino stayed on his bench. The three black kids entered a different car.

Except for an old man reading a newspaper, their car was deserted.

Two stops later, the old man left. Nobody else entered.

Finley, hanging onto an upright pole and smiling down at Wayne, said, 'Sure are a lot of strange customers in here.'

'Guess it's our lucky night,' he said.

Helen patted his thigh. 'I'm glad you're with us, anyway. I feel so much safer.'

For the rest of the ride, nobody else entered their car.

They stepped out at the Times Square station.

'We know our way from here,' Cora said as they gathered in the rain at the top of the stairs.

'I've come this far,' Wayne explained. 'I might as well see you safely to the hotel.'

'It's only a few blocks. We'll be fine.'

'No, really. I don't mind.' He started off, Helen staying close to his side.

Christ! Abilene thought. Why won't someone tell him to go home?

'What the hell's he up to?' Cora muttered.

'I don't know,' Abilene said. 'But I don't like it.'

'He's just being helpful,' Vivian said.

'You always were too trusting,' Cora told her.

'It looks like the guy's adopting us,' Finley said.

'How are we gonna get rid of him?' Abilene asked.

'I'll take care of it,' Cora said.

Wayne opened the door for them, followed them into the lobby of the Hilton and walked with them to the elevator bank.

Elevator doors were open, cars waiting.

Nobody entered one.

'Well,' Vivian said, once again shaking Wayne's hand. 'Thanks so much.'

'Glad to be of service.'

'I don't know what we would've done without you,' Helen told him. She offered her hand. Wayne took it, squeezed it and let go.

Cora opened her purse. She took out her billfold, saying, 'We'd like to give you a little something for all your trouble.' She plucked out a ten-dollar bill.

Wayne held up both hands to ward it off. 'No, please. I don't want your money. Gosh. Put it away.'

Cora blushed. 'Please. Take it. If nothing else, use it for a taxi home.'

'The subway's fine.' He patted a pocket of his jeans. 'Already got my token.'

Cora put the money away. 'Okay, if you're sure. Anyway, thanks so much.'

'Yeah, you were a lifesaver,' Finley said.

'Thank you very much,' Abilene added, realizing she had misjudged him. 'You really helped us out.'

'You're all very welcome. Now, I guess I'd better . . .' He started to turn away, then stopped and grimaced. 'You don't suppose I could . . . use your facilities before I start back?'

Uh-oh, Abilene thought.

'I really hate to ask, but . . .'

'I'm sure there's a john here in the lobby you could use,' Cora said.

'Yeah. Probably so. Okay, I'll . . .'

'For Godsake!' Helen blurted. Scowling at Cora, she grabbed Wayne's arm and pulled him toward an elevator. 'Of course you can use our john. Come on.'

'I don't want to impose.'

'You're not imposing.' She pulled him into the elevator.

The others stepped aboard.

Helen jabbed a button for the twenty-fourth floor.

The doors slid silently shut and the elevator began to rise.

'I really do appreciate this,' Wayne said. He was leaning back against the rear wall.

Cora turned to face him. 'I'm sorry, but you'll have to use the toilet in the lobby.'

He frowned.

'Cora!'

'I mean it, Helen. Wayne's been very nice to us and helpful and everything, but he's not coming into our rooms. That's final.'

'It's not fair!'

'I only want to use your toilet,' Wayne said. 'It'll only take a minute, then I'll be gone.'

'I'm sorry.'

'We could at least vote on it,' Helen said.

'We aren't taking any Goddamn vote,' Abilene snapped, stepping close to Cora's side. 'We've gotta be sensible, and it's stupid to let a stranger into our rooms.' Looking Wayne in the eyes, she said in a softer tone, 'I'm sorry.'

'What do you think I'm going to do, attack you all or something?'

'We just don't want to take any chances,' Vivian told him.

'Sorry,' Finley added.

As the elevator stopped, Wayne shook his head. 'You gals are sure something.'

The doors rolled open. Cora glanced over her shoulder and punched the button for the lobby. 'Just stay here. We don't want any trouble.'

'This is the thanks I get, huh?'

Cora, backing away, pressed her shoulder against the side of the doorway to keep the doors open. Abilene, Vivian and

Finley stepped out. Helen stayed at the rear of the elevator. She folded her arms across her chest. She shook her head. 'It isn't right,' she said.

'Damn it, Helen.'

'I'm not budging.'

'Come *on*!'

Wayne turned his eyes to Helen. He slipped his arm across her shoulders, and she looked at him. 'I'm afraid your friends aren't going to give in on this. You'd better go with them, now. But thanks for trusting me.' He squeezed her shoulder, then withdrew his arm.

Helen, nodding, walked toward the opening. 'I think it stinks,' she muttered. As she approached, Cora moved out of the way. The doors slowly began to roll shut. Helen stepped out of the elevator. She looked back at Wayne.

'So long,' he said.

And she leaped through the gap between the doors.

'No!' Abilene gasped.

Cora rushed forward, but she wasn't quick enough. 'Shit!'

Abilene punched a finger against the call button. The plastic disk lit up, but the doors remained shut.

The lights above the elevator blinked from 23 to 22 to 21, marking the descent of Helen and Wayne. Below the twentieth floor, the elevator was an express to the lobby.

Abilene felt as if her stomach were dropping along with it.

'What're we gonna *do*?' Vivian asked.

'She'll be all right,' Finley said. From the look on her face, she didn't believe it.

'We should've let him use the john,' Abilene muttered.

'Don't be ridiculous,' Cora said. 'If we'd let him into the rooms, there's no telling what he might have done.'

'Maybe we ought to go down to the lobby,' Vivian

suggested. As she spoke, an elevator arrived. Its doors opened for those who had called it to this floor.

They all glanced over at it.

'We wouldn't get there in time,' Cora said, returning her gaze to the numbers above Helen's elevator. 'Whatever he's doing to her, he'll be finished by the time they reach the lobby.'

Abilene groaned.

'She wouldn't leave the hotel with him, would she?' Vivian asked.

'She's not that stupid,' Cora said.

Above the doors, the letter L lit up.

'What if he forces her to go with him?' Vivian asked.

'No way,' Cora said. 'All she'd have to do is yell, security'd take care of him.'

'I sure hope you're right,' Abilene said.

The L remained bright.

'What the hell's . . . ?'

It went dark.

They waited. They didn't talk.

Please, Abilene thought. Please, Helen's gotta be on it. She's gotta be all right. Please.

Finally, 20 blinked on and off, followed by 21, 22, 23. Then the 24 lit up.

The doors slid apart.

Helen, crouched in a corner, looked at them with tears in her eyes. Her face was red and wet. Her hands were clutching her upraised knees. The back of her skirt shrouded the floor, baring the undersides of her thick, pale thighs.

Cora blocked the doors open and the others rushed inside.

Though they asked if she was okay, asked what Wayne had done to her, Helen only shook her head and sobbed. They lifted her, and she staggered with them out of the elevator.

'Let's get her to the rooms,' Cora said, leading the way. 'I'll call security.'

'No,' Helen gasped. 'Don't.'

'Do you need a doctor?' Abilene asked, hugging Helen against her side as they rushed her along.

'No. No!'

'Did he rape you?' Finley asked.

'Jesus, *you people!*'

'What the hell did he do to you?' Cora demanded.

'He . . . he kissed me,' Helen choked out through her sobs. 'He *kissed* me. He was so sweet and . . . and you were all so mean to him.'

Chapter Thirty

Lashing the anchor rope to an upright of the raft's ladder, Abilene shouted, 'The gun!'

Cora let go of the oars. They were lifted out of their locks and carried away on the waves as she knelt in the sinking boat. She dragged the shotgun out of the water and swung it by the barrels.

Abilene caught hold of the shoulder stock. Clamping it against her side, she scooted on her rump to the highest corner of the platform. She grabbed the edge and braced herself with her feet flat against the slippery boards.

Cora came up the ladder. On hands and knees, she scurried over the lurching raft and flopped beside Abilene.

She hooked an arm over the side to hold herself in place.

Moments later, Vivian sprawled beside her.

Finley climbed the ladder. Smiling, she called out, 'No sweat!' She sat down, her back to the others, and wrapped her legs around one of the uprights.

Abilene slumped forward against her knees.

We made it! Thank God. We're all safe. Not quite ashore, but not in any real danger.

Peering through the heavy shroud of rain, she could make out the end of the dock.

Nice to be there instead of here.

But the span of lake separating them from the dock was a gray, flinging turmoil.

Better not to risk it if we don't have to.

No risk, no fun. She wondered if any of them would ever express that notion again.

That's the idea that got us into this mess. We could've all drowned.

And she remembered, suddenly, that Helen was dead.

Still in the shower room.

And she felt guilty when grief didn't overwhelm her. She supposed that she must be just too thankful that the rest of them were still alive. If she'd been any less quick to grab Batty's arm, Finley might be dead now, a knife in her back. If the boat had capsized in the middle of the lake . . .

It didn't. We're okay.

Shouldn't have gone back to Batty's.

But it turned out all right. And we got the gun.

She swung the shotgun out from under her arm and lowered it in front of her. As she wedged it into the space between her belly and thighs, the rain stopped pouring down.

'Hey!' Finley called. Twisting around, she turned an open hand toward the sky.

Vivian and Cora rolled over, sat up.

A few more drops fell as the wind dwindled. Soon, the raft settled to a gentle, rocking motion.

As the clouds scooted away, the sun came down so bright that Abilene had to squint. She watched the dark thunderheads fly over the tree tops beyond the shore. Though she could see rain falling into the forest, it no longer rushed down in a torrent. She saw no lightning, heard no thunder.

Almost as if the storm was meant just for us, she thought. Almost as if Batty had created it to drown us.

Ridiculous.

Turning around, she peered across the brilliant water. She spotted some willows along the distant shore, but couldn't figure out which might be the one below Batty's cabin. There was no sign of Batty.

'Well,' Cora said. 'Shall we get going?'

'What about this?' Abilene asked, lifting the shotgun. 'I don't think we can swim with it.'

'We aren't gonna leave it here,' Finley said. 'Not after all we went through to get it.'

'Will it still fire?' Cora asked.

'A little water shouldn't hurt it,' Vivian said. 'I'm not sure about the shells, though.'

Finley dug a hand into her pocket. She pulled out one of the bright red cartridges and rolled it between her fingers as she studied it. 'Looks like the thing's plastic or something. Whatever, it seems watertight.'

'Okay,' Cora said. 'We take the shotgun.' Standing up, she plucked the clinging seat of her shorts away from her rump. She scanned the water. Pointed.

Abilene saw an oar floating on the swells. It bobbed gently, its shaft rubbing against a piling at the end of the dock.

'Back in a second,' Cora said, and dived off the raft.

'Anybody feel like diving for the ax?' Finley asked.

'Be my guest,' Vivian said. 'I don't want it. I'd rather not even have to look at it again.'

'Are you the one who nailed the pussycat?'

'You didn't see?'

'I was otherwise occupied at the time. But I noticed the aftermath. You really . . .'

'Stop, okay? I don't want to hear about it.'

'The cat had it coming,' Abilene pointed out. To Finley she said, 'If you're going down for the ax, see if you can find my shoes. They might still be in the boat.'

'Just leave the ax,' Vivian muttered.

'It might come in handy,' Abilene said. 'We could haul it up with the anchor rope.'

'Viv doesn't want it. *I* don't want it. Do you want it?'

'I've got Batty's knife,' she said. 'I suppose I can get along without my shoes.'

'Shouldn't have taken them off.'

'I try not to go swimming in them.'

Their attention turned to Cora as she splashed closer, pushing the oar along in front of her. Finley lay down beside the ladder. She grabbed the oar and pulled it onto the raft.

Still in the water, Cora said, 'Let me have a knife.'

Finley shoved the oar over to Vivian, then pulled her knife and handed it down.

Standing up for a better view, Abilene saw Cora duck below the surface. The taut anchor line wobbled, then went slack. A moment later, Cora came up. She held the knife in her teeth while she plucked open the knot securing the rope to the ladder.

She brought the section of rope onto the raft, sawed it in half, and used the two pieces to bind the shotgun to the oar.

'That should do the job nicely,' she said.

'Do you think we should bother with the ax?' Abilene asked. 'Nobody seems to want it, anyway. And hauling it up wouldn't be easy.'

'I guess we can get along without it,' Cora said. 'The shotgun's the main thing.' Dragging the oar and shotgun along at her side, she scooted down to the sunken corner of the raft and eased into the water. The oar and weapon slipped beneath the surface. Instead of disappearing from sight, however, they slowly rose.

As Vivian and Finley followed Cora into the lake, Abilene said, 'I'll be along in a minute.' She dived off the side of the platform, plunged into the lake and kicked her way toward the bottom. The rays of sunlight slanting down through the water were cloudy with swirling motes. So much debris had been stirred up by the storm that she couldn't see past the wrists of her outstretched arms. But the boat should be straight below her unless it had glided away after Cora cut the line.

Slimy tendrils suddenly slid over her hands, up her forearms. Weeds. As they lapped her face with slick tongues, she shut her eyes and groaned.

Screw the shoes.

She swept the weeds away from her face, arched her back, and kicked for the surface.

Moments later, she was sucking fresh air into her lungs. She trod water while she fought to catch her breath, then began to swim with an effortless breast stroke.

The others had already reached the end of the dock. Cora

mounted the ladder there. She waited on a low rung, water to her knees, while Finley cut through the ropes binding the shotgun to the oar and thrust the barrels up at her. Cora released the ladder with one hand, grabbed the weapon, and hoisted it onto the dock.

They were all sprawled on the weathered planks by the time Abilene climbed to the top of the ladder.

'No luck with the shoes?' Finley asked.

'Too many weeds down there.'

'I had to go barefoot last time,' Vivian pointed out. 'It wasn't that bad. The socks help.'

Abilene sank to the boards and lay back, folding her hands under her head. 'Somebody always ends up shoeless when we visit Batty,' she said. 'Ever notice that?'

'I managed to leave my tire iron behind,' Cora said.

'At the cabin?' Abilene asked.

'I put it on the floor when we sat down.'

'You would've lost it in the drink anyway,' Finley said.

'Probably.'

Abilene shut her eyes. There seemed to be no breeze, but the heat of the sun felt good. For now. Especially good was the feel of flat, motionless wood beneath her back. She heard the quiet lap of water against the pilings.

'I wonder if Batty'll come after us,' Vivian said.

Finley let out a soft laugh. 'Probably hot-footin' it through the woods right now, hot for our blood.'

'I doubt it,' Cora said.

'Too bad I missed.'

'You wouldn't want something like that on your conscience,' Vivian told her.

'Oh yeah? Try me. The weird fuck tried to kill me.'

'We were stealing from him,' Cora pointed out.

'Him? He had boobs. Did you see that? Shit. A hermaphrodite.'

'I really think he's gonna come after us,' Vivian said. 'Maybe we oughta get going.'

Abilene didn't want to move. She felt too weary, too comfortable sprawled on the dock with the sun warming her. Keeping her eyes shut, she said, 'Batty won't come after us. Probably too busy calling down another curse. Plans to let the forces of magic nail us.'

'I guess we're doomed,' Finley said.

Though Abilene couldn't help smiling at the remark, she was surprised to hear Cora and Vivian laugh.

'Next thing we know,' Finley went on, 'we'll have flocks of birds dive-bombing us.'

'More likely bats,' Abilene said.

'I think maybe we should get out of here,' Vivian said.

'Batty can hex us till hell freezes over,' Cora said. 'It's just bullshit.'

'That storm wasn't bullshit,' Abilene said.

'It was just a storm. Batty didn't *make* it happen.'

'You sure of that?'

'Christ, Abby.'

'More things in heaven and earth, Horatio . . .'

'That's not what I mean, anyway,' Vivian said. 'It's not curses and hexes that . . . I think maybe we should get out of here before something else happens. I mean, we could've drowned. Finley almost got stabbed. Cora, you got torn up by that damn cat. *I* killed it. We attacked that poor freak. Abilene broke his arm. Finley, you got so crazy you actually took a shot at him. It's all . . . out of hand.'

'It's out of hand, all right,' Finley muttered. 'Someone murdered Helen.'

In the silence that followed Finley's words, Abilene rolled over and pushed herself off the boards. She sat cross-legged, facing her friends. They were already sitting up.

'You want to *leave* leave?' she asked Vivian. 'Not just go back to the lodge, but . . . really leave? Hike out of here?'

Lower lip clamped between her teeth, Vivian nodded. Her green eyes looked solemn, thoughtful. 'Nothing we do is going to bring Helen back,' she said. 'If we stay . . . I'd rather get out of here alive, with all of you, than stay and try to get revenge. Look what just *happened* to us. Just so we could get our hands on a shotgun.'

'We got it,' Finley said.

'And a lot of good it did us when the boat sank.'

'I guess I go along with Viv,' Cora said. 'Hell, I was ready to walk a couple of hours ago until everyone talked me out of it. You included,' she told Vivian.

'Things have changed. I never realized . . .'

'We always got payback,' Finley said.

'Nothing ever got this heavy,' Cora said.

'Nobody ever butchered one of us before. I want to kill the son-of-a-bitch that did it to her. And now we've got the gun. All we need to do is stay the night and ambush the bastard when he shows up. A piece of cake.'

'Right,' Cora said. 'A piece of cake like stealing the gun from Batty. Let's just call it quits. I want the four of us to make it out of this alive.'

'What about you, Hickok?'

'I've had enough.'

'God! You're all gonna woos out on me?'

'You were one second from having a knife in your back.'

'Sure, but you . . .'

'You would've been as dead as Helen. If I'd been looking

625

the other way. If I hadn't been quick enough. It was just too close.'

'Like they say, close only counts in horseshoes and hand grenades.'

Nobody smiled at her remark.

'Besides,' Abilene continued, 'now we've got Batty on our case. I don't know if he's got any special powers. It sure did look like that storm was meant for us. But, regardless, I don't think he's gonna just leave us alone after all we did. He'll want to nail us one way or another. So we've got Batty *and* the killer to worry about.'

'Batty might *be* the killer,' Finley pointed out.

'It was that kid,' Vivian said.

'We'll never know if we don't stay and find out.'

'Then we'll never know,' Cora said. She wrapped a hand around the shotgun barrels and stood up. 'We'd better get started.'

'This really and truly sucks,' Finley muttered.

'It's the only smart thing to do,' Vivian said as she got to her feet.

'I don't feel good about it either,' Abilene said, forcing herself to stand. 'But we've already pushed our luck. Let's just hike out and let the police handle things.'

'A lot of good the cops'll do.'

'Come on, Finley,' Vivian said.

Finley frowned at the three of them. She shook her head. She muttered, 'Shit,' then stood up.

Cora in the lead, they started walking over the weathered planks of the old dock. Abilene felt tired and stiff and achy. It would've been nice to rest a while longer.

But, God, we've got a long way to go.

Miles and miles.

At least we're getting out of here.

At the end of all those miles, there would be a motel. Eventually. A motel. A cool, soft bed.

If only we'd done this *last* night.

Helen would still be . . .

A plank gave out beneath Cora's foot with a sound like a cracking whip and she gasped 'Fuck!' and pitched forward, her foot trapped. Her outthrust arms crashed the shotgun against the dock. Crying out in pain, she slammed down on top of it.

As the others rushed forward, she pulled her fingers out from under the gun. They were red and shaking. She wiggled them a bit, apparently to see whether they still worked. Otherwise, she didn't move.

She lay there, left leg thrown out to the side, right leg straight out behind her but twisted, caught at the ankle between two boards.

Vivian stepped over the gap, knelt at Cora's side, and stroked her head. 'Are you okay?'

'Just great.'

'You'll be all right.'

'Sure. *Damn* it!'

Abilene and Finley crouched over the opening. The heel of Cora's shoe was wedged under the board behind the one that had broken.

'We'll have it out in a second,' Abilene said.

'Be careful.'

Finley let out a huff. 'Yeah. God knows, we might get careless and bust it.'

'Very funny,' she muttered. She flinched when Abilene eased her knee sideways. She let out a long groan when Finley, holding on just above the top of the sock, pulled her foot out from under the edge of the plank and lifted it free.

627

Around Cora's ankle, the sock bulged like an inflated balloon.

Vivian, watching, wrinkled her nose.

Finley whistled and said, 'Nasty.'

Feeling sick, Abilene said, 'I hope it's just a sprain.'

'Don't bother,' Cora told her. 'It's broken.'

'So much for hiking to civilization,' Finley said.

Chapter Thirty-one

Cora rolled over slowly and sat up. She scowled at her misshapen ankle. 'Just great.'

'Does it hurt much?' Vivian asked.

'It hurts like shit.'

'*Now* what'll we do?' Abilene asked.

'Sit here and wait for it to heal,' Finley suggested.

Ignoring her, Cora said, 'I guess I can use the shotgun as a crutch. But we'd better start by stabilizing my damn ankle. I don't want it flopping around. We'll need some splints.'

Abilene stretched out flat on the pier. She looked down through the gap and saw the splintered ends of the plank that had snapped under Cora's weight. Still nailed at the top, the two sections of board drooped toward the water. She grabbed one, pulled it up, and jerked it from side to side. The nails squawked as they were torn from their moorings.

She stood the slat upright. With Batty's knife, she split it down the middle. She broke each board across her knee.

When she was done, she had two usable pieces of wood, each a couple of inches wide and nearly a foot in length.

'Perfect,' Cora said.

Grinning, Finley said, 'Hickok, you're a regular Boy Scout.'

Taking the makeshift splints from Abilene, Cora pressed them against both sides of her ankle. 'Now we need to bind them in place.'

'Belts,' Finley suggested. She lifted the hanging front of her shirt, looked down at her waistband, and frowned.

'You took it off to tie up Batty,' Abilene reminded her.

'Oh, yeah. So where the . . . jeez, did I leave it there?'

'I guess so.'

'Well, shit.'

'That's all right,' Abilene said. 'I've still got mine.' She unbuckled it.

As she pulled it from the loops of her denim skirt, Vivian said, 'Batty's got my shoes, Finley's belt . . .'

'Improving his wardrobe,' Finley said.

'Cora's tire iron. Anything of yours?' she asked, looking at Abilene.

'Not unless you count the water bottle.'

'The old bat's got quite a collection of stuff,' Finley said.

'That's what *I'm* thinking,' Vivian said.

'While you're thinking,' Abilene told her, 'give me your belt.'

Vivian unfastened it and pulled it from the loops of her white shorts. 'Can't he use that kind of stuff for casting spells? You know, personal possessions of people?' She passed the belt to Abilene.

'Here we go with hexes again,' Cora said.

As she buckled her belt to Vivian's, Abilene said, 'They use things like fingernail trimmings and hair. I've never heard of working black magic with someone's shoe . . . or tire iron.'

'It's not my tire iron, anyway,' Cora pointed out. 'Came from a rent-a-car, remember?'

'But you were carrying it.'

'Could we just forget all this *curse* shit? We've got real things to worry about, okay? Like, for instance, my ankle.'

'Should we leave your shoe on?' Abilene asked.

'Yeah. It'll give me some extra support.'

While Cora held the splints in place, Abilene wound the connected belts around them. She overlapped the leather end to secure it, then worked her way downward, wrapped the strap a couple of times under her heel, worked her way back up the ankle and shoved the end buckle between two tight layers of leather.

'Pretty good,' Cora said.

'It might come undone after a while, but . . .'

'As long as it'll get me back to the lodge. Plenty of stuff in the car we can use to bandage it better. Let's get moving.'

Vivian lifted Cora from behind while Finley and Abilene pulled her up by the arms. Braced on her left leg, she tucked the shoulder stock of the shotgun under her right armpit and put much of her weight on it. With Abilene supporting her from the other side, she turned around.

'We'll go ahead,' Vivian said. 'Try to step where we step.' She put an arm around Finley. Side by side, they matched strides and stepped together onto each plank. Abilene and Cora followed them, Abilene struggling to hold Cora steady, Cora hopping along on her good leg, the shotgun barrels clumping each time she planted them against the wood.

'You doing okay?' Cora asked.

'Just a little nervous.'

It's like walking across a frozen lake, Abilene thought. Feeling the ice give a little every time you step down. Hearing it groan and crackle. Knowing it's going to collapse. Waiting for the drop.

She was awash with sweat, panting for air, and muscles all over her body seemed to be twitching. Partly from the exertion, she thought. But mostly from fear, from expecting the drop.

Vivian and Finley, only a short distance in front of them, took one final stride and stepped ashore. They turned around to watch.

'You'll make it fine,' Vivian said.

'No sweat,' Finley added.

It felt to Abilene like a miracle when she finally placed a foot on solid ground.

'Let's make it to the top,' Cora gasped. 'Then we'll rest.'

Abilene grunted in response. Vivian and Finley stepped aside to make way for them. The ground was level for a few feet, then slanted upward toward the edge of the forest. The boards of the dock had been nearly dry, but the grass and weeds were still wet from the rain.

They struggled slowly up the embankment, being careful not to slip. The muzzles of the shotgun sank into the moist earth, and Cora had to yank them free after each step. Like Abilene, she was panting for air and drenched with sweat. Her right side, bare where Abilene clung to it above the armhole of her tank top, was hot and slippery. Her left arm felt like a massive weight across Abilene's shoulders.

They were halfway to the top when hands pushed against Abilene's rump. She couldn't look around, but realized that Finley and Vivian must've decided to help.

It's like when I was towing the boat, she thought.

Cora no longer felt quite so heavy leaning on her and the slope seemed less steep.

When she reached the top, a pinch through her denim skirt revealed the identity of her helper.

'Ouch! Fin, you creep!'

'Couldn't resist.'

The three of them lowered Cora to the ground. Then Abilene flopped down beside her. Though twigs and rocks poked against her, the grass felt cool and wonderful. She lay there, struggling for air.

'That was probably the worst of it,' Vivian said, sitting down nearby. 'The rest'll be pretty level.'

'It won't be easy,' Abilene said.

'I'll take over for you,' Vivian told her.

'Yeah,' Finley said. 'We can trade off every few minutes.'

'Who's gonna trade off with me?' Cora asked.

'You're the jock around here,' Finley said. 'This oughta be a snap.'

'Thanks.'

'Too bad it wasn't one of us,' Vivian said.

'Speak for yourself,' Finley told her. Abilene didn't look up, but she was certain Finley must be smirking.

'Would've been better,' Vivian went on. 'Cora's the biggest.'

'And heaviest,' Abilene muttered.

'Hell, yes,' Finley said. 'That's how she broke the pier.'

'You guys are a riot.'

'If one of *us* had the busted ankle,' Vivian continued, 'Cora could've carried us out.'

'Maybe Batty planned it this way,' Abilene said, and wondered if she was kidding. 'To keep us from leaving. Broke the board under Cora to disable the strongest of us.'

'Get real,' Cora muttered. 'It broke because it broke.'

'None of the others did,' Vivian pointed out.

'I guess that proves it,' Finley said. 'Old Batty's gone and put the whammy on us. We're doomed for sure.' This time, nobody laughed.

Abilene unbuttoned her blouse and spread it open. She felt a mild breeze stir over her skin, cooling the sweat. 'Whammy or not,' she said, 'we've sure been running into a lot of crap ever since we went to Batty's place.'

'My friend,' said Finley, 'the crap started before that. Just ask Helen.'

They made their way slowly through the woods, Cora hobbling along with the aid of the shotgun, Vivian supporting her. They didn't get far, however, before the belts came loose and Abilene had to rewrap Cora's ankle. They continued their trek, Finley hanging onto Cora. When the belts came undone a second time, Abilene fixed them, then knotted her blouse tightly around the straps. 'That oughta hold things together for a while.'

She was staggering along at Cora's side when they finally reached the edge of the forest and she saw the lodge at the far end of the field.

'Let me down,' Cora gasped.

Abilene lowered her to the ground. She wanted to flop, but hated the idea of having to get up again in a couple of minutes. So she bent over and clutched her slippery knees. Sweat dripped off her nose and chin, streamed down her neck and back and sides and chest and legs. Her skin felt crawly goosebumps. She was shaking all over.

'And you thought nothing could ever be worse than climbing the Statue of Liberty,' Finley told her.

'This . . . is . . . almost as bad.'

'I can't go on,' Cora said. She was leaning forward, kneading the muscles of her left leg.

'We're almost there,' Vivian said.

'I can't. Not right now. Gotta rest.'

'Yeah,' Abilene gasped. 'What's the hurry? We're . . . not going anyplace . . . once we get there.'

'*I'm* going in the pool,' Finley said. 'I don't care if it is hot water. It's gotta be an improvement. Might drink it all down, while I'm at it.'

'I'm so thirsty I'm spitting sand,' Vivian said.

'Why don't you two go on ahead?' Cora suggested. 'Bring back a water bottle. I'll be okay in a while.'

'It's not a good idea to split up,' Vivian said.

'We can keep an eye on you till you get to the lodge. It's an open field. Nothing's gonna happen. Just go right around to the car and hurry back.'

'What about you guys?' Finley asked.

'We've got the shotgun.'

'I've got Batty's knife,' Abilene added. She straightened up and patted its handle. 'Go on. We'll be all right. And get me some shoes. And a blouse or something.'

'Anything else while we're there?' Vivian asked.

'How about flashlights?' Finley suggested.

'Get going,' Cora muttered. 'And keep your eyes open.'

'You too,' Vivian said. 'Be careful.'

She and Finley started across the field, walking side by side. Abilene watched them. The sunlight out there looked very bright, very hot.

'Glad it's them and not us,' she said.

'Our turn'll come. I'm just glad to have Finley out of my hair. What a pain.'

Abilene smiled. 'I'd really start worrying if she stopped being one. Did you see how she acted after Batty grabbed her boob?'

'Yeah. She didn't make a crack for all of ten minutes.'

'I think it made her a little crazy.'

'That's for sure. Christ. When she's not being a wiseass, she's dangerous.'

'Viv's taking everything pretty well,' Abilene said.

'I don't think I've ever seen her lose her head, you know that? Even when stuff hits her hard. She could be torn to pieces inside, but she always keeps her cool. She'll complain about shit. She'll cry her eyes out sometimes. But she always gets on with business. Never flips out. Smart, gorgeous, *and* she's got balls of brass. I could kill her.'

Abilene laughed.

Vivian and Finley were halfway across the field now. Walking slowly as if the sun were pressing down on their shoulders.

Finley looked around.

Abilene raised a hand.

Finley nodded, turned to Vivian and said something. Vivian elbowed her.

Abilene swept her eyes across the rear of the lodge, then up and down both sides of the field. Satisfied that no one was approaching them, she turned to Cora.

'Are we gonna need those flashlights?'

'I'll be ready when they get back. I think. Get a load of this,' she said, and raised her right arm. The skin of her armpit was red, abraded raw by the stock of the shotgun.

'God,' Abilene muttered.

'My leg might last long enough to get me to the lodge. I hope so.'

'We'll get you there, one way or another.'

'I'm not gonna be hiking to town, that's for sure.'

'Maybe we can find the car keys.'

'Sure.'

Abilene sat on the ground beside her. She was tempted to lie down, but knew she wouldn't like the feel of the weeds and twigs and leaves against her bare back. She crossed her legs, then folded her hands behind her head and stretched, straining her arms backward and arching her spine. It felt so good that she moaned.

'How would you like to stay with me?' Cora asked, looking her in the eyes.

'Huh?' Abilene lowered her arms.

'Somebody'll have to go for help. I figure Finley'd be good for that, but she can't go alone. I don't want anyone going *anywhere* alone. I thought maybe Vivian could go with Fin and you could stay with me. It's up to you. If you don't want to, that's fine. It'd mean spending the night around here someplace. God knows what might happen.'

'There's gotta be another way.'

'If you can think of one, I'd be glad to hear it.'

'We should all at least try to get off the grounds of the lodge. Down as far as the road, maybe.'

'I don't know about making it down that driveway.'

'You could roll.'

Cora grimaced at her. 'You're almost as bad as Finley.'

'What was your plan?'

'Hide somewhere in the woods, I guess. Like last night.'

'Are you sure you'd rather have me than Vivian?'

'I think so. If something goes wrong, I think I'd rather have you with me.'

'Really? How come?'

Cora shrugged. 'You're quick to use your head. You usually seem to know right away what needs to be done, and you go ahead and do it.'

'Well. Thanks.'

Looking out across the field, she watched Vivian and Finley vanish beyond the corner of the lodge.

'So you'll do it? Stay with me?'

'Sure. Hell, it'd beat walking all night.'

'Scoot over a little closer, would you?'

The request perplexed Abilene, but she did as asked. Cora put an arm around her back, gently caressed her bare side.

Her heart started thumping.

What's going on?

She can't be . . . gay. She's *married*, for Godsake! Got married only three months after the New York trip. (What does that prove?) She *can't* be.

'Just relax,' Cora whispered, her breath tickling Abilene's ear. 'Just act like everything's normal.'

'Cora . . .'

'There's somebody in the bushes right behind you.'

The words slammed through her chest. 'Who is it?'

'I don't know.'

'Batty?'

'No.'

'Oh God.'

'It's okay, it's okay. Act normal. We're gonna nail him.' Cora patted her side. 'Let's get going,' she said in a louder voice. 'I'm tired of sitting here.'

Fighting her urge to look back, Abilene got to her feet.

Someone watching us.

Helen's killer?

She glanced toward the lodge. No sign of Vivian and Finley.

A great time for us to be split up.

She bent over and clutched Cora's left arm.

She saw her blouse knotted around Cora's ankle. Not that she needed reminding that she was half naked.

I don't believe this. Shit!

As she pulled, Cora pushed herself up with the shotgun. 'Let me see if I can walk on my own. Stand back.'

She let go and took a couple of steps away. She watched Cora, keeping her eyes from the bushes where the stranger supposedly lurked.

Cora stayed up. 'See? I can get along without you.'

Pivoting on her left leg, she shouldered the shotgun and swung its barrels toward the dense foliage beside the trail. 'Come out of there or I'll blow your fucking head off!'

Abilene heard a gasp, but couldn't see anyone through the green tangle.

'Come out!'

'Don't shoot! Don't.'

The head of a teenaged boy rose into view. Abilene recognized his long dark hair, the almost pretty features of his smooth face. He was the kid they'd seen yesterday in the pool, the kid who'd fled into the woods.

Helen's killer?

Abilene pictured her friend sprawled dead in the shower room.

She pulled Batty's knife from the sheath at her hip.

The kid's terrified eyes stayed on Cora as he came out from behind the bushes.

He was shirtless and skinny, wearing cut-off blue jeans low on his hips. The jeans, too big for him, were held up by a couple of ropes that came down from his shoulders like suspenders.

His stomach was smudged with bruises. Had Helen done that to him? Punched him as she struggled for her life?

Halting in front of Cora, he shook his head. 'I didn't do nothin',' he said. 'Ya ain't gonna shoot me, are ya?'

'More than likely,' Cora said.

'No, please! It weren't me. I didn't touch her!'

'Oh you bastard,' Abilene muttered. The kid's head jerked sideways. He looked at her. She saw his eyes lower to her breasts but she didn't care. 'You killed her. You butchered Helen, you filthy maggot.'

'No! It weren't me!' He shook his head wildly from side to side. 'My brother done it! He's crazy, my brother. I didn't do nothin' but try 'n scare ya off!'

'Bullshit,' Abilene said.

'I swear it! I swear it!' Facing Cora, he blurted, 'Don't shoot . . . hey.' His mouth fell open. He ducked his head close to the muzzles and squinted. 'Them barrels is all plugged up,' he said. 'Ya go and shoot me, the whole gun's gonna blow up, more 'n likely.'

Cora frowned. She glanced at Abilene.

The kid drove an arm forward, pounding his hand against the double muzzles, ramming the shotgun hard against Cora's shoulder.

The blow knocked her backward. The barrels swung toward the sky. Even as she tried to catch herself with her right leg and cried out, Abilene knew she was going down.

The kid bolted, looking over his shoulder at Abilene. She was rushing him before Cora hit the ground.

He raced into the field.

Abilene sprinted after him, flinging her legs out long and quick, pumping her arms, the blade of Batty's knife flashing beside her face each time her right arm shot up. In seconds, she was wheezing for breath. Her muscles burned.

The kid got farther and farther away from her.

And he was running along the edge of the field, not across

it, not fleeing toward the lodge. He'd been watching. He knew that Finley and Vivian were in that direction.

Abilene looked toward the corner of the lodge.

No Finley, no Vivian.

Where are they?

He's gonna get away!

Turning her head forward again, she fixed her eyes on the kid's gleaming back. He was fifteen, twenty feet ahead of her. Closing in on the woods at the corner of the field.

Can't let him.

Can't let him get away.

He killed Helen.

Abilene staggered to a halt. She turned the knife around and clamped the blade tight between her thumb and the curled side of her forefinger. She cocked it back over her shoulder and threw it.

Not a chance, she thought.

But she *knew* she couldn't chase him down.

The knife tumbled end over end. At first, it seemed to be whipping straight for the kid's head. That's where she had aimed, figuring that even if she wasn't good enough to make the blade stick, the handle might at least connect and stun him.

But the knife began to drop.

Gonna fall short.

Expecting it to hit the ground behind him, Abilene wanted to be there fast to retrieve it. She forced herself to run. And only took a single stride before the blade sank deep into the back of the kid's left thigh. He twitched and cried 'Yeeah!' His leg jumped upward instead of striding out. He dived at the ground as if sliding head first for a base.

He reached around. He grabbed the knife. He yanked it

out of his leg an instant before Abilene smashed down on his back. He grunted under the impact. Abilene hooked one arm across his throat and squeezed. Her other arm stretched out sideways and grabbed the wrist of his knife hand. She tried to keep it pinned to the ground as she choked him.

He bucked and writhed, slippery beneath her. He shook his head. He dug his chin into her forearm. He shoved himself upward with his right arm. Abilene felt his body rise and tilt. Starting to slide, she swung a leg over his hip.

Together, they rolled. He came down on top of her. Though she could barely breathe under his weight, she kept her grip on his knife hand and tried to tighten her stranglehold. She hooked her legs over his.

When he shoved her arm away from his throat, she jammed her mouth against the back of his head. His hair was wet and oily, so thick that she thought she might not get through it. But her teeth found his scalp.

He yelped and let go and drove his elbow down. It smacked into her just below the armpit. At the shock of pain, her mouth sprang open. He got his head away from her teeth, but she clutched his throat again. The elbow punched her a second time. And he kept on pumping it down, pounding her side. Each blow seemed to steal more of her strength.

She was helpless to stop him when the kid pushed her arm away from his throat, freed his knife hand from her grip, kicked his legs out from under hers and rolled off.

She lay on her back, struggling for air.

He got to his hands and knees. The knife in his left hand was pressed against the ground. He was gasping just as hard as Abilene. Raising his head, he looked at her through cords of wet hair that had fallen over his face.

'I . . . didn't . . . do it,' he panted.

He suddenly raised his head higher. His face, red and dripping behind the strands of hair, twisted with despair.

Abilene could guess why.

She wondered if she had enough energy to turn her head so she could watch Finley and Vivian racing to her rescue.

She was still thinking about it when the kid scurried to her side and pressed the knife blade against her throat.

Chapter Thirty-two

On his knees by Abilene's shoulder, hunched over her and holding the knife against her throat, the kid stared up at Finley and Vivian. They halted just on the other side of Abilene.

Finley had the old, rust-speckled knife in one hand, a water bottle in the other. Vivian was holding Abilene's moccasins and a plaid blouse.

'Go away,' the kid said. 'Leave me be.'

Finley dropped the knife. 'Just take it easy.'

'Where's Cora?' Vivian asked.

'She's . . . okay,' Abilene gasped.

'I only just wanta go home,' the kid said. 'I never hurt no one.'

'What's your name?' Vivian asked.

'Jim.'

'I'm Vivian. This is Finley. That's our friend, Abilene. We don't mean you any harm. Why don't you put your knife away? You can leave. Nobody'll try to stop you.'

'Yeah, ya will. Ya think I killed that girl.'

'Did you?' Finley asked.

'I already said. Weren't me. My brother, Hank, he's the one. He's crazy. All I done, I tried to scare ya off. Didn't want him doing that to none a ya.'

'Are you the one who threw our stuff in the pool last night?' Vivian asked.

He nodded. 'To scare ya off. I didn't take nothing. Honest.'

'It's all right,' Vivian said. 'We don't care if you took something.'

'Well, I didn't.'

'What about the car keys?' Finley asked.

'I didn't see no keys? Didn't take no keys.'

'What *did* you take?' Finley asked.

'Nothing!'

'Damn it, Fin,' Abilene blurted.

'He's lying.'

'He's gonna slit my throat, you dumb shit.'

'No, he won't. Don't worry. If he does, I'll kill him. You don't want me to kill you, do you Jim? What did you take?'

'Nothing.' He sounded as if he might start to cry. 'Just a . . . thing. It weren't yours. Ya don't wear 'em.'

'A bra?' Finley asked.

'Yeah. Hers.' He looked at Vivian. 'I only just . . . borrowed it.'

Vivian grimaced, but only for an instant. She managed a smile. 'That's fine, Jim. You can have it.'

'Ain't got it no more, anyhow. Hank took it off me.' His lips started to tremble. 'He made me tell where I got it.'

'When was this?' Finley asked.

'Last night. I didn't wanta tell, but he made me. I knew he'd come over. I figured he'd kill ya all. But he only just got the fat one. I sure wish he hadn't.' Jim started to weep. 'I *tried* to scare ya off . . . ya just wouldn't *go*. He's . . . gonna get the rest of ya if ya stay, too. Ya gotta *go*.'

Jim lifted the knife away from Abilene's throat, then leaned away from her. As she sat up, he let the knife fall to the ground. He knelt there, head down.

Abilene braced herself up. She was glad to get her back off the ground. It itched horribly, but she felt too exhausted to do anything about it.

Every muscle in her body seemed to be trembling. Her skin, dripping with sweat, was rough with goosebumps like before. She noticed that her nipples were erect. Great, she thought. She glanced up at Finley and Vivian. They were staring at her, frowning. She expected a remark from Finley.

'All that blood better be his,' Finley said.

'Yeah,' she muttered, glancing at her outstretched legs. They were smeared bright red. 'All his.'

'Did he do anything to you?' Vivian asked.

'We . . . just wrestled.' She wanted to tug her skirt down to cover her panties, but she couldn't bring herself to move. 'I think . . . all he wanted was to get away.'

'What'll we do with him?' Finley asked.

'Let him go,' Vivian said.

'That doesn't seem like such a hot idea,' Finley said. She crouched and picked up the knife she'd dropped. 'No telling what he might do.'

'I won't do nothing,' Jim said, his voice high and shaky.

'He's hurt,' Abilene explained. 'I got him in the leg with my knife. And bit his head.'

'Are *you* all right?' Vivian asked her.

'I'll live. But my back. Itches like crazy.' She knew it must be scratched some and littered with bits of field debris clinging to her skin. Vivian crouched, wadding the blouse. Figuring what she had in mind, Abilene shoved at the ground and leaned forward. Vivian began to rub her back with the blouse.

Abilene moaned as the itching faded to mild soreness.

'Hey!' Cora's voice.

Abilene looked up and saw her at the edge of the field, standing on one leg, propped up by the shotgun.

'What's going on?' Cora yelled.

'Everything's okay,' Abilene answered. 'We'll be over in a minute.' Vivian gave the blouse to her. Putting it on, she looked over at Jim. He still had his head down. She picked up the knife. 'You can leave if you want. I'm sorry about . . . going after you. Hurting you.'

He wiped his eyes and looked at her. 'I don't blame ya none.'

'All the same . . . I thought you'd killed our friend.'

'How do we know he didn't?' Finley said.

'I believe him,' Vivian said.

'He could've cut my throat,' Abilene explained. To Jim, she said, 'If you want to come along with us, that's fine. We've got a first-aid kit at the car. We can bandage you up.'

'Okay,' he muttered.

Abilene stood up. She straightened her skirt. She slipped her feet into the moccasins that Vivian had brought for her, then took a drink from the water bottle.

Jim got slowly to his feet. He winced when he put weight on his left leg. Bending over, he clutched the back of his thigh.

'Can you walk?' Vivian asked him.

He gave it a try. Hand clamped to the wound, he took a few hobbling steps. The back of his injured leg was sheathed with blood. Some had gotten onto his good leg as well.

Abilene expected to find blood all over his hair and neck and back, but there was none. Apparently, she hadn't bitten his scalp hard enough to break the skin.

Of course not, she thought. I would've gotten it all over my face.

Finley took over the lead, walking backward, holding the knife at her side and keeping her eyes on Jim. Abilene and Vivian walked behind him.

Cora, up ahead, had lowered herself to the ground. When the others got to her, she asked Abilene, 'Are you okay?'

'The blood's his. I got him in the leg.'

'He didn't hurt you?'

'No, I'm fine.'

Finley gave her the water bottle and she took a long drink.

'He says his brother's the one who killed Helen,' Finley said.

'A likely story,' Cora said.

'He could've killed me, but he didn't.'

'He knows I would've nailed him,' Finley said.

'I think he told the truth,' Vivian said. 'He admitted throwing our stuff in the pool last night. He said it was to scare us away so his brother wouldn't get us.'

'Where was this "brother" then?' Cora asked.

'Back home,' Jim explained.

'The thing is,' Abilene said, 'the brother apparently didn't know we were at the lodge until later last night. He caught Jim with Vivian's bra.'

'Fuckin' pervert,' Finley said.

Jim stood there with his head down, his hand clasped to the back of his leg.

'I never even noticed it was missing,' Vivian said. She

646

sounded apologetic, as if she blamed herself for luring the killer to the lodge.

'The brother took it from him,' Abilene continued, 'and made him tell where he'd gotten it. Apparently, he beat Jim up.' She flapped a hand toward the dark blotches on Jim's stomach. 'That's how you got those bruises, isn't it?'

'Yeah,' he murmured.

'How do we know Helen didn't do that to him?' Finley said.

'I never hurt nobody.'

'That's what you keep telling us.'

'What were you doing at the lodge in the first place?' Cora asked him.

'Isn't that obvious?' Finley said.

'It's . . . I just like to go there. It's quiet 'n nice 'n . . . I go there all the time. Just to swim and stuff. Ain't nobody ever there. Till yesterday.'

'And you liked what you saw,' Finley said, 'so you came sneaking back last night.'

'That ain't it. Figured ya'd be gone. But when I seen ya was still there, I tried to scare ya off. Hank, he goes there sometimes. He's crazy. He'll go and stay the whole night, sometimes. It's 'cause he done stuff there when he was just a kid . . . killed some folks 'n . . . done stuff to gals. He likes to . . . stay in the lodge 'n run it all through his head. Ya hear him, ya'd think it was just the finest thing ever . . . what he done that night. So I knowed what he'd do if he come across ya. That's how come I thrown your things in the water. Just to spook ya off.'

'If you were worried that way,' Abilene said, 'why didn't you just come out and talk to us, explain the situation?'

'I don't know,' he muttered.

'He was having too much fun,' Finley said.

'Were you afraid of us?' Vivian asked.

'Not much. I . . . liked ya.'

'I'll just bet you did.'

'Quit it, Finley.'

'Oh, come on. The kid's a voyeur. He was getting his jollies spying on us.'

'That may be,' Abilene said, 'but I think he's telling the truth about his brother.'

'Brother or not, he got Helen killed. If he hadn't been spying on us and decided to fuck around with our stuff, we never would've lost the car keys and we would've gotten outa this shithole last night and Helen'd still be alive. If he hadn't swiped Viv's bra, his fucking brother wouldn't even've known we were *here*.' She suddenly lunged at Jim. Arms outstretched, she rammed her hands against his chest. He staggered backward, dropped, and landed on his rump. As he looked up with surprise and pain in his eyes, Abilene sprang at Finley. She grabbed her friend's arm and tugged, but not quick enough. The toe of Finley's sneaker punched Jim under the chin. The kid flopped backward, his head bouncing off the ground.

'Christ, Fin!'

She yanked her arm free of Abilene's grip, but didn't go after Jim again.

Vivian hurried over to him. She crouched by his side. His eyes were shut. For a moment, Abilene thought he might be dead. Then she detected the rise and fall of his chest. Vivian looked up at Finley. 'Good going,' she muttered.

'He had it coming.'

'You could've killed him.'

'Tough. Serve him right.'

'You didn't have to do that,' Cora said, 'but maybe it's just as well. Let's tie him up before he comes to.'

'What the hell for?' Abilene protested.

'So he doesn't run off.'

'He came with us on his own.'

'But I don't think he'd want to stick around for what I've got in mind.'

Finley didn't need any more urging. She dropped to her knees beside Jim and plucked at one of the ropes that was knotted to a belt loop at the front of his jeans.

'What *do* you have in mind?' Abilene asked.

'We keep him till we're outa here.'

'Keep him prisoner?'

'I believe "hostage" is the appropriate term,' Finley said. 'Good plan, Cora. Wish I'd thought of it. Nobody's gonna fuck with us as long as we've got the kid. Give me a hand,' she told Vivian. Together, they rolled Jim onto his stomach. He moaned quietly, but didn't struggle. Finley picked at the other knot.

'I'm not sure it's such a good idea,' Abilene said.

'Sure it is,' Finley said. She got the knot loose and started to bind Jim's hands behind his back.

'He'll be our insurance,' Cora explained.

'The brother might come looking for him.'

'That'll be just fine,' Finley said. 'We'll blow his head off. That's what we wanted to do in the first place. Now we'll have Jimbo for bait instead of one of us.'

'What if the whole family comes?' Vivian asked.

'They won't attack us if we've got Jim,' Cora said. 'We'll threaten to kill him. They'll leave us alone.'

'Not if we shoot the brother, they won't,' Abilene said. 'Not if Helen's story was true about what they did to the lodge people.'

'It was true, all right,' Vivian said. 'You heard what Jim said. Hank was one of them. So this is the family that did it. We oughta just leave him and get outa here.'

'How do we go about that?' Cora asked. 'I'm not going anywhere. Not unless somebody comes up with the . . . check his pockets!'

'We already asked him about the keys,' Abilene said.

'Check!'

Finley, done tying his hands, patted the seat pockets of his jeans. Then she jammed a hand under his right thigh while Vivian did the same on the other side. 'Nope,' Finley said. Vivian shook her head.

'Shit,' Cora muttered.

'Maybe Hank's got 'em,' Finley suggested. 'He took the bra from the kid. Maybe he took the keys, too.'

'Jim told us he never saw the keys,' Abilene said.

'You believe everything he says, Hickok?'

'My God, he admitted taking the bra, and that embarrassed the hell out of him. He doesn't know anything about the keys.'

'Hank still might have them,' Cora said. 'If he didn't take them from Jim, he could've gotten them when he . . . found Helen.'

'We'll find out when we bag him.'

'And suppose he doesn't have the keys?' Abilene asked. 'Then we'll be stuck here and the whole damn clan'll want our blood.'

'Not to mention Batty,' Vivian added.

'This really sucks,' Cora muttered.

They were all silent for a while. Jim raised his face off the ground, pulled a bit at the rope around his hands, then lowered his head again and didn't move or speak.

'I still think we should keep him for insurance,' Cora finally said. 'We'll find a good hiding place in the woods. Abilene and I, we'll hang onto him just in case while you two go for help.'

'Who two?' Finley asked.

'You and Viv.'

'No way. I'm not leaving you guys here. Not a chance. I aim to be around when Great Big Billy Goat Hank comes looking. I wanta be the one to drop him.'

'For Godsake, Finley, the important thing is getting out of here alive.'

'Speak for yourself. I'm not going anywhere till Hank's dead.'

Cora sighed. 'All right. Then you stay with me, and we'll have Abilene and Vivian go for help. *Somebody's* got to, or we'll be here forever.'

'We'll have a better chance if we all stick together,' Vivian said.

'Fuckin'-A,' Finley said.

Vivian nodded. 'I'm not leaving.'

Cora looked at Abilene.

'Me neither. I don't want to come back with the cops and find you guys … hurt. We can worry about getting away from this damn place *after* we've … taken care of business. When there isn't any more threat.'

'If we go down,' Finley said, 'we all go down together.'

Chapter Thirty-three

Jim made no effort to escape as Vivian, holding his arm, led him across the field toward the lodge. The other three followed them, Abilene walking along with the water bottle while Finley supported Cora.

Jim's cut-off jeans, held up only by the single rope over his shoulder, hung at a slant that bared the top of his left buttock. The way he looked reminded Abilene of the guy in New York City. Wade? Wayne. That guy had been shirtless, too, with his jeans low. She remembered how Wayne had led them back to the hotel, how she'd suspected he might try to pull something, and how upset Helen had been when they'd refused to let him into their rooms. Only Helen had trusted the guy. Only Helen had been right about him.

She wondered what Helen would have to say about their treatment of Jim.

He just wanted to help us, and look what we've done to him.

Hell, maybe he actually saved our lives. We'd fully intended to spend the night in the lodge. And that's where we would've slept if he hadn't thrown our stuff in the pool. Maybe Hank would've come along, just as Jim had feared, and gotten us all.

Instead, we hid in the woods. And he only got Helen. And *she* would've been okay if she hadn't gone back on her own to grab a snack and go looking for the keys.

Maybe we should be thanking this guy.

Instead, I nailed him with my knife and tried to choke him and Finley knocked him down and now we've got him limping along with his hands tied and his leg bleeding.

To ease her feelings of guilt, Abilene told herself that Jim might've lied about everything.

He might not even *have* a brother.

Jim could be the one who butchered Helen.

His story had certainly sounded true, but he might've made up the whole thing.

We'd be fools to trust him.

But we didn't trust Wayne that time. We should've.

At last, they entered the shadow cast by the lodge. 'Let's stop at the pool,' Cora said. 'I wanta soak.'

Vivian kept Jim standing while Abilene and Finley helped Cora sit on the edge of the pool.

'I'm not sure *hot* water's the thing for swelling,' Abilene said as Cora lowered her feet into the water.

'Maybe not. But it feels good.'

Finley jumped in.

'What about us?' Vivian asked.

'He's not getting in here with all that blood,' Finley said.

'We need to do something about his leg.'

'I'll watch him,' Abilene offered. 'Why don't you go up and get the first-aid kit?'

'Not alone,' Cora said. She plunged the muzzles of the shotgun into the swirling water. 'Finley, go with her.'

'Let him bleed.'

'I'll go by myself.'

'No. Finley!'

'Shit.' Finley boosted herself out of the pool.

'Why don't you take those with you, too?' Cora said, nodding at Helen's sneakers and the bag of chips propped between them.

Dripping, Finley picked up the shoes and bag. Then she strode ahead of Vivian toward the corner of the lodge.

'Come over here,' Abilene said. She took Jim's arm and led him to the narrow drainage channel that led from the outer pool toward the woods. 'I'll clean you up.'

She helped Jim to sit down. He eased himself onto his back, then rolled over. Crouching beside him, Abilene cupped up water with both hands and began to rinse the blood off his injured leg. The wound was a raw vertical slit a few inches above the back of his knee. It leaked fresh blood as Abilene gently cleaned the skin around it.

'I'm sorry I did this to you,' she whispered.

'Don't guess I blame ya,' he said. 'Ya thought I'd killed yer friend.'

'Does it hurt much?'

'Ain't so bad. Just wish I wasn't tied up, is all. I ain't gonna run off.'

She saw the way the rope was pressing into his wrists, then looked over her shoulder.

Cora, still sitting on the edge of the pool, had her little finger up one of the shotgun barrels. She twisted it around. When she pulled it out, the finger was dark with mud.

'The rope's cutting off Jim's circulation,' Abilene said.

'It's gotta be tight or he'll get loose.'

'Sorry,' Abilene told him. 'We can't take any chances.'

'Ya gonna keep me till Hank comes?'

'That's the idea.' She cupped up more water and spilled it onto his leg, watching it turn pink as it mingled with his blood.

'Yer gonna kill him, ain'tcha?'

'Maybe.'

'I can help.'

'Help us kill your own brother?'

'I hate him. Hank, he's always tormentin' me. 'Sides, I

don't want him cuttin' ya up like he done the fat one. Don't want him cuttin' up none a ya. I think yer all pretty nice, 'n . . .'

'Say cheese,' Finley called.

Even before looking up, Abilene knew she was being taped. Sure enough, Finley stood at the corner of the lodge, the camcorder to her face while Vivian approached with the first-aid kit.

'Quit screwing around and come over here,' Cora called to Finley.

Abilene rinsed off the leg once more as Vivian knelt across from her. Then she leaned forward and used the tail of her blouse to dry the area surrounding the gash. She held the cloth there until Vivian had a bandage ready. When she took it away, Vivian covered the wound with a wide, adhesive strip.

'Thanks,' Jim said. 'Both a ya.' He started to roll over, but Abilene held him down.

'Just a minute. I'll wash off your other leg.'

He nodded. Abilene scooped up more water and began to rinse the smears of blood off his right leg.

Vivian picked up the first-aid kit. 'We oughta patch your back,' she said, heading for Cora. 'And there's an Ace bandage in here.'

'Later,' Cora said. 'I'm planning to soak a while as soon as I've got this taken care of.'

Finished with Jim, Abilene got to her feet. She slipped out of her moccasins, pulled off her socks, and stepped into the drainage channel. The warm water washed over the tops of her feet. She bent down and splashed it up her legs. As she rubbed at the blood stains, she watched Cora break open the shotgun, remove the two shells, and peer down the barrels.

Finley dug a fresh shell out of a pocket.

Cora took it from her, slipped it into the breech, then replaced the unused shell and snapped the barrels back into place. She tossed the empty shell. It tumbled through the air and landed silently in the grass.

Finley patted Cora on the head. Grinning, she said, 'Loaded for bear.' Then she jumped into the pool.

'Why don't you take a peek inside?' Cora suggested.

With a nod, Finley waded over to the archway.

'No funny business,' Cora warned.

'Who, me?' She leaned into the opening. After a few moments, she backed away. 'Nobody there.'

Cora looked around. Apparently satisfied that Hank was nowhere in sight, she set down the shotgun alongside the pool and lowered herself to the submerged ledge. She winced a bit as her shoulders sank below the surface. 'Damn cat,' she muttered.

'You coming in?' Finley asked Vivian.

'No way.'

'Feels good.'

'I'm sure it does.'

'I took a good look around inside. No sign of that headless body floating around. Ghost or otherwise.'

Ignoring her, Vivian walked toward Abilene. 'You can get in, if you want.'

'Bring the kid over,' Cora said.

Together, Abilene and Vivian helped him up. They led him to the near side of the pool and held him steady while he sat on its edge and lowered his feet into the water.

'If one of you wants to loosen the rope a little,' Cora said, 'go ahead.'

'What's the big idea?' Finley blurted.

'It's too tight,' Abilene told her.

'He won't try anything.' Cora reached out and patted the stock of the shotgun. 'You *won't* try anything, kid. You'll just sit there.'

'I'll take care of it,' Vivian said, and crouched behind Jim's back.

'For Godsake,' Finley muttered.

Though eager to get into the water, Abilene waited while Vivian picked open the knots and removed the rope. Jim flexed his hands, wiggled his fingers. Both his hands were stained with dry, rust-colored blood. She hadn't thought to clean them. And didn't want to bother now. She watched Vivian retie the hands.

'How's that?'

'I guess better.'

Vivian fingered the binding, then glanced up at Abilene. 'I think that'll hold him.'

'Looks okay to me.' She stepped over to a corner of the pool, sat down, and eased herself into the water. She sighed as the heat soothed the itches of her skin. She dunked her head. She rubbed her scalp, raised her head out of the water and swept back her hair.

She didn't want to sit beside Jim's dangling legs. Cora and Finley were seated across from him. That left only the shelf opposite the archway. She waded over to it, scanned the rear grounds of the lodge, then turned around and lowered herself onto the granite ledge. She slumped down until her chin touched the water.

And found herself staring through the opening at the inside pool.

She could see straight across the shadowed surface. She could see past the far side of the pool to the stairway. Just off to the right, barely blocked from her view by the edge of the archway, would be the door to the men's changing room. To the showers. To Helen lying dead in the darkness.

She quickly turned her face away.

And met Jim's eyes.

'Ain'tcha gonna tell 'em?' he said.

'Tell us what?' Cora asked.

'He says he wants to help us. He says he hates his brother, Hank, and wants to help us kill him.'

'That's right,' Jim said. 'He's crazy 'n mean.'

Finley smirked. 'And you want to kill him, huh?'

'Sure do.'

'When did this urge suddenly come upon you?'

'Huh?'

'How come, all of a sudden, you feel like wasting the bastard? Seems as if you would've had plenty of opportunities before now. I mean, he's your brother. I assume he lives with you. If he's all that bad, why haven't you ever nailed him in his sleep, or something?'

Jim lowered his head. 'Hank ain't normal,' he muttered. 'He don't sleep like regular folks. He don't shut his eyes. Can't. Ain't got no eyelids.'

'He *what*?' Vivian blurted.

'Born that way.'

'Bullshit,' Finley said. 'No eyelids? Gimme a break.'

'That's how come I can't do nothing to him when he's asleep. He'll be snorin' away, and starin' right at me, 'n they're the awfulest eyes. They're blue in the middle, this real clear blue, but where they're white on other folks, they're red on him. Like they got blood in 'em.'

'My God,' Vivian murmured.

'He's making this up,' Finley said.

'Ain't neither. The worst thing is, he has me lick 'em.'

Vivian gaped at Jim. 'His eyes?'

'I can't get anywhere near him but what he makes me lick his eyes. Every day. Every night. They's dry 'n sticky, 'n the way they slide around on my tongue . . . It's enough to make ya sick. But he beats on me if I don't.'

'No wonder you want to kill him,' Vivian said.

Abilene felt sick. *This* was the man who'd forced Helen into the shower room, who'd ripped her with a knife, who'd probably raped her?

Did he make Helen lick his eyes?

She suddenly felt too hot in the water. She pushed herself up and sat on the ledge and crossed her legs. The hot air felt almost cool after the greater heat of the water.

'That's about the most disgusting thing I ever heard,' Cora said.

'It's just awful, bein' his brother. The only good thing's when I can get away from him. But sometimes, he don't let me go. Cause he can't go out, hisself. Not in the daytime. And he don't wanta be left all alone. So I gotta stay with him in the cabin. And he won't allow no light in. We got the windows covered, and the door shut, and it's just so dark and smelly in there, and he's always wantin' me to lick him. And then when I do, he gets all carried away, 'n . . .'

'Wait,' Cora said.

'. . . does stuff to me.'

'What kind of stuff?' Finley asked.

'Don't wanta tell.'

'Wait,' Cora said again. 'He can't go outside in daylight?'

'Hurts his eyes too bad.'

'So he isn't going to show up here? Not until after dark?'

'No. Huh-uh.'

'Thank God for that,' Vivian muttered.

The news cheered Abilene. If it's true, she thought, we can relax for a while. We'll be safe till after the sun goes down. 'What is it, about three now?' she asked.

'Three or four, I'd think,' Cora said.

'Shouldn't be really dark until about nine.'

'Gives us plenty of time to get ready for him.'

'We could go to *him*,' Finley said. 'Stage a little surprise attack.'

'Yeah, right. I'm not walking anywhere. The three of you want to go off after him and leave me here?'

'Forget it,' Vivian said.

'Where's your place?' Finley asked.

'Other side a the lake.'

'And he's there alone?'

Jim nodded.

'What about the rest of your family?' Vivian asked him. 'All the others. Don't you have . . . a lot of kinfolks?'

'Just me and Hank.'

'We heard it was a whole bunch that attacked the lodge that night. You said your brother was there.'

'Yeah. We had us a right big family, back then. The rest of 'em, they all died off. The fever got 'em. Now there's only just us two. Wish the fever'd gotten Hank. Him 'n me was spared, though.'

'Too bad about that,' Finley said.

'So he's the only one we'll have to deal with,' Cora said. 'And not till after dark. This is looking better and better.'

'Waiting's gonna be a bitch,' Abilene said.

'It'll give us time to get ready for him.'

'We should probably eat and rest up,' Vivian suggested.

'Is the sun over the yardarm yet?' Finley asked.

'We oughta lay off the booze,' Cora said.

'A couple of drinks can't hurt.' Finley grinned up at Jim. 'How about you? You look like a guy who could use a libation.'

'He can't drink with his hands tied,' Abilene said.

'Somebody could hold the glass for him. How about it, fella? Do you like tequila?'

'I don' know.'

'Good stuff. It'll put hair on your chest.'

His chest was darkly tanned. It was smooth and hairless. *You* don't need any hair on your chest, Abilene thought. And she remembered that she'd spoken those very words. Only last year.

Chapter Thirty-four
Cora's Choice

They gathered in San Francisco exactly one year after the Big Apple adventure. But they hadn't come to see the city. This was Cora's turn to choose, and she had no interest in exploring urban attractions.

They took connecting rooms at a Quality Inn on Van Ness, had pizza delivered, drank margaritas and ate while they talked about all that had happened since they'd been together for Cora's wedding.

Abilene showed off the engagement ring that Harris had given her.

Helen announced that she'd met a terrific guy named Frank.

Vivian told them about being signed to do ads for Tipton shirts.

Finley recounted tales of her adventures as the assistant director for *Zombie Zone*. Then she said, 'I've got something interesting I want you to see.' She got busy hooking up her camcorder to the room's television.

'Your movie?' Helen asked.

'Hold your water. You'll see.' Done with the wiring, she slipped a tape cassette into her machine. 'I meant to have this for last year's reunion, but didn't get around to it.' She turned on the TV, then fingered the Play button on her camcorder.

On the screen appeared Finley wearing her old gorilla head and a green silken evening gown. 'Greetings,' she said, her voice muffled by the mask. 'Fill your glasses, sit down, shut up and get ready for fun. What you're about to see is a documentary laboriously pieced together by the Fin-man from hours upon hours of tape. This is the authorized, uncensored version of what I like to call, *Daring Young Maids*.'

'Oh, no,' Vivian muttered.

'It all begins on a hot September evening . . .'

It began with Finley showing herself in a mirror just inside the restroom of Hadley Hall. She wore the gorilla head, a tank top and shorts. She was holding the video camera to an eyehole of the mask. She vanished from the screen as the camera swept across sinks and toilet stalls. Abilene heard faint, hollow-sounding voices. Watched a shaky, jumping view of the dressing-room entrance as Finley approached it, entered, and turned toward the shower room. Then she glimpsed Helen, herself, Vivian and Cora, all naked in the steam, shocked and wet and shouting as the camera rushed by. Cora lunged forward, reached out, fell. Her rump slapped the tiles. Her feet flew into the air.

'Beaver shot!' Finley blurted through the laughter of the others.

Then Abilene was in front of the camera, blocking Finley's escape.

'Ooo, you look pissed!' Helen gasped.

Abilene's breasts filled the TV screen.

'Hot stuff, huh?' Finley said.

'Bitch,' Abilene said when the camera lowered to show her belly and pubic curls.

And everyone cracked up as her voice came from the television snapping, 'You bitch!'

She suddenly vanished. Walls, ceiling, floor. Then Helen straight ahead, face grim, huge breasts swaying as she swung a fist. Quick tumbling views of tile and girls. A jolt. Then a steady view of bare feet. Mine, Abilene realized.

The laughter in the motel room stopped when Cora slammed Finley against a wall of the shower room and punched her in the belly.

'You gals were not very nice to me,' Finley commented.

'You got off easy,' Cora told her.

'All my friends thought you over-reacted, when I showed this at a party last month.'

'You *what*!' Vivian blurted.

Abilene felt her skin go hot. She saw Helen turn a bright shade of red.

Cora scurried across the bed and got a head-lock on Finley.

'Just kidding! Hey! Nobody's seen it.'

Cora released her.

'Touchy, touchy,' she said. 'Come on, you're missing the epic. Settle down.'

'We oughta *burn* the epic,' Cora suggested.

'This is just a copy.'

663

'Hey, quiet,' Vivian said. 'Get a load of this.'

On the TV screen, Vivian was talking to a guy in the doorway of the Sig house.

Finley rushed forward and pushed a button on her camera. Vivian, Cora, Abilene and Helen, all in evening gowns and carrying beer bottles, stepped quickly backward – away from the frat house door and up the walkway.

They started forward again, moving at a normal speed but staggering and weaving as if drunk. Finley returned to her seat on the corner of the bed.

'We looked pretty sharp,' Abilene said.

'God, I was so scared,' Helen said.

'You and me both. I wanted to hightail it.'

'Shhh,' Vivian said when the door opened. Her voice from the TV slurred, 'Do y'know who I am?'

They watched.

They watched and commented and laughed, distracting themselves again and again from the scenes of their past so that Finley kept bouncing up to rewind. Often, they asked her to go back so they could take a second look. They ended up missing nothing, but saw much of the epic two or three times.

They watched themselves dance for the Sigs, dump their bottles of gasoline on the carpet and flee as the flaming bills fluttered down. They watched themselves party in Hardin's office and paper it with the glossy nudes. They watched Vivian vomit on the floor. They watched Cora make her phonecall to Hardin's home. They watched themselves attack Wildman and leave him tied beneath the bridge in Benedict Park. They watched the antics of the Merry Halloween Team, and Abilene got a special kick out of witnessing her first encounter with a zombie named Harris. Then they were trashing the house of the mean guy who'd yelled at the kids.

And Abilene found herself looking at the horror in the wheelchair.

'You were gonna erase this,' she said.

'Couldn't. It was too weird, you know?'

'Jesus,' Vivian muttered.

'That fella's mother definitely hit him with an ugly stick.'

'It's not funny,' Abilene said. She shut her eyes as the camera lingered on the hideous face. Then came Finley's voice, 'Say cheese.' And the low voice answering, 'Cheese.'

'The good, the bad and the ugly,' Finley said.

Abilene got over feeling sick when she saw herself with Harris in Benedict Park. They were pretending to be those characters in the 'Mess Hall' story. Soon, she was down on the ground with Harris on top of her.

She was there again, feeling the twigs and leaves under her back, feeling the weight of Harris's body, feeling the way his trapped erection prodded her through her panties.

'You should've gotten an Oscar for this,' Vivian said.

Cora laughed. 'That's not *acting*.'

Helen nudged Abilene. 'Getting hot?'

'I *was* till the peanut gallery chimed in.'

'Want me to rewind?' Finley asked.

Cora chuckled. 'We'll promise to be quiet. We'll just sit here and watch you pant.'

'I could be home with him right now.'

'Getting a taste of the real thing,' Finley said.

'Here comes that asshole, Baxter,' Helen said.

Abilene watched, growing apprehensive, as Baxter killed Harris and took her away in the car, as he dragged her into a clearing and tied her under a tree, as he tormented her with the knife.

'Couldn't you maybe fast-forward through some of this?'

she asked when Baxter started licking her chest. 'This is a stroll down Memory Lane I could do without.'

'Yeah, but you really nailed him good,' Finley said as Baxter started kissing Abilene. 'You wouldn't want to miss that, would you?'

'Finley.'

'Okay, okay.'

Finley was on her way to the TV when Baxter broke the strap of Abilene's bra and grabbed her breast and she kneed him in the thigh.

In fast-forward, Baxter pulled her skirt up, yanked her panties down, was flung backward by Helen, and barely hit the ground before Helen, Cora and Vivian, dressed as zombies, pounced on him.

'Hey,' Helen protested. 'We're missing the good part.'

'Fine with me,' Vivian said. 'It was awful, beating up on him like that.'

'Fucker deserved it,' Cora said.

But Finley didn't stop fast-forwarding until the TV showed their farewell party at Belmore. They were lounging around the living room of their apartment on Spring Street, dressed for bed and holding champagne glasses. 'Just act natural, babes,' Finley advised them. 'You look great. What was your big idea, Viv?' Later, she said, 'One of these days, we'll get together and watch all this stuff and have a few laughs.'

'Was that a threat or a promise?' Cora asked.

'I came through, right?'

'I wouldn't have minded missing some of this,' Abilene said.

'I think it's great,' Vivian said. 'Most of it, anyway.'

'Come on,' Helen protested, 'we're missing stuff.'

Finley got up and rewound.

The farewell party came to an end. Then it was the next morning, and they watched tape of their tearful departures.

Finley appeared on the screen. She had removed the gorilla head, but still wore her formal green gown. 'And thus ends,' she said, 'the saga of the Belmore girls. But it was not the end of the Daring Young Maids, or our adventures. True to our word, we gathered one year later. This time, we were far from the hallowed halls of the university, and eager to take our bites out of the Big Apple.'

'What corn,' Cora said.

They watched Vivian struggle to yank a suitcase off a carousel in the baggage claim area at Kennedy. Then she and Finley were apparently in the back seat of a taxi. There were views of the driver's head, and some scenery along the way to Manhattan. They'd been the last of the group to arrive. Finley was ready with her camera when Cora opened the door to their room at the Hilton.

'We oughta fast-forward through *this*,' Cora said. 'Hell, it was only last year.'

'And it's getting late,' Vivian said.

'Don't be party-poopers. There isn't all that much.'

'Have you got my wedding on here?' Cora asked.

'But of course.'

'Let's just move on to that.'

'Fine with me,' Helen said. 'This New York stuff'll just remind me of what you people did to Wayne.'

'We didn't do anything to him,' Cora said.

'He's not on the tape, anyway,' Finley explained.

'Even so, it's making me think about him.'

'Okay, okay.' Finley went to the TV and pushed the fast-forward button on her camcorder. Scenes of their days in New York City flashed by.

667

'It would've been stupid to let him into the room,' Cora said.

'He was a nice guy.'

'Maybe he was and maybe he wasn't. We were just playing it safe.'

'Maybe we misjudged him,' Abilene said. 'But who knows what he might've done if we'd let him into our rooms?'

'He could've been a rapist,' Vivian explained.

'Helen had her hopes pinned on it,' Finley said. 'But I would've called firsties.'

'That's not funny,' Helen muttered.

Finley, shaking her head at the television's speeding images, said, 'It was *almost* a waste of tape. Nothing happened. It's like looking at a travelogue.'

'Maybe *my* choice of activities will turn out to be more interesting,' Cora said.

'I sure hope so.'

'He was a nice guy,' Helen muttered.

'Let's have some quiet,' Cora announced as the scenes of her wedding began.

The next morning, they rented a Pathfinder recreational vehicle, loaded their sleeping bags, luggage and supplies, and headed north across the Golden Gate.

Following Abilene's directions, they took the turn-off to Mill Valley. She pointed out some of her favorite places as they drove through the town. Her parents had moved to Flagstaff three years ago, but she wanted to see the old house. Unfortunately, the final stretch of hillside road was too narrow for the RV. 'No big deal,' she said.

'Looks like Wolfe was right,' Vivian said.

She laughed. 'Can't go home again . . . not without a tiny car, anyway.'

They retreated to wider roads. 'Anybody want to visit Muir Woods or the top of Mount Tam?' she asked. 'They're on the way.'

'Have you got your heart set on it?' Cora asked.

'I'm gonna bring Harris over here on our honeymoon. Give him a guided tour of where I spent my callow youth. Unless you guys are interested, we can skip 'em.'

'I guess I'd rather get on over to the coast,' Cora said.

Abilene navigating, they made their way along twisty roads and down the side of Mount Tamalpias to the town of Stinson Beach. In a shop there, Cora selected a wetsuit and a surfboard. 'I'm the only one gonna surf?' she asked.

'You can count me out,' Finley said. 'I'll record your wipe-outs for posterity.'

'I'll borrow yours if I get the urge,' Abilene said. 'Which I doubt.'

'*I'm* not going in the ocean,' Helen said. 'There's sharks out there.'

'This'll do it for me,' Vivian said, holding up a string bikini.

'You're planning to wear that in public?' Abilene asked.

'If Cora's right, there won't be any public. Right?'

'That's the idea,' Cora agreed. 'That's why I decided we should go north. Miles and miles of deserted coastline. If we stop in the right places, we'll have the water to ourselves.'

'Because it's too cold for sensible people,' Abilene pointed out.

'That shouldn't bother any of you pansies,' Cora said. 'Sounds like I'll be the only one going out in it.'

She purchased her surfboard and wetsuit. Vivian purchased

her bikini. Then they returned to the RV and headed north on Pacific Coast Highway.

They stopped for lunch in Bodega Bay. Helen was thrilled. This was where Hitchcock's *The Birds* had taken place. Their table at the restaurant overlooked the very same stretch of water that Tippi Hedren had been crossing in a motorboat when a bird had swooped down and pecked her head. 'I can't believe I'm actually here,' she said, and took an eager gulp of her Bloody Mary.

Abilene laughed. 'Last year, Grandpa Munster's. This year, Bodega Bay. You've really been lucking out.'

'Yeah,' Finley said. 'Even if the rest of the trip turns out to be a total bust, you . . .'

'It won't,' Cora interrupted. 'We'll have a great time.'

'Watching you ride a surfboard?'

'It's great so far,' Helen said. 'And next year's my turn. We'll go some place really cool.'

'Lining up a haunted house for us?' Abilene asked.

'I'm still working on it. But you can bet I'll find some place just dripping with spookiness.'

After lunch, they went to a market and stocked up on supplies: groceries, soft drinks, booze, ice, sun block, and fresh batteries for their flashlights.

Before leaving town, they drove past the old school-house that had played such a prominent role in *The Birds*. Helen gaped out the window at it. 'Fantastic,' she muttered. 'Incredible.'

'You'll have to come to L.A. sometime,' Vivian told her. 'Fin and I'll take you to Universal, and you can see the Psycho house.'

'Yeah! Neat!'

Then they left Bodega Bay behind. In the late afternoon,

the fog came in. It had been lingering over the ocean, but moving slowly closer until its white, smoky fingers began creeping over the edge of the bluffs and scurrying across the road ahead of them.

'You'd better start looking for a place to pull off,' Abilene warned.

'Gotta find a way down to the water,' Cora said, and kept driving. Soon, the fog was so thick that it blocked out the sunlight. They were moving through a murky grayness that hid the ocean and the cliff at the left edge of the two-lane highway and the rocky slope to the right. The pavement itself seemed to dissolve into fog. Its yellow, center lines faded and vanished only a few yards in front of the vehicle. 'Can't see shit,' Cora finally said.

'Just get off the road,' Abilene said. Peering out the passenger window, she saw the vague shape of a low stone parapet. 'But not here. I think we're on a bridge.'

'Great.'

'Slow down,' she said as the end of the wall passed her window. 'There's gotta be a pull-out, or . . . here!'

Braking, Cora swung to the right. The smooth pavement went away. The camper rocked slightly. Its tires crunched along the gravel shoulder.

'Get as far over as you can,' Abilene suggested.

Cora steered more to the right, then stopped.

'We aren't gonna *stay* here?' Helen said.

'Would you rather go off a cliff?' Vivian asked.

'Some real excitement for a few seconds,' Finley said.

'The fog probably won't lift till tomorrow,' Abilene explained. 'It's just one of those things, when you drive the coast up here. But we've got everything we . . .'

'Is it a mirage,' Cora broke in, 'or is that a road there?'

Abilene leaned closer to the windshield. Just ahead and to the right, the gravel area seemed to flare out. 'Might be.'

Cora drove toward it. 'A road, all right.'

'If you can call it that,' Abilene said. The lane was unpaved, rutted, and angled downward for a brief stretch before disappearing in the fog.

'Is it wide enough for us?' Vivian asked.

'Let's give it a try,' Cora said. 'Maybe it goes down to the shore.'

'I hope it's not someone's driveway,' Helen said.

'I doubt it,' Abilene told her.

'This'll be fun,' Finley said.

'What if we get stuck?' Helen asked.

'You worry too much,' Cora told her, and started forward.

'Be careful,' Abilene muttered.

Cora inched the camper down the road. On her side was a steep, rocky slope with a few scraggly bushes. On Abilene's side was nothing but fog. She suspected that a wrong turn in that direction would send them plummeting to the bottom of a ravine.

The camper bounced and shook. Sometimes, Abilene heard the squeak of bushes scraping against its side.

She spent much of the time gritting her teeth. And clenching her thighs through the corduroy legs of her pants. And holding her breath.

We're getting lower all the time, she told herself. Eventually, we're bound to reach the bottom. Or at least a nice, broad area of flat ground where we can stop for the night.

Eventually. If we live that long.

A hairpin turn reversed their direction and put the hillside close to Abilene's window. She felt a little better, having it there – almost near enough to touch.

'I don't like this,' Cora said. Apparently, *she* didn't enjoy having the abyss beside her.

'You're doing fine,' Vivian told her.

'Maybe the rest of you should get out and walk ahead.'

'The worst is over,' Abilene said. 'We've gotta be almost down, by now.'

'Just think,' Finley said. 'If we do get to the bottom in one piece, we'll have to go back up again.'

'Sooner or later,' Abilene agreed.

'Not today,' Cora said. 'No way. Wherever we end up, that's where we're gonna stay till the fog goes away.'

'Driving back up won't be nearly as bad,' Abilene said.

'Maybe we're lucky we can't see what we're doing,' Finley suggested. 'We might not've had the guts to try it if . . .'

'All right!' Cora blurted.

Abilene looked to the left.

Where the gray void had been, she saw a blurry dark shape beyond the roadside. A treetop?

They continued downward, and more trees appeared. Each seemed taller than the last.

Turning to her window, she watched the desolate slope recede.

Soon, there was level ground on both sides of the camper.

She reached over and slapped Cora's thigh.

'A piece of cake,' Cora said.

'Ya done good,' Finley said.

'God,' Helen said, 'I didn't think we'd make it.'

'Can we stop now?' Vivian asked.

'Let's see where it goes,' Cora said. 'I think we're heading back toward the water. We might as well get as close as we can. Maybe we'll run into the beach.'

She drove slowly onward. Out the windows, all that Abilene

could see beyond their strip of road were nearby pines and thickets, fallen trees, boulders and fog.

That was all.

Until, gazing through her side window, she glimpsed the rear end of a pick-up truck. It loomed for an instant – green paint and rust, a broken brake-light, an open tailgate – and then they'd left it behind.

Chapter Thirty-five
Cora's Choice

'Did you see that?' Abilene asked.

'What?'

'That pick-up truck.'

'You're seeing things, Hickok.'

'I saw it, all right. It was parked back there by the road.'

'Anybody inside?' Cora asked.

'I don't know. I couldn't even see into its bed. It was kind of a wreck, though. It might've been abandoned.'

'Oh, well,' Cora said. 'Big deal.'

'I don't know,' Vivian said. 'If someone else is down here . . .'

'If you think we're leaving, you're nuts.'

The road ahead of them widened out. It seemed to cease being a road at all as it joined a broad, flat area.

'What've we got here?' Cora asked, driving forward.

'A parking lot?' Abilene suggested.

'Looks like . . . Yep,' Cora said when a pale log loomed out of the fog, barring their way. She stopped at it, shut off the headlights and killed the engine. 'Well, gang, here we are.'

'Wherever that might be,' Vivian said.

'I hope it's not private property,' Helen muttered.

'I just hope the natives are friendly,' Finley said.

'Why don't we climb out and scout around?' Cora suggested.

Abilene opened her door and jumped to the ground. A layer of sand carpeted the solid earth. Though she couldn't see more than a few yards in any direction, she heard seagulls squawking. She also heard the distant, muffled sounds of the surf tumbling, washing up the shore and withdrawing.

'We made it to the water all right,' she said as the others joined her.

'We're probably under that bridge,' Cora said.

If so, the bridge was out of sight.

Finley stepped onto the log barrier and walked along it, arms out for balance. At its end, she leaped to another. A few more strides and she was gone.

'Don't go wandering off,' Abilene called.

The fog seemed to deaden her voice.

'Just exploring, Hickok.'

'We oughta get back in the camper,' Vivian said, 'and explore a bottle of tequila. It's cold out here.'

'And creepy,' Helen added.

'I thought you liked creepy,' Cora said.

'It's nice and cozy inside.'

A dark smudge in the fog became Finley. 'It is a parking area,' she called from her log. She kept moving. 'So far, it looks like nobody's here but us.' She vanished again, this time hidden by the camper, not fog.

'Let's stick with her,' Abilene suggested.

'Yeah.' Raising her voice, Cora said, 'God forbid we should lose *Finley*.'

'Ha ha,' came a disembodied reply.

Helen curled her upper lip.

'What is it?' Abilene asked.

She shook her head. 'Nothing. I was just thinking. What if we did lose her? You know? What if she just went roaming off into the fog and we never found her again?'

'No such luck,' Cora said.

'Her tapes might fall into the hands of strangers,' Vivian pointed out.

Cora's mouth fell open with mock alarm. 'My God, I hadn't thought of that. Fin!' she shouted. 'Hold up!'

They went after her. Cora in the lead, they stepped over the log and followed it past the front of the camper. No sign of Finley.

What if she *is* gone? Abilene thought. Ridiculous. But Helen had given voice to her own fears and made them seem less far-fetched.

Anything, anyone, might be lurking in the fog.

'Finley, say something!' she called.

'Guys?'

Her voice sounded eager, as if she'd made some kind of odd discovery. It had come from somewhere not far ahead, but slightly off to the right – in the direction of the ocean.

They quickened their pace.

Abilene spotted a blurry, indistinct figure through the shrouding fog. *Two* figures.

Her stomach seemed to drop like an express elevator.

Finley. Finley and someone else. Someone big.

'Oh my Christ,' Helen gasped.

Finley, clear now, looked over her shoulder at her approaching friends. 'Gang, this is Rick.'

'Hi.' Rick raised a hand. He smiled. He appeared to be seventeen, maybe eighteen, years old. His crew cut was matted down, his face dripping. His face was tanned so dark that his teeth and the whites of his eyes almost seemed iridescent. He was well over six feet tall, powerfully built. He wore a black wetsuit with pale blue piping on its sleeves and legs. A surfboard lay in the sand near his bare feet.

Studying him, Abilene felt her fears slip away.

He's just a big kid, she thought. A very big kid. And a hunk.

'A friendly native,' Finley explained. Reaching out, she patted his chest. 'You must be freezing, Rick. Why don't you come on along with us? You can warm up in our *recreational* vehicle.'

'Oh, I wouldn't wanta barge in,' he said, frowning down at the sand in front of his feet. 'I'd better get going.'

'Do you have a pressing engagement?'

'Well, no, but . . .'

'He says he wants to leave,' Cora said, giving Finley a quick look.

'Lighten up. This is an actual California surfer. He could give you pointers. Besides, where can he go in all this fog?'

'Do you live nearby?' Vivian asked.

'Palm Springs.'

'Jeez,' Abilene said. 'You're a long way from home.'

'We don't have much of a coastline in Palm Springs.'

'Are you by yourself?' Vivian asked.

'Yes, ma'am.'

'Ma'am?' Finley chuckled.

'It's Vivian. Just Vivian.'

He glanced at her, gave her a nervous smile, then looked down again.

'Is that your pick-up truck?' Abilene asked. 'We passed one coming in.'

'That's her, I suppose. Just on my way back when I ran into Finley.'

'You're not planning to drive off, are you?' Finley asked. 'In this fog?'

'I'd intended to stay overnight. But nobody was here then. I don't know.'

'You sleep in your truck?' Vivian asked.

'There, or on the ground if it's nice out. But I guess I'll move along.'

'You don't have to,' Cora said. 'For now, I think you should just come along with us. You can at least warm up for a while before you go back to your truck.'

Helen rolled her eyes upward. 'Whatever happened to "playing it safe!"? Christ! You gave Wayne the bum's rush, and now all of a sudden it's open house.'

'This is different,' Cora said.

'It's not New York, for one thing,' Vivian added.

Rick held up a hand. 'I don't want any trouble. I'll just be on my way.'

'No, you won't,' Finley told him. 'Helen!'

'I don't have anything against you, Rick. It's just the principle of the thing.'

'I understand.'

Abilene put a hand on Helen's shoulder. 'I really think he's all right.'

Helen knocked her hand away. '*Wayne* was all right. I liked him. I *liked* him, damn it!' Suddenly, she was crying. She whirled around and strode away. Just before the fog enveloped her, she looked back and blurted, 'It's okay. He can come in.'

'I think she liked Wayne,' Finley quipped.

'Not funny,' Abilene said.

After a little more urging, they talked Rick into coming along with them. They found their way to the camper. He propped his surfboard against its side and followed them in.

'Welcome aboard,' Helen said. Though her eyes were red, she was smiling. 'By the way, I'm Helen.' She shook his hand. Cora and Abilene introduced themselves to Rick.

They turned on lights and the heater. Cora hopped onto a swivel chair behind the driver's seat, and the others sat on cushioned benches that faced the center aisle.

'It does feel good to get out of the cold,' Rick said.

'I'll second that,' Abilene said. 'And I'm not even wet.'

Finley laughed. 'You were born all wet.'

'Let's get some booze in us,' Vivian suggested.

She headed for the kitchen area to get it. Finley went after her and returned with a towel. 'Get out of that frog suit and dry off,' she said, handing the towel to Rick.

She sat across from him. He rubbed his head with the towel, then unzipped the jacket of his wet suit and peeled it off. His chest was muscular, nearly hairless, and deeply tanned. He had goosebumps. After drying himself, he draped the towel over his shoulders. 'That's a lot better. Thanks.'

'You oughta get out of those pants, too,' Finley said.

The suggestion gave Abilene a flutter in her stomach.

'That's okay,' he said, blushing through his tan. 'I'll keep them on.'

'Aren't they uncomfortable?'

'Not much.'

'Oh, I get it. You're not wearing any trunks.'

His blush deepened.

'We don't mind, do we, guys?'

'Cut it out, Fin,' Cora warned.

Vivian arrived carrying a box full of bottles and plastic glasses and packages of chips. She stepped by carefully, avoiding feet, and set it on a small round table between the swivel chairs. 'Don't listen to Fin,' she told Rick. 'The girl's an inveterate wise-ass.' She went off again and came back with a bag of ice. 'If you don't want any hard stuff, we've got some Pepsis.'

'I don't know.'

'Tequila's good for you,' Finley said. 'It'll put hair on your chest.'

'He doesn't need hair on his chest,' Abilene said. Rick smiled at her, and *she* blushed.

'Rick is obviously a minor,' Cora reminded everyone.

'So what?' Finley said. 'We'll contribute to his delinquency.'

'I guess maybe a little tequila wouldn't hurt,' Rick said.

'Won't hurt at all.'

Finley and Vivian prepared drinks for everyone. The drinks consisted of ice cubes, tequila, a splash of Triple Sec, and a capful of Rose's lime juice, stirred with a forefinger.

Helen tugged open a foil bag of nacho-flavored tortilla chips.

They drank. They munched chips. Rick explained that he'd been traveling up the coast from Santa Barbara, surfing along the way, moving steadily northward in search of less crowded shores and rougher waters.

Cora explained that she had never surfed before. She'd always wanted to give it a try, and this was her turn to be in charge of the annual gathering of her old college friends, so here they all were. Maybe, in the morning, Rick could give her a lesson.

'Be my pleasure,' he said, and rubbed his legs as if they were getting itchy trapped inside the wetsuit pants.

'You oughta take those off,' Finley said. 'It's hot in here. You'd be a lot more comfortable.'

'Can't do that.'

'You can cover yourself with the towel.'

'No need to be shy around us,' Helen said.

A corner of Rick's mouth curled up. He looked around at everyone, his expression vague and confused as if he didn't know how to handle the situation and hoped for some advice.

Abilene felt squirmy inside.

What the hell's happening here?

'You don't have to do anything you don't want to,' she heard herself say.

A real voice of protest, she thought.

'Whatever you want,' Vivian told him.

'It's no big deal,' Cora said. 'I'm sure you *would* be more comfortable.'

Rick's comfort, Abilene knew, was the farthest thing from any of their minds. They just want to get him naked. What's wrong with everybody? Why are they doing this?

We. Why are *we* doing this?

'I'll give you a hand,' Finley said. She knelt on the floor in front of Rick, reached up and slipped the towel off his shoulders. She spread it across his lap. 'There you go,' she said. Her hands disappeared beneath the towel.

Helen, seated on the bench to Rick's right, took the drink from his hand. He mumbled, 'Thanks,' and held the towel to his waist. Though he muttered, 'I'm not so sure about this,' he cooperated by raising his rump off the seat cushion.

Finley peeled the rubbery pants down his legs.

Abilene took a sip of her drink. Her hands were trembling. She looked at her friends. They were all gazing at Rick and Finley. Their faces were flushed and moist. Helen's mouth hung open. Vivian had her lower lip clamped between her teeth. Cora held her glass close to her chest, her wrist pressing against her breast.

Finley tossed the pants aside. 'Now that's better, isn't it?' she asked, returning to her seat beside Abilene.

'I guess,' Rick said. His legs were red and shiny with moisture. The blond hair on his shins glistened like gold filaments. Bending forward over the towel, he rubbed his hands up and down his shins and calves. 'Feels a lot better,' he admitted.

Helen and Vivian, on either side of him, were staring at his back. The way he was hunched over, their view had to include some of his rear end, as well.

'Feels a lot better,' he admitted. He straightened up and sighed. Helen returned his drink. He polished it off. 'A little embarrassing, though, I guess.'

'Don't worry about it,' Cora said. 'Nothing shows.'

'Still,' Finley said, 'he's the only one here without his clothes on. That *would* be embarrassing. I bet Rick would feel a whole lot less embarrassed if he weren't the only one.' She set aside her drink and began to unbutton her red flannel shirt.

Rick gaped at her.

'Finley,' Abilene murmured. 'Jeez.'

Finley gave her a quick smile. She pulled off her shirt. 'You don't mind, do you, Rick?'

His head shook slightly from side to side. The towel across his lap was suddenly rising like a tent, and he crossed his legs in an effort to conceal the growing bulge.

'Am I the only one doing this?' Finley asked as she pulled off one of her sneakers. 'Come on, gang. Get with the program.'

'It is awfully hot in here,' Helen said. Her crimson face disappeared inside her sweatshirt. A moment later, the sweatshirt was off.

Abilene couldn't believe it. Timid Helen, always so self-conscious because of her weight.

At least she's wearing a bra, Abilene thought. It'll probably stay on, too.

Rick glanced at Helen. She gave him a sheepish smile. His return smile looked a bit forced. He turned to Abilene as if to see what she might be taking off.

Abilene just shook her head.

Finley was working on her shoes and socks. He checked Cora. She sat on the swivel chair, arms folded across her chest. 'Not me,' she said. 'I'm married.'

He looked ashamed. Accused. 'I didn't mean you should,' he said, a note of pleading in his voice. 'This is all . . . strange.'

Vivian, not saying a word, got up and stepped past the others and walked away toward the rear of the camper.

That's what I should do, Abilene thought. Walk away. All this is just too weird.

But she couldn't move. She sat there, a little breathless, heart pounding hard, ashamed but fascinated and excited.

God, I hope Harris never finds out about this.

I'm not doing anything, she told herself. And I won't. I won't.

Finley slipped her jeans down her legs. She kicked her feet free, then leaned back, naked, and patted her thighs. 'Don't you feel a lot better?' she asked Rick, 'now that you're not the only one?'

His head bobbed. He squirmed on his seat. He darted his eyes this way and that, either hoping for others to join the party or trying not to stare at her.

'You look nervous,' Finley said. 'Why don't you have another drink?'

Before he could respond, Helen took his glass. He watched while she went to the table and made his drink and brought it back to him. 'Thanks,' he murmured. His hand shook badly. He took a sip as Helen sat down beside him. 'I . . . I really should get going.'

'Don't you like it here?' Finley asked.

'I don't know. Nothing like this . . . it's like I'm dreaming, or something.'

'A good dream, I hope.' Finley slid her hands slowly up her thighs and over her hips and up her belly. She cupped the undersides of her breasts. Her thumbs stroked her nipples. She spread her knees wide apart.

Groaning, Rick writhed and looked away.

'Stop teasing him,' Cora said.

'Who's teasing?' Finley asked. She stood up, stepped through the pile of discarded clothing, and stopped in front of Rick. He gazed at her. He was gasping for air, blinking.

Finley took the plastic glass from his hand. She gave it to Helen. He made only a feeble attempt to hold on to the towel when she plucked it away. Before he could cover himself with his hands, she took him by the wrists.

She drew him forward, guided him down to his knees, placed his hands on her breasts, then gripped his shoulders as she slowly squatted and impaled herself.

My God, Abilene thought. Oh, my God.

It seemed unreal, impossible. It seemed inevitable.

Right here in front of us all.

Except Vivian.

Sank right down on it. Planted it into her. Abilene could almost feel the thick hardness inside herself, slick and thrusting.

It was over very fast, but it wasn't over. They started squirming together in the narrow aisle, kissing and squeezing and groping.

I could be next, Abilene thought.

No. No no no.

There's Harris. It wouldn't be worth the guilt.

Besides, Helen obviously intended to be next. She'd already unleashed her breasts. They were swaying wildly as she struggled to get out of her pants and underwear.

Soon, Rick was sandwiched between Helen and Finley.

'Join the fun,' Finley gasped.

Cora, looking dazed, got up from her swivel chair and stared down at the writhing bodies. 'I need some fresh air,' she said. She turned away and went out the front door.

'Come on, Hickok. You're not married yet.'

Rick pushed into Helen. She let out a shaky whimper.

'More the merrier,' Rick gasped, and plunged deeper into Helen.

Abilene could feel it.

She wanted it.

She realized she was squirming and her hand was inside her blouse, kneading her breast.

Nobody'll ever know but us.

She stood above the thrashing bodies and unbuttoned her blouse and took it off and strained her arms up behind her back to release the catches of her bra and the wrongness of it all struck her with numbing force.

Rick was a kid. A big kid and they'd lured him into their

camper and given him booze and seduced him. He never knew what hit him.

He doesn't seem to be complaining, she told herself.

But that didn't make it any better.

And even if Harris never found out, *she* would know. She would have to live with the guilt.

Abilene put on her blouse and hurried down the aisle to the rear of the camper.

Vivian was there, lying on a cushioned bench with her knees up, hands folded on her belly.

'You're missing out on the orgy,' Abilene said, and sat down across from her. 'You got out of there just in time.'

'Avoiding temptation.'

'He's a good-looking guy.'

'I noticed. Christ. Are they *all* at him?'

'Finley and Helen. Cora went outside.'

'I guess I can't blame Helen much. I mean, she doesn't have much luck with guys. Finley, though. Sometimes I wonder about her.'

'She can get a little nuts.'

There was a knock on the back door. Abilene got up and opened it. Cora climbed aboard.

They sat down.

'How come you didn't join the party?' she asked Abilene.

'Not my style.'

'You looked like you were getting awfully horny.'

'Yeah, well. Guess it was contagious.'

'I'll say. Shit. Helen sure caught it. I thought she'd fallen in love with that Frank guy. How can you be in love and drop your pants for a stranger?'

How, indeed? Abilene thought. I came damn close, myself.

'Just lost control,' she muttered.

'If this sort of stuff's gonna start happening, I'm not so sure we should keep on having our little adventures. Hell, maybe we oughta just go home.'

'This is the first time things've really gotten out of hand,' Vivian told her.

'It's once too often.'

'We could've stopped it,' Abilene said.

'But we didn't. That's what worries me. We all went along with it. We let it happen.'

'I don't think we should call it quits and go home, though,' Abilene said. 'Let's just keep a tighter rein on things from now on.'

'Keep Finley away from men,' Vivian added.

'Though, actually,' Abilene said, and hesitated. From the front of the camper, she heard grunts and quiet laughter. 'I know we really abused the kid . . .'

'Raped him is more like it,' Cora said.

'But, honestly, I think he's having the time of his life.'

'He'll be back first thing in the morning,' Finley said when the others returned to the front of the camper. She seemed chipper as she stepped into her jeans. 'I think he was disappointed you three woosed out. But tomorrow's another day.'

Helen, her naked body draped by the towel, was sprawled on one of the cushions, gazing at the ceiling. She looked grim. 'We shouldn't have done it,' she muttered.

'Oh, lighten up. It was a blast. The guy thought he'd died and gone to heaven.'

The next morning, Rick didn't show up.

'Probably hung over,' Finley said. 'I'll go find him.'

'Don't,' Cora said. 'Just leave him alone.'

Finley flapped a hand at her, then headed off into the fog and vanished.

The others caught up with her.

'You're not going after him alone,' Vivian said.

'And you're not going to touch him,' Abilene added.

'Gimme a break.'

They wandered up the dirt road.

They found tire marks where his pick-up truck had been. They found a mat of drying vomit. But the pick-up was gone.

They didn't quit and go home.

After the fog lifted that morning, they went to the shore. Abilene stood on the beach, watching while Cora experimented with her surfboard. Vivian sunbathed in her new bikini. Helen, stretched out beside Vivian, read a new William M. Carney paperback. Finley wandered off down the beach by herself. She climbed an outcropping that jutted into the ocean, and sat down on its summit. And stayed there.

Finally, Abilene climbed the rocks and stood beside her. 'Mind some company?' she asked.

'Pull up a chair.'

She sat down. A crashing wave hurled up spray that showered the outcropping just below them.

'It's neat here,' Abilene said.

Finley looked at her. The usual mischief was missing from her eyes. 'Am I a real jerk?' she asked.

'Most of the time.'

'You know what I mean.'

'Yeah.'

'I just couldn't help it. You know? The minute I saw Rick, all I could think about was getting him to fuck me. Nothing else mattered. Just something about the guy. Now everybody's pissed at me.'

'I think we're pissed at ourselves, too. Especially Helen.'

'Shit, she wanted him as bad as I did.'

'I have a feeling we *all* wanted him.'

'Well, it's not gonna happen again. No more guys for me. Not on this trip anyway.'

'Not worth the guilt?'

The old, normal gleam appeared in Finley's eyes. 'You've gotta be kidding me. It was worth the guilt and then some. It was *tremendous*. But if I tried something like that again, you guys would probably trounce me.'

Abilene smiled. 'Probably.'

'I just don't wanta get myself trounced. Especially not by my best friends.'

Chapter Thirty-six

Finley, shoulder deep in the small pool, glanced from Jim to Cora. 'If we get enough booze into our friend here, we won't have to worry about him running off. We might even be able to untie him for a while.'

'Get him stumble-down drunk, you mean?' Cora asked.

'Exactly. Anaesthetize him.'

'Forget it,' Cora said. 'I know what you're thinking. It isn't gonna happen.'

Finley's face darkened. '*What* isn't gonna happen?'

'You know damn well.'

'Oh, real nice. *Real* nice. Helen's fuckin' *dead* and you think I've got the hots for our friendly local hillbilly? For all we know, he's the bastard that did it.'

'It weren't me,' Jim muttered.

'Sure, sure.'

'I just wanta help ya.'

'And he won't be much help to us if we get him bombed,' Vivian pointed out.

'Why not? We're just gonna use him for bait. He doesn't have to be sober for that. Doesn't even have to be alive.'

Jim raised his head slightly. He looked at Finley as if she'd just told him there wouldn't be a Christmas this year.

'That kind of talk isn't necessary,' Abilene said. 'Jeez, Fin.'

'We're not going to do anything to you,' Vivian assured Jim.

He tried to smile, but it was a miserable attempt. 'She might,' he said.

'Durn tootin',' Finley said. 'You just never know about the crazy Fin-man. Loses her head, she does. Maybe she'll try to fuck you. Maybe she'll kill you for kicks. You just never know.' She bared her teeth like a lunatic grinning or ready to bite. 'Neither do they. They all know I'm mad. No tellin' *what* I might do.'

'Cut it out,' Abilene told her. 'It's not funny.'

'Of course not,' Finley said. 'Madness is serious business. *Deadly* serious,' she blurted. And bolted from her seat and charged through the water and reached up for Jim, yelling, ignoring the shouts of her friends.

Jim's mouth fell open. His eyes bulged. He tried to drop away from her, but she sprang up in front of him and grabbed the rope at his chest and tugged. With a gasp, he jerked forward and plunged off the ledge. Finley disappeared beneath him as water exploded.

Abilene flung herself into the pool. Currents from the thrashing bodies buffeted her legs. Ducking below the surface, she saw Finley and Jim tumbling in a froth of bubbles. Finley, on top, shoved the kid toward the bottom by his rope suspender and the waistband of his cut-offs. He could do nothing but kick and squirm and shake his head. There was terror in his eyes.

Abilene grabbed Finley by the hair and pulled, dragging her head up.

Finley blew a spray of water from her lips. She blinked at Abilene. Her shirt had lost buttons in the struggle with Batty, and now it hung off her left shoulder, exposing her breast.

'Let him up!' Abilene snapped.

'Join the fun, Hickok.'

Abilene slapped her hard across the face.

An arm darted up, flinging water, and Finley's fist hammered Abilene's cheek. The blow snapped her head sideways. She staggered backward a step and started to fall. Finley lunged at her. She cringed, expecting another punch, but Finley grabbed the front of her blouse with both hands and a rough yank stopped her fall.

'You okay?' Finley gasped.

Behind her, Vivian jumped into the pool.

'You *hit* me,' Abilene said.

'You hit *me*.'

'Knock it off,' Cora snapped. 'For Godsake. Give Vivian a hand.'

They both looked at Vivian. Who'd refused to let the pool water touch her since hearing Helen's story about the headless body. But who'd jumped in to help Jim and was now completely submerged.

As they waded toward her, she broke the surface. She pulled Jim up by the same rope Finley had used to haul him off his perch. He emerged face first. Water spewed from his mouth.

Vivian scowled at Finley. 'Just stay there. Haven't you done enough?'

Finley didn't come back with a crack. All she did was lift her shirt back onto her shoulder.

Vivian helped Jim to his feet. He stood in front of her, gasping and coughing. She put her arms around him. She drew him against her and patted his back. 'It's all right,' she soothed him. 'You'll be all right.' Still embracing him, she looked over her shoulder at Abilene. 'Come over here and untie his hands.'

'Hey!' Finley blurted. 'Fuck that!'

Abilene ignored her. She made her way through the water and stepped behind Jim. She fingered the rope around his wrists and began to pluck at the knot.

'Don't do it,' Finley warned.

'Go ahead,' Cora said.

'Are you nuts!'

'I'm not gonna leave him tied up,' Abilene said, 'so you can jump him every time you get the urge.'

The knot loosened. Jim worked his hands free and Abilene lifted the twisted rope out of the water.

He put his arms around Vivian.

'Isn't that sweet,' Finley muttered.

Abilene tossed the rope out of the pool. She stepped backward and sank down onto the submerged shelf. She fingered her face, wincing as she touched the knot of swelling at her cheekbone.

Finley didn't do this to me, she realized. It had been Batty's work with the skull.

But Finley had struck her in the same place.

It felt hot and sore.

I hit her first, she told herself. I had it coming.

As she gently rubbed the sore lump, it occurred to her that Finley, though right-handed, had punched her with the left. Just a matter of convenience? she wondered. Or had Finley swung with the left to spare her a stronger punch?

If she was taking it easy on me, why'd she use a fist?

Finley sat down beside Abilene. 'Are you all right?'

'I'll live.'

They both watched Vivian and Jim. They were still embracing. Jim was breathing hard, but no longer coughing.

'Sorry I slugged you,' Finley said.

'I hit you first. I'm sorry, too. But what were you doing, trying to drown him?'

Finley didn't answer for a while. Then she muttered, 'I don't know.'

Then Vivian eased Jim away from her. He didn't resist. She guided him to the side of the pool, and he lowered himself onto the shelf. Vivian sat next to him.

Meeting Finley's eyes, she shook her head.

'Okay, I was a bad little girl,' Finley said. 'So crucify me.'

'Just leave him alone from now on,' Vivian said.

'We've got enough to worry about,' Cora added, 'without having to keep an eye on you.'

'Yeah. Right.' Finley climbed out of the pool. Without another word or a look back, she started striding away toward the corner of the lodge. Her sneakers made squelching sounds.

Ol' yellow foot, Abilene thought, and felt a rush of sadness.

'Where are you going?' she called.

'That's my business.'

'Come on back. Jeez.'

Finley kept walking.

'Let her go,' Cora said.

'She'll be all right,' Vivian said.

Probably, Abilene thought. Hank won't be coming along till after dark. If Jim's been telling the truth.

Still, she didn't like the idea of Finley going off by herself.

'We've been kind of tough on her.'

'She's been acting nuts,' Cora said. 'Ever since Batty's place.'

'It freaked her out, being grabbed like that.'

'You'd think she would've enjoyed it,' Cora said. 'Being Finley.'

'Hey, come on.'

Jim raised his head. He frowned at Abilene. 'Ya had a run-in with Batty?'

'Did we ever,' Cora said. A corner of her mouth turned up. 'Broke his arm, killed his cat, stole his shotgun and boat.'

'Do you know him?' Vivian asked.

'Or her, as the case may be,' Abilene said, and realized it was the sort of remark Finley might make.

I oughta go find her, she thought.

'Batty does conjure stuff,' Jim said. 'Ya don' wanta make him mad at ya.'

'Too late for that,' Vivian said.

'Batty's the one let us know about Juniper. My sister? Hunters from the lodge here, they done killed her dead. We didn't know nothing 'bout it, but Batty saw it all in a vision and come over 'n let us know. Then he made us up a poison we used on them folks.'

'We?' Abilene asked. 'Were you in on it? Were you with them at the lodge that night?'

A sick look on his face, he nodded. 'They made me. I was only just a kid, but they made me go along. I didn't hurt nobody. But I was there. It was . . . just the awfulest thing. Seein' what they done. 'N how Hank carried on with the gals. How he cut 'em up 'n how he . . . done stuff.'

Cut 'em up. Done stuff.

Helen. Oh, Helen.

Abilene, suddenly feeling trapped and suffocated by the hot water, shoved herself up. She sat on the granite ledge and scooted backward, lifting her legs from the heat.

Vivian looked at her, then at Jim. 'You weren't with Hank last night, were you? When he killed our friend?'

'No! Honest! He shut me up in the shed out back. After he beat on me. I begged him not to do nothin', but he just laughed 'n tossed me in the shed 'n locked it up. I guess he knowed I'd try 'n interfere. But I couldn't get outa there. Then he come back just before sun-up, and told me what he done. It just made me plain sick.'

'What did he say?' Cora asked.

Vivian gave her a frantic look.

I don't want to hear this! Abilene thought. *Jesus, no.*

'He told me all how he done her, but . . . ' Jim glanced at Vivian, at Abilene. He shook his head.

'Tell us,' Cora said.

'I'm gonna go see about Finley,' Abilene said.

'Don't you want to know?'

Scowling at Cora, she shook her head. She started to stand up. 'I'm not sure. And besides . . . if we're gonna hear something like that, Finley should be with us.'

'You're right,' Vivian said.

'I want to make sure she's okay,' Abilene explained. She took a step away from the pool, then looked back, wondering whether her two friends would be safe, left alone with Jim. His hands were free. What if he went for the shotgun?

'Go ahead,' Cora told her. 'We'll be fine.'

'I ain't gonna do nothin',' Jim said.

Abilene started away. Stopping beside the drainage channel where she'd washed the blood off her legs, she picked up her socks. She stepped into her moccasins, then walked alongside Finley's trail of wet dribbles and shoeprints. As she stopped at the stairway leading down from the rear porch, she looked back and saw Cora boost herself out of the pool.

Even from here, she could see Cora's nipples through the thin wet fabric of her tank top.

Jim's sure getting an eyeful, she thought.

Cora's legs came out of the water, Abilene's blouse knotted around her left ankle.

Which is just where it had been when she'd chased down Jim and wrestled with him on the ground. God, she'd been all over him.

She felt a blush heat her skin.

No wonder the kid wants to stay.

The first time he laid eyes on us, *all* of us were naked. Except Helen.

Jim must figure he's died and gone to heaven.

Maybe he's not interested in that kind of thing.

Could be gay, she supposed.

Could be he's *very* interested, secretly thrilled by the whole thing, but smart enough to act oblivious of it all.

She watched Vivian wade across the pool and stop at Cora's feet. With her back to Jim. Cora, braced up on her elbows, had no view of him either.

The kid stayed put.

Vivian tossed Abilene's blouse aside.

She's unwrapping the ankle.

By the time the belts were off and Vivian was lifting away the makeshift splints, Abilene decided that Jim had no intention of jumping her friends.

She stepped around the porch stairs, turned the corner of the lodge, and began to climb the steep pavement toward the rear end of the Wagoneer.

No sign of Finley.

Not until she'd trudged higher and she spotted her friend through the windows, sitting on the hood.

When she came up beside the car, Finley said, 'Can't a gal have any privacy around here?'

'Nope.' Abilene dropped her socks to the driveway, then hopped up and sat on the hood.

Finley's legs dangled over the front, her feet on the bumper. Her hand was wrapped around the neck of a tequila bottle. She glanced at Abilene, then hoisted the bottle and took a drink.

'I wanted to make sure you're all right.'

'What's that, your goal in life?'

'Hey.'

'I'm fine. Just fine. Why don't you go back to the pool before Jim kills our trusting pals?'

'They can take care of themselves.'

'And I can't, huh?' She gulped some more tequila.

'Save some for the fishes, huh?'

'If I wanta have a drink, it's my business.'

'It's my business if you hog the whole damn bottle. Gimme.'

Finley looked at her, smirked, let out a quick laugh, and handed it over.

Abilene took a few swallows. She shuddered. She took a deep breath and gave back the bottle. 'It's better with mixers.'

'Yeah. I just didn't feel like wasting time with 'em.'

'You don't really think Jim's the killer, do you?'

Finley shrugged. 'Hell, I don't know. I guess not. That shit about his brother's pretty hard to buy, but . . . I guess I believe him. Sort of.' She took a drink and passed the bottle to Abilene. 'I guess if I really thought Jim was the bastard that murdered Helen, I would've gone ahead and killed him by now. But the kid pisses me off.'

'So I gather.'

'It's mostly his fault, even if his brother *is* the guy who actually did it.'

Abilene took a sip of tequila. 'We never should've come to a place like this.'

'It was Helen's pick.'

'We didn't have to go along with it.'

'Sure we did. That was the deal. Besides, nobody knew what was going to happen. And if we'd gone somewhere different, she might've gotten killed anyway. No place is safe. We might've had a head-on, and *all* gotten wiped out.'

'Coming here is what did it, though.'

Finley took the bottle from her, tilted it up and drank. 'Sooner or later, something was bound to happen. Five gals going around looking for adventure.'

'Yeah.'

'Looking for trouble. Taking all kinds of risks. The surprising thing is that nobody ever nailed any of us till now.'

'We were pretty lucky.'

'Damn lucky.'

'I guess the luck stopped here.'

'For Helen, it sure did.'

They were silent for a while. They passed the bottle back and forth. It was Finley who finally capped it. 'Don't want get so polluted I miss my chance to waste Hank,' she said. 'Gotta buy him a farm.'

'We gotta keep alert,' Abilene agreed. She was feeling a bit numb.

'I used to keep a lert. Had a little cage for it. They make damn fine pets.'

'Wonder if we oughta head on down, see what's happening?'

'Left my camera down there.' She leaned forward, braced her elbows on her knees, and hung her head. 'Guess it doesn't matter. The epic's all done. Gone with the fuckin' wind. Never even got around to adding last year's stuff. Figured it'd just remind everyone of . . . what I did with that surfer guy. As if they need reminding. Shit. And now . . . nobody'll ever want to look at the thing again. Me included. Wouldn't be able to stand it. *Daring Young Maids*. Minus one. Maybe I'll burn the whole fuckin' thing.'

'Naw. Don't.' She patted Finley's back. 'We might wanta see it again. Someday. Just to see how we used to be.'

'Maybe won't be any of us left to watch it, anyhow. Just be a bunch of dead gals on the thing.'

'Cut it out. We'll be fine.'

'Sure.'

'Come on, let's go on down with the others.' Abilene stood on the bumper, jumped to the driveway and staggered forward, waving her arms for balance. She managed, just barely, to stay on her feet. She turned around carefully. 'Rough waters,' she said.

Finley didn't jump. Instead, she lowered her legs and slid down the front of the car until her feet found the pavement. She stood up straight. She wobbled a bit. 'I'm afraid we'd better not attempt to descend the treacherous dri . . .'

'They're gonna save us the trouble,' Abilene interrupted as the others appeared at the bottom of the slope.

Jim was carrying Cora piggy-back. A good trick, Abilene thought. A very good trick, especially since he had a leg injury himself and Cora must outweigh him by twenty or thirty pounds. But he seemed to be doing just fine.

Cora kept her right arm across the top of Jim's chest to hold herself tight against his back. She gripped the water bottle in her left hand. Both her legs were hugging Jim's hips. He held them there, hands hooked beneath her knees. Her dangling feet swayed. Her right ankle was wrapped with an Ace bandage, and the splints were gone.

Jim looked as if he might lose his cut-offs. Heavy with water, supported by the single rope, they sagged at such an angle that Abilene could see matted pubic hair. The crease at the side of his groin showed, too. He paused a moment, huffing, then resumed his trudge up the slope.

Vivian walked behind the pair, carrying the shotgun and Finley's camera. Her clinging white polo shirt was nearly transparent. The two belts that had been used to secure Cora's splints hung across her chest like bandoliers. Abilene's blouse was tucked under the waistband of her shorts.

'You got everything?' Abilene called.

'No thanks to you two,' Cora said.

'You could've waited for us.'

'We did. We figured you weren't coming back.'

'Just on our way,' Finley said, coming over to Abilene's side and flinging an arm across her shoulders. With her other hand, she waved the bottle at them.

Cora, her face bobbing above Jim's head, frowned at them. 'Are you two drunk?'

'Had a few wee sips,' Abilene said.

'We're perfectly fine 'n dandy,' Finley added.

'Terrific,' Cora muttered.

Abilene stepped out of Jim's way and took the water bottle from Cora's hand.

Finley met Vivian and took the camera.

Where the pavement leveled out in front of the car, Jim eased Cora down. She clung to him and stood on her left leg. Abilene, hurrying forward to help, saw a patchwork of Bandaids on her neck and back and shoulder. The worst of the scratches and bites were covered.

She set down the water bottle and clutched Cora beneath the armpits. With Jim's help, she lowered her friend to the concrete.

He pulled up his drooping cut-offs, then bent over and held his knees as he struggled to catch his breath.

'I'll have some of that,' Cora said, reaching up toward Finley.

'Don' overdo it,' Finley warned, and gave her the bottle. 'Moderation in all things. Thas the secret to a long 'n happy life.'

Chapter Thirty-seven

Cora only had a few sips before setting the bottle aside. Vivian brought the shotgun to her, and she kept watch on Jim while the others unloaded food and supplies from the Wagoneer.

Vivian lit the stove. Abilene opened cans of chili and dumped them into a pot. Finley got out rolls and Pepsis.

While they waited for the chili, they helped Cora to the car so she could sit on the hood with her legs dangling.

Soon, the chili was bubbling. Abilene ladled it into cups and passed it around.

Finley perched on the hood beside Cora. Abilene and Vivian sat on the pavement near Jim. They ate in silence. The chili was hot. The Pepsis were warm. The rolls were hard. Everything tasted very good to Abilene, but she ate slowly. She didn't want the meal to end. She *dreaded* for it to end. Because, when it was finished, there would be nothing left to do but get ready for Hank. She had a second cup of chili, not because she was still hungry, but only to prolong what seemed to be a final piece of normalcy.

When everyone was done, she volunteered to do the dishes.

'Why bother?' Cora said. 'Let's just throw them in a box. We won't be eating again.'

'That's what *I'm* afraid of,' Finley said.

'You know what I mean. As soon as we've taken care of Hank, you're gonna hike out of here and get help. You and whoever else wants to go.'

'Wouldn't hurt to clean the dishes, anyway,' Abilene said. 'Besides, it'll give me something to do.'

'Walk off your drunk,' Finley said.

'In that case,' Cora told her, 'you oughta go along with her.'

'I'm feeling pretty damn sober,' Abilene said. 'Unfortunately.'

'You and me both.' Finley slid down from the hood. 'Let's do it. Beats waiting around.'

Abilene and Finley gathered the dirty pot and cups and spoons. Taking along a roll of paper towels, they headed down the driveway. At the rear of the lodge, they came to the pool's run-off channel. They followed it into the woods where it flowed into a brook. And where the shadows were deep enough to remind Abilene that night was coming soon.

She and Finley crouched on rocks and began to rinse the utensils. The water, probably as cold upstream as the water in the lake, was warmed with the run-off from the hot pools. It felt good on Abilene's hands. And crouching like this felt good. Hunching against her legs, reaching way down between them.

Comforting.

Almost a fetal position, she realized.

It would feel *very* good to curl up in a dark place and hug her knees. And stay that way until morning.

'Are you scared?' she asked.

'I don't like the waiting.'

'I just wish the whole thing would go away.'

'It'll be fine once we've taken care of Hank.'

'You're the one who said we might all be dead.'

'I was . . . just in a mood. The booze and everything. We'll be fine. We've got the shotgun. We'll blow the fucker's head off. He won't have a chance.'

'I hope you're right. But something can always go wrong.'

'You worry too much, Hickok.'

'We could use Hickok tonight. Or at least a couple of his six-guns.'

'Hell. Batty's over 'n under'll do us just fine.'

They wiped away the remaining chili and grease with wads of paper towels, then piled the cups and spoons into the cook pot. Abilene clamped the paper roll against her side. She picked up the used towels so they wouldn't be left behind to litter the shore.

Then, Finley in the lead, they walked out of the woods into the evening's golden glow of sunlight.

* * *

At the top of the driveway, they found that Cora had abandoned her perch on the car. She was stretched out on the pavement, hands folded on her belly. Vivian sat crosslegged, the shotgun resting across her thighs. She was facing Jim, who sat with his arms folded around his knees.

Someone, probably Vivian, had already put away the stove and supplies. On the hood of the car was a box containing the empty cans. Abilene tossed the wet, dirty balls of paper into the box. Then she braced a door of the Wagoneer open while Finley climbed inside with the roll of towels and the pot full of cups and spoons.

'Need anything while I'm in here?'

Ducking, Abilene looked in. The back seat and rear storage area were heaped with clothing, swimsuits, shoes, purses, sleeping bags, food and gear. 'See if you can find the flashlights,' she said.

'They're in here someplace.'

While she watched Finley dig through the mess, she considered getting in and hunting for her sneakers and fresh clothes. Sneakers would be better than the moccasins she was wearing.

Especially if I have to run.

It would feel good to get into dry clothes. But the way she was sweating, anything she put on would very quickly be just as moist as what she was already wearing. Besides, this skirt and blouse were already ruined. No point wrecking anything else.

The others hadn't changed, either, though the back of Cora's tank top was snagged and torn and half Finley's shirt buttons were missing. If anybody needed fresh clothes, they did.

Finley handed out two flashlights.

'See if you can find my sneakers,' Abilene said.

'They're right here. I just saw them.' She turned away to look for them.

'Are you gonna wear what you've got on?'

'You think we should dress for the ball? Who are we trying to impress?'

'Guess not.'

'These're my fightin' duds,' Finley said, and crawled out backward with the shoes.

Abilene put them on, tossed her moccasins into the car, then trudged to the top of the driveway and joined the others. She lay down on the pavement. She folded her hands beneath her head and crossed her ankles and shut her eyes.

Nothing to do now but wait, she thought.

It felt good to be lying down.

If I could only fall asleep. Get away from all this. At least for a while.

'Maybe we should have Jim tell us about Helen,' Cora said.

'What about her?' Finley asked.

'Hank told him . . . how he got her.'

'Jeez,' Finley muttered.

'I don't think I want to know,' Vivian said. 'We *saw* what he did to her. We don't have to hear about it.'

'Not sure I wanta talk about it anyhow,' Jim said. 'Made me just sick, him tellin' me. Had me lickin' his eyes, 'n he was moanin' 'n rubbin' me the whole time. It was awful. But that's when I made up my mind I had to save the rest of ya. I'll help ya kill him, if ya let me.'

'We'll do the killing,' Finley said.

'You've already helped us a lot,' Vivian said. 'Just by telling us about him. Now we know who we're up against.'

'Especially about his eyes,' Cora added. 'It's good to know he can't operate in light.'

'He can see like a cat in the dark,' Jim said.

'We oughta go for his eyes with the flashlights,' Finley suggested.

She really does believe, Abilene thought.

And pictured herself and Finley shining flashlights into Hank's eyes. He is a huge man, pale in the darkness. Very pale. An albino. Did Jim say he was an albino? And hairless. And holding a big knife. He is wearing a loincloth. Like a redskin from the movies, but he's white, not red. White as the belly of a fish.

When they shine the light in his eyes, he roars and staggers backward and flings up his arms, trying to block the painful brightness. He acts . . . like *The Thing*. Not The Thing from the remake, but the real one. James Arness. When he's being zapped. Bellowing with rage and pain, writhing and twitching like a lunatic dancer.

Doing the Mash.

The Monster Mash.

'The Monster Mash is a graveyard . . .'

Abilene flinched awake, opened her eyes, and what she saw made her insides shrivel.

Vivian. Crouched beside her. A hand on her shoulder.

Vivian. But not the way Abilene wanted to see her. Not at all.

Her tangled hair, usually auburn gleaming with red and gold highlights, looked dull brown. The whites of her eyes were blue like snow in evening shadows. Her sunburnt face was dusky, her white polo shirt gray.

But not as gray as the sky.

'It's time,' Vivian told her.

Not what Abilene wanted to hear.

'Time to rise 'n shine, Sleeping Beauty,' Finley said.

Abilene groaned. She pulled her hands out from under her head. They felt lifeless. So did her rump. Even her feet, crossed at the ankles, were a little numb.

She uncrossed them, sat up and shook her arms and legs.

'Guess I conked out for a while,' she muttered, and felt shivery as hot, prickly sensations spread through her feet and fingers and buttocks.

'More than a while,' Cora said.

'You didn't miss much,' Vivian told her, standing up.

Abilene got to her feet. She hopped a few times, wincing. She rubbed her rump through the damp denim skirt. 'I don't recommend falling asleep on concrete,' she said.

'Pins and needles?' Vivian asked.

'With a vengeance.' Also, her skin felt itchy under the knife scabbard. Even though she hadn't been sleeping on it, the moist leather had been tight against her hip and thigh ever since she'd taken it from Batty.

She drew out the big knife. Its sheath remained against her skin as if glued there. She reached beneath her skirt and pulled, grimacing as it peeled away.

She slid the blade into its holder, then rubbed her irritated skin.

'At least you got some rest,' Vivian told her.

'Wish *I* couldn've fallen asleep,' Finley said. She was sitting on the hood of the Wagoneer, her feet on the bumper. The shotgun rested across her lap.

Who let *her* have the shotgun? Abilene wondered.

'I guess I must've missed *something*,' she said. She shoved the covered knife under the waistband at the other side of her skirt. Its tip caught her panties and pushed them down. Turning away from Jim, she hitched them back up. Then she frowned at Finley. 'How come you've got the gun?'

'Just lucky.'

'I'm a bit handicapped,' Cora explained. 'Wouldn't make sense for me to be the shooter. Vivian doesn't want to be.'

'Screwed her up just chopping the cat,' Finley said.

'I'm not sure I *could* shoot at a person,' Vivian said.

'Whereas,' Cora added, 'Finley has already shown herself capable of that. Even if she did miss.'

'Hey, I was in a moving boat, for Godsake. Batty was probably out of range, anyway.'

'And Finley wants to be the one,' Cora said.

'Fuckin'-A-right.'

'So unless *you* want to do it . . .'

Abilene shook her head. She rubbed the sore backs of her hands.

'Didn't think so,' Finley said. 'Besides, it was my idea from the start – sticking around to bag the bastard. I wanta do the honors.'

'Fine,' Abilene told her. But she didn't like the idea. Finley had shown herself, more than once, to be a hothead. With the shotgun in her hands, no telling what she might do. The weapon should be kept by someone with better self-control.

Who, though? Cora was right. With her ankle broken, she wouldn't be able to maneuver worth a damn. Vivian didn't *want* to shoot Hank or anyone else, and neither did Abilene.

Certainly can't give the shotgun to Jim, even if he does claim to hate his brother.

That leaves Finley. Like it or not.

'What else did I miss while I was snoozing?' she asked. 'Any other major decisions?'

'Don't get so huffy,' Finley said. 'You were zonked. We didn't want to wake you up.'

'You know the balcony that overlooks the lobby?' Cora asked. 'We figured we'd position ourselves up there. It'll give us a good field of vision, and we'll be hard to get at. Hank would have to come upstairs.'

'He couldn't possibly sneak up on us,' Vivian added.

'Jim'll be our bait,' Cora said. 'He'll be down in the lobby in plain sight. When Hank goes over to him . . .'

'Bang!' Finley blurted.

'It sounds like a good plan,' Abilene admitted. She liked, very much, the idea of being above it all. Out of reach. Even if Finley should miss, she'd have plenty of time to reload before Hank could climb the stairs and get to them – especially if they were all the way at the far end of the balcony.

'The trick,' Finley said, 'will be getting Hank into the line of fire.'

Cora nodded. 'We've got no idea where he might enter the lodge. He might come in anywhere; through the pools or even on the second floor. But we want to get him down there in the lobby area.'

'I'm gonna call out to him,' Jim explained. 'Soon as I figure he's around, I'll start callin' out. I'll get him to come on over to me.'

'And then it's *adios*, asshole.'

'Sounds really good,' Abilene said. 'If it works.'

'It'll work,' Finley said.

'What if *he* has a gun?' Vivian asked.

The question stunned Abilene. She hadn't even thought of *that*.

From the looks on the faces of her friends, they hadn't either.

After a moment, Finley said, 'I'll just have to nail him before he brings it into play.'

'*Will* he have a gun?' Abilene asked, frowning at Jim.

'Maybe. We got us some rifles. But he didn't take one along last night. Just went out with his knife, is all.'

'And he left that in Helen,' Cora said, her voice grim.

'Oh, he's got more. He's got *lotsa* knives. That's what he likes . . . to cut on folks. I don't spect he'd wanta ruin all his fun by shootin' any of ya.'

'Isn't that charming,' Finley muttered.

They were silent for a while.

Thinking about Helen? Abilene wondered. Or wondering how it might feel to have a knife blade shoved into them?

A hot, shocking thrust into the belly.

Or maybe it'd feel cold. Ice cold.

And maybe it wouldn't be your belly he stuck it in.

'We'd better get at it,' Cora said, and Abilene was glad to have her thoughts interrupted. 'The sun's down. He might already be on his way.'

The lodge was much darker than the evening outside. Abilene, entering first, halted and swept her flashlight across the lobby. Here and there, support posts blocked its beam and cast shadows that flitted over the floor. She felt goosebumps scurry up her spine and the nape of her neck. Her scalp prickled.

'Don't just stand there,' Cora said.

'Pretty sure he ain't here yet,' Jim said.

Abilene hurried to the left, shining her light on the stairway. It looked clear. But she didn't like the shadows thrown by the banister. She sidestepped and looked at the others. Jim was close behind her, Cora riding on his back. Following them was Finley with the shotgun. Vivian entered with the second flashlight and eased the door shut.

Abilene started to climb the stairs backward, lighting the way for Jim.

'Are you doing okay?' she whispered as she made her way higher.

'Ain't bad.'

'Just don't fall.'

'I'll second that,' Cora said.

They were several stairs below her when she reached the top. She wanted very badly to swing her light away and check the balcony, imagined herself doing just that and imagined Jim tripping in the sudden darkness. A gasp and he's falling backward, Cora screaming, both of them colliding with Finley and the three of them tumbling down the stairs, taking out Vivian, all four coming to rest in a broken heap at the bottom of the stairs.

Just because I was scared somebody might be up here.

She managed not to check behind her. Even after Jim made it to the top of the stairs, she kept her light trained on the floor in front of him while she backed her way along the balcony.

Hoping no one would grab her.

Then the balcony rail was there for Jim, so she whirled around. The bright beam showed only a long empty stretch afloat with dust motes between the banister and the wall with its three closed doors.

Satisfied, she lit the way for Jim and sidestepped, keeping her back near the wall.

He could heave Cora right off here, she thought.

Finley'd probably shoot him, though.

Hell, he's been untied for hours. He's had plenty of chances to jump us. Or make a break for it. He's in on it with us, just like he says.

Unless it's just that he's scared of the shotgun.

Scared of his big brother, Hank, that's what he is. Wants us to do the dirty work for him.

And Finley'll be glad to comply.

'Okay,' Cora said. 'This is far enough.'

Abilene halted only a few strides from the end of the balcony. Jim lowered Cora. She released her hold, got her good foot on the floor, pivoted and grabbed the top of the split log railing.

'This'll be perfect,' she said.

Vivian squeezed past Finley. She and Jim clutched Cora by her upper arms and eased her down. She sat with her legs outstretched and hooked an arm around one of the uprights.

Finley brought the shotgun to Abilene. 'Keep us covered, okay?'

'Don't mess around down there. He might be anywhere.'

'Won't take long.' She started away. 'Let's go,' she said, and gave Jim a pat on the flank. Vivian went first, lighting the way.

Abilene watched the three of them hurry along the balcony. She lowered the shotgun until its stock bumped softly against the floor. Its barrels felt cool and slippery in her hand. She hoped she wouldn't need to use it, but knew that she could if she had to. Her dad, immersed in the lore of the Old West, had trained her not only in the art of the quick-draw, but in how to hit what she aimed with sixgun, rifle and shotgun. He'd even taken to calling her 'Dead-eye.'

Good thing Finley never caught wind of *that*, she thought as she watched her friends descend the stairs, Jim between them.

They came back through the lobby, the light swinging from side to side like the headbeam of a miniature locomotive. Abilene kept her eyes on it, half expecting it to reveal Hank leaping out from behind a support.

Then the light darted up at her. She squinted and turned her face away from its glare.

'Right about there's fine,' Cora said.

The light slid away. Abilene stepped closer to the railing and looked down. They were directly below her, eight or ten feet beyond the balcony's overhang.

Jim leaned back against a support beam. He hitched up his drooping cut-offs, then put his arms behind the post. Finley pulled a rope from a front pocket of her shorts. The one they'd used before? The last time Abilene had seen that rope was when she'd untied Jim down in the outside pool.

Maybe someone had gone to get it while she'd been asleep.

One more thing I missed, she thought.

Finley stepped behind the post. Vivian aimed the light back there while Finley tied Jim's hands.

'Not too tight,' Vivian said.

'I know, I know.' When she was done, she asked Jim, 'How's that?'

'I guess okay.'

'If it was any looser, it'd fall right off.'

'It's okay.'

'All right. Good luck.' She gave Jim's shoulder a squeeze.

She's sure done a turn-around, Abilene thought as Finley followed Vivian back toward the stairway. Not so long ago, she'd attacked Jim in the pool and even threatened to kill him. Now she was treating him like a pal.

She must've finally decided he really is on our side.

Or maybe she'd started to find herself attracted to him.

Wouldn't be the first time she'd gotten the hots for a young stranger.

He was a dim shape down there against the post. Even with his deep tan, his skin seemed pale compared to his cut-offs and the darkness around him. He had a strip of very white skin below his waist. Because of the way his shorts hung crooked, it was narrow at one hip and got much wider as it crossed his belly.

Abilene supposed she couldn't blame Finley for warming up to the guy.

He was slim and handsome and you sure couldn't miss the fact that he wasn't wearing much. On top of that, he'd apparently spent all his years in the wilds. There was something of the primitive savage about him. But he seemed vulnerable, shy and friendly.

Also, you couldn't help but feel a little sorry for him. His whole family was dead except for his maniac of a brother. A freak who makes Jim lick his eyes and does God-knows-what-else to him. Molests him, apparently.

He'd had a tough, strange life.

Part of you feared the wildness in him. Part of you wanted to hug and comfort him. Part of you wanted to slip that rope suspender off his shoulder and climb all over him.

No wonder, really, that Finley had started treating him nice.

Abilene switched her flashlight on. She aimed its beam down at Jim. He squinted up at her. His skin was gleaming as if slick with oil. 'Are you doing okay?' she asked.

'Yeah. Thanks.'

Then Finley and Vivian were coming along the balcony. Abilene turned off her flashlight. She gave the shotgun to Finley.

Finley stepped past her, leaned against the railing and peered down.

Vivian lowered herself to the floor on the other side of Cora.

Abilene sat cross-legged near Cora's feet. Gazing between the uprights, she could see Jim down below lashed to his post like a prisoner of Indians about to be tortured or burned at the stake.

Or like a witch waiting for the same kind of end.

A male witch is called a warlock, she thought.

She wondered what that made Batty.

And felt a tremor as she remembered Batty's threat to kill them all. *Get me plenty a fresh items for m'stock.* Including one of Finley's breasts. *I'll cut me this one right off.*

This is all bad enough without thinking about *that*, she told herself.

I broke Batty's arm. He can't hurt us. She can't. *It* can't.

Unless with magic . . .

Forget it.

Just worry about Hank.

Chapter Thirty-eight

The windows at the front of the lobby, which had been rectangles of dim gray a short while ago, now were nearly black. Abilene watched them through the gaps between the uprights of the balcony railing. She tried to watch the door, too. She knew just where it ought to be, but she couldn't see it.

I'll see it if it opens, she thought. It'll let in darkness, but that's bound to be brighter than what we've got in here.

She doubted that Hank would enter the lodge from the front, anyway.

Sometimes, she scanned the long room below her from the foot of the stairway to the fireplace at the other end. Not that she could *see* the stairway or the fireplace. All that she could really make out, down there, were the vague shapes of the support beams. Probably a dozen of them. A few were visible against the lesser darkness of the windows. She could distinguish the others, just barely, because they seemed to be a shade lighter than the wood of the walls and floorboards. A very slight degree of a shade lighter, so that they almost seemed not to be there at all, and appeared to melt away if she tried too hard to see them.

She didn't like looking at those posts. Didn't like it at all. The way they shifted and vanished. The way she kept expecting someone, hiding among them, to slide into view and scurry from one to another.

Every so often, when her nerves needed a rest from the vigil, she looked at Jim.

Some time ago, he'd slid down the beam and sat on the floor.

She could see him there, now, his legs stretched out. Only his bare skin was visible, blurred and dusky. His head hung forward so that his dark hair concealed his face. Where his cut-off jeans covered him, he didn't appear to be there at all. He looked like a torso and legs, as if the section from just below his hips to part-way down his thighs had been severed and thrown away.

Not a pretty idea, she thought.

She wondered if he would be all right down there.

He'll be fine, she told herself. Hank won't do anything to him. The creep's after us, not his brother.

Unless he figures out, somehow, that Jim has thrown in with us.

He's got no way of knowing.

Besides, Finley'll shoot him the moment he shows up.

Finley, some time ago, had stopped leaning against the banister and sat down. She was silent at Abilene's left, the shotgun across her thighs. The tan of her safari shirt and shorts matched her skin so well in the darkness that Abilene couldn't tell where her clothes left off and her skin began. As Abilene was looking at her, Finley turned her head. In the blur of her face were muddy white eyes. A row of teeth, as dim as her eyes, showed for a moment when she smiled.

I wish we could at least talk, Abilene thought.

She reached over and gave Finley's knee a brief squeeze.

'Don't get fresh,' Finley whispered.

That brought a smile to Abilene, but either Cora or Vivian went 'Shhhhhh.'

Abilene turned her head toward them.

Cora's right leg was still extended, its bandaged foot almost touching Abilene's thigh. Her left leg was bent, its knee raised. She had let go of the railing and eased herself backward so her head was on Vivian's lap.

Both of Cora's legs seemed to end high up her thighs. Like Jim, she looked as if the tops of her legs and her pelvic region had been lopped out. But her shorts were skimpier than his, so less appeared to be missing.

The shorts, Abilene remembered, were red. For a few moments, she couldn't recall the color of the tank top. Yellow or . . . no, pink. Pale, faded pink. The fresh blood on Cora's back had been bright red on pink. Now, the shirt was a shade of gray somewhat lighter than the skin of Cora's chest beyond the low scooped neck and around the shoulder straps.

Cora's face was a dark oval smudge against the white of Vivian's shorts. Of course, the shorts didn't look any whiter than had Finley's eyes and teeth. They were dingy gray, the same as her knit pullover. But that gray seemed to be brighter than anything else in sight.

Vivian's clothes almost *glowed* in the dark.

Her legs were crossed and she was leaning backward, braced up with dim arms.

Her shirt looked very much like a ghostly apparition floating at an angle above the floor, nobody in it at all.

The Tipton Shirt without the Tipton Girl.

This isn't a Tipton, she reminded herself. It's a Ralph Lauren or something.

And awfully damn visible.

If I can see it this well, Abilene thought, anyone can.

Including Hank.

That outfit could blow us all out of the water.

Why the hell didn't she change her clothes!

Too late for that. Way too late for that. Shit!

Oughta make her take 'em off.

Calm down, she told herself. It's not like Viv did it on purpose. It simply hadn't occurred to her that she would stand out like this.

Hadn't occurred to the rest of us, either.

Any of us might've ended up dressed in white. The whole idea of trying to blend in with the darkness simply hadn't come up.

718

She'd blend in a lot better if she *did* take off those clothes. They're a hell of a lot brighter than her skin.

Abilene considered suggesting it.

Oh yeah, she thought. Right. Ask her to strip down. Sure thing. We're up here waiting for a Goddamn homicidal sex pervert to show up and I calmly ask Viv to get naked. Brilliant. Forget it.

Too bad Finley isn't the one in white. She'd be delighted to shuck off every stitch.

Abilene looked down at herself. Her own plaid blouse was dark, her skirt as black as the night. But the short skirt was rucked up high because of how she sat. She saw that she, too, was wearing white.

I'm *not* taking off my panties.

Besides, nobody down below could possibly be in a position to see the small bit of pale fabric.

For that matter, she realized, Vivian was far enough from the railing that no one on the ground floor should be able to see *her* white clothes, either.

Only if Hank were actually up here . . .

Abilene peered into the darkness beyond Vivian. She saw nothing.

He could be right there, right now.

We would've heard him, she told herself. You can't take a step in this old place without a floorboard creaking.

But maybe *he* can.

We should've prepared better, she thought. Why didn't we bring the trash box with us? If we'd set up empty cans and bottles across the balcony floor, they'd be kicked over by anyone sneaking toward us.

Or we could've strung a rope across it to trip him.

We don't have enough rope for that, she realized. But we

719

could've used belts or something. *Anything* to make him trip or at least make noise.

Too late for that kind of thing, now.

Unless a couple of us want to hurry back to the car.

And that's *exactly* when Hank would show up.

If he's not already here.

Standing just on the other side of Vivian. Wearing something dark. A knife in his hand.

I'd be able to see his eyes, she thought. Without lids, they must look huge. There'd be big white orbs . . .

No, they're red. Jim had said they're red.

Cora's shorts were red, and you can't see *them*.

Abilene reached down, fumbled in the fold of denim on her lap, and wrapped her hand around the flashlight. She raised it and aimed it past Vivian.

Before she could thumb the switch, her left arm was grabbed. She flinched and gasped.

'What're you doing?' Finley whispered.

'I've got to *see*.'

'Shhhh,' came from her other side.

'He might be here,' Finley warned, ignoring the shush. 'Keep that light off.'

'Shit.'

'Shhhh.'

Abilene lowered the flashlight to her lap. She sighed.

He probably isn't up here, anyway. Probably. We probably would've heard him. And he probably wouldn't just stand there, watching us. He'd have *done* something by now. Like plunge his knife into Vivian's chest and slash Cora's throat.

So he's not here.

Not yet.

Probably.

Abilene finally calmed down.

As time passed, she saw others shifting their positions. Cora lowered her knee, stretching out her leg. She sat up and hooked an arm around a baluster and peered down. Vivian's tilted shirt sank down until its back met the floor. Her knees rose like a couple of dim peaks. Finley stood up for a while, then squatted like a baseball umpire.

Abilene realized that her own rump and legs had become numb. She scooted away from the railing, uncrossed her legs and pushed herself backward. Instead of meeting the wall, she was stopped by a door. She slumped against it and stretched out her legs.

Much better.

For a while, she suffered pins and needles. But the hot tingly sensations soon passed.

From here, she had no view of the ground floor.

Neither did Vivian, lying down the way she was.

But Cora and Finley were keeping watch on the area below. And Jim was down there.

Hope he's not asleep, she thought.

But even if he's wide awake, he'll be the last to know if Hank comes in up here.

The whole plan falls apart if Hank decides to climb the outside stairs to the second-story porch. He might enter through the door at the end of the corridor. Or he might use the broken window and get into that room, just as Abilene had done yesterday. The squirrel room.

He could come out of it, sneak into one of the rooms on this side of the hallway, and open one of *these* doors. Then he'd be right here with us on the balcony.

Abilene wished she hadn't thought of that.

All the doors are locked, she reminded herself.

What if he has a key?

He doesn't. He *probably* doesn't.

And he sure couldn't break into one of these rooms without us hearing him.

He might be in the one right behind me.

No way.

But now that the idea had come to her, she found herself waiting for the door at her back to swing inward, dropping her across the threshold. She saw herself falling, saw Hank crouch out of the darkness and grab her arms, felt him pulling, dragging her into the room. Before the others even knew what was happening, he would slam the door. Locking them out. Locking her inside the black room with him.

Crazy.

Don't think about it.

She couldn't *not* think about it, so she leaned forward to get her weight off the door, then scooted sideways until her back found the safety of the wall. One of her feet accidentally nudged Finley's rump. Finley let out a quick gasp, popped up from her squat as if springs had been triggered, and glanced around at her.

She's jumpy, too, Abilene thought.

Of course she is. She's got more guts than any of us, but you'd have to be a damned *robot* not to be scared at a time like this.

'That you?' Jim's voice in the stillness shot ice through Abilene's body.

Finley's back stiffened and she raised the shotgun to her shoulder.

Cora, twisting sideways, grabbed two of the railing uprights and peered down.

Vivian sat up fast, her pale shirt a moving blur.

Abilene drew in her feet. She grabbed the flashlight, then straightened her legs, sliding her back slowly up the wall as Jim said, 'Over here. They got me tied.' Shaking all over, heart slamming, she took a step forward. A floorboard creaked under her weight. Praying that Hank hadn't heard it, she took another step.

Finley was already up against the railing.

Vivian, at the other side of Cora, was on her feet.

Abilene took one more step and felt the split log push against her waist. She gazed down into the blackness. She could see enough of Jim to realize he no longer sat on the floor. He was standing up. Probably looking toward Hank, but she couldn't make out which way his head was turned – or whether it was turned at all.

Then a black shape slid across Jim, and Abilene could see nothing more of him. She aimed her dark flashlight down at the place where Jim had been standing only a moment ago.

Where he's still standing, she thought.

Only someone's in front of him.

Jesus, this is it. This is it!

With her empty hand, she squeezed the top rail to hold herself steady as terror sucked the strength from her legs.

'Where's them gals?' Little more than a raspy, dry whisper. 'I want 'em, Jimmy.'

From Abilene's left came a solid metallic *snick-clack*. Finley thumbing back a hammer of the shotgun.

'We're right here, asshole!' Finley yelled.

Abilene thrust the flashlight switch forward. Apparently, Vivian did the same, for suddenly two bright beams were slanting downward, lighting the intruder who stood in front of Jim.

He was skinny. He was naked. He was red. A savage in gory warpaint.

He looked as if he'd moments ago climbed out of a bathtub full of blood – or dumped a bucket of it over his head.

He carried a long white bone with joint knobs at each end.

His other arm hung limp, swaying at his side.

And Abilene knew this wasn't Hank.

She knew in an instant, even before Batty spun around and squinted up into the light and the thunder of a gun blast clapped her ears.

Chapter Thirty-nine

The load caught Batty just below the neck. It bit out a big chunk. Blood exploded from the cavity. The red sacks of Batty's breasts jumped shoulder-high. The bone flew into the darkness and his broken arm leaped, flopping, as the blow slammed Batty backward.

The old lunatic's head pounded Jim in the belly. It bounced off the muscles there, which knocked it sideways.

Batty crashed to the floor and lay motionless, head between Jim's feet.

Abilene gazed at the spread-eagled body, stunned. She thought vaguely that she ought to look away from it, but she couldn't.

Blood was spraying out of the chest hole. It came raining down, and if not for the ringing in her ears, she knew she would've been able to hear its soft patter on Batty's skin.

One breast rested neatly on his ribcage, but the other

draped an armpit. She glimpsed his rigid penis, and that was enough to make her look away.

Finley still had the weapon up as if she were contemplating a second shot.

Abilene shone the light in her face. 'That's *Batty*.'

Finley nodded, squinting.

'What'd you *shoot* for?'

'God, Fin,' Cora said.

'I thought it was Hank, okay?'

'Are you blind?'

'Gimme a break. That was *supposed* to be Hank down there, and I fired. Anyway, what the fuck was Batty doing here? Looking for us, that's . . .'

A belchy coughing sound stopped her words. She leaned forward to see past Abilene. They both looked. Vivian was bent over the rail, heaving. Abilene saw the vomit gushing from her mouth, heard it splatting the floor far below. She gagged, herself, and looked away. But she could still hear it. Then all she heard from Vivian were gaspy sobs and sniffles.

'Ya okay?' It was Jim.

'Yeah.' She sniffed. 'Guess so.'

'Why didn't you tell us it was Batty?' Cora called down.

'Didn't know. It was awful mighty dark, just couldn't see *who* it was. Thought it was Hank, though. Till he talked.'

Abilene pointed her light down. Batty was still sprawled at Jim's feet, but blood no longer flew from the wound. Jim was looking up, frowning. His belly was smeared with blood where Batty's head had bumped him.

'It's just as well ya got him,' Jim said. 'He weren't up to no good.'

'He didn't even have a weapon,' Abilene muttered.

'Batty don't need 'em. Had his magic bone. I seen how he

works. He only just gets naked when he's fixin' to work his meanest spells. He meant to kill ya all. That's how come he had the blood on him. That's his bat blood, 'n he don't use it less he's aimin' to do a murder hex.'

'See?' Finley said. 'I saved us from a whammy.'

'Yeah,' Cora said. 'And we *still* have Hank coming after us, and a deaf man could've heard that gunshot a mile away. If he's already here, he knows right where to find us.'

Abilene and Vivian both started probing the darkness with their flashlights. They checked the length of the balcony, the staircase, the foyer. The support posts cast shifting shadows against the wall and floor, and the windows that weren't broken gleamed bright reflections as the lights swept back and forth.

'Shine it over here,' Finley said.

Abilene turned the flashlight toward her and watched Finley break open the shotgun, pluck out the spent shell, replace it with one from her pocket, and snap the breech shut.

'Okay,' Cora said. 'Now, kill the lights.'

Two switches snicked. Darkness clamped down.

'What're we gonna do now?' Abilene whispered.

'Wait for Hank,' Cora answered, her voice low.

'Get him the way I got Batty,' Finley said.

'But he knows we're *here*,' Vivian protested.

'Maybe,' Cora said. 'Maybe not.'

'Ya oughta move Batty outa the way,' came Jim's voice from below. 'Hank ain't gonna come walkin' right up to me, long as the body's here.'

'He won't be able to see it,' Cora said.

'He'll see it. He can see like a cat.'

'Jim's got a point,' Finley said. 'If Hank *does* spot the body,

726

he'll know something's up. All we've gotta do is drag it off. Maybe hide it behind the registration desk.'

'We'd . . . have to touch him,' Vivian whispered.

'Doesn't bother *me*. Look, I'll go on down and take care of it.'

'Not alone,' Cora said.

'I'll go with you,' Abilene offered. Though she hated the idea. She wanted to stay right here on the balcony, out of reach from below. And she sure didn't want to help drag Batty's body anywhere.

'I've got a better idea,' Finley said. 'I'll do it on my own. Just give me your flashlight so I don't trip and fall down the stairs or something. You keep me covered from up here.' She held out the shotgun. Abilene took it with one hand and passed her the flashlight.

'I don't like this,' Vivian said.

'Neither do I,' Cora added.

'Hey, what can happen?'

'Hank could jump you, that's what,' Abilene told her.

'If he does, shoot him. Just don't hit me.'

'There might not be a clear shot,' Cora warned.

'I've always got this.' Finley lifted the hanging front of her shirt and pulled the knife from her waistband.

'A lot of good that'll do you,' Abilene said.

'Shit. I don't think Hank's down there, anyway. For all we know, he might not show up for hours.'

'Maybe he won't even come,' Vivian whispered.

'He's gonna come, all right,' Jim said. 'Ain't here yet, though, pretty sure a that.'

'Okay,' Cora said. 'Go on and do it. But make it quick.'

'And be careful,' Abilene told her.

Finley turned on the flashlight and made her way past the

others. Vivian lit her back as she jogged along the balcony, then swept her beam down the stairway before Finley got there.

As Finley started trotting down the stairs, Abilene lifted the shotgun to her shoulder. Her left hand swung the barrels up. She crouched slightly, and braced her elbow on the railing. Head up, she watched Finley bound off the bottom stair and take a few steps and halt.

Knife in one hand, flashlight in the other, Finley turned all the way around once, apparently to make sure nobody was creeping up on her from the corridor or the open room beyond the stairs. Then she walked slowly through the middle of the lobby, head swiveling, her light joining Vivian's in skittery sweeps of the area surrounding her.

She is being careful, Abilene thought.

But why doesn't she *hurry?*

She won't be safe till she's back up here with the rest of us.

Gazing over the shotgun barrels, Abilene glanced from post to post, half certain that Hank would leap out from behind one. Her forefinger stroked the front trigger. She brushed her thumb across the upper hammer, tempted to pull it back but resisting the urge.

Don't want to flinch and shoot Finley.

Halting beside Batty, Finley moved her light up and down the body. Then she shone it on Jim. 'How are you doing?'

'Okay, I guess.' A moment later, he looked down at his stained belly and said, 'I don't much like the blood on me. Makes me itchy.'

'I'll be back,' Finley told him. She turned off her flashlight and stuffed it into the rear pocket of her shorts. She threw her knife down. It stuck in Batty a couple of inches below his navel.

'Jesus H. Christ,' Abilene muttered.

Finley smirked up at her. 'Want to keep it in easy reach.'

'That's sick,' Vivian said.

'Hey, I don't hear Batty complaining.' With that, she stepped over to his feet, crouched and grabbed his ankles. She straightened up, raising them. Ankles clutched against her hips, she walked sideways. The body turned, then began to slide as she staggered backward, dragging it.

Abilene glimpsed the smears left on the floor.

Batty's arms trailed behind as if raised overhead in surrender. His breasts wobbled. Then darkness masked him as Vivian's light went away to illuminate the area beyond Finley.

Abilene was glad she couldn't see him now.

He was here to get us, she reminded herself. But that didn't help the heavy sickness she felt.

He wouldn't have *wanted* to get us if we hadn't gone to his place and robbed him and killed his cat and hurt him.

We did this to him.

But maybe he was evil and maybe we did the right thing, killing him.

I didn't kill him, she told herself. It was Finley's doing.

Finley knew it was him, but she shot him anyway.

Maybe we're lucky she did.

But it's all so horrible. And disgusting. And maybe we'll end up paying for it.

Maybe Hank's the one meant to collect.

With the thought of Hank, Abilene's guilt and revulsion were submerged by fear. She swung her shotgun toward Finley, who might have been a character from one of those plays Vivian had taken them to in New York – a girl struggling to drag a body across the stage, illuminated by a single spotlight.

In front of the registration desk, Finley straightened up and let go of Batty's feet. The legs dropped. Twin thuds as the heels struck the floor.

Finley stood over the body, panting for breath. 'This is . . . far as he goes.'

'That's fine,' Cora said. 'Get back up here.'

'In a minute.' She lifted the front of her shirt and wiped her face. Then she bent over the body. She pulled out her knife and wiped its blade on a leg of her shorts. 'Don't go anywhere, Batshit.'

'Cut the comedy,' Cora said.

Finley grinned up at her.

'Come on,' Abilene said.

'Hold your water.' Finley headed back the way she'd come. Vivian's light stayed on her, and she didn't bother to take out her own flashlight. Nor did she bother to look around. She strode boldly toward Jim as if she'd forgotten all about the possibility that his brother might be lurking nearby.

'Keep your eyes open,' Abilene warned.

'Hank's not here yet. He would've jumped me by now.'

She's probably right about that, Abilene thought.

'He might show up any second,' Vivian said.

'If he does, Hickok'll blast him. Right?'

Finley stopped in front of Jim. Standing there in a puddle of Batty's blood, she took off her shirt.

'What the *hell* are you doing?' Cora snapped.

'Just gonna clean him up a little,' Finley said, and slid the knife down the waistband at her hip.

'Are you out of your gourd?' Abilene blurted.

'Christ, Fin,' Vivian said.

'Get back up here,' Cora ordered.

'In a minute. Don't get your shorts in an uproar.' She

started rubbing Jim. Her back blocked Abilene's view of exactly what she was doing, but she seemed to be mopping his belly with the wadded shirt. She stood very straight. Her shoulders rocked a little with the movement of her arms. The skin of her back, shiny with perspiration, slid over undulating muscles and shoulder blades. Her hips swayed slightly from side to side.

She's taking her sweet time about it, Abilene thought.

This is more than just wiping off the blood.

The balled shirt came out from between the bodies, wrapped around Finley's left hand. It disappeared behind Jim. Finley's other hand caressed his cheek. Tilting back her head, she eased herself forward.

'She's *kissing* him,' Vivian blurted.

Not just kissing him – writhing, sliding herself against his bare skin.

'Damn it!' Cora blurted. 'Finley!'

She ignored Cora.

'Somebody better go down and break them up.'

'Yeah,' Abilene murmured.

Jim's arms went around Finley. His hands drifted up and down her back, caressing her. They slipped inside her shorts.

'He isn't tied,' Cora said.

Doesn't seem to bother Finley, Abilene thought.

'He wasn't tied up all afternoon,' Vivian whispered.

'I know, but . . . Finley!'

Jim's hands came out of her shorts, caressed her back, her sides.

The fingers of his left hand wrapped her knife.

'Watch out!' Abilene shouted as Jim started to draw out the blade.

Finley grabbed his wrist, clamped it against her side. Her

mouth broke away from his. 'Jim!' she gasped. 'What're you . . . ?'

Jim drove her backward, right arm squeezing her tight to his body. Finley squirmed, kicked wildly.

Abilene thumbed back the shotgun hammer. But the only target was Jim's face beside Finley's head. She held fire and then it was too late to shoot.

They were both out of sight beneath the balcony's over-hang.

'Fuck!' Cora yelled.

Abilene leaned over the railing. Couldn't see them.

Jump?

Vivian had already thought of that. She had one leg on the railing.

'Don't!' Cora warned.

From below came sounds of a struggle: gasps, grunts, quick smacks of skin against skin, thuds of bodies striking the wall or floor.

'Get down and help her!' Cora blurted. 'Quick! But don't jump, for Godsake.'

Vivian swung her leg back down from the railing and started to run.

'Take this.' Abilene shoved the shotgun, stock first, into Cora's hands. 'Cover us.' She rushed past her and raced along the balcony behind Vivian.

'*Cover* you?' Cora called.

'Hank!' she shouted.

Hank? If there *is* a Hank.

She wished she'd kept the shotgun, but she was already leaping down the stairs. Too late to go back for it. And Hank *might* show up. Cora can watch our backs for us.

Vivian grabbed the newel post and swung herself away

from the stairs. She dashed across the lobby, the beam of her flashlight bouncing through the darkness ahead of her.

She hasn't got any weapon at all, Abilene realized.

Remembering her own, she grabbed the handle as she jumped off the last three stairs. She couldn't see the floor. But it found her feet, almost knocking them out from under her. She stumbled, regained her balance, then jerked the knife from her skirt and ran toward Vivian's skittering light.

She switched the knife to her right hand.

God, what if we're too late?

Finley's a wildcat. Maybe she's already nailed the bastard. Maybe she's dead. Split open like Helen.

A support beam rushed out of the darkness. Abilene tried to dodge it. Her left shoulder pounded it. She cried out as the blow spun her around. She staggered backward, fell. The floor hammered her rump. Then she was up again, running toward Vivian's light.

The light was steady, now. Motionless. Casting a bright cone on Jim and Finley.

She stopped running. There was no longer any need to rush.

She halted beside Vivian. The floor under her shoes was slick with Batty's blood.

'What's going on?' Cora asked.

Vivian raised the light. Cora was looking down from the balcony straight in front of them. She had gotten up. She was leaning over the rail with her elbows on it, the shotgun in her hands.

Nobody answered her question.

The light returned to Jim and Finley.

He was on his knees behind her limp body. She lay on her back, eyes shut, her head raised off the floor, held up by Jim's

733

fist clenched in her hair. His other hand pressed the knife blade against her throat.

Abilene saw no blood on Finley's skin or on the floor beside her.

He hasn't cut her, she thought. Not yet.

But he'd done something to her. She was out cold.

Or dead.

No, not dead. Her belly was moving slightly up and down. She's breathing.

'Is Finley okay?' Cora asked.

'I think so,' Abilene muttered.

'Drop yer knife,' Jim said.

Throw it at him?

She'd tried that before, but only managed to wound his leg. If she threw it and missed, he would cut Finley's throat.

Even if I hit him, she thought, it won't kill him fast enough. He'll still have time to kill Finley.

'Drop yer knife,' he told her again. 'Do it!'

She opened her hand. The knife fell and clattered against the floor in front of her.

'Kick it off somewhere. Get rid a the thing.'

She stepped forward and swept the knife away with her foot. It skidded spinning across the floor and vanished in the dark. 'Now stay put,' he said. Tilting back his head, he glared at the underside of the balcony floor. 'Cora, don't ya try nothin' or Finley gets herself cut open. Ya hear me?'

'Yes.'

'Come on over here, Vivian.'

'What do you want?' she asked, her voice trembling.

'Get under here with me. Do what I tell ya.' He pressed the knife tighter against Finley's throat. The way it dented her skin, Abilene expected blood to pour out from under its edge. But this is Finley's knife, she reminded herself. The one tugged from the top of the totem pole.

Dull as it might be, she thought, it'll do the job if he tries harder.

Vivian took a step forward.

'Don't go,' Cora warned from above.

'He'll kill Finley.'

'He can't get *you*. Not if you stay put.'

Vivian looked up at her, then started forward again.

'Don't!'

She didn't halt until she was standing beneath the edge of the balcony. 'I'll do whatever you want,' she told Jim. 'Just leave her alone.'

He lowered Finley's head to the floor and freed his fingers from her hair, but kept the knife against her throat. 'Come here 'n gimme yer light.'

She stepped up to the side of Finley's body, bent down, handed the flashlight to Jim, and straightened up. Then she took a step backward.

'Don't go nowhere.' He shone the light on her. 'Just stay put 'n take off yer stuff.'

'What stuff?'

'I wanta look atcha. All over. Like I seen ya yesterday.'

Vivian balanced on one foot to pull off her shoe and sock.

'Did you kill Helen?' Abilene asked.

'Sure did.'

'What about Hank?'

'Ain't no Hank. He's deader'n hell. Killed him my own self three summers ago.'

Vivian switched feet and pulled off her other shoe.

'You killed Hank?' Abilene asked.

'Killed the whole bunch.'

'Your own *family?*'

Vivian peeled off her sock and let it fall.

'Some fun, huh?' Jim said. Though Abilene couldn't see his face beyond the flashlight trained on Vivian, she knew he must be grinning. 'Ain't had that kinda fun since I was a kid. But I guess this is gonna be a whole bunch better. Now get yet shirt off, Vivian. Whatcha waitin' for?'

She pulled her shirt up, drew it over her head, slipped her arms out of it and tossed it aside.

'Yeah,' Jim said. 'Yeah. Yer the best a the lot. Nice. That other, she was a pig.'

'You're the pig,' Abilene said.

The light swung away from Vivian. Abilene squinted and turned her head away.

'Gonna take care a *you* later. Gonna save *you* till last. Ya hurt me, ya bitch. Gonna hurt *you* till ya squeal.'

The threat turned her insides hot and squirmy.

He can't get me, she told herself. Not if I stay right here. He comes out for me and Cora'll blast him.

'Come and get me,' she said.

'I ain't stupid.' His light returned to Vivian. 'Who told ya t'stop?'

She unfastened her white shorts. She bent over, pulling them down. She stepped out of them.

'Ya ain't done yet.'

'Why are you doing this?' she asked.

'The fun of it. I been achin' t'do you. Just achin'. Get 'em off.'

Vivian slipped her panties down to her ankles.

The light roamed slowly down her body. 'Yeah. Yer a real beauty. Never had me a gal the likes a you.'

The brilliant disk of the flashlight's head rose higher off the floor.

He's standing up.

He aimed the beam downward. It lit his legs and Finley's motionless body as he stepped over her.

'Cora!' Abilene shouted. She clapped her hands. 'Viv, down! Hit the deck!'

Chapter Forty

Jim gasped, 'Hey!' His flashlight followed Vivian as she flung herself sideways, diving for the floor, and Cora launched the shotgun.

Abilene braced her legs. She reached high. The shotgun came down at her fast, stock to the left, muzzles to the right. It smacked her hands. She grabbed hold as the impact knocked her back a step.

Light stabbed her eyes.

'Oh *no* ya don't!' Jim yelled, charging her.

She clamped the stock to her left side, searched for the trigger, swept the barrels toward the blinding light only a yard in front of its muzzles. Found the trigger at the same instant something hit the barrels with a ringing clang and the light went dead.

The shotgun lurched sideways as she pulled its trigger.

The detonation crashed, stunning her ears.

In the muzzle flash, she glimpsed Jim leaping at her, the barrels off to his side, his arms up, the dark flashlight in his right hand, the knife in his left.

Even as she caught the brief look at him, the recoil of the blast was ramming the shotgun up and back, jerking its forestock from her grip, snapping her trapped index finger with its trigger guard. She cried out in pain and then Jim hit her.

The weapon flew from her side.

Jim plowed her through the blackness. She felt his arms wrap around her. She slammed the floor, the knife and flashlight pounding into her back. She grunted with the impact. Jim gasped and she knew he was hurt – at least a little – at least his fingers.

'What's going on?' Cora's voice, sharp with alarm. 'What's happening down there?'

She got no answer.

Jim struggled to pull his hands out from under Abilene.

She punched the side of his face.

The knife turned. Its edge pushed against her. She bucked, trying to throw Jim off. And shrieked as the blade ripped across her just below the shoulder blade.

'Abilene!' Cora called.

The flashlight was still under her back but the knife was gone.

'Viv? Finley?'

She flung her arm up, hoping to ward off the blade, not knowing where it was.

From off to the side came quick footfalls and huffing breath.

Jim yelped and tumbled off her. There were thumps, gasps.

Abilene rolled over, scurried toward the sounds.

A smack like a fist hitting flesh. A grunt. A whimper from Vivian. More sounds of blows landing against skin.

She hurled herself forward, arms spread. Her cheek

bumped something. She clamped her arms tight around the body in her way, realizing her mistake when she felt breasts against her left arm, realized that Vivian had been on top of Jim.

Together, they plunged through the darkness. A quick thud jolted Vivian. She flinched and went limp, but fell a little more before the floor stopped her and her shoulder rammed Abilene's cheek.

Abilene's left hand was trapped under Vivian's armpit. As she pulled it free, wincing at the pain of her broken finger, she reached up with her other hand. Touched Vivian's face, her hair. Found the wood of a support post.

I drove her right into it!

'Hold on!' Cora called.

And Abilene felt fabric rub against her shin. One of her legs was on Vivian's leg, but the other, she suddenly realized, was stretched across Jim.

Why hadn't he grabbed her yet?

Had Vivian been up there, pounding on him so hard that she'd dazed him?

He must *still* be out of it!

Pushing herself off Vivian, she scurried backward and dug her knee into the denim. Jim let out a grunt. As she crawled onto him, she heard a distant thump, a surprised cry of pain, then loud tumbling sounds.

'Cora?' she shouted.

'Shit! *Shit!*'

She straddled Jim. He squirmed, but so far he wasn't striking at her. She slid her hands over his chest, felt it rising and falling as he panted for air. The rope suspender didn't seem to be there, but that wasn't what she was searching for. She found his shoulders.

The knife had been in his left hand.

'What's happening?' Cora called. Her voice sounded shaky.

Abilene ran her right hand down Jim's left shoulder and along his arm. The arm was sticking straight out away from his side, bent at the elbow. She slid her hand up the slick skin, past his wrist to his bunched fingers. She didn't need to feel the knife to know it was still in his fist. She pinned his wrist to the floor.

'I think I've got him,' she said.

'Hope so,' Cora answered. 'Wrecked my other fuckin' leg.'

'Just stay put. I've got him.'

'Where's Viv?'

'Over here. I think she's knocked out.'

'Shit.'

Keeping Jim's knife-hand tight against the floor, Abilene hunched down and pressed her left forearm against his throat. She pushed.

'What're you doing?' Cora asked.

'Strangling the bast . . .' The blow caught her just above the hip. Her breath burst out. She felt as if her side had been caved in, but she stayed on top of him. When he started to buck, trying to throw her off, she dropped down against his chest and thrust her arm as hard as she could against his throat. He punched her again, this time hammering her rib cage.

And his knife hand got free.

In an instant, the blade would be driving down into her back.

She flipped herself off Jim – away from the knife – and hit the floor rolling.

Jim growled. She heard him scuttling after her.

She rolled over again and again until a post blocked her

across the belly. She dropped onto her back, sat up, glanced into the darkness toward the sounds of Jim rushing closer, then hurled herself over to her knees and scrambled up and ran.

Ran and saw twin patches of dim gray light off to her left and dashed toward them.

Windows.

The two at the rear of the dining area?

She wasn't sure, didn't care. They were a way out.

If Jim doesn't get me first.

She could hear him huffing, pounding the floor, gaining on her.

The gray window straight ahead grew.

She couldn't see whether it was a broken one.

If it's not, I'll be cut to ribbons!

They do it in the movies.

In the movies, it isn't real glass.

But Abilene knew she would rather risk glass than face the certainty of Jim's knife.

Arms hugging the sides of her head, right hand clutching the nape of her neck, she dived at the window. She rammed through. Glass exploded. Her head and neck got outside before the shards began to drop on her. She felt them bite and slice through the back of her blouse. The denim of her skirt seemed too heavy for them to penetrate, but they got her bare legs.

The dive took her clear of the window. She glimpsed the moonlit floor of the porch. Then its edge. Then the ground far below. She yelped 'No!'

Her lips and thighs pounded the floor, skidded. She flung her arms back, hoping to grab hold. Her fingertips brushed the edge of the porch as it slipped away. She dropped headfirst. Her legs flew up. Her heels struck the railing.

Oh, my God!

Then there was only the warm night air rushing around her.

This is it.

She saw the pale strip of granite along the rear of the lodge and wondered if she would miss it. As her legs swept down behind her, she saw the shadowed wall of the lodge and then the porch above her . . . the porch with its damn railing that she'd dived right under . . . then the second-story porch, then the edge of the roof. The moon was straight above her face when the ground crashed her rump. Her legs and back slammed down. Her head smacked.

Lights flared behind her eyes.

You *do* see stars, she thought.

Not just in the cartoons.

There was a roar in her head. A roar and a blazing pain. Her whole body seemed to be roaring inside.

She wondered if this was how it felt to get hit by a car.

No. It's how you feel if you go through a window and fall a story.

She wondered if she was conscious.

I must be. I'm thinking.

Maybe dreaming I'm thinking.

At least I'm alive.

And I got away from him.

Jim!

She opened her eyes. Standing at her feet, naked and pale in the moonlight, was Helen.

Helen. Though the handle of a knife jutted from her belly, Abilene saw no blood, no guts spilling out, no rips at all in her skin.

Joy welled up through her agony. It was followed quickly

by terrible sorrow, for she knew this couldn't be Helen. Not really. She was either dreaming or hallucinating. Helen was dead. Had to be.

'Rough night, huh?' Helen asked.

'My God.'

'How you feeling? Pretty shitty, I guess.'

'You . . . you're alive?'

'No such luck.'

'I don't . . .'

'Don't you know a ghost when you see one?' She smiled. 'I couldn't find a white sheet. But this is okay. It's a pretty hot night.' She raised her arms and looked up at the sky. 'A gorgeous night.' Her arms lowered. Her smile slipped away. 'But look, you haven't got much time. You've got to pull yourself together before Jim shows up. He didn't want to hurt himself following you through the window, so he'll be coming out the kitchen door. Any second now.'

Groaning, Abilene pushed at the ground with her elbow. She braced herself up.

'Come and pay me a visit,' Helen told her. 'I've got something that'll help.' Her fingers closed around the knife handle. She slipped the long, thick blade from her belly. It came out, leaving no wound behind. 'It's his, after all. You can give it back to him.'

And Helen was gone.

And Jim lurched across the porch and rushed down the stairs. He'd lost his cut-offs. But he hadn't lost his knife. It jumped up and down in his right hand, flashing silver moonlight.

Not *his* knife, Abilene thought as she struggled to her feet. Finley's knife.

His is in Helen. In the shower room.

I'm supposed to get it.

But how?

Jim leaped off the last stairs and turned toward Abilene. *Between* her and the outer pool. But he no longer seemed to be in a hurry, maybe because she wasn't running.

'Gotcha now,' he said.

With each step Jim took toward her, she sidestepped away from the lodge. Moving slowly further into the field. Limping, every muscle hot and sore, her broken finger throbbing, each cut afire with pain. Her blouse hugged her back, sodden with blood that slid down and soaked her skirt and panties. Blood dribbled down both her legs.

She wondered if she would have enough strength and quickness to get past him.

Probably not.

Gotta give it the old college try.

She kept stepping sideways, circling away from Jim as he walked toward her. Soon, he was no longer in the way of the pool. She was tempted to go for it. But he probably wouldn't have any trouble cutting her off.

She had circled far enough that every step now carried her closer to the pool.

If we keep this up much longer, she thought, I won't need to run past him at all. I'll end up right there.

But he's going to get tired of this game.

Any second, he'll come running at me.

Abilene whirled and broke for the pool. She raced for its edge, arms pumping, legs striding out long and fast. Pain surged through her head. Her back sizzled as if fiery grease had been splashed on all the nicks and gashes from her shoulders to her ankles. She knew she couldn't outrun her agony. She only hoped she could outrun Jim as he closed in on her from the side.

Sprinting full speed, glancing to her left and seeing Jim almost near enough to touch, she didn't wait for the pool. She dived.

Déjà vu.

Just like diving through the window, but no glass this time. And no porch floor rushing out from under her. This time, it was granite and she *hoped* her plunging body would clear its edge.

She hit the surface flat out, arms extended. It smacked her, enveloped her.

She knew she'd entered at an angle that would collide her with the side of the archway, so she rolled and kicked to the left. Her breasts scraped something. Her belly bumped. She twisted away and met no other obstruction as she glided forward.

She heard a hollow, muffled splash.

He's in.

Sure that she was clear of the archway by now, she rolled face down and started swimming underwater.

Stay down here? she wondered. I could veer off and maybe lose him.

Cat and mouse in the dark pool.

Cat and mouse. Jim would like that. He'd been playing with all of them right from the start.

Sooner or later, he'll find me.

Gotta go for the shower room, go for the knife.

Straight ahead.

She kicked to the surface and swam with all her strength. The sounds of her own splashes reverberated like water churning, erupting inside an echo chamber. She couldn't hear splashes from Jim. But he had to be back there, had to be coming.

Does he know how to swim? she wondered.

If not, he might be wading. That'd slow him down plenty.

More likely, though, he was gliding silently toward her below the surface.

She tried to swim faster. Her sneakers felt heavy. They dragged at her feet, slowed her down. She wished she'd gotten rid of them, but couldn't waste any time doing it now.

I've got my shoes slowing me down, she thought, but Jim's got the knife to hamper him. He can't possibly swim full speed with that in his hand.

And I can outrace him, shoes or not, as long as I'm up here and he's down below.

Even though she told herself that, she half expected with every kick to feel the clutch of Jim's fingers around one of her ankles.

Her right hand, darting out, jabbed a hard surface that curled her fingers and scraped her knuckles. She drew it back fast, flung up her other arm and lunged against the pool's side. Her feet found the bottom. She leaped, shoving at the granite, knowing for sure Jim would grab her now.

But he didn't.

She got both knees on the edge and scrabbled away from the pool. She thrust herself up. She ran. The smack of her rubber soles resounded through the silence, horribly loud, but not so loud that she didn't hear a *swush* of disturbed water behind her or the wheezy gasp of Jim sucking air into lungs that must need it badly.

Abilene knew she had to be very close to the stairway. She slowed to a walk, rolling her feet to quiet the sound of her footsteps, bending forward and sweeping her arms in search of the banister.

She heard Jim panting, but no new splashy sounds. He's

still in the pool, she thought. Standing in the water, listening for me.

Her right hand hit wood.

And she had a sudden urge to rush up the stairs. She didn't *want* to go into the shower room, to be in there in the blackness with Helen's savaged corpse. If she could get back up to the lobby, maybe she could find the shotgun. Maybe Cora already *had* it. Or Vivian or Finley might've regained consciousness by now and maybe one of *them* had the shotgun.

They could blow the bastard away.

I'd be leading him straight back up to them, Abilene thought.

They're safe up there. For now. As long as he's down here after me.

If I can nail him, they'll be safe perm . . .'

Water swished and flopped.

Here he comes!

Abilene turned away from the banister. Following a mental picture of where the door marked Gents should be, she crept through the darkness with her arms outstretched. She found the wall. As she felt her way along it, she heard water dripping onto the granite floor. And footsteps. Slow, quiet pats.

He can't see me, she told herself. Doesn't know where I am.

She touched the doorframe. Two more sideways steps, and she knew she must be in front of the door.

She pushed.

The hinges squawked.

Rushing footfalls slapped the floor.

Abilene lunged forward, whirled and threw the door shut. It slammed with a crash.

She backed away from it fast, angling to her left and hoping she wouldn't trip over the bench. Its edge brushed the side of her knee, so she knew she'd cleared it. Knew that she should miss the bank of lockers, too.

The door hinges groaned.

Reaching out, Abilene touched cool metal.

I'm at the end of the lockers.

She couldn't remember if there was a bench on the other side of them.

But the shower room was there.

She could smell it.

That's Helen.

Christ!

Imagining the diagonal path she would need to take, she spun around and ran.

She flung her arms out, swept them ahead of her as she charged through the blackness. The stench was like a foul, putrid rag rubbing her face. She tried to hold her breath. Something hammered her right foot out from under her.

As she plunged, arms out to break her fall, she realized it must've been the raised threshold of the shower room that had tripped her.

The floor smacked her palms, her knees. It knocked them out from under her. It hammered the breath from her lungs but she managed to keep her head up as she skidded.

Wheezing for air that clogged her nostrils and throat with its heavy reek of corruption, she belly-crawled until her hands slipped on gooey muck.

'Gonna end up same as yer fatso friend,' Jim said from somewhere behind her.

She thrust herself up to her knees and scurried forward. Her hands swept across the mat of congealing blood, but didn't find Helen.

'How'd ya like yer skin peeled off? I'll do that for ya.'

Did he move her? Abilene wondered. Where the hell *is* she?

Then her right hand jammed beneath something tight against the floor. Whatever it might be, it was too heavy for an arm. She must've pushed her hand under Helen's side or leg. With her other hand, she reached out higher. She touched something sticky and yielding that made her want to pull back. She resisted the urge and felt along the mushy bulges.

She flinched, cried out, as her left foot was stomped.

The pain jolted her body. Her left hand rammed down into glop. Her right hand wedged deeper into the crease between Helen's body and the floor, fingertips poking something that clinked.

Keys?

'Guess I gotcha, huh?'

The weight lifted from her foot. Fingers clutched her ankle and pulled. As her knee began sliding backward, she jerked her right hand out from under Helen and hurled herself forward. She dropped across the body, flung her arm out and grabbed hold. Her fingers hooked into cool flesh. Helen's side? Her rump?

Clinging to it as Jim tugged at her leg, she pulled her left hand out of the clinging slop and groped along Helen and found the knife.

Her swollen forefinger wouldn't close, but she wrapped her other fingers and thumb around the upright handle.

Clutching it hard, she released her grip on Helen.

She yanked the blade out as Jim dragged her backward.

She didn't resist him.

She slid off Helen's body. The floor pounded her chest. As she skidded along, she raised both arms overhead. She passed the knife from her left hand to her right.

Does he know I've got it?

He must know he left it here.

But maybe he isn't thinking about that. Not yet. Maybe.

'I'll do whatever you want,' Abilene gasped. 'Just don't hurt me. Please.'

'Please please please,' he mocked her. 'That's what *she* kept sayin'. Gal sure didn't wanta come in here.' He stopped dragging Abilene. He twisted her foot. She yelped and rolled over quickly onto her back.

'I really like you, Jim.'

'Ya won't much when I start ya' squealin'.'

Her legs were nudged apart. She felt the knife blade scrape along the inner side of her thigh. It eased higher. She sucked in her breath and shuddered.

Dear God.

Get him now!

A swing and a miss and you're out.

But the blade went away. A sharp tug at her skirt lifted her buttocks off the floor for a moment before the fabric split. The point pushed under her waistband, then tugged again.

'Ain't very sharp,' he muttered. 'Gonna hurt like hellfire, skinnin' ya with it all dull.'

'You don't want to do that,' she said.

'Sure do. But I gotta pork ya first. I don't pork dead folks.'

He moved forward, his knees nudging her thighs farther apart.

She felt both his hands on her belly.

Where's the knife?

Between his teeth, maybe.

He ripped open the front of her blouse.

She heard buttons skitter across the floor.

His hands slid up her body. They clutched her breasts, squeezed.

A swing and a miss and you're out.

She swung.

She swung her right arm up from her side as hard as she could and the knife lurched in her grip as its blade struck something in the dark beyond her chest and kept on going.

Jim squealed.

His hands leaped from her breasts.

She felt a bump against her belly. His knife. He'd had it in his mouth, all right.

'My *eye*!' he shrieked.

Abilene clamped her legs tight against him and sat up fast. She felt his knife slide down her belly to her groin. She grabbed its handle. Her three-fingered grip wasn't much, but it was good enough.

She drove the blade forward. It punched into him and he bellowed and blood washed over her knuckles. It was still buried in him to the hilt when she slashed the darkness with the knife in her good right hand. The knife jerked when it hit him. His bellow changed to a gurgle. A hot stream hosed Abilene's right breast.

The body viced between her legs twitched and writhed.

She pulled out the other knife.

She rammed both into him at once and the impact threw him backward. As he fell away, the blades came out of him.

She scurried clear, then crawled back to him. A thrashing foot kicked her face, but she didn't mind. She straddled him, sat down across his hips. His twitching body thrust up against her. She heard him choke and gurgle. She heard his limbs smacking the floor.

She pounded her knives down.

She jerked them out and hit him again. And again. And again.

Soon, he was only moving because of the blades jolting him.

Sometimes, they got stuck in bone. But Abilene always managed to yank them free.

Finally, a blade broke.

Chapter Forty-one

'Hickok!'

She was gasping for breath. Instead of trying to speak, she tossed the handle of the broken knife. It clacked against the floor.

'You in here?'

'Yeah!' she blurted.

Quick footfalls.

'Where's Jim?'

'Here.'

A beam of light criss-crossed the darkness beyond the shower room entrance.

'Don't do anything to her, Jim,' Vivian pleaded. 'We won't hurt you.'

'Not if she's okay,' Finley added.

Abilene squeezed her eyes shut when the brilliant glare hit her face.

'Holy shit,' Finley muttered.

Vivian said, 'My God.'

'I'm . . . okay.'

'*He's* not. Holy shit.'

The light on the other side of her eyelids dimmed slightly, so she opened them. The bright beam was aimed down at Jim. She groaned at the sight of him. He glistened with blood. His left eye was a slashed, bleeding pit. The left side of his neck was split by a gash that crossed the front of his throat. All over his chest and stomach were raw-edged slots. From one in his ribcage jutted the handle of a knife. A wedge of broken blade showed, sticking out an inch from a wound below his right shoulder.

Abilene started to get off him.

Vivian gave the flashlight to Finley, then hurried toward her. She was barefoot, but no longer naked. She wore the white shorts and shirt that Jim had made her take off under the balcony.

She grabbed Abilene's arm and helped her up.

'Man,' Finley muttered.

Abilene looked down at herself. Her blouse was no longer plaid. Below its short sleeves, her arms were sheathed in blood. The open front covered her left breast and felt glued there. Her right breast was bare and looked as if it had been dipped in a bucket of red paint. The rest of her chest and belly were splattered and dribbling, but she could see a few places that the blood had missed. Her skirt was gone. Her panties were sodden with crimson blotches, her thighs splashed and runny.

'How much of that's yours?' Finley asked.

'Not much. It's my back . . .' She turned around.

A hiss of indrawn breath came from Vivian.

'Nasty,' Finley said.

'You'll need stitches in some of those.'

753

'Did you get all that going through the window?'

'Mostly. One's from his knife.'

'Well, you sure gave him payback,' Finley said. 'For all of us.'

'How'd you know about the window?'

'Cora told us.'

Abilene faced her friends again. 'You were both out of it.'

'Don't I know it,' Finley said. 'The shit played basketball with my head.'

'I don't know *what* hit me,' Vivian said.

'I did. Sorry about that.'

'Cora was just telling us what'd happened,' Finley explained, 'when we heard a door slam. Sounded like it came from down here.'

'Christ, what took you so long?'

'I thought we made pretty good time. We had to find the shotgun. And Viv, of course, had to get dressed.'

'If you'd kept your shirt on,' Vivian said, 'none of this would've happened.'

Abilene saw that Finley hadn't bothered to put it back on. Hardly surprising.

'He had me fooled,' Finley muttered. 'Shit.' She looked down at Jim's body. 'He really had me believing in that crazy fuckin' brother of his.'

'He had us all believing,' Abilene said.

'Yeah. Right. But I'm the only one who *made out* with the scumwad. If I hadn't gone over and started messing around . . .'

'It would've happened differently,' Abilene told her. 'That's all. He was planning to get us. He would've made his try sooner or later. *He* knew Hank wasn't gonna show up.'

'Can we get out of here now?' Vivian asked. 'It's . . . awful in here. And Cora's gotta be wondering.'

'She'll be thinking we're all dead,' Finley said.

'How is she?' Abilene asked.

'She won't be walking out of here on either leg.'

'Maybe she won't have to.' Abilene turned toward Helen's body. Finley lit the way for her. 'I think Helen found the keys before . . . he got to her.' She stepped carefully over the mat of blood and crouched. 'I touched something when . . .'

'Did Jim bring you here?' Vivian asked.

'He came in after me. I was here for the knife.' She shoved her right hand beneath Helen's thigh.

'The knife he used on Helen? Good thinking, Hickok.'

'It wasn't my idea. I had a little help from a friend.'

She closed her hand around the key case and pulled it out.

Finley and Vivian stood by the edge of the pool, watching over Abilene with the shotgun and flashlight. The water turned pink around her. When she finished washing, she climbed out and looked down at herself. Her skin looked ruddy and clean.

She left her bloody blouse and panties beside the pool, and followed Finley toward the stairs.

Vivian, behind her with the shotgun, said, 'You're bleeding all over the place.'

'You can patch me up when we get upstairs.'

'I can try.'

'It doesn't matter. We'll be out of this place in a few minutes.'

'The four of us, anyway,' Finley muttered.

They began to climb the stairs.

'But not Helen,' Vivian said. She sounded as if she might start to cry.

'I don't know,' Abilene said.

They didn't ask what she meant by that. Just as well. This wasn't the time to talk about such things.

Wait till we're out of here.

'That's just about the best sound I've ever heard,' Cora said when the Wagoneer's engine roared to life.

Vivian and Finley had left her stretched out on the porch, then headed for the car.

They'd gone there once before and returned to the lobby with the Coleman lantern, a bundle of clothes, and the first-aid kit. By the bright glow of the lantern, they bandaged the cuts on Abilene's legs. There weren't enough bandages for all the cuts on her back, but they'd come prepared for that. They folded two sweatshirts into heavy, square pads and lashed them to her back with belts and Jim's ropes. When the pads were secure, Abilene had dressed herself in shorts and one of Helen's big blouses.

She'd led the way outside, carrying the lantern.

After Vivian and Finley had lowered Cora to the porch, they'd taken the lantern and hurried away to bring up the car.

They'd been gone a long time. Abilene, standing beside Cora, had started to wonder if something might have gone wrong.

What could go wrong? she'd told herself. Jim's dead. Batty's dead.

Someone we don't know about?

What if Jim had been lying about Hank?

They're probably just clearing off the back seat for Cora, she'd thought.

But with the noise of the racing engine, she knew that everything must be all right.

She looked toward the sound and saw headbeams slant

into the night from beyond the far corner of the porch. The bright paths slipped lower as the car nosed into view at the top of the driveway. When it turned, the beams swept sideways and lit the pavement that stretched like a road across the front of the lodge.

The approaching car looked almost as good as home.

It swung over close to the porch and stopped. The engine went silent. The headlights went dark, but a light came on inside the car as the front doors swung open. Vivian and Finley hopped out.

'Anybody feel like a ride?' Finley asked, pulling open the back door.

If only this had happened last night, Abilene thought.

If Jim hadn't thrown their clothes in the pool. If she'd been more careful dragging Helen's shorts up from the bottom. If they'd kept on hunting, afterwards, until they found the keys. If Helen hadn't gone off by herself to look for them.

If if if if.

If they'd simply driven away after their first encounter with Jim down at the pool.

If they hadn't come to this damn lodge in the first place.

It was Helen's choice.

A different choice, and she might still be alive.

But maybe not.

Maybe things would've turned bad even if they hadn't come here. Maybe it was just time. Maybe Helen's number was up, no matter what.

Abilene stepped out of the way as Vivian and Finley crouched beside Cora. They pushed their arms under Cora's back and rump, lifted her, and rushed her down the porch stairs. They sat her down on the back seat. Then Vivian hurried around to the other side of the car. She climbed in and dragged Cora backward while Finley carefully raised her legs onto the seat cushion.

'You get in front,' Finley said, looking over her shoulder as she shut the door for Cora. 'Vivian's riding in back.'

Abilene made her way around to the passenger door. She climbed into the car, wincing as she lowered herself onto the seat, groaning when she leaned sideways to pull the door shut.

Finley got in behind the wheel and slammed her door. She started the engine. She pulled a knob on the dashboard, and the headlights shot out into the darkness. 'I hope the peedunk town has a hospital for you guys.'

The car lurched forward.

'Ow!' Abilene blurted.

'Shit!' Cora snapped from the rear. 'Take it easy.'

'Don't be such wooses.'

'Just drive carefully,' Vivian said.

Abilene caught a last glimpse of the Totem Pole Lodge before the car swung away from it. She thought about Helen down in the shower room, and suddenly wished they hadn't left her there in the dark with Jim.

Helen isn't there, she told herself.

It's just her body.

Helen is somewhere else.

Maybe here with us. Or maybe out roaming the night. She'd called it 'a gorgeous night.'

The Richard Laymon Collection Volume 2

Richard Laymon

THE WOODS ARE DARK

In the woods are six dead trees. The Killing Trees. That's where they take them. Innocent travellers on the road in California. Seized and bound, stripped of their valuables and shackled to the Trees. To wait. In the woods. In the dark . . .

OUT ARE THE LIGHTS

The Vampire movie came first, then the story of the Axeman. This was the horror movie series to end them all. Cinema buffs admired the grainy, amateur camera work – it suggested the action was the real thing. But it couldn't be – could it?

'If you've missed Laymon, you've missed a treat' Stephen King

'A brilliant writer' *Sunday Express*

'This author knows how to sock it to the reader' *The Times*

0 7553 3169 9

headline

Coming soon in the **Richard Laymon**
Collection and available from your bookshop
or *direct from his publisher*.

FREE P&P AND UK DELIVERY
(Overseas and Ireland £3.50 per book)

Volume Four:
Beware! & Dark Mountain   £7.99

Volume Five:
Flesh & Resurrection Dreams   £7.99

Volume Six: £7.99
Funland & The Stake

TO ORDER SIMPLY CALL THIS NUMBER

01235 400 414

or visit our website: www.madaboutbooks.com

Prices and availability subject to change without notice.